LAKE SPARK

The Complete Collection Volume Three

EVEY LYON

THE LAKE SPARK WORLD

CONTENTS

SHOULD HAVE BEEN

SHOULD HAVE KNOWN

HARLOW

I tap my perfectly manicured dark red nails on the counter next to the bell. The receptionist behind the desk is too busy typing away on his computer to check me in. Which is probably why my eyes have traveled back to the man leaning casually against the desk next to me. He's too easy on the eyes by far, and he seems familiar, but I can't pinpoint from where. Why is he smirking at me?

Are his lean and toned arms peeking from under his white t-shirt even real? I think I could bounce a quarter off his body. His hair isn't bad either. I like short in the back and a wave on top, his brown eyes to match, with a glint of curiosity. An instinct has me thinking he knows more than I might expect.

How I ended up in Lake Spark, Illinois at a place called the Dizzy Duck Inn, I'm not entirely sure. Well, that's a lie. It was my publisher insisting that I should attend this writers' retreat. And so far, the town seems quaint. Summer is over, yet September brings out a sharper blue in the sky against the backdrop of pines and a deep blue lake.

A steady beat. That's what my nails are doing as I'm in a standoff with Mr. McBroody.

"Can I help you with something? Normally eyes on me aren't a bad thing, however, you kind of feel like an asshole who's about to say something I won't like," I tell him, having no problem being blunt.

He just simpers and propels himself off the desk. "Can you go any slower, Stuart?" he asks the college-aged receptionist as he glances over his shoulder. Jock man returns his gaze to mine. "Harlow Olive, right?"

A smile spreads on my glossed lips. "That's me." Ah, he's just a guy who probably has a sister or a girlfriend who reads. "You're familiar with my books?"

He snickers a breath. "You mean, unrealistic romance novels that you probably don't even write because you're too busy picking out what heels to wear and posting smoothie photos on your social media?"

I glance down to my black stilettos. I only wore them because I like to dress well when traveling… plus, I do need some social media content before I throw on my flats.

But wait a second, what an ass for just saying what he did.

My hand lands on my hip that I tip out. "Aren't we judgmental," I counter.

"I'm confident this writers' retreat is for people who actually form a plot."

My head perks up. How does he know about the retreat?

He straightens his posture, clearly having read my mind. Then he has the audacity to offer me his hand to shake. "Stone Madden." I blink, as the name means nothing. "Doesn't ring a bell?" He idles in his arrogance. "The former hockey player now a successful author," he presses. "We have the same publisher."

I look unimpressed before my own scoff of disbelief hits me. "You're him? You are the guy who writes about fictional hockey with a little mellow drama. I've heard something about that. Just assumed you were some guy who lives in the woods somewhere and chops his own wood while wishing he was someone else."

"Hey there, doll. I would look amazing in plaid and using an ax.

Besides, there are a hell of a lot of facts woven into my books," he clarifies.

I chuckle under my breath, scanning the room to see if this is some kind of joke. Sports jock is actually a writer. Huh.

"Stone, do you want me to give you the lakeside view or are you tired of looking at it?" the receptionist asks him, as if he is partly unnerved.

"I'll never get tired of the lake; plus, if I face the woods, then I'm positive I'll just end up seeing two raccoons going at it."

I look between them peculiarly. "Uh, I believe you were working on my check-in," I reiterate to the receptionist, with his Stuart name tag that I want to rip off because my flight from the warmth of Florida has made me a little edgy, and, okay, the heels hurt my feet like hell.

Stuart throws me wide eyes. "Yes, but Stone is a new local to Lake Spark, so we must give him the full welcome, plus…" His eyes land sharply on Stone, and Stuart's face falls. "He tried to get me fired a few days ago."

Stone gives him a contrite smile. "Just keeping it real."

My eyes swim between both of them. "Local?"

Stone gives me a satisfied smile. "You see, Harlow. Our publisher loves me, maybe it's my name. Not to mention I have a little investment in this fine establishment."

"Then you should talk to someone about that ridiculous moose head on the wall." I don't blink and tip my head in the direction of the fireplace in the lobby.

He stifles a laugh and ignores me. "Anyhow, the organizers were far too eager to set up this retreat in my new hometown at this spectacular boutique hotel that's home to weddings, baby showers, events —you know, that kind of thing. I'm just not staying at my house as I want the full retreat experience."

I blow out an aggravated breath. "Great. I'm blessed with an arrogant asshole who probably uses a ghostwriter to turn out his books."

"Watch it there, feisty firefly. Please tell me you don't write hockey romance. I bet you've actually never even been to a game."

What a jerk. "I have… does it matter?" Damn it, he sees through me. My understanding of the sport could probably be improved, but I don't write about hockey, so who cares.

"Mr. Madden, your room is ready. Would you like a welcome cookie?" Stuart offers him a wide smile.

Stone gives him a neutral glance. "Nah, it's okay."

"How's your brother and the baby?" Stuart asks, as if they are now suddenly old friends.

Stone gets comfortable again, leaning against the reception desk. "Great, thanks for asking. Vaughn is busy on the road now that hockey season has started. Isla and the baby are doing well. She's the cutest kid too."

"Go, Spinners hockey." Stuart gives a little fist pump in the air.

Are we for real?

I wave my hands between them. "Yoo-hoo, tourist here waiting for my room. What kind of welcome to Lake Spark is this? You're treating him like he's some kind of royalty." I jerk my thumb at Stone. My annoyance is about to blow sky high.

"Oh, Ms. Jelly, don't worry. I ensured you got a corner room near the squirrel garden. There is also a fruit basket and local treats from the town too, not to mention a Spinners t-shirt. Welcome cookie?" Stuart gives me an overdone, albeit sincere smile as he magically holds up a basket of cookies from behind the desk.

Great. Squirrels and carbs.

"Lovely." I'm not at all serious.

Gah, I hate that he said my legal last name.

"Yeah, I would change my real name to a cocktail garnish too." Stone chuckles under his breath, and that deep sound causes something inside my belly to flicker. What the hell?

"See you at the afternoon session, Harlow. Let me guess, you're going to go curl your hair and freshen your makeup." His eyes draw a line up and down, assessing me, and his eyes on me feels like a sin.

Still, I stay strong and point a finger at him. "You are a judgmental jerk. Shouldn't you be on the ice playing hockey or drinking a protein shake or something? I'm sure your ability to think is the size of a puck."

A short chortle escapes him. "Aren't you a cute little fiery thing. See ya, firefly." He walks away with a swagger that irritates me because my eyes linger a little longer than they should on his exit.

"Are you sure you wouldn't like a cookie?" Stuart breaks my attention, and I glare at him.

This is going to be a long retreat.

———

I'LL SHOW HIM.

Stone Madden will be proven wrong with his critical accusations.

Staring in the mirror of my room, I double-check my black yoga pants with a dark olive-green sweater with matching converse shoes with olive-green sparkles. The memo for the afternoon instructed us to arrive in comfortable clothing for the welcome session. I fluff my hair and begin to leave my room but stop abruptly and lean half of my body back to catch one more glance at my appearance and decide that despite my makeup mostly being off, that maybe I should throw on a little highlighter on my cheeks and smear on lip balm. It's not clear why that hunch hits me, as if I need to impress someone.

By the time I'm down in the conference room, a small group is scattered around the place. A few people are already sitting on the circle of chairs, and a few are perusing the snack table off to the side.

I decide water is a great start and head straight for the table, saving introductions to the group for after I'm hydrated. Truthfully, this retreat is kind of what I need. My writing nights are sometimes consumed by a mix of distraction and a flinch inside of me that I still can't seem to escape. Sleep isn't for me.

Grabbing my bottle, I notice someone in my peripheral vision, studying me.

"Wow, does it hurt not to be in heels?"

Ugh, the guy who pretends to be an author graces me with his presence.

I bark a laugh as I turn in his direction. "I don't know. Does it hurt not to be in a room where your sweltering gaze distracts the world?" Oh shit, why did that roll off my tongue? Subconscious hell is hitting me earlier than normal today.

Stone's brows raise a smidgen, and his lips stretch into a line of satisfaction. "Natural looks are natural looks. Something you hide behind your alter ego."

"Are you saying I have natural looks?" I'm wary yet slightly honored.

Someone claps their hands, indicating we should all join the circle, and it breaks our comments, meaning I don't get a reply.

"Welcome to the club, Harlow," he whispers as he walks away. I guess he gave me my answer.

My jaw drops slightly before I shake my head and join the circle.

We are a group of six.

A lady in her mid-fifties stands and greets us with her bright smile. "Hello, everyone, I'm Gloria, and I'm excited for our next few days. We will study some writing techniques, soak in inspiration, and also take some time to relax because health is key for great writing. You're all here because your publisher sent you. Doesn't mean you need to improve, you can only grow and become better here. Each of you represents a different genre too, which enables you all to share a different perspective."

We all seem to be listening without judgment.

"Let's start with a quick introduction round, then we will dive right into our activities." She indicates for the woman next to her to start.

Turns out we have a sci-fi writer, historical fiction author, a fantasy author, plus women's fiction, whereas I write the romance that I'm sure my hypothetical future daughter one day will roll her eyes about.

Stone smiles at the group. "Hey, I'm Stone and a local to Lake

Spark. I used to play hockey, and my little brother is the general manager of the Spinners. So yeah, it's only logical that I write fiction about hockey, mostly about a coach who finds himself in moral dilemmas. Loosely based on a coach from way back. I absolutely do write my own words. Every. Single. One." He zips an unfavorable look at me.

"Great." Gloria turns her attention to me. "Last but not least."

I swallow and give everyone a curt wave. "Hi, I'm Harlow, and yes, that's really my first name. I write romance, just the, well, steamy kind. Uhm, I live in the Florida panhandle, so the temperatures here are a bit nippy, but the start of fall in this small town seems perfect for writing. Complete Gilmore Girls vibes."

"Aren't you the author who makes all those olive-green-themed videos next to green drinks?" Jennifer, the women's fiction author, asks.

I shrug my shoulders. "Yeah, that's me. Marketing, unfortunately, comes with the profession."

"Unless you're me. It's amazing what being a former MVP of a hockey team does for selling books." Stone casually drinks from his cup of coffee that seems to be filled with a giant dose of ego.

I roll my eyes. "Right, because that must work when everyone buys because of your looks." I'm doubtful, and damn it, that just spun out of my mouth.

His smirk is subtle enough to cause something inside of me to pulse. Luckily, he seems to let me off for my slip-up. "If I can write or not is an air of mystery that people love. It's great. Eases the pressure and allows me to focus on my writing and gym sessions. Not to mention, hitting up Jolly Joe's in town that gives you coffee with little jellybeans inside. Oh, you might like that. They say the olive-green ones bring luck. You can take a picture of it and post it online." Now he throws me a fake smile.

"Cute. An arrogant writer. We just love those," I retort.

Frank, the sci-fi writer, looks at us, confused. "Have you two dated or something? You seem like a bickering couple with a torrid past."

Jennifer snaps her fingers. "They are totally giving off those vibes."

My mouth gapes open, amazed that anyone would assume that. "No. I just met the guy this morning when the staff rolled out the red carpet and treated the rest of us like peasants," I inform everyone.

"Hey, that's a step too far. I heard Stuart offered you a cookie," Stone coolly mentions, not fazed by the accusation flying at us.

Gloria smiles awkwardly. "Well, aren't we all getting side-tracked. Let's get back to the agenda."

I groan quietly to myself; this is not how I imagined these tranquil few days would go. I quickly whip my head to Stone to give him one more glare for good measure, and the hockey ass just winks at me.

"I want everyone to use either their journal or online project tool, whatever you use, a few times a day to check in with where your thoughts are. I've also included a list of questions to guide your gratitude and future goals. Of course, you all have time to write your current work-in-progress each day. We have a lot planned in the next few days but plenty of downtime. Tomorrow will be about descriptive writing and editing. Today is inspiration. So, I've teamed you up with another member of the group to go on a long walk on various routes for a few hours. Soak in nature and let your thoughts wander."

We all seem to be on board with that plan. Sounds like a great start.

"Okay, so I've put you two together." Gloria stands and points to Jen and Brett, the fantasy author. Then Frank and Greg, the historical author. Gloria hesitantly looks between me and Stone. "Uhm, you two." I hear her grumble something as she walks on. "Hope I don't regret this."

"What kind of luck is this?" I rub the back of my neck, frustrated.

"What a gift." Stone is not at all serious. He turns his head sharply to me. "Five minutes, meet you by the bench swing overlooking the lake."

"Yes, sir." I salute him, but it just causes him to tip his head to the side and a wry, devilish smile appears.

Oh no, did he think there was innuendo under that, in calling him sir? Now it's a thought in my head.

"Well, well, aren't we eager."

I growl a sound before we both stand to head off to get ready for our forced bonding session.

2

STONE

I hear someone walking toward the bench swing. I've been waiting for her with my arms crossed as I admire the lake, lost in thought.

"Yoo-hoo. I've arrived for my taste of misery." Harlow waves a hand in front of my face, and a prickle spreads along my body.

My train of thought about why I'm in a fog of peculiar confusion over a woman is broken. I wasn't expecting Harlow today, with her manicured nails, bouncy strawberry-blonde hair, and tight jeans and heels. She's every bit a reminder of the women who used to throw themselves at me when I played hockey. Except… she has a bite to her personality and seems to be able to stand her ground.

She surprised me by arriving at our welcome session in comfortable clothing, albeit glitter on her sneakers, and without a care in the world that she's in yoga pants. A hint that maybe she isn't her alter ego. But Harlow simply seems different to what I anticipated when I saw her name on the list. Sure, she's a little uptight. Yet, there does seem to be a casual persona hidden underneath, and it has me curious. I'm also not one to deny when someone is attractive.

I smirk when she mentioned misery. "The feeling isn't mutual." I stand taller, and my eyes lock with hers with a seriousness that feels sincere. I wonder if I have a glimmer in my eyes due to interest. Maybe she feels a small jab at her chest, and it's not as annoying as it should be.

"What does that mean?" Her voice scrapes from her throat because her breathing changes, shaking off her disapproval of me.

I need to take the high road, otherwise this will be a strenuous afternoon. Fine, I'll be the one to admit defeat. "We got off on the wrong foot. Speaking of feet, I might be blinded by the glitter on your shoes."

"Don't care," she volleys.

I clear my throat, ready to continue. "We're just opposites. We have a long walk ahead of us. No point in making it more difficult."

Yay me for taking the mature road.

She doesn't seem to be expecting it or that I don't play the game of life as everyone would anticipate. She regresses and drops her shoulders, maybe realizing that I have a point. But just then, a woman comes jogging up to us as she leaves the gym at the spa.

Oh shit, Florence.

Florence flicks her dark hair behind her shoulder and throws on an overdone smile then arches her tits out that are barely contained under her tight running t-shirt. "Stone, I thought that was you. Good to see you. Did you get my text the other day?"

Glancing to my side, I see Harlow's eyes bug out slightly.

I awkwardly scratch my cheek. "Oh, did you text?" I lie.

Florence touches my upper arm, giving my muscle a squeeze. "Totally. We should meet up soon for an after-dinner drink."

"Uh, I'm kind of busy the next few months or years." I remain composed.

Florence doesn't get the hint and just giggles before she waves goodbye to continue her run.

Harlow stands there, entertained with crossed arms. "Wow, she's perky. Sounds like someone is getting some action. Playing the field. Keeping a woman on the backburner. Probably adding her as a notch on your belt," Harlow lists.

I flex my jaw side to side, realizing this isn't helping the situation. "For your information," I say tightly, "in her wildest dreams would it happen. I'm new to town. It's not my problem the single women here are piranhas."

Harlow studies me for a second. "Trust me, my image of you hasn't changed… yet."

"Ah, so there's hope."

She huffs and rolls her eyes. "You're right, this is going to be a long afternoon. Fine. Call it a truce, and we'll start over."

I nod once, thankful we're moving on. "Hi, I'm Stone. The hockey player you think can't write." I offer her my hand.

She looks down and slowly hesitates but gives in. "Hi, I'm Harlow, the supposedly superficial woman you assume can't write."

"Seems like we have a lot in common then."

Her mouth begins to curl up into a smile. "Perhaps."

The moment our fingers touch, a spark that should be a warning hits me. I want to retract my hand instantly, but I move past it, and we shake quickly with subtle smiles on our faces.

"Come on, you're lucky that I know the area. We can follow a few shortcuts and head to Main Street so you can look at boutiques and probably grab green ice cream or something for you to take a photo of."

Now she seems amused because she can tell that I'm teasing her. "Funny."

I nudge her shoulder as we begin to walk into the forest. "We should take a detour. I really just want a milkshake," I admit.

She seems to ease, and I decide maybe our walk won't be so bad. "Do they have oat-milk smoothies, maybe with a little spinach in it?"

My face screws up. "Really? You want to go to a soda-shop-styled place with a jukebox in the corner and order a damn smoothie?"

"Yes," she says, remaining firm.

I take another deep breath, reminding myself of our truce.

When we walk farther and are under the trees, I glance over my shoulder to see the hotel is nowhere in sight and I inhale the fresh air.

"Do you actually believe in your romance crap? What the hell are the tropes again?" I ask her. My expectations are low for the genre.

"We can all escape to a fictional world, and maybe there is a lot of truth behind it. Well, actually, I'm not sure true love happens," she admits.

"Yeah, you sound convincing," I respond flatly.

"Maybe we haven't met anyone to make us believe," she strikes back.

"Hmm, maybe. I'm not sure my history with women has given me any outlook on the matter. It's a wild ride when people discover you are an overly handsome retired hockey player." I can tell she grasps that my cockiness is only half serious. I'm not that big of an ass.

She gives me wide eyes. "There you go. You just need someone to prove you wrong."

I scoff a laugh. "Not many options in Lake Spark."

"Really? I had bouncy back there pegged as wife material."

I look at her, unimpressed.

"You're living in a small town. That's romance subgenre number one." She raises a brow at me. "A lot of fictional men live in small towns."

I shake my head at this. "So, tell me, Harlow. Why don't you just write romance, you had to take it up a notch and write the dirty stuff?" I don't mind. It makes me want to unlock the filthy thoughts that must be floating in her head. I bet she has a wild side.

She stops right in her tracks, and a tightness seems to hit her entire body. I get the feeling she isn't going to tell me, and if she opens her mouth, then anything she says will be a lie.

Secrets can be fun. It gives me something to unravel.

"For two people who went into this walk a little shaky on how the mood would go, you sure are inquisitive." She brushes past answering and diverts us into a different road of our conversation as she begins to pick up her pace.

"Sorry if I'm trying to get to know my inspiration partner." I follow hot on her heels, except she's in sneakers, and still they suit her. I'm still chill as a cucumber, so I bite into my apple that I took out of my pocket.

"Why do you write? Surely, playing hockey would have set you up for life." I sense a tad of sarcasm in her words.

I chuckle at her thought as she continues to walk in front of me. "Listen, sweetheart, did we not just agree to start on a new foot?" Truthfully, it made me financially set, but I wanted to keep busy.

Harlow pauses again and glances over her shoulder, a small grin forming on her luscious lips. "We did. My bad."

"My guess is you are bad, *very* bad."

She laughs at my sentence. "Gosh, am I going to have to listen to romance jokes all day now?"

"My guess is you will throw back hockey jokes just as fast."

"Maybe." She's playing coy.

"Now come on, aren't we supposed to walk?" I mumble as I chew on my fruit.

I tread past her to take us to the trail marked with a green dot on the signpost. It will be way faster than the yellow dot that the retreat suggested.

"Do you want to be in town in twenty minutes or do you really want to do this whole two-hour indicated trail?" I ask, as I'm up for anything. "I kind of love hiking. Walking is the best exercise."

"Despite what you may think, I love hiking too."

I give her eyes that indicate *really?*

Harlow grins to herself. "Really, I do… Okay, I don't. I'm more of a Zumba kind of girl. Besides, perusing Main Street counts as inspiration, right?"

"I think so. Plus, we'll need to walk there and back, so that amounts to something."

We both have a wistfulness on our face, all traces of earlier hostility fading away. "Do you think we'll get in trouble with Gloria?" she wonders.

My lips quirk out. "You're the girl who literally loves to write bad girl on a daily basis, so something tells me you don't mind."

She playfully swats me. "Har, har. And… it's good girl."

I crack out a laugh because this woman has a good sense of humor.

"Okay, to milkshake, disgusting smoothies, and perusing," I announce and begin to walk the track, with the sticks and leaves crunching under our feet.

Throwing my apple core to the side without a thought, I'm met quickly with a sharp scolding sound hitting my ears.

"Hey! Pick that up."

My head half circles to face Harlow who doesn't appear to be joking. "What did the apple do to you?"

"Pick up the apple." Her voice is stern and adamant.

"It's an apple core." I lift my shoulders up.

Harlow gawks at me, while her hands land on her hips. "And? Are you trying to kill a deer?"

My face scrunches into confusion. "Kill a deer?"

"Yeah. Mr. Deer could show up and eat the apple then choke." She is so serious with conviction that I can't help but chortle a sound, which leaves her unimpressed.

I step closer to her, ready to debate this. "Choke on an apple?" I repeat her question, very confident of what's about to go down.

"Yes. Wouldn't you hate to be responsible for having Mr. Deer die, and then his entire deer family is without the patriarch?" She stands tall, ready to dispute me. "If it's a baby deer, then I'm sure that you're going to hell, too."

My lips press together before raising the corners of my mouth. "That's, uh… some travesty. Yeah, I should definitely think of my life mistakes." I feign concern as I bring my fingers to my chin to contemplate.

"Fine, don't take me seriously. Still, pick up the apple," she demands again.

"Harlow, why don't you pull up your phone and literally type in 'What do deer eat?' I'm sure you will find that science is on my side here, and besides, you can't live in Lake Spark without having studied the billions of deer crossing signs in the area and wonder why local people have not yet taken out the overpopulation of deer in the area with apples. Reason one is apparently they love their apples, so unless we want to go fairytale magical fruit on those creatures, then sorry, but apples are a no-go for killing the deer."

"Fairytales? As in the poisonous apple? That's a bit cruel."

I cross my arms. "Search the internet," I one-tone so we can wrap this up.

Her brows knit together before she hesitantly slides out her cell from her sweater pocket then types quickly. Her lips roll in, and she cranes her neck as she delays a response. "Okay… so it appears that deer may… eat apples." Her face falls as she realizes her error.

I smirk from accomplishment. "Oh dear, look at us having our first quarrel."

Harlow rolls her eyes and walks past me. "Fine." She throws her arms up in the air. "You're right."

Walking by her side, I keep my cheeky grin fixed. "I like hearing that roll of your tongue. It's a statement that you might be repeating often."

She shakes her head ruefully. "I would probably push you into the woods if it wasn't for the fact that underneath your exterior, I can tell that you're not that cocky." She shoots me a glance. "Doesn't mean you should have littered in the woods, though."

I hold my hands up in surrender. "I shall obey."

"Great."

"Let me guess, you're a vegetarian."

"Let me guess, you eat a lot of meat," she counters.

"I need my protein," I respond.

"Well, there are other ways to get your protein." Harlow stops again, and she winces when she realizes her word choice could be completely inappropriate, and because it's me, then of course, I only heard the inappropriate version. "I mean oats, nuts, beans."

"Nuts, hmm."

She shakes her head, getting exhausted from me. "I don't eat meat, okay… well, unless it's a warm beef sandwich with melted cheese and this special sauce. But that doesn't really count."

"I won't tell anyone," I tease.

We continue on our walk and occasionally throw a look at one another, with light smiles on our faces.

This feels like an unusual day. Can't exactly figure out why, other than the breeze feels different, lighter, new. Harlow seems to play a part. That's a little crazy considering we only just met, and we didn't make a great first impression either. However, as the day moves on, I'm beginning to wonder if maybe everything this morning happened for a reason.

Harlow intrigues me. And lucky for me, she's someone worth looking at.

"See up there?" I point to where the row of trees ends. "Main Street isn't far."

"What made you move here?" She's curious as we continue our stroll.

"I was living in Chicago, but I wanted a quieter life. I've been out here a few times, as there are a lot of hockey camps and training sessions at the sports complex in Lake Spark, and the Spinners train there. I may be retired, but I'm still very much passionate about hockey."

Her face brightens with surprise. "A true loyalist."

"Perhaps. Anyhow, when my brother became general manager for the Spinners, then he moved here recently, and we're close, so it was a no-brainer. Not to mention that I have a baby niece now."

Harlow looks at me with a soft fondness hinted on her face. "And wildlife too." She nudges my shoulder with her own. "Winter this far north scares the hell out of me. I need sun, smoothies, and a beach. I'm an only child, and my parents moved down to the Virgin Islands when they retired."

"Sounds lonely."

She smiles gently. "Nah, I have my book boyfriends."

I roll my eyes, and we continue to walk until we pass the gazebo on the grass along the lake and hit Main Street. To my surprise, Harlow doesn't want to stop inside any of the boutiques; instead, she follows me until I lead us straight to Jolly Joe's. They have great coffee and delicious ice cream, and perfect grilled cheese too. It's a

Lake Spark essential, however the jukebox in the corner seems to be reserved for tourists.

When we walk inside, Harlow quickly excuses herself to use the restroom. It's perfect timing, as I see my brother's girlfriend waiting for something to-go.

"Hey, Isla," I greet her as I arrive to stand next to her.

She looks up from her phone and gives me a warm smile. "Oh hey, thought you were at your writers' retreat thing."

"I am, but my partner for the day and I decided we should break a few rules, so here we are to order milkshakes."

"You and rule-breaking. Sounds about right." Isla hasn't been with my brother Vaughn for long, but she gets me. "Vaughn is away at the game down in Dallas next week. Want to meet up for dinner?"

We've been meeting up quite a bit lately, since my brother is away often, and Isla is alone with my baby niece. "For sure. We can do dinner and invite Nora, make it a long night with the three of us. The usual party you can expect with us," I say with a bit of humor.

"Perfect. I'll text you. Have to run to relieve the babysitter and attempt to shower in peace. Enjoy the retreat." Isla grabs her drink from the guy behind the counter and touches my shoulder in passing.

"Talk later," I say then turn around. I nearly run into Harlow who has a blank face and seems taken aback. "Everything okay?"

A sound cracks from her mouth. "Uh, yeah, totally, uhm, sounds like you're in for a party."

It takes a few seconds to try and figure out her train of thought, but then that sly grin takes over when I realize. "You have a very dirty imagination. I thought I confirmed it already, but this just cements it. What do you think you heard?"

She appears flustered now. "It's none of my business. I'm sure you and your *friend* have an… eventful relationship."

"Wow… have you not figured out that I'm single at any point today during your attempts to flirt with me?"

It gets a rise out of her. "Whoa there, Iceman, I was not flirting. You were."

"Agreed." I slip that in before continuing on my quest. "Yet just now, your mind conjured that I'm setting up… what is it?"

Her face doesn't move an inch. "As I said, none of my business." She darts her attention to the menu on the wall. "Oh, look at that, an array of milkshake choices."

I gently touch her elbow to guide her sight back to me. As amused as I am, an overbearing need to clarify hits me. "That was my brother's girlfriend, mother of my niece, local resident, Isla. Most definitely nothing going on there. We meet up for dinner when my brother is out of town, and we do invite someone else to join us… my baby niece, Nora. And because of my baby niece, then dinner can take a long time. Who knew babies needed a schedule of bath time, milk, and a pajama routine. It all makes me dizzy."

Harlow realizes what she mistook as probably my setup for a threesome. She smiles to herself awkwardly. "That does… make a lot of sense."

My head tilts to the side as I observe her and rock my lips, getting comfortable. "You like to make a lot of assumptions, and you get kind of cute when you admit when you're wrong. You easily find yourself at a loss of words, which is odd, considering you're a writer."

She bites her bottom lip, clearly enjoying the conversation that floats between us. "You seem to bring out this abnormal side of me. I'm normally a nice, clear-thinking human, I swear."

"I'm not entirely convinced."

"Hmm, what can I do to change your mind?" Her voice is 100% flirty, nearly sultry, which is why yet again she realizes the error of her ways. "Let's just, uhm, get a shake, right?"

"Depends, is that before or after you change my mind in unusual ways?" I love teasing Harlow, it's more rejuvenating than a smoothie.

Harlow studies the menu. "You're trouble, Stone." She focuses ahead. "Are we only partners today?"

"I might be able to bribe Gloria with my charm if you would like day two with me. Unless you really want to bond with Frank the sci-fi geek." I join her in reading the menu, even though I know what I want.

"I think I might just be persuaded to insist you charm Gloria," her voice slightly drifts.

Ah, so I'm not alone in feeling this connection that travels between Harlow and me. She doesn't want our day to end, nor do I.

"I'll shoot that promise straight into the net, even if it gets me sent to the penalty box," I promise.

She stifles a sound. "I'm surprised we made it this long without a hockey reference."

"Yeah, because you were too busy saying dirty things to me by accident and attempting to speak on behalf of the deer union."

Harlow drops her face into her hands, entertained. "Can we just forget about all of that?" Her eyes draw back up to meet mine. "Oh, they actually have it. A spinach and banana milkshake please, with non-dairy milk. You're buying."

"Sure. Save us a seat, and I'll be there in a sec."

"Perfect."

After ordering my usual milkshake of chocolate and cherry, I head to the booth where Harlow is staring out the window onto Main Street.

"Finding your creativity?" I interrupt.

She smiles as she brings her sight back to me. "Something like that."

"Penny for your thoughts," I pry.

Harlow rests her forehead against the glass and returns her gaze back outside. "I'm just thinking that this is the kind of small town that writers dream about. And all I seem to think is how wonderful that it's light out and the people seem to be in a safe bubble, truly happy."

I squint my eyes as I soak in her simple statement that feels as though there is more underneath the surface. She's still a mystery.

Her attention zips back to me, and the corner of her mouth raises but weakly. Until our eyes meet and the shift in the air brings an excitement inside me that, for once, isn't just fueled by a need for temporary relief. It feels as though she finds me thrilling too. That's what unexpected things do, right?

"Why do I feel like neither one of us have followed the assignment?" I softly say aloud.

We both marvel in this moment, with a gently giddy look on our faces, in agreement that we are acknowledging our start.

"Maybe because we found something better," her voice is a whisper to herself, yet she doesn't seem concerned that I heard.

I couldn't agree more.

And I'm beginning to wonder if she's the key to solving my own secret.

3

___

HARLOW

___

Gloria walks back and forth as she examines our group sitting in a circle. Her fingers steepling as if she is debating her next move.

"Well," she sighs. "It seems our plans need to change."

Yep, we're all in trouble.

She continues, "It seems that our afternoon of inspiration took a turn. Brett and Jennifer got lost, and it required the forest ranger to save them. Frank and Greg decided that saving a lost dog, although noble, was their mission for the afternoon." Gloria stops in front of Stone and me. "And you two decided to ditch the trail and head into town for milkshakes." I open my mouth, but she raises her finger to stop me. "Yes, I saw you two cozied up at Jolly Joe's while I was exiting the general store with supplies."

Stone raises his hand to calm her. "Whoa there with the accusations."

Jennifer gently pats Brett's arm. "See, I told you they had vibes."

Stone and I scan the room, kind of in surprise that we've become the gossip of the group. Stone ignores everyone. "Jolly Joe's is an establishment full of inspiration. Just the other day Sheriff Carter had a breakup with the new nurse in town. I'm sure in Harlow's world she's already concocting a reunion in her head."

"Yeah," I state a little too boldly. I don't, but fine, I'll roll with this.

Gloria doesn't look amused and instead claps her hands together and surveys the room again. "Well, I think that our change of plans calls for self-reflection time and writing. We'll reconvene tomorrow morning bright and early, ready to share how our word count went this evening. We'll head straight into editing techniques tomorrow morning to avoid any of you veering off course."

Stone leans into me to whisper, "This no longer feels like a retreat. Did we just get schooled?"

"Tell me about it. I'm questioning ditching tomorrow and heading to the spa."

Everyone begins to stand to depart the room.

"Want to grab dinner? I have connections to get us a good table at the restaurant here. There is normally a waiting list," Stone asks, maybe a little too hopeful.

To my surprise, the day took a turn, and it was an enjoyable afternoon with him. A click between us that I can't ignore. As great as that sounds, though, it's all the more reason to take a step back.

"I'm kind of stuffed from that shake, and evening is my prime writing time. Maybe a rain check?"

"That would imply you want to see me another time."

I sputter a sound. "Well, we are stuck together for a few days, so it does seem likely."

"Lucky me." He flashes me a suave grin before he heads off.

I can't help but smile to myself. He's a peculiar soul. For sure, at first appearance, he seems like a stereotypical athlete with a personality problem. But when you scrape the surface, he has a few specks of softness and something else, I can only determine it to be confidence. It crossed my mind what he would be like with a woman, but as soon as that thought entered my mind, I pushed it away out of habit.

But I'm not sure if it's a habit at all.

By the time I get to my room, I'm tired and eager to strip out of my clothes and take a shower. I don't head into my pajamas, though, and instead opt for jeans and a t-shirt. My social media posts will have to wait for tomorrow morning because I did nab a quick photo earlier of my shake.

Taking a seat behind the desk, I bring my knee to my chest as I open my laptop and prepare myself to write. Admittedly, the inspirational walk in the woods, although rules were broken, fulfilled Gloria's goal. Ideas are swirling in my head. I don't write small-town romance, mostly billionaire assholes, but our publisher insists I maybe need to head into another direction. I'm dreading that.

I have one problem tonight, though.

I'm supposed to be writing a spicy chapter. This is my ultimate escape. Where I can do anything I want through a fictitious character. Tonight, it just seems to be a problem, because halfway through, Stone enters my thoughts.

A picture of him pinning my arms above my head against a wall with one hand, while the tips of his fingers glide up my thigh, dragging my skirt with. Our eyes connect while he gives me a warning smirk before crashing his lips onto mine.

I close my laptop in a flash, also with a little force.

Shit.

But wait...

A relieved smile begins to stretch on my lips as a sting forms in my throat from emotion when I realize that he's invading my thoughts in a good kind of way. It's been a long while since I've experienced that.

I search the room, and the dim lights constrict my chest for a short moment, and although I see a comfortable bed, I know that sleep won't really happen, just as it never does.

I glance at the clock I see that it's only eleven, which means the hotel bar must still be open.

Grabbing a sweater and my key, I head straight for some alcohol.

By the time I'm walking into the bar, with its chestnut interior and leather chairs, I've decided that a red wine is calling my name.

Just as I sit on a stool at the bar, I notice the occupant next to me. Maybe it's a coincidence or fate just leading us.

Stone looks far too sexy in jeans and a tight dark tee.

"Oh, look at that, Harlow is here. Probably hoping that I was enjoying a drink too." Stone doesn't look at me, but I can see his lips tighten around his beer bottle as he takes a sip, and it's clear he's grinning.

I indicate to the bartender for my order. "Clearly you read my mind," I play along.

He turns to me, pleased with my arrival. "What brings you down here?"

I focus on Stone. "I'm not the greatest sleeper, so I'm hoping the wine helps," I admit. "You?"

"Writing wasn't really calling to me, and after my workout, I decided to enjoy an excellent IPA."

"Nothing to do with checking out the staff of your hotel?"

He shakes his head. "I only have a tiny stake in this place. It's my buddy Holden who runs the show. There is Nash who owns 10%. His parents used to own the joint. They insisted that they would only sell if 10% would stay in the family. He's gone rogue, though. For me, this is purely an investment that one day I can use to impress some-one. Otherwise, nobody knows about my role here."

My eyes scrunch. "You told me," I point out.

His eyes brim. "Call it instinct, and I wanted to piss you off a little more when Stuart was arranging your squirrel-hut room."

I now find that comical. "Well, your secret is safe with me. How did you get into writing? We kind of skipped the conversation that we probably should have had when we were debating the civilization of deer." I don't mind making fun at my moments of crazy. I own it.

"Believe it or not, I was valedictorian in high school. Mostly because creative writing managed to get me a few awards. Mix that with hockey and I was the dream kid for colleges to offer me a schol-arship. Great at hockey, and they didn't have to worry about me struggling with grades. Even during my hockey career, I would write recollections of games I played, little things I noticed. Then there was the occasional best-man speech where I had the guests laughing, then in tears."

My cheeks rise at his admission. "See, you might be more of a romantic than me."

He shakes his head. "Anyhow, my hockey career ended a few years after going pro. Some asshole hit me behind the knee. Despite physical therapy, I didn't have it in me to play anymore."

I nod my head to thank the bartender for my wine but keep my focus on Stone. "I might have searched you on the internet to grab a few facts."

Stone raises his brows. "Ooh, you know I'm going to bug you about that for a long time." He turns to look behind the bar then nudges my shoulder with his. "But I kind of searched you too."

I take a sip of my wine. "Find anything interesting?"

"Nah, just pictures of books with juices and enough olive green to blind me."

"That is Harlow Olive's life," I agree.

He glances sidelong me. "Why do you write?"

My lips slide side to side, as the reason is one that I've rehearsed many times. "It's an escape. Sometimes ideas enter our heads, and we have to get them out, otherwise we'll get consumed. Plus, romance is fun and gives people a few hours of relaxation."

"You must have had a great love life to lead you to romance, no?"

"The opposite. I had a few long-term boyfriends years ago but nothing serious in retrospect. Actually, they were kind of jerks, so maybe I'm writing my dream guys to compensate," I joke.

"I really need to buy one of your books and then ask you to high-light the good parts for me."

We're back to flirting again. "You mean the dirty parts."

"If you insist."

I can't help but smile. "You have a sense of humor, I'll give you that. So why are you on this retreat?"

He rubs his stubbled jaw because it's the end of the day, and it just makes the image of him more sweltering. Made worse by the fact that he seems to have no clue of his appeal that makes many women melt, I'm sure. But I do my best to sit here casually. "Simple. Our publisher says I need to change up my view on my plot. So far that plan has kind of gone to shit in terms of why I'm here. You?"

"Same, they think I need to clear my head and change direction."

Stone's face goes puzzled. "You mean write about hockey players?"

"I don't know, but sports bore the hell out of me." And writing about sports just kind of irritates me. I choose my own direction, not somebody else's.

"You said writing is perhaps a distraction, so you don't really believe in it all, do you?"

I huff out a sound and sigh. "Truthfully, I'm not sure, but some things, yes. Second chances, for example."

His head bobs side to side. "Okay, maybe that makes sense. Not that relighting a flame with an ex would ever cross my mind."

"You can be attracted to your opposite. Your enemy can seriously become your lover, that's why people have hate sex all the time," I list.

A cheeky look returns to his face. "Are you saying that I might become your lover, considering this morning you really wanted to throttle me?"

A blush hits me in full force, and my face instantly warms from his sentence. It's an image flashing in my mind now, and I feel a wave of sensitivity between my legs. "No, uh… of course not." I swallow his statement to shake it off.

"Keep going," he encourages.

"Accidental pregnancy is another," I add.

He laughs and seems ready to give me another shocker. "You're going to love this. My brother Vaughn and Isla had an accidental pregnancy… but she didn't tell him until she was about to deliver the baby."

My jaw drops. "What? Like a secret pregnancy kind of thing?"

"Totally, but they're together now and finding their way."

This is like discovering gold. My hands splay out. "See, maybe it's all realistic, and I have it all wrong."

"Ah, you still seem kind of unconvinced." He remains firm.

I've nearly finished my wine because time seems to be flying, but I don't want this conversation to end. We could talk for hours.

"Did you get your goodnight cookie?" Stone asks to change the topic.

Twisting the stem of my wine glass, I focus on that to avoid the handsome man next to me. "I did. A warm chocolate chip cookie, nearly heaven, except sleep might be better." If only I could.

"You should try sandalwood oil if you have trouble sleeping. They say it can send you into a deep sleep and chase away bad thoughts. My brother's girlfriend stands by having a dreamcatcher above their daughter's bed too. Won't let her sleep without it."

My brows lift softly. "I'll try it. Thanks." I've already attempted everything else.

He quickly brushes us past the topic on to new things. "Holden, the guy running the Dizzy Duck Inn, is also a retired athlete," he notes.

I'm in awe. "What's with this town? It's like 'Welcome to Lake Spark. We have crossing signs for deer, ducks, and hockey players.'"

A deep chuckle roars from the back of his throat. "Something like that. But ever since The Spinners decided to leave Chicago to train with more focus, they settled here in Lake Spark where the owner lives. Naturally, it draws retired players here, and they fall in love with the charm."

My lips quirk out. "I guess that makes sense."

"You'll have to come back to examine all of us in our habitat. That should help with your writing."

I laugh. "There is that hilarity again."

"Trust me, when it comes to other things, I'm anything but." He sips from his beer and realizes what he just said could be taken out of context, and I already did.

"Aw, so you're serious and dominant when it requires a lack of clothing." I have no problem saying that as a matter of fact.

He leans in closer to me, and the heat of his presence brings a wave of warmth that flames along my body. "Yes. But you don't always need to take the clothing off to find satisfaction. I'm sure you write about that too."

I want to move closer to him, as I have an unexplainable need to touch his cheek with my fingers. Alas, I refrain myself.

"This is probably my cue to escape," I whisper with an edge in my voice. I'm uneasy, partly because he's enticing.

"I'm a gentleman, believe it or not, and I respect that move." He turns to the barman. "You can put her wine on my tab. Then again, this is my place, so no need to have a tab anyway."

"That's considerate of you," I tell him.

"I guess for you, I can be. Other than for my family and you, it seems, I'm a grumpy-as-fuck guy. Stuart at reception normally takes my wrath."

"Poor kid." I stand and softly touch his shoulder. "Thanks for today. Even if you were an irritating jerk this morning. You didn't stay my enemy for long."

"But I'm not your lover." He's referencing our trope talk, except there is a hint underlying.

"Time will tell." It barely escapes my lips, and again, I awkwardly pop my mouth, as it feels like the hundredth time today that innate honesty has escaped me.

He smirks and chooses not to tease me back. Inside he's probably fulfilled by his effect on me. "Sweet dreams, Harlow."

Our eyes hold for a second longer, a rope unwinding between us, with my body easing.

"You too, Stone."

Walking away, I feel his eyes on me. It flickers an unfamiliar feeling inside of me. I'm not sure why this guy fell into my world.

But it's hopeful.

Stopping to get one more glimpse of Stone, a twitch hits my lips.

Silly me for thinking I could ignore the facts during this week. They are still there.

I'll never tell Stone my secret. I have to ignore this unrealistic optimism that maybe Stone Madden will be the one to unravel it.

4

STONE

Throwing my pen onto my leatherbound notebook, I heave a deep sigh. This lady needs to get laid or loosen a notch somewhere to ease up. Gloria is my new enemy number one.

Who the hell makes a group write in their notebooks at a great restaurant? I'm grateful that the waiter just brought a few bottles of wine to the table to end the tyrant's demands of stirring our thoughts.

We're at Catch 22 here in Lake Spark for dinner with the retreat group. Apparently bonding on day two was on Gloria's agenda, after a day of workshops about deep narrative and editing your manuscript before you send it to your editor. Sure, some people are finding it useful and writing up a storm on our breaks. Me? Meh, I use breaks for breaks.

But luckily, Harlow ended up sitting next to me most of the day, not that we could talk much as we listened to Gloria. Just a shame that we're not alone now as the sun sets over the lake. Catch 22 is casual enough, still with enough classiness for a good ambiance, with its dock outside. A lot of the locals come here for lunch or evening dates. Why that thought comes to my head, I kind of know why.

Harlow is completely under my skin. She's beautiful, and I judged her wrong. Doesn't mean I can't tease her that she's wearing long earrings and taking a picture of her notebook next to a candle on the table.

When her head tilts to the side to offer me a subtle look that informs me that she's content, I'm even more entranced.

"This isn't turning out like I imagined. I mean, well, the retreat," Harlow mentions. "I've been stuck with you, and if I hear the words escape or inspiration one more time from anyone, then I might just throw my laptop into that lake." She chuckles to herself.

I grab the bottle of white wine, ready to get this evening started. "I'm not sure that would work. The lake might be too shallow to give your laptop a proper goodbye. Might want to add a few weights to the thing."

She laughs and her face brightens. I hate how her lip gloss is a little too much. She doesn't need it, yet it completes its goal, drawing me in to stare at her mouth.

"So, what's good here?" She seems chipper.

"You mean your rabbit food?" Harlow throws me a playful scowl. "I've heard the beet salad with goat cheese is not bad, and for the main entrée, the pumpkin cranberry loaf is in season, with this apparently mouthwatering sage-butter sauce. I'm not much help, as I normally grab a steak for dinner… need to fuel these guns." I flex my biceps.

She squints her eyes. "Oh yeah? I didn't notice that you work out." She's sarcastic, and that's not something many women I've been around have managed to pull off.

"What was your word count today?" Jennifer attempts to make conversation from my side.

"Only 1200," Harlow replies.

"Am I supposed to be counting?" My tone is flippant.

Jennifer grins. "You're making this whole trip a bit more eventful, Stone. Saving us from Commander Gloria over there." She indicates to the head of the table.

"Offer Gloria *lots* of wine," Harlow suggests.

"I bet you by dessert we can get her slipping up with a few embarrassing stories from her college years. Something tells me she's a wild one," I mention.

"Hopefully." Jennifer turns her attention back to Frank sitting next to her.

Harlow leans back in her chair to examine me. "Do you ever have a serious moment?"

"Trust me, I had enough to last me a lifetime," I assure her. "Childhood, ending my hockey career, to name a few."

She grabs her wine glass. "May I ask about your upbringing?"

I drop my head before lifting it back up because this woman somehow feels easy to talk to. "Our dad bailed, and our mom did it all on her own. She's married now and focuses on her life in Arizona. And my sports career? Nobody wants to see something like that end early."

"What happens in life only makes us stronger," she remarks.

That's the right mindset to have. "I believe that. What non-happy memories make *you* stronger?"

Harlow stalls for a second and then bites her bottom lip. "Uh, not drinking a good wine. We should focus on enjoying this evening." Again, an air of mystery surrounds her.

The waiter arrives to take our order, and I hand over my menu after I tell him a Caesar salad and steak medium done. Harlow seems to have listened to my advice and orders what I suggested.

I lean to the side to speak low. "You seem like a woman who listens well." My voice is sweltering with a desire I can't deny.

It's been a while since I've spent the night with a woman. My bedroom style tends to be a little too dominant, and I'm not used to wanting something without diving in full force on the physical front, then I just leave it all there, I don't need more. With Harlow, slow seems to be my calling. That isn't really my character, but I can't seem to shake that feeling.

Her face flushes to a pink that I've seen a few times today, as if her cheeks are burning.

She clears her throat, and her eyes dip down. "I can only imagine that's what you like."

My eyes bug out that her train of thought is on the same wavelength, and she has me figured out.

"Either you read me well or you've simply written that scenario far too many times. Actually, I know you have. I read a passage from one of your books earlier today, the one about a billionaire who needs a fake fiancée."

Harlow's head whips in my direction. "Oh?"

"Your imagination is by far dirtier than I could have guessed. Is it rope or handcuffs that you enjoy more?" Fuck, her scenes get me hard, and I can picture her in every single one.

She coughs from nerves. "I should feel completely uncomfortable right now. But I don't mind admitting what I write, I have nothing to be ashamed about. I'm just not used to a man relaying what he thinks about my writing."

I take another sip of wine. "Trust me, I skipped the parts about almost-kisses and tension-filled elevator rides. Went straight to the good stuff. However, from what I read, you have talent."

Harlow slides her tongue across her bottom lip then settles on the corner of her mouth, trying to figure out how to reply. "I'm kind of happy wine is present. Ah, I read the opening page of your book that you shared earlier in the workshop. Admittedly, kind of boring, but the words flow, and I would never guess a guy who spent so many hours on the ice could create such a page." She holds her hand up. "Yeah, yeah, yeah, I know I'm stereotyping."

"Nice of you to admit that."

Her eyes roam the room and land on the floor-to-ceiling windows overlooking the lake.

"Want to get some air?" I suggest.

Her gaze snaps to me, with her eyes agreeing. "A good idea."

We both take our wine glasses and stand to leave the table. After we slide open the door to outside, she walks straight to the railing to soak in the view of twilight, the stars gracing us with their presence. It's a halfmoon this evening.

Harlow wraps her arms around her body, as it's a little chilly out.

"I always thought the moon in fall is special. It has a different hue. More profound and a warning of change in the months ahead," I comment.

She turns to rest her back against the railing while I still look forward, leaning onto the banister. "That's a whimsical thought."

I lift a shoulder then sink it back down. "Maybe that's why I moved here too. The sky is clearer and encourages a blank slate in your mind. I heard people here go a little overboard around Halloween, the pie competition gets out of hand, too."

Harlow smiles, and the hanging lights outline her peaceful eyes locked on me. "The night can be many things, Stone. It's good that you see it in a way that is hopeful."

I want to stroke my thumb along her cheek and slide down to trace her bottom lip. It's an innate need inside of me that I choose not to act on, considering I'm sure our group is eyeing us through the window. I don't mind, though; it would be impossible for them to miss the connection that's a current between Harlow and me.

"I'm happy that I came to this ruse of a retreat," she admits. "Maybe a piece inside of me needed to break away, and it took this to do it. I'm ready to let the words flow."

"Is it the ruse of the retreat?" I'm going to dig until she confesses that she's feeling this aptitude to stay close to one another.

A wry smile hits her lips, and she shakes her head once side to side. "Nah, it's the company we keep."

"Isn't that a movie?"

"No clue. It just sounds fitting."

We stare at one another, getting lost in a moment that keeps occurring. "Do you think you will come back to Lake Spark?" I wonder and may even be optimistic.

Harlow shrugs. "Don't have much reason to. Without this retreat, I never would have known this town was on the map."

My eyes widen. "Your hockey research needs improvement then. The Spinners are kind of making waves in the league."

"Oops. I better listen tomorrow during Gloria's research workshop," she quips before silence falls on us for a few ticks. "To answer your question, I kind of have a busy schedule happening the next few months. The publisher planned a few signings for me."

"I see." A slight disappointment flinches inside of me.

Now an awkwardness breezes into our air as we pause for a moment.

"Well, we should probably head back in. Looks like the waiter arrived with the food," she notes.

"Probably a good idea."

After we head inside, there seems to be a shuffle of seat assignments, and the seat next to me is now occupied by Brett, while Harlow is across the table listening to Jeff. Still, Harlow's eyes catch with mine for a mere second before she goes back to pretending to listen to Jeff talk about zombies or the equivalent of a snooze fest.

Maybe Harlow is placing a little distance between us. Doesn't mean the zap of attraction lessens even the slightest. I'm afraid that it only ups the ante.

Dinner goes by slower than I hoped. It's a welcome ending when Gloria taps her glass of sherry with a few giggles because she seems to have proven us all right that her handle on alcohol is minimal.

"I hope everyone got a chance to turn off their writing minds for a few hours, and that alone helps rejuvenate your juices—for writing, of course." My face scrunches at her odd choice of wording and wonder where she is taking us direction wise. "You should have a long night." All of our heads tilt in surprise at Gloria's boldness. "I mean, a long night of sleep and rest." Right, sure, totally, that's what she meant. "Anyhow, I'm sure everyone will get back to the hotel safely. We can share a few taxis, or you are free to explore town. The walk isn't too far either. Just remember the first session tomorrow is 8am."

The lady seems a little pale from embarrassment, but I'll just add this to the memory bank of retreat good times.

Everyone shuffles around the table, and a few of us decide that walking around Main Street sounds like the best way to round off the night. Even though the center of Lake Spark is small, Catch 22 is a bit more out in the surroundings, creating a little distance, but we can follow the sidewalk along the shore.

And that's when it happens.

Harlow gravitates back to me as the others walk up ahead of us. I believe on purpose, we trail behind.

"So we meet again," she greets me.

"It's not a coincidence," I confirm.

She shakes her head. "I think not."

"I have no complaints."

"I guess neither do I."

We stroll slowly along the sidewalk, side by side, with my hands in my pocket as my eyes map out the steps we take forward. I try not to count how many it takes until I get to touch her.

"Is this what you do on your evenings in Lake Spark? Walk around?" Harlow tries to make conversation.

"Not so much. My friend who handles the day-to-day running of the Dizzy Duck, we often meet for drinks. Nonetheless, we tend to drink at the bar there. When my brother is in town, then the schedule kind of revolves around my niece, so we hang at their house."

"Still sounds tranquil. Where I live in Florida, there are great art expos and cafés, but I sometimes feel it's missing that community coziness or charm."

"But at least you have the warm weather."

She scoffs a laugh. "A writer would tell you that a cold winter is all the more reason to be stuck in a cabin together."

I laugh. "Sounds about right. Let me guess, he's a billionaire or brother's best friend?"

Harlow swats my arm, and I pretend to be hurt. "I'm pegging you as a secret lover of the genre. You have nailed down every cliché."

"It's kind of easy to figure out. Anyway, ready for your last day tomorrow?"

She hums a sound. "I'll be out of the clutches of Gloria's stern eyes. However, I will miss the fact that I can get away without thinking about much right now."

"Just admit it, I've been the key to turning your work retreat into a delightful vacation." I bring a hand to my heart.

"Oh yes, Stone. The true highlight." She's being sarcastic.

The banter between us has been an instant click from moment one. I'll miss it.

I get a glimpse of Harlow at my side, and she's wrapping her hair around her hand and sweeping her locks to one side.

"May I ask what you were writing about in your journal? It's a classic journal, and the pages have a sort of crinkle that gives the book a mature artistic flare. But it's your eyes focused on your fancy pen while writing that has me interested," she notes.

"Hmm, so you've been watching me." It's all I heard, ignoring the fact that the contents of my pages are for my eyes only.

"Don't do that. We both know we've been observing each other when we think nobody is looking." She's going the honesty route, not sugarcoating a damn thing.

My head dips down, but I peer up to focus on her angelic face. "Why, whatever will I do when you leave? I'll have nothing to stare at except for maybe a deer eating an apple."

She nudges my arm with her own, enjoying my humor. "You'll be fine. You said it yourself that you keep busy with your family."

We resume our slow walk, ignoring the rest of the group way up ahead as the pavement curves through the gazebo square at the start of Main Street. "That is true."

"Do you want a family one day?"

My eyes bug out. "Wow, we took a serious turn in our investigation of one another." She chuckles, and the sound seeps into my body and floods my veins. "I think one day. It's not really on my radar, to be honest."

"Same. I'm indifferent."

I'm trying to stay calm, but Harlow makes me anxious in the best possible way.

The group ahead looks back at us. "We're going to head back to the inn, will you two be all right?" Frank asks.

"I'm a local, remember? We're fine," I call out.

They're already heading off when Harlow throws a frown at me. "Deciding our agenda for the night? Speaking on my behalf?"

I growl under my breath at all the ways our night could go. "Just doing what I do best… leading."

That bashful flush hits her cheeks again. It's kind of unexpected. I just assumed her sexual confidence would be above average considering what she writes. However, all indications have been that she's shy, yet interested in how I could worship her.

My eyes stay transfixed on her, and I wish I could kiss the breath out of her. Every time her lashes flutter, I'm digging myself further into a hole of need. Yet, I'm not sure why, but something tells me not to push.

We continue to walk and take in the night. It's quiet except for a few people. All the store windows have picturesque displays, which brings a special ambience to every evening in Lake Spark.

"I've heard when they head into the winter decorative light season, they have horse-drawn carriages."

She looks at me strangely. "Is this place like a fairytale or something? Will I wake from a dream?"

I chuckle before we grow quiet for a beat. "It's a great night for a stroll."

"Yeah. It's been a while since I've done this," Harlow explains. I notice how she's absorbing this evening with what feels like a fresh view. Her breaths are deep and relaxed.

"I should do it more often, I guess."

A short laugh escapes her. "Before your arctic Illinois winter, why yes, you should."

"Sure beats hurrica—"

Without warning, a noise catches us off guard, as I don't see the teenager until I partially turn to see him coming out from the alley behind us with a trash bag for the curb. He must work at the general store.

But it doesn't matter.

Harlow's gripping my arm tightly, and her gasp could cut the air.

Her body tenses, and her immediate change in demeanor is noticeable.

"You okay? It's just a kid. It's Lake Spark, we only worry about pissed-off raccoons."

My words seem to fall on deaf ears. Examining Harlow, she's in near shock, and her breathing turns heaving.

Her arm wraps tighter around mine, and her breath only gets heavier. Is she having a panic attack?

"Can we just get out of here?" She sounds terrified, with an urgency in her voice.

My inclination tells me not to question or even try to comfort her. Still, I'm kind of taken by surprise. "Yeah, sure." I have to ignore my thoughts and just follow her cues.

We say nothing on our entire walk to the inn, with her arm bound to mine. I just detect how Harlow is agitated, with her eyes frozen.

The moment we arrive at the Dizzy Duck, she's through the front door so fast that I'm nearly struggling to keep up.

But I don't let her out of my sight and follow her up the stairs until she's at her room door, fumbling with her keys because the hotel uses traditional keys.

A puzzle piece hits me.

I gently touch her arm and ease the key out of her fingers as she stares blankly at the door.

"Let me do that for you," I offer softly.

I jiggle the key into the hole, and when the door is slightly ajar, she doesn't take a step.

I patiently wait for a clue what I should do. "Harlow… are you okay?"

She takes a deep breath, and her eyes slide to meet mine. While my eyes are trapped in observation, hers are pooling with tears.

"Congratulations, you discovered my secret," she says before she disappears into her room, closing the door, with thoughts stirring inside me that cause my chest to still.

The puzzle piece was a discovery.

The reason she writes.

Because sometimes we write to conquer our fears of past events.

Inside I crack for her. It's sympathy for sure, anger at whoever did something to her, and the overpowering need to not walk away.

I may have discovered her secret, the one she probably wouldn't want me to know.

So I'll offer her my own.

A secret for a secret.

5

HARLOW

The ripples in the lake mirror my mood in this moment.

It's mid-morning, and in one sense I feel numb, but maybe deep down, and I hate to admit it, I feel relieved that someone sneaked a peek into the side of my life that is sometimes lonely.

I'm not sure that I wanted it to be Stone. The connection that has been developing between us has been an uplifting surprise. Now, it's been ruined by my own fears that I can't seem to shake.

There is a reason that I hate the night and withdraw into a room behind a laptop.

The night brings out demons that I can't seem to shake.

Except the last few days, I've gotten a glimpse of near normal. At least when a certain former hockey player is nearby.

The feeling of someone approaching should make me tense, but I know it's him.

Stone.

Arriving at my side, he offers me a coffee. "Hey, you missed the morning session."

"I don't drink coffee," I say as my eyes lift up to admire the view.

"Learned a new fact about you then. More for me." Stone's voice sounds slightly delicate which causes me to jolt my sight to him as he sets the cups down on a nearby table next to the wooden seats.

"I'm not going to break if that's what you're worried about."

His lips purse out, and his subtle comforting smile for once doesn't feel like pity. "I don't think you are."

A silence overtakes us, as we're both unsure of what to say.

I might as well halt the conflict of that predicament. "I write for reasons that nobody understands." He listens patiently. "And before you ask, yeah, it's probably what you think. What can I say? People have an evil side to do things to others."

His head drops down, and he sighs. "I wasn't going to ask, but the dots kind of connected."

My cheeks stretch out from the air blowing from my mouth. He must think I'm a victim who has issues.

He reaches his fingers out to touch my shoulder softly. "Your secret is safe with me." I don't say anything. "I discovered one of yours, so I think to keep it fair I'll share mine. A secret for a secret."

Surprise flares in my eyes as I trap myself in our usual tied-together, unexplainable way.

"You don't have to," I offer.

"I want to. It's not really in comparison to yours, not at all actually. I have writer's block. My editor is expecting something in a month, and I keep getting stuck because of baggage that I should have let go of years ago. After my hockey career ended, I pretended it was some sort of fate. In truth, I was so depressed about it. What's worse is I kept thinking of my asshole dad who left me and my brother. Having nightmares that he was standing on the ice, smirking, that he expected no less from a fuck-up of a son."

I'm not sure what to make of it. Appreciative for sure that he's opened up. Yet it's not clear what I should say.

He continues, "Parents have an uncanny knack of screwing up our thoughts early in life if they're not careful. Truthfully, everyone has moved on except me. My mom with her husband and Vaughn with fatherhood, that I'm sure he's more capable of than I could be.

And here I am with the pressure on, thinking I wanted someone to notice me while everyone gets their happy ending… it all lacks the confidence that I normally carry."

It seems he has self-analyzed his own life to a T. I ask instead, "Your writer's block is stirring it all up?"

He nods.

"I'm sure your words will come back," I assure him.

Stone tucks his hands into his jeans pockets to turn his attention out to the lake. "Probably, but I have a lot of people building this up as some former hockey star writing this amazing book. The pressure is there."

"Sometimes finding a corner to be alone and writing everything that you wish would happen is the best way."

"That's what you do? Write what you're afraid to do in real life?"

"It's a bit more than that. It's my safe space. I'm not scared of anything that happens on the page. No risk of a panic attack or feeling guilty for what I would want if I was capable."

He draws his breath in, and yet again he is at a loss for words. Stone indicates his head back to the inn. "Want to ditch another session and do that walk we probably should have done on our first day?"

A change of scene is probably the best solution for this morning full of mixed emotions.

My mouth twitches. "Sounds perfect."

The comforting smile he offers sparks a feeling of safe calm inside me that's been flickering the past few days… because of him.

We both head straight for the entrance to the forest.

"Let me know if we need to stop for wild animals and leave them a note when their town hall meeting is. I heard humans are out to get them, and they must take action at once," he teases.

An honest smile begins to haunt my lips for the first time today. "You're really never going to let that go, are you?"

"Not a chance. And I would certainly never imply that we will cross paths again, because you're suggesting that I will have more opportunities to taunt you." I could swear there is optimism hidden behind his statement.

"Maybe so." I hope so too.

We continue our walk, this time ditching the shortcut into town. The tall trees act as protection from the sky, or rather the gentle breeze that requires a sweater.

"Tell me something I don't know," he says.

I chortle. "I hate bread that's been in the freezer. It feels like a crime."

He laughs, and it's deep and hearty, masculine and strong. "Maybe I agree, unless it's bagels. That's totally cool to freeze."

"Hmmm, maybe. Something about you?"

"I have a thing for cactuses in my house. Not sure how that came to be."

I look at him strangely. "I guess it's the manliest of plants."

"I'm also a baby whisperer. I can get my niece to calm down in four minutes and fifteen seconds flat." He snaps his fingers. "Yeah, we've timed it."

I'm impressed, and he must observe it on my face. "Whoa. You have a cuddly side."

"Nah, I just enjoy quiet, and the screech of a baby can be a headache," Stone says, trying to downplay it.

I kick a pinecone out of the way. "I have a thing for animal crackers shaped as dinosaurs. They're so good." He bursts out laughing. I shrug "What?" My voice rises. "You asked, and I'm delivering."

"Okay, you should probably question that more. But hey, I have a thing for deep-frying turkey for the holidays, but at least that's a normal thing. I do it all the time with my brother."

"Poor turkeys. Contributing to Stone Madden's protein diet." God, my chest feels empty of any ill feelings. It feels near jubilant. I'm not thinking about anything but the decent conversation we're having. It's keeping me occupied in only having a better day.

Stone leads the way, and we turn onto another pathway that has a steady incline. "Not going to lie, I'm circling us back to the inn.

We'll sneak past Gloria who probably gave up on us already yesterday."

"Why are we heading back?"

"Rain's coming. You can feel it in the air."

I chuckle. "Are you a boy scout or something?"

"Nah, but it sounded legit. Plus, I have a better idea."

"What would that be?"

He flashes me a mischievous frown. "You'll meet me at the indoor pool."

"I didn't bring a swimsuit."

"Doesn't matter." My eyes go wide, and his smoldering gaze hits me. "No, naked only crossed my mind for a second, maybe three. But that's not happening."

Now, I'm intrigued, which is why I agree. "Okay. I'll follow your wicked ways and ditch the rest of the day."

"You always listen to me." There is that sizzling innuendo again, causing my body to warm a degree or two, with my nipples growing sensitive and tingly. I'm forgetting about my lack of sleep and numb morning before he came along.

———

STARING at Stone as we stand next to the pool, shoeless and with my sweater removed, so I'm only in leggings and a t-shirt, I'm waiting for an explanation.

Luckily, we're all alone. The pool is a gorgeous turquoise tile, with a pattern on the bottom of the clear water. It seems to be heated, as a thin level of steam grazes the water's edges.

"Do you trust me?" he asks, and his hand shoots out, inviting me to take it. Without hesitation, I do. "Jump in with me."

My face puzzles. "We're wearing clothes."

"Makes it all the better. Jump in with me," he encourages, firm in tone, as if he won't give up on me.

I squeeze his hand. "This is unusual, probably crazy, but... I'm in."

"Yeah, we are."

He yanks me with him, causing me to jump into the water with him. The warmth envelops me until my feet touch the bottom of the pool, not so deep that my head goes under. It happens so fast that I can't even adjust to this scene, until I can, and my face shades to elation.

"Really, what are we doing?"

"We're going underwater. Then you can scream as loud as you want without anyone hearing."

"Won't you hear?"

Stone shrugs. "Do you mind?"

I shake my head no; I want to follow his guidance. "What's the point of this?"

"Releases tension, any shitty feelings that you might have. A way to get rid of negative energy, because I sure as hell don't believe in that energy-of-the-moon crap."

"Oh? That surprises me," I deadpan.

A droll smile spreads on his mouth. "Are you in, Harlow?"

I roll my eyes. "I'm in a pool in my clothes, might as well make this worth it."

"Good. On the count of two."

"Why not three?"

"That's too expected."

That answer fits perfectly. Nothing goes as planned in life.

"Okay."

"One. Two."

We both drop under the water, and nerves hit me as I try to figure out if this is ridiculous or not. But when he holds his fingers up to count, I follow.

I scream.

The muffled sound hits my ears, which only encourages me to yell harder. Then a current swims down my veins, hitting my chest. Anger hits me, and I scream more.

I focus on letting out every negative thought that hit me today, maybe even from the past two years. It feels so damn helpful.

Even when my breath begins to lose steam, swimming up feels as though I'm leaving bricks at the bottom of the water.

Gasping for air, I'm met with Stone's wry smile, and I know my own face must appear exhilarated. "That was…"

"What we needed," he finishes my sentence.

"Do that often?" I wonder.

"All the time," he states simply then snickers. "Actually never. Just thought it was a good idea."

I splash water at him. "Seems like you are full of ideas. It will come to you—what to write, I mean."

"I just needed some inspiration." It barely escapes, and his jaw ticks, his eyes locked on mine.

That overwhelming air circles around us. "Turns out this retreat did what it was supposed to do," I say softly.

"Yeah." It's delicate. Stone seems to realize he is lost in his gaze and shakes it off. "Gloria should be fired, though."

I chuckle. "Probably." I push the water around me with my arms. "As much as standing in a pool is fun. I believe we now have to head back to our rooms dripping wet." His head recoils, and my eyes close from my choice of words. "That just happened again… sentences taken completely out of context."

"It's your intuitive thoughts. I'm just along for the ride." His smug look signals victory before he begins to walk to the steps of the pool.

My head lolls to the side then bows down, as I enjoy our banter that it seems my soul needed.

"I guess I'll change, and I think I want to write for a while. Ideas have kind of hit me."

He grins even more as he leaves the pool. "I'm your muse. Don't deny it."

Yes, but I wish you weren't.

He will forever cross my mind when I write scenes that I will now imagine involving him.

Following him out of the pool, he hands me a big fresh white towel from the shelf at the side for guests. We both pat our bodies, even though it's pointless, as we're soaked through.

Then it sputters out of my mouth. "Want to grab dinner later?"

A cheekiness ghosts his face. "I thought you'd never ask."

———

It was actually difficult to grab a table at the Dizzy Duck Inn. There is normally a waiting list, as the chef has won many awards. Luckily, having a claim in the hotel has its benefits. Throughout the meal, it felt like we talked about every hobby under the sun, our opinions landing on every opposite there could be.

We decided to skip dessert and instead grab a chocolate chip cookie from the front desk, usually reserved for evening turndown service, after Stone gave Stuart a strong glare. I've noticed when Stone clashes with someone, then well… it's a strong conviction. The cookie travels to my mouth for a bite. Probably an insult to the gourmet meal we just ate, but damn, those cookies are delicious. Besides, we had no plans to turn down and needed some fuel as we opt to head out to the end of the dock.

The moment our feet hit the stone pathway outside that leads to the dock, I notice Stone hesitate.

I know exactly where his mind went. "It's fine. I don't mind night when I know where I am and there is no chance of any unwelcome surprises. Plus… I'm with you."

The corners of his mouth tug from my answer. What feels right is interlinking our arms together as we walk, and I initiate that.

When we reach the water's edge, with lit candles outlining the length of the dock, we both take in the night.

"Tomorrow, I leave." I'm sad about it.

Stone sighs. "Figured we couldn't keep you in Lake Spark forever."

"Yeah…" No more hours of conversation and subtle looks. "You can send me letters that arrive by boat, taking the long way down the

Illinois River into the Mississippi to the Gulf, which means I maybe won't get them for weeks."

"How very old-fashioned of us. But why not?"

"Or email works just fine… I've heard it's faster."

He turns to me and seems pleased with my suggestion. "Sounds like a perfect idea."

Stone steps closer to me, and my entire body anticipates what his mission may be. I'm wishing for it. Should I be?

"Tell me it's okay?" It's a plea more than a question.

I'm with him on what he is insinuating, and I gently nod in agreement.

"I want to kiss you," he states, his voice soft.

"I think I want you to kiss me too."

Lines form on his forehead. "Think?"

A smile begins to form. "I would appreciate it if you kissed me."

"Appreciate?"

He inches closer, now aware that I'm playing coy with him, and his head tilts as he prepares to take charge.

Now my smile is in full force. "I undeniably want you to kiss me and have been thinking about it all day."

"That's better."

His grin doesn't get a chance to shine as his hand slides along my cheek until his other hand follows on the opposite side of my face. Stone cradles my head, supporting me to ensure I don't lose the strength in my legs, because that's what is beginning to happen. I'm weak from his touch, with his thumb tracing my lips. I press against his finger with my lips to encourage him not to stop.

Stone dips his head down and slowly his mouth meets mine. Closing my eyes, my senses magnify. His kiss is soft at first, allowing my body to adjust to what's happening. It's electrical, awakening things inside of me that may have been dormant. Wait, no, that's not true. This is all new. Different to anything before. A kiss that will be far too memorable.

I murmur into his mouth, inviting him to explore with his tongue. He groans when he angles the kiss in a different way, capturing more of my desire for this man who I only met a few days ago, but it feels as though we were meant to cross roads.

Kismet is apparently real.

We part, only to feather one another's lips. A delicate brush that I feel all the way down to my toes.

Then another kiss, this time deeper. More together.

An intensity takes over. Enrapturing me into a space that feels enticing, and I want to explore more. How far can I go to give and take?

Then it hits me.

I'm broken goods. This man needs someone to match his needs and persistence.

I'll just ruin it for us somehow.

Which is why I break this kiss, even though I think that I could ever stop. But I can't lead us down a lane with no clear ending.

"Tomorrow I Ieave, but maybe it's better to part now… Goodbye, Stone," I whisper.

"Harlow," he warns before I walk away, our fingers only letting go at the very last moment.

I don't look back.

I should have known that it wouldn't stop Stone Madden.

HARLOW

The Florida sun provides the vitamin D I need. It's supposed to lift your mood, isn't it?

Instead, I've been wallowing around, trying to shake the days that I had with Stone.

I wish there was another way. Alas, I'm back to where I was before the retreat. Sitting at my desk with a veggie wrap that I picked up from the deli down the street and my screen open to a Word document mid-chapter.

Maybe I should head to the beach. The Gulf is still warm from the summer, yet there are fewer tourists. But somehow, a spurt of fictional ideas has been uncontrollable lately.

The ping of an incoming email doesn't faze me, until I notice the name on the corner of my screen. His name strikes me within, and curiosity pumps up to full swing. I click it open after waiting a few seconds, as there is no way that I can be patient enough to wait.

Harlow,
You said email was faster. Speed of light would be better. How are you?

-Stone, Murderer of Deer

I hate yet love the smile hitting my lips and the fact that my fingers begin to type so eagerly.

Stone,
Can we stop with the animal talk? Irritating Jock Who Breaks the Rules is by far better. I'm okay, and you?

Signed,
Harlow, Who is Sticking to Traditional Signatures

P.S. Email is the way to go. Text messages feel too average. Hand-written letters on worn paper would imply romantic endeavors, and even my characters can't handle that.

Then it happens again a few minutes later.

Harlow,
That's a shame, I was going to go buy paper at Pioneer Village, that kids' park outside of town where they pretend it's pioneer times. Aw, shucks. Anyhow, I realize that I never teased you about your last name... Jelly.

And I'm not exactly okay. You left.

-Stone

The longest sigh hits me, and pain builds in my throat. I wait a few hours, debating what to say. Maybe I should wait another day to reply, but my body refuses to do that. Guilt hits me that I left, and I hate it.

Stone,
It's what I needed to do.

-Harlow

P.S. It's Harlow Grape Jelly actually… Okay, kidding about the middle name. Nonetheless, you shall under no circumstance repeat my last name.

————

Harlow,
Hmm, Olive is probably better.
And as for what you needed to do, I could argue that. You like to listen.

-Stone
P.S. Yeah, there is a hidden meaning there. ;)

I SNORT A LAUGH. Why is he letting me off so easily?

Stone,
It seems we're writing to one another now? I guess we did talk about it. You're the initiator, leading us to mischief, as always.

-Harlow

I could go back and forth for hours. I'm slipping back into the comfort and ease of talking to him. Missing his voice but enjoying his typed words too. Writing can sometimes be even stronger than voice.

Harlow,
Isn't it obvious what we're doing? You know, there is this German movie about two people who write to one another and never meet. I don't speak German, but I'm sure it's award worthy. Lucky for us, we've met, but it made me think of you and how email is better than nothing.

By the way, my baby-whisperer skills have taken a turn. It now costs me four minutes and forty-five seconds. I blame you for that. You're in my head.

-Stone

Now I want to cry. The guy has a romantic flare to every email. Better than nothing... it's dangerous yet true. It's amazing how not facing one another makes it easier to be honest. Which is why I admit the truth a few days later.

Stone,
You're perhaps in my head too. Have you been able to break your dry spell? Shit, I mean with your words, no, that's not... Wait, let me try again. Have you managed to work on your book? Phew... that's better.

-Harlow

His email back has a few shocked emojis and one that winks.

Now, now, Harlow, you're not playing fair. You know people always write what's subconsciously underneath it all (our thoughts, not clothes).

And yes... half a chapter, thank you very much.

-Stone

Then it begins. Every few days we exchange emails. Short, but they feel bittersweet. I should stop, but I don't. Nor does he.

Harlow,
Tell me you watched the hockey game last night? I know you've been watching old videos of me. Don't deny it. Yeah, yeah, yeah, you'll tell

me that it's for the sake of understanding the sports news. Lies. It has something to do with me, your favorite former athlete. Anyhow, my brother's team slammed Las Vegas. You can often see him on camera, yet we all know that I'm the better-looking one. Lucky you.

Have you found a bottle of sandalwood yet? It might help…

-Stone

With my dreams and sleep, he means. He mentioned it once, and I'm surprised he remembers the little things.

Stone,
Let's not question my research tactics. And no, I haven't bought the oil yet. I'll go this afternoon straight to the shop that sells oils, potions, and insists that I should write my dirty scenes around the position of astrological signs.

-Harlow

I do go to the shop, and my fixed smile doesn't seem to fade. Every night when I place a few drops of oil on my wrist, I think of him, and I lie in bed in a blissful state. Sometimes letting my fingers explore my skin, moving lower, reaching between my legs and thinking of Stone. I feel it in my bones that he would want to use his tongue before he slams into me with his cock. The mere thought brings more sensitivity to the little bundle of nerves between my thighs. I imagine him at that very moment lying in his own bed, stroking his length in his hand, wishing it was me. Some nights, I could swear we are coming at the same time in different places.

The thing is, when I'm alone, I'm completely comfortable fantasizing and touching myself. It's when someone else is present that it changes. With Stone, though, something within me feels altered. There is a boiling of sensual urges. If I wasn't broken, then I would have already been in his bed naked... if only I could let myself breathe.

Every email, he seems to circle us back to sweet, just when I'm tempted to hear him beg to try and touch me in every single way. We're not even writing anything remotely near sexting. Even if I wish we would, that isn't fair to him. I'm just not sure he is patient enough.

Another week goes by, and another email pops into my inbox.

Harlow,
Has it helped? The oil?

-Stone

I type back without much thought.

Hey there,
Over days, the nightmares only lessen, but do they ever go away? I believe they do, want to believe they will, anyhow. You got me to open that door of possibility.

-Harlow

Then he goes bold on me. Innately, I knew it was coming.

Harlow,
Don't you want to meet again? Our trails are bound to cross.

-Stone

———

Stone,
Sometimes what we want isn't what we need. Besides, I'm traveling

for the next few weeks. Marketing has me at a few signings, ending in Seattle.

Hope your writing came back in a tsunami.

-Harlow

I DON'T HEAR from him again. Not for a few days and not even a week or two. Time passes. I assume his impatience must have eventually worn out. Waiting can wear people down. Waiting for nothing is a deeper wound.

———

FORTUNATELY, my mind could be occupied. The publisher kept me busy with meetings, signings, pictures for social media, causing my need to take an hour to put on makeup and curl my hair. Between it all, I write better than I ever have and try to write in spare moments.

It's all left me exhausted, though. I walk down the hall of my fancy hotel in Seattle with my heels hanging from my fingers. I rub the back of my neck, eager to get my makeup off and throw on some pajamas. When the door's green light flashes from my key card, I'm already celebrating relief.

Sliding my key into the wall switch, the lights flicker on, and I let the door close behind me. Dropping my shoes to the floor, I walk into my room to grab my pajamas.

Then I spot it.

On the small table in my room there is a basket... full of apples.

That's a little strange, but an inkling hits me.

There is only a small card on hotel stationery from the concierge.

This was delivered without a card. With kindest regards, Reception.

A soft knock on my door causes me to instantly dart back to the door. I peek through the viewer and squint my eye, but I see nothing as another guest walks by, blocking my view.

It feels safe enough with other people around, but it doesn't matter anyhow because I'm certain who is here.

Opening the door, I'm greeted with a smirk as Stone leans against the opposite wall with his ankles crossed, and he's holding up a single apple, with his other hand in his pocket. He's wearing dark slacks and a dark blue button-down shirt. Not entirely sure why he's on the formal side, but his appearance is sexy as hell.

"I believe you're missing one," he informs me before he tosses it up, only to catch it.

My face eases into a happiness that I've been keeping on the offside. "You found me," I rasp.

Stone steps forward. "Had to. One of us didn't want to admit that they wanted to see the other."

A sharp breath hits me. It's me, completely me.

"The thing is, Harlow, you miss me. I know you do."

"Stone, I…" What should I say? I want to run and not ruin this moment at all. But I want this moment, every second, and what comes next too. "If I say yes, then what?"

He steps closer, and his eyes narrow in on me, they darken, have me in a hold, and I get that glimmer that I've had a few times when Stone Madden has a strong desire to ensure he gets what he wants.

He glides the back of his long finger along my cheek. "I believe our kiss scared you away, and our emails only solidified that you ran when you didn't want to."

My chest rises, and I want to crumble and admit the truth. A shaky nod is all I can give.

Another step closer and the back of his hand brushes my cheek, and I nuzzle my face into his hand, breathing in his scent that has a hint of cardamom, taking in this natural movement between us.

"I want to scare away your bad dreams," he whispers.

My lips part, and I struggle to form a word, but somehow, I manage to invite him in.

———

STONE SITS on the chair in the corner of the room, reading on his phone while I quickly head to the bathroom to throw on my pajamas and take off my makeup. Taking a few extra moments to examine myself in the mirror, I feel the flutter in my chest. It's the special kind that is comforting yet exciting.

I'm literally about to enter my room in pajamas to meet a man that I should be wanting to impress, except we're already past all that. We've seen one another drenched from a pool, with my mascara running. Most of all, he's seen me in a few of my dire moments.

I could have suggested that we head down to the hotel bar, but intuition has me planting my feet here. Plus, I'm not sure I can handle noise and people. I am really tired.

Taking a deep breath, I open the door and enter the room. Stone's eyes flick up to survey me, and the corners of his mouth curve up subtly.

"Hope you don't mind; I've been in restrictive clothes all day."

He stands and grins. "Although still gorgeous when I arrived, the real you is even better."

Another deep breath escapes my lips, then I have to smile to myself. "Uh, how did you find me?"

Stone laughs. "Our publisher let me know where you were staying. Coincidentally, my brother is at the hotel since the Spinners have a game here tomorrow. How I managed to get your room number, huh, should I admit my crime?"

"Yes," I say, amused.

"I leaned over the counter to look at the screen when the receptionist had to collect a bag in storage for another guest, and she forgot to lock the screen, which by the way, would never happen at my fine establishment, the Dizzy Duck."

I smirk at his tendency to cross lines when he wants… except with me. He seems to treat me like I'm fragile, only he's waiting for a signal to throw a different side of himself at me.

"Typical Stone Madden."

He scratches his cheek, and I notice the stubble on his chin is just short enough but already adding to his appeal.

"Here we are," he begins.

My lips press in as we both stand there in the middle of my room, curious to see what the night will bring.

"I'm just here to be with you, nothing else," he assures me.

Half a smile hits my mouth. "I know, you're always a gentleman." I step forward to tap his arm with mine. "Want something to drink?"

He groans a sound and rubs his face with his hands. "I've had enough. I had a heart-to-heart with my brother for the past hour or so. He has romantic woes and is working on his grand gesture, as you call it."

My brows rise from curiosity. "Is that so? Sounds like my plots aren't so crazy after all. I hope he works everything out."

"Vaughn will; he's as determined as me. A cursed genetic trait that makes us slightly edgy when needed." Stone can't tear his gaze away from me, nor can I with him.

My hands begin to fumble with one another out of nerves. "I kind of thought, I don't know, we stopped our emails for a bit."

Stone throws me a promising wry smile as his fingers softly brush hair behind my ear. "Nah, I just thought you might have needed a little space, and then I had this plan. Felt the element of surprise was better."

I close my eyes to let out relief that I didn't know was so large inside of me, but it releases and my shoulders ease. In the corner of my eye, the apple basket is right where I found it.

Stepping away from Stone, I slowly walk to the apples and begin to list. "Apple pie, apple butter, apple cake, apple sauce, baked apples, apple muffins, apple juice, caramel apples, so many things one could do with an apple." I pivot to glance at Stone who is amused, waiting for me to finish. "You can do a lot with apples... Except, I guess I never told you."

"What?" He seems mesmerized.

I tip my head and attempt to hide my smirk. "I fucking hate apples."

Stone bursts out laughing. And this feels like the icebreaker we needed to relax from our heightened emotion this evening.

"Of course, you would. The one time I thought I could be romantic, and I fail miserably." His head falls but the grin stays glued to his cheeks.

"You're being romantic?" My voice is delicate, but I know the answer. It's been obvious from the moment I opened my door.

"I'm trying."

I begin to walk until I find myself at the foot of the bed. Stone watches me, unsure what I'm doing. I sit down, and Stone follows my cue and sits next to me when I pat the mattress.

"Is it crazy that even though we only met for a few days that it feels as though every word we write is binding us more?" It's a scary admission.

He swallows, and I notice the way his throat bobs. "You're right. In truth, you have me upside down. I'm not used to being the one who wants to push forward and want something more than physical, it's normally the other way around. But you don't leave my mind, and I'm about to lose it." His hand rests on top of mine on my lap.

"I'm not sure what to do, Stone. For once in the longest time, I want to open up, but it's a lot of bricks to break down." His thumb caresses my hand, and it's soothing.

"Doesn't matter. Just focus on now." He sounds confident with his words, and I have no choice but to believe him.

The tranquil calm arrives again as the feeling of him nearly consumes me. My entire body is heightened in awareness that he is close.

"I didn't pack the sandalwood oil, I forgot. Tell me how you plan on scaring my dreams away. I wish we could talk all night, but I'm so ridiculously exhausted."

"What can I do?"

I glance to the pillows on my bed then swim back to Stone. "There are no Dizzy Duck Inn cookies here, but maybe I don't need them to persuade you to lie with me for a while?" My voice rises slightly.

This is what I want. I wouldn't be able to sleep knowing he was nearby, yet not close to me.

Stone observes the pillows then checks in with me to make sure, and he must see that I'm behind my suggestion 100%.

"How could I be so careless with what I'm doing?" He sounds serious, and my stomach drops, thinking this is the end of tonight. We're both giving mixed signals, aren't we? "I should have brought cookies on my journey here." A smirk breaks out on his lips, and I grin as air escapes me.

We both fall back onto the bed, laughing.

But I stay true to my request and crawl up the bed to move the duvet and tuck myself in and prop my head on the fluffy pillow. Stone gets comfortable next to me, lying on his side to focus on me, with his fingers instantly weaving through my hair as I rest my head on my hands under my cheek.

"I'll let myself out when you're deeply asleep."

I say nothing. Just sink into the bed, realizing that I'm sharing an intimate moment with someone and how it opens a door that I've had closed.

"I'm sorry I pushed you away. I left after the kiss and maybe even reiterated via email that we would be a bad idea. I'm not great at lying, so that all seemed like the answer. This is all new to me again," I whisper.

"Shh, close your eyes, Harlow."

I grip his shirt and slide an inch closer to him. My breath is warm as I lean in, and the heat of his body causes any thought in my head to blur because I'm attuned to my feelings. Taking the initiative, I brush my lips along the line of his jaw, feathering up to touch his lips with mine, before pressing gently to signal that he can give back what I desire. The tip of his tongue seeks entrance, which I give because I want it on my own. His fingers glide through my hair, as he is the one to possess me. I'm not sure this man would ever let me take the reins in this moment, and I don't mind one little bit.

My murmur is more sensual than perhaps I intend, but it comes naturally. It's a shame that air is a necessity, but when we part, our mouths stay as close as possible. "I didn't kiss you hello," I murmur against the corner of his mouth.

A hoarse sound from the back of his throat informs me that he approves of my move. "Well, hello then." I feel his fingers caress the curve of my forehead, and he kisses the top of my head. "Sweet dreams, firefly," he whispers. He's called me that once or twice now, and I like it.

My heavy eyes begin to close as I nestle closer to his body. Maybe when he believes I'm asleep, he begins to stir. But I'm not sleeping, and I reach out to grip his wrist.

"Stay. Just lie with me tonight. You don't need to go," I request.

Stone's eyes are set on my hand, but only a second later, he responds by getting comfortable again. He brings my body closer to him and his arm tighter around my middle.

"Night, Harlow. I'll be better than sandalwood oil, I promise."

His whisper warms my heart.

If anyone can scare my bad dreams away, then I'm beginning to believe it might be him.

7

STONE

I wonder if she knows how peaceful she looks when she's sleeping.

Even though I woke up half an hour ago, Harlow is still in a deep slumber. I'm sitting up in bed, admiring the sun streaming in, even though I can tell that clouds will arrive soon. Maybe it's the morning light that makes her appear softer and striking.

This isn't me. Not in the slightest. Going slow. Is that what we're even doing? Are we heading somewhere, or are we just friends who have an elevation of something more? Either way, I'm not used to any of this. I'm the guy who has dated with clothes off on date one, and normally by date two, we've upgraded it to more provocative physical activities, and date four or five, I let her loose to avoid attachment from their side.

But now, I'm drawn to Harlow and apparently have patience and a side of me that's gentler than my persona would suggest or than I believed possible.

Harlow begins to stir and groan as she wakes up and stretches her arms over her head. I wonder if she realizes a smile is fixed on her mouth. Her heavy lids begin to lift until her eyes open.

It takes a few seconds, but then she soaks in her surroundings and shoots up in bed.

"Morning." I have to smirk because maybe she forgot I was here.

Harlow adjusts her body until she's looking at me. "Morning," she rasps, and her smile changes to one of more ease and euphoria. "How long have you been up?"

"Not long. You were out like a light."

Her face puzzles. "I was?"

"The whole night. I woke up a few times. That pillow should be burned for what it does to people's necks," I explain as I begin to massage the back of my neck.

"I slept? The… whole night?" she whispers.

"Yeah."

Harlow's eyes widen slightly. "I slept a whole night," she repeats to herself, almost as if this is profound.

My hands splay out. "See? I kept my promise." Our eyes lock, and a bittersweetness shades across her face before her smile widens.

"It's been a while. And I feel… rested."

I slide off the bed, energized. "Good. Shall we order some breakfast?" I'm unsure if I should let her ponder on the significance of this moment or keep her mind occupied. Turning the television on, it opens to the hotel channel, and I quickly use the remote to get to the room service menu. For some reason, I don't want her to overthink this. Maybe it only brings up everything she wants to forget. "Croissants and fruit if we want continental. Eggs and bacon, even fake bacon, if we want to go all out. Ooh, oat pancakes. I bet you love those."

Harlow makes her way out from the covers, clearly content to start her day this way. "You're right. Oat pancakes sound great."

"Perfect. I'll order us some things, and I will quickly head to my room to get dressed, unless you don't want to be alone."

She chuckles. "It's fine, you can disappear for a little bit. Ah, you actually made a reservation here."

"I wasn't going to assume anything."

"You just deliver apples. And yeah, sounds like a plan."

We stare at one another, realizing that we entered a new realm. At least for Harlow. Me? I'm still kind of in shock that I'm in a patient state and wish I could make all her bad thoughts vanish, so I'll just try.

Harlow's lips twitch, and her eyes tell me that she's thankful.

I nod once before I head out.

By the time we're sitting around the table in her room eating a breakfast that admittedly is more food than we probably need, I want to plan the rest of the day.

"What's on the agenda for today?" I ask.

A sound from the back of her throat escapes. "I don't know. I wasn't expecting you, remember?"

"You never were," I rasp to myself, and I don't mean just last night, instead the first moment we met. And I know I feel the same about her.

Harlow seems to grasp the meaning behind my words as she quirks her lips to the side. "Thank you."

"For what?"

"Making me sleep." Her eyes dip down to the fork that she's fiddling with. It's the way her voice weakens that makes me not answer her, as I feel she wants me to patiently wait and listen.

Her mouth parts open and a sound scrapes from her throat. "It was two years ago…" She doesn't seem sure where to look until she flicks her eyes to me. "I-I…" she quivers then swallows, gathering courage. "It was late, and I was walking to my car, when out of nowhere, this guy… he was too strong." She blinks her eyes rapidly. Not wanting to remember yet, she wants to share. Harlow avoids looking straight at me. "He took advantage of me in the worst possible way. I didn't just end up with ripped-up clothes. My world was ripped away from me, and my life changed after that. "

I wasn't going to push for her to share, but she has, and it feels like a rock hits me between my stomach and heart with every word she says as she relays the events of that night. I appreciate that she's opening up, but I honestly don't know what I can say. The rage inside of me is hard to simmer, even though my intuition has already prepared me for how dark this memory for her would be.

She must pick up on that. "The police never found him, and I let it go after a while. Completely shutting out the thought that he's walking around somewhere was my first step to finding a sliver of normalcy. Maybe I've moved on for the most part. Well, I mean, stopped being angry or asking why. Yet the panic attacks still hit when I least expect, and the feeling of suffocation just restricts me at moments that I can't predict. So, there you are. You don't need to try to piece the details together, and we never have to replay it again."

I stare at her blankly, in awe that she unwrapped the mystery to me. "You didn't need to explain, but I appreciate that you did. Doesn't mean I hate that it happened any less."

Harlow dips her gaze down before striking back up. "I never really talk about it… except with you it seems. My friend Flo knows and the therapist I tried a few times only seemed to overanalyze. Why are you, Stone, a key for a lock I thought could never open?"

I reach over the table to touch the top of her hand. "I'm not sure. But I am."

Her eyes catch mine again, and they seem heavy yet optimistic.

We shouldn't sulk in this serious conversation for too long. I want to see her smile again and to relax or be distracted. Diversion seems to be my talent today. "Hey, you've never seen a hockey game, right?"

Harlow sniffles a sound as she rolls her eyes. "Remind me of my failed book research. But no, never have."

I cluck my tongue. "Let's go to a game tonight. My brother can easily get me an extra ticket. I was going to watch it anyway."

"Uhm, sure, why not?" Her mood inches up the ladder to a barely-there smile appearing as she agrees.

"Awesome, and before then… we could walk around?"

Her smile crawls a little wider. "Sounds perfect."

———

THE SOUND of the crowd keeps us stuck in the adrenaline of the hockey game. We're sitting where there are a lot of Spinner fans, and the curses at the referee and other players that quickly changed to cheers could give anyone whiplash.

We spent the afternoon walking around, holding hands, because suddenly I've gone a little chaste, and checking out Pike Place Market. Then, after heading to a coffee hotspot where Harlow had tea—sweet of her to tag along for my coffee needs—we headed back to the hotel and took a cab to the arena.

"I don't quite understand." Harlow is studying the ice where players are heading toward the attacking zone.

"It's called a power play. Because someone on the Seattle team got sent to the penalty box for two minutes, they are one man down. Which means the Spinners have more players on the ice. Therefore, a better chance to score," I explain as I look forward, only to glance up to the VIP boxes where I see my brother busy looking out the window and speaking to a man next to him.

"Okay, that makes sense. But why are there literally like twenty people on the bench when only six play on the ice?" Harlow grabs another handful of popcorn from her box.

"Because you never know when someone will get hurt, tired, or the coach needs to swap players due to performance. Especially, if the goalie gets hurt, then they need to have another player ready. That's why you have alternates."

She brings a finger up to the air. "Okay, I think I'm getting this. And the captain isn't an official role but pretty much is the lead on the hierarchy of players on the team. More, a morale booster who just so happens to play exceptionally."

I laugh. "You're doing well. I should give you a test after all this."

Harlow lolls her head to the side when she gives me side-eye. "Truthfully, this is all kinds of exhilarating. It moves superfast and is kind of entertaining. It's almost like if you blink, you miss something. Although I would hate to be sitting behind those clear wall thingies down by the ice. You're too close to the fights."

I curl my arm around her shoulders, and she doesn't seem to mind. "It's called the boards, and it's probably one of the best seats in the house. You are aligned with all the action, as if you're on the ice. Not to mention, you have more chances of getting a few words from the player when they leave the ice. When I played, I mostly focused unless a kid was there with a sign pleading for anything, a stick, a puck, a wave. There was also an old lady once who had a sign saying it was her first time at a live game after sixty years of waiting, which was kind of cool."

Harlow gives me a knowing look. "Miss it more than you thought?"

I contemplate for a few seconds. "I always will, but it's the hockey part which I can still do in my free time, just not with a group of guys that are a team with a close bond. I don't miss the schedule, the training, chance of being traded, the media, and how it's all kind of grueling. But actually, back in Lake Spark, a bunch of retired players get together a few times a year, mostly for charity games."

"I bet that's fun to watch." I notice Harlow scanning the arena.

"You're searching for girlfriends and wives of the players, aren't you?" I state with a flat tone, yet feeling a grin break out.

Her head tilts side to side. "Guilty."

"Most of the away team's wives or girlfriends aren't here. They tend not to travel with the team. As for Seattle, they're most likely up in a box on the other side of the arena or maybe watching closer to the ice, though I haven't seen them appear on the screen."

She chortles a laugh. "Just look on their social media and I'm sure you can solve the mystery."

"Probably."

"Hey, Stone," she affectionately says my name.

"Hey, Harlow," I return the sentiment.

"Thanks for arranging this. It's been fun."

"*Fun* fun? Or fun as in you're now a fan and will be turning on the game when your schedule allows?"

She gives me a short laugh. "Probably the latter, to be honest. Just need to find someone in Florida who will join me to watch with wine in hand." My arm loosens and drops. I don't enjoy that thought. Harlow pinches my arm playfully. "As in a friend. Maybe one of the girls from my Zumba class or something."

I blow out a breath, relieved, but she raises another point. "I guess I live in Lake Spark, so I won't be much help."

An awkwardness comes over us. "Right." Her T is tight. "We don't live near one another. Not even close."

Fuck distance.

And fuck the crowd for erupting into celebration because Seattle just got a goal. The noise completely ruins any hope of discussing a tiny practical matter between Harlow and me, because I'm cursing the referee's decision on that play; the forward should have totally had the ref on his ass. I'm enjoying my time with Harlow, but hockey is hockey.

———

WALKING down the hall of the hotel, Harlow surprises me. She brings her fingers to mine to interlace so that we're holding hands.

I'm completely gone.

This is saccharine, yet I'm all in. The thought of pushing her against the wall and slipping my hand up her thigh until I feel her heat and sliding along her slit… I've tucked that thought behind a wall in my head, hoping it will eventually come to fruition.

We approach her room, and I assume this is where I bid her good night.

"I'm happy we got out of the hotel and played tourist before you made me a hockey fan," she tells me.

"It was a great day." And I feel the pull toward her even stronger. "I should probably let you head to bed since you have a morning flight back to Florida." I'm choosing the safest option to round off our night.

But she surprises me when she yanks my fingers closer to her.

"Sleep in my bed again." A wry smile doesn't falter on her lips. She wants this.

I swallow, reminding myself that I have to keep it down a notch from how I want to touch her, lick her, and make her moan. The willpower and desire to fulfill her wishes overpower me, which is why it doesn't take long for me to answer. "Yeah, sure." I'm trying to be casual about this, but I was hoping that she would invite me in. I mean, we've done it already.

Her smile turns to a beaming one before she turns to swipe the keycard.

I follow Harlow into her room, and when we arrive in the middle, she turns sharply to face me, nearly running into my chest.

"There is one more thing," she mentions.

"What is it?"

A smirk appears on her face as she takes a sensual step forward and plants her hands on each side of my face. "Kiss me again," she whispers.

She doesn't need to ask again. I lower my mouth and brush my mouth along hers until the hint of her lips parting has me firmly imprinting onto her. I wrap my arm around her middle to pull her to me flush as I kiss deeper. Harlow murmurs an indistinct sound, but I'm not worried, as she hooks her arms around my neck and sinks more into our kiss.

Our position slants, and I take the opportunity to slip my tongue past her lips to greet hers. I nearly growl from how good kissing her is. All day I've wanted to do it to her. But I honest to God have no clue what we're doing or what our lines are.

We kiss and kiss some more until both of our mouths tip back and our noses scrape one another.

Harlow breathes out a long panting breath. "It's better than last time."

I scoff and grin in unison. "Just don't run away this time."

Her eased face turns slightly serious, and I realize that my choice of words might have just ruined the moment.

"I won't run away," she assures me. "It's just a shame we live on opposite ends of the country, and tomorrow I have a flight back."

A logistical nightmare.

But I'm selfish, and I bring my finger to her lips to shush her. "Let's not think about that right now."

Harlow circles her mouth, with my finger staying right where it is, as if she is using me as a paintbrush, right before her lips pucker out to kiss my fingerprint gently. "You know, I think about you in ways that if I were someone else, then you and I would have been naked already last night. I just…"

I pull her close to me to give her a firm hug. "I'm not going to lie. It's taking a lot of endurance to keep myself in check. But I'll do it for you. I'm like a man tethered to you."

Harlow's head retreats back slightly, and she peers up at me. "You know, tethers can break if someone has too much strength and persistence."

I hook a finger and glide it along her cheek. "It also means that someone is holding onto the rope, and they have the power to pull back when needed or loosen their hold. Most of all, it means that you're in control."

Her eyes light up again. "Stone…" She stammers. "I don't believe you have hardened edges that everyone seems to assume you have. Am I getting a side of you that's new?" She seems bewildered.

"Yes," I say point blank, and it makes her chuckle.

"Okay then, let's get to bed."

She quickly goes to the bathroom while I take off my shoes and empty my pockets. Sleeping in clothes isn't ideal for my comfort level, which is why I debate if I should take my shirt off. I begin to tug on it but then stall.

Harlow enters the room, entertained. "It's okay, you can take it off. Your jeans too if you want." I want to bring a fist to my mouth to hold in any temptation, but I follow her lead.

Throwing my shirt to the side, Harlow walks straight to it and quirks her lips out. "Can I wear it to bed?"

The corner of my mouth hitches up, it feels like high school, yet more endearing. "Sure. I'm kind of honored that you enjoy my scent," I say to lighten the mood.

I have to turn away when she throws off her own pajama top to put my shirt on. Someone upstairs should give me a gold star or at least a step back from the gates of hell for not sneaking a glimpse.

By the time we're in bed, the heightened tension in the air completely vanishes into our own bubble of complete harmony. Nothing about this feels odd at all.

Even when Harlow rolls onto her side and slings a leg over mine. I wrap my arm around her as we stare at one another. I clear my throat as the smoothness of her skin on her legs melts onto mine.

She grins. "I take no offense if you have a hard-on at any point tonight and need to go shower," she assures me.

I snort a laugh. "Thank you. I was wondering how this might go down. It's a struggle not to be tempted by you and have my way. But I respect you too much."

"I'm not made of glass, I won't break. I'm just waiting until I know that it will be indestructible."

I begin to comb her hair with my fingers. "Glass is always destructible, no?"

"It's not if you're in control, because then it doesn't matter what happens. When it's your own doing, if it breaks, then it's because you broke it yourself so nobody else has the chance to shatter it."

"You have a lot of strength, you know," I inform softly her as our eyes dance in this sentimental aura that has that tether pulling me closer to her.

"I think so. But my point is… I'm waiting for the sign that I can let all my inhibitions go and feel again."

"Have you found a sign yet?" I'm curious.

She nods ever so tenderly. "I'm closer than I've ever been."

I feel it in my bones that it's me. I lean in to kiss her forehead, but she moves to kiss my lips, giving me the confirmation I needed.

"I wish we had more time." I can't get enough. I'm addicted, and there has to be a way around all of this.

"Stone, I'll write to you. I promise."

My chest sinks. "Traditional has never been me."

"Me neither, but distance isn't on our side."

"I don't want this to be the end."

Harlow hugs me tighter. "I don't have answers. Just hold me, please."

Bringing her closer, our bodies mold to one another, and we lie there in silence, but our breathing synchronizes, and when she is blissfully asleep, I stare at the ceiling because I never expected any of this. I'm now a reserved man that's unfamiliar.

Which is why I sigh and come to the conclusion that I'm not going to let go quite yet.

I finally know what building an attachment means.

It's just that the wind has been knocked out of me because the bond with Harlow is stronger than I could have contemplated.

8

HARLOW

We find ourselves in a predicament.

Those are the words of Stone's email a few days after we ended our time in Seattle.

Walking along the beach with a smoothie in hand, I recall what those few days with Stone were like. Then a tinge of disappointment hits me that I had to return to Florida, and him to Illinois. Then a smile begins to hint on the corner of my mouth.

I slept.

I was held.

I wanted more.

His arms around me felt like a new heaven, and his scent I could inhale a thousand times, a sort of subtle crisp shower-fresh smell. I wore his shirt, I kissed his lips, and I wished his hand would have traveled up my thigh to touch me in those sensitive spots that pulse when he's near.

I kind of curse his respectable boundaries, because if anyone is going to knock down my bricks, then I'm beginning to realize that it's him. And my body is taking tiny steps to be closer to him.

Pulling out my phone, my thumb scans the email again. It's refreshing to communicate email letters and not text messages.

Harlow,
We find ourselves in a predicament, and you know why. Distance
does crazy things to people. But our biggest quandary... Did I just
say quandary? See, I'm already going out of my mind. You've made
me unrecognizable, and I'm not sure how I feel about that. Nah, I
kind of enjoy it. It was about time I became a gentleman.

Did you study what a hat trick is? I'll send your hockey-knowledge
quiz soon.

-Stone

A deep exhale leaves my body. There isn't one word he wrote that I could disagree with. It's horribly true that distance might make feelings grow fonder. That could bring a little misery to my life.

Glancing at the ocean, I used to feel like my life was crashing down just like the waves. Now, I feel a new sensation, similar to new waves forming.

At the line where hard, wet sand turns to soft, I sit down to type back.

Stone,
It seems we do have a problem. You know it's dangerous to write.
Words make a connection grow. We should probably take some time
before jumping into... Wait, what are we jumping into? Are we even
jumping? Gah, don't you hate when an unexplainable connection
doesn't have a label?

A hat trick: Something like a player scoring three times in the same
game. I noticed that the internet tells me that you had many hat
tricks in your career. You've seen me two times now. The retreat in
Lake Spark with Commander Gloria, and Seattle. You haven't quite
scored a hat trick yet when it comes to us.

How is your Illinois weather? I'm in the high 70s, with sun, thank you very much. Are you freezing yet?

-Harlow

Sighing yet again, I decide to head back home. Get down a few chapters about a billionaire who gets his secretary pregnant. Sometimes my plots are ridiculous, but it's the sex scenes and happy endings that are the escape that everyone needs. This billionaire is demanding. He pulls her hair and won't stop until she comes, before he stuffs his cock inside of her. What he doesn't know is his office affair, where he bends her over his desk while he's on a conference call, will end up with a little surprise that she doesn't plan on telling him, because he's a cocky asshole who doesn't want a family. Pfff, that will change by chapter twenty.

It's the next morning and three chapters later, and I notice that Stone emailed early. Does he sleep?

Harlow,

Huh, you could be my hat trick as you're someone who is one long game. Never thought of that, but it makes me a little more resolute. It just means that I have to see you again. I've thought of hopping on a plane to surprise you. But I've already surprised you once. I think the apple is now in your basket, in terms of taking steps.

Low 40s here, but it doesn't matter because late autumn is too breathtaking to complain about weather. The leaves are in their last weeks of orange, yellow, and red. They will turn to that weird brownish-gray color soon and be extra crunchy under your feet. Then the town becomes colorful, with holiday lights and overdone shop windows with little trains riding around fake cotton snow. The farmer's market gets vicious about who sells the best candles, stockings, and cookies. We're not even at Thanksgiving yet, but the battle is on.

It's my niece's first Christmas. I need to outdo Isla's brother for the uncle-of-the-year award. Presents for sure, but my secret weapon is a stocking with Nora's name embroidered from the knitting club in town. For my piece de resistance, I'm getting her an overly expensive snow globe with dancing bears inside. I'm going to nail it.

Lake Spark is a perfect time to visit... hint, hint.

-Stone

I laugh out loud. This guy is sometimes ridiculous, but it lights up any day. And the undertone that I should visit is something I've thought about. But is an attachment to someone where it can't really go anywhere a good idea?

It will fuck up somehow. We have too many miles between us, and the possibility that I'll freak out when he's sliding into me and making me see stars. I never know when it'll hit me. That feeling of constraint in my chest that causes me to gasp for air.

Stone could never be just a friend. Friends don't kiss or want to strip one another naked. We're moving slowly in an unknown direction with no map. But then I imagine the moment I could snap and give into this unbearable feeling that I need more of him physically. I'm confident he would take his time, kissing every inch before his tongue finds my pussy, and I comb my fingers through his hair as he's doing it. I would beg him to be inside me, and he would comply.

I shake my head of the fantasy and decide to hold off replying. Until two days later.

Stone,
Shall I already order the trophy for uncle of the year? Damn, you're going to extremes. I think I need to follow this journey until the big day. You do realize that she has no clue what's going on. You'll need to take photos as proof and tell her when she's older. You've turned into a Lake Spark local if you are overly enthusiastic for the holidays.

I got your hint. It makes me ponder. Oh God, it does.
If you could get inside my head, then you'd have to touch yourself
and think of me.

-Harlow

I hit send, then realize what the hell I just wrote. I've initiated a world that I probably shouldn't, leading us through a labyrinth of more confusion, like fuel thrown on this emblazing fire.

Bad me. Very bad me.

Almost as bad as the email I get a few hours later.

Harlow,
Have you picked out a gravestone for me yet? I think I just died.

You've shared the secret of your thoughts. One that I was confident I already knew, but that's beside the point.

You think of me. How my mouth would glide along your skin and cause a ripple through your body. Your lips would part, unsure but wanting, which is why you would let me drag the edge of your shirt up with my teeth while my fingers sneak under the waistband of your jeans and slip into your drenched pussy to stroke. You'd clutch tight to my hair because my tongue wouldn't leave you until you shudder underneath me.

I've thought about it with my cock in my hand, and I know you do too when you touch yourself.

I feel safe to write that. Hell, I'm surprised I have it in me to write this. Maybe I should reconsider my genre and begin to write a series on billionaires. You know, the kind when he has a one-night stand then discovers later that she's his new employee. Yeah, I read Billionaire and His Intern. *You nailed it on the dirty parts... Nail... see what I did there?*

My point is, you have it in you. You're allowed to want it off the pages.

How is the pondering going?

-Stone

The heat in my body is domineering as I tuck my hand into my underwear and my finger gets soaked in my arousal. If he were here now, he would be on his knees and parting my thighs open to enjoy the view before he insists on taking over with his tongue. Then with his hands around my wrists, he would yank me up to kiss me before he guides me to the bed and opens me wide, with a quick tease of his cock before he slides right into me.

His searing eyes would drill into me.

Just as they do when his hands aren't on me.

I pant while an orgasm takes over my body, leaving me breathless.

It's a cold shower and contemplation that clears my head.

———

A WEEK LATER, I find myself at a smoothie bar with my friend Flo. We went to high school together way back, and not only is she my friend, but she also reads my books in the rough stages, not to mention she owns a beauty salon, and I may get a discount.

Flo twirls her sun-kissed blonde hair around her finger. "Listen, Harlow, I'm not sure what's going on, but your newest book is… different. No offense, but compared to your other books, this is quite a step up. The steamy scenes have turned to five-pepper levels, and to be honest, there is more… finesse to the story. You're steering away from over the top to… emotions." She takes a sip from her straw.

My brows raise. "Is that so?" I kind of already thought it.

"Yes. Was it that writer's retreat? See, I knew it would help."

I scoff a huff. "Gloria, the organizer, was…" I wave her off. "Never mind."

"Yeah, you mentioned that she's eccentric and probably has a yappy little dog that she carries in a basket when she's not working. But it seems to have sparked something in you. I searched the web, and Lake Spark is just gorgeous."

My mouth hitches up in acknowledgment. "It is a quaint little town."

"I bet." She smiles, and then it drops. "Now, chitchat over. What the hell is changing your direction?"

I try to look anywhere but across the table, then I admit defeat. "Uhm, you see…" I nervously tuck hair behind my ear. "I kind of met someone at the retreat. A hockey player who is writing a book…"

Flo drops her jaw. "What? Ooh, I bet he could be prime research if you want to write a hockey romance."

I shake my head. "Or not." I'm not even going to attempt it.

"Okay, well, Mr. Hockey Guy is sparking your creativity. Is he hot?"

I take a long sip from my green drink. "Maybe." I shrug.

"Oh yeah?" She raises a brow. "First, you know your texts indicated that you hated that retreat, but I guess the organizer did something right… She brought you together with Mr. Hockey Hottie Guy. Your muse." Flo grins wide.

If only she knew that it was slightly more. Stone is the guy who is making me come alive off the pages too.

"What's your point, Flo?" I want to wrap this up. Couldn't she just focus on the weather forecast or something?

"Go back to Lake Spark. Clearly that little town fueled your creative juices. Seriously, go there."

Oh, now… this is… a nudge or a big push.

My thoughts turn sharply in my head.

"Uh." I croak a sound. "Is that really a good idea? I mean, hockey McHottie is there."

She reaches across the table to touch my hand resting in the middle. "I think… if this is the first sprinkle of normalcy with a guy in a long time, then… explore that." Her sincerity punches me in the gut because she's been through it all with me, more an observer of my aftermath, so maybe she has a point from a different lens.

"I don't want to treat him like some experiment, you know? Oh, Harlow can finally take a step, let's use him to explore." I mock my own words. "He… surprised me in Seattle."

Flo brings her arms into the air with shock on her face. "What the hell? You were keeping this news from me? Holy cow, that is just… you have to go to Lake Spark." Now she pleads and looks like a jumping bean in her seat.

"I'll think about it."

He's in my head. He touches me even when he isn't present. Wild thoughts enter my mind and an inkling has me wanting to make a move.

"Don't think. Just do it," Flo insists.

I can only flash a weak smile.

———

Finishing up at the smoothie bar, I take a stroll into town. I'm lucky it's tourist central here, which means everything is near to one another to make it easy. It's quieter than normal because it's low season. I don't need anything at the grocery store, but I buy an avocado and a bag of dinosaur crackers anyway.

On my walk back, a realization hits me.

I've been scared, but that doesn't have to be me anymore, which is why I open my laptop to write as soon as I get home.

Stone,

It's been a week since I've emailed. I was contemplating, but it's over.

It seems the thoughts swirling in my head won't give up. Apparently, it's been confirmed that my recent inspiration has come from… Lake

Spark. Or you. But let's not make a big deal about that, and don't get cocky either. So, Lake Spark is where I will go.

Damn it, now I need to rummage for a hat and gloves in the back of my closet. They're behind my flip-flops and sun hats because winter isn't that exciting here, except for a lower ocean temperature.

You don't happen to know a place where I can stay? The Dizzy Duck doesn't seem to be my calling this time around. Plus, I'm watching my chocolate chip cookie intake. Totally not cool.

-Harlow

––––––––

Harlow,
You already know my answer but how polite of you to ask. My home needs its first guest to get my five-star review. Breakfast is included, with non-frozen bread and no coffee offered. If you're lucky, I might even carry your suitcase up the stairs to…

…my room? Only if you want. To sleep is fine.

-Stone

––––––––

I SNORT a laugh at what I hope is sarcasm in his email. I want more. The thoughts in my head of his lips trailing my body and his fingers guiding my jaw to ensure I look at him are something that I can no longer ignore. A flicker of hope and a push of courage for a safe haven that involves his body is apparent that I can follow through. My lips tuck into my mouth as I repeat in my head the sentiment that I've felt as the days go by.

Letting out a deep exhale, I type.

Stone,

Please make my reservation. I would like to book your room. I just don't know if we will need the do-not-disturb sign or not. I'm sorry. I just…

Something tells me that it doesn't matter. We both want to see one another anyway.

I'll send you my flight info and times when I will visit. Does my reservation include airport pickup? I'm not a great driver. Those duck and deer crossing signs along the winding road scare the hell out of me. Are warnings every quarter of a mile really necessary?

See you in a week or two.
Harlow

P.S You said a connection with me is one long game. Three visits for us… It would appear that you'll get your hat trick.

9

STONE

I give a sharp glare at Stuart behind the front desk of the Dizzy Duck Inn.

"Are you sure these cookies will be okay tonight?" I ask for the second time.

He gives me an odd look. "The kitchen said yes. As mentioned, they were baked this morning, and you can always warm them in the oven."

I glance down at the box tied with a ribbon then slide my eyes back up. After thinking it over, I decide it's time to give up. "Fine."

"Leave the guy alone. You're such an ass sometimes." I hear a deep voice from behind me, and I know when I turn that I will be greeted by Holden. He played sports during my own years as a professional athlete. But our paths always crossed, and I consider him a friend, which is why I wasn't hesitant to invest in this place.

Pivoting, I throw on a grin to match his. The guy never wears a suit, only dark jeans and button-downs. "I'm only a jackass when it's important."

Holden indicates with his head to join him in the lounge on a low couch. My eyes squint, as they do every single time, at the moose head over the fireplace. "For the love of God, get rid of that thing," I plead. "This isn't a hunting lodge."

He chuckles. "I know. Next summer, I'm getting an interior designer in." Holden leans forward and rests his elbows on his knees. "Tell me something exciting. I'm tired of listening to my pre-teen and ten-year-old argue and complain." He has two kids with no wife or mother for his kids in the picture, only a constant flow of nannies.

"Yikes." I reach over to pat his shoulder. "No envy there."

"Really? You had a one-night stand with my ex-nanny way back," he deadpans.

I wince, as that wasn't my proudest moment, nor are my womanizing ways of the past.

"Anyway, what's with the cookie demands?" he quickly changes topics.

I roll my shoulders back. "It's a nice Dizzy Duck touch. Everyone raves about them." Holden doesn't believe a word; his face informs as much. I give in. "I have someone visiting and thought it would be a nice surprise."

His brows raise. "A woman?"

I nod. "Met her here at the writers' retreat we had a while back."

"Ah, so you have a new girlfriend."

I chuckle. "Not exactly."

"Seeing where things go?"

"Maybe." I shrug. Harlow is right, there is no definition for us. Other than that, I want to make every second with her count and surprise her in ways that are creative, even for me. I don't feel I need to impress her, our ease with one another doesn't call for that.

Holden seems fascinated. "I'll be damned. Someone is under the influence of feelings."

"Funny."

"Who is it? Does she live nearby?"

I shake my head. "Harlow doesn't live here. She's flying in this afternoon, and I'll pick her up."

"Harlow... a cute name."

"She's beautiful and... knocked the wind out of me."

Holden grins at me. "Sounds promising."

My lips quirk side to side. "It's a little complicated, and now I'm in a totally new realm. A new side of me has opened up, and quite frankly, my patience is confusing me. Never in my life have I had that. Normally, I demand, and I get. But here I am."

He crosses his arms. "That's a sign. Will I get to meet her?"

I snicker. "Hell no. I'm not bringing her to lunch with you. Last time I tried to enjoy a meal with you, your nanny number six called to say she quit because your kids are little devils. We can't even sit through a normal meal."

Holden gives me an awkward look. "True. Hopefully, they will calm down as they get older."

"Yeah… good luck with that."

I glance at my watch and know I need to head out. I want to clean my house a little and pick up a few flowers from The Flower Jar on Main Street. It's cheesy as hell, but I know it will make Harlow laugh until her stomach hurts.

"Gotta head out." Holding up the box of cookies, I tell him, "If these don't hold up to my standards then you best believe we're having a corporate meeting," I joke.

"Do that and I'll play hardball. Say goodbye to your access to the gym and pool, buddy."

I ruefully drop my head. "See ya, Holden." I get up and begin to walk away.

"Hey, Stone." I glance over my shoulder. "Nothing is ever as it seems. Tread carefully," he warns.

I ignore everything he says, except there is a small pit somewhere in my stomach that tightens slightly.

———

Waiting outside on the tarmac of the small regional airport, I'm confident with how this is going to go. It just doesn't mean the nerves I feel are any less.

The moment Harlow steps off the plane, she stills, our eyes lock, and a gentle smile appears on her lips. She has a beret on, and her scarf matches, with complete Paris vibes. But it doesn't matter, it's our frozen moment that is the starting line for the next few days that has us entranced.

That is until the passenger behind her must grumble to speed up, so Harlow walks down the steps.

Her slow walk toward me causes a pounding in my chest.

What the hell are we doing?

What abyss are we heading down together?

And why is neither one of us running?

It's when she is within touching distance that all thoughts leave my head, and I reach my fingers out to skim along her arm as she surveys the small bouquet of red carnations, because roses seemed too romantic, wilting in the cold. As expected, she bursts out laughing.

"What a welcome," she says as she reaches to take them from my hands. "You clearly read one of my books that you called garbage when we first met."

"Ha-ha."

Her laugh fades away, as does the hesitation for us. We step into a deep hug where I rub her back and she squeezes me tightly. I wish I could inhale the smell of her coconut-scented hair, but the cold air won't allow it.

Neither of us let go and our heads angle slightly. It feels natural to kiss, which is why we do it. A soft gentle kiss, near a peck, until we meld into a stronger sealing of our mouths. It's a welcome and nothing crazy. It just leaves us with droll smiles, and we break our embrace to keep our day moving.

Reaching down, I swing her bag over my shoulder.

"What service," she teases.

"You have no idea," I nearly mumble, and admittedly, I have thoughts in my head that have been on a constant rotation. I want to do a lot of things to her if she'll let me.

We head to my car, and on the fifteen-minute drive back to my house, we keep conversation simple about her flight, weather, and the latest in Lake Spark. Thanksgiving passed, and Harlow spent it with friends, while I spent time with my niece, as my brother had an away game the day after.

When we get to my house, that heightened feeling from earlier returns. We head in, and she surveys my house. It's a condo that is by no means modest. Everything is new, and the three bedrooms and four baths are something I probably don't need. There are a few cactuses to contrast my mostly light gray interior.

"Bachelor pad," she states. Harlow saunters to the room off the living room with opened French doors, and she realizes it's my office. I lean against the doorframe to observe her. She circles the desk, with her fingertips brushing along the books and paper, then stops at my closed laptop to tap twice. "So, this is where you write your emails to me? Or is it upstairs in your bed?" Her voice is floaty, sultry, and our eyes catch.

Now I'm curious what's going on in her head.

I rub my thumb across my jaw. "I'll let your mind run wild there."

She swallows. "Uhm, speaking of upstairs. Can you show me? We should probably … put my suitcase there." Now she's just toying with me.

I have to roll my eyes. "Good idea."

Every step up the stairs strengthens that thumping in my chest. I watch her sway as she moves, as if she's always belonged here. It's a challenge because I know I need to be patient, but that tether that she's had me on is getting too short.

She figures out which room is mine right away, as if it was a magnetic pull that led her that direction. We enter my room, and we both stall.

Harlow breaks the tension yet again with the laugh that fills the room as she marches forward. "Wow. A good start to earn your five stars." She heads straight to the edge of the bed where a folded towel rests with the box of cookies with the Dizzy Duck Inn logo. She pauses, and her fingers trace the outline of my folded shirt on top of the towel. She glances up at me. "You left me a shirt to sleep in." Her voice is delicate, and the gesture causes her lips to press while she smiles gently.

"I have high standards of what a hotel should offer."

She turns to me then throws her arms around me. "Thank you."

Fuck, that need to not let her go and rip her clothes off returns.

The thought is intercepted when I hear her mumble something against my chest, and as she backs up, it's now clear as day. "Stone, I don't know what it is, but the flight over opened a gate that I've tried to keep closed since I met you. I'm incredibly weak for you, and the thoughts just become… no words to describe it."

"What are you saying?" I caress her cheek.

Her eyes sideline toward my bedroom window. "How about I freshen up and we can grab something to eat before I burst out with words that would've been far easier to write… I wish I thought of that."

Now I have to clunk my tongue. "Alright, Harlow. I'll follow your lead."

"You do that a lot."

I tip my nose up in agreement. "I'll give you some space. The bathroom is over there. My top drawer is fair game for your curiosity," I say to brighten her beaming smile even more.

She chuckles and swats me away. "I'm not that nosy… today."

Our banter apparently continues even outside of our emails.

That's a relief.

Which is why I head downstairs, content and positive that today is different to others.

———

HARLOW SETS her wine glass on the counter, causing a satisfying clink noise.

"That was delicious. The eggplant parmesan was mmm, chef's kiss." She kisses her fingers.

"Unlucky for me, I wasn't the chef, and we can thank the general store. That place is a gourmet store with a whole deli of food to take away and heat at home in the oven, then pretend you stood over the stove for hours," I quip.

She licks her bottom lip, amused.

I'd already decided this morning that going out for dinner wasn't really appealing. Being alone and catching up without people around was more our calling. Harlow couldn't have agreed more.

"Want some dessert?" I offer.

"Absolutely not. I had about two cookies pre-dinner plus wine, so my sugar intake is at its limit." She looks around, figuring out which topic to switch us to. "Considering Christmas is in a few weeks, you're not very much in the festive cheer."

"I bet you have a small tree that is in decoration overload. We can decorate a cactus tomorrow if you want," I propose.

She chortles. "Nah, it's okay. And yes, I do have a festive tree."

I run my hand through my hair. "I just live off my brother's house to fulfill the holiday-decorations quota."

A fondness appears on her face. "You're very close with him."

"We've always been close. Now that he has his own family, I think subconsciously I'm interwoven into their world, and they've only had a baby for a few months; they are new together themselves. But it feels like a family. One unit with all of us. We never really had a big family with aunts and uncles growing up. I want to be there for him, especially since he has to travel with the Spinners so much," I explain.

"Sounds like something special."

"It is."

That silence hits us again. Only for a few moments, though.

"Do you think we can head upstairs?" Harlow asks. "It's been kind of a long day."

"Yeah, sure." Actually, this is kind of cruel, she's throwing me morsels, but fine, I digress.

Upstairs in no time, we get to my room and get ready for the night. It seems to be natural for us, as if we live together. Once we're in my bed, we turn to face one another on our sides, not ready to turn the lights off.

"Hi," she greets me delicately, and her eyes nearly sparkle.

"Hey," I reply.

I'm broken by her lips landing on mine in a passionate and deep kiss. It takes me by surprise, but no complaints.

She pulls away. "I kind of wanted to do that."

"I kind of noticed." I smirk. I'm too lost in her eyes to register that her hands find mine, until she begins to lead them slowly down.

Her look is a confirmation that she's comfortable with something, but I'm not sure what.

"Touch me," she rasps softly as she brings my hand to her thigh.

I want to hesitate, but I can't. I'm at her mercy, and I'm following her. Instead, I give in to an urge that I've been doing a damn good job suppressing. My fingers swirl on her bare thigh, and her lips part open gently. Her eyes close for a second before they open with approval.

I swipe my fingers further up slightly, to test the waters as our eyes hold. Harlow gently nods her head. She does more than that; her hand stays on top of mine, and we move together until I pause by the cloth of her panties; they're damp, and I want them off.

Her hand doesn't desert mine, which is why I slip my finger underneath her panties and feel her soaking pussy, and she gasps. We don't say any words, but our eyes remain locked. I stroke, I circle, I explore her, and she releases a moan. I feel as though she will combust far too soon. I begin to slide my body down then pause.

"I want to taste you," I whisper.

She's taken aback, but she doesn't seem to be closing the book on that idea. But then she traps her bottom lip between her teeth, and her cheeks rise from a smile she's trying to hold back.

I coast down her body until I'm lying on my stomach between her thighs that naturally seem to part for me, and I tug the fabric to the side. I would much prefer to rip them off, but in a way, that feels as though it's too big a step. I peer up at her, and Harlow seems mesmerized as she watches. I then focus on my task and lick the tip of my tongue over her in one lap, up and down, then I find her clit to circle and flick. Her head falls back, and she struggles to lie still on the bed, but it's the best kind of hips swirling. I go slow at first, but her sounds only encourage me to pick up my speed. I take a moment to study her taste, distinct and perfect.

Resting my palm on her belly to ease her down, I continue to stroke her with my tongue, devouring her, and her murmurs are the perfect sound in my room. Somehow my hands travel to hers, and we interlace our fingers while my head stays put between her legs.

"Stone," she breathes heavily.

It only causes me to smile against her flesh. She's experiencing pleasure, and it's because of me which is why I'm on my quest to bring her to an orgasm.

Her body feels so damn close. Normally, I wouldn't be satisfied with making a woman come so quickly, but I can imagine it's been a while for her.

"I'm going… to—" she pants softly.

Then it happens. Her body begins to convulse and vibrate against my mouth. Harlow clasps my hands tighter as her body shakes it all out. When she's calmed, I lift my lips away to look up at her with a grin on my face.

Her blank look seems to be due to an uncertainty of how she should feel, but then her lips tip up.

"I… I can't believe I…" Harlow's speechless.

I grind up her body to lie next to her again on my side. "You don't need to say anything. I think I found my new favorite hobby. You're beautiful when you let go." I brush a few strands of her hair behind her ear.

Her hand moves to touch my cock, but I'm quick to grab her wrist.

"I should…" she begins.

Returning the favor is not going to fucking happen. She deserves to enjoy her step.

"Don't worry about it. I'll survive," I downplay it.

She seems unconvinced but still slants her lips to the side. "For tonight, anyways."

I nod with a closed-mouth smile and reach to turn off the light before we cuddle into one another.

———

HARLOW STEPS one foot in front of her and then the next.

"Uhm, you should try skating instead of stepping. It's the whole point of being on the ice," I tease her.

We slept in, had yogurt, then I decided to take her to the ice rink since the Spinners are away for a game. But ice-skating Harlow is, well… a disaster. She has not one ounce of skating talent.

"Listen, hockey player, I'm ensuring I don't fall on my ass because a bruise would ruin my bikini lines," she responds.

I circle around her body. "I gave you figure skating skates. It would probably be worse if I gave you hockey ones."

"There are two different types of skates?" Her voice rises.

I shake my head, disappointed. "Did you not study this for your hockey exam that I still have yet to give?"

Her wide smile forms quickly. "Kidding. I know there's a difference."

I take hold of her hands as I skate backwards and tug her along. "The first ten minutes are the hardest, and then your body gets the hang of it," I promise.

"Until I need to brake to stop," she deadpans.

I chuckle. "Damn, this plan for our daytime activity really was not my best idea."

She ignores watching the ice and stares at me. "Nah, I kind of enjoy seeing you in your territory. You're like a child at a toy store."

"Keep talking to me," I encourage.

Lines form on her forehead. "And say what? It's cold, and there are girls here skating around in t-shirts and gloves, which makes no sense."

"It makes sense. The temperature actually isn't that cold when you move around."

"Tell that to someone who believes you. So tell me, how many hours would you be on the ice when you played?"

"On average, 12 hours of training per week on the ice and a hell of a lot of hours in the gym," I explain.

Harlow hums a sound. "Do you miss the scuffles with other players?"

I laugh. "Truthfully, yes. It's good to get out some aggression, and I was right defense, so I had to defend my turf," I attempt to make her smile.

She chortles in response. "I can't imagine you being aggressive. You're kind of soft."

My eyes grow into saucers. "Whoa, whoa, whoa. I'm only soft around you and a baby, a true exception. If you only knew how I was with other people and in the bedr—" I stall, because I just don't want to put any pressure on her.

She doesn't flinch, and I know I need to distract us to another topic.

"Look at you skating," I inform her.

She was so lost staring at me and in our conversation that she didn't realize she's no longer stepping on the ice. I might be pulling her along, but she's skating in a way.

Harlow looks at the ice and then around, as if this isn't happening. "Oh, so this is how it goes? I've been skating."

"Ready to let go? You're no longer taking steps," I say, and if only she knew the underlying meaning.

But her face relaxes, and she's on the same wavelength as me.

"I'm ready," she softly announces.

I let go.

…and she falls instantly onto her ass.

Turns out she still needs me to help her along.

———

WE WALK into my room after a day of ice skating and a dinner which was takeout from Catch 22. We're tired, so our plan is to just relax in bed and maybe put something on TV.

But as soon as we're in the middle of the room, Harlow twirls to face me.

"Kiss me," she demands.

It's my favorite nighttime routine that we've developed. No reason to argue, I do exactly as she requests. I cup her face and pull her into a slow, hard kiss that seems to absorb whatever thought or nerves are running through her.

When she pulls away, her eyes gleam with intent and a plea. "The thing is, I don't want to sleep. I don't want to think. I just know that for once I feel safe, and this desire is so over my head that I can't ignore it. It twists inside of me until I might burst. Do you understand?"

My eyes narrow in on her as I digest what I believe she's thinking. "What are you saying?"

"I don't want to sleep, Stone. Nor can we tiptoe around what I know you've been patiently waiting for, and so have I, if I'm being honest."

Now I wonder if it's me who is getting the sympathy.

Harlow grabs my hands confidently, setting them on her obliques, ensuring that our eyes hold before she inches my palms lower to her waist. "Something more and now," she rasps, her eyes vulnerable.

For some reason, I'm going to follow her cues, but also not. It makes no sense. I just know somehow one of us will lead the way.

I could scream finally, but I know this is a profound moment for her.

And truthfully, for us too.

10

HARLOW

I shiver because this feels like a leap off a cliff. But exhilarating, a giant swoosh of anticipation enrapturing me.

Stone reaches out and grazes his fingertips down my arms. Slowly and barely a touch but enough to cause my nipples to tingle.

He's about to check in if I'm sure, I can read his face, but I cut him off before he has the chance. "Yes," I say, adamant. The last few weeks I've been treading carefully further along a trail, taking tiny steps. And for the first time, I don't take two steps back.

Which is why in this very moment, I make the move forward.

His fingertips trail to my waist before he plants his hands firmly on the sides of my hips. We don't blink because our eyes are in a strong embrace. Maybe there is a hint that he's still studying if I'm okay. I am. I really am.

Stone is safe and makes my pulse race in a way that isn't panic; it's freeing.

We move closer, my breath picking up, as my nerves are still there, but I don't care.

He reaches up and slides his hands through my hair to bring my mouth to his for a kiss that's cementing, lustful yet soft. Warmth floats around us from this electricity that traps us in a current. I close my eyes to sink into the touch of his lips skimming my mouth.

I take this opportunity to circle my arms around his neck because I have an overbearing need to bring our bodies tighter together.

Stone tilts his head back slightly, his eyes dipping down to take in the look on my face where there's a ghost of a smile. It's his gaze that has me captivated because his eyes darken with a determined glint that he will do everything I ask, even if he has a far more powerful side that he's keeping locked up.

He catches me by surprise when without warning he lifts me up, and I wrap my legs around his waist instantly.

"I'm going to lay you on my bed, but you're going to have to trust me on this," he tells me softly.

"I do."

Stone keeps to his word and lays me carefully on the bed, ensuring my head lands on a pillow, then he slithers down my body with his gaze tipped up. I watch every second as my body melts under his touch. The next moment, he's on his knees working to remove my skirt and tights, which he peels down in a swift tug. Something lodges in my throat that I recognize as eagerness, especially when he parts my legs open.

He kneels down, with our eyes still tied by an imaginary rope, and he begins to kiss slowly up my skin, from my knee to my thigh.

My breath. Why does it grow heavier, and I don't want it to stop?

"Don't lie to me, Harlow. The moment you feel we need to—"

I rise to lean against my propped elbows to get a better view. "Don't say stop. I need this. I don't want to stop. Trust me when I say that. I want you."

He offers me a gentle smirk before he's back where he left off.

My pussy is throbbing from a desire that's so damn needy that my hips rock up to encourage him to give me more.

Stone gets the hint, and his tongue darts between my legs, giving me one stroke that already causes me to moan. His tongue maps out where to go, and when he lands on my clit, I'm a wanton woman who writhes and twists because it feels too good.

He flicks the tip of his tongue over my clit before drawing circles, and my eyes slide to the back of my head as I get lost in this fleeting moment. His hand splays below my belly button to keep me down so he has a better canvas to work with.

"Fuck, Harlow, you taste sweet. I don't think I'll ever get enough." His voice has a satisfied underlying tone. He may have done this last night, but he is ravishing me as if this is our first time.

My hand comes to my head to check that I'm still on planet earth. "Don't tell me that, it just makes me more desperate for you to make me come."

Stone chuckles softly deep in his throat. "That's kind of the point," he rasps.

I have to smile to myself at his remark. But it makes me realize that I'm in a light mood that's taken over my mind and body.

"I-I think…" I begin to stammer. A release begins to barrel down my body, twisting in my pelvis. My only answer at this point is to comb my fingers through Stone's hair to hold on and keep me safely against the mattress. My moan is a sound I didn't know I could make; it's honest. This is by far better than any fantasy that's been lingering on a loop in my thoughts lately.

He slips a finger Inside of me, and I whimper a pleased sound, enjoying the surprise as he slowly pumps, and my walls tighten around him. I'm in such a frenzy between his tongue and fingers that heat spreads across my skin, a near burning feeling.

"I want you to come on my tongue, Harlow," Stone murmurs his demand against the apex of my thigh. His slightly stubbled jaw drives me wild again.

The aching of my clit is too much to bear, and then it hits me like a tidal wave, and I vibrate on his tongue just as he requested. He doesn't leave me just yet and keeps his tongue on my clit until the convulsing fades away and my labored breath begins to calm down.

My heavy eyelids indicate my drowsy and spent state. I'm not complaining, but I need to come down from my orgasm. I smile when Stone studies me to check that he succeeded at his job.

"You're beautiful," he informs me as he moves to lie on his side next to me. Stone captures my chin with his finger to tip my mouth up, and he kisses me. I taste the proof of his talents on his lips, and he slips his tongue inside my mouth. I hum a sound in my relaxed moment.

My hand roams down his body to find the button on his jeans, but his hand wraps around my wrist to stop me, and then my eyes shoot fully open with confusion, as I can feel he's hard as a rock.

"Not now." His face is light and doesn't have me worried. "No need to rush." The feeling of the back of his finger gliding along my cheek is sweet, but I know where his mind really is.

Still, I nod once.

Stone pulls me closer to his body, and his leg lands around my waist to cover my bare lower body. I don't feel vulnerable that I'm the one half naked. We lie there with our arms entwined for a few moments in silence.

But it only makes me ponder a lot of thoughts floating inside my head.

I can't take it.

"Your shirt. It has to go," I request with a firmness in my tone. I'm in control of this evening, aren't I?

Stone's eyes widen and again he examines my sincerity. I'm about to scream that he doesn't need to check every other minute, but he gets the hint when we're in a stare-off and I don't give up.

His eyes are just as daring as mine, but he obeys and sits up to take his shirt off.

"Jeans too," I add.

Stone shakes his head, charmed by my insistence. He listens and follows through, stripping down to his boxer briefs while I peel my shirt up and off, leaving my bra on, and I'm not sure why.

His body is defined, and the small tattoo of hockey sticks on his chest just one-ups the sexy factor. I've seen it before, but it's even better when he's nearly naked.

I don't waste time and sit up to splay my hands along his chest then travel down. I watch my fingers trace the lines of his warm body, and again, that beating inside of me nearly drowns my ears as emotions coil between my ribs.

Please don't ruin this, I pray to myself and close my eyes in a long blink.

Stone watches as I skim along his skin until I grip his length through his boxer briefs, and he groans from the touch. He feels large and ready. Most of all, I just can't get over this demand within to have him inside me. I sneak my hand into his boxers to wrap around his cock, and our foreheads touch as we both soak in the feeling of my touch on him.

"Damn it, I'm not sure how long I'm going to last waiting," he mutters.

"You don't have to wait. Please," I whisper a plea as I encourage him to take every scrap of clothing off, which he does in a flash.

He sighs. "You don't want to know the thoughts in my head, Harlow. You'll only run." There is something underlying, and I can only imagine it's fantasies that would make my legs buckle until I'm on my knees to obey whatever he demands. He sounds nearly sinister, but it just pools more desire between my thighs.

Stone isn't an innocent man. I have a sixth sense when someone is anything but vanilla in the bedroom. He would be rough and fast. He knows exactly what he wants. Stone leads the way with dark eyes to possess you, I can see it already.

Yet right now, he's giving it all up for this moment with me.

"Sit on me, Harlow. Straddle me and stay on top," he instructs as he reaches over to the bedside table to grab a condom.

With me sitting on top, I feel like I'm about to explode. It happens, my worst fear. The underlying fear, and an image flashes in my head that makes me freeze. Then warmth and calm slides down my spine. That's new. I glance down to see that Stone and I are wrapped around one another.

I breathe a deep breath.

"Harlow, you have to tell me if you wan—"

My finger flies up to hush his mouth. "Don't say it."

Stone's hands quickly land on my cheeks to hold my head in place. "Listen to me, you're in control. We don't have to do anything. And if you want, bite my shoulder if you need to, squeeze my body tight, just don't worry about disappointing me."

That's the last thing I want to do.

"I want this now, please." I'm getting aggravated by his insistence to check in.

It only makes him smirk yet again, right before he rips open the condom wrapper and sheathes himself.

Then it happens. I feel him align himself along my opening and the tip of his length slides along my wetness, flicking my clit and wanting more.

My head falls to his shoulder, and I close my eyes with my mouth firmly tucked into the curve of his neck.

The moment he enters me, emotion nearly takes over me.

"Fuck," Stone breathes. "You feel too good. Tight, and I'm trying to take you slowly, but you fit snug around my cock." He tips his body up to hit me deep.

My nails claw his back, but I don't want to stop.

This is different, I repeat in my head.

Maybe I had more fear than I thought, because a moment overcomes me where suddenly a new air warms within. One where I can finally feel someone inside of me and smile to myself.

Our breaths begin to sync. Stone's more a grunt and mine a long moan. I do my best to slide up and down on his cock, and his hands guide my hips.

We move together on every thrust, completely in rhythm and lost as air wraps around us that feels like a steam shower. Our lips find hard and long kisses, only adding to our breath growing heavy. His mouth explores my cleavage, only to draw a line back up to my mouth.

Our eyes connect, and I'm not entirely sure what clicks, but we both barrel toward an orgasm that hits us in a mind-blowing moment only a few seconds apart.

By the time our breathing hollows out, I'm not sure if we can untangle from my body draped around Stone.

He kisses the top of my head. "I'll be right back."

I mumble okay, and then it registers he needs to get rid of the condom.

Gathering strength, I move the covers to tuck myself under the duvet, with no plans to do anything else. Instead, I lie on my back staring at the ceiling, realizing what step I just took and how it feels kind of amazing. An uplifting key to unlock what I deserve to have again.

I touch my face before I touch my stomach, slowly dragging my fingers in a near sensual way. I'm not dreaming, and my lips press together.

Stone is soon back and slides under the covers. "Penny for your thoughts?" His head rolls to the side to watch me.

"Trust me. When I say unexplainable, I mean it," I say softly.

He wraps his arm around my middle and drags me to his body until I'm resting my head against his chest.

"What do I say?"

"Nothing," I answer blankly.

"Sleep. We both need sleep."

I smile against his skin. "That's probably the last thing we both want. However, two orgasms later and maybe you're right."

"Of course, I am," he teases.

My fingers draw on his chest. "The thing is… now that I got over a wall, then I might need to do it again." Because this feels good and right. And it's with him.

Stone is quick to roll me to my back. "I was hoping you would say that."

I nearly squeal as I soak in this night that was exactly how I hoped it would be.

It's later when he climbs out of bed to dispose of yet another condom and I see his glorious naked body walking to the bathroom, his ass a crime to humanity how impeccable it is, that I realize something else.

I was on top, again.

Stone Madden is hiding. He hasn't unleashed his inner inhibitions. But it bothers me, and I'm well aware why.

Which is why I have to make another request later. I'm comfortable with it.

I'm just not sure he will agree.

The soft stretch of Harlow's mouth hasn't seemed to fade all morning. Even when her lips press against the rim of her mug of tea, it doesn't falter. I'm not going to deny that it swirls a feeling inside me that is brighter than I'm used to when I'm with a woman. I dare say that there is a real feeling behind the last 24 hours, not just physical.

We're sitting at the Dizzy Duck Inn for brunch in the restaurant, partly due to the fact that we skipped the breakfast hour and slept in. Having her long hair splayed against one of my pillows is a fantasy that any guy would dream of, yet I get to live it.

We sit by the big bay window to overlook the lake that is partly frozen with the cloudy sky in the backdrop. We're taking it easy and not rushing the morning.

"What?" She's near bashful. "Why do you keep staring at me?"

"You have a glow," I state bluntly. "It's good that you ordered more than toast for breakfast, you seem a little exhausted." A half-smirk hits the corner of my mouth.

She smiles. "That would be for a good reason. And don't criticize my breakfast choices. Toast is an important start of the day, but it has to be just soft enough to ensure your knife doesn't make the scraping noise. Halfway between not toasted and half crunchy. The butter will melt better that way, then a thin layer of jam, preferably strawberry or apricot, is the finishing factor."

I laugh. "Wow. I didn't realize there is an art to toast and that Harlow Olive treats it like a sport. No wonder you have a hate for frozen bread."

"It ruins the toasting process," she retorts.

The waiter arrives to leave us with Harlow's toast and a basket of breads and croissants then quickly scurries off.

"Right on time," I say. She quickly grabs the croissant, and I feign shock. "You're cheating on your toast?"

Harlow grins. "We should probably exit this ridiculous discussion on carbs."

A teenager enters the dining room with his parents and gives me a wave and seems excited.

Harlow quickly looks over her shoulder after I wave back. "Who's that?"

"I don't remember his name, but he was at a hockey weekend for the local prep school's hockey team not too long ago," I explain.

"You help with kids' hockey?" She seems surprised.

I pick up my cup of coffee and take a quick sip before I answer. "I volunteer, yeah. Next summer, I'll help with the development camp here at the Spinners training facility for rookies and also the camp for inner-city kids."

Harlow's jaw drops a little, and she brings a hand to her heart. "Swoon."

I chuckle at her response. "Wasn't expecting that?"

"You never mentioned."

"I guess not. Probably because we're still getting to know one another. We've only seen each other a handful of times."

Her eyes dip down to the tablecloth, and she grows silent as she seems to be occupied with a thought, and her lips tuck into her mouth. Now she seems different. I study her, but honestly, I have no clue where her head is at.

"About that." Her eyes drift up so our eyes can lock again. "I kind of... hmm, you see..." Harlow can't seem to bring her words together.

"Yes?" I draw it out as I wait patiently, which is why I grab my coffee cup again.

"Last night was great."

"Way above average," I correct her, and it earns me a smile that she's pleased.

"You don't need to treat me like a delicate flower."

Hmm, not sure where we're going with this, but I will take a wild guess and tread carefully. I scan the room, and it's only half occupied with people; still, I lean in, as Harlow is sitting beside me at the square table.

Lowering my voice, I manage to figure out what to tell her. "Harlow, I think, considering the circumstances, it was better that your fir —" God damn it, I shouldn't say that. "It was just better that you were in control, okay?"

"Maybe, but also not. The thing is, I know you're keeping your..." This time she checks the room. "Inner inhibitions locked down." Her voice is uneven.

I snicker, and my eyes widen, but I can't help but smirk. "You want to talk about our sexual desires at 11am in the very public restaurant of the Dizzy Duck Inn?" I can't help but tease her.

She carefully tucks her hair behind her ear, and it brings my attention to her fingers that I want to tug away from her head to interlace with my own; instead, I grab my orange juice and sit back and enjoy whatever direction this conversation could be going in.

"I've overcome the mountain, so you're free to be as dominant as you want." She strings her words together at record speed.

I nearly choke on the sip of juice that I just took. Harlow should be proud that she's caught me slightly off guard.

Setting my glass back on the table, I readjust my body then grab the arm of Harlow's chair and yank her closer to me so she's nearly sitting by the corner of the table.

"Why would you think I want to dominate the fuck out of you?" I recognize the heat in my voice because she's cracking that box of want that I've been keeping locked lately. The kind of want where I demand she opens her legs while I pin her arms over her head. I lead the way, and she obeys. Flip her, slide into her, nibble her skin, and spank her. That's the Pandora's box that she's telling me to open.

My eyes, I can imagine, are forming a gleam full of warning.

A sexy smile ghosts her mouth. "Because of the way your hands hold my hips, the way you pistol your way inside of me, going hard, but then the moment you realize, you slow down because it's me. More importantly, when I first met you, well, you had this devilish appearance. I don't think I've contorted an unrealistic image in my head."

My cock twitches at her words.

I bring a hand across my jaw. "And if I say it's true?" I challenge.

She scoffs a gentle breath. "Then I'd answer to do it. I want to… do it all, because for some reason you dropped into my life, and it feels as though the chemistry is uncontrollable, and I just… you lead the way tonight. I enjoyed last night, and it was special in a way that not many people will understand." She touches my elbow, and I swallow because that box is now partly open. "You're in control now."

Her eyes haven't blinked once, and I can tell that she's dead serious.

I click my tongue on the top of my mouth as I consider my next move. But my body moves of its own accord, and my hand slips under the table to quickly find her knee. Our eyes lock, and my fingers begin to trail up her leggings because this woman slays in a long sweater over a thin fabric that's doing a half-ass job of warming her legs.

Her breath hitches slightly because she doesn't anticipate that my fingers slide straight up to the middle of her thighs, and I feel her warmth.

I bring my lips closer to her ear. "Harlow, you need to be 100% sure, because sometimes I can be gentle, but sometimes, so help me, I want to be demanding as hell until we make one another come not just once during the night or day, and you best believe I have no problem taking you behind a tree or on a beach. As much as you're free, I want to shackle you down, and I'm beginning to think it's because you drive me so damn crazy and should be punished for that."

Harlow's eyes blaze and her mouth opens, her cheeks rising, which tells me that she's satisfied with everything I say.

I give her no opportunity to answer, and instead, I circle a finger around her pussy, not caring that it's covered. My head lolls slightly to the side. "My guess is that you're soaked, because you feel damp. Is that what you are?"

She nods slowly.

"Words."

"I'm soaked," she confirms as she nibbles on her bottom lip.

I kiss her cheek. To anyone in here it would look innocent and sweet, but inside me it's sweltering a desire to ignore everyone in here and take Harlow right here on the table from behind.

Squeezing her thigh, I wish I could make her come right now, but I see our waiter walking toward us, which is why my hand returns to her knee, and I throw on an overdone smile and straighten my back to welcome our interrupter.

"Eggs Benedict with a side of bacon for the sir." A sound escapes from Harlow because she has a dirty mind, and our dear clueless twenty-year-old waiter has no clue that his choice of title means something else.

The waiter's face turns partly puzzled before he sets down the other plate with a returned smile. "The Belgian waffle with fruit and crème brûlée topping. Enjoy, you two."

The moment he turns his back, I bug my eyes out at Harlow. "Trust me, I hate the word sir."

Her face flushes before she sighs and creates space between us by scooting her chair back into place, causing my hand to fall from her knee.

"Okay, so… you agree with my request?"

I stare at her for a second more than I should, my gaze turning to sweltering and determined. "It's not a request that you made, it was a plea." She gently shakes her head, thinking I'm joking. But my face remains serious. "It was. I much prefer begging, though. Tonight, Harlow, if you're sure—because seriously, you're unleashing a side of me that's a bit heated—then yes, you will have your hands firmly planted against a surface while I fuck you from behind."

"I am sure. Sometimes unleashing something only brings more passion." She states it so simply.

But my mind meanders to the underlying meaning. Because normally, it's a few-days fling or a mutually beneficial situation. In this case, this is a longer commitment because I don't see this thing between us ending anytime soon, nor do I seem to mind.

She's giving me permission. I was beginning to fear that I would have to compromise when it came to us, in the bedroom at least. Now she's erased that boundary, which means there are no boxes unchecked except for that not-so-little factor of distance and unclarity of what the hell we are.

Nonetheless, our possibilities are now a little more endless.

"Tonight then. Now eat your waffle before it gets cold," I say casually.

I'm a hot-blooded man who has every intention of fulfilling her begging request, because I'm relieved to be crossing a threshold to a world where the door has been closed for a while.

Now I'm just wondering what I'm unleashing.

12

STONE

There is definitely a glint of excitement in Harlow's eye as we walk along Main Street, which means that she was completely serious about what she requested back at the Dizzy Duck Inn.

Thank the fucking heavens.

Does that make me an ass? Should I be questioning this more? Pressuring her is the last thing I want to do. But now she has thrown in a yellow card and flipped the pace on me; damn, maybe that puts the weight on me.

She flashes me a closed-mouth smile before she turns her head to observe the store fronts decorated for the holidays.

I just admire her because I've seen Main Street a thousand times.

"I'm sure if Santa were real that he would be very proud of the Lake Spark citizens for their efforts to turn this place into an overdone North Pole," she jokes.

I snort a laugh. "I'm kind of scared for Easter, but I heard they go crazy for St. Patrick's Day. It must be weird for you in Florida to see holiday decorations amongst palm trees."

Harlow shrugs. "It's all I've known." She leans in to whisper,

"Shh, don't tell my family, but it looks a thousand times better with snow, except I'm not sure I can feel my toes."

I instantly wrap my arm around her shoulders as we walk together. "I can probably fix that."

"I'm sure."

Her eyes squint. "Oh, I think I noticed last time I was here, but it's a bit more confronting when I see blue and silver lace." She tips her head in the direction of the lingerie boutique in town.

"By all means, explore." No, she really *should* explore.

Harlow nudges my arm, and alas, we move on.

My phone goes off, and I quickly pull it up to see a message from my brother.

"What's giving you a bright smile?" Harlow wonders.

"My brother wants to up the betting pool for Christmas. We always watch football the next day, a sort of tradition. Mostly college ball," I explain.

"Your face really does change when you talk about him. The bond must be nice between you two."

What the hell? Why did it just flicker in my brain that I should introduce her to the family?

I breathe out a long gust. "Did you ever wish you had a sibling?"

"Nah, I don't know what I'm missing. It's my friends and routine as the reason I've stayed in Florida. Anyhow, aren't I supposed to be writing while I'm here? I haven't gotten a single word in, you devil you," Harlow chides.

I look behind her and scan her ass, which she notices. "It's fine, you've been researching."

We both stop in our tracks. "I meant what I said. I'm not fragile."

My lips purse out. "In hockey, we speed ahead, and sometimes we look back after and realize it was the wrong play."

It takes her aback. "Ah, you think I will think I'm fine, only to freak out?"

I say nothing.

"I'm in control of my desire, don't you think?"

I need to lighten the moment. "Desire now? Hmm, I thought it was fulfilling that fantasy of sleeping with a hockey player." Harlow shakes her head. "You have to promise that you will give me an indication if something doesn't feel…"

"We're making promises now?" she teases back, but then after a moment, her face turns serious. "Just don't do anything that makes me feel like I can't breathe, well, except the orgasm part, but I think you know what I mean."

I nod that I do.

"So…" She swirls her foot on the ground, waiting for me to take the lead.

"Come on, Harlow. We should probably warm you up. Your poor body isn't used to real winter. Lucky for you, body heat is a perfect way to solve that."

Harlow makes me nervous. Not because of the dynamic of her life but more so because she feels different. How many times can a guy say different? It's more she's the flick of a switch inside of me that maybe I was waiting for in life.

But I always deliver, and I refuse to give her anything less.

The moment we both manage to get our coats off, I twirl her body and push her against the back of the door, feeling that primal need take over. Her breath hitches from surprise, but a satisfied look begins to form.

Our eyes lock, and I'm quick to pin her wrists against the door.

"I promise I have a plan to devour you." My voice boils, because any thought except how to rip her clothes evaporates from my mind. Her hips jut out and then press harder against my body; she's all in. "Wrap those legs of yours around my waist," I demand right before I crash my lips onto hers, ensuring it isn't light, instead sending a message that I might be a little rough, and I have every intention to do as I please. The keening noise from the back of her throat is an indication that she doesn't mind in the slightest.

I feel her one leg slide up the back of my thigh before she repeats the same move with her other one until she's wrapped tightly around my waist. I instantly walk us toward my bedroom upstairs, confident that the stairs are no obstacle. Instead, when we reach the stairs, I feel her nails dig into my shoulder blades as we continue to kiss fast and urgent, my lips skimming down to tease her neck when her head falls back.

Harlow's hair is perfect down; I'll be able to wrap it around my hand even better. My door is slightly ajar, and I kick it with my foot, not even hearing the noise because our kisses and murmurs are the champions of the room's soundtrack.

Heading straight to the mirror, I set her down and swirl her until we're both staring into the glass, with my fingertips on her hips.

"Too many clothes, Harlow," I seethe a whisper near her ear, and I feel her shudder instantly, and it makes my cock twitch, desperate to get rid of my jeans, but I need to wait because I have plans.

I slide my hands to grab the hem of her sweater and the shirt underneath to yank up in a swift move with absolutely no grace. Her eyes glow with anticipation, and the sweater quickly drops to the floor, and our eyes lock in the mirror. Damn it, another wild card. She teased me about silver lace earlier, and my mind imagined it, but now I'm living the dream as I stare at her in the mirror. The cups of her bra perfectly lift her cleavage, and the panties leave little to the imagination, a detailed piece of fabric, but it will be easy to move aside. Everything about her in the moment is a vision of perfection. She'll never be allowed to change in the bathroom in the morning ever again if I'm around.

I tsk a sound both in approval and letting her know that her game is a bit naughty.

"Hmm, I thought I would throw it on," she hums in accomplishment.

My fingers quickly move up to grab her jaw and squeeze in a way that isn't too comfortable, nor too coarse. "Harlow, I much prefer when you're the good girl."

She breathes heavily, and I drop my hand until the back of my fingers drag down the side of her body, careful to trace the band of her pants before gliding back up to swirl the cups of her bra. Feeling her tremble only makes me harder.

I bring my mouth near her, with the heat of her body making me dizzy. I nuzzle my nose against the skin of her cheek. "See how fucking perfect you look." Our sight hasn't left the mirror. "Tell me that you're eager, Harlow."

Harlow's jaw slides side to side softly. "I'm eager," she repeats.

"Take off your leggings. You're still too covered."

She fumbles around her waistband but manages to pull them down, with her ass bumping into the hard bulge of my cock. Does she know she's driving me equally crazy? I believe she does.

Heading straight between her legs, I feel her hot and damp through the lace. Swirling my finger, we both seem to whimper together.

"Someone wants me," I mumble into her hair as I splay one palm down on her belly and my other hand explores her pussy, ensuring I never sneak under the lace. She's so fucking wet that the lace feels as though it evaporated into her flesh.

"I can't wait to taste that. Only after you get on your knees for me."

Harlow lets out an uneven breath. "Is that what you want?" She glances over her shoulder. "Me on my knees?"

"Absolutely." I pull her panties to the side to give her pussy one stroke and swirl around her clit before bringing my fingers to her mouth that willingly opens. "Suck, Harlow." The tightness of the pressure against my digits only encourages me to move this all along faster. "Good girl, your mouth is going to feel good around my cock." I pull away from her mouth to stick my fingers in my mouth to suck the cocktail of her juices mixed with the taste of her tongue.

I'm taking her up a rollercoaster, with full intention to ensure the drop will be mind-blowing. Unhooking the clasp of her bra, I kiss the curve of her shoulder, her skin soft as silk, sliding the straps down until the bra lands on the floor. "Keep your eyes on the mirror, Harlow." My voice now has a bit more edge as I recognize that my carnal need for this woman only rises with every second and with an overpowering need to control her until we both get our release. Cupping her breasts, a murmur leaves her mouth, and she continues to watch in the mirror. Her body curves slightly into me as I press my thumb and index finger around her nipples to squeeze and twist, her moan only adding to the heightened sexual tension in the air.

"I want to drag my lips around these, swirl my tongue until I suck them, and I want to come on them." That earns me her bottom lip getting chewed on by her teeth.

"Then do it," she rasps.

Releasing her tits, I quickly wrap my hand into her hair gently, pulling her head back slightly. "I decide what we're doing, Harlow," I remind her against the skin of her neck, and a flame fills her eyes, and she releases a sound of agreement. Letting go of her hair, I step us backward to the bed where I turn her and urge her to sit on the edge of the bed. "Unzip me."

A satisfying look flashes across her face, and she submits to my demand, with the feeling of her fingers dragging the zip lower. She peers up as though checking that she's obeying right. And she's tormenting me with the slow drag of each tooth of the zipper. I only feel slight relief when she slides my pants and boxer briefs lower, and her hand wraps around my length.

A few strokes is all I let her do. "Mouth," I order.

Harlow's eyes drift up and stay on mine as her lips cover my tip, and she makes a point for me to watch as her tongue swirls to taste my pre-cum. Her moan is slightly overdone, but I like her a bit overzealous and wanting to drive me wild. She moves lower and takes me into her mouth. I wrap my hands around her hair to guide her forward until I'm fully in her mouth, hitting the back of her throat. I'm proud that I'm by no means lacking on the size front, which means that she struggles slightly, but it doesn't matter as her mouth waters even more on every pump.

"That's it, take me deep," I encourage her. "I bet you want my cum to slide down your throat, don't you." It's a statement, not a question. She nods with her mouth stuffed. "Keep going, I'm going to fill that dirty mouth of yours."

Her moan sounds like a groan, but she keeps going until the pressure under my navel drives lower down until I explode into her mouth, and I ensure she can't leave by holding her head firmly on me until every last drop is in her mouth and sliding down her throat.

"Fuck, you suck good," I breathe to myself. A flash of worry breezes across my mind that I'm pushing her too far; we've been moving at a snail's pace the last few months, only to dive in deep. But when she pulls off and there is pride in that sexy smirk of hers, I know she's content. I don't give her much time to soak in her accomplishment. I guide her up the mattress by hovering over her, with the corner of my mouth hitched up, and her soft smile indicates that she is enjoying every second of this.

A sound hides in her throat yet is still enough for me to hear pure heaven, encouraging me to open her legs, as we're not going to waste a second to take in this moment. I'm on my stomach, ripping her panties down her legs and throwing them to the side. My tongue finds home, and she writhes under the pattern that I trace on her pussy, taking extra time around her clit.

"That feels really good," she exhales.

I press her stomach down when her hips try to rock up. "It will be even better when I'm fucking you hard and deep." A lazy, low, muffled laugh escapes from the back of her throat. It just makes me dip a finger inside her warm heat then add another to pump a few times. "You're soaking, and I need your snug pussy on my cock."

I abandon between her legs to linger over her, careful to give slight space between us to ensure we're not too tight in this position, allowing her to breathe and for me to soak in the glint of her eyes. I kiss her lips, and she gives back what I offer. It's an instant of calmness, sinking into a moment, a break from fucking her. Even though I'm beginning to think this isn't fucking at all, which is why I end the pause and sit up on my knees to flip her to her belly, pulling her hips up until her ass is in the air, and my pants come off in record speed. I'm not sure making this too sensual and sentimental will be great for my heart; I feel it weakening. Hard fucking is safer.

"Hands over your head against the mattress and don't move them," I say, right before my fingers dig into the muscle of her ass, wanting to spank her but deciding this isn't the moment; instead, I palm the flesh and admire her firm behind. "I swear to God, one day I'll take you like this right after I throw you over my lap to spank you, and you'll take it because you like it." *Save me,* she tips her ass up more to show off.

"Fuck," Harlow pants.

"Exactly, fuck," I quickly reach over to the table to grab a condom and get it on, wishing I could take her bare.

It's a quick tease through her pussy before edging her entrance and sliding right in, feeling her squeezing along my length. I hiss out a breath because this is nearly an out-of-body experience where my entire body wants to race toward coming, just because I think it hurts how much I want her and need relief. I reach forward to grab her arms and bring them behind to hold them across her back in a hold that again has me wondering.

"You okay?"

"Yes," she mumbles against the mattress, almost sounding aggravated that I keep checking in.

I continue to thrust inside her, speeding up my movement, going a little harder until I have nowhere left to go. I have plans to live inside of her all night. How could I not? "You take my cock perfectly. The right fit."

One hand stays firm on her wrist while the other one sneaks under her body where there is space to play with her. She has to come around my cock, I want her to vibrate around me before I thrash and jerk to come inside of her.

We seem to lose track of time, but I get my wish, and a loud moan of my name fills the room while she shakes around me. I don't give her the opportunity to calm as I follow her, and I come shortly after before I fall forward, careful not to squish her. Instead, I kiss her back, drawing a line down her spine. My heart throbs, and my body glistens with sweat.

Having to leave her to get rid of the condom is not what I want. Exploring her back while she lies in a blissful state is by far better.

By the time I make it back to bed, Harlow hasn't moved an inch and instead lies in a state where a drowsy smile is permanent on her lips. I slide in next to her and continue where I left off, painting her back with my touch.

"I like you that way,"

Harlow partly turns her head. "Like what?"

"Obedient," I say.

She giggles gently. "I like you that way… dominant."

I do too. But I like slow with you too.

I interlink my hand with hers before I kiss her shoulder. Harlow twists her head slightly more to capture my mouth for another kiss; it's warm and deliberate. I'm not a cuddler, except with her it feels right.

She's far too beautiful for my bed. She molds to me in all ways, and most of all, I don't want her to leave. I wonder if she feels this connection, this rope that is no longer long. I care for her for sure, but I can't pinpoint what else is brewing.

"A shame you're not staying longer. Now I just have to take you in the shower, on my kitchen counter, and again in my bed with you reverse cowgirl at record speed."

Harlow rolls to her back like a pancake getting tossed. "Well, I'm not a Lake Spark citizen, and you have Christmas with your family and I'm going to visit my own parents."

My lips close tightly because I hate time and space suddenly.

"Maybe you can visit me after the new year?" she asks.

Now that sounds like a good idea. "I will take you up on that."

Her thumb begins to caress my cheek as we lie here naked, with no plans to cover ourselves. "You have to write too. It's old school, but what kind of writers would we be if we didn't?"

I chortle a laugh. "Very true. By the way, has this been an inspiration for your writing?"

Harlow snuggles close as my arm snakes around her body. "Completely, which might be a problem, as I'll just think of you and walk around wet all the time."

"I should buy you new lace panties, which came from the offside, by the way. Naughty you."

She laughs again. "Nah, naughty me would be occupying your head and never leaving."

I'm already there.

I give her a tight smile. "Tomorrow, will we have breakfast here?" I suggest to change the topic.

Harlow nods once. "Only if I get to watch you writing in your office. Something tells me that might be sexy as hell."

Now I'm amused. "Ditto."

A silence overcomes us, and we stare at one another, both lost in thought.

Her face turns vulnerable but elated, nonetheless. "I'm happy I've unlocked what I've been waiting for."

I fear that's all I am. A sort of therapy for her.

"That it's with you feels even better… as if it was always meant to be you," she adds.

That answer is by far better.

I swipe her hair behind her ear to kiss her cheek because suddenly chaste is me. "A secret." She begins to broaden her smile. "I wanted to hear that."

We kiss longingly which can't help this confusion.

Yet again she reads my mind. "What are we doing?" Her whisper is near desperate.

"I'm not sure," I reply honestly.

Our answer is only to roll together in an embrace and feel each other again in a way that seems to be strengthening us into an uncertain future that neither of us want to end. Maybe it's a collision course, something will be thrown our way.

For now, we don't seem to have a care in the world.

HARLOW

Hey, Harlow,

Happy we both survived the holidays; I mean with our families. Albeit, my brother and I timed the turkey frying wrong, yet we all came out in one piece. It was a surprise to see your social media post where you staged your bikini on a mattress next to a towel and your book… an olive-green bikini. How original. That's good you're back in writing action. Just double-checking, you don't basically write what you and I do, right? And if so, I should just make it dirtier between us.

So, I was thinking. Well, not really thinking, since I hit that button on the screen at high speed, but I booked a ticket to Florida. We have no clue what we're doing and left things unexplainable last time, although we couldn't stop grinning. That's a good sign.

I'm assuming I have a place to crash and can save my money for a lingerie shopping spree. Don't worry, I'll head straight for the olive-green section so you can take a photo of the lace lying on your bed for social media before you give me a private showing.

I would say that I hope you don't mind my not giving you a choice on having me as your houseguest, but I know you enjoy being commanded.

-Stone

———

Uh-oh, Stone,

Someone is very presumptuous. But of course, mi casa es su casa. And you're right, we are two clueless souls.

Is this all like a hockey pinch? When you attempt to make a gamble as you want to win my puck? Yeah... I can already hear you saying that you will literally pinch me.

You're in luck. I don't think I want to be alone in my bed, and if you are offering your services, then I'm not sure you need to bother with lingerie, I just plan to stay naked. On the other hand, my wrists might need to be constrained...

-Harlow

———

Tsk tsk, the belt tying was going to be my surprise.

-Stone

———

I could re-read his emails a thousand times. We're not a texting couple, we write letters because we are a sappy couple, apparently. Text messages are for practical reminders. Letters are for words that will carve into your heart.

My heart. Why does that come to mind?

Blowing out a deep breath, I wait for Flo to work her magic as I lie down.

She whistles, impressed. "You were sure in a rush, demanding I fit you into my schedule for your wax. Someone has plans," she remarks as she gets the wax ready.

I prop myself up on my elbows. "Well, Stone is coming in a few days, and I'm sure we have plans."

Flo snorts a laugh. "I'm sure he will be coming."

I gawk at her for her joke, but admittedly, it's funny.

The holidays have passed, and I think he got his uncle-of-the-year award. I saw my folks down in the Virgin Islands and kind of kept myself busy the past few weeks with writing. When Stone wrote that he had booked a ticket to come see me, it was an easy decision. I can't wait to see him. I'm happy he's making the effort, even though I'm not sure what the effort is for.

"You know, Harlow. I think it's really great that you have a brightened face and more bounce to your step. Who knows, maybe it can go somewhere."

A feeling dips in my stomach. "That's the hard part. We're more than a fling but nothing serious."

I flinch when I hear a rip and there's a brief sting against my skin, but this is all in the name of a good cause.

"Whatever it is, then enjoy it. Will I get to meet him?"

I shake my head. "Probably not. He's only here for a few days, and, well, I kind of hope that we are occupied, except for maybe a walk on the beach and having dinner by the ocean."

"I bet."

A thought stews in my head as I stare at the ceiling. "Maybe this is all another blow from fate. Throwing me another obstacle. Giving me a preview of what a normal relationship could be again, only to tear it all away for some reason."

I turn my head to see Flo contemplating with her lips pursing out, maybe even hesitating to say anything, but then she does. "Nobody knows what will happen, Harlow. That doesn't mean you shouldn't take a chance. What if you miss out on fate throwing you the perfect card?"

"I'm not sure I'm so lucky."

Flo works another waxing strip off with a little more force, and I yelp. "Sorry, trying to knock some sense into you." She flashes me a contrite smile.

I can't think about it all anymore. Time is ticking anyhow, and before I know it, Stone will be here.

———

MY HOUSE IS VERY different from Stone's place. Mine is one story, with two bedrooms, and a few blocks from the beach. It's simple in style yet with a few knickknacks. Stone follows me in, as I picked him up from the airport, and in the car, we caught up and I gave him the window tour. The greeting kiss knocked me off my feet, literally, he tipped me back to kiss me deeply.

But now the air has thickened because we have privacy.

"This is my humble abode," I say as I throw my keys into the basket on the side table. "I figured tonight we can eat in and tomorrow book a table somewhere. You eat seafood, right? I normally just order a salad or veggie burger. My friend Flo is desperate to meet you, but I figured we could save that for another time maybe." I do my best to avoid his eyes because I'm a little nervous. The good kind that sends butterflies to my stomach.

Stone sets his suitcase down and kicks it gently to the side. "Good plan." I begin to walk toward the kitchen, but he is quick to touch my arms from behind. "Show me the bedroom, Harlow." His hot breath hits my ear, and boom, I'm sinking into the arousal that's been building. "Now," he grits out.

"This way, please," I play along.

"You said please. You might need to say that again when you're begging," he informs me.

I want to laugh, but he isn't joking.

The moment we get to my room, he turns me around, only to push me onto the bed. "I need to be inside you. My hand has been working overtime lately." Stone is already whipping his t-shirt off, and I'm quick to follow by taking off my own clothes.

Taking a moment to admire his body, my jaw goes slack. "God, you have a body that I very much enjoy seeing every single time as though it's the first time." I begin to back up on the duvet until I'm near the headboard.

I want him inside me just as impatiently as Stone wants it. He crawls onto the bed naked, and even though I left my panties on, I did so with purpose; I like it when he rips them off.

My knees come up, and I rest my feet on the mattress. My intention is to tease him by dragging my fingers down to my breasts. "Touch me, Stone."

His eyes glimmer with mischief, and he tips his head slightly to the side. "Not until I watch you play with your clit to show me what you do when we're apart."

We kiss hungrily before our game continues.

I wasn't expecting that, but I'm here for it. My fingers slowly move lower until the tips of my nails circle along the edges of the fabric while my knees butterfly out. My eyes align with the vision of Stone stroking himself.

Bringing the fabric of my panties to the side, I catch him by surprise. He inspects it closer, and his brows rise. "Fuck me, you are… unexpected."

"You like?" I say as my long finger begins to circle around my bundle of nerves.

"I'm not complaining." His knees meander forward slightly as he closes in, as if I'm prey. "I'm going to demand one day that we video chat so I can watch you play with yourself while thinking of me."

I slip a finger inside myself, and his eyes darken with more heat. "I much prefer you having a closeup in person." I hum a moan.

He tuts once before taking hold of my legs to roughly drag my panties down right before he rests my ankles on his shoulders. "I much prefer licking you before I fuck you." He dives down to plant his tongue between my folds, and I feel more arousal dripping from me as my clit throbs. I'm nearly there, and then he stops. "Fast now, slow later."

He grabs the condom that he threw on the bed earlier, and I'm woozy in ecstasy when his tip begins to explore inside me, getting covered in the proof that I need him. Then Stone plunges into me.

He groans, his face gratified. "You always fit me like a glove. Tight because you've been waiting for me all these weeks."

My hips begin to roll, and his palms hold me still before guiding me with him. I moan, and my back arches up. He's pumping into me as he sits on his knees and I'm lying on my back. We're joined purely by my legs wrapped around him and his cock inside of me.

"I need more," I rasp.

I begin to clench my walls around him, and Stone drops his head. "Harlow, you are a *very* good girl. Milking me because you want me to come while I'm inside of you. Is that what you want?"

"Mmhmm."

"Say it, Harlow." His gaze pierces me.

"I want you to come so hard while you're inside of me."

He smirks before his two fingers reach down to toy with my clit to help me along the ride.

Having Stone inside me feels a million times better than any substitute in my drawer or my own fingers. I don't want to leave this bed while he's here. I'm addicted, and I'm a woman free to explore.

All the reasons I barrel down a hill into a crashing orgasm, with Stone following quickly behind. He takes a moment before he lowers his body, staying inside me, while he rests his arms by my sides to hold his weight while he floats above me.

"I've missed you," I breathe as I feather my fingers through his hair.

"I plan on making you prove that all night. I've missed you too."

I look down, and he peers up to ensure our eyes hold, right before our grins grow until they hurt.

"No point in showering. I need you on all fours in a few minutes."

"At your service, Stone."

———

WE WALK ALONG THE BEACH, hand in hand. Maybe it's too sweet for us, but when I interlaced our fingers, Stone just squeezed tighter.

"Admit it, you're a snowbird, relieved to have some low 70s weather," I tease him.

"Nah, even in cold weather I'm able to trace the tan lines on your body. Surprisingly, it's not my tongue but my fingers that I enjoy sketching those lines with. I think it's more sensitive against your skin. Not that it matters, you're always drenched around me."

I swat him gently. "Anyhow, I'm happy we are taking a break to get some fresh air."

Before we can continue our stroll, I grin to myself when I notice Flo pretending to go on an evening jog, heading straight for us. I texted her that Stone and I would be going for a walk, as I wanted to know the name of the new restaurant on the pier.

"Oh, hey there," she waves to us then slows her pace to stop.

I shake my head, amused. "Stone, this is my friend Flo. *Clearly,* she's taken up jogging as a hobby."

"Now, now, Harlow. We all need to try something out of our comfort zone. Plus, you forgot that you have me on that tracker app because we believe in safety first." Flo raises her brows at me, and I sigh because I forgot about that.

Stone looks between us with a goofy grin. "Hi, Flo, nice to meet you."

"The feeling is mutual." Flo turns to me and mutters, "He's way hotter in the flesh. Those online photos don't do him justice."

In the corner of my eye, Stone dips his head and rubs his thumb across his jaw with a wry smile on his mouth. He seems to be preening from Flo's statement.

"A romantic sunset walk, points for effort," Flo tells Stone. "No bonus points since you didn't bring a picnic."

"I assure you that I'll make it up to Harlow later." Stone is now a little smug.

Flo flashes her eyes at me. "I bet you will."

"You've now seen him in the flesh. Anything else, Flo?" I try to move this along.

"I mean, I have about a thousand questions, but I don't want to ruin this moment between you two, and I need to head to the grocery store."

"Well, be on your way then. I'll see you at Tuesday's Zumba class," I encourage her to scoot away, with my words nearly gritted out.

"Hint taken. Nice to meet you, Stone. Harlow talks about you a lot."

He glances at me with swagger. "Wonderful to hear."

"Go," I say, giving my friend a curt tone. Flo only giggles and walks away. "What happened to your run?" I call out.

Flo quickly throws me a look. "Fuck that. I hate running."

Stone attempts to hide his chuckle, and I just smile awkwardly.

When we're out of earshot, Stone's eyes meet mine. "Well, cross meeting the crazy friend off the list," I inform him.

"It's good. It seems we have a list." He drapes his arm around my shoulder to direct me to continue our walk.

Stone searches for a shell with his toe as we slow our walk. "I'll be handing in the last round of edits next week." His tone maybe has a hint of soberness.

"That's great, no?"

He glances at me with a soft smile. "Actually, yes, I'm just struggling with the ending."

"Well, what is the ending for a hockey player? Do you mean the next steps in your character's career or life in general?"

"Both. You have to take the competitive aspect out of your life," he notes.

I glance off to the calm waves as the sunset's hues reflect off the horizon. "I know we've talked about it before but I think it plays a big role in your life. Do you miss playing hockey on a team? I mean, even though it was only a few years, I'm sure it left an imprint in your life." My head turns back to him to notice his face remains stoic.

"It's a bitter pill to swallow sometimes. For years, you're building up and hoping for a career as a professional, then you get a taste and…" He snaps his fingers. "It's gone, just like that. I'm grateful for the few years that I had out in Colorado, but half of me didn't want to give it up and the other half knew better. I'm lucky that I have another hobby."

"Lucky indeed." The corner of his mouth lifts from my statement. We wouldn't have met unless we crossed paths; I sure as hell wouldn't have met him at a hockey game.

Stone loops his arm around my body as we continue to walk, the sand feeling cool between our toes. "You know, my favorite play in hockey is actually a pinch."

I sputter a laugh. "I would like to think that you're making innuendo, but you're not. Maybe that makes it more endearing."

"Trust me, I'm not a commendable guy. Someone is probably writing a book about my antics on and off the ice. If only they knew that a plot twist just entered my life."

My heart patters in an unusual beat. It's Stone. He's seeping inside of me. I bite the inside of my cheek, trying to let a shade of crimson spread. I do agree with his assessment, though.

We take a few steps before sitting down to watch the sun go down. The wind breezes through my hair, and I take a deep relaxing breath. "You know, I normally don't come here, unless I'm with a friend. There is no way I would come here alone when the sun sets and the night descends."

Stone pulls me closer to his side. "But you're here now."

"Because there are strong arms around me… Speaking of which, how many pushups *do* you do a day?" I try to bring lightheartedness to this conversation, even though another traumatic past event seems to be breaking away, and that's profound.

"Do you think it will ever go away, the feeling?" he wonders.

I shrug. "It's getting better slowly. But probably not. I remember fewer details, if that's any consolation." Every time we talk about it, I notice Stone tense, his jaw tightening as if he would kill someone. I touch his knee to assure him. "New topic. The dinosaur animal crackers at the store were on sale, so that made my week."

"I thought it was me," he retorts.

"But they have pink frosting with sprinkles." I pretend to pout.

"Well, in that case," he rebuffs.

My head falls onto his shoulder. "We can hit the bar after this if you want. I think there's a hockey game on the TV there. Take it easy and don't make it too late. If we don't wear ourselves out, then maybe we can try writing in the morning."

"As much as a joint writing session sounds like a delight, with my iced latte that everyone here seems to drink while rollerblading or pretending to have run five miles, I'm confident you would just be a distraction."

"Hmm. Would it be better if we were at my house and just take it easy, with you writing shirtless and me in your shirt, knowing full well once we get 500 words in then we can rip everything off and end up on the living room floor?" I suggest while throwing on my sultry look.

He kisses the top of my head. "Yes. Now come here."

Stone indicates for me to sit between his legs as we both look out across the ocean.

"You're tearing down the boundaries I thought I had, and I'm not complaining. I want you to break more."

He scrapes his lips near my earlobe. "Harlow, you're making me create boundaries I didn't even realize I'm capable of."

"Perfect opposites then."

We take in the sunset, but the sun might as well run away. It's the feeling of Stone's body wrapped around me like a blanket and his lips skimming my cheek to whisper sweet nothings in my ear that has me mesmerized in this moment.

It turns out that I might be lucky.

But nobody is that lucky.

I know.

STONE

nd so it continues.

Stone,

Well, that was fast. It's only been a few weeks and now I find myself on the way back to Lake Spark. To write, of course. How horrible of a liar am I? Hmm, I appreciate that you said I could bring my bikini for an afternoon at the Dizzy Duck Inn spa to go swimming and enjoy the jacuzzi, even though you said I don't really need one since you can trace the tan lines of my bikini with your tongue. However, you are ever the gentleman to make the offer.

My hockey term this time is playmaker. The player who is so fast, he can create chances for a win because he reads the room (okay, ice). There is more chance of a win if he sets up another player for success.

Are you proud of me?

I can't help wondering if you are our playmaker. Are you trying to create a chance for us to get a goal that we both want? Even if I'm shaky on the idea that it's possible?

Yeah, I'll leave you with that.

Okay, see you soon!
Harlow

MY FINGERS TRAIL over my phone screen, outlining the email that I've already read a few times. I can feel my mouth slant to the side in an uneven smirk, only to be distracted when a hand begins to wave in front of my face.

"Uhm, earth to Stone. You're supposed to be catching up with your brother while we enjoy the fireplace under a dead moose," my brother Vaughn reminds me.

My eyes tip up, and I give him a smile. We're sitting in the lounge area of the Dizzy Duck Inn. He has exactly two days free before he is on the road again. He and Isla are using the opportunity for wedding planning since they got engaged at Christmas, and after the cake testing, Isla ditched him for a massage. We both quickly glance at Nora, my niece, sleeping in her stroller, before Vaughn and I focus on one another again.

"Sorry, I'm a little distracted," I admit.

"Harlow?" He looks at me, amused. I've always kept him up to date. We're close, even when his schedule is chaotic.

I growl to myself. "You know the answer."

"Don't you think at some point you both need to address that you're basically in a relationship with one another? I mean, you've now seen each other more than a few times. You're turning into a couple that travels distances to see one another."

I sigh, as he's saying my thoughts out loud. "Trust me, I think we both realize the obvious, but we're choosing not to confront it."

"Have you hit the ice lately? That normally clears your head."

That and writing. About every two weeks, I skate or help out at the training facility nearby, just to remember the good old times.

"Yeah, and speaking of which, how is that going for you, Mr. General Manager of the Spinners? Heard you had to trade Murphy."

Vaughn scoffs. "He threw a chair at me. That's how that went," he answers mundanely. "Don't change the topic. I need to meet Harlow."

My lips roll in, and that idea actually feels good. "Maybe. You're doing Sunday brunch before you fly in the evening?" He nods, and I give him a little fist pump in the air. "Yay, you know how I love burnt eggs, because apparently you and your fiancée are the couple that manage to do that," I tease him.

"Exactly. We'll be simple and not make a big deal about meeting the woman who's been making you a gentler soul the past few months." There's a pause between us. "I want to be happy for you if this all works out. We both deserve to have a better life than the one we grew up with. Even a shitty upbringing can do a 180 when you're an adult. Besides, one day you will have it all like you were meant to."

I roll my eyes. "Hell, let's not make it one of those conversations." I adjust my body on the sofa.

He chuckles. "Confronting reality is fun, isn't it?" His brows rise as if he's a wizard of knowledge.

In the corner of my eye, I see Holden, and he is quick to sit down uninvited, nor do we mind. He heaves a breath. "Don't mind me."

My brother and I study him then wince. "You look like hell," I say bluntly.

Holden stretches his neck, clearly agitated. "Another nanny quit."

"What the fuck?" I'm quick to respond. "Is it you? Because no kids are that devilish to make you go through as many nannies as you do."

Holden's lips purse out. "Oh yeah, this time was totally me, I admit—well, it was her. She tried to come on to me. No interest from my end, and this morning she quit. Leaving me yet again stuck to juggle meetings and school drop-off."

My brother tries to suppress his laugh. "Just find wife number two and then all of your problems are solved," he says, sarcastic.

"Then, at least, I would have someone to fuck on a daily basis to release my stress from parenting alone with a pre-teen and a ten-year-old who doesn't stop talking." He loves them, really.

My head drops at his half-honest sentence.

Vaughn holds his hand out to stop Holden from speaking. "Try and move on with your day." He points his thumb at me. "Harlow is visiting him again."

Holden looks at me, impressed, before throwing an arm over the back of the sofa to get comfortable. "Oh yeah? No wonder you demanded a dozen chocolate chip cookies and the best table at our restaurant." He clicks his fingers in the air. "Which reminds me to tell you to stop being an ass to the intern at reception."

I flash him a tight smile. "Excuse me for trying to have an enjoyable experience at our establishment."

"Geez, Stone, look in a mirror and accept that you are in relationship territory," my brother nearly scolds me. "She writes romance; surely, this must all be obvious to her too."

"He's right," Holden adds.

Defeat is building inside me. "Fine. I'll address that elephant in the room." After we have reunion sex and I stare into her eyes that lighten in my presence and it feels like the hours of the day vanish quicker than the clock can tick.

My jaw tightens, and I attempt to stretch it side to side as I gently nod that I've heard them.

———

HARLOW CIRCLES MY DESK, her usual olive-colored nails tapping my closed laptop, a habit she has gotten into the few times she's been here. After picking her up at the airport, we slid into an ease because we're comfortable around each other. It felt like I couldn't get us back to my house fast enough.

"You'll check emails first thing in the morning when the sun rises. I'll write for an hour and a half, then we can feel relief that we've actually been productive," she states firmly.

I step to her and come to sit on the edge of my desk, and I lower my eyes and spin my globe once. "That's not how sunrise is going to go. Why make us suffer? If we have to leave the bed before morning sex, that's just cruel."

A subtle smirk appears on her lips. "Or tonight makes us need a rest tomorrow. Besides, I need my breakfast fix at Jolly Joe's. I love watching Main Street in winter. The displays in the windows are overdone in red and pink for Valentine's Day. Not many towns get in that spirit for a holiday that was created by greeting card companies."

I have to smile at her humor. "Fine, I'll make your wishes come true."

My retort causes her to pause and for her smile to fade slightly. "Wishes come true." It sounds earnest. "I guess you kind of have. A fire has been lit again inside me." It's barely a whisper, but I hear her, the woman she used to be.

"That's good, because I'm riding the train with a destination that I'm not quite sure of, nor am I complaining about."

She sets her hand on my shoulder before gliding it down my arm. "Interesting. Seems our minds have conspired with one another on the not-quite-sure front. Maybe we can address it, but not today."

I pull Harlow to me between my knees to hold her head in my hands. "Why do I feel like we're in trouble?" I don't mean it in the literal way, more a fun way, with only a hint of reality underlying.

"Focus on tonight." Her cheeks rise, and I'm positive she's gearing up to say something that she's afraid to. "So, do you think… well, I'm ready."

"For what?"

The tip of her tongue hits her top teeth for a brief moment. "I know you are even more, uhm, adventurous." Her voice rises slightly. "In the bedroom. You've been holding back still. It's okay, we can stretch the boundaries."

I stare at her blankly before a closed-mouth smile spreads on my mouth. I'm not sure if I should feel lucky or proud of her, or both. She seems to want that. Harlow is confident in this moment.

"Uh, I'm on board with that."

Her face turns more elated, and a grin crosses her face. "Good."

She's waiting patiently while I bring my thumb to my jaw and debate what I'm going to do with her. Which fantasy I want to unravel with her.

"Upstairs now," I direct, with my voice firm. I lift her up as I stand, throwing her over my shoulder like a fireman trying to save someone, except she doesn't need saving. Not anymore. Instead, it's me who is getting in too deep with this woman who swept into my life unexpectedly.

Her joyous squeal brings me back to the moment, and how can I not be happy about that?

———

"ARE YOU SURE?" I double-check, as I have Harlow down to her lace olive-green panties and matching bra. A for effort and the fact she's keeping to her brand.

She stands before me with her lips in a pout as she contemplates, before her eyes squint and study me. "This isn't what I was expecting. Kind of thought you would be a little rough… but this is new for me."

I laugh rather sinisterly. "Oh, I'll be a little rough," I promise as I dangle my phone in the air. "This is just an added element. Ups the foreplay."

"So, we make a video, and then what?"

I step closer to her, closing in, assured that she's under my spell. "We can either watch it, delete it, or save it for when I need to watch you but you're not here."

She chortles. "Okay. We delete it. You're right, it's upping the ante a bit. Wait… is this something you do on a regular basis?"

"No." I'm point blank and honest.

"Then let's do this." Her voice is husky, and a seductive look appears on her face.

I twist my upper body and prop my phone up on my dresser, hitting play before focusing back on my prize.

Slowly, I stride to her before I cup the curve of her lace bra. "I bet you're already soaked from the pure idea," I rasp. Her head barely nods. "I knew you were a dirty girl like that."

I squeeze her breast, and she jolts from the touch. Then my entranced state turns to power. My fingers sneak under the straps of her bra to yank them down, causing the cups of her bra to lower too, her nipples hard. I give both a quick twist between my fingers. Only a preview of what is to come.

Pushing Harlow onto the bed, her eyes haven't left me, as I'm in command. I take my shirt and jeans off before sitting on the bed and inviting her to lie on her stomach across my lap, and I yank her drenched panties to her knees. Quickly, my hand rests on her ass, preparing her for what I'm about to do.

"Tell me you want this. Beg for it."

"I want this, please," she coos.

One spank, then a second one with a little more force, her yelp turning to a sultry breath. "You are a bad girl for making me wait for you. I need your pussy to lick and to fuck with my cock, at my beck and call." Another spank. "Your pussy wants to be touched?"

"Yes, Stone, I'm not sure I can wait."

I dig my nails into her flesh and squeeze. "You didn't say please." I rub along her skin and examine her fine ass.

"Please," she breathes.

I slide a finger between her legs, not bothering to give her the slightest relief by skimming her bud that appears to be pulsing, begging me to circle with my finger. Instead, I plunge a finger inside of her.

"Damn, you're already ready." I pump a few times then add

another finger. "But you're going to have to suck me before I fill you up."

Bringing my fingers out, I jam them into her mouth, and she sucks, making a sound that ensures she's enjoying it.

"Stomach on the mattress and take my cock out, Harlow."

She obeys like the good girl she is. Harlow enjoys giving as much as she receives. The feeling of my cock gloved by her hand causes my eyes to close as I lean back on my hands. The tip of her tongue sends a new wave of sensitivity to my groin.

"That's it. Deeper, Harlow. You need to earn my cock inside of you."

She sucks and swirls her tongue, bringing me to a near edge. I focus on unhooking her bra that's been stuck around her ribs, and she pops her mouth off of me, eager for the next step.

"More, Stone."

"Greedy," I grit out.

Sliding my boxer briefs completely off, I then lift her hips and guide her on all fours. Bringing her ass into full view of the camera, Harlow glances over her shoulder, realizing what I'm doing.

"Eyes forward, Harlow. Or I might need to spank your ass until it's red."

I love when she groans, and it sounds deprived. "Do what you want with me, just touch me and fuck me, please."

I roughly turn her hips so we're side view to the camera, then I jerk her sides until she's in a perfect position on her knees and hands. Leaning down, I lick her pussy from behind, and she moans in relief. Truthfully, I'm about to give up and give her whatever she wants. She's more than ready. But I don't relent, and when she pushes against my face, I just hold her hips down to still her.

"Stone." My name is a pure pant from her lips.

"Harlow, I'm going to flip you to your back, open your legs, and stuff you so hard that you won't be able to say my name without struggling because I'm fucking you so deep. You'll be squeezing my cock the whole time, and even if you begin to come, I won't let you stop, even when your eyes blur."

She mumbles, "Fuck me," in a way that is more excitement than an actual request.

I flip her body then open her legs, remembering that I need a condom and wishing I didn't. Grabbing one from the side, I watch as her fingers skim across her breasts and down to her clit to toy with.

Condom on, I lean down and pin her arms to the mattress and don't give her warning before I delve inside of her. We both grunt at the same time as we get used to the position. It's not at all sweet or slow. It's that way for a bit before I decide we need to change positions. I lie on my back.

"Come sit on me, your back to me, and look forward."

"You want my pussy in full view of the camera as you slide in and out of me." Her voice is full of a sensual agreement as she adjusts her body.

"Exactly that."

The moment she slides on top of me and brings her feet and hands to settle in a supporting position, I guide her to pick up speed by holding the sides of her stomach, occasionally reaching up to grope her breast before returning down.

"That's right, fuck me, Harlow." I touch her clit, eager to bring her to a moment where she shakes around me.

We move faster, our thrusts sharper. Sweat breaks out, with our breaths and pulses on fire.

Then we get there, the room feeling as though it's spinning as we nearly roar together with an orgasm that bursts with pleasure. It takes a moment until she falls back onto me while I stay inside of her to come down from my orgasm.

We lie there for a few moments before I indicate for her to get off. I leave the bed to turn off the camera and get rid of the condom in the bathroom.

I return to my bed, with Harlow in a blissful state, her body like a stone in my bed, unable to move. My hand comes to her head as she makes a sound approving of what just went down and her lips curling into a fulfilled grin.

I can't help but mirror her state when I fall onto the bed next to her, and we both stare at the ceiling, completely naked above the covers with our hands finding one another between our bodies.

"That was…" she begins. "There are no words."

"We suck at writing then if we can't form words," I tease her.

It causes her to roll to her side to study me. "I'm still alive, right?"

My eyes assess her up and down. "Yes, and you look perfectly fucked."

"You have some good ideas in that head of yours," she compliments.

"Didn't even get the rope and blindfold out." I'm dead serious.

She grows silent and brings her hand to draw along my chest as I recover my breath and feel my pulse slowing down. "Is it wrong of me that I actually enjoy things like being rough and adventurous, considering my past."

My eyes strike to the side to meet hers. I know what she means, and it has nothing to do with me. "Absolutely not, and you should get that idea completely out of your head then throw it into the ocean, or even better, burn it away, if we could do that with thoughts."

I feel too much for Harlow, and I encourage her to rest her head against my chest. I'm not letting her dive into a bad thought on my watch or in general.

"I thought so, just needed to hear it I guess," she whispers.

"Harlow, you're past a lot. Don't look back, you don't need to."

"Because of you, I'm beginning to believe that."

I kiss the top of her head before tangling my fingers in her hair. "I like hearing that." I tighten my hold on her.

"I hate that there is a blank slate when I look to the future," she mentions.

"Mmm, you can also attempt to help the future you want along by having a plan. Even if nothing goes as planned. We both know that. I intended to have a hockey career, living in a city, and here I am in a small town, writing books, with a beautiful woman in my bed."

"Very true. You do have a beautiful woman in your bed." There is humor in her voice. "But yeah, we can give indications to what we want in the future."

"Is that what we're doing?"

"No clue."

I blow out a breath. "I need to take you slowly now. I won't let our night be dictated by a wild session. That's what I'm planning for our future right now."

"I think that's exactly what we need. Your eyes never leaving mine makes life feel promising."

Fuck me, I wish that were true. I hope it will be, at least.

Is it so wrong that I want her to take a jump off a cliff with me, because a long-term relationship between us does feel promising?

My only answer is to roll us until she's beneath me, with her eyes glimmering a connection that we can't seem to shake away.

15

STONE

Harlow looks good in my button-down shirt, with nothing else on except her panties underneath. My shirt drowns her slightly, but it doesn't matter, as her knees are pulled up where she's leaning back against my sofa. She's got my laptop, with her facial expressions changing occasionally. She's reading the early copy of my book that my editor sent over a few days ago.

We've taken it easy today. Grabbing breakfast at Jolly Joe's, hitting up the pool and jacuzzi at the Dizzy Duck, followed by stopping at the store for some groceries so we can just stay home for dinner and drink wine with the fireplace on.

I don't particularly care if she wants to read all 80,000 words in one sitting because I could watch her all day. Her eyes strike up from the pages, noticing I'm mesmerized by her.

"I'm not a museum exhibit. Stop watching me." Her toes dig into my side, attempting to create distance.

"Sorry. I'm trying to come up with a plan to unbutton that shirt with just my teeth."

She shakes her head, entertained, and ignores me as she snaps the laptop closed and sets it on the coffee table. "I'm not into sports fiction, but this is good. At first, it seems dramatic, but then it feels like character development."

Ah, she must be referring to the fact that my hockey player has a conscience and leaves his immoral coach and returns to vineyard belonging to his father, a veteran, when he loses faith in the sport.

I shrug my shoulders. "It's not too soft, considering this caters to the male demographic? I mean, the ending." My main character, despite receiving major sports offers, decides to live a quiet life on his dad's vineyard to help, since his family sacrificed so much.

"Not at all," she says with sincerity, then a smirk curves up her lips. "All you need to do is add the ending where he's in town picking up supplies and catches the eye of the bakery owner, then women will flock to your book."

I shake my head, appreciative of her lightness. "It's not my best."

"Maybe you need a break from writing for a while. Writer's block is a real thing. Plus, straightforward fiction doesn't always have the same structure as romance."

"Right, no ridiculous tropes." Not entirely true, I can think of three when it comes to Harlow and me.

She swats me. "I'll prove you wrong."

"Okay." I straighten my posture and wait for her explanation.

Harlow counts on her fingers. "We've already discussed small town, enemies to lovers, accidental pregnancy, secret baby, second chance… instant attraction." She nibbles her bottom lip.

"You mean us?" Because I agree.

She scoots closer to me. "Uh-huh."

"Alpha male? Yep, unlike you who is slacking in their hockey research, I did mine in the romance genre."

Harlow giggles under her breath. "I could agree with that, but I consider that a character trait. We are traditional and doing the whole pen pal, long-distance thing." Another one of her fingers flies up. "Hmm, I think we can end this conversation, as it's cheesy as hell."

My eyes widen. "See? You don't actually believe in what you write."

She rolls her eyes. "I do, I just… never mind."

"One day, you're going to have to explain yourself." I pretend to give her a stern voice.

She blows out a breath, and our eyes hold for a beat before she gently tugs on my sweater. "What's on the agenda tomorrow? We can attempt to walk in this cold."

"Hell no. I may be from colder climates, but that windchill factor is brutal. I do have an idea, though."

"Oh?"

"It's no big deal or anything. Casual, even. But we can head to my brother's for brunch tomorrow." Harlow seems taken aback. "Really, it's not a big thing. They always burn toaster waffles, and the baby normally makes a mess at some point. Nothing fancy," I assure her.

Her mouth opens as she seems to be evaluating what to say, but she catches me off guard. "Hmm, okay," she answers, near bubbly.

My head and neck straighten, like a goose, at her answer. "Alright then, I'll let them know. And really, totally chill. Bringing-a-friend kind of thing."

She laughs before she gets up off the sofa to head toward my kitchen. "Friend kind of thing. Something tells me your brother knows that you're sleeping with said friend."

I follow her, with the orange glow of the fireplace highlighting our faces. "True. We're close like that."

Harlow grabs the wine bottle from the counter. "It's obvious. I'm that way with Flo. We see through each other. Then again, we've known one another for years."

"That's good. Friends are essential for life too." I slide over our wine glasses that are sitting on the counter, empty from our last round, and she pours the red liquid into the glass.

"Good wine, right?"

Her face blazes in agreement before she circles the bottle to study the label. "Blisswood. Hmm, didn't know Illinois produces wine."

"Not much, but there are a few vineyards, mostly all family owned. The Blisswood brothers have family here in Lake Spark."

"Nice."

I pull Harlow to me by the waist, as we both have our wine glasses in hand. "I'm happy you're here."

"Me too. Uhm… how often do we plan on doing this back-and-forth thing? Hate to burst the bubble, but well… I should probably point out this tiny detail."

I glance away, hating the ping in my stomach that feels uneasy. "Until it fizzles out?" But I don't believe it ever will.

"Right," she barely whispers before she sips her wine. I can't for the life of me figure out if she was expecting that answer.

"And if it doesn't…" I'm throwing this discussion back in her corner.

I notice that Harlow takes a long exhale. "We may be doomed." It sounds painful but true.

"There must be a way around it."

She chortles. "Are we serious? Isn't this the conversation that couples have when they are contemplating marriage or something?"

"Again, you're the romance writer. What would your fictional characters do?" My tone is mundane, because as ridiculous as it sounds, it's completely true.

Harlow throws me a near glare. "We aren't fictional." She holds her palm up. "Okay, you made your point. What I write is completely unrealistic. I'm not a believer." The sound of the glass hitting the counter confirms that she's frustrated.

I whistle out a long sound because I've been proven right, yet hate it all the same.

"Let's not get too worked up about this. We can just focus on enjoying our time together." I follow her to the middle of my living room and grab the back of my shirt to force her to turn to me. I hook my finger under her chin to tip her face up to meet my gaze, ensuring she has no escape. "Relax, Harlow, let me just kiss you right now."

The moment I end the sentence, she's up on her toes to ensure our mouths press together even faster.

I hope we're not caught in quicksand together.

But in this moment, we will let any worry leave us so we can end up a tangled mess on my living room floor.

————

"I THOUGHT you said this would be casual?" Harlow mumbles to me.

We arrived at Vaughn's big and freshly furnished house that bought a few months back, let ourselves in, and headed straight to the kitchen where Isla was busy making a pot of coffee and Vaughn was swaying my niece on his hip as he grabbed a piece of cut-up melon from the patterned display of fruit on a tray. Which is right next to the box of fresh croissants and donuts, not to mention a plate of eggs that look edible, and bacon and veggie bacon that seems to be the right texture to actually eat. Don't get me started on the mimosas that have been poured into flutes.

"It normally is casual," I grit out to Harlow under my breath.

We both throw on overdone smiles.

"Welcome." Vaughn walks straight to us. "Nice to meet you." He waves my niece's little arm. "This is Nora." Damn it, the cute little baby with chubby cheeks is calming my desire to kill my brother.

"Hi." Isla waves from the kitchen. "I'll join you guys in a sec. We have these new specialty teas, so I want to boil some water." Really? I mentioned once that Harlow doesn't drink coffee, and here we go with an all-out effort to impress.

Harlow side-eyes me, confirming our suspicions that this is no casual brunch. Still, my girl stays strong. "Hi, everyone."

"Make yourself at home." My brother hands me my niece to hold, and I notice Harlow cock her head to the side, trying to decide if I'm melting her soul, because I can't lie, I'm aware that I look good holding a baby.

I lean to the side. "Do you mind if I go have a moment with my brother?"

Harlow looks between me and my brother who has plastered a cheeky smile on his face. "Oh yeah, totally. I'll see if I can help Isla." Her eyes are slightly bold with humor.

"Shall we go check out Nora's new toys? Yeah, we're going to do that," I inform him.

Vaughn is still entertained as he follows me to the other side of the living room in the open floorplan. "What's up?" he asks, acting casual.

"What the hell happened to having a normal brunch, at which we normally eat and you and Isla look like a trainwreck because of a teething baby?" I glance down at Nora whose little fingers are clawing my shirt.

"Simmer down. You're holding precious goods."

My eyes give him a pointed look. "Yeah, so I can't murder you for making this a big deal."

Vaughn sighs. "Excuse me for wanting to make an effort."

"By adding more fuel to the fire by putting pressure on defining Harlow and me?" My voice squeaks out.

He smiles tightly. "That's a good thing. Now you can check meeting the family off the list of relationship etiquette."

"Or just bringing on more confusion."

He pats my shoulder. "Trust me. You'll thank me."

I blow out a breath to calm myself down. There is no escape from this house at the moment. "Let's just get through this brunch."

Vaughn raises a shoulder toward his ear. "At least we have some damn good food. Having my brother stuck in a romantic cloud brings out the best of Isla and me... we made an effort in the kitchen."

I roll my eyes before we saunter back to the kitchen area. I'm quick to hand my niece back to my brother to ensure I'm not trapped into any more shenanigans. Harlow smiles at the baby who squeals a sound.

"You like Lake Spark, I hear?" Isla begins our conversation.

"Yeah." Harlow swirls a tea bag in her mug. "It's quaint and gives you a warm fuzzy feeling. Not sure how you all survive winter, though."

"Summer makes up for it. A total opposite, and fall is just, wow, the colors changing, and Halloween feels different than in other places. There's a sort of smell of wood in the air," Isla gushes.

"I could see that. I should come back then for writing inspiration."

My brother looks between all of us with awkwardness, and I

internally groan because I know what he is about to do. "*So,* that means you plan on coming back more often?"

Harlow smiles self-consciously. "Uh, I'm not sure, probably. Who knows," she strings a sentence on the go. "Those donuts look great, I love old-fashions with glaze."

"Wonderful. I wasn't sure if you were vegan or just vegetarian so got both options." My soon-to-be sister-in-law is a little chipper and oblivious to my brother's investigation.

"Oh," Harlow seems taken aback. "Wow, you guys seem to know a lot about me."

Isla nods her head with a bright smile. "For sure. Stone mentions you all the time when we meet for lunch or dinner." Geez, Isla, please stop digging me into a hole.

"Kind of cute, don't ya think?" My brother is leaning against the counter bouncing his daughter on his hip and wearing a proud smirk.

Harlow chortles to herself. "Definitely," she plays along.

I clap my hands together. "Right, everyone, let's eat." And move us the fuck along.

A few minutes later, we're all sitting at the table, with my niece in her highchair.

"Freshly squeezed orange juice, anyone?" Isla asks, holding up a jug.

Holy hell, this effort thing is now ridiculous. "Absolutely, why don't you throw on an apron and some pearls, and then we're all set with this future-housewife thing." I'm not at all serious.

"Now, now, let's not talk about my fiancée's and my role-playing fantasies at this moment. After all, there are little ears present," my brother jokes, or maybe not, and I just shake my head.

Glancing to my side, Harlow is desperate to burst out laughing. I can tell.

"Well, thanks for taking this morning to a new level of weirdness," I comment.

"Trust me, I haven't even asked if Harlow enjoys our family enough to see us again, which would imply that she's not going anywhere in the future as far as you're concerned."

I will punch him. Then get him in a headlock like we used to when we were kids. Even better, have a rumble on the ice because he seems to be in his good-old-days phase.

For the first time, Harlow now has a shade of no longer entertained. A little sigh escapes her as she realizes that we probably can't keep avoiding the obvious.

———

HARLOW LETS GO of our interlaced fingers, barely a brush, but nonetheless a loss of her touch. She heads straight to the couch in my living room and falls down with an exhausted sigh. I slowly take a few strides in her direction, relieved when a faint smile appears on her lips.

"Sorry about all that." I scratch the back of my neck.

She holds her hand up. "Don't. That was hysterical. I will never forget that. No brunch will ever be the same." She splays out her hands.

A lopsided look hits my face. "Well… that was my family." I slide next to her on the cushions.

"They…" Her face softens. "Are wonderful. You can see the connection and love for one another. Teasing is part of having a tight family."

I play with a strand of her hair while she nuzzles into my touch. "You didn't really have that, did you."

She shakes her head. "My parents are great, we just weren't playful or took time to have moments together. I love visiting my parents, but they are a bit reserved and struggle to show emotion, ya know?"

"I'm lucky."

We pause for a beat and both get lost in a stare, knowing the time has come.

"And here we are," I rasp.

"The big conversation." I can't figure out her tone.

It's a stalemate for who will lead this conversation, until I decide to be tribute in what I'm scared could specifically be an ending, even though we feel closer than everyone.

"I don't want to let you go."

Harlow snickers. "Stone, nor do I. But we both know we have a few obstacles in our way."

"We can either continue as we are and see where we land or accept that we drew the bad card and that nothing is realistic." My throat feels tight, with a near salty taste from emotions that I'm not used to. My next words seem lost in the back of my mouth.

She scoots closer to me, taking both of my hands into hers. "I'm lost. Scared. Wishing I would be fortunate that the one thing I need would drop from the sky; clarity. But I was lucky that you entered my life, even if for a fleeting moment across the map, and maybe that's all I get."

"I don't think luck had anything to do with it."

"I enjoyed meeting your family, it's what even friends do. But I'm aware that it's more than that. Discovering pieces of you is better than finding a new kind of freedom in my life." Her eyes dip down, and I see sorrow.

My stomach churns, and the future suddenly seems bleak, yet a glimmer of hope that we can take hold of us is in sight.

"Harlow, I wish you didn't experience the things you did, but I've only ever seen you as broken." I pull her close, tight against my chest, to kiss the top of her head. "Let's not give up."

"You live here, I live there. Maybe eventually in a moment, we'll get tired due to an atlas."

"Damn it, Harlow, I think our biggest concern is that you hate apples," I say in an attempt to bring her smile back.

A line draws on her mouth as her eyes strike up to me. "Fine, it's the distance that will drive us apart. Won't it?"

I let her go to hold her strong by her upper arms with pure reverence, giving her no opportunity to look anywhere but at me. "If we didn't have distance between us, then what obstacle would we have? I don't think anything would be in our way. Without that factor, tell me what you want."

An honest smile brushes her lips. "You."

"Then that's what you get. We're still fresh, we don't need to make any jumps, it's just that it seems the next step would be..." Moving, which she has already connected in her head.

Her bottom lip gets attacked by her teeth. "It's not new, Stone. We were meant for a chapter together the moment we laid eyes on one another."

"It's stronger between us, isn't it? Not a momentary click."

She nods. "We've laid out the risks."

"I'm willing to take them. I'll do it for both of us."

Her tongue slides to the inside of her cheek as she seems to be suppressing a grin. "Okay... I think we've laid out what we're both avoiding."

My brows furrow. "And?"

She breaks from my hold and circles her arms around my neck. "Facts are out, and now we have discussed it like responsible adults. We don't have an answer yet. Which only means we should pat ourselves on the back for at least listing the obvious and then do what we want."

I wasn't expecting that. "Which means?"

"Stone Madden, take me upstairs and fuck me as though it really matters."

My lips reach hers due to our magnetic pull. I ensure we skim one another's mouths, reminding us we are capable of sensuality. "It's always mattered, Harlow. So you'll just have to settle with slow and staying in my arms all night."

She instantly crashes her lips on mine before I lift her off the sofa, and she hangs off me. We find solace in a night that in no way feels like a goodbye yet.

I stare at my blank white screen, desperate for the words to flow. It's been three weeks since I've seen Stone. Days too many. We've exchanged our usual emails and have done video calls, all the things people in a long-distance relationship do.

But the routine seems to be burning out. Or at least, the last few days a sour feeling hits my stomach then travels up to tighten in my chest. I care for him far too much, and it's making it hard. It's more than caring, it's… everything I could want. But nothing comes easy in life.

Apparently, the expression *distance makes the heart grow fonder* is the truth.

I wish I could wake up and he'd be here. Or meet him at a restaurant because we decided to have a last-minute dinner together.

Then there is a part of me that's staying strong, desperate to hang on. The knot we created to tie to one another is very tight. It would be hard to untie.

Stone doesn't have the opportunity to visit anytime soon, and our publisher is keeping him busy. They're throwing a wrench in our works.

Which is probably the reason why I get positive apprehensions in my stomach when I see a new email.

Harlow,
They are taking St. Patrick's Day to a whole new level in Lake Spark. I was at the Dizzy Duck the other day, using the gym, and I was nearly blinded by the green decorations. I guess your alter ego would love it. Maybe I'll grab one of your books and stage it next to a leprechaun hanging off a mug handle as if it was a casual day.

By the way, I told you about this woman, right? I want to ravish her body that molds to mine with perfection. She hums when I scrape her ear with my teeth while I slide into her warm pussy too. Most of all, she always has a euphoric smile on her face when our eyes meet.

If you didn't get the underlying meaning, I'm saying I miss you. See? I've turned into a sappy man, just like your billionaires. Now all I have to do is own some media company or a major real estate company and I've turned into your fictional man.

-Stone

———

Stone,
The thing is, I don't need fictional when I already have you.

I've run into a problem. I loved every second with you last time. But then I got home, and over the week, reality hit me like a brick. Distance somehow creates a feeling that I'm not used to. No, I take that back. I've never had it. Every word tightens our tether. I guess tethers only end if someone breaks it.

But you uplift my day and provide those fantasies in reality. I wish I could grab your hand right now and we'd go for a walk to talk about our days. Then when we get home, I would set your hand on my breast, giving you the indication that I'm wet and need you to touch me. Home. I'm not sure if it's yours or mine.

We don't get a middle ground.

-Harlow

———

Harlow,
In my head I'm on my knees, waiting for you to tell me exactly what you want in a breathy whisper. You would say my tongue, and I would obey, but I wouldn't indicate how many fingers I plan on plunging into your soaking and snug pussy while my tongue flicks your clit. That's only after my hands would be quick to tug your panties down because you wear skirts a lot. I wouldn't pull lightly, instead a forceful drag down your legs. Then I place a kiss on your inner thighs and part you open.

I wish I could do that every day after we pour a glass of wine and talk about the latest hockey game we've watched. You'd look good in my old jersey.

Between the blue lines in hockey, it breaks the offense and defense zone from one another on the ice. A sort of crossroads, except with some broody guys in helmets.

Is that where we are? With the area between the blue line keeping us at bay? Or rather you?

-Stone

———

WALKING out of Zumba class with Flo, we find a seat on a bench in the changing room, ignoring everyone around us while we drink from our water bottles.

"You seem… down," she remarks.

I close my bottle. "I am, and I'm not."

"Okay, let me be blunt. Since your last trip, you've been down."

A smile is instant on my face, as it always is when it involves Stone. "It was a wonderful few days. Better than I could have imagined. Therein lies the problem." I sigh. "I feel so close to him, it hurts to be away for long periods. Those are all promising signs when it comes to being with someone, yet I can't help feeling that we are in a spiral that will never end. That's what I hate and has me down."

"Ah, the classic 'why am I doing this if I'll only end up in pieces' kind of philosophy?"

I zip up my light sweater that was in my bag. "It's hitting me. We ignored it last time we were together, but maybe we were too easy on ourselves, you know?"

Flo gives me a knowing, closed-mouth smile. "Blinded by affection is what you're saying. Except… well… I think it's more than that. You're not sure if he's the guy you're falling in love with or the guy who in a way has helped you heal."

"I don't want to confuse those two things."

She raises her finger in the air. "My guess is you already know the answer, you're just looking for an excuse. You two are not the first couple to do the long-distance thing, but people do it because they don't want to let love go. Sure, eventually they have to find a landing place. You don't need to be there now, though. You met the guy like six months ago."

That strong current swirls inside me again. "Sometimes that's all it takes to feel as though the world is different when they're not around. Hell, people marry in shorter times than that."

We pause our conversation when we stand up and leave. Deciding to walk two blocks, we grab a table at a café for a late breakfast. Although we made small talk on the walk over, the moment after I order my juice and bagel with avocado, Flo picks up right where we left off.

"So, what's your plan of action?"

I gently shake my head side to side. "I'm not sure. All options hurt. It just appears letting my feelings for Stone grow, it means a harder ending."

Flo puffs out a breath. "Now you're just being a pain in my ass. There doesn't have to be an ending."

My shoulders roll back, as I need to release stress and that seems to be my body's way of dealing with it. "I can't even think straight."

"Have you tried talking to him about this?"

"I'm sensing that he's feeling it too, but Stone is relentless, that's just his nature and temperament. We're also not very good at finding clarification." I pick up my lip balm from my bag to smother a layer on my lips. "I should probably give us a little space to get our thoughts in order."

Flo's face screws up. "I both hate and like that idea. But ultimately, it's your call."

"I need to think a little more, find my feet before I figure out what's best. All I know is I wish I didn't have to do anything. He's… special." And I feel the bottom of my heart growing an ember into a flame.

Flo gives me an empathetic look which doesn't do much to ease my mind.

––––––––

Stone,

Sorry it's been a few days since I emailed, and maybe I kind of ignored your few texts too. I'm completely, well… It's just that I'm enamored with you. There is nothing I don't like about you. From your mind down to your fingers to your cock… your legs, meh. The point is, what is one to do when you're holding on, even though it might be a sinking ship?

-Harlow

————

You grab a life vest.
I'm not ready to let you go.

-Stone

————

Stone,
I figured you might say that. Gosh, I can see your serious face, with
your Adam's apple rising then dropping because you swallowed,
trying to keep it together. If I were there, then you would wait
patiently before you grabbed my arms, not letting me move an inch
so you can say your viewpoint and force me to listen.

Which leads us to yet another problem on the list. I enjoy it when you
do that. You have strong viewpoints and hate the word no in the most
respectful way. In fact, you would be adamant to lead me to agree
with whatever you say. Right before you make a joke that makes me
laugh until my stomach hurts.

Were we fools last time? I'm probably going to vote for that. We tend
to get lost in lust around each other, then throw in a bucketful of feel-
ings now.

-Harlow

————

Harlow,
Can you hear me chuckling under my breath from there? We are a
little past the bucketful of feelings, and you know it. I'm also begin-
ning to feel dizzier than the concussion I got when I played St. Louis

and two defensemen had me in a hold, before my head hit the boards and my helmet came off.

If I'm comparing you to that, then you know how much you have me in a chokehold right now.

-Stone

———

TEARS STREAM down my face because nobody wants what I'm about to type. Most of all me—well, not true. Stone won't be happy. And I think a piece of me is already breaking, but it would shatter more if we wind even tighter around one another, sinking in the current. Which is why I do what I need to do.

Perhaps a little break is what we need. A game suspension or something. Nobody wants it, but we have to in order to regroup. It might save us.

-Harlow

I get a simple sentence back that touches me in the center, somewhere near a window to my soul.

Don't you remember? You don't need saving. You never did.

17

STONE

I'm staring into my whiskey glass as someone pats my shoulder in passing in acknowledgment, but I don't take much notice. I should be enjoying myself amongst the publishing team at this evening event for authors. On a top floor in a fancy hotel in downtown Chicago, the dusting of clouds with a peek of city lights from surrounding buildings brings a mellow feeling as I glance around the floor-to-ceiling windows.

Space.

That's what Harlow asked for a few weeks ago, and I've been miserable since. I've done my part and not reached out to her. I'm just hoping that she finds clarity.

"Well done with the latest book," my editor Ashley says, arriving in front of me.

I offer her a weak smile. "Thanks. I believe you played a part." My eyes dip down to see her growing baby bump. "How long?"

"Ten more weeks."

"I hope your replacement is only temporary. You're the magic to my words."

She snorts a laugh. "That's not true. You've had something else in your life lately that acted as a mystical spell on you and changed the mood of your writing in the best way. It really is top-notch what you handed over to me. What was the secret?"

Harlow.

I sigh. "Just… someone I met."

"Harlow Olive?" My eyes pop out slightly which causes her to chuckle. "Her editor and I talk sometimes at staff meetings. Gloria was once our special guest at a meeting, and she mentioned that you and Harlow were partners in crime at her writing retreat that we sent you on. So, I'm going to put two and two together."

I trace my thumb along my jawline, as I enjoy the vision of people connecting me with Harlow. I'd be proud if she were by my side.

"Well, there is maybe some truth to that."

Ashley smiles at me as she touches my bicep. "I'm surprised she's not next to you."

I take a sip of my alcohol, needing it to ease my depressed mind. "Why do you say that?"

She indicates with her head to the side, and my sight moves to scan the room, settling on a figure across the crowd. I close my eyes tight before opening them, aware that I should have known better. Maybe I feared it, too much of a confrontation.

"I'll leave you be. I need to grab a snack and then sit down." Ashley touches my shoulder as she walks behind me.

I'm left to pierce my gaze at Harlow who is chatting with a woman who I can imagine is her own editor. Damn it, Harlow is dressed in a black shirt with elbow-length sleeves, accompanied by a flowy olive-green skirt that will haunt me in my fantasies. There isn't a day that she isn't stunning.

I would be a fool not to recognize the obvious. Harlow seems as though the happiness on her face is a façade for the solemn mood that's underlying. I know her body too well now and see the way the corners of her lips tick to the side, only to falter back to neutral.

She's faking her attention to the topic that the woman next to her is discussing. It's when Harlow drinks a sip of her wine and her eyes slide in my direction that the strike of electricity sparks between us.

She seems to do a double take, then an honest brief look of happiness hits her face.

I just stand firm, taking a swig of my drink. I had a hunch that Harlow would be here, I just imagined she would write me a warning. That alone causes me to expect that this night isn't going to go in my favor.

Harlow excuses herself from the conversation and slowly saunters in my direction, hesitant yet initiating our reunion that I wish would go the way I want.

"Hey, Stone."

"Hey, Harlow."

She briefly looks to her side then back to me. "I wasn't expecting you here… or maybe I was. My mind isn't, well… it's a little chaotic."

I need to touch her right now. "So how is that game suspension going for ya?" For some reason, I've managed to stand and speak in a neutral tone, showing no hint of my frustration. She gently dips her eyes low. "Here we are, Harlow. I'm not sure what you want me to say. Ignoring you isn't particularly me, and telling you that you're wrong isn't right either. I'd rather be with someone who is sure and willing to fight than run away."

She soaks in my words and seems to not want to confront them either, instead an attempt to smile arrives on her face. "It's hard to talk to you right now either way. You look very good in a suit. I might be distracted."

It earns her one laugh from under my breath. "I can't really complain about that comment."

"You know… I had an inkling that we would end up in this conversation, and I'm sorry I didn't caution you about my attendance tonight. I'm happy for you, that the book stuff is going well. Either way between us, I'm proud of you," she says, sincere.

"Praise isn't what I want. I could think of a million other things when it comes to you that would be even better." I set my empty glass on the tray of a passing waiter.

Harlow seems to be caught, guilty even. She nervously drinks her red wine. After a few seconds of standing in our bubble, with my fingers desperate to touch any inch of her, she breaks the silence. "Okay. You're right. This situation is all on me. I'm not great at assessing my feelings."

I stare at her blankly. "You literally write it for other people."

Her lips quirk out. "To be fair, they're not real."

I roll my eyes, getting aggravated. "If there was no one here then I guarantee that you and I would be in a debate now." I evaluate the room and notice that nobody is taking notice of us. "What's your plan? Keep me in suspense? Talk over cheese puffs?"

She heaves a breath of exasperation. "I wanted to wing it and see what my inkling was when I saw you. What to do, I mean. Which I now realize was a horrible idea."

I step closer to her, feeling the warmth of her body, and for a moment I allow myself to stare at her collarbone that is enticing and just causes me to want to scream that she's a temptress.

I do the next best thing. I bring my mouth close to the spot between her cheek and ear, dragging her hair behind her shoulder.

"Tell me, why would it be a horrible idea?"

When I notice the slight shiver running down her body, I move away to leave her patch of skin cold.

Her lips open, while her eyes try to avoid mine, but it's pointless. "I have an overpowering need to kiss you and touch you while you make me laugh."

Why must she answer what I was hoping for?

I ease a notch. "Me too," I admit. "But you're the one in the lead here, and I'm going to walk away right now because it's nearly impossible to be around you without forgetting my gentleman card right now."

A weak half-smile forms on her mouth. "Then one of us should go now. I… really, I'm happy for you on the professional front."

"Sure." In defeat, I walk away, wishing in a way that she wasn't here.

In one hand right now, I have her near, and in the other she's slipping away.

———

THE SWOOSHING of the revolving door is my sign that I can loosen my tie and leave this miserable attempt at socializing. But my eyes flick up when I notice Harlow waiting for a taxi. Her hands are in her pockets as she's looking up at the sky, which are the lights of skyscrapers in place of stars.

Most of all, I notice her nerves, and it has nothing to do with me.

It's night.

Without me, I think she might still hate them.

I can't walk away now. My feet won't even attempt to step away, I'm permanently protective of her.

I curse to myself that it may be my fate. I'll never shake that feeling away, no matter the distance or how we end up.

"Harlow." My voice is low.

She side-eyes me then does a double take. "Oh, hey."

That may be a disappointing greeting to most guys, but it has nothing to do with me. "Heading back to the hotel?" She sounds almost nervous for my answer.

"Yeah… I guess we're all at the same place." Our publisher arranged everything.

I hail down a taxi that's approaching. "Come on, I'll ride with you."

Harlow looks at me, unsure yet appreciative, which is why I hold the door open to let her slide onto the backseat first. After I inform the driver where we're going, I sit back, only to notice the space between Harlow and me.

Awkward cab ride here we come, it seems.

"Uhm… so how's your niece?"

Ah, break the silence by sticking to chitchat. Classic.

"She's good." I pull out my phone to show her a photo of Nora using a Labrador as support to stand. The dog appears to be patient with her clawing of hair. The scene is completed with a giant, drooly grin on Nora's face. "Standing up and giggling like crazy." When Harlow leans in to steal a glance, her fingers feather my wrist, and my entire body wants to jolt from the urge to yank her closer to me on the backseat.

"Adorable," she nearly mumbles. Harlow must feel the heavy air wrapping around us as she slowly leans back.

"How're photos of green-colored olive flowers next to a book going?"

Now she chortles and gives me a humorous glare as we both realize our ability for neutral talk is an epic failure.

Which is why I don't care and bring my finger to draw lazy circles on Harlow's hand, resting flat on the middle seat. I stare down, acknowledging that this touch isn't enough; I need more.

Her breath catches from the connection as her eyes rush to look out the window. "Stone, I'm not sure what to—"

"Shh, I don't need to hear you say it again. I got the picture. Your thoughts are all muddled."

A short laugh escapes her. "A mind reader, are you?"

"Yeah, something like that. Or my intuition is heightened around you."

As we approach the hotel, my fingers retreat from her hand to grab some bills from my pocket to pay the driver. I'm out of the car first, and Harlow follows behind me. I hold the door for her, and as she stands, our eyes hook in a serious way. It's both sensual and a warning.

Closing the door, we stand on the sidewalk and can't seem to part.

"I'll walk you to your room." It's not even an offer, it's going to happen. Not even in a hopeful way. I simply want to walk her to her door.

She understands my undertone of being a gentleman and nods in agreement.

But that heightened tension between us only follows us. The lobby is a struggle, the elevator nearly unbearable. Even when she asked me about the latest Spinners game that I watched, I had a short response, not wanting to discuss.

And now as we walk to her door, luckily not far from my own

room, I notice she walks purposely slow, as do I. We're trying to prolong the moment.

Arriving at her door is our end point.

"Well… this is me."

"So it is," I say as I rock on my heels, with my hands in my pockets.

"Thank you for the ride and walking me to my door." The corner of her mouth lifts then falls.

I step to my side, prepared to make my dreaded return to my own room. This isn't how we were meant to be. Never was.

Pivoting back to her, I shake the last few hours off. "Fuck it, Harlow. I'm not going to pretend that your needing space makes sense. A few days, fine, but a few weeks? If that's the case, then we were nothing at all. But you and I both know that's not true." I'm about to unleash, and she doesn't even seem taken aback.

"We weren't, or are, nothing at all." She blinks a few times.

I step closer to her. "Do you know what I think?"

She holds my stare. "You're going to tell me anyway."

I smirk and step closer, causing her to move back, only for the door to support her. "You're scared as hell. You don't want it to end but you think it will. Even more, you're scared that we could be something permanent."

"Stone," she pleads. "What do you want me to say?"

I lean against the door with my forearm framing her head. "The truth. You miss me and hate this space."

Her eyes glaze over, but I can't help but notice how her body is subconsciously curving into mine. "Yes," she breathes.

My other hand slides up her arm to find home on her jaw, not too rough. It only intensifies the lust floating between us. "Just speak your mind, Harlow. I need to know so I don't feel like a hole has been dug somewhere inside of me."

A sound cracks from her lips, and a flicker passes between us because now she is the one aggravated. "Okay, Stone, yes, yes, yes, okay? I have strong feelings for you, you don't leave my mind, and I'm miserable when you're not around. I suddenly hate maps, even though when I was younger, I believed that an atlas gives us roads to possibilities. But you and I?" She breaks away from under my pinned arms and takes a few steps away from me, causing me to turn to face her. "Our road seems to go back and forth."

"It's better that way. Nowhere else to go, I guess."

"I'm scared… I've never felt this way."

"Ditto."

Harlow scoffs. "Yet you seem calm and not a mess like me."

"I don't mind you being a mess."

Harlow claws her hair and blows out a long breath. "I'm always spinning in a circle around you. I don't want to be. I just want to close my eyes and…"

I don't let her finish. I interrupt her sentence to kiss her, placing my hand on the back of her neck. My kiss must have caught her by surprise because she murmurs a sweet sound into my mouth, but she gives in and reciprocates back. Not only that, but her arms circle around my middle, pulling me tighter.

Breaking our kiss, both of us with heavy breathing, I warn her. "Harlow, I'm not leaving you alone right now. I have a point to prove. Do you understand me?" My eyes widen, ensuring that she grasps that I won't be sweet.

She mouths yes.

Grabbing the keycard from her hand, I haul her to me and at the same time open the door. The moment we're both inside, I kick the door closed. Harlow stops in the middle of her room by the foot of the bed. Striding straight to her, I'm sure I must appear cunning, as I'm about to have my way.

"Harlow, I plan on fucking you until you repeat over and over what you feel for me."

I rip the buttons of her shirt off then I push her onto the mattress. She yelps slightly and breaks her fall with her elbows. Harlow watches as I throw my suit jacket to the side and quickly unbutton my shirt then remove my pants. Her eyes are hungry when I splay open her blouse to admire her black satin panties and bra.

Balancing over her, I steal another kiss and feel her knees rising to my hips, encouraging me to take more.

"Tell me all you think about is having me inside of you," I whisper into her ear.

"All I think about is having you inside of me," she breathes out, her hands exploring my back.

"You don't want us to end," I make my next request.

She moans as I press myself against her center. "It's true, I don't want us to end."

"You've made me crazy, I swear." My voice swelters, and I move to flip her onto her stomach, taking her by surprise. I grab her hair and yank gently with my other hand, pressing her back down. "You've made a mistake, Harlow. You shouldn't run. Understand?" I hiss and scrape my nose against her elongated neck.

For a second, I'm not sure if I'm taking this a step too far with this position and my words. But she throws me a half-smirk as her face is smooshed sideways to the mattress. She knows we can always stop it with one word.

Letting her hair flow down, I glide down to yank her panties off, leaving her in her bra. I stroke a few fingers through her folds for a few strokes. All the worship of her body will have to wait for later. Lowering my boxer briefs, I drag her forward and raise her hips before my tip finds her entrance. I feel her heat and arousal, and I just want to sink further inside her. One inch, two inches. I close my eyes and groan a sound because she is heaven. Harlow hums and pushes against me, drawing me deeper inside.

But then I freeze.

"Harlow, wait. Shit, condom."

Harlow breaks the moment to rest on her forearms and flash me a look. "It's fine, I'm on birth control. I want you like this."

Her conviction has me slowly twisting her body until she's on her back. With her feet resting on the mattress and knees up, I force one knee wide, then the other. Our eyes connect, and I realize slowing down is in our calling.

Sinking back into her, I delve my lips back onto hers. Softly once then hard twice. She grips onto me, and her hair is splayed across the mattress. She holds me tighter, and I pump deeper.

"You feel too much, but it's right. Tell me," I husk.

"I do feel too much, but we're right," she pants.

Our mouths seal with a kiss because this moment is ours, not some confused thought.

———

I REST my head on my arms crossed behind my head as I lean against the headboard with a sheet draped around my waist. Saying I'm calm and sated would be an understatement right now, even though I'm trying to recover from that orgasm. When I see Harlow exit the bathroom, I can tell she's at peace, but a crack in her thoughts still lingers.

"Don't think about it, Harlow," I nearly growl.

She smiles to herself before she joins me back on the bed. I encourage her to rest her head on my chest.

"Let me be in this moment. I want you and always wi—" She stalls.

But I can only smirk.

A forever.

That's what's been scaring her away.

HARLOW

He's right.

Be in this moment.

I'm guilty as hell for taking what I can, knowing this will only make us spiral into the unknown.

I move to straddle him then lie forward, our bodies tight and my head resting against his chest.

"Stone, well, this has been a twist to the night," I comment mundanely for humor.

There's that scoff from his lips that always weakens my knees. "Did you really think this wouldn't happen?"

A smile begins to stretch on my mouth. "True. It's just a little confronting."

That's when he cozies up to my body to flip me under him and be on his side, I have to smirk because he is about to unravel my thoughts the way he manages to do.

"You mean…" His finger caresses the spot just above my breast, and I refrain from looking at him. "You want us, but you're not sure how we can make it work?"

My head bobs side to side. "Something like that. We established that I actually really enjoy your personality and the way we click, not to mention you're not too shabby in bed either. So yeah, you nailed it before you nailed me. I've missed you, and I'm scared."

"I'm a little wounded that you didn't contact me before we saw one another, you knew it would happen."

"I look for easy ways out, only to make it more complicated." I give a weak fist pump in the air. "Yay, point for me," I say, completely sarcastic.

Stone's face skews for a second. "I'm not complaining, but why did you insist I took you bare?"

My eyes strike up to meet his. "I only want you closer, to feel you inside me a little longer… Call me selfish."

His thumb travels up to my cheek and swirls my skin softly. "If you're selfish, then it seems we meet eye to eye."

"What the fuck now?" I growl yet can't help but smile.

Stone slides out of bed stark naked, and we seem to swap roles as I grab the sheet and sit up in bed. "Now we eat."

I laugh at his demand and sadden a bit when he throws on a robe from the bathroom. "Wine and dine. Look at us planning a future," I tease.

He chuckles and turns on the TV and presses the room service button. "Ooh, ouch… apple à la mode is on the dessert menu. Looks like you need your knight in shining armor to save you from that."

I roll my eyes at his humor. "A bottle of white wine and maybe some fries will suffice."

"Sounds good." He types in our order on the screen, and it should be a little bit before it arrives, but he notices the TV guide indicates that the evening highlights of today's hockey games are on. His head tilts and his jaw slides side to side. Stone's trying to keep the night between us, but it's a struggle.

Grabbing a spare pillow next to me, I throw it at him. "Don't need to have chivalry now. You can turn it on. Hockey is you. Just like green smoothies are me."

Relief hits him, and he is as fast as the speed of light to change the channel and sit on the edge of the bed with great interest on the screen. "Ah, a woman after my own heart," he mentions without turning his head.

Maybe it's in jest, but why does my entire body wish and hope it's true?

I want his heart.

Oh fuck, that internal war inside me is building again. A desire to fight for a future that seems difficult to achieve.

The thought I keep to myself as Stone groans and grins when the scores for various teams appear and a few major highlights are replayed. He grins when Vaughn, his brother, has to speak to the media about what the Spinners will do with a player who just got banned for two games in the middle of the playoffs. The brotherly affection for one another is always there on Stone's face, and a text to his brother will happen in the next ten minutes.

Because Stone is a family man who will never leave them. Being near is part of his life.

Blowing out a breath, I bury the thought for tomorrow morning. "Since your brother's team seems to have somehow won, does that mean you will come back to bed soon? This northern climate is shaking me to my bones."

Stone looks over his shoulder, amused. "First off, it's the end of April. Illinois weather has been warming up a bit."

"It's 55 degrees, with a prediction of tornadoes outside the city," I deadpan.

"Totally a warm spring. Plus, a storm front is coming through later to bring a change of temps. We're all good."

"Oh, really." I give him a pointed look.

Just then there is a knock on the door. Wow, it seems hockey and contemplation of my love life took longer than I thought. Stone quickly hops off the bed and heads straight to the door. He doesn't let room service come in to set the stuff down since I'm literally draped in a sheet.

For that, I have to laugh when he walks in with a tray after he closes the door with his foot. "What?" He looks like I'm crazy. "I'm a little protective, with no plans for anyone to ever see you with anything less than actual clothes."

Now I just burst out laughing. "I have no plans to live my life covered from head to toe. Besides, I'm proud that I have a body to show off."

Stone straightens his posture. "Fine. I'll have to deal."

"Why thank you, master."

His brow rises, and I see sin in his eyes. "Master, huh?"

I roll my eyes. "Later."

"You're right. First, we need to talk about how you're using the weather as a ruse to avoid hard talk."

A deep breath hits me in a flash.

Stone gets to work on the bottle of wine as he patiently waits for me.

Having this talk while I'm in bed naked under a sheet is not wise. Taking a moment, I leave with the sheet wrapped around me to grab a robe from the bathroom. The moment I tie a knot around my waist, a strong feeling hits my stomach.

The few paces that my feet take is like a trek through the desert; difficult.

"Come on, Stone, long-term we both know this isn't sustainable. We're two mature adults talking about what the future could bring, to see if we can go anywhere. Distance and…"

He turns around to lean against the desk, only to cross his ankles and arms. Stone is like a rock; he has no plans to move. Instead, he will stay firm with perseverance.

"Can we ban the word distance, because that's not the only issue," he states.

Then panic hits me in the chest, as if I'm about to suffocate. Throwing my hands up in the air, an overwhelming fear is about to spew out of my mouth. It's impossible to hide from him. "I'm a disaster waiting to happen. I'll only disappoint you when a panic attack that I shouldn't be having hits me, when a memory that has faded from my mind somehow returns. Hell, I can't even walk at night unless I'm with someone. That's what you will have to deal with. You could have any woman you want. They fall at your feet. Yet, someone you want, the one who might still...” I don't know how to define it.

In record time, Stone propels from the desk and charges at me to grab my upper arms; he's firm with a storm in his eyes. “That's the biggest bunch of bullshit. You're not a fucking mess, and even if you were, I'd still be standing right here. I'm very well aware that it's difficult to shake away the shitty things in life, but that's not a reason to run away.”

“But...” I quiver.

“No buts, Harlow. I'm here, and I'm not afraid. You've got to accept that. I'm not the one running away. It's you. Even when I tell you that there is nothing to escape from.”

“I don't want to disappoint you.”

Stone chuckles in astonishment. “Again, you're adding thoughts that are not true to your pot of crazy that I'll happily prove wrong... I mean, I'm hoping we could add something sweet and spicy to your caldron.” He shrugs. “But that's up for discussion.”

A weak softness spreads on my face, relaxing my cheeks, and a chip of calm falls inside of me.

“Stone—”

He brings a finger to my lips to hush me. “We all deal with things in our own way. But this isn't even a factor on my list.”

I give him a gentle nod, but I'm not 100% sure I believe that my mind has caught up.

“Can we maybe save the rest of this conversation for tomorrow? My brain is spinning, and I could use a little wine before we head to bed.”

“Of course.”

Stone's jaw ticks, and I'm certain he hates how this night is going as much as I do.

But we both ignore it, and 20 minutes later we find ourselves back in bed with our bodies entwined and a consuming need to have him inside me as he peppers kisses all over every inch of my body within reach of his lips, while he lazily pumps inside of me, because all we want is slow while our sight remains attached to one another. Every time we wake up during the night, we repeat what we can't seem to stop doing; getting lost in one another with the flare of fire that we share, not simmering down in the slightest.

———

I DO my best to shake Stone off as he attempts to keep me in the shower. It's tempting, but I'm a little worn out, plus I have a flight later this afternoon.

"Can't I just hold you a little longer while you spread soapsuds across my back and my cock rests against your middle, ready to slide into you?"

I throw him an amusing glare. "How have I not trained to keep up with for your sports stamina that translates to your sex drive?"

"You'll catch up one day."

My head falls from his humor, and I walk out to dress. When I'm working on my earring, Stone emerges then quickly throws on his clothes from yesterday. He ditches the tie and suit coat and keeps a few buttons open at the top of his white shirt.

Sexy as hell. I could repeat that statement a thousand times.

As he's rolling up the sleeves of his shirt, he sighs. "*So…* for us to work long-term, then the obvious thing is that…"

I huff out a breath and drop hopelessly onto a chair by the tall light. "One of us will eventually have to move. That's how I see it. Long-distance relationships might work for some, but most of the time, they eventually find a destination together."

Stone wipes a thumb across his chin. "Exactly."

"It's a big step."

"But kind of necessary. We are well past being a fling. Maybe we are two people in a serious relationship who eventually need more together."

My eyes widen. "Wow, we're not just in the 'find a place to live near one another' stage. It's the whole possible 'moving in together stage' too."

He isn't impressed with my statement. "Really? You seem surprised."

My entire body slackens, and I rub my hands down my face as I take a beat. "No… I'm not. We didn't just meet yesterday and falling in love often involves getting to know one another beyond a schedule of flights," I admit. I stand, giving up on sitting; it doesn't feel right when we're in a faceoff, yet equally agreeable that this is the conversation that we need.

Love. That's what this feeling is. I mentioned it, but he just brushed past it.

Nerves seem to hit him. "Harlow, you know what I'm about to say."

Licking my lips, I remind myself that this is about honesty. "You won't leave Lake Spark."

His shoulders slant up then drop. "My family is there, helping on the ice is there. It's a great little town."

I swallow. "And I'm not sure about leaving Florida."

The last step he takes has Stone tangling his fingers in the ends of my hair. He focuses on his fingers, only to meet my gaze a second later. "The thing is… I believe that you would love it in Lake Spark. Instantly, you have me who is kind of the greatest gift to humanity." Still, he tries to make me smile before he turns serious again. "But there are people there who would welcome you instantly. A support network readily available. A place that goes holiday crazy with great summers and cold winters that many would say are romantic as hell. Who doesn't love the smell of wood burning?"

I can't suppress the wry smile on my lips. "I've only ever known where I live now. I have friends. It's a big step. Maybe even a sacrifice. I'm not sure. It's just…"

"Damn," it draws out of his mouth. "If you say you're scared then I might be out of strength to argue yet again right now. That's a word that should be buried with no chance of resurrection."

My head falls back as I take a deep breath. "I can't decide right now. You wouldn't want me to either if I wasn't sure."

Stone's face falters into disappointment. "I agree. It's just that closing the distance means someone has to take the leap. I'm deciding that it can't be me. This is the one thing that I can't even debate on. I'm standing firm. My entire life, I've lacked a father, but Vaughn and I have been united by that fact. I have a niece, and one day, if I ever have a family of my own, then Lake Spark is the place I would want to raise them."

"See?" I protest. "We haven't even discussed kids. Maybe I never want that."

"Really?" he challenges dryly.

My head goes on a slight roller coaster from side to side. "Okay, I do want that one day."

"I'm sorry, Harlow, but…"

My palm flies up. "It's clear."

"Will you think about it?"

Getting attacked between my teeth, my lip takes a beating as I figure out my words. "It's that or run away."

In a flash, Stone kisses me, and naturally I kiss him back with the same devotion and murmur as his hands hold my head while his body pulls me tightly close. It's long and deep, never-ending, the way I love.

Then he pulls away, his lips brushing against mine. He whispers against them, "I should go." I can't answer, especially when he creates space with one last hold of our eyes. This time he is giving me a seriousness that I've never seen before.

Watching him walk away, a mixed feeling stirs inside me.

Only made worse when he stops short, his fingers on the door handle. He half turns to give me one last glance.

"I'm surprised you haven't realized that we get another signature trope from those romance books you write."

"What's that?"

The corner of his mouth hitches up slightly. "He falls first."

Then he's off.

Leaving me to ponder a future with him.

19

STONE

"It's complicated," I say to my brother as the group of his friends stands to leave us alone outside. It's Vaughn's wedding, rain clouds left us and the night is descending with a clear sky overhead. We've been sitting on the terrace of the Dizzy Duck smoking cigars and enjoying whiskey.

And what an ass I am for dredging it all up.

My brother gets comfortable in his lounge seat, because apparently, he is okay with leaving his bride inside while he gives me a moment to hash out my current woes. Except, it won't take a moment; I could go on forever.

"You were hoping Harlow would be here as your plus-one?"

I sigh, and my head lolls to the side. "We're kind of in a confusing place, but I still sent her an invite."

It went something like *Harlow, Can we call a pause on making decisions for a second? Vaughn's wedding is coming up and a plus-one only feels right if it's you.*

To which she replied, *Maybe.*

He smirks. "I'm aware that you were planning on having a plus-one since I gave you the green light to bring someone on your arm and the extra seat for your guest was all planned. There was a group of women in my living room discussing the dinner table seating map for the wedding, and it was beyond exhausting. Wow, some real truths about people were shared. I wasn't even involved, just grabbing a beer from the fridge, and it felt like a freaking reality show episode." I can tell that he's not even joking.

"Maybe I shouldn't have asked. Space is probably what I should give her, especially since I only got a one-word answer, and I didn't want to press." I take a decent swig from my whiskey glass, leaving the bottom dry.

My brother evaluates me for a good few seconds. "I think that... you're both trying to navigate what to do. At this moment, it still feels promising. Nobody has walked away yet. You're in a confused state, probably because you both want to put in the effort *to have* a future."

"One could hope. Anyhow, she isn't here, and it's your big day. It was a beautiful and short wedding, and your kid might have stolen the show." I throw him a grin.

Vaughn has a hint of fondness over his face, and it only grows as he sips from his whiskey then sets the glass down. "You'll have all of that one day. I'm sure of it. Give it a little more time, and if it's too unbearable, then what's the saying? If you let it go, maybe it will return… or some shit like that." He stands and loosens the top button on his shirt.

"I probably shouldn't be asking you. You are in a loved-up and optimistic mood today, with a wedding night about to go down." I wink at him and stand.

Vaughn squeezes my shoulder in passing. "Shouldn't that all be hopeful for you?" His eyes seem to be searching for Isla through the window, and he spots her as his lips curl. "By the way, you should check out the cake. Chocolate with white cream cheese icing. The cake of dreams."

I watch him walk away, and I look out at the lake that is lit up with hanging lights and lanterns along the dock. Damn, they did good with their magical nuptial setting.

My feet pivot, and when I'm inside, I beeline for the bar to order another whiskey. While I wait, I turn to lean against the counter and take in everyone having a good time.

But then I notice someone, and I do a double take while my jaw lowers from surprise.

Next to the cake table is a woman standing in a light green dress with short off-the-shoulder sleeves, her hair down in waves.

Harlow.

She's here.

And she's standing patiently by the table and surveying the room, hopefully searching for me. No wonder Vaughn told me to check out the cake.

My feet don't move, instead I stay put to take in the view of Harlow, and when our eyes meet, a smile sweeps across her face. Her cute little wave appears, as if she's nervous, and hell, maybe I am too. We haven't exactly been in a clear frame of mind lately.

I give up on the scotch and stride straight to her. "You're here."

"Yeah." Her voice sounds delicate. "Thought I would be a wedding crasher."

"I don't think it counts as being a wedding crasher if you're invited."

"I guess not. Anyhow, I wanted to be here earlier and surprise you, but my flight was delayed. When I got here, Stuart seemed to have a soft spot for me, so I smiled sweetly, and he let me into your room, ignoring protocol. You mentioned in your email that you're staying here so you can drink and avoid duck crossings at night." She's almost rambling, yet her face stays straight.

I step closer to her, inhaling her flowery scent, still in doubt if she's here in reality. "I'm not hallucinating, right? The expensive whiskey might be good but not so phenomenal that it has me imagining you're here."

Harlow blushes, and her shoulder pops forward while she glances down to hide her happiness, only to drive her eyes back up to meet mine. "This might count as crazy, considering we've been on a… pause. Then suddenly I'm here as though all is well. I'm not sure—"

I interrupt her. "It's a wedding, rules can be bent."

Her eyes sparkle, hopeful. "In that case, will you kiss me already?"

I chuckle before I run my hand through her hair to pull her mouth to mine and kiss her warmly and longingly.

Logic and our blurred status can go out on the lake in a canoe, because tonight we can just be in a moment.

My tongue slips into her mouth, and I kiss her deeper, pulling her snug against my body. She begins to smile against my lips as she drags her mouth away with a struggle.

"Wow, the best man has some skills," she rasps against the corner of my mouth.

"You have no idea," I growl with a low tone.

Keeping her in my hold, I soak in the fact that she's here. "I hadn't heard from you and just assumed you weren't coming."

Harlow plays with the buttons on my shirt. "Yeah, well, wedding dates are neutral territory, and I didn't want to leave you hanging despite where things are between us. Sorry I missed the vows or speech if you gave any or the critical flower toss."

I lick my lips. "They didn't do the bouquet throwing yet, so you're still in the running," I tease.

"What a shame I haven't been practicing my catching skills." Our eyes lock with an underlying hope of something we haven't talked about but would probably want one day. "So, what does a wedding date have to do to get a dance around here?"

My fingers sweep across the bare curve of her shoulder. "Well, probably not wear this dress which is a fucking distraction." She laughs, looking proud that she got that reaction from me. Glancing over my shoulder at people making fools of themselves to some ridiculous club tune, I decide that isn't for us. "I have a better idea." I offer her my hand that she easily takes with an intriguing glint in her eyes.

"Uh-oh, Stone has another mystery in store for me. Last time I ended up fully clothed in a swimming pool."

We head in the direction of the terrace. "A damn shame it wasn't swimming naked, but ah, another time."

Harlow giggles as she follows me outside, and I notice her confused facial expression when we walk past the terrace and straight to the dock.

"But seriously now, what are we doing?"

My brother and Isla thought of every detail for their wedding, including rowboats for guests to have some time on the lake. Grabbing a lantern hanging on one of the poles, I hold it up. "A cruise on the lake."

Harlow stares blankly at the boat, unsure if I'm for real. "As in…"

"Come on." I don't wait for her reply, and I'm already stepping into the boat, with my hand held out, waiting to help her into the boat.

"You're crazy." Nothing about her tone informs me that it's a bad thing. She likes me a little spontaneous.

When she's sitting across from me, I hand her the lantern to hold because I'm busy grabbing the oars so I'm able to row us to the middle of the lake. It's a clear sky with a bright moon.

"You didn't have too many scotches, right? This isn't like drunk rowing or anything, is it?"

I rumble amusement and continue to row with even strokes. "Not at all. Even if I had, I think you made me sober as soon as I noticed you next to the tower of icing."

"I do have magical abilities," she responds proudly.

We both admire the scene, even when we reach a point where I stop far away from the Dizzy Duck Inn, but the twinkly lights are still in the backdrop. Locking the oars, I move to sit next to Harlow and take a moment to find a position that will be comfortable enough for both of us to lie down and keep the lantern secure on the bottom of the boat.

The moment we settle into our spot, we cling to one another, and that amazing feeling of her head on my arm while I kiss the top of her head hits me like a drug.

Staring up at the night sky, we both seem to relax and breathe out.

"I wasn't expecting this. Kudos for your romance A-game." Her nose nestles into my neck.

"I'm kind of weddinged out. We just need to watch for mosquitos, but the lightning bugs are an extra nice touch to our *warm* Illinois summer."

Harlow playfully pats my chest. "Point proven. We don't have as many lightning bugs down in Florida. They seem magical. People also call them fireflies." She admires the sky without giving me a glance.

I pull her tighter, if that was humanly possible. "We blew bubbles. To celebrate the bride and groom walking down the aisle. They popped in the air, just like your last chapter closes and vanishes into history."

"They have a new chapter."

"That and the Dizzy Duck prohibits throwing bird seed or rice," I quip.

She chuckles against my chest. "I'm actually not a huge wedding person other than writing them in fiction. I would like to believe that a wedding equates to a clear and lasting future, but doubt seems to stick a pin into that. I was at a wedding a while back for an old high school friend, and it was blatantly clear they would be divorcing in a few years. Does that make me a horrible person?"

"Nah, I just hope your sixth sense isn't about to put a damper on my brother's wedding."

"If anyone could last, it's them. They burn toast together and still laugh about it."

My eyes squint at her logic and look down at her, content in my arms. "Burnt toast is the key to a lasting marriage?"

Harlow shrugs. "Why not?"

"We should probably stop the talk on marriage… it's a little much for tonight."

She walks her fingers down my chest before swirling around my belly button. "There isn't some weird fish that is about to jump up and kill us, is there?"

"Harlow, chillax. It's just us and the sky. The stars are out, and my favorite star is in my arms."

She slings a leg across my body and props herself up, with her hands against my chest. "Ooh, that was a smooth line."

My hand forms a fist, and I bring it to my body in celebration. "*Yes.*"

"I think I can top you, though." The lantern highlights her face.

"Go on then."

"You can love someone like Pluto. The farthest planet."

"It's technically a dwarf planet," I deadpan.

She fakes a pout that she's unimpressed with my attempt to ruin her moment. "Shh. Let me continue. Pluto is the farthest planet, which means there is nothing beyond."

"A galaxy," I blankly state, yet can't hide my smirk.

"Smartass. I'm trying to say that I love you like Pluto because it's the farthest, and it means there is no farther place to go because we have it all." She strings a sentence together, only to freeze.

I instantly sit up while not even her lips twitch.

She said it. She loves me.

I fucking knew it. My ears didn't fail me last time.

"Inner truth escaping ya there?" Satisfaction and a smug grin possess me, trying to keep this casual, but I know I will fail.

Harlow's mouth closes, only to pop open as she realizes what she just said.

I sit up and hold her hips to keep her firmly in place with no escape. "That's a good fact to know, considering I already told you I've fallen for you."

"It just… came out… I—" she sputters, still in shock.

"Since I love you too, then I sure hope it wasn't an accident what that mouth of yours just did." I'm unable to turn away from her blank face, only to see her relax as a smile begins to form.

"Okay, it's true. I do love you. I wasn't necessarily planning on telling you that tonight, but it seems I've taken a detour, and here we are on a boat in the middle of the lake with lightning bugs and a possible big fish about to jump up. We're completely ruining the fact that you should be celebrating your brother's wedding, and instead we are making this about us and a big step that we just seemed to take."

I blink a few times to check that I understand her amazing tangent of the night. I laugh to myself as my head falls from this perfect moment. "It's kind of romantic this way. Plus, if we tip over into the water, then we've said it before the killer trout gets us."

The corner of her mouth tilts up. "Will you stop making me beam so much that my cheeks hurt and shut me up with a kiss?"

Doing my best to ensure we don't lose balance in the boat, I hold her by her sides and lean in to kiss her the way she deserves, in the middle of a lake under the night sky that she once feared, but that thought has been thrown into another time that will never return.

Our mouths seal with no attempt to breathe because it would break our kiss. It's placid and tender, making me dizzy in bliss and wondering how in the world I've never been able to kiss like this. I've been missing out, but it only makes sense that this is possible with Harlow.

We tug and relent until we have no choice but to gasp for air, but we keep our lips close and brush along the crease to keep us connected. Her hum is the perfect sound.

"I'm kind of regretting I did this, I mean the boat. Now I have to row us back, which means we waste precious seconds of me undressing you to show you how much I love you."

She purrs into my jaw. "You'll just have to work extra hard then to make up for lost time." She turns her head, yet she keeps our cheeks smashed together. "The lightning bugs are dancing around us in celebration."

"Actually, you said they're magic, and they are. If you see more than one at a time it means that you're not alone on the journey. And if you see even one, they are a reminder of bravery in darkness." I'm serious, and she picks up on that.

Her breath catches from the fact. "Is that so?" She swallows.

"Seems like you found your spirit animal."

I can feel her mouth rise then weaken. "I guess I have," she rasps.

We let the evening air float around us. Her eyes search around our boat, and her lips press together but the line spreads.

"Come on, I should actually say goodbye to my brother before you and I disappear to our room." I kiss her one last time near her ear. "Hold the lantern, and I'll work my strong arms."

Harlow seems quieter than she was, but not somber.

By the time I make my rounds and Harlow wishes the bride and groom well, we head upstairs hand in hand. Although she's been quieter in the last half-hour, I have every plan to break her down until she's underneath me and repeating her proclamation over and over.

A reflective look graces her face when we reach the door to our bedroom, as if he is putting the key in the door to open a gate to possibilities.

"Harlow, Harlow, Harlow," I tsk. "How am I supposed to let you sleep now?"

Her brow rises, and her eyes fill with lust. "You don't."

I've never used a key so fast in my life.

It's on.

She jumps into my arms, and I lift her up with her legs wrapping around my waist as I carry her into the room. The sound of the door abruptly closing hits our ears.

I drop her onto the bed, and we both swiftly claw our clothes off. I'm over her, our mouths finding one another. It's rapid and raw, with my hand sneaking between us to part her legs open.

"Say it again," I grovel an order.

Her eyes twinkle. "I love you."

I kiss down her neck with no direction and feel like we're drowning in chaos, as hands and mouths go everywhere. We're hungry for one another.

"I'll never get tired of you saying that." My voice is thick.

I use my fingers, exploring her pussy to see that she's ready, but it was a pointless move, as she's soaking, and instinct reminds me that I knew she would be.

"Please," Harlow keens.

I slam inside of her with so much purpose, and she whimpers. Her back arches off the bed, and her legs align around my waist, bringing us closer.

"I fucking love you." I kiss her once more before pumping into her with reverence and a strong desire to sear her so she'll always be mine.

We move together with labored breath and bodies heating up.

I'm conflicted if hearing her say the words for the first time or saying it while I'm deep inside her are better. I can't think about it right now; we're getting lost in our own bubble, with her moan being a curse because it only levels up my plans to never let her go. That pesky detail of next steps in our relationship are only a speck in my head right now because my focus is on Harlow underneath me, her eyes wistful and trapped with my own.

We whisper back and forth the words that I didn't imagine I would hear earlier today but had buried inside me behind the defensive wall that I had temporarily built in case our relationship never went anywhere.

After an explosion from what feels like the confirmation that we're in too deep, I collapse onto her and bear my weight on my arms. I stay inside of her, completely spent, with her heart under my ear and her fingers fumbling with my hair.

"Give me tonight. Over and over," Harlow whispers.

It's reassuring, but I can't help but notice there's a looming disaster at the root of her words.

20

HARLOW

Glancing to my side, I'm well aware that Stone is in a good mood, and to be honest, so am I. We walk side by side down Main Street after grabbing a coffee to-go for him and an iced tea for me. Our shoulders occasionally touch as a natural current flows between us.

Last night felt as though I were in a dream. Everything I would never expect yet apparently exactly what I wanted. I don't think either of us can stop smiling. I'm surprised the muscles in my cheeks haven't strained from the constant stretch of elation on my mouth.

But then I feel guilty, very guilty. I truly wanted to be there for Stone last night for his brother's wedding. However, I think I had an underlying motive. I need to observe Lake Spark once more. When Stone and I last saw one another, it was blatantly clear that our future would hang on a choice. He's staying firm on his decision, which means that I'm the one making the leap.

"It's great weather today. Want to go to Catch 22 and grab a table by the water?"

I grab his arm to loop through mine. "I am slightly famished, although I enjoy taking in my surroundings too. I haven't checked out the sale at the lingerie boutique or glanced at the schedule at the dance studio, maybe they have my Zumba lessons."

Stone gives me a peculiar look. "Those are must-dos. But let's take a seat over there by the gazebo and I can finish my coffee."

"Sounds good."

I'm surprised that the park isn't busier. There are only a few picnics between families or friends happening and a father and son kicking a soccer ball between them.

"It's calm here," I reflect.

Stone rests his arm on the back of the bench. "It's Sunday. Most people are at this tiny stretch of beach on the other side of the lake or out on a boat or SUP board or something. A lot of hikers in the forest too."

"Those are all good activities, especially since feeding ducks bread is off the list." I point my nose at a sign that forbids giving snacks to the birds.

Stone chuckles. "You love it all." I shrug but say nothing, instead sitting back and breathing in the light breeze, yet I still feel Stone's eyes fixed on me. "Harlow, as much as I'm loving every second of this weekend, I sense that something is on your mind."

I press my lips together. "We probably shouldn't have this conversation here in public with the knitting club president walking by. Isla warned me that she spreads gossip like wildfire."

My quip only makes Stone more uneasy, and I can sense he is about to boil. "She can say what she wants. I only care what you're about to say."

I stand up to pace in front of him, unsure where to begin, as I'm nervous and recognize the necessity of this all the same. "The thing is, Stone… you've asked me to make a big jump."

There it is.

He's fuming.

Stone stands to stay level with me, but he keeps a few feet of distance. "Holy shit. Did you seriously come here this weekend and tell me that you love me, only to end things?"

My hands fly up to stop him. "No, not to end things. I'm just not sure that…" It hurts to say it. I wish I didn't have to, especially when I see how steamed he is. "I can't make a decision about moving."

The back of his finger sweeps across his upper lip, and I can tell his mind and body are going into overdrive. "What the hell is keeping you back? I know it's a spring off a cliff, but is it something else that you don't want to admit?"

I attempt to connect our hands, but he only rebuffs me. "Don't you think we are moving a little fast? I mean, we already talked about wanting a baby one day, yet I don't even know which shirts of yours go to the dry cleaner."

Stone looks at me blankly. "Does any couple actually know that?" His voice cracks.

"Okay, what about Thanksgiving? I have no clue if you like cranberry sauce or not."

He only gets more aggravated. "Who the hell doesn't, Harlow? It's a necessity for turkey and stuffing." He is dead serious, but his voice still squeaks.

This is so ridiculous, all of these little things, but aren't people in love aware of the tiniest details?

"My point is that moving across the country is… how do we know we're compatible to live together? What if it doesn't work and then my life is uprooted."

His eyes grow into saucers. "Harlow, it doesn't matter if I lived a fucking mile from you. Not knowing if we are compatible, living with one another, would be exactly the same."

A valid point, ugh.

Stone rubs his forehead while I stand in my spot with the world's biggest frown, and my heart racing in panic. I'm making up excuses when reality is that a future with him could be amazing, and that terrifies me. What if I fail him or become unworthy?

"I'm trying to be honest."

Pain shades his face. "Did you come to Lake Spark to investigate or to really be with me this weekend?"

I attempt to tug his arm to me, but he makes no effort to move, however he doesn't shake my hand away. "A tiny part, yes, I wanted to experience again what it feels like here. Because *I am* seriously considering the move. But mostly, I wanted to be with you because I'm miserable without you, and I'm happy that those three little words slipped out of my mouth. We can't hide our secrets forever."

Stone's eyes lighten slightly. "Why would you want it to be a secret?"

My head bows. "I wasn't lying last time I saw you. I'm scared that we could be everything but I'll just screw it up somehow. All it takes is one second."

His body squares off, and he straightens his shoulders to focus on me. "Except now you discovered you are a firefly."

For the first time in minutes of our somber faces, I have a hint of a weak attempt to smile. "Right, the bravery-in-night thing."

I take one step forward and I feel the warmth of his body. His fingertips trail up my arms. "I believe the future between us is what we've been waiting for. I just need you next to me to make that happen."

He always says the right thing. His words are comforting and wrap around my body and soul.

As confident as this man is, his eyes mist with the start of tears. "I'm going crazy, Harlow. I feel like a yo-yo. We take one step forward and one step back. I freaking love you, but I might break if we can't stop taking steps back."

My breath stops short. "I understand, and I agree. I'm just not... I guess I'm confused. I'm trying to push fear away to let us in."

Stone's lips slide side to side right before he kisses me hard on the mouth without warning. It's his way to shut me up and prove a point. I press against his lips because I'm hoping this kiss is the glue to ensure I can't run away.

But it's only a quiet confirmation that he wants me to think.

"Come on, we'll head back to my place since you have a flight tonight."

"Sure."

A flight sounds like the worst thing on the planet right now.

———

WE WERE quiet most of the afternoon, except for the occasional kisses. Stone and I were both considering the ups and downs of this weekend. My theory of ruining something good between us already seems to be proven as fact. Today, we should have been basking in the glow of last night and enjoying a day with a new horizon. Instead, I opened my mouth and let out my thoughts that swing from all directions.

The regional airport means Stone can wait on the tarmac with me as it's such a small plane and only two commercial flights take off each day. Stone drops my carry-on next to my feet. "Well… I guess this is the end of our weekend."

"Yeah." I assume this is what heartache feels like. "Stone, I do love you."

"I love you too."

"Give me a little more time. I promise, I'm considering and want to ensure my answer is honest."

He glances away, only to draw a line right back to me, his eyes conflicted yet cold. "That's fair." We both look down when he slides his fingers between mine and brings them up between us with our fingertips in the air. He looks down at our connection and studies it with affection. "But, Harlow…" He swallows and seems to be hesitating. "I can't take the back-and-forth or I might as well throw my heart onto the ice until it melts. It's miserable when you don't have clarity, not when you want to give so much."

"What are you saying?" An ache builds in my throat.

"Next time I see you, it's either to embark on our future or to say goodbye."

A tear drops from the corner of my eye.

I feared he would say that.

21

HARLOW

I haven't taken one sip. The green juice in front of me, my favorite that even has kiwi in it, isn't even appetizing today. Nor has it been for the last two weeks while Stone and I have taken some space—all my doing, by the way.

Flo's on the other side of the table as we sit outside in the late morning sun. She's been patiently waiting for me to say something, but I come up blank on how to filter all of my emotions and thoughts.

Her nails tap in a steady beat on the glass before she takes a purposely long sip of her red smoothie, ensuring she slurps with extra emphasis to ensure that I begin to spill the tea.

I sigh in aggravation. "What the fuck have I done?"

"Ooh, that's a start. I was worried that you'd taken a vow of silence."

"Stone thought that I went to Lake Spark to spend a night with him as a goodbye." It hurts that the thought even entered his mind, however looking from afar, I understand how it may have seemed.

"Harlow, at some point, not deciding *is* saying goodbye. The guy has every right to set his limits. He's smart, and it's a classic move to be the one to lead when you feel as though doom might be on the horizon."

Panic spreads across my face. "It's not doom… it's just…"

"It's just you're scared, and your inability to make jumps is understandably warranted, but Stone is literally standing before you telling you being scared isn't a problem. Jump, he'll be there to catch you."

Finally, I give in and take a drink of my juice to hydrate as my thoughts are creating a workout in my head. "The crazy thing is that I think I've laid out all my fears and concerns, it's not that I'm hiding anything from him."

I notice Flo looking over my shoulder and getting distracted. I do a 180 and grumble as there is a guy working out over on the beach. "Can you stop checking out guys right now and focus?"

Her eyes circle back to me, and she gives me a contrite smile. "I don't need to focus. It's obvious what you want, but you're waiting for a push. One that can only come from yourself, actually, since you need to be walking into his arms, ready to pick out new towels and writing grocery lists, completely sure of your decision."

Blowing out a breath, I become agitated again. "It's just, moving, and here and—"

"There is nothing here for you. As much as our cherished smoothie sessions and Zumba classes should be a national treasure, it's not a reason to keep you back. I'll visit and hope Lake Spark has a police officer that I accidentally run into, and he spills my coffee and promises to buy me a new one, with his cute little dimples." I flash her appreciation for trying to make me smile. "Look, your parents no longer live here, you can write anywhere, and I'm still not entirely sure why you want to be here, considering…" Compassion crosses her face.

I hate sympathy.

"Don't say it," I urge.

Flo gives me a pained look. "I'm going to. Do you ever think that… well, this is crazy and maybe I'm coming from left field here, but… you found your feet again here alone, as proof that someone didn't kill your soul, and despite having had an uncontrollable fear, you're still here, and it's a point that makes you proud. But now… you have to face a new fear which isn't even for something horrible, it's amazing. A guy who wants to be there for you. You're no longer doing anything alone."

Doing my best, I tightly hold in the tremble of my lips that wants to erupt and keep the sting behind my eyes in check. "I'm not used to it, you know? It feels like forever since I could breathe and laugh and have something spectacular without a care in the world." I jam the straw in my juice a few times to let out frustration. "I would be devastated if that just vanished. I don't think I have it in me to rebuild yet again."

Flo gently reaches to pause my destruction of the straw. "That's an if. And you're forgetting the not-so-tiny factor that you're the one preventing what could very possibly be a spectacular future that lasts forever."

"I know." I have to smile softly to myself. "I love him."

She nods slowly. "It's obvious. You're just overthinking it, when all you need to do is check in with what you're feeling."

My face screws. "Since when have you become a romantic guru?"

Flo chortles. "I've read almost all your books. How the hell does this all sound surprising to you? You literally write this stuff on a daily basis."

"It's make believe," I protest.

"Yeah, all the more reason to hold on and never let go, since it isn't a fantasy."

I claw my hair and groan. "I am aware of that. Even if I run right into his arms, I still feel guilty for making him wait, probably in agony too."

She laughs and it's vibrant. "Isn't this where your grand gesture comes in?"

I snicker at her thought. "If I decide to move, then yes. Whatever my decision, I'll see him. He'll always be the man who changed my life."

"Then run. Straight to him."

And yet again, I'm preoccupied with my thoughts.

———

Sitting in my living room, giving up completely on any work tasks that I planned on doing, I decide to turn my phone back over. Swiping my screen, I pull up photos.

My lips twist when I see the pictures of Stone and me in my gallery folder that seems to have grown as the months together progressed. Content is the first word that comes to mind. That and the love in our eyes when we look at one another with no effort. A natural filter that is fixed to every one of our pictures.

Opening my laptop, I pull up his name to write.

Stone,

I promise I'm thinking. I guess it's not about the brain, though. Probably more to do with the heart.

Needless to say, I've been in a "lying on the bed and staring at the ceiling" kind of mood. My current music playlist is kind of melancholy.

Whatever happens, happens. I'll come to see you one last time or for the start of forever.

Have you put me in a power play, where the game is down to one player and one team has an advantage to win? The answer to that is very clear.

I love you.
Harlow

P.S. Letters are our thing. Okay, emails. Damn, I wish for the times when you would write by candlelight with a feathered quill that you need to keep dipping in ink. The good ole' days. I'm sure a modern couple would actually use text with weird eggplant emojis. That's not us.

————

Harlow,
Well, eggplant emojis are reserved for couples who remind one another to pick up toothpaste at the grocery store on their way home and not to be late because they have plans tonight.

Anyhow, that still doesn't sound like a decision.
I'm not sure goodbye is in my vocabulary. You would have to explain in great detail how that makes sense to either one of us.

You don't want to see my music playlist right now. It's taken a dark turn because I'm trying to distract myself from imagining how I would pin you against a wall right now and shake you until you let your heart lead.

And yeah... a power play, that's what I've put you in. Taking the league cup then retiring into bliss could be all ours.

Love you too.
Stone

————

WHAT THE HELL am I doing? I'm throwing us into a pit of turmoil, only leading us to more misery by prolonging the inevitable. That's a dark thought but realistic.

My hands shake while hanging at my sides, and I pace my living room, gathering courage to do what I'm about to do.

I'm never going to be enough, and I'm only ever going to feel far luckier than I deserve. My only choice is to believe in Stone's testament that I'm so damn wrong and he'll still be right there. The other option is to walk away.

I jerk my body and nearly march straight to my laptop, not even bothering to sit down.

Stone,
No more waiting. We need to talk.

I'll book a ticket as soon as I can.

-Harlow

22

STONE

I skate solemnly on the ice as my brother stands on the side, watching me with a somber face, probably concerned. Allowing the puck to slide side to side, this is probably my most pathetic moment on the ice, even more than the day my career ended.

For the last few days, I've felt sick to my stomach. Harlow is coming to Lake Spark to talk, which is often code for parting ways.

"Damn, get it together, Stone," my brother says.

I don't even need to slow down, I'm moving at nearly a snail's pace. I was hoping that the ice would clear my head, it always has in the past. Well, a lot of fucking good this is doing.

Braking by Vaughn, I step off the ice to go sit on the bench, and he follows. He looks at me with sympathy before he leans over to rest his elbows on his knees, waiting for me to say something.

"She's coming to break up with me," I say, deflated, and sigh.

"Are you sure?"

I flash him an unamused look. "Get there faster with the clues, Vaughn. Talk, visit, we've been floating in and out of what we want. Eventually a crossroads must come. Seems that moment might be now."

He chortles at me. "Some roads never end. You said it yourself."

"But directions normally lead you to a destination too."

Vaughn blows out a breath. "Since when did you become Mr. Negative? This is kind of depressing. Either be optimistic or accept what's coming and be mentally prepared for that. I refuse to let you walk around for weeks or months in pieces." He pats my shoulder and squeezes for encouragement. "You once helped solve my relationship woes. It's because you were meant to solve your own problems one day."

I break away from his touch to lean down and unlace my skates. "I gave her an ultimatum, Vaughn, probably one of the worst plays in history. I brought this on myself."

"Truthfully, it's a winning move. Without clarity, you'll both be miserable and uneasy. All the more reason to be calm about her visit. You know all the scenarios on the table."

The pit in my stomach is stabbing, and I want to refuse the possible outcomes, but I know it's what I needed to do, and I am at peace with wanting to stay near my family and welcome Harlow into that fold with open arms. It's belief that a life with her would be better here. I can't call it selfish, even though they say follow someone to no end, but if she took a step back and evaluated the big picture, then I'm positive she would see that the pros for moving to Lake Spark outweigh me moving down there.

But transplanting her life isn't the issue.

She's scared of love.

Harlow just needs to admit defeat and come to that realization on her own.

I throw my skates into my sports bag, not having one care in the world that ice skates should be treated with respect, like a bottle of fine wine.

"This is hell," I state blankly.

"Put on your big-boy pants, Stone," Vaughn says, staying firm that I need to get it together.

In the corner of my eye, I see Holden stepping down the stairs with his daughter. While his daughter looks excited, Holden looks ragged and tired.

"Slow it down," he tells Lori.

She looks over his shoulder. "I need to get ready for practice."

"Yeah, yeah, yeah." Holden flops down in the stands behind us. Before we can ask him anything, he rubs his face in exasperation. "Shit, forgot her snack for after her figure skating class. Ugh, add this to the list of how life is not going as planned."

Vaughn and I look at one another with questionable intrigue. "I would love to hear what's going on, but I have a team meeting in ten. See ya, guys." Vaughn stands. "Even though it sounds like you're in a shitty mood, give my brother a pep talk, will ya? I tried my best."

Holden has a bewildered look on his face as my brother walks away. He turns to me with brows furrowed. "Something you haven't told me?"

"So…" I'm not sure what to say anymore. "Harlow is coming to visit."

He nods slowly. "I know."

"You know?"

"Yeah, I was in the lobby at the desk looking for a package that arrived for me, and I heard Stuart answer the phone when she checked on her reservation."

My body freezes, and my mouth goes dry. "A reservation? At the Dizzy Duck? Without asking me to arrange?"

He nods. "Fuuuck." I swipe my hand across my jaw and do my best to let a long breath try to calm me.

"Is that… a bad thing?" Holden asks, clearly confused.

I side-eye him. "She's staying at the Dizzy Duck instead of my place. That's a bad sign. Astronomically bad. Besides, she knows that at the snap of my fingers I can throw in my stake-in-ownership card to get us a room at our beck and call."

Holden groans. "Not really. The hotel is kind of busy these days and…" His casual tone changes when he notices that I'm not amused. "Come on, why is this such a bad end-of-the-world kind of sign? When I heard mention of the reservation, I just assumed you two were going to have a romantic night or something."

Shaking my head, my frown turns into a scowl. "No. It means for sure this is our ending. She said if we were to break up, it would be in person, and I'm sure she doesn't want to stay at my place, as that would just be awkward after she rips my heart out."

He swings his palm side to side in the air. "Whoa, wait. Why do you think she's going to do that?"

"I gave her an ultimatum. Last time we were together, at my brother's wedding. I felt like we've been going in circles. The reality is that one of us has to move. It can't be me. As much as we're told to follow your heart, it's utter bullshit. Logistical reality of day-to-day operations has to be considered, and my life is here. It's far easier for her to move."

"Your relationship isn't a business plan. Maybe she took the time for reflection and…" Holden can't give me an answer that I want to hear. "Hey." He smiles. "Maybe she just wanted to book a room to admire the moose head for writing inspiration."

I stare at him blankly. "Really? Yeah, totally. She decided to come to Lake Spark and the inn to admire a dead moose and squirrels on a tower before she breaks up with me."

"I was trying to make you laugh. Besides, the moose head is by far better than a duck head which would just make all the guests feel awkward, considering it's called the Dizzy Duck Inn."

"Seriously, let's get our focus back." I throw him a hardened look. "Maybe I shouldn't give her the chance, and I should just take the lead. End things to ensure I'm in control. It could soften the blow."

Holden tips his head toward the ice. "You never stopped trying to win when you played hockey. Why stop now? There must be a realization that she hasn't connected to yet that would be the gamechanger for her life."

If only he knew.

Harlow has had things thrown at her. Horrible things…

…but amazing things too.

Our bond and attraction.

"You're right. I'm just… out of ideas on how to handle this."

"Don't overthink it. Just lay it all out from the start. Accepting her answer isn't an option. She'll come around if you two are the real thing. If not, then I'm sorry to say that she'll be the one that got away."

Abruptly, I stand and grab my bag. "I should go simple is what I think you're trying to say. Forget the dozen roses and romantic dinners on the rooftop of the Dizzy Duck. What I would write, I just need to tell it to her face."

"I was not saying…" It drags out. "Yes, I was totally saying that. A great idea. One that I most definitely came up with myself and not you on your own having a realization." He smiles tightly.

I snap my fingers. "I should go. I need to meet Harlow at the airport later."

Yes. I'll practice what I'm going to say the moment she gets off that plane.

———

STANDING ON THE TARMAC, I'm waiting for her with a present, a stack of letters in envelopes tied with string. I wait anxiously as the flight attendant opens the door. This feels like a moment from an old movie, because I know Harlow will probably have a cute little dress on with a sunhat, her hand trying to keep it down in the wind.

A subtle smile cracks on my lips when my theory is proven right, and our eyes meet for a moment that feels as though a key is turning in a lock between us, and I could be on either side of the door. The corners of her mouth tilt up, then she takes a few steps down the stairs, and it feels like eternity.

When she's at the bottom, we both mosey and meet in the middle. Harlow glides the strap of her bag down her shoulder, and it falls to the ground.

It doesn't matter what's about to happen. Our arms of their own accord naturally find their way to wrap around one another, and I pull her tight, afraid to ever let go. I kiss the top of her head, inhaling every fiber of her body that I can.

"Stone." My name escaping her lips sounds like a yearning that I wish she would let me solve.

Creating some space between us, we still don't part ways; instead, our hands stay firm on one another near our elbows, with the envelopes hanging by a string on my finger.

"Harlow, we're not going anywhere until I tell you that I don't want you in my life as a lightning bug that flies away. You're a light, but more a perfect little permanent star that deserves her own night sky. It's just… I believe that I'm meant to be there too. This is nothing I planned to say in my lifetime to anyone. But damn, woman, you have me in knots, and I kind of hope I don't unravel, because you're wrapped up in that. I have no plans to let you go." Her mouth parts open, and the way her eyes twinkle in daylight is all the more reason that I'm certain I make her feel alive. "So, you can say what you were planning to say. Stay at the Dizzy Duck Inn." I notice her face puzzle, and she flutters her lashes. "And I know I told you that we have choices to make, but I've made mine, you know where I stand on us, my family, a future. Is it so bad that I plan on getting on my knees to beg you to see what we have?"

Harlow places her fingertips against my chest then gently pushes me back. "Stone… are you done yet?" A smile grows.

"I'm not sure. I'm kind of winging it here. I would keep talking if it meant that I don't have to hear your words of disaster."

She chortles a sound. "I believe you said you would get on your knees."

I cock my head to the side. "True." We both stand there, lost for a few seconds. Our eyes fixed with what I see as true love. Which is why I grab her arms to keep her firmly in place, adamant that we have to start the difficult days ahead. "Just say it. Tell me what you came here to do so I know what I'm up against, before I convince you that you should have known when we first laid our eyes on one another that we could never be just a fling. Tell me."

Her eyes widen slightly, and her lips roll in, as if she's

suppressing humor which feels kind of cruel. "Well, as much as I loved hearing every word that you just said, I am afraid to disappoint you." That's it, my heart is hit with a bow and arrow. "I was just going to tell you that you're going to have to buy me a winter coat."

Huh, what?

"A winter coat?"

She nods, as if she is waiting for me to solve a riddle. "Also, I kind of need your muscles today. I packed a little heavy on the luggage front."

"Heavy luggage?" My dry throat seems to ease.

Her head moves again in confirmation of my questions that are now clearly statements. I stand there trying to connect the dots, but Harlow can't wait and bursts out in the brightest smile I've ever seen. "I'm moving to Lake Spark." Realization hits me, and she playfully pushes me. "To be with you."

Instantly, I crash my lips onto hers, as if the weight on my shoulders fell off a cliff, never to return. The present that was hanging by my fingers falls to the ground. I'm not sure who is smiling more, which interferes with our kissing skills, by the way, but we don't stop our kiss. I pick her up and twirl her around, only to set her down and seal our lips together right where we left off.

When my head angles to scrape my lips along hers, I murmur, "I'll buy you five coats, and if you're a good girl, then I'll get you boots too."

Her head falls back in laughter, and I take the opportunity to kiss her neck on offer. "I love you," I repeat a few times between kisses.

"You've mentioned. Remember, you fell first?" She's teasing me because I see that mischief in her eyes, but she's oh so right.

My eyes rocket up as I lightly groan for how I got it all wrong, and hope vanished to relief.

"Stone?" Harlow waits until I draw my eyes up with a goofy smirk.

"Harlow?"

"I love you, and I'm sorry it's taken so long to end up here with an answer, but you're not just the guy who healed me. You scared me in the best possible way and made me believe a forever with someone was possible. And it turns out that I'm strong enough to close the map since I've reached my destination." Her voice is fragile but so firm at the same time, the perfect magical chemistry that seems to be possible between two people.

"It *is* very possible." I cup her face between my hands, and with the pad of my thumb, brush along her jawline. "I thought you came here to end things. Your email sucked."

Her face screws up. "I guess… I'm coming to Lake Spark and we need to talk was a bad choice of words," she reflects.

"No shit."

Harlow's eyes drift down to the ground and puzzles as she notices the envelopes. "What's that?"

I'm quick to pick the gift up. "It was yours in case I needed to convince you or give you a parting gift." Her fingers trace the string. "It's every email we've written to one another, printed out on fancy paper with traditional writing, because that's the magic of modern times. Every letter… except your last one because that was just brutal."

She laughs, and her eyes glaze with love. "This is special. I'm happy it's not a parting gift."

"Me too. Me too, Harlow."

We get caught in a confirming look until she begins to giggle. "In a way, I wanted to surprise you with this life-altering news, and you're still the one to surprise me. We should probably head out of here."

"Agreed."

"Obviously, we need to figure out how to actually move stuff. But you know… seriously, I did pack extra in my suitcase, and it weighs a ton," she informs me.

"Good thing I have strong arms then." Then it dawns on me. "Really, I was a mess the past few days, and when I heard you made a reservation at the Dizzy Duck Inn, then—"

"What?" She looks at me blankly.

"You made a reservation for a room at the Dizzy Duck Inn?"

Harlow's mouth quirks out. "No, I didn't. I called to see if we could get a table in the restaurant for a little celebration dinner."

"But Stuart told Holden—" I groan. "Fucking Stuart. Completely incapable of doing his job."

"Or just making your life hell." Her closed-lip smile stretches.

I kiss the tip of her nose. "Love the idea of dinner, as you'll need to refuel for what's about to go down in my bedroom."

"Oh yeah?" She has a sultry voice. "Does my new roommate like to play games in the bedroom?"

I scoff a sound as I lead us with my arm draped around her shoulders. "You mean your new bedmate? Yeah. Yeah, he does."

"What a coincidence. So do I."

We grab her luggage which is no joke a workout in itself, then drive back to my place with our hands perfectly interlaced on the middle console.

I'm lucky. More than.

Her damn books apparently warrant some merit in reality.

I laugh to myself at that notion when we slide out of my car. Deciding that I'll get the luggage later, we walk to the door, and I unlock it before I quickly swing her up into my arms to carry her over the threshold, as if we just got married, which will happen one day—this is just practice.

"As soon as we're on the other side and the door closes, you'll never be able to go back."

Harlow's affectionate look slays me. "Turns out, I should have known that you'd be the only door I'd want a key to."

Her answer warms my heart, and I kick the door open but don't move, instead stealing a kiss.

"Turns out I was holding onto it for you." She likes my answer because I sense that she's melting in my arms. But I love teasing her and seeing that smile of hers. "You'll get your actual key tomorrow. I need to find you a deer keychain."

23

HARLOW

Looking at my eighth cup that I pull out from the box, with a straw and cute imprint on the front, I quirk my lips out, contemplating if I really needed to pack this many smoothie cups. Meh, Stone will just have to deal. I set it on the kitchen island then tuck my hands into the back pockets of my jeans while I explore the house with my eyes for the hundredth time.

After getting the logistics of the move sorted out, I find myself a new Lake Spark citizen and living with Stone. The butterflies in my stomach have subsided, mostly because after a few days, this has felt very right.

A smile curls on my lips from that thought, and my body relaxes in this house that is beginning to feel like home.

The sound of someone entering through the door by the garage has me turning my head, very aware that Stone is back from town. He slows his pace and examines my unpacking skills, then his sight bounces to my row of cups while he tosses his key onto the counter and sets a bag down with his other hand.

"Well… I guess it cuts down on daily dishwasher needs?" His strained look fades to humor.

I shrug my shoulders. "Cups and mugs are crucial when working from home. We can't go to Jolly Joe's every day."

"Yes, we can," he says adamantly. I think it's part of his daily routine.

Stone dives into the cloth grocery bag to pull out a few items, then he tosses me a bag of chocolate candy. "What's this?" I ask.

"Halloween candy."

"Uh… that's not for like another two months."

He chuckles. "Yeah, but it's Lake Spark. We gotta prepare early for the beloved pumpkin season, because the day after it's straight into winter festivities."

I laugh as I open the bag, since a little treat sounds good right about now. "Do you get a lot of trick-or-treaters?"

Stone grimaces when he steps forward to pull me close by the hips while I chomp on my mini chocolate bar. "You mean, do *we* get a lot of trick-or-treaters?"

I won't get tired of hearing about our house—well, technically, Stone owns it, but semantics.

"Hmm, I thought I was being held captive by a reclusive author who has talents in bed and gives me pop quizzes on hockey. If I fail, then there is most definitely punishment."

Stone growls and is quick to dive down into my neck to nibble my skin, his stubble tickling me and creating a sensitive sensation down to my toes. "Watch it, Harlow," he warns.

"Oh dear, did I cause something to stir and press right into that spot between my legs?" My voice is sultry and my look trouble.

"My restraint is on a ledge right now. I just want to rip everything off you and take you on the living room floor because you're too bad to deserve the kitchen counter," he husks. My entire body comes alive with a desperate need, and I grind against him, encouraging Stone to do more. Instead, I get a devilish growl when he steps back then sweetly kisses my forehead. "Now, now, Harlow, you know we're on a schedule," he tsks.

Ugh, Gloria.

Still ruining our moments like a plague.

"Yes, the Dizzy Duck and writers retreat, yada, yada." My enthusiasm is low. Gloria asked us to stop by for her new group to give tips. We are literally the last people who should be doing that. Did Stone and I actually do anything last year on that retreat, other than escape into our own little world? Yikes, this might be a disaster.

"We'll make it a half-hour tops," Stone promises. I look at him, puzzled. "Okay, it might be a little longer than that before we can escape." He urges me forward with his fingertips on my arm.

I groan a few more times for good measure.

———

THIS WOMAN still has the power to make me feel as though I'm in high school again and in trouble for ditching class.

Gloria smiles brightly at us sitting at the front of the room after giving our introduction. Her eyes shift to her new group of prisoners that walked in to what they thought was a relaxing week of workshops.

Her hands come together. "I'm so happy that Harlow and Stone could stop by to give a few tips and reflections from last year. I'm sure they have some great advice on how you can make your week ahead productive."

Stone and I look at each other awkwardly.

"Go on. Stone, you're first," she suggests.

A croak escapes his dry throat, and he glances at me for a signal of what to say, but I gawk at him to keep this show rolling.

He claps his hands together. "Last year, Harlow and I were partnered together for most of Gloria's life-changing and empowering retreat." I try to keep my chortle in, as I sense the underlying sarcasm, while Gloria just eats this up. "The first day, the walk you are about to embark on will…" Stone's lips tick up before his eyes sweep in my direction with fondness. "Lead you on the path you are supposed to be on. The destination might not be clear, but you'll get there in the end. Well, at least the part where you were meant to be.

Endings are for the reader or yourself to figure out, a future that everyone leaves for their own interpretation."

My quip that I had planned for this event doesn't seem fitting anymore. Apparently, this is a sentimental day, and my lips seal together while my mouth stretches up.

"What advice would you give for the first day?" Gloria asks.

Stone stares directly at her. "Abandon the walk and go into town for coffee at Jolly Joe's." He's dead serious, and Gloria isn't thrilled, especially when a few of the authors in the group chuckle.

"What about your moments of writing, didn't you find solace and be productive?"

His face grows tight. "Nope." His deadpan expression causes me to rub my forehead, as Stone has no plans to appease Gloria. "Probably the least productive days in terms of writing in my life. But hey…" Stone throws on an overdone smile. "You paired me up really well. You matchmaker you."

"You two are together?" a woman in her thirties from the circle asks.

I pipe up. "Actually… yeah. That was the best part of that week. We met."

"That is so sweet," she coos.

"What?" Gloria nearly spits out. "*Together* together?"

Stone and I face one another with a shrug. "Yeah. Didn't you figure that out yet?" he outlines the obvious. We interlace our fingers, and Stone sets our hands on his knee. This is more of a statement, yet the pad of thumb rubs a circle on my palm.

"We really are the worst people to ask back to talk to everyone," I tell her. "I mean, we literally ditched half the workshops, didn't even show up to a few lunches, and ran away to Main Street a few times too. Not to mention, we had a late-night drink at the bar, which obviously affects your clear head and writing," I list.

Gloria's face is blank, and her jaw already dropped about ten seconds ago.

"I mean, I assumed you asked us here since you knew we were both in Lake Spark. Kind of thought you got the memo that Harlow is my girl now." Stone playfully brings an arm around my shoulders and squeezes me as I smile tightly.

Gloria seems to puff as if she's a fish and even turns a shade of red. "You two are impossible. From day one, you were trouble, yet out of everyone, you didn't require saving from forest rangers, so I thought okay, we can ask Harlow and Stone back since they both had books released this year." Her tangent leads to a lot of hand gestures.

I hold my hand out, indicating for her to calm down. "If it's any consolation, by bringing Stone and me together, it gave us inspiration in the long run. Yay, you… nailed it on the life-changing experience." I smile brightly.

"Sounds like he nailed you," a man from the circle mumbles, and my eyes whip in his direction.

Gloria growls again. "This is a disaster."

"No, it's not. I'm sure this little crew here…" Stone throws a thumb over his shoulder. "Will leave with a new outlook on life, just as we did. It's not always about tasks."

Gloria's demeanor seems to brighten. "I mean, I guess I did sense that your personalities would be a great match for the retreat."

"Exactly," I assure her.

"And I did give you both a scootch to deviate from the schedule. The walk was all my idea."

"You must have mystical powers," Stone adds.

Gloria straightens her posture and seems to be in better spirits. "I knew I was good for something." A proud grin appears on her face before she snaps her gaze to us with a pointed look. "You two can go, this was still kind of useless." She shrugs.

Stone is quick to stand up and yank me up with him. "Great. Have fun. Let's go. We'll consider you for the invite list for the wedding. Good luck, everyone."

We are out of that room so fast that my laugh is uneven and mumbled.

The moment we get peace down the hall and head toward the lobby, we calm down, and Stone and I face one another in an embrace.

"That was a real delight."

Stone widens his eyes to get his bearings before blinking a few times. "What a highlight of our day," he says, cynical.

"It kind of was. I mean, how are we going to top that, unless you have plans to tie me to your bed again," I retort.

Stone half-circles us to lead us on. "Not a bad idea."

I pat his shoulder. "Plan that out in your head while I ask Stuart for a batch of cookies."

"He might poison them."

I pinch Stone on his side. "No, he won't. He likes me."

Two minutes later, we're sitting on the sofa in the lobby while we wait for cookies. Stone and I face forward and study the moose on the wall.

"Do you think it's possessed?" I wonder.

"Maybe. He doesn't seem to leave, no matter how many times Holden says it's going to go."

"Does he have a name?"

"Dead Animal on a Wall."

I wince. "Ugh, I don't need that image."

Right on cue, Holden approaches us. "Heard you two were here."

He takes a seat on a chaise lounge near us. I met him at Vaughn's wedding.

"Welcome to Lake Spark, Harlow." He smiles.

"Thanks. So far so good, except this moose on the wall seems to be an evil spirit."

Holden rubs his face with his hands. "I know. When we had a flood downstairs a month ago, it set us back on the interior designer front, so we were pushed back by four months. I hired a woman to do a full project of this place. The daughter of an old coach of mine, Lexi, but she was in college back then."

"Great. You can finally swap hunters' paradise for something to actually represent Lake Spark," Stone comments.

"Or swap it with a dead duck," Holden counters.

Stone and I both appear terrified, even though Holden rolls his eyes that we would even consider him to be serious.

"Anyhow, it's nice to see that you're shacking up with Stone. I'm sure he's a real delight to live with. You can soften him a bit, and maybe he'll finally leave Stuart alone."

"Nope. His passionate dislike of your receptionist will never disappear."

"He shows no respect," Stone is quick to defend himself.

Holden stands and straightens his rolled-up shirt sleeves. "On that note, I'm going to go bury myself in financial numbers. Good to see you, Harlow."

Stone salutes him away while Stone's phone vibrates in his pocket. He pulls it out only to huff a sound.

"Well, seems like tomorrow's brunch with my brother has returned to normal. Isla texted that she attempted to make muffins and a casserole for tomorrow and she burned them all."

I smile to myself. "Huh, I guess now that I'm here, they don't need to impress me. Everyone can be themselves."

Stone pecks my lips quickly. "That's a good thing. But still, remind me to pick up donuts tomorrow morning so we don't starve." He nods to someone behind me. "Your cookies are ready. Be right back."

As he heads off, I reflect to myself.

This feels so damn perfect. Stone Madden was always right. We were always going to be something. We were always going to have a life together. In Lake Spark too.

Maybe if I would have realized earlier then it would have gone so easily, but then it might not feel as amazing as it does now. Hurdles make us stronger.

The only thing I will always hold on to inside of me with strong conviction is that the moment Stone's eyes met mine with the strike of a flame would lead us here.

In that moment, I should have known that it would always be him.

EPILOGUE: STONE

Well, that plan went out the window.

The whole "have a few days at the Dizzy Duck Inn with my secret motive" plan.

We have people in to repaint my home office and add another wall so Harlow and I each have some space to work. It meant that we needed to be out of the house for a few days.

Perfect. We could stay at the place where it all started. Use my investment card to get us a great room too, except that's under renovation, so we had to settle on a smaller chic room.

And now, Harlow is lying on her stomach with her head near the edge of the bed, and although I think she has drool escaping from the corner of her mouth, she still looks beautiful.

Her groan fills the room. "Stone, I can't take this. Take me out to the pasture and kill me."

I snort a laugh and come to kneel down next to her, my fingers instantly finding home on that spot behind her ears. "Well, that's a bleak outlook. It's just a virus. It will pass."

Yep, a romantic few days got obliterated by a virus that's taken her down for the count.

"Is the room spinning?" she mumbles.

I pretend to evaluate the room. "I don't think so." She growls from that answer. "Just rest." I reach for the thermometer and take her temp; it's one of those forehead gun ones. "Yikes, you should probably take off a layer or two to get the fever down."

Her hand rises then flops back down. "You want to really try and get me naked right now?"

I grin. "Oh, how I wish it would be for the reason I want. But that's not what's happening." Harlow murmurs into the mattress, and she looks miserable. "At least we ruled out that we didn't fall into the accidental-pregnancy trope. That's, I guess, a bright side." Not that we don't want kids, just not now. We both agreed we wanted to enjoy life with just the two of us before adding a little one to the mix. Until then, we can dote on my niece.

"My head hurts."

"Sleep, Harlow," I order before I adjust the pillows.

"So bossy." She still manages to tease me, which tells me that she must be on the mend.

By the time she's fast asleep with a little snore because she's ill, I take a moment to recall how my master plan has failed.

I walk to the corner of the room, shove my hand down the inner pocket of my suitcase, and pull out the envelope. A letter that screams special. It's closed with melted wax, our initials imprinted. On the inside, the letter is written in the beauty of a fountain pen that uses actual ink. You can imagine a quill and a lantern nearby.

Trapping the envelope between my fingers, I sigh because I didn't get my moment.

But I guess that's us. Our road together tends to have corners and twists and turns until we land right back where we started; together.

Blowing out another breath, I toss the letter onto the table since Harlow won't be leaving the bed anytime soon.

Later that night, I'm struggling to sleep. I'm constantly waking to feel her forehead or check if she has chills or is sweating. There is no way I could fall into a deep sleep.

When morning comes, I wake up and order room service, ensuring its freshly squeezed orange juice. I feel like I can be an ass to the new part-time receptionist this time because I know the kid, as he was training at the development camp in the summer, hoping to turn pro.

Since Harlow is still sound asleep, I decide it's my moment to take a shower, as one of us has to hold it together today.

My shower is good, a little extra long as I take in my moment of solitude, as if I need to meditate or some shit. I've always liked leaving a shower with the bathroom full of steam. The kind where you have to use your forearm to rub the mirror kind of steam. At least that's a sign that I'm starting the day right, it's promising.

Opening the door with a towel around my waist, I circle around the corner to find Harlow sitting at the table with a white robe wrapped around her body. The table has two trays of food plus a basket of croissants. Staying in a boutique hotel also equates to fancy trays, with a flower in a glass vase and freshly squeezed orange juice.

Maybe that's why Harlow smiles before she brings a tissue to her nose. "Hey, they dropped off breakfast. For some reason the guy on the other side of the door had this snarly look and then brightened when he realized it was me. He even mumbled that it was his lucky day, which I would assume is because someone is a little grumpy with the front desk here." Even pale and with a hoarse voice, she manages to scold me in a way that I'll never get tired of, but then she rewarded me when she heard me tell Holden to give the staff bonuses.

I throw her a weak smile while I head to my suitcase for clothes. "Shouldn't you be in bed?"

"I'm famished," she says while she picks up her fork, then throws me a quick glance over her shoulder. "Stay in your towel. Nothing else. Do it for me. It gives me strength and encouragement to persevere with this virus from hell."

I chuckle then give up on finding a shirt. "Well, if you put it that way. And someone must be feeling a little better."

"I am. My throat is a little tender, and my nose could use a steam bath, but perhaps the end is in sight."

Still, I lean over from behind to give her a quick kiss on her forehead before sitting across from her at the table with the towel taut around my waist. Pouring myself a cup of coffee, I survey Harlow to really evaluate if she's feeling better. The verdict is that she's a tad better.

"Mmm, I love this omelet." She sucks her fork during her bite.

"I wish I was your fork right now," I tease.

She laughs before she sets her utensil down, and something draws her attention. "Oh." She finishes chewing. "I must have gotten a letter at reception."

I nearly choke on my coffee, and she looks at me oddly. "Wow, that's piping-hot coffee," I lie.

Lines form on her head. "Take it easy. We would hate for your tongue to be burned. Could totally set you back for sensual activities." I love how she speaks so seriously, but it's just part of our banter.

What I don't love is that I forgot about that envelope.

It's too late, as Harlow sniffles her blocked nose before she begins to open the dark blue wax seal. There is no stopping this now.

Her head tips to the side with curiosity. "Strange. Your initial and mine are on the stamp. Huh." She's now intrigued and begins to read it aloud.

> *Harlow,*
>
> *We need to add another letter to our pile of envelopes.*
>
> *You and I have only ever been on a path forward...*

I begin to speak as I repeat the contents of the letter I wrote, sitting across from her with an enduring facial expression that will be unreadable to her. "Which is exactly why you knew that one day you would become my wife. I should probably ask you first… Will you marry me?"

When her mouth gapes open, with the corners of her lips tight and eyes glistening with a new energy, I have to give her the grin that I've been holding in.

"Uhm, first, yes. Absolutely, yes." Harlow speaks as though this is a normal day, then she holds her finger up before she sneezes into her arm. "Holy shit, you proposed while I'm sick and look like a complete mess."

I get up and circle around the table to kneel down in front of her, sneaking my hands between the flaps of the robe to settle just above her knees. "I wasn't exactly planning it this way, but hey, at least it's at the place where we met. Points for us."

Tears begin to rain down her cheeks, and she smiles uncontrollably. I tip my head up and stretch to kiss her lips, and instantly she revolts.

"I'm snotty and eww. I'm going to get you sick."

I chuckle. "I don't care. You just said yes. Besides, we can both be sick together in bed. All the more reason to have sex like it's medicine."

She swats me playfully before she touches my face with a caress, her thumb circling right where my stubble ends. "I love you."

"I was certain about that, hence the ring." I indicate with my head behind me. "Which is hiding in my suitcase since nothing is going as planned today."

"Really?" she one-tones. "I hadn't noticed, considering I'm sitting here with my fiancé in a sexy towel on his knees, while I have snot and tears, and I'm 100% positive I feel a fever returning."

I wince, and the back of my palm lands on her forehead. "Shit, you really need to get back into bed."

"I might be persuaded if you show me the ring," she muses.

I drop my head in humor before I walk on my knees to pull out the box from my bag, then wobble back because casual is just how we are playing this today.

Attempting to give it to her, I pause then pull it back. "In bed without the robe?"

She rolls her eyes, feigning as if it's a discomfort. "Whatever you say."

Grinning, I open the box to show her the ring that is a little shinier than I'm sure is her taste, but I need to make it clear to the world that she's taken.

Harlow gasps, and her hands cover her mouth as she takes in what's about to slide onto her hand. "It's gorgeous. I'm blinded."

"Whoa, whoa, whoa, isn't this what you write? See? Reality."

She laughs as the ring finds a permanent spot on her finger.

"You're going to be my husband." Her voice strains due to her sore throat. Still, she studies the ring by holding up her hand.

"That's the idea."

Her bright grin returns before she hugs me again, and I inhale her hair, never getting tired of her embrace.

"Can I share my germs with you just for one quick kiss?"

I cock my head to the side to pretend to think about it. "Depends. Do I get a little tongue action?"

She doesn't even answer as our lips meet and stamp together, a husky murmur in the back of her throat encouraging more. One quick flick of our tongues and then she pulls away, only to cough.

Her palm flies up. "Okay, as much as this is a wonderful moment and it had my favorite question of all time, I have to put my foot down. I can't wipe out my fiancé, he's one of the only people in civilization that I enjoy," she jokes. "I need to go back to bed."

I stroke her cheek with the back of my hand. "Good idea. I'll go grab more medicine from the store, and I expect you to be in a blissful dreaming state when I return."

Harlow stands and then wobbles back to bed. "I have nothing to dream about now since you made it a reality."

I help her get tucked under the covers. "I think we'll have many more dreams to come."

She becomes groggy, her eyes becoming heavy. "True. I need a dog, a trip to a warm climate, and a baby at some point."

"Sounds perfect." I kiss her forehead then leave her to rest.

Grabbing my keys, I head into the hall and walk down toward the elevator until I abruptly stop because a guest opens their door to exit their room.

Except that's no guest.

Holden is busy fixing his collar, his shirt ruffled around his waist, and he looks a little flushed.

"Holden?" I'm confused.

He looks up and freezes. "Oh, hey there." He swallows.

"Uh, what are you doing?" I cock my head to the side as I notice something. "Did someone bite your neck?" Right, he was doing *that*.

He clears his throat. "Just… a meeting." He realizes his lie wasn't even an attempt.

"You know I'm not buying that." Instead, I lean against the wall and cross my arms and ankles to wait patiently for his story. My grin must unnerve him.

His eyes swim side to side, and his jaw flexes. "You know how we have that new interior designer for the hotel?"

"To get rid of that ridiculous moose head, yeah. Lexi, your former coach's daughter, right?"

He smiles tightly. "Exactly. I might have…"

The door swings open. "I'm off, need to meet with the tile guy." Lexi is finishing buttoning her blouse, completely oblivious to me, then she stops in her tracks. "Oh, hi." She frowns.

"You remember Stone?" Holden awkwardly asks Lexi.

"Yeah, for sure." She attempts to give me a polite smile. "Nice to see you again. I'm not here. Have a great day." She is quick to walk away.

"Don't forget that my daughter has figure skating practice after school," he calls out.

She grumbles and doesn't even give him any attention. "It's Tuesday, so she doesn't, and how many times do I have to remind you that I'm not your nanny?"

"Yeah, but that was the deal when you moved in," he reminds her.

She groans again before disappearing into the elevator.

Holden's lips push out, and his head tilts because he's checking out her ass. He makes no effort to hide it. He swings his tight smile to me, and I greet him with an entertained look.

"Someone has some explaining to do."

He blows out a long breath. "I might have… blackmailed her into living with me for a bit."

My eyes bug out. "Wow, she's really getting the five-star treatment on the personal-attention front."

Holden rubs his face. "*Yeah*, so we might be encountering a little problem with that…"

SIX MONTHS LATER

My heels patter down the pavement as I tug my fiancé along, and he nearly steps on my feet. I huff out a breath, knowing this conversation isn't over.

Stone grabs hold of my elbow and stops my walk, and it causes my eyes to drag in his direction, but I still sulk.

"Come on, Harlow. You're supposed to believe in big romantic weddings." His grin and the persistence in his eyes *nearly* has me caving.

"Ugh, Stone. I'm positive this is the way we should do this. I don't want a big wedding, and it's better if it's just you and me, exchanging our own words." I roll my eyes and land on the vision of the courthouse right in front me, only to have Stone pull me flush and nuzzle my cheek in that way that screams he will win me over.

"Harlow." Yep, the devil is seeping through his words but oh so very damn sexy. "A wedding with nobody else here? My niece would love to drop some flowers on the ground, and I know you want Flo to visit."

I wave a finger in front of him. "No. I want it to be just us. We've talked about it, and you agreed. So here we are in wedding casual and ready to rock." We give each other the once-over and both approve. He's in dark jeans with a dark shirt, and I'm in a short lace dress that flares at the waist. My nails are olive green, of course. But this is all how I want it.

"Cake after?" he pleads.

Nibbling my bottom lip, I know I have to give a compromise, and to be honest, my sweet tooth is kicking in. "A milkshake like our first day together."

Stone loves that idea, I can tell by the way his cheeks rise and his eyes dip. "I like that."

He agreed to a quick wedding, and maybe I was being selfish in this request. It's just that I love sharing extremely special moments with only him. But I'm no fool, marriage is a balance, and I will give him something.

"Now, shall we go lock one another down or are we just going to stand here…" I pretend to be annoyed.

Stone sputters a laugh. "Come on, time to make you an honest woman."

I tsk him. "Says the man who attempted to break open the box from Piper's boutique without me noticing." I raise a brow while his mouth opens, but he struggles with his words. "Yeah… I figured that out."

It's white lingerie for the wedding night. We have to keep it traditional somewhere today.

When we're inside and waiting for our turn, we sit in a calming silence. The tips of our fingers dance with one another as I lean my head against his shoulder.

"You might have had a good idea," he whispers.

Quickly, I glance at him. "Why is that?"

"Without all the fuss, I can marry you faster. No need to entertain guests, we just thrust ourselves right into it and say what we legally need to."

I snort a laugh. "Thrust? Really? That's your word choice?"

"Such dirty thoughts, Wifey."

The man in front indicates that it's time. I stand and offer Stone my hand. "I'm not your wife yet."

It's a while later when we've said the necessities and have been declared husband and wife that we make our way to the Dizzy Duck Inn. Stone guides us toward the restaurant, only for me to tug on his wrist to follow me another way.

"What's going on? We have a reservation. The chef is preparing us a special five-course meal." He looks at me, perplexed.

Throwing him a sultry stare, I love this man and everything that is about to happen. "He can wait a few minutes. There is something we need to do first."

Stone raises his brows with intrigue. "Oh yeah?" He wraps his arms around me with heat in his voice.

I swat his arm while I smile. "Not that, although tonight will be special. But follow me. Your wife has plans, and you should always follow her lead." I'm being sarcastic.

"Alright, Mrs. Madden. Lead me away."

We hold hands as we walk, and by the time we reach the entrance to the spa and stand outside the door to the pool, Stone is officially confused.

Stopping, I ensure we focus on one another. I take a deep breath. "Stone, you once took me here and made me jump into a pool with my clothes on. We have our letters, and we have our kisses, so why not do something different for our wedding day. You surprised me then, so I'll surprise you now."

He licks his lips. "I'm all for this, whatever this is."

I swoop in and take his other hand in mine. "We were once here, and you told me to get rid of my negative energy. It was fun, crazy, and special. So here we are, but this time, it's to soak in the positives. Happy wedding day, Husband."

Grinning at him, I use my back to push the door open, and the moment the humid air hits us, he blinks a few times. This pool is beautiful, lit up like art and deserving of calm. It's not intended for kids or pool parties. It's a spa pool, but today, we're breaking the rules.

"Surprise!" everybody yells.

His brother, sister-in-law, Flo, Holden, and Holden's girlfriend are all in the pool in their swimsuits, and Stone's niece is fluttering her feet in her floaties. At the side table there is a cake and champagne.

Stone takes in the scene, and I'm quick to explain by whispering in his ear, "It's our wedding day. How could I not let you celebrate? A pool party seems different and romantic."

He kisses me, and it's with so much love and longing. That's just us. Always catching the other off guard but doing every little thing from pure promise of a future. I give up. It's true. We're hopeless romantics.

"This is… crazy, but thank you." He takes hold of my hand and squeezes extra tight to walk us to the edge of the pool, exchanging congratulations with everyone.

But then he throws me an awkward glare over his shoulder. "Uh, swimsuits?"

I chuckle. "We don't need them. You made me jump in fully clothed, remember?" Stone stands tall, assessing if I'm serious or not. I do my best to keep a straight face, but it's a fail. I sputter out a laugh. "Relax, we have a bag so we can change."

"That's actually a shame. I wanted a reason to spank you tonight," he mumbles, but his brother clears his throat, having heard.

Now I just giggle. "That will happen anyway." I wink.

Stone tickles me, winding me closer to his body. "I love you."

"Likewise. Now let's get into our wedding-day swimwear, grab some champagne, and play Marco Polo or something like that."

We both lean in for a kiss, aware that the rest of our lives will be strong and amazing, no matter the highs or lows. Stone is my rock, and I'm not quite sure why I haven't repeated that to make us laugh at the reference. But I can't laugh… because it's true. Which is why I'm never letting go, and the ring on my finger promises he won't either.

SHOULD HAVE RUN

1

HOLDEN

I'm doomed.

If one more thing goes wrong with my schedule, then I'm absolutely unlucky. My eyes slide past my laptop on my desk and land on the photo of my two little devils—my kids. They are such joyous creatures, causing chaos in my life. Okay, I do love them. A lot, actually. I'll always have a soft spot reserved for them. Lori, my twelve-year-old, and Harry, my ten-year-old. I want to believe they make me a better person. That's fatherhood, right?

But holy fuck, they are challenging me in a game I'm not sure I know how to play. I'm good at games. I played professional hockey for twelve years. I win, always. Except with them… I don't.

I huff out a deep exhale and decide to look out the window of my office to find some tranquility in the scene of Lake Spark on this spring day. The blue sky and the bright sun would be perfect, except Illinois in March can be unkind on the temperature front, and it's a solid high 40s with a breeze.

The Dizzy Duck Inn is my post-pro-athlete life. It was something different and fun. There are so many professional athletes in this town and people escaping Chicago for a weekend away. It's a prime business opportunity that I snatched up when the old owners wanted to retire, then I packed up and moved my family here a year ago. I have two investors, but it's me running the show. Lake Spark is a calm little town with an excellent private school nearby that was an extra draw for parenting my kids. After all, my ex-wife decided to exit the picture long ago, leaving me to do it all.

I can be Superman.

Just not lately.

I think I'm on nanny number six in the last year alone.

I sigh as I lean back in my chair and interlace my hands behind my head."To be fair, I ignored all their attempts to flirt," I say to myself. Well… that might be a tiny lie. There was one a few years ago who seemed like a good one-night kind of drunken Christmas party thing, my bad. But I've been a perfect boss since then. My little angels? Not so much.

I shake my head, knowing that I need to focus on some numbers before the interior designer shows up to start the project of freshening up the look of this hotel. It's not that it's in bad condition, I just want to rejuvenate the atmosphere. With the spa and wedding venue here, I want to step it up to ensure guests have to book well in advance. We already have an award-winning chef.

My attention is drawn to the door when I see my friend and business partner Stone Madden peek in. We're from similar hockey circles, though we never played on the same team. We just hit it off at some charity fundraiser way back and have been friends since.We have one other smaller investor, but he takes zero part in almost everything, as it's purely the old owner's wish that his son kept a stake.

"Hey, Holden, you alive?"

I chuckle. "Today, yes. What brings you by, considering you firmly said that you would invest in this place, but I quote, 'don't want to do one fucking single thing in regards to management, nor do I want to hear about it.' End quote."

He quickly holds his palm up. "I won't deny that, but I also said I would invest so that one day if I needed to impress someone, then I could slide in this little fact to gain me points."

My expression flattens. "And?"

"I'm using my part-ownership card. Harlow and I are taking a room for a week or two while the contractors redo our house."

"This place is getting a makeover too."

He shrugs. "Yeah, but this place has charm."

"We do our best." I grin cheekily.

"By the way, your old coach's daughter, Lexi, starts today, right? Met her a few times at various sponsor gigs long ago."

"Something like that."

I have examined her portfolio, and it's what I need. Apparently, she had grandparents that lived around here when she was younger, and she has a best friend, Summer, that lives here in town who I see around. Summer also recommended Lexi. I've met Lexi a few times. After all, her dad was my coach up in Michigan. Let's just hope she's changed since I saw her last, which was a few years ago after she graduated college. I remember running into her once during her college years. A true sorority girl who valued social life just as much as academia. I'm hoping she's a calm adult now, with baggy jeans and an oversized t-shirt. It's what I need to keep me concentrating on the task at hand. I can't afford distractions.

Besides, once you leave hockey, the team rules still apply; stay away from the coach's daughter.

"Good luck, or rather, keep it locked in. See ya, buddy." He waves his fingers in the air.

I tip my nose up in acknowledgment, and the moment the door shuts, I'm back concentrating on my task. I must lose time though, because as I'm busy typing away and clicking my mouse, I hear a soft knock on my door.

The door cracks open. "Hi, Holden." Lexi's voice sounds chipper, or excited at least. I'm sure she wants to do an excellent job on this massive project ahead.

"Hey, Lexi," I say as I glance up from my laptop while I press save on my screen. But the moment my eyes hit the image at the door, I instantly do a double-take.

Oh no.

No. No. Nope. Fuck no.

I'm cursing to myself inside my head as I attempt to keep my face neutral.

Well, wish one is a massive failure. Lexi's in jeans, except they're tight, which isn't ideal. Wish two, a total miss too. She's in a sweater, even a turtleneck, but unfortunately for my dick that suddenly twitched, it's not a baggy shirt. Instead, it highlights her tits and taut body. I didn't even predict her long dark blonde locks that frame her face. Confidence oozes all around her.

She is what I recall, yet with less makeup, which makes her hotter… and now she's older, too.

Bad. This is bad.

She's supposed to be that college kid that I remember when I was in the height of my career and way past the early-twenties stage. It seems that she's turned into a woman that turns heads even when dressed perfectly respectably.

I swallow and throw on a polite smile. "Good to see you again."

"Yeah, I guess it's been a while. I ran into Stone in the lobby. It's like déjà vu seeing everyone from the hockey world again." She doesn't even wait for me to invite her in. Lexi strides straight in with poise and heads to the chair in front of my desk to sit down.

Oh yeah, we're supposed to have a meeting. Not me staring at her and studying the shade of gloss on her lips. Professional Holden. Yep, that's who I am now.

"Figured it was safe to hire you without an interview since you're not a stranger to most of us." I attempt to lighten the mood, and it causes her to give me a grin, with her lips that look welcoming for my co—

"I guess being the coach's daughter has its advantages," she replies, breaking my thought.

Sure, think that, sweetheart. Screw the team rule of not going near her for life. It can go out the window. I'm a grown man anyhow. Wait, why am I even thinking all this?

I can't sit in front of her face to face, because her brown eyes seem as though they will turn me into the smug man I know I can be when I find prey. Standing, I walk to my window to divert my attention to other thoughts. "Everything good in your life?"

"Can't complain. I'm sitting in front of you for a project that's any designer's *fantasy*."

Her tone, I can't pinpoint it, but it causes me to snap my sight to her and find that she has a smirk, which confirms to me that she might have grown into a little spitfire.

And her mind seems to be not as straightlaced as I hoped. That's a relief, sort of. Looks like we might have a few shared interests.

Taking the high road, I keep my wry smile fixed. "And non-work life?"

She folds her hands on top of her thigh thrown over her opposite knee. "Different to last time you saw me. I'm no longer in a sorority, and I keep my weekends busy with sophisticated wine drinking and attempting to find the latest dinner hotspot."

I lean against the window. "Except you've never been here with your boyfriend. I should be offended that the Dizzy Duck Inn didn't make it to your hotspot list."

Lexi's head tips slightly to the side as she purses her lips. "It did. It was before you became owner. No boyfriend. I went with my father." New fact on availability. Noted.

My jaw ticks as her eyes are somehow possessive and cause me to feel slightly uncomfortable. "Of course you did," I mutter.

Her mouth gapes open, and she fakes shock. "Implying I'm a daddy's girl? That's not cool. Back when he was your coach, and even to this day, his team takes priority, and you know that."

I take a few steps back to my desk and hover over it by placing my fingertips on the hard oak, which could potentially be as hard as my cock might be soon. "I'm happy you're doing well." I'm sincere about that.

This time it's Lexi who stands and strolls over to the window to steal a look at the spring scenery outside. "How are you? Lori and Harry?"

I forgot that I brought them to a team holiday party when they were much younger. "Let's see…" I pop my lips and debate the best answer. "Since I last saw you, that messy divorce was finalized from the ex-wife from hell who decided motherhood wasn't for her, and my two great kids cause so much mischief that I'm beginning to wonder if I have Satan as an ancestor. But hey, gotta love them."

My light tone causes her to laugh. "Sounds like you have your hands full and not the way you prefer." Her smirk is sultry. I've been around enough women to know the differences of mouth positions.

And damn, she's at it again.

Does my expression make it that obvious that she can read that she's caught me off guard and isn't what I expected? My head retreats back as my cheeks tighten and rise up. I don't remember her having this sassy boldness, but it's quite a positive attribute to have. "Something like that. But it seems like that might change soon." That's my subtle warning. This time it's her face that has surprise or concern, I'm not sure which, but her brows rise. "With this project, of course." Bullshit, but I do need to discuss the re-design.

She clears her throat and returns to the chair in front of me, and we sit down. Our eyes lock in this unusual meeting. I'm not sure what's in the air that surrounds around us, but I'm doubting it's professionalism.

The thing is, sometimes you have an instant click with someone. That's how attraction works. Noticing someone across the bar isn't a made-up lie. Being familiar with one another just adds that extra element. In a way, it's added value to the flirting game. And I see no problem with flirting as long as the door to exploring that flirtation is deadbolted shut when it comes to my younger interior designer. I didn't think of her this way before, but now she's sauntered into my office as a woman grown and changed.

"Okay, so, I have clear steps to attack the re-design," she begins.

It seems one of us can shift to work mode as fast as a light switch.

I shut my laptop screen that I forgot I left open. Might as well save some battery, right? "Take me through the steps."

"First, I already sent suggestions to your staff manager so they could arrange logistics, and she sent back some feedback on your behalf. After we have a walkthrough, I want to start by bringing in samples. I understand we need to attack the lobby first. Already noticed the moose head on the wall." She cringes.

I chuckle. "You're not a fan of Caesar?"

She chuckles, and it's cute. "I doubt anyone is, especially if you named him after a salad."

Swiping a hand across my rough but short-shaved jaw, I fall into a more relaxed state. "Although a tradition to the inn, nobody is a fan, so you have my full permission to knock him down before an animal lover sends me an angry letter."

Her shoulders lift up then down. "Perfect. No debate there then. So, after samples—"

Lexi is unable to finish her sentence because my phone vibrates on the desk. I reach to ignore the call and turn my phone to silent, but I pause when I see the name across the screen.

I hold my finger up. "Sorry. I just need a sec."

She doesn't hesitate. "Of course."

I hit the green button as my entire body fills with dread. "Principal Johnson," I attempt to sound pleased for her call.

"Mr. West, we seem to have a little problem at school," she begins on the other end.

I clench my jaw in an attempt to keep myself calm. "And what might that be?"

"Today it's Lori. She made quite a scene at afternoon pick-up. Lori decided to speak… disrespectfully to one of her classmate's moms when Lori and her classmate were in a little… debate." I can hear that she's trying to be delicate in her approach.

I snicker while my sight lands on Lexi who patiently waits. "Seriously? You're phoning me because my daughter spoke about a parent outside of school hours?"

"Mr. West." Principal Johnson sounds surprised. "Everyone by the sixth-grade door heard her. It left Gemma McClearly in tears that her mother was being called such things."

Damn it, Lori has been having issues with Gemma. From what I hear, she's a little brat with parents that could use a parenting book or two. And her mom? The parent committee president on a power trip to make up for her recent divorce.

"I'm sure she had a reason. You're well aware they are not the best of friends," I highlight.

"She called Ms. McClearly a gold digger looking for a husband, then decided to add that plastic isn't the look you go for, which means she must have been referring to you." Her tone is unamused.

Even my jaw drops from this incident. "I could see… how that might… be a…" Ah damn, I have no words.

"Mr. West, Gemma was in tears, and the other parents who heard were none too pleased with Lori's lack of manners. Lake Spark Academy, of course, upholds our values of kindness and respect very seriously. Lori is in my office, and you need to pick her up. I'm losing my patience with her, Mr. West."

I blow out an exhausted breath. Great, perfect, swell, exactly what I need today. I pinch the bridge of my nose, attempting to avoid an oncoming headache. "Of course, I'm on my way."

Hanging up my phone, I hear the clearing of a throat, and I glance at Lexi who's awkwardly sitting there. "Everything okay?"

I stand and grab my keys off my desk. "An urgent matter has come up."

"Oh, I hope it's not too serious." She sounds concerned as she stands, realizing this meeting has reached a close.

"Nothing but the usual. I need to get to my daughter's school. We'll have to finish this meeting tomorrow. Let's do the morning so you can get started. Stuart at the front desk will get you your room key, as I know you wanted to stay here for your creative flow."

Her hand flies up. "Don't worry. I'll figure it out. And tomorrow sounds like a plan. I'll meet you here when you figure out a time."

A near sinister sound escapes from my throat. "Not here. Meet me at my house. Early. Seven even."

"Your house?" she questions the unusual request.

I walk to the coat rack and grab my jacket. "Yeah, Stuart can give you my address."

"Your address?" she repeats, as if she's checking that she heard me right.

Throwing her one last grin, I kind of enjoy that I've thrown her off. "Don't worry, I don't bite… at least not at breakfast, anyway."

Her eyes blaze with slight fear. And that's fair enough, because a vision of bending her over my desk just flashed into my brain.

Tomorrow. I'll be on my best behavior. For sure, it's possible… I mean, impossible.

Shit, tomorrow.

2

LEXI

Please don't let Holden wear a tight button-down, and his eyes that probably pop with a forest-green shirt with jeans.

I stare up at the clouds in the sky at seven in the morning, as if someone is listening and can save me. *Please just do that*, I wish. Nor can he wear that cologne that is crisp to the nose. And as an extra hope, maybe he got rid of that wave of brown hair that I want to rake my hands through.

Anyone in the sky, please. I beg of you.

Holden must know that I'm here, as the security guard of the subdivision let me past the gate to a street with gorgeous lake houses. I raise my finger to press the doorbell, but before I can touch the button, the door soars open, catching me by surprise.

My eyes drop to a little boy that is the spitting image of Holden. His face is soft as he stares at me, then the corners of his mouth hitch up. He's a lot taller than I last saw him when he was maybe two or three.

"You're pretty." He smiles.

"Uh… thanks." I return his smile, as he is cute.

"Don't throw your charm at our guest." Holden arrives behind his son and sets his hands on Harry's shoulders, and oh no, it's a white t-shirt today, giving me a glimpse of the muscles on his arms. "Hey, Lexi, come on in."

I follow and take in my surroundings of a big modern house with an open staircase. It's all industrial feel and clean, with the floor-to-ceiling windows overlooking the lake. Holden continues to walk toward the kitchen, and I seem to follow in tow.

I'm always up for spontaneous adventures. It's why I've spent time traveling and going where life takes me. If there is something I like, then I make a point not to hide it. I'm not a shy person in the slightest, nor am I afraid of many things.

Walking into Holden's house after he got my pussy excited yesterday? This has me slightly nervous.

"Are you sure this a good time to talk about the Dizzy Duck?" I ask, skeptical, as Harry hops up onto the stool at the kitchen island.

Holden opens a cupboard to pull out a box of cereal. "I don't have many options today. I need to head down to Bluetop to sample new wines at the Blisswood winery for our new cellar at the Dizzy Duck," he explains as he hands Harry the box of chocolate cereal. "Besides, I lost a nanny last week, so I need to get the kids to school."

I blink a few times, attempting to absorb the situation happening around me.

"Lori, on the double," he calls upstairs.

"You'll have more luck calling her on her cell," Harry says with a full mouth.

Holden drags a hand through his hair. "Except, she lost phone privileges due to yesterday's little stunt." Holden looks in my direction, as if it's normal that I'm here. "Coffee?" He points to the machine.

I haven't even taken my coat off. "Uh, no, thanks. Again, are you sure about right now?"

His chuckle is low, humorous, and sexy as hell. "No choice, remember? Now tell me the game plan." He grabs a carton of juice. "Lori!"

I shake my head, accepting that this is how this is going to go.

"So, uhm, I need a room to keep samples to compare to the existing fabrics and colors. I'm thinking we need to minimalize the use of carpet and focus on area rugs and use bright wood for the walls."

Holden checks on his son who is chomping away. "Lori, seriously, we have twenty minutes!" His attention returns to me. "Timeline?"

I survey the scene of chaos then question the thought in my head about why Dad Holden makes my stomach tighten below my navel. "Right, timeline. We will start with the lobby, which could take a week if we have the right team of contractors. It's just that furniture orders can take a while."

"We'll pay for priority orders," he notes.

"The bedrooms will take the longest, as we will give the larger rooms more of a luxury suite feel. I think the rooms will need a month. We can work in a wave so you still have a few rooms available at all times."

"Great."

Is he even listening?

"Are you going to say yes to everything?" I wonder.

Holden's eyes slice straight to me as he pauses in preparing his kids for their school day. "Probably. I'll trust you with this, just tell me when the budget goes haywire." His gaze snaps to the clock on the oven just as a girl with braids set on the top of her head passes me and grazes my arm without concern.

"I'm here. Can I have my coffee now?" Lori slides up onto a stool next to her brother.

Holden smirks to himself. "No, because you're only twelve."

She scoffs. "So unfair. I'm no longer a kid."

He gives her a doubtful look. "Oh, I know. You've been trying to prove that for weeks. Hence, why we lost the nanny last week."

"Ugh, not my fault. She wouldn't let me have my space," Lori protests.

"She was nice," Harry voices his opinion.

"You both put her bras in the freezer," he deadpans, and my eyes bug out. Then Holden smiles tightly. "Well, we get nobody new since the wonderful antics of you two have gotten us banned from the agency list." I'm beginning to feel awkward standing here. Then Holden remembers I'm present and his demeanor returns to normal. "You have the budget, and the contractor will meet you later today to go over initial ideas."

"Great," I say flatly because I'm still trying to digest this show in front of me.

Lori glares at me. "Who is she?"

"The hotel's new interior designer. You don't remember her, but you've met her before when I played on the ice up in Michigan for the Golds. She's Coach Moore's daughter," he explains.

I give her a weak smile and a curt wave which causes her disdain to intensify.

"Fantastic. Another one to put you on a pedestal," she says sarcastically.

Holden brings his hand to the back of his neck and tries to de-stress with utter failure.

"I need my recorder for school. We have music class today," Harry reminds Holden.

Holden now rubs his hand over his face. "Maybe… in your room or the TV room? Check there."

Harry stands up, ready to search. "Don't forget my lunch." Harry runs off while Holden looks like he is about to melt in frustration.

"Fuck me, lunch making. What the hell goes into that? The nanny normally did it," Holden says to himself, and he massages his temples.

"Well, look at that. Someone curses and sets a perfect example for his kids," Lori berates him.

My eyes gawk because this girl has some attitude. Now I understand why Holden is about to lose his cool on a daily basis.

"Okay." He snaps his fingers. "Let me think. What does the nanny throw into a bag?"

Really? How does he not know? It's simple logic what a child eats for school lunch. Isn't it?

Ah damn, I shouldn't get involved, but I know Holden well

enough, and I'm bold in my life encounters, not always needing approval. Which is why I step forward and walk straight to him then search for the lunch bag and spot it near the fruit bowl. I'm going to assume Lori buys her lunch at school since there's only one bag.

He doesn't seem to notice what's happening, as he is in a daze. "So yeah, just do what you need for the Dizzy Duck. I want to have a reveal in a few months and invite a few photographers and writers for blogs and magazines."

I throw an apple into the bag then grab bread from the bread box. My eyes scan the kitchen for where a knife might be. Maybe I should be questioning what I'm doing more, but thinking can happen later. "In the moment" is my philosophy. But I should examine why I'm working in sync with the man in the room.

"We're still on the deadline that you indicated originally?" Now I'm the one caught in an odd moment of multi-tasking.

"Three months," he states while I pull out a peanut butter jar from a cabinet.

Spreading jam and peanut butter on bread, I continue our conversation. "Fine. We should have weekly meetings to check in, too."

"Sounds good."

Now I'm attempting to find some other snacks. I spot the pantry and head straight there. Opening the door and walking in, I examine the shelves then find a granola bar, water bottle, and small bag of crackers shaped as fish.

We say nothing as he watches me, unsure what is transpiring. After tossing everything in, I zip the bag then pass it to Holden by slamming it into his chest. "Here. How can you not know how to make a school lunch?" I'm brazen with my astonishment.

His eyes are saucers, unprepared by my tone of slight disapproval.

Harry walks to his father and takes his bag, oblivious to who worked their lunch-making magic and assuming his dad suddenly became a sandwich wizard. "Thanks. I'll meet you in the car."

Holden and I seem to be in a stare-off, ignoring his children as they slide backpacks off chairs and walk toward the hall where I think the garage is.

I cross my arms, not sure why I'm not afraid to level with Holden, even if he is my semi-boss.

"Wow. Someone isn't afraid to be bold." His eyes remain locked with mine.

"I'm not some shy girl, if that's what you remember of me. In fact, I've never been scared of everything I do in life," I defend, speaking my mind.

He scoffs before his tongue darts out to sweep across his bottom lip. "Everything?" The innuendo is there, I'm not reading it wrong.

Heat swims through me. I wasn't thinking about the broader spectrum of everything, including the X-rated kind, but it's also the truth. Standing taller, I will own this moment. "Yes, *everything.*"

Holden snickers. "Thanks for the insight, and just FYI, I know how to make a lunch. You've just caught me on a day when my mind is somewhere else, and last time I checked, we're all allowed to have one of those mornings. Come on, meeting done. You can leave via the garage." His tone is curt before he turns on his heel, and yet again, I trail along, not sure if I pissed him off.

But then halfway down the hall, he stops in his tracks, causing me to bump into his back and get a whiff of the cologne that I'm sure will soak into my coat fabric. His instant turn brings us close, with our bodies brushing as his eyes dip down, and I peer up.

"You owe me," he says, his tone serious.

I frown in surprise. "I owe you?"

"Yep." His P is sharp. "Remember, one of us has an IOU, and it isn't me." I'm confused, and he must see it. "I believe I was out with the team once, and I caught you at the bar when you were twenty and you were attempting to buy a drink with your friend. The bartender was about to card you, but I stepped in and told him that you were a friend of mine so he wouldn't ask."

I do remember now, but still my mouth opens at the ridiculousness of this. "And?"

"I joked that you owe me, and you agreed."

"That was said in jest," I rebuff.

His finger comes up to wave side to side as he shakes his head. "Nope. In your appreciative state, you asked the bartender for a pen then wrote on a napkin." He pretends to search his memory. "Oh yeah, 'I owe Holden West a favor one day, signed Lexi Moore.'"

Crap, it rings a bell and is something I totally would do. "What? Nobody would take that as fact. It was having fun in the moment," I justify.

Holden gives me a satisfied smirk. "Putting it in writing kind of cements it. *So,* Lexi, I'm calling in that favor now."

My entire face squinches from adjusting to the feeling that he isn't joking one single bit, but still I play along. "What might that be?"

"I don't think staying at the hotel for so long is ideal, especially with the room next to yours getting a leak fixed. It could get loud. Treat the hotel more like an office."

"And? Where do you suggest I stay?"

The lines of his mouth stretch so far that his wide smirk nearly makes me want to swipe it off his face by any means possible because it's infuriatingly annoying, cocky, and a little too sexy for seven in the morning.

"My guesthouse."

My entire body must show that nothing about that sentence feels normal. Especially as his tone is so simple.

"Why would I do that?" Because seeing him a bit more than I should feels kind of dangerous.

"That favor you owe is the reason. You can pick up Lori and Harry at school for me once in a while, maybe even do a few drop-offs. I need to find more permanent help, but I have to find a new agency that doesn't know the history of the employment turnover in my house."

I'm nearly dizzy from shaking my head. "No." I continue to shake. "I'm not a nanny, and that's more than one favor."

"You owe me, and we'll count this as the IOU," he repeats.

Returning to a normal stance, I hold my hand out low. "Here's you helping me buy alcohol when I would have charmed my way with the bartender anyways." Then I bring my hand up high. "And here's you asking me to drive your kids around. Not exactly even on the favor front."

Holden tsks. "Lexi, if you could have charmed the bartender, then why didn't you?"

"Because it wouldn't have been as enjoyable. It is by far better to say a 27-year-old pro-hockey player bailed me out. My sorority sisters had a thing for you." I'm maybe too honest around him.

"Well, you did rely on me, so a favor owed is where we are. Plus, with all the redecorating happening, then I could use all the extra rooms I can get for guests, and not to mention that your dear old dad mentioned you were once an au pair in England. See? You love kids. There are many reasons why this isn't a big deal. I might even throw extra budget your way for redecorating and give you a reference for an upcoming hotel deal that I might have."

My eyes widen, and my hip tips out with my arms crossing over my chest. "Bribing me now?"

"Call it extra incentives for following through with your favor. So, what will it be, Lexi?"

Hearing my name on his tongue seems to swirl desire, and everything about him in this moment is a turn-on. I don't need that. My brain even bypasses his mention of extra budget and references, which is an added bonus for my dream job. I desperately need a clear mind to get out of this situation.

But that's not in my cards today. Instant clicks with people are a weakness to me and always sink me into full commitment mode.

Because I blurt out, "Fine."

What the hell? I'm free-spirited, but this? I clearly don't have the backbone to use a one-syllable word that begins with N.

My finger comes up to point to him, as I feel the need to justify my impulsive decision. "I'm doing this because I'm a good Samaritan to civilization and a caring, thoughtful person. Not to mention I hate being bored, and I doubt that happens here."

He claps his hands together with an overdone smile. "Wonderful.

You just dropped into my life when a hotel refresh is essential and I still need to balance my little heathens, aren't they cute?"

My fingers come up to rub my temples. "This is…" I have no words.

That exhilaration inside of me bubbles again, especially when Holden steps once forward and it closes our space. "Totally not a good idea, but I'm kind of out of other options right now." He's straightforward, at least.

"Wonderful. Bad ideas," I deadpan.

His grin is full of accomplishment and trouble. "I love how you are very agreeable."

"Well, I aim to please." I'm being sarcastic, but it's too late. I close my eyes at my choice of words. This is, oh no. I blow out a breath and open my eyes to find Holden eyeing me up and down, which isn't helping me keep my body from crossing all the wires.

"Duly noted." He tilts his head before he turns and heads straight to the garage, and I trench behind.

Duly noted. Yeah, let me just add a warning in my head and between my legs to that list.

3

LEXI

"*Poof*." I gesture with my hands. "All normal human logic just vanished in a few seconds."

As I explain my situation, Summer smiles weakly at me. We're sitting in Jolly Joe's, the local hotspot that fills our needs, from coffee to burgers to ice cream. A throwback to a soda shop, complete with a jukebox in the corner. And Summer? We've been friends for years, and whenever I visit Lake Spark, I head straight to her.

"Remember when you were in Austria and you met those two backpackers, then later that day you ended up paragliding? You've always been spontaneous and impulsive," she reminds me.

I sigh as I stare at the menu to keep myself occupied. "I know, it's just… This is on a different level. Damn, I haven't seen Holden in a couple of years, and suddenly in the span of 24 hours, I've nearly drooled at his hot dad look and complied with his ridiculous demand."

She snorts a laugh. "Well, if it's any consolation, I've heard every single mom in a ten-mile radius is trying to discover his favorite food so they can casually stop by and offer him a store-bought cookie that they pose as their own baking. So, the sexy look doesn't seem to be in your imagination."

Licking my lips, I tip my head slightly to the side. "I hope it's my brain going on a break, because the vibe between us just seems… I can't pinpoint it."

Summer smiles softly before glancing out the window onto Main Street. "That's a good thing to have. I can't wait to watch this all unfold."

"Nothing. It's nothing. Besides, Holden has a chaotic life. His kids? Holy crap, wild."

"Well, it makes staying on his property all the more entertaining. You're still the woman who has no desire to settle down, so maybe that can be your strength to stay in line."

"Hopefully. Besides I'm not sure what I'll be doing once this project finishes. My lease for my place in the city was up long ago, and I've just been housesitting various places while I traveled. I'd love to be near you more and have a change of scene, I'm just not sure there are many opportunities for me here."

She clucks the inside of her mouth. "Ah yes, Lexi is still a wandering soul. Still, I'm excited for the unfolding of your predicament." Summer has a cheeky smile.

I scoff at that encouragement. Then it dawns on me that my ludicrous change of events in my life are minor compared to her life. After a pause for a few seconds, I lean across the table to place my hand gently on top of hers.

"Uh, how has it been?"

Her eyes slide to me as her lips quirk out. "You mean, with a husband?" Summer eloped with her best friend, Zac, for reasons even I don't quite understand. It was recent and sudden, and all I can do is give her an ear. Coincidently, her now in-laws used to own the Dizzy Duck.

I shrug. "Yeah, I guess."

A wry smile emerges. "I'm not exactly sure what I dragged myself into, but for some reason, it feels right."

Squeezing her hand one last time, I then let go. "I don't know what to say. One day you're going to have to explain."

"When it's clear to me, I will let you know." She sounds at peace with whatever is happening.

I don't press her further, especially when Summer's gaze seems to tip up and over my shoulder, with the corners of her smile lengthening. "Someone just arrived, and this might be my entertainment of the day."

I turn my head to catch a glimpse of what she's looking at. Or rather who she's looking at.

An opportunity to pull in some clarity to my brain just vanished as Holden slowly strides to our table with a sly grin. "Grabbing a coffee to gather strength before you pick up your suitcase to move on in?"

Summer snorts a laugh as she watches this scene progress.

"Why, of course, dear master."

Both Summer's and Holden's eyes grow wide at my sarcasm. Because, of course, when it's me, then everyone takes my words out of context.

Holden now keeps his smirk fixed then tips his head behind his shoulder. "The usual," he tells someone behind the counter.

My face puzzles. "You get coffee here?"

He looks at me as though I'm crazy… and maybe I am. Holden even shares a look with Summer who seems to agree.

"It's the best damn coffee around, and I need one for the road before I head down to Bluetop," he explains.

"But you own the Dizzy Duck, shouldn't that be the best coffee around? You're a traitor to your own hotel?" I'm bewildered.

Holden chuckles as he crosses his arms. "Nah, ours *will* be the best. Just ordered new machines, and I'm waiting on the import of beans from Colombia. They need to have a soft taste for cappuccinos but a sharper hit to your tongue if it's an expresso."

I nod in agreement. "That's fair enough. I guess you must need to consume a lot of coffee after what I saw this morning."

Noticing the way his tongue darts out to sweep to the corner of his mouth, it draws my eyes to his lips, and it causes a simmering warm wave to travel through me. "Well, problem soon solved by your presence," he reminds me.

"Not a nanny," I firmly inform him yet again.

"Of course, you're not. You will just be living on my property—"

My palm flies up. "*Guest* on your property."

"Sure. A guest who might casually notice morning routine gone to hell and say, 'Hey, Holden, anything I can do to help before I head to the Dizzy Duck?'"

"Absolutely, because compliancy was on my resume when you hired me to *interior design* your inn, *not* nanny."

Holden grabs the to-go coffee that one of the staff hands him, except Holden doesn't give the woman even a drop of attention because his eyes are fixed on me, or rather, glued in a gaze with mine because I can't tear away from the view either.

Then he leans down, every inch closer causing my nipples to peak even tighter. "But I believe your words were… I always aim to please." His voice is nearly husky with his breath even breezing into my space.

As much as I should be scared because it feels like a caution, I only smile. The kind that informs him I'm having fun, although my words are difficult to muster in this moment.

Holden stands and switches his attention from me to Summer. "Good to see you."

"Surprised you noticed I was here." She chortles a laugh.

Holden finds that amusing as he takes a sip of his coffee. "Any chance your brother-in-law has broken his radio silence and might actually return to Lake Spark to take interest in his 10% that your in-laws were so intent were mandatory for the hotel sale?"

Summer's face hardens a tad, her smile strained. "I'm the last person to ask about Nash," she grits out. "And you probably know just as much as I do."

Mentioning Nash's name around Summer always seems to cause her to tense. Nobody knows why, and that unfortunately includes me, too.

Holden doesn't pause for a tick because maybe he too noticed Summer's demeanor change, but then he brushes past the subject anyhow. "By the way, we have a job opening coming up. I need someone to handle the staff and the bookings. It's part-time, but the last manager is moving to California due to her husband's work. When your father-in-law dropped by recently, he mentioned that it might be your forte."

Her lips quirk out. "Huh. Maybe. I kind of like working for the city council, though."

Holden shrugs. "Well, if you change your mind."

"First I need to see how you treat your interior designer, since you are her current *boss*." Summer flashes her eyes at him.

Holden's jaw tenses, and he smiles awkwardly. "I like to think of Lexi and me as equals in a partnership… to improve the Dizzy Duck."

I want to hold onto the table for stability because I think my mind just tricked me into hearing allusions of underlying meanings. My eyes sideline to Summer, and her look informs me that it is not in my mind.

"Well then, good luck with that, or rather her." She indicates me with her head.

Holden's sexy smirk is back. "I think that I can keep her in line. See you around, ladies." He walks toward the door. "You even sooner, Lexi," he calls back.

When the bell dings to inform us that he's left, I notice Summer's mouth has gaped open. "Uh-oh, someone is in for a wild ride. Wow, you guys have chemistry."

I roll my eyes. "Yeah, I know. His sweltering gaze needs to be locked in a box."

Summer brings her cup of coffee to her lips. "I'm sure you will find a box for that… probably in his bedroom."

I huff a breath. "Well, now you know my predicament."

"This is going to be fun. I get to be the bystander that watches from the offside." Now she has a bright smile that's good to see.

Sliding out of my seat, I say, "Happy to provide entertainment.

Now, if you will excuse me, I need to get to the inn to talk with the contractor."

"Keep me updated."

I wave her off.

———

AFTER INFORMING the contractor how I want to redo the fireplace mantel in the lobby, yet preserve the stones and also keep the original wood where we can in the inn but paint over or polish, I feel good about where I can take this immense project. I have so many ideas, but my vision is clear for what will make the best statement when someone walks through the door.

But now I find myself closing the door to Holden's guesthouse behind me. Stuart at reception gave me a key. To be fair, this little place, although missing a kitchen, is a great location behind the house, getting an even better view of the lake. The interior is simple but with a few added colored pillows so the white is taken down a notch.

Again, my mind is spinning with how fast the last day has transpired, but Summer was right when she reminded me that I am a spur-of-the-moment kind of person. I'll just go with the flow and follow the direction of where this rollercoaster takes me.

Opening my suitcase, I search for clothes. It's getting late for dinner, but I'll just order something in, although I'm positive when Holden is back from his meeting he will welcome me to his property like the gentleman I'm sure he isn't. My instinct tells me that he won't let me go to sleep without a reminder of his smug assurance that he has me wrapped around his finger, or at least in his head.

Walking to the window, my eyes wander to explore my surroundings. There is the lake with a dock for a boat, and there's a hot tub near the house. Then there is a tire swing on a big tree and a basketball hoop near the back of the garage. When I admire the stone patio, my eyes draw a line up and I land on a window upstairs. A big window with the curtains open.

The same window where I can see Holden walk into the room. He must have just gotten back, and he quickly yanks up his t-shirt. Oh no, my entire body energizes in a way that seems to be on repeat lately. My eyes refuse to take my sight and mind back to my own room, and instead, my feet stay planted as I study his shirtless chest. The man keeps himself in shape, that's clear.

I hear my soft gasp that I get to see this, but then I deeply question if I owe him privacy when he unbuckles his jeans. Fuck that, I deserve a prize for doing this favor for him. His black boxer briefs appear when he slides down his jeans, and I see his thick and toned thighs.

Am I drooling yet? Nah, that's not me. I'm a confident woman who has no problem allowing herself a peek. He isn't a stranger to me. Although it's been a while, I've known him for years, I guess. Back then, of course, I thought he was hot with a lot of swagger. It didn't matter that he was a dad by twenty-five, he still went out when he could just like any other guy in their twenties. Now? He's aged well, and he still has an aura that pulls you in.

I should question this appraisal more, especially when he turns around and the boxers disappear too, which means I have a clear view of his ass. My brows rise, as I'm not at all complaining about his body. My fingertips glide down my neck, unsure if I should touch myself or hide further behind the curtain. Holden grabs a white towel, and the pool forming between my legs is my sign that I too should hit the shower.

Desperately, I now need relief, but I'm scared that I'll imagine him in the shower with me. His lips cascading down until he's on his knees, his tongue eager. I wouldn't last long because I'd want to be on my knees before him too.

Shaking my head, I walk to the bathroom and whip off my shirt and notice the stack of folded towels next to the sink. I reach out to twist the knob in the shower.

Nothing comes out.

I twist the other direction.

Nothing comes out.

Strange. I turn and do the same thing with the sink knob.

Nothing.

Grumbling, I'm not happy about this. More because I have no clue where a switch or something might be to turn the water supply on. He must have turned it off to ensure water doesn't freeze the pipes in the winter if nobody uses this place.

Okay, I'm not going to be able to fix this by myself. Throwing my yoga pants back on and a fleece sweater, I head to the house. I hug myself because it's nippy out as I cross the patio.

Opening the sliding door, I hear pop music is getting overshadowed by a squeaky recorder that might hurt my ears, even though the kids seem to be upstairs. Man, does Holden have to listen to this every day? Another point of sympathy goes onto the scoreboard.

Remembering that Holden was in the shower, I walk to the kitchen to wait. I might as well steal a cookie; I notice the chocolate chip ones from the Dizzy Duck. The ones they leave on guests' pillows at night or offer as a welcome. It's a great touch to the inn, and the cookies are damn delicious and soft, too.

It's a few minutes later when I hear someone come down the stairs as I sit at the island. I know it's Holden because the steps are heavier than what a child's might be.

Strolling into the kitchen, he greets me with a smile, but my eyes only dip down with dread because he's in a fresh pair of jeans and a white fitted t-shirt. "What brings you in? Everything okay?"

I snicker but give him a smirk because I do love our interaction. "Actually, the water doesn't seem to be on in the guesthouse, or at least no water is coming out. I'm not sure where the pipe nozzle is outside."

He licks his lips, and his grin is tight. "This isn't good."

"Why?"

Holden walks to the fridge and pulls out a bottle of beer then pulls out wine to offer to me. Waving my hand no, he places it back in the fridge. Opening his beer, the cap snap fills the silence between us as I patiently wait for his answer.

He takes a long sip as the line on my lips stays permanent with entertaining fear that his response won't be easy.

"I thought for sure that had been fixed," he begins. "I guess not. The plumber did mention if the water doesn't come out, then it's blocked somewhere, and the water can't get through."

My head falls into my hand because this kind of feels like bullshit, but I'll play along. "Is that so?" I cast doubt.

He shrugs his shoulders. "Plumbers don't lie."

I stand up and begin to walk toward him as he leans casually against the counter near the fridge. "Hmm. So, what is the solution to this issue? May I please go back to the Dizzy Duck?"

One step closer and he doesn't flinch; instead, he casually takes another sip. "Nope. I have alternative sleeping arrangements."

My journey lands me close to him, desperate to reach out and touch his chest. I loll my head to the side, ready to soak in this tension between us, except it isn't tension… it's a game where we're on par in our equal level of flirtation.

"Where might that be?" My voice is a soft husk.

He leans down because I'm shorter. "Congratulations, Lexi. The guest room near the laundry room is calling your name," he whispers.

I feared something like this was coming. "Lucky for us we have your kids as the perfect middle line to keep us on good behavior."

A sound escapes his throat. "Is that a 'yes, Holden. What a great idea. Please can you get my suitcase?'"

My mouth seems to dance around his but not enough to graze. "It's a 'yes, Holden. Get me…'" I pull back, and my voice grits out, "A hell of a lot of wine."

We both create space, and his hand combs through his hair, and I notice that he frowns. "There wasn't a please," he teases.

I laugh to myself. "Just move me in because logic doesn't exist around me anymore, unless it's related to paint colors and shellac walls."

He reaches for his cell phone on the counter. "Good that you stay focused on the Dizzy Duck. Now, do you take extra cheese on your pizza?" Now he is ordering pizza for everyone as if the last five minutes didn't happen.

Throwing up my hands, I figure I might as well eat. "Get me whatever. I have a feeling your kids won't be happy about this."

Holden's demeanor completely changes to a sort of fondness, but it isn't for me, it's for his children. "They'll be okay. You're not actually a nanny, so that's a positive step in their book. Lori will be feisty, but that's with everyone. Harry is actually quite innocent. Having you around will be better than me running around like a headless chicken anyhow. Don't get me wrong. I've got my shit together, but *lately*..." He winces. "I could just use even the smallest of favors to relieve some pressure."

His jaw slants to the side and holds as he registers what I'm completely interpreting his sentence to mean.

"Relieve pressure... huh." My nails tap against my hips.

He returns his focus to the screen of his phone. "I can be tame if I choose to be. It might be good for me to have a breath of fresh air in the house that doesn't involve a disgruntled nanny."

"I'm not a breath of fresh air," I point out. He looks up at me. "I'm a hurricane that's about to turn your life upside down."

He laughs. "I can handle you. After all, in the span of 48 hours, you've called me Master and Sir."

"Wine, Holden. Get me that wine faster," I answer dryly.

"Say please and I will."

I shake my head ruefully.

Most fires only start if you light it.

I should probably hide the matches.

HOLDEN

My daughter flops her piece of pizza onto her plate, her frown never fading. "So, she's just going to stay here?"

I set another piece of pizza onto Harry's plate while Lexi observes everyone, not saying much. Fair enough, I've dragged us down a hole.

Something snapped when she showed up yesterday at my office. An immediate inkling to push her limits, and there is nothing to rein me in. I didn't lie, I'm desperate for a little help when it comes to Lori and Harry. Losing another nanny created a total shuffle of my schedule, and I'm struggling to figure out the little things, such as what the hell goes into a lunchbox, because that was a lie when I told Lexi that of course I know how to. But, truthfully, lunch-making is my nemesis, and it's such a simple task too.

"Lexi will stay here for a little bit. She has to work on the Dizzy Duck, but we're short on rooms there, and now the water in the guesthouse is off. We're lucky enough she can give us a hand or two, and she isn't a stranger to us."

"But I'm not a nanny," Lexi chirps, then sinks into her seat in case she's out of line.

Lori and Harry shoot her a stare as if they forgot she was here even though we've been talking about her.

"It's cool. She seems nice." Harry isn't fazed as he enjoys his pizza. My son has a kind heart, and even if he pulls a prank, it's because he wants to make someone laugh and not out of vengeance… but if it pushes a nanny away, then he doesn't mind that either. He has a softer personality than I ever had. Sports don't really seem to be his thing, and sometimes I'm not entirely sure if I'm getting it right in trying to relate to one another.

He continues to speak with a full mouth. "It'll drive my teacher crazy when a not-ugly nanny shows up to pick me up." God, his single teacher who lays it on thick at parent-teacher meetings.

"Not a nanny," Lexi reminds us all again, her tone now exhausted from her repeated memo to the table.

Lori shakes her head and grabs her cell phone that somehow made it out of my discipline attempt. I said it was only for communication to text *one* friend for the night before taking it back. But that plan went to hell when every kid her age uses their phones for everything, and it's my lifeline to connecting with her. Lori is perhaps my biggest challenge as of late, but she's also not, because her stubbornness and independence are good attributes as she grows older. It's just… can't she give me one clue that we're alright? At least before boys enter the picture? Give me an opportunity to save up a little energy before we have to deal with the teenage chapter?

Lori doesn't even part from her screen. "As fun as this little conversation is, I'm sure our *guest* is aware that my room is off-limits."

Lexi quickly answers, "Of course. Besides, I have no plans to be here every second of the day, so do your thing. I'm only sitting here right now because pizza seemed like a way to refill my strength and hopefully bring back reason."

I'm on board with Lexi's humor, it means not a dull moment that isn't exhausting. My hand slides across my face, not allowing myself to think any more about Lexi as I deal with my daughter. "No, Lori? Can't even be polite for maybe three minutes?"

She studies Lexi up and down, then she grumbles before sliding off her chair. "I'm going upstairs. My nail polish color doesn't match my outfit for tomorrow." Off she goes with her signature hair flip as a statement. I hate it, as much as I try to suppress a smile that wants to form. My daughter has a backbone.

"Great conversation," I call out and unenthusiastically give myself a little fist pump. Glancing to Lexi, she offers me a pained sympathetic look.

"Will you make me a peanut butter sandwich for school lunch tomorrow but use cashew butter?" Harry plays with the cheese on his pizza.

"Why cashew butter?" I'm confused, he loves peanut butter.

"Because Mrs. Crawl said it's a new school rule in the email you should have read that we need to use cashew or almond butter because of allergies."

I snicker as I see Lexi contemplate that logic. "Sure, let me dig it out of the pantry."

"What a bummer. They're ruining a classic American sandwich," he groans.

I reach over to nudge his arm with my fist. "How about we make peanut butter and jelly cheesecake soon?"

His face instantly lights up. "Really?"

"Yeah, it's the only thing I know how to make, and lucky for me, it happens to be my son's favorite." I smile because it does the trick every time. It's a pain to bake because it takes hours, but I always knock it out of the park. Not even sure how I found the recipe in the first place, but it's my golden ticket. "Anything else?"

He shakes his head, still smiling. "No, I'm going to go read my book now."

"Sure, kiddo." I'm both relieved and sad that we're past the whole storybook and tuck-in phase. It was a time drain, but now I'm wishing I could turn the clock back. Those were guaranteed moments of bonding. I watch Harry leave as I recall it all.

It's only when I hear a stifled laugh that I turn to see Lexi desperately trying to suppress a laugh.

"Yes?" I wonder what the hell could be so amusing.

"No offense, but your kids are hysterical and are totally giving you a hard time because they can. I even have a feeling that one of them will add something awful to my morning coffee, and still, it's kind of funny."

"Are you serious?" Lexi nods up and down in response as she stands to collect plates. "You don't need to do that."

"Oh yeah? You know where the dishwasher is?" Her joke causes me to break out in a smile. "By the way, what is this sorcery of peanut butter and jelly cheesecake of which you speak?"

I follow her in clearing the table and head straight to the sink with pride on my face. "It's my gateway to happiness for children and adults. If you haven't had it yet, then your life isn't complete."

"It sounds delicious and the last thing that would have been on my radar of what to expect from you. But peanut butter squishes all doubts."

"As it should. You know, I… have no clue why I'm dragging you into this."

Maybe it's a game? Everything in my life might feel like a mess, but this is a fun escape I still deserve. Except I'm not sure where our blue line is. Flirtation is okay, but crossing the lines, probably not.

Lexi clears her throat, breaking me away from my thought. "Can I ask, Holden?" She seems to hesitate, and I think I know where this is going. "I know that you were married and the divorce was kind of ugly, but…"

Grabbing a kitchen towel, I turn to lean against the sink. "It was more than ugly. Michelle was, well… a bitch, to put it bluntly, and I don't use that word lightly."

Her lips roll in then her boldness returns. "Was it always that way between you two?"

I scoff a sound and stare ahead of me at the wall. "It was. Lori was an accident, and I will always be grateful it happened. But marrying because of an unexpected pregnancy isn't always the right move. I learned that the hard way," I reflect.

"But you stayed together long enough to bring another child into the world."

"Damn, Lexi. You're not afraid to be forward. But to answer your question. We always lived separate lives in our marriage, as in even separated. Michelle didn't have much interest in being a mom, but I still wanted it to work for Lori's sake. Still, it got to the point when divorce was the only way, but one night I had a thought of pure desperation that we could try one more time to make it work for Lori, and then Harry entered the picture. And I'm 100% sure that Michelle planned it that way to string me along. After Harry was born though, I still asked for a divorce, especially when she…"

She gently touches my elbow. "You don't have to say. You've already shared a lot."

Why am I? I don't really talk about this. Especially with a woman who dropped into my life. Still, intuition has me knocking down a block. My eyes whip to hers. "You're easy to talk to."

"It seems so."

"Michelle didn't want to be a mom. Simply said, she got pregnant with the hope that it would bring her the life of luxury she wanted. When motherhood hit, then reality came crashing down. How someone can walk away like that, I don't know. But I had hoped co-parenting could still happen. So, yeah… that divorce was fun." My head drops, and I bite my bottom lip from the recall of events. "Funny how people are. She has no interest in being a mom, yet she wanted a hefty settlement in order for me to have full legal custody of the kids. I thought that would at least keep one door open if she asked or made an effort to be involved."

Lexi winces at my story, and her hand slides up my arm to land on my shoulder to give a few squeezes to show comfort. "That never happened," I state somberly.

But even though I'm talking about the misery of divorce, a weightlessness comes over me, and I think it's because of her touch. I can't help but follow the path of where her palm traveled.

"I'm sorry that happened. Lori and Harry?"

A long exhale escapes me. "Harry was too young to remember,

and Lori was almost four. Maybe it's why she's a little extra… difficult."

Lexi smiles gently. "Oh, I assure you that it's pre-teen angst too. You're not the only parent to be going through this. I was rebellious and utter hell when I was her age… well, until now too, but you know what I mean."

I chuckle and enjoy that her hand hasn't left my arm, even if it's platonic. "I'm sure your dad loves that."

Now she lets go, and her gaze circles to the floor. "I think we can all agree that hockey is number one for him, and I'm a distant second. My dad, I mean sure, he loves me and is protective, but his time is consumed by hockey."

"Protectiveness, for sure. The first pep talk of the season was always for everyone on the team to stay away from you. It's supposed to be a lifetime oath." A small grin forms on my lips.

Her mouth slants halfway up as our moment holds from my words. "Well then, oaths are not meant to be broken." It feels like she is testing me.

I'm not sure what to say except, "Want more wine?"

Lexi softly shakes her head. "Nah, it's okay. I'm going to go use a shower that actually works and get some shuteye. The carpet guy is meeting me at nine tomorrow."

If my kids weren't here, then I would storm right after her to help her undress and join her in the shower so I can get a little relief. I'm not immune to having someone on call for physical gratification, but it's been a solid few months since I got laid.

Attempting to gather some composure, I decide to be the exemplary older one. "Of course, and thanks."

"Anytime. Communication isn't breaking an oath… even if it's dirty. Night-night." She wiggles her fingers at me, pleased with her closing sentence.

The moment she's gone, my upper body collapses over the counter, desperate to do everything to her that's in my mind right now.

———

WALKING into the Dizzy Duck after school drop-off, I debate if it's good for morale for my staff to see me carrying coffee from another establishment, but I think they understand the need for real caffeine.

I glance at Stuart behind the reception desk as he's typing away on the laptop. "We're going to switch to tablets soon to give this place a sleeker feel."

Stuart looks up. "I know, but some things only really work on laptops."

"Solid point." I have to agree. "I'll be in my office," I say.

Starting my walk, I only manage to get a few steps before I backtrack to look at the empty spot on the wall. "What happened to the moose?"

"Lexi had it taken down. You know, she really has great ideas. She should have her own television show. She's hot enough for—" I shoot him a sharp glare, and he must get the sentiment of my scowl. "Or not." He swallows.

Pursing my lips, I decide to find the woman of the hour. It doesn't take long, as she's in the hall that leads to the private reception room. I missed the detail that she's in skinny jeans and heels, since she left before I made it downstairs this morning. The carpet guy is getting a gift to his eyes since Lexi's ass is in the air as she leans over to check two swatches against the wood.

She's completely unaware. "No, let's still do wood. The carpet doesn't work."

For some reason, a wave of protectiveness hits me. Partly because I am a territorial motherfucker when it comes to a woman that I shouldn't pursue but probably will anyhow.

Clearing my throat, carpet guy looks at me and meets my warning glare. He adjusts his posture and slides his eyes away from Lexi.

"Lexi." Saying her name seems to surprise her, and she looks over her shoulder from the samples that the man way below her league is observing.

"Oh, hey." She stands up to greet me with a smile.

I crook my finger to gesture her over. "A word."

Lines form on her forehead. "Excuse me for a second," she tells the guy. Her saunter to me is nearly in slow motion. "Yes…" she leans in quickly, "Master," she whispers her taunt.

My face remains stoic, trying not to let her have the upper hand. "The moose is gone."

"Yeah, because you said it could go."

"Where is it?"

"A closet, why? Does it deserve a ceremonial funeral or something?"

I'm being absolutely ridiculous. "No…" *I just need a reason to bother you.* "Let's just save it for sinking it to the bottom of the lake or something when the Dizzy Duck is all remodeled."

She nods. "A good idea. We could even get a special buoy to mark his resting place." Is she teasing or is she serious? I can't tell.

"The room warm enough for you? Enough bounce to the mattress for your special time? The drawer the right size for your supplies to get you through the moments when you have some frustration to work out?"

Lexi's face flushes red, with her eyes blazing as I stand in front of her casually drinking my coffee.

"Uh…"

"The old first-floor guest room of the inn for your designing stuff, of course." Absolutely not. "You wanted to keep your supplies and samples there. I can imagine you just use the bed as a shelf and probably tuck some scissors and tape measures in the drawer. Naturally, being a good boss, I wouldn't want you to freeze in there. Why? What did you think I mean?"

She attempts to avoid my gaze, but I only step closer. "Do I make you nervous, Lexi?" I speak so only she can hear. The tension between us causes a shiver for us both, but we try to keep our bodies in check.

Lexi partly opens her mouth but only a croak escapes, then she gathers her thoughts. "No."

My voice turns rather chipper. "Thought so, considering you were spying on me yesterday when I went to take a shower." I get to enjoy a second of her jaw dropping before I turn to leave on that note.

Because yeah, I've been holding onto that fact.

My phone dings with a reminder, and I swipe my screen while juggling my coffee. Lucky me, each of my kids are at a sleepover with friends tomorrow.

Oh, look at that. Seems to mean I'll be alone with my house guest.

(5)

LEXI

My nails thrum against the desk in the large bedroom at the Dizzy Duck. Most definitely, I'm going to refurbish this. I've surveyed the inn to see what pieces of furniture we could keep and revamp with a new look. I'm really going to bring in the elements of history from around Lake Spark and tie it into a mix of farmhouse and cabin feel, using whites and painted wood to keep it bright. There is a park nearby, literally called Pioneer Park.

But my fingers change their beat because of a lightbulb moment of finalizing my plan forward. Instead of celebrating, I have irritation. With certainty, Holden is now adding me to his flavor-of-the-month list, or at least, that's what it feels like. Every word that slides off his tongue is a torturous taunt where it feels as though he has the upper hand.

It's fun, sure. Doesn't mean I want to give him a piece of my mind any less.

I breathe to myself, trying to inhale a relaxing breath as I straighten my shoulders, before I glance at my phone lying on the desk to see the time. It's nearly two, which means it's time for a break.

Leaving the room, I walk down the hall then the stairs to find myself in the lobby, but instead of heading to the table that offers refreshments for guests at all times, my feet plant down, unable to move. I tip my head back to get a glance of the office near the hall and the private party room, I guess because I'm subconsciously thinking of what to do with the fact that the door is ajar, and it's Holden's office.

Oh, fuck it.

I charge in his direction with my heels clicking against the wood. Storming into his office, I close the door behind me without a thought. My abrupt entrance catches him off guard as he glances up from his laptop, with lines creased on his forehead.

Pointing my finger at him, I stop due to the desk being a barrier. "So what? I watched you undress and head to the shower. I am sure it would happen if you used the sauna in the spa here too. No big deal."

Amusement gleams on his face, a fine line stretching on his lips. Ugh, why must he have a little rough stubble today?

No, Lexi, I will not be distracted. I'm confident.

He holds a finger up as he leans back in his chair, relaxed as can be. "One, Lexi, a towel is a necessity in the sauna here at our spa, it's optional if you use it to cover yourself or sit on. And two, you know it's not exactly *not* a big deal. You've seen the goods, and it's quite the opposite, it's a large deal."

My lips part open, entertained by the repartee being tossed around between us. "Holden, I only saw your immaculate ass, so the size of your dick is still a guess."

Holden licks his lips as he chortles. "Are we really going to go back and forth about this?"

I bring my hand to my hip. "No. I just find it interesting that you didn't tell me yesterday that you knew I saw you."

His hands come behind his head and his chest stretches, which has an added benefit since his button-down is fitted, so I see a few outlines of his muscles. "It's more fun to catch you off balance."

"I'm sure. Let's just keep everything aboveboard, shall we? I have your hotel to decorate."

Holden stands, completely unfazed by my request, as he bypasses me and heads straight to his coat rack, and my eyes follow him. I'm intrigued by what he's up to now.

He swings his coat off the hook then slips it on. "Sure. Anyhow, I need your help if you don't mind. I need to take Harry to get his supplies for his science project, and Lori needs to get to the ice rink for her figure skating lesson. Would you be a doll and help me?"

"I'm not a child carer," I reiterate for the thousandth time, my tone flat.

Holden has a droll smile. "So you've said. But please, can you help get Lori to her lesson?"

I blink a few times. "What does this entail?"

"Pick her up from school, listen to pre-teen angst for ten minutes, then drop her off at the ice rink. I'll pick her up later," Holden explains as he steps slowly in my direction.

I have a weakness for helping people in a crisis, and in a flash, I remember the disaster of his morning routine with his kids. Maybe it's pity. "Fine." I don't sound enthused, but I am agreeable.

Holden reaches with his fingers to touch my arms, sending a buzz throughout my insides, especially when I notice his eyes dip low to my body then jump right back up. "Thank you."

I roll my eyes but then nearly laugh to myself that he keeps wrapping me around his finger. But this time, it's me invading his space, reaching out to his open coat. I pull on the fabric to catch the start of the zipper. His eyes become glued to my fingers that are maneuvering his zipper. Slowly, tooth by tooth, I drag the zipper up as our eyes meet. I do my best to give him a sultry look because I know it drives him crazy.

The sound of the zip stops when I reach the end of the line, and I bring my palms to his chest. I smooth out the fabric, pretending I'm sweeping off some lint, then pat near his shoulders. "I would hate for you to get cold." I pretend to pout with concern.

Holden purses out a breath, fully invested in our tit-for-tat. He caught me off guard with his knowledge of what I saw, and now I'm causing his pulse to pick up a beat because I have the power to weaken him purely by a tantalizing touch.

He clears his throat, but his straight-lined lips that have a hint of entertainment returns. "You're so considerate," he comments dryly.

"I know, and that's just me being a completely normal person." A breathy husk comes out of me. "I'm a giver, what can I say?"

Holden clasps the tip of my hair resting on my collarbone, and he rubs the strands between the pads of his fingers. "I'm a taker, so it seems we have a match."

After a brief pause, we both lock our eyes with soft smiles appearing.

Breathe, I remind myself. Everything inside me wants to be touched, and I'm desperate to pull him close to relieve me.

"Thanks again for helping with Lori."

"Sure."

It feels as though neither one of us wants to leave, but the clock keeps going even if you want it to stop.

———

LORI SLIDES onto the front seat of my car, closing the door a little harder than I would prefer. Even though Holden texted her about my limo service, she still looks none too pleased.

"Hey there." I do my best to attempt to start out with a hopefully pleasant conversation, even offer a smile.

Her eyes roll to me as she snaps her seatbelt in with aggression. "He roped you into carpool duty now?"

"No," I answer, as though her question couldn't be further from the truth, even if she's right. "I'm happy to help, and your brother has a science project."

"Because he's a nerd like that. Bet my dad wishes Harry would play hockey."

I turn the engine on, and we get on our way. "But figure skating is pretty cool. I did it myself when I was younger."

"Really?" There almost seems to be a faint sound of interest, but I can't tell.

"Yeah, did it for seven years actually. But I didn't like competitions and somehow lost my interest in skating." I focus on the road.

"So, you're a failure." Lori seems to be happy about my revelation.

And here is why I knew a pleasant conversation wouldn't be happening despite my best efforts.

"Aren't you honest," I say, sarcastic. "I don't think I'm a failure, I just grew up and found other interests. Anyhow, how long have you been skating?"

She begins to play with the buttons on the dashboard for music in the car. "Since I was seven. I think I'm good."

"So modest," I mumble to myself. The sound of pop-country fills the car. "Nice choice in music."

"Tell that to my dad. I've been begging him to use his connections for concert tickets for my birthday."

I shrug. "Sounds like a reasonable request."

Lori rests her head against the seat then throws me a look. "You know, he loses interest easily. Just because you're staying with us, that doesn't mean you're different."

I nod, trying to think of what to say. "Your dad and I aren't like that." Somewhat true. No kiss or further bases have been taken. Fucking via eye contact doesn't count.

I glance quickly to my side to see that Lori is studying me, then she hums a sound. I'm sure she has a theory or opinion; she seems very intuitive for her age.

"You're weird."

My eyes pop out from her forwardness. "Uh, isn't that a good thing?" My voice is uneven from lacking certainty.

"Maybe. You're the one chauffeuring around kids you barely know."

"I've met you before, you just don't remember. Your dad would always show photos of you guys growing up too. It's just been a while since I've seen him. And I'm not a child caretaker." I feel like I need to get a sign to hang around my neck.

"Fair enough. I'm an adult anyhow. I think my dad still tries to have someone care for us because of Harry. He's a bit sensitive."

"Really?" I focus on the turn on the road.

"I don't know, I'm not a therapist," she responds.

I chortle to myself. "We're almost there. Do I need to come in with you?"

"Of course not." Lori looks out the windows to investigate where we are. "How did you know how to get here?"

"My grandparents used to have a lake house here. I'm not new to the area."

A sound escapes her lips. "So you actually know the area and knew us from before. I'll give you points for that. Most women start from zero when they try to grab my dad's attention."

I come to a stop outside of the rink just in time. "Oh, but I'm not —" She's already opened the door with no interest in hearing my defense and grabs her bag from the backseat.

She leans in through the open window. "Thanks for the ride. See you at home. Remind my dad that I need new cucumbers for my eyes, he always forgets. Something tells me that he'll listen to you."

"Why is that?"

"He actually lets you near us. That's rule number one in his book, don't let his *friends* around his kids."

She walks away, and despite her attitude that needs a strong adjustment, Lori is quite… insightful.

And I'm not sure why a sprinkle of a special feeling forms somewhere within my body.

I watch Lexi as she compares paint samples against the wall next to the fireplace mantle in the lobby. Last night, I think she was hiding from me, as she went to Summer's for dinner then retreated to her room as soon as she was back. Like any sane person, she avoided breakfast in my house before school, too.

But now I do owe her a few words. I approach her slowly, as she seems completely unaware that I'm behind her. My inkling has me believing that we both experience a sort of electricity around one another that heightens the tension in the air, but it only causes us to have relaxed smiles because we both enjoy it.

"Hey there."

I startle her, and she drops the paint sample sheet. "Oh, hi, I was lost in my thoughts and didn't notice you were here."

We both lean down to save the swatch, and our arms graze in the battle of who will pick it up first. Our eyes connect, and I hiss a breath. "Thoughts about me?" I tease her, and her cheeks heat.

Even though I managed to beat her at collecting the swatch, we remain kneeling, lost in a simple touch and my enjoyment of the gleam in her eyes.

"Wishful thinking, Holden, since my thoughts normally only

include how to use mason jars in staging a room or debating in my head what *is* the best position for nighttime activities." Her breathy rasp is a taunt that I'm here for.

"Mmm, if it is designated to only nighttime, then he is the wrong man for you." We both stand as she stifles a laugh, and I hand her the paint sample. "Anyhow, before my indecent thoughts go any further into the gutter, I should probably keep us on neutral ground."

Lexi looks at me with interest. "Oh yeah? That's a sudden one-eighty," she flatly states.

I love when I smirk, it's good for the facial muscles. "The thing is… I owe you a massive thank-you for helping yesterday with Lori. I know she's, well…" I love this kid, but I need to accept her current state. "Feisty and moody. She probably even slammed the car door for extra effect."

Lexi relaxes in her stance as her enjoyment of my presence doesn't seem to fade. "It's… not a problem, and I hate to be the one to remind you, but it might only go downhill from here until she heads to college. It's the joys of pre-teen and teenage life."

Blowing out an exhausting breath, her words instill fear in me. I really need to step up my plans to prepare for all of it. But I have no plans, I'm just going with the flow. I bring a finger to my chin and rub for a few seconds while I follow Lexi to the couch in the middle of the lobby and then notice that the coffee table is already gone.

"You're really speeding along with everything," I compliment.

"Of course, you need the lobby done ASAP. It's your statement room for making first impressions. Plus, we're packing up so they can sand the floors and walls before they paint. I managed to get some of the furniture to arrive next week, a friend owed me a favor," she explains as she grabs her coat slung over the back of the couch.

I really am impressed with her ability to dive deep into this project. "Sounds great, a lucky friend to have, I guess." I fill my jeans pockets with my hands to keep them occupied and in check, because how I would love to touch her ass right now.

She begins to button her coat. "I guess. I went on a few dates with him a couple of times, and I assume that helped." Lexi isn't even attempting to keep me on edge, she's simply relaying a fact.

My body tenses, and for the life of me, I'm not entirely sure why a wave of possessiveness is like a match when she said that. "Oh? Is this recent?"

Lexi stares at me and then nearly snorts a laugh. "Subtle, are we? And no, not recent. Like, two years ago maybe."

Stepping forward, I want her whole body to feel my presence, which is why my hands come up as I invade her space, and her breath hitches. I even sense a shiver when I reach around to grab the belt of her coat. Slowly, I wrap the fabric around her waist.

"Good. That topic's closed." Our eyes are fixed to one another as I continue to tie the belt. "Any plans for tonight? It's Friday, but it is Lake Spark, so…" My voice drops low, and without regard for Stuart at reception who is our audience, I tie Lexi's belt.

Lexi gulps a breath. "I think I'm going to take it easy, you know a glass of wine or read a book."

I yank on the knot to tighten, and it causes her to press against me and yelp from surprise, and her hands can't help but find a resting spot on my shoulders to ensure she doesn't lose her balance. "There is a hot tub at my house if that's your thing."

Her head tilts slightly, and here we go, I know that sexy-as-fuck look forming on her face, her mouth about to retort with a comment I will appreciate. "You own a spa here at the Dizzy Duck. I think I would rather use the hot tub and pool here."

"*Yeah…* but tonight is an unusual night at my place."

"Why might that be?" Her voice is hoarse.

"I'm going to order in Chinese food if you like that. You must get hungry for dinner."

She rolls her head and looks defeated yet doesn't let go. "That is true, and I do love sweet-and-sour chicken."

"Great, I'll order."

"As long as Lori and Harry enjoy it then sounds good."

A gruff humorous sound rumbles under my breath, and it causes Lexi's eyes to flood with alarm, clearly waiting for an explanation.

"Except Lori and Harry are away for sleepovers at their friends' houses."

She backtracks at record speed, creating space between us as she steps away. "Come again?" She blinks.

"Again? Geez, let me first make round one happen."

Her eyes roll at my demeanor that must be driving her crazy. "This is not…" Her face falls into her hands and then appears again with her lips in a grin. "What the hell, fine. Dinner, and then our best behavior in the hot tub, and we can talk furniture ideas."

I begin to walk away without even looking back, instead taking satisfaction from my triumph. "Agreeable as always."

———

WITH HESITATION, Lexi walks down the hall then slows when she reaches the kitchen. I don't give her much notice as I'm unpacking white boxes from the bag, the smell of Chinese food hitting our senses.

"Here I am." She's still in jeans from the day but has replaced her blouse with an old Hollows University t-shirt.

"Got eggrolls and fortune cookies."

She grabs the packet of chopsticks to prepare. "Then I won't be running away."

I circle around the island to join her on the high stools. Sitting at the dining table would be too formal, and the couch would just be a mess.

"You weren't going to run away anyhow," I confidently inform her.

Lexi's eyes have a glimmer of something that I can't quite describe, but it feels positive for me. "Maybe true. Now pass the eggrolls before I get cranky."

I do as I'm told, and we decide to ditch plates and just eat from the boxes. "Eating Chinese food without plates. I feel like this calls for sitting on the floor, eating behind a coffee table," I state.

A peculiar look floods her face. "That is not what I expected you to say, but I couldn't agree more."

"Want to do it then?"

Her shoulder lifts. "Why not, the rug is the perfect material for sitting on," she notes.

We both grab a few things and head to the living room. I manage to grab the bottle of wine and glasses too since she's carrying the brunt of our dinner.

Once we are settled on the ground, I pour some wine for us, and then an odd silence hits us when our eyes catch, and her face turns soft and shy.

"What are we doing, Holden?" She gets straight to the point.

Honestly, I'm not sure. It's just too fun and exhilarating to have a connection that streams between two people. I know I have kids relying on me, and I shouldn't be distracted, but…

"There was an instant click between us, and you're familiar with my situation. In a way, it's refreshing to have someone who doesn't assume I'm one way purely because they've never met me."

Lexi swirls some food with her chopsticks. "It has been quite a few years since we saw one another, and it's different circumstances, but I do like this time around better."

I take a sip of my red wine before setting the glass back on the table. "I'm an asshole for flirting with you. I'm not sure why you're not running."

"Because a retired hockey player doesn't scare me." This conversation doesn't even faze her as she brings a piece of chicken to her mouth.

"The thing is, it's okay to flirt with someone; it's crossing the parameters of flirting when things can get a little murky," I warn her.

She buries her chortle while she swallows her food. "Is moving your flirtation into your house not beyond the parameters already?"

My head bobs side to side. "Meh. I need the help right now, and you're up for the challenge."

"A few days and then I will go back to the Dizzy Duck. I'm not sure us being around one another is good for either of our blood pressures," she explains while she picks up another piece of chicken.

I shrug. "Your loss."

"Maybe. I do appreciate how you threw my father's demand for the team to stay away from me out the window."

I intervene. "As much as I want to be loyal, I also don't give a fuck. I have other issues to deal with, in case you haven't noticed." I don't frown about it, and instead smile.

"You most definitely swagger around to your own tune. But what I mean is Lori and Harry are around, and that's where your attention lies, as it should. I'm not sure us adding underlying innuendo is the way to go."

Neither is being lonely in the coming weeks when I don't need to be.

I look at her with fondness, as she has strong shoulders with realistic expectations, and more importantly, she cares about how my life revolves around my kids. In the past, the women I might have had a hookup with were always well away from anyone and discreet. Now? Lexi is in close waters… yet still, I'm ignoring the lifesaver that I should probably consider using.

"You are extremely right, except tonight, they are not here," I remind us.

Her face swings in my direction. "I've noticed."

I nudge her shoulder with mine. "Relax, we can eat and have adult conversation. Other than eating with Stone, my ability to have adult discussions at dinner is limited. This is a refreshing change."

"I ran into him this morning when I stopped by to hit the gym. He gave Stuart a hard time about cookies."

I chuckle. "That's always the case."

"It's a little insane the number of athletes, retired or not, that live in this town. I know the Spinners train here, but still. Do you miss playing?"

Nobody has asked me that in a while. "Hmm, let me think," I pretend. "No. Which might sound strange, but I feel like everything was meant for that chapter. I always knew that I would retire young, as most athletes do, so I made those the best years possible. Not to mention that fatherhood hit me earlier than I probably would have planned. But now I have a completely different life. Do I wish Harry would be more into sports? Sure, but he has other interests. Do I get excited when Lori is dancing on ice? Yeah. Because the ice brings good memories."

Lexi steals some of my sesame chicken, and I appreciate that we're comfortable enough around one another to do something like that. "I would never have expected you to end up owning the Dizzy Duck Inn, but it's a great story." She gently swats my arm in excitement. "Actually, I have an idea that I wanted to run by you."

"Shoot."

"I was thinking we could hang some photos of all the athletes and sports stuff from here in Lake Spark. I could get some frames to match the feeling of the Dizzy Duck. Everyone appreciates those little touches."

"I like it, and I'm sure our guests would love it, including the owner of The Spinners when he eats there with his wife. We have a lot of team dinners happening all the time too."

"Perfect." She sounds accomplished with her thought before she picks up her wine.

I grab an eggroll, but I'm eager to keep our conversation going. "Other than design, what has life looked like for you in the last few years?"

"Well, I worked on a few projects. Homes mostly, which I love, because your home is where you return to and it's the base of your life, therefore you should make it cozy and full of personality," she gushes.

"Heart in the home or something like that."

She's completely enthusiastic. "Totally. And after a few projects, I backpacked around Europe and then Costa Rica. I even went up to do a tour of Alaska. Basically, I'm not afraid to get lost somewhere in Austria because I ended up on the wrong train or ending up in unusual situations that find myself eating Chinese food on the floor in Lake Spark." She smiles proudly before popping food into her mouth.

"Don't worry, adventurous and self-assured were the first two things that came to my mind when you walked into my office."

Her grin turns shy as she sets the box down, deciding not to eat. "I guess you're kind of my client. And yes, I have no qualms admitting that I wasn't going to keep quiet about my attraction, it would have been obvious anyway."

"You were not subtle, nor was I." Setting my food on the table, we both have empty hands, and we should probably efficiently use them for other activities. "Again, I feel obliged to point out that I'm the guy that plays games, and I just haven't figured out which one I'm playing with you."

With purpose, Lexi leans across me, ensuring her body presses against mine as she reaches for something. Her eyes sizzle with a sexy glint that is roping me in, only made worse because her mouth is within inches of mine. I take in our mingling breaths and debate if my hand should slide up the side of her body, but I don't get a chance to decide because she begins to drag her body back to sitting next to me.

Lexi holds a fortune cookie up. "My favorite part of the meal." Her voice is a hoarse whisper.

"Meal, sure, but once that goes into your mouth then the meal is over."

Her brows rise to throw caution at me before she cracks open her cookie to read the paper. "Run while you can or accept your fortune."

I lick my lips, completely enamored by her humor that is on par with my own. "Fitting," I say before I nab my own cookie. Breaking it open, I read aloud, "You should touch the woman sitting in front of you." I throw the paper over my shoulder and move in to glide my hand along her cheek, urging her to move closer.

"It didn't say that." She grins.

"You're right. It only said, 'you will have a good year.' But my version is better and by far more likely to come true."

She presses her lips together but doesn't let go of her smile. I'll cross the line because I'm completely tempted by her. From her fun personality to the way she tucks her hair behind her ear, I'd be angry if I never got the chance to touch her the way I want.

"I've walked into your life when I probably shouldn't," she chides.

"Don't think, Lexi. We're all allowed a little escape," I whisper.

She breaks away and stands abruptly, with her palms smoothing over her clothes. She busies herself with cleaning up the table which disappoints me and confuses me, but I follow her lead.

Walking to the kitchen, she sets the boxes on the counter with her back to me and her hands planted on the edge of the quartz counter. She appears to be in deep thought.

It doesn't feel like I should say anything, so I don't. Which is good, because Lexi spins on her toes, and the speed of her eyes flicking to me transmits the message perfectly.

I'm not sure who makes the move first, but we both take the step to crash our mouths together, her hands quickly finding their way to hang onto my elbows as my hands discover the curve of her hips, because we're in for a long kiss.

Maybe even more.

7

LEXI

Was he really anxious that I would just walk away and avoid a kiss?

Nah, I just wanted to keep Holden in suspense a little. Draw it out to ensure he doesn't get cocky with the idea that I would be easy at the click of his fingers.

Our ability to play around one another is equal. We both have that skill and on the same level.

Holden's lips are near bruising, and I love it, which is why I give back as good as I get. My arms slide up his then slow so my hands can trace the curve of his shoulders until I link them behind his neck. He is a little taller than me, so I rise on the balls of my feet. The ability for my body to find the right position of its own accord while I kiss Holden is a talent because it means I can sink into this heavenly kiss.

We both seem to murmur when our mouths tilt together to get more. His lips are firm but caress mine just right. The short afternoon stubble around his mouth is the perfect combination to remind me how much of a man he is.

Sparks fly through my body, and my heart quickens as we gently part to gather some air to breathe, right before our mouths find each other again, a little slower this time. The tips of our tongues greet one another with a little dance. Heat skims down over my obliques to settle on my waist, and gosh, his hands framing my body is what I was craving. It brings stability to the kiss that has me wanting more.

Holden almost growls when we pull away, with his eyes connecting with mine, only to dip down to my swollen mouth then strike up back to my eyes. It's sexy and inviting. He has plans for me, and I'm willing.

"That was fun." His voice is gruff but assured.

"Was?" I ask, with a smile covering my fear that this was it.

But he chuckles. "Not a damn chance."

My smile widens right before he dives down to kiss me again. We begin to step together, circling around as we move toward the couch. During this travel of anticipation, he pulls on the edge of my t-shirt before peeling it up with vigor, only for me to take over when his arm wraps around my middle to keep me close. He only takes one moment to admire my pink lace bra, and it seems to fuel him, because the moment we are back at the couch, he lifts then twirls me until I'm on my back underneath him.

"Tsk, tsk, Lexi," he tuts with a devilish smirk. "You made us go to the kitchen, only to return to where we started."

I chortle as my hands play with his t-shirt, wanting it off already a minute ago. "I'm not that easy, Holden. I may be another one of your conquests, but by no means am I falling at your feet."

A wave of uncertainty glazes over his eyes, and I don't have a clue how to uncover his thoughts. "Huh, conquests. But you have the best mouth I've ever seen that spits out retorts at record speed. Now let me touch you more." He sounds desperate, and confidence and excitement bloom inside me.

My leg drives up to pull his body even closer to mine. "Only if you're nice." I fake a pout.

"I'm never nice, but I am demanding, and something blazes in your eyes that you want that anyhow."

I breathe out a knowing breath but don't answer because I don't get a chance. His mouth is trailing down my neck to my breasts, and my entire body lifts to offer him more. I'm buzzing with a need so strong that I really wish the clock would speed up.

Which is why my hands sneak between us to work the button of his jeans. When his mouth kisses and nibbles at the valley of my breasts, his hand joins me in loosening his jeans to slide down his hips. Instantly, my palm covers his cock underneath his briefs, and I softly gasp. His stiff cock feels very big, and that excites me even more.

The feeling of fingers unbuttoning my jeans ups the anticipation, but I won't wait and slide them down as fast as I can. I'm not sure that Holden even looks, he just pursues his crusade to fuck me, and I'm ready to surrender.

A moan hits me as his finger grazes over the damp lace near my clit. A few strokes and I'm already halfway on the road to trembling.

"Lexi, your pussy seems to be eager for me to play. My mouth will have to wait, because since you walked into my office the other day, I've thought about fucking you senseless for round one."

A noise tunes a short melody under my breath. "I don't think I'll mind."

Quickly, he no longer hovers over me, and instead, he stands to offer me his hand. "Come on, your room. I don't think the sofa with popcorn stuck behind a pillow is the place for this."

Ah, and he's right. This is where his family spends their relaxation time, and it would be a little odd for him to take his hookup on his couch, wouldn't it?

I comply, and he yanks me up with power. I don't expect Holden to keep my hand firmly in his as he tows me along, but the off-guard sweetness kind of sends a twinkle somewhere inside me. Luckily, the guest room and bathroom are off the study, so we don't need to go far.

He kicks the door shut behind us and then pushes me onto the bed, and we are back to the same position that we were on the couch. My toes now dig into his ass to press his cock to my pussy. I'm not sure if I can wait long.

"Condom," he says into my neck.

"Mmmhmm," I hum.

"No, I mean, I don't have a condom here. It's in my jeans back in my wallet in the other room."

"Oh." I come up to my forearms. "I think I have one in my bag somewhere." He lies to his side to allow me to hop off the bed, and it takes me a few big steps or rather jog to the bathroom to grab one from my makeup bag. Appearing at the door, I hold it up. "Lucky us." Then I dive back onto the bed.

He studies me with concern. "Had plans for your time in Lake Spark?"

I swat him. "Oh yeah. I was totally going to head to Main Street to see who I could convince to join me in my wicked ways, even heard the sheriff is single again," I tease him.

Holden flips me until I'm on my back and he is on his side. "Looks like you upgraded." His hand pulls my thigh to the side, with the back of his finger drawing a line up my skin, creating a sensitive wave throughout my body.

"Don't go off topic, we need clothes off and the condom on," I usher us along.

The corners of his mouth hitch as he's entertained. We both work off any fabric that remains on us, and he rips open the condom wrapper with his teeth, quickly sheathing it on. The moment he settles between my legs, I think my clit is in pain I'm so desperate for Holden to fill me up.

When he begins to nudge his cock inside me, I moan from a release of patience.

"Fuck me," he grunts. "You're perfectly tight yet taking me well." He pushes further and slowly until he's in deep. I twirl my hips a few circles, only for him move up, pin my arms above my head, and open me wide. "No, baby, you'll lie back and watch as I take you hard and deep."

A sound of pleasure draws out from my mouth when I look down to see his cock sliding in and out of me, glistening with my arousal.

Holden pumps and pumps, and I clench and meet him on thrusts. We go faster, harder, until I'm not sure how long it's been because I'm lost. "Fuck. Almost. Fuck. So good," I moan breathlessly.

"I know," he grunts.

His thumb on my clit brings a near scream from my lips as I reach my orgasm that overtakes me as I shake around his cock, and my head spins. It feels like I'm not even on earth when a few moments later Holden follows me with an orgasm that rips through him and causes him to nearly roar.

He takes a few seconds to recover before he withdraws and falls onto his back.

We're both perfectly spent.

———

I LEAN on my side with the sheet covering me loosely and my head propped on my arm as I watch Holden reappear from the bathroom after having taken care of the condom.

There is a droll smile on his face as he walks naked back to the bed and then joins me under the covers.

"That escalated quickly," he jokes.

"It seems so." My lips quirk out. "I don't think you particularly care, though."

He glances at me. "Not really. Should I? I think we both know this was a release for one another, and there will probably be a second time or third."

"Is that what you do with the others?"

He snorts a laugh. "You really have a great interpretation of me." He sounds almost offended, but his relaxed face doesn't fade. "I haven't had sex with anyone for a few months, believe it or not."

"Well, I mean, I guess you still know what to do," I taunt him, and it earns me Holden gently tackling me until he is on his side looking down on me.

"You are kind of a sunshiny, almost annoying woman, so fortunately for you, I appreciate your humor."

I lick my lips. "Likewise. It's nice seeing very adult Holden again. Last time I saw you, well, you were an adult but with a lot of chaos in your life and not the good kind. You were so distracted that everyone kind of gave you some space," I explain, and it's honest.

Sure, even I wasn't immune to his looks, but it never crossed my mind that he would be a contender since he was way beyond my years in terms of life experience. Now? The moment I walked into his office, a light went on, and I could see maybe more in him, completely unexplainable.

"My life is still chaos," he reminds me honestly.

I smile softly at him. "The good kind." We both lie on our backs, and I tip my nose in the direction of a canvas photo on the wall of Lori in a tutu. "It's a great picture."

He follows the line of my eyes. "Yeah, she was maybe eight there. She used to dance more but figure skating is her hobby of choice now. Lori still goes to one ballet class a week because her coach says it will help on the ice." The smile of affection and love on his face is apparent. "She's good. I'm happy it brings me to the ice rink on a frequent basis, and memories hit me." Holden points to another picture on the wall of his son playing in shallow water at the lake. "As much as I dreamed of raising a little hockey player, Harry is our science and music guy. I've accepted that one squeaking instrument at a time. A great kid when he's on good behavior."

I begin to draw on his arm with my fingers. "You love them. Any fool could see that. One day, you will look back at this chapter and laugh at some of their tricks."

He chuckles as his own finger begins to swirl on my thigh under the sheet, not even in a sexual way. "You're completely right. If you are firm on that theory, then I'm sure you will roll into motherhood with a breeze."

I shrug. "Maybe, not sure I'm ready for that now, though, if ever."

"Hmm."

I roll back onto my side and tuck my hands under my head. "Can I ask? If it's too personal, then don't answer. But do you think they are acting this way because, well, their mom isn't in the picture?"

He ponders. "First off, with you, I don't seem to mind talking about this stuff, which is new for me. But I'm not sure, at least they never mention it. At some point, it must cross their mind that their mom doesn't want any involvement. I sure as hell have tried to make up for that by being two parents in one… You just caught me on a bad month… or year. It's been a wild ride for the last year or two."

"Growing pains," I assure him.

Holden has a serious look when his eyes greet mine. Maybe for a moment I think it's appreciation. "I should probably go."

It's nice not being alone for a night, but I follow his cues because we need to keep this simple. "Yep."

Neither one of us moves.

There's a tension that can't be ignored.

Then he throws the sheets off us. "Fuck it. One more time."

I giggle as we head into another round.

Meaningless sex is not new to me. You just have clear guidelines, and when it runs its course, then you move on. Except staying and working with the man while you enjoy mind-blowing sex?

That's new.

And I'm not sure about the rules or limits.

Even worse, I've been known to only accept intuition when it's too late.

Grabbing my glass of orange juice, I notice Lori and Harry looking at me strangely. Is it because they sense that their father did dirty things to me? He just arrived and went straight to the coffee pot. We aren't obvious. We are putting in effort to be the opposite. That's how passion can work in a platonic way. You can switch it off when needed.

Why are his kids quiet? Hmm.

Bringing the juice to my lips, I take a sip and nearly gag. I swallow with great difficulty while his kids laugh hysterically. "Oh God, what the hell?" Holden whips his sight to me to see what's happening. "There is tabasco sauce in here." Seems my suspicion of spiked coffee was a misjudgment, and I should have given care to other beverages.

In unison, Holden and I snap our eyes to his kids, knowing who the culprits are. He begins to shake his head as his mouth tightens.

"This again?" Stern-voice Holden, here we come.

"Again?" I croak out.

Harry shrugs. "It's a classic move."

Holden drags his hand across his jaw. "Great way to start the day." He takes the juice from my hand and walks to the sink to pour it down the drain. "I'm sorry, Lexi. I thought they got the memo that you are *not* the nanny." His kids receive a serious warning glare. "You don't do this when your aunt stays here. Lexi is a house guest, so treat her the same."

"But she seems like she can handle it," Lori explains before bringing a spoon of cornflakes to her mouth.

"Doesn't mean you won't say sorry because A) it's not cool, and B) how am I supposed to ask her to do me a solid and drop you two off at school because I need to meet with my accountant?"

"It's fine, really. I'll just start a tab at Jolly Joe's, and they can send it to you, since I have a feeling that I'll be eating a lot of safe breakfasts there."

Holden looks at me with pleading eyes. "Deal. But I need to ask…" His face squinches.

I sigh. "Fine. I'll take your little criminals and bring them in their chariot to school."

He smirks and brings his hands together in prayer. "Thank you. I owe you one." The glint in his eyes informs me that there is some innuendo there.

I have to ignore it if I want a chance to get on with my day. "Okay, shall we go in five minutes? I need to grab my laptop," I tell the kids.

"Fine," Lori groans.

Won't this be a fun ride.

———

ARRIVING at Lake Spark Academy after a quiet drive, since Lori had earplugs in and Harry seemed to be reading something on his tablet, the conversation was simple, actually minimal, except the random pointing out a deer or sign about the upcoming market. Apparently, Harry loves a good market churro stand too.

Coming to a halt in the drop-off lane, I shiver from the mom holding the sign. She looks like she's completely on a power trip with her ability to call us all out for stopping too long.

Easing up the line after the lady waves for me to continue, before I barely brake, Lori is already unbuckling. "Thanks, houseguest." Now she's just teasing me, which seems hopeful for no future pranks.

"Have a good day. I think your dad is picking you up for figure skating."

"I don't have skating today. I have ballet." She slams the door then hurries to a group of girls waiting on the sidewalk.

I glance over my shoulder to see that Harry isn't so eager to exit. "Enjoy school," I tell him, giving him the clue that now is the time to head out of my car.

He sighs deeply and opens the door. "Yeah, sure. Thanks, houseguest." I guess that's my new name.

Now he's off, and I can head straight to Jolly Joe's because I'm starving, and I need carbs because screw my health kick. I've found myself in a situation that is beyond normal. Probably, I should avoid adding houseguest to my name before this turns into a muddled mess with Holden that I willingly agreed to.

Driving off, I glance in my rearview mirror and notice Harry walking slowly before two boys come up to him, and my stomach churns when I see them shove him. They clearly are not friends.

I shouldn't involve myself. Harry and Lori must already be confused by my presence, but Holden really does seem desperate when it comes to them.

"No, Lexi, don't do it," I mumble to myself aloud. But that's only a mere second before I decide fuck it, bullying is bullying.

I slam the brakes and swing open my door, not a care in the world that I'm blocking the car line of fearful drivers at the mercy of the traffic cop. As I storm over to Harry, I hear the traffic lady yelling at me to move, but I don't care.

On my approach, I hear one boy. "You should be good at hockey like your dad, but instead you're weird. You shouldn't even be here. This is a sports school, weirdo."

I arrive and place my hand on Harry's shoulder who is staring at the ground. "Everything okay here, boys?"

The two boys look at me strangely. "We were just telling our friend that science class will be great later, weren't we?"

Before Harry can answer, I pull him back closer to me. "Sure you were." My skepticism is in full force.

In my peripheral view, I see another mom arrive, and her tight dress is distracting. I can't even imagine what the guys from the high school football team must think. "Everything okay here? My son and his friends are just speaking with Harry." She throws me a fake bright smile.

"Yeah, sure. These little youngsters over here are holding up the values of Lake Spark Academy to the highest standard." My disapproval runs strong.

The lady holds her hand out to shake. "I'm Kate McClearly, I don't believe we've met."

That name rings a bell, not sure why, but my weariness is on alert. "A pleasure." I'm sarcastic and don't offer her my hand.

Her hand falls, and her face screws up. "You must be the new childcare for the West kids."

"I am not." I don't bat a lash.

"Oh?" She wasn't expecting my answer.

Harry speaks up. "She's my dad's houseguest."

Yikes, that came out with many ways to interpret.

Kate straightens her posture, clearly agitated. "I didn't realize that Holden has a new… *friend*."

I just stare at her and keep my face straight. "Shall we focus on these boys with demon qualities?"

Her jaw drops. "Demons is a little harsh, considering the children that you must be around as Holden's…. guest," she says rather dryly.

I keep my hands on Harry's shoulders to stay calm. "So, what about those Academy values? Would you like me to find the principal to discuss these boys' exemplary behavior or would you prefer to talk to these boys about showing kindness and respect?"

She brings her hair to her side. "We know how boys are at this age. It's just a little back-and-forth."

"If that's what you would like to tell yourself due to your bad parenting, then by all means repeat that mantra. Wait…" I snap my fingers. "Aren't you the mom that Lori had words with?"

Kate's face shades with disdain. "Yes, my daughter is in her class, and it was Lori who exemplified bad parenting." Her smile is now contrite.

"Okay, maybe she didn't say the right things, but she didn't shove you. So swallow your pride about your child's shitty behavior and take the high road, lady."

She gasps, and I notice kids and a group of moms congregating around us. "You have some nerve. You do one school drop-off and now you are the expert of these fine students at our school?"

I bring a hand to my hip as Harry walks to Lori who joined the circle. "Let me guess, you're a PTA mom."

"Head of it, actually."

"Great. So do something about your son and his friend. "

"They are being kids." She raises her voice.

I shake my head. "Doesn't make it okay. So please rein in your son and his friend, because I'm sure Harry's dad would love to chat about this with the principal."

"I'm sure Holden and I could discuss this without the need of the principal." That thought seems to excite her.

I roll my eyes. "I'm sure he will be busy." Her mouth gapes open, and again the interpretation of my words do not give me points. "I think these kids should get to class. Education and all, don't ya think?"

Kate just holds me in a death stare, but I take a moment to glance to my side and see Harry steps out of the way close to Lori, her fingers feathering his elbow, and I'm sure I see the corner of her mouth twitch in approval. I know they can stand up for themselves, but maybe they need to know that someone else will too.

"Go on, get to class. Your dad will pick you up," I offer Harry, and flash Lori a comforting look.

The crowd disperses, except Kate who stays put in her snooty stance. She can't say anything because traffic mom arrives. "You need to move your car, otherwise I will give you a parking ticket."

I look at her, bewildered. "As in a fake ticket, considering your only power is your sign?"

She straightens her shoulders. "We're allowed to give tickets; this is private property."

I look between them. "Shove it."

I blow out a breath and stop when an older woman blocks my way. She doesn't look happy. "I don't think we've met. I'm Principal Johnson, and perhaps we should have a chat." The moms behind me try to cover their satisfied looks.

Studying the principal's face, I close my eyes for a second, cursing internally.

Shit.

———

WALKING INTO THE DIZZY DUCK, I see Holden waiting for me. He is leaning against the front desk with ankles and arms crossed, wearing a stern look. It makes me feel uneasy if I'm honest.

"Someone is in trouble. The principal phoned, and to my surprise, it's not because of my kids, which is refreshing."

Oh. He's already aware.

I step forward, ready to defend my actions. "I'm sorry, but those two little punks were being such an ass to your son. I couldn't just drive away like nothing happened. His mom just glared at me with disapproval and words of stupidity." I hold my finger up. "I'm like 100% sure she is more pissed that I was there on your behalf, ruining her chances to get in your pants if she plays her cards right."

Holden just stares at me with his lips pressed together. He isn't saying anything, why isn't he saying anything?

My eyes search the room to see if I'm making a scene. Stuart just pretends to be reading mail, and Holden seems to be enjoying his current state of hanging this situation over my head.

But then his stern phase vanishes into thin air as he uncrosses his body to step in my direction. He reaches out his fingertips, and they land on my shoulders to square me off.

"Thank you," he simply states. We agree that I'm not the villain. "I'm happy you did what you did. I want to throttle a few people, but it seems you put them in their place. Most of all, you were watching out for my son."

I gently loll my head to the side, trying to avoid his praise. "It was nothing."

"It was everything." His appreciation is apparent.

"I-I… He's a good kid. You raised a sweet boy."

Holden rubs my shoulders as he half smiles. "Thanks. Maybe I needed to hear that before I storm into the principal's office tomorrow."

I grin. "Uh-oh, someone is going to get it."

"Maybe you too but in a different way."

Now that twisting ache begins to form at full force between my legs, but maybe I should throw in caution. "Don't you have work to do? I should really focus on a few orders of accessories, and I'm not sure where we're going, but… we should tread carefully."

Holden steps back, not thrilled with my sentence. "Maybe you're right."

"I'm sorry if I caused problems. I'm not sure why you send them there."

He tilts his head to the side. "They have had a few tough times lately with select kids, and the principal isn't thrilled with those kids, either. But for the most part it's a positive place, hence why the principal keeps reiterating values to all of us. Harry loves the science club where he has close friends, and Lori has some great friends she coordinates her daily outfits with. You've just caught us all on a bad week or two. Besides, my donations kind of shut everyone up when needed and gets me out of the parents auction too."

That part I can see him doing. "As long as you feel everyone is happy, then…""

Holden steps forward and plants his finger over my lips. "Shh, you were calm compared to what I would do. I bet you are kind of hot riled." His finger drops.

"Now that would land you in detention for sure," I respond. He gently shakes his head, and my lips roll in as I do my best to avoid his gaze. "See ya later."

But as I walk away, I still feel his eyes on me.

———

RUBBING the back of my neck, I try to focus, but it's useless as I work in my room office. Maybe I should just take a few hours off, get some fresh air, pack my bags, and return to the Dizzy Duck on a longer basis. I groan from the situation that spins around me. I took another step to intertwine with Holden's life, and I shouldn't have.

The knock on the door breaks my thoughts. I go to open it, and as soon it's even a crack ajar, it's pushed open, with Holden charging for me and slamming the door behind him.

No words before his lips are on me, hands hoisting me up by the hips to encourage me to hold on. I'm in this moment with all previous doubts now dispersed into history. My inner inhibitions win.

We don't break our kiss, even when he lets go with one arm, and I hear him clear the desk with his arm with items falling to the floor. He plops me down on the wood as we tear at one another's clothes, as if we're two lovers who haven't seen each other in years, though it's only been 72 hours since the last time he made me weak underneath him.

"Fuck everything. I'm starving for you." His fingers hurry up under my skirt, and I try to yank him closer to unclasp his belt.

My breath grows heavy, and my face burns as he kisses my neck, with his fingers touching my pussy.

"Don't stop," I plead.

Holden slithers down my body, throwing me a mischievous warning. "No plans to. I need to taste you before I fuck you so hard that the people on the other side of the wall will question if there's an earthquake."

I gasp, desperate for it all.

9

HOLDEN

This isn't good. Well, this is kind of *excellent*.

But no, I shouldn't be crossing our lines again, but Lexi can handle the reality that we're only two people who have needs and her brazen attitude does something to me. Add in the hint of her caring nature toward my kids, then I'm a man in a crazed state.

I'm on my knees then jerk her forward so she's on the edge of the desk. Everything is happening fast, but we're both feral in demanding each other. I wobble one step to ensure my mouth aligns with her cotton panties. Most guys hate cotton, but on Lexi, it blasts away any impressions of innocence. It doesn't present any obstacles to slide the fabric to the side either.

My mouth prints kisses along her silky skin while her hands run wild through my hair.

"I wanted to do this more to you the other night," I husk when my eyes jump up to check in.

Her sly smirk shows approval. "You were rather disappointing on that front."

Now she's just toying with me, which is why I bite her inner thigh, and she yelps. "I would spank you right now, but I need to lick your glistening pussy that clearly doesn't look disappointed when I'm around."

Lexi hums a laugh as her body rocks in my direction. The tip of my tongue licks a taste, and she's fucking luscious. I need so much more. I draw a slow teasing line from her entrance all the way to her clit. I hold her thighs wide and feast on her, with my tongue circling and my lips pressing. Adding a finger, I have her at my mercy.

"Fuck, Holden," she moans.

Another flick and I need to be inside of the woman. Fast and hard is the way I like it with her. Not that fucking has been a pattern for us, but maybe it's becoming one. I knock that thought out of my head, especially as Lexi begins to convulse and curses out my name. My tongue doesn't move, and instead I press until she comes down from her orgasm.

The moment she does, with her breath now rapid, I shuffle back on my knees with her wetness on my mouth. "On your knees."

"Whatever you say." She slides off the desk while I stand and unzip my pants where she had managed to already unbuckle me when our hands were roaming of their own accord.

Lexi's eyes appear eager to please, ensuring I'm staring down at her when her mouth begins to wrap around my length, slowly taking in more with her tongue firm underneath to join the journey.

I grab her hair to hold her the way I like it and to have control of her. Her decadent mouth drags from root to tip, sucking and pumping until she's in a rhythm that I'm guiding. She wraps her fingers around me and grips the base of my cock to give her ample playing field.

"That's it. Just like that. I'm sure you can take it a little deeper." I want to push her limits. Does that make me a selfish man?

A slight gag doesn't seem to bother her as she repeats several times, her mouth salivating and her muffled sounds of pleasure mumbling in her throat.

"Want my cum to slide down that throat of yours? You would take every drop, wouldn't you?"

She nods with her mouth full of my cock.

I'm in a dilemma, though, as I want that sassy mouth to make me come, but I need to be inside her pussy, and I'm not sure I have time for both.

"Sit on the desk," I instruct, and the loss of her mouth around my cock is anything but enjoyable, but in ten seconds, I will have something better. Lexi follows orders well, and I search for a condom in my wallet on the floor with my pants. I notice in the corner of my eye that Lexi's panties are at her ankles, and she kicks them off.

Returning to her, our hands run wild again when our mouths meld into a deep kiss, our tongues twisting around one another. We take a few seconds to soak in our kiss, only to part. I glance down to ensure the condom is on correctly, and I feel teeth scraping down my neck, only to latch onto some skin and bite.

"Fuck," I growl, but my grin doesn't fade, even when she sucks and sinks her teeth tighter. "You're a bad girl. Next time it will be extra spankings."

She throws her head back in laughter. "It's not punishment if I enjoy it, Holden," she taunts.

With my cock in one hand aligning to her center, my palm lands on my stinging neck. "Is this payback for going hard the other night?"

"Does it matter? Now fuck me."

She's my undoing. A perfect quick fuck, even if she leaves me longing for another round.

I enter her while our mouths steal each other's breath, moaning in sync from her pussy clenching around my cock. A few slow pumps, but then I'm at it like a wild animal, only encouraged by her legs wrapping tighter around me and the desk shaking on every thrust.

"Is this how you like it? Hard? Your craving pussy has been desperate for my cock since last time."

"Yes," she whispers.

"You touch yourself when I'm not around? Thinking of my cock?" I lock our eyes because I would be able to see a lie.

The corner of her mouth twitches. "Yes."

Slamming my lips down onto hers again, I bring her closer to my body until we are tightly wound and pumping together.

More. I need her deeper and to make her whimper.

"Come all over my cock, Lexi. Get what you fantasize about," I breathe into her neck as heat explodes in my body, traveling down to my navel, and I know what's impending.

My thumb finds her clit to help her ride the wave with me, and we both get what we need until it leaves us draped around one another with panting breaths.

"If that was a thank-you then I'm scared what will happen if I disobey." Her voice is a labored breath.

I chortle a growl. "You'll figure it out soon enough," I warn.

Because I'm adding another round with her. Not sure when, but it's on the horizon.

"Get me naked next time, will ya?"

Her snark makes me scoff. I wonder if she ever has a moment where she's anything but a woman who takes things in stride with a smile.

Pulling out, I head to the bathroom to get rid of the condom, knowing damn well that I'm late for a meeting with the hotel manager for filling in her closing paperwork, with information for when she leaves.

It seems Lexi is also in a hurry. We both begin to throw on the few clothes that we took off. I should probably explain why I stormed in here.

"Hey, Lexi," I grab her attention, and she glances up from tucking her shirt into her skirt. "Thanks again. With Harry, I mean."

Her smile is simple. "No big deal." Because kindness is imprinted in her personality, so it's a normal day for her, I guess.

"I should get going," she says.

"Me too."

Then that's us.

A quick tryst, complete with no regrets.

"I'll head out and give you a second," I say.

Lexi doesn't seem to know what to say or do. "Yeah, sure, great."

I grin at her because she's kind of cute when flustered.

Leaving, I open the door, ensuring nobody gets a view of Lexi just royally fucked. I'm straightening my collar, feeling a little flushed myself.

"Holden?" I hear Stone's voice.

I glance up and freeze then gulp. "Oh, hey there."

"Uh, what are you doing?" He cocks his head to the side, and his face is puzzled. "Did someone bite your neck?"

Damn, that's a giveaway. I'll need to hide the evidence later.

I clear my throat as I cover the mark for a second, feeling the broken skin. "Just… a meeting."

"You know I'm not buying that." He grins as he leans against the wall, crossing his arms, waiting for a better explanation.

I do my best to avoid his gaze, and my jaw flexes, but he's a good friend, so what the hell. "You know how we have that new interior designer for the hotel?"

"To get rid of that ridiculous moose head, yeah. Lexi, your former coach's daughter."

I tightly smile. "Exactly. I might have…"

The door swings open right on cue. "I'm off, need to meet with the tile guy." Lexi is smoothing her blouse, completely oblivious to our spectator. Then she stops in her tracks.

"Oh, hi." She frowns.

"You remember Stone?" I awkwardly ask, because of course they know one another, even ran into each other a few days ago.

"Yeah, for sure." She attempts to give him a polite smile. "Nice to see you again. I'm not here. Have a great day." She is quick to walk away.

Shit, forgot to ask something about the kids. "Don't forget that my daughter has figure skating practice after school," I call out.

She mumbles a sound and doesn't even give me any attention. "It's Tuesday, so she doesn't, and how many times do I have to remind you that I'm not your nanny?"

"Yeah, but that was the deal when you moved in," I remind her.

She grumbles again before disappearing into the elevator.

My lips push out, and my head tilts because, damn it, despite these circumstances, I still have time to check out her ass. I'm not even trying to hide it. I swing my tight smile to Stone, and he still seems to enjoy my quandary.

"Someone has something to explain."

A long breath escapes me. "I might have... blackmailed her into living with me for a bit."

His eyes bug out. "Wow, she's really getting the five-star treatment on the personal-attention front."

I rub my face. "*Yeah*, so we might be encountering a little problem with that..."

"As in..." He encourages me to continue.

"I didn't exactly blackmail her, more a favor owed. We lost another nanny and needed some help. Not my fault Lexi tried to buy alcohol way back, and she needed Prince Charming to save her. Alas, favor now owed."

"So, she's living with you?" Stone seems confused, as he should be.

I bobble my head side to side. "Yeah. Just to help out every now and then until I can find another solution for my lovely kids."

He gives me a knowing look. "Just so happens you added other favors..."

I laugh to myself. "Can you blame me? She has good banter, and she's hot. We both know what it is. Nothing around the kids either. It's just some fun. I need to destress, and she's the golden ticket."

Stone brings his fingers to his jaw, thinking for a hard long second. "Uh... I give it a few weeks before this blows up in your face. You don't let women around Lori and Harry. Let alone take up residence in the guesthouse."

Shit. My face stills, and I say nothing.

The problem with close friends is they see straight through you. "Yes?" It drags out.

"Guest *room*, the guest room," I correct him, and his eyes widen. "Water problem in the guesthouse."

"Really? This just got complicated. The only way this could get worse is if you turned off the water on purpose or something." He huffs a laugh.

And face freezing moment number two.

Stone's jaw drops. "No fucking way. You turned off the water, didn't you?"

I step forward. "Keep your voice down," I hush him as I scan the hall. "That part she doesn't know."

"Are you a little psychotic? I mean, we've all known that you have wild ways. You're the guy who hands out candy to the kids and alcoholic beverages to the parents during trick-or-treating. You're also an impulsive guy. But why the hell would you do that?" He raises his voice.

I comb my hands through my hair. "Honestly? No clue, other than that woman seems to have possessed me to do crazy things. Hence, why I called in a favor due to a ridiculous bar napkin. And her appeal doesn't exactly lose any points either."

Stone blinks his eyes a few times. "Seriously, Holden, first-glance connections can raise a flag of caution to what you think is a simple situation. Harlow and I were an instant attraction, and here I am with a fiancée."

I take us out of my lecture. "Fiancée, eh? That's great, man." I knew he was going to ask soon; I guess the time came.

He looks elated. "Yeah, she said yes." He sounds so happy, but then his look falters. "Now back to you. This is my warning that feelings are brewing behind a wall that you didn't realize you have. On the other hand..." His lips quirk out. "You seem kind of content despite your hooligans stressing you out. I'm also assuming you've thought about the kids, so… why not. Have fun with whatever odd game this is." Stone gives up.

I rub my temples. "I should consider your sound wisdom… but I won't. Let me ride this situation out while I ride her. When it begins to get gray, then we'll bench this and be done. We can be friends. She and I both know the score."

"Sure, you do." He doesn't sound convinced.

My phone dings, and I bring the screen up to see that I'm five minutes late because I'm standing in a hall discussing my predicament that I think I'm kind of addicted to.

I've always been a little reckless, and it's been a damn while since I've allowed myself to enjoy that trait.

"Really gotta head out. Tell Harlow congrats." I begin to walk away.

"Will do. Let me know when you need a beer to reflect on your situation like a normal human soul," he calls out.

I flex my neck before straightening my shoulders. "It will be fine."

My phone chimes again, and this time I see a calendar reminder for an upcoming business dinner. They are really into making it a family affair, hence why they want Lori and Harry present.

That might be a headache.

So let me just add asking Lexi to attend as another checkmark on my list of things I probably shouldn't do but will.

‌

10

LEXI

Fumbling with the keys in my bag, I'm only aware that someone is behind me from the crunching of gravel on the ground of the Dizzy Duck parking lot.

"Where do you think you're going?" Holden is messing with me.

"Not that it's any of your business—okay, it might be, but I'm heading to an antique store about thirty minutes from here. It's only open a few days a week, and today just happens to be one of them." *Got them* I pull my keys out and turn to Holden who is smirking under this bright day with a cold nip that hits your skin with a chill.

Lines form on his forehead. "Really? For the Dizzy Duck?"

"No, my billion-dollar house on a tropical island," I deadpan.

He scoffs. "Can't believe you never told me about that. Kind of brokenhearted that you haven't given me an invite." For theatrics, he brings his palm to his heart.

My smile spreads wider as I move away from our playful chat. "But yes, for the inn."

Holden glances at his watch. "How long do you think you'll be?"

"Hmm, I don't know. Probably two hours or so, depends on what I find."

He steps forward and snatches my key fob. "Great. I have time, so let me drive us there."

I take in this change of events. "Drive us?"

He's already heading toward his SUV, expecting me to follow as he pulls his key out of his pocket and hits the unlock button without so much as checking over his shoulder. And, well, I've learned that I'm weak when it comes to his surprise plans.

"Antique stores are a new realm for me, and I have a bigger trunk if you want something. Plus, if it's for the inn, wouldn't you want my credit card?"

All logical. No way to counter.

"Valid points." I eagerly open the passenger side door.

The engine revs up, and he begins to press buttons on the dashboard. "Address, please."

I swipe my phone screen to draw up the address and show him, then he types everything in to the GPS. Off we go, and I'm still trying to grasp what the mood is between us. Friends with benefits means said friend can accompany you on one of your favorite activities, right?

"It's in an old barn that the owners spruced up. We most definitely don't need them, but they even have old wagons and barrels." My voice is cheerful to bring us to neutral topics.

Holden chuckles under his breath. "Then into the cornfields we go."

"Could be wheat," I quip, and his head turns slightly in my direction, clearly amused. To avoid his eyes, I glance out the window and stare at the woods that circle the lake. The duck-crossing sign reminds me of this quaint town that is a special place for many. "Actually, Illinois is 75% farmland."

"Someone is studious."

"Nah, I just wondered once when I left the suburbs to see an old college friend and boredom kicked in after thirty miles with no change of scene. Unless you get off a highway and go to a small town that is along a river or freight railroad track. There is, of course, Route 66 which has its quirks."

He laughs as he keeps his hands steady on the wheel. "Ah, so you were a nerd by day and party girl by night all those years ago."

My head lolls to the side against the headrest to appraise him. "Eight years ago, to be exact, that's when you got your favor napkin, and yes, I'm highlighting that you're older yet not wiser," I joke.

"Watch it. I'm beginning to tally how many spankings you'll get next time."

Sprinkles of anticipation begin to burst throughout my body. "Looking forward to it."

The corners of his mouth tug in approval. "Let's focus on this drive, shall we?"

"Agreed." Otherwise, we might not make it there without stopping for a quickie in the back of his car.

Another half-hour goes by until we're driving onto the grass and dirt parking lot where only two other cars are stationed. We both hop out and walk side by side. Holden with curiosity and me feeling like a kid in a candy store.

My sight lands on the outside stand selling fresh carrots and asparagus. "Yum. What are the chances your kids would like those?"

"About 25%, maybe 45% if we slather a bunch of butter on it."

I swat his arm. "Then we shall try." Speeding up my walk, I beeline it to the wagon with fresh apples and glass bottles of cider. This is fantastic, we can use the bottles after the cider is finished.

Holden watches with a blank look. "Didn't we come here for antiques in the large barn?" He steps forward and places his hand under my elbow to guide me away.

Throwing my finger over my shoulder, I reluctantly give up on my crusade, though I still point out the obvious. "But there's jam." I pout.

"Damn, you are like a woman possessed."

He manages to lead us, and we enter the barn where my exhilaration grows. Right away, I spot a few pieces that would be ideal for the inn. It doesn't take long for me to find myself next to a dresser, and my palm slides against the wood.

"This would be great for the large suite." I bend down to inspect further. "Need to re-sand and then paint it white, but it's perfect."

My eyes are unable to tear away from the furniture, but a blurry vision in my side eye shows me Holden picking up a jar and examining it purely to keep his hands busy.

"But there is only one, and we have several rooms," he points out.

I stand up, with my elation never fading on my face. "It doesn't matter, as each of the large suites will have their own feel. We're not going to be cookie-cutter, as every room will be distinctly different."

He sets the jar down, clearly entertained with my enthusiasm. "Who will be sanding it?"

"Me," I state proudly.

"You?"

My exploration goes on, and now it's Holden being tugged along. "Yes. I sand and upholster all the time. I can even use a hammer."

He hisses a whistle. "Oh, hammering I'm aware you can do."

I throw him a fun glare. "Shall we focus?"

"How? You're all over the place. I'm scared you'll tell me the chest over there is the key to real treasure."

My eyes widen, and then I nearly run. "This one is great." I'm serious.

"Really?" His voice is unsure.

"Of course. Place it at the end of a bed." I set my hand on the curve of his shoulder. "You have great ideas," I add.

His face is purely confused. "I don't sense sarcasm in that." Holden pretends to search around him. "I should probably take you down a notch. Make out with you behind the long mirror over there?"

I step forward, coming face to face with Holden, calming down as my fingers gently crawl up his shirt along his chest. "Could be an option," I say, my sultry voice in full swing. Another step and his body rises to attention, and if we're not careful then his cock will join in. But then I drop the cruelty of leading him along by patting his chest before I return to business. "There are 1920's light fixtures over there, perfect for candles."

Holden groans and steps back. "Don't test me, Lexi. We have an entire ride back, and if we get bored of farmland, then we can stop so I can fuck you in the backseat."

I titter as I survey further. "So inappropriate, in public and in the presence of our elders too," I tease.

He laughs. "I don't think I'm ever going to forget today. On a scale of ridiculous yet entertaining, this, well…" His voice softens the end of his sentence, and it raises my attention, only to see a glint in his eyes. "It's nice. My mind has kind of shut off, and it's been a while."

Trapping my bottom lip between my teeth, I try to dissect his words and what they really mean. "I guess you've been busy with life," I begin, and he nods subtly once. "You're welcome. I guess this is an odd outing. There's even Amish furniture over in that corner that they brought up from central Illinois." I bounce my shoulders as I try to lighten the mood of his realization.

Our eyes hold, in a moment that lets go of the back and forth of our constant wit, and instead, we're soaking in a new atmosphere between us. But it's dangerous, and I'm not even sure that I've blinked.

"Well, how does this work?" Oh, he's going right into the *us* discussion. I nearly lose my balance. "Do we just pay and they can deliver?" A tinge of disappointment hits me when I realize he meant logistics of our outing.

"Uhm." I tuck a few strands behind my ear. "Yeah, we can do that." My returning smile might appear pleasant, but it feels weak to me. "But the asparagus, tomatoes, cider, and jam, plus the homemade bread that I saw, we can take in the car."

"Casually threw in the jam, didn't you?"

We're back to normal us. How we can already have a normal when it's only been two weeks since I entered his life? I'm not quite sure, but I've always been one to ride the flow between people. I'll just continue that.

———

TWO DAYS later after avoiding the man of the week, I return to Holden's for the day. The cleaner is exiting the front door after she finished her weekly visit, and her intense study of me is a bit daunting. I'm relieved with a faint line on her mouth appears before she moves on without any use of words.

"Goodbye to you too," I mumble.

I really need a snack; an afternoon boost is always key to continuing the day. The view of Harry working on his homework is a welcome scene.

"How's my favorite scientist?" I greet him.

His sight jumps up once before he returns to writing in his notebook. "Not bad. Math is too easy. We're working on decimals, but I've been a pro already for a year. I have stocks to maintain."

"What?" I sputter out.

"My stocks," he tells me, as if I'm an idiot.

"Can kids even buy stocks?" I'm now bewildered.

He shrugs. "Not exactly, but my dad set them up, and I just do the heavy work. A bummer that the NASDAQ has been down for two days."

My jaw drops open because this is a complete shock, and I mouth *what the fuck* to myself. What ten-year-old talks finance?

Shaking my head, I make a note to check the internet later about this phenomenon. My eyes drift down to where he's writing. "Cool, kids are still using a notebook these days."

He continues to write. "Oh, don't worry, this is only a list of companies that I'm interested in investing in if the dollar-euro exchange rate picks up. At school, we have to hand all homework in via our portal app. We're entirely digital. I mean, why would you use paper for that?" He shakes his head.

Holy shit, I feel ancient.

I can't handle that realization, and it's going to take a few hours before I recognize that I'm staying with a whiz kid. This calls for a granola bar, a mini cake in a package, and I might throw in a small bag of crackers too.

Holden enters the kitchen, scruffing Harry's hair in passing. "What's up, kids?"

"You seem far too happy for my liking, there must be a catch." Lori arrives with her mundane tone, expressing that she heard her father.

Holden gives her a contrite smile. "And what if I am, no catch?"

Lori's eyes swim between Holden and me, trying to connect dots perhaps as her nose rises slightly before she drops her demeanor when she glances down at her phone.

Holden arrives next to me while I rip open a snack cake. "Your son has stocks," I say dryly.

His smile is beaming. "Great, huh? In a few years he can probably handle my entire portfolio." Is Holden joking? I'm not sure.

"Right. So, uhm, hey, the delivery from the antique barn arrived." I survey the room and feel that leaving to get another round of fresh air seems like the way to go. "Tomorrow I'll be sanding, so I'm going to run to the hardware store to pick up gloves and a sander. You guys have a yummy dinner."

"You're not joining us?" Does Holden sound kind of disappointed or am I losing my mind?

"Nah, I'm dying for a little quiet time to search the latest blogs for trends while I gulp down a milkshake and maybe throw in a salad."

He stuffs his hands into his pocket. "Oh, yeah, sure. Quiet time."

"Yep. Off I go." My feet are glued to the wood while Holden and I are stuck in a trance.

"Completely ready to get in my car and check off that list."

Blinking a few times, he blows out a breath. "Let me walk you out. I may need to move my car so you can back up. Not enough space maybe."

"Of course." My lips twitch, as I'm not sure how to act right now with extra pairs of eyes on me.

My awkward attempt to leave leads us outside, staring at my car, both of us with hands in our pockets, me in a coat and Holden in jeans. "I guess the cars are good. I did get home after you, as you were well aware of back in the kitchen," I note.

We both continue to look straight forward at our cars. "I did perhaps know that."

A long pause again, the fifth now, but who's counting?

"I heard the ducks are a killer this time of day." *Yikes*, I realize what I just said. "I mean, not that we want to kill the ducks. Or rather they aren't getting killed, just they overpower the roads in the masses, and we have to stop every quarter of a mile because they normally travel with baby ducks as a family," I ramble.

"Yep, those ducks." His tone is neutral.

I roll my eyes because this conversation is a cover for other things.

"Lexi?"

"Yes, housemaster?" My tone is simple.

Even after our assurance that our cars haven't moved, our standstill continues. "I want to kiss you right now and bend you over the hood of your car."

I chortle. "Thought so. Because I'm sure you've read my mind."

"Another time then."

"Indeed, another time. Not when we have little eyes at the window behind us." The one moment I slightly tilted my head to the side, I saw them in my vision.

He chuckles. "Thought that would be the case. Have fun enjoying your moment of solitude."

"I'm beginning to think solitude is overrated."

That is what breaks our standoff, and we at last turn to one another with wry smiles.

"My chaos of a life is growing on you." He tries to suppress his smile.

"Maybe." Because truly I am unsure, or rather scared that he is right.

His lips push out, and he thinks for a moment. "Be careful. And that's a warning to us both."

HOLDEN

I watch Stuart behind the front desk opening boxes with a box cutter. I'm not sure what surprise will be in this box.

The lobby is looking great, and in the banquet hall, the floors were spruced up with polish, which meant we had to use the patio doors by the restaurant to let the few guests we have in. It's not exactly an issue since the view of the dock and lake are some of the best in Lake Spark, unless you're hiking up in the small hills. But now with the floors done and the walls receiving a new paint color, I imagine furniture can be placed by the end of the week.

Lexi has been busy, which is why we haven't seen one another much the past few days, which is strange considering she's in my guest room. That's probably for the best, so my brain and dick can cool down.

"I think these are sheets," he guesses.

I assess the contents of the box and see the packaged linens. White with a lace pattern. Huh, not my choice, but I will trust the designer's take, as I promised before I realized my interior designer was a woman who sucks cock well.

The sound of two women giggling hits my ears. I glance up to see Lexi gently touching Summer's arm as they walk into the lobby.

"Oh, hey." Lexi smiles when her eyes lift up to greet me.

I step in their direction as Lexi twists her hair and uses the elastic around her wrist to tie it back. Summer… just observes me with a crooked smile. Of course, she knows what new hobby I've started.

"What are you ladies up to?" I play it cool and pull out my phone to have a quick peek and to appear calm and cool.

Summer clears her throat. "Lexi was just showing me one of the finished bedrooms, then we stole a cookie or two that just came from the oven. I love how, hammers aside, the Dizzy Duck is still upholding their fresh warm cookie tradition."

Actually, she doesn't seem to be covering up what they were probably talking about… me. They probably did nab a cookie.

Lexi and I share a gaze again, with our eyes lingering for a few seconds. "There are…" I scratch the back of my neck. "Sheets that arrived."

Her fingers drop from her ponytail, and she claps her hands together in excitement. "That was fast."

"Dated the hotel sheet supplier too?" I quip.

Summer looks between us, and her lips roll in to keep her laugh in.

Lexi doesn't seem fazed by my comment. "Nah, the woman on the other end mentioned you two go way back, so thanks for that," she rebuffs.

Love her little fabrications. It always leads to her face creating a portrait of pure trouble.

"Lucky us then. Anyhow, we need to talk sheets."

Both the women's brows furrow. "I think this is my cue to leave," Summer awkwardly mentions.

I turn my attention to Summer, ignoring the atmosphere that is boiling into a need for me to push Lexi against a wall. "Have you thought more about that job? To be honest, I doubt I'm going to get anyone new in the coming month or two. The job market is slow around here."

"I'm still in the appraisal of staff treatment phase, but thanks, Holden, for keeping me in mind." She smiles warmly at me.

"Any time."

"Well, bye, you two. Good luck with whatever is going… I mean, sheets. Have fun with serious sheet discussion."

I grin. "Towels are somewhere in that conversation too."

Summer smiles then leaves us be. Lexi and I watch her walk away, but the feeling of Lexi's arm grazing mine brings my thoughts back to her.

"I might give her a good recommendation on your boss skills in your effort to recruit," she mentions. I choose not to answer, and I press my lips together as a long pause floats between us. "So, sheets? Is there a problem?" She trails away.

"They're white," I say bluntly as I follow her behind the desk.

"And? You've signed off on it. White with colored pillows. What's wrong?"

I watch her examining a package. "I do trust you, but can't you see every little thing on white?"

"As in?" She stares at me, waiting for an explanation. "A lot of hotels use white. Makeup comes off in the housekeeping laundry, and if red wine is spilled then we have backups. The mood is more important than concern for wine or any other bodily fluid, if that's where your mind is at."

The painter walking by coughs into his arm, clearly having heard. I turn slightly to ensure nobody else is in an earshot then give Lexi a warning grimace, but she seems not very concerned.

"You just took us down a very inappropriate route."

She smiles tightly as she crosses her arms over her chest. "And you love it." I roll my eyes. "But seriously, is this really an issue? The curtains will match the throw pillows, as will the candles. That's going to be a great splash of color."

"Candles in bedrooms, as in a hotel room?" My voice nearly breaks. "That's a fire hazard that I'm not sure we can get rid of."

"No, Holden, those are the touches couples want when they stay here for an expensive room and romance. This isn't a big hotel, and although there are many great things here, such as the spa and lake, it's still a boutique hotel, and as such should have the qualities of a traditional inn, even with a cabin feel, including candlelight. This is the land of Lincoln and prairies, after all."

"Okay, fine." I give up on our discussion. "You have some valid points."

"Great." Her bubbly voice returns. She kicks the box to slide it along the floor. "I'll ask one of the guys to move this to the design headquarters, otherwise known as the spare bedroom of indecency, which is an HR nightmare should I work here on a regular basis."

Her wit never fades, and I love that.

"I would offer to carry the box, but I need to change and head to Catch 22." The other great restaurant in Lake Spark. It may not have won awards, but it's still a decent evening that is worthy of frequent visits.

Lines form on her forehead. "Eating at the competition again?"

I chuckle and pull my phone out of my pocket to keep myself occupied with checking my inbox. "I don't want to show this place until the final touches are in place. It's a meeting with an old sponsor, he's in hotel development. Old money who potentially wants to invest in opening an inn similar to the Dizzy Duck elsewhere. He wants to have dinner with my kids included, as he seems to be into wholesome and doubts a former pro-athlete is on the straight and narrow. I thought of asking you to come but then realized that I'm pushing the limits on the not-a-nanny quota."

Her laugh sounds good. How can anyone not enjoy the melody? "That's very true. Could be a great opportunity for you, and if you need an interior designer…" She splays her hands out.

"You'll be the first I ask," I assure her.

Her eyes glint at me, unsure of where to carry our conversation. She slouches a bit as she ponders her thoughts. "I don't want to intervene, so it's better that you bring your very-well-behaved offspring who most definitely will not be bored at the dinner."

I groan at the reminder of my wonderful children who I adore but know this might not be easy. "Thanks." I recoil.

"I kind of want to have an early night, as there's a flea market tomorrow between here and Bluetop."

My lips push out as I understand her logic. "Sure, of course." I'm still slightly disappointed, though. "If you change your mind, then well…"

"I know." Lexi takes a step forward to touch my arm. "Good luck, Holden. My fingers are crossed for you."

"For the meeting or my kids?"

"Both."

Her smile as she parts from our encounter is so incredibly platonic and caring. Because despite her wicked ways, she has heart. Not often do you come across that combination.

———

WE'RE SITTING at Catch 22 next to the big windows, displaying the dark sky, as we pass around a basket of bread. I glance to my side to see my kids less than pleased to be here. They've dressed up when all they want is to be in jeans, and they're counting down in their head until this dinner will be over. This isn't the first time we've done this. I used to have a lot of meetings with sponsors, but now they're a little older, so saying they can play on their tablets while the adults talk doesn't exactly work.

Ordering their kiddie cocktails with extra cherries only brought me five seconds of hope.

I get it. I do.

I'm able to give them a great life through love… but also money that provides them many things.

"Into hockey, Harry?" John Colbie asks my son. John is in his sixties and as honest and genuine as you can get. That's how I've always remembered him. He's very much a family man, too.

Harry looks up almost in fear of disappointment. "No. I enjoy music."

"Ah, music isn't half bad. It's never too late to start ho—" His attention hops up to behind me.

"Sorry I'm late, I told Holden I couldn't make it but moved some things around." Lexi's voice and her hand landing on the back of my chair is a welcome relief.

When I turn to smile my appreciation, I bite my lip. Because she arrived in a dark red sweater dress with knee-high boots. It's completely appropriate, but the shape of the fit captures the attention of every man sitting in this room.

A bombshell with snark. Lucky me.

Now it's not just my kids counting down the time until this dinner is complete.

12

LEXI

I shouldn't involve myself. I shouldn't even be here. I most definitely need to tamp down my free spirit that seems to want to explore situations that I've never been in.

Still, I'm standing behind Holden with a polite smile coating my face for a man across the table as old as my dad, and Lori and Harry are staring at me peculiarly from around the circular table. But when Holden offers me a faint smile, a mixture of surprise and gratitude, then I know why I'm here. He didn't ask outright, but I could sense that this night might be better for him if I was here. Such a crazy impression considering whatever we're doing.

"Lexi." Holden stands, ready to offer introductions. "John, this is Lexi, our interior designer at the Dizzy Duck. I thought she would be a useful addition to the discussion and your ideas." Holden pulls the chair between him and Harry out like a gentleman, multi-tasking while indicating to the waiter for an extra wine glass for me. Holden and John already opened a bottle and are halfway through a glass of white.

"It's so nice to have you join us. I can't wait to see the end result at the Dizzy Duck. I hear there will be a big grand opening. Holden did share some preliminary photos, and I enjoy what I see." John seems pleasant. I could imagine Lori and Harry wouldn't find him riveting, but these days some folks just brush off any extras to the conversation in favor to talk purely business.

"I'm sure you must be excited for the prospect of another inn. Will it have a spa too?" I attempt to insert myself into the conversation, but really, I am interested too.

Holden's eyes find their way back to me. "No spa, but he mentioned a pool. He wants it to be more family friendly."

"You should have human-sized Jenga blocks," Harry pipes up.

"As opposed to alien-sized blocks? We're all human," Lori snipes.

Holden smiles nervously. "I think what Harry means is large, outside-sized blocks," he attempts, to defuse his kids' bickering.

John chuckles. "That's a great idea, Harry. This is why I wanted you here. I have a lot of grandkids, but they all live out in Colorado."

"Well, wonderful kids are here," Holden gushes. He has hard times with them, but he also relishes every moment he's in. That's the balance of fatherhood, right?

My wine glass arrives, and Holden pours from the bottle. I take a sip, noting to pace myself, since I drove here. "Don't let my arrival disrupt wherever you were discussing," I say. I use taking a sip of my drink as a cover for the fact that there are fingers swirling over my thigh under the table—fingers that aren't mine. A pleasurable ache spreads down my skin.

"We should talk about timelines of what you're thinking," Holden suggests to John.

"I'll be back, going to the bathroom," Lori excuses herself, and nobody takes much notice.

I wink at Harry who picks at his bread roll out of boredom. Grabbing the basket next to him, I offer him one more, but he shakes his head to decline. More for me, I'm a little famished. I search for the butter because who wants a bread roll without it?

"A year and half could maybe be realistic, depending on the

construction," Holden discusses, and I clearly missed part of the conversation.

"Are you building from the ground up?" I wonder, as that's quite a project.

John shakes his head. "Oh no, dear, I'm on the search for a historical property. It will probably need a lot of renovations."

My whole body lights up. "Historical buildings are the best for charm. But you mentioned family friendly, which means you would for sure need to be cautious of interior choices."

"No candles in bedrooms," Holden volleys.

My sight whips in his direction, and a mischievous smile ghosts on his face, with his eyes narrowing on me, almost a message to prepare myself for being devoured or spanked later.

They continue their conversation, and after a few more minutes, I notice that Lori has been gone a while. Probably made an escape. Still, I should probably check, as John and Holden seem to be lost in numbers.

I quietly excuse myself and make my way to the restroom. When I open the door, it's quiet, too quiet considering I didn't come across Lori on my travels here. Walking in, I check the lock signs by the knobs of the stalls and see all are open except one. Bending over, I see Lori's shoes and hear a sniffle.

Oh no. Tears. I don't do well with tears. It makes me either cry like a waterfall or become dry as an alligator. There is no middle ground. It always depends on the person.

I bring my knuckles to the door. "Knock, knock, the houseguest I haven't figured out if you like or hate is here," I announce.

"Go away," she says, her voice muffled.

My face screws up, aware that I'm going to have to reach her chip by chip. "No can do. The table conversation is kind of boring, and you seem to have found a great hiding place."

"It's a toilet," she deadpans.

Well, her mood is still the same. That's a start.

"I might as well freshen up my makeup. Want some lipstick?" I offer and meander to the mirror to color my lips.

"Your lipstick doesn't match my dress."

I twist up the stick. "Good point. I ordered the chicken Alfredo. You ordered before I got here. Did you order that or go for the chicken breast with potato?"

"Go away." Her voice is even more disgruntled.

"Not a good idea if I do. Otherwise, I have to tell your dad that you're crying in the bathroom—"

"Don't," she cuts me off.

My eyes meet my reflection in the mirror, congratulating myself for grabbing her attention enough that I can stay. "Okay, then are you not feeling well?"

It's a long silence, but then I hear the click of her door, and it opens slightly. I turn my body to see what her next move is, but nothing happens.

"Do you… you… have something?"

I step forward. "Uh, what do you mean?"

"Something. You know, *something*."

I circle my eyes as I try to decode, and then it hits me. "Oh, I—yeah." I begin to search my purse. "I think I have a tampon."

"I…" Lori sounds petrified.

Then it dawns on me again. "Is this your first time by chance?"

Another sniffle, and I have my answer. I flinch and my body tightens. It's her first period and she's stuck with me in a bathroom. I wasn't prepared for this, nor was she.

"I think it's better if we get you a pad, let me think." I'm beginning to panic because I don't see anything around. Stay calm, Lexi. Do it for the almost thirteen-year-old who is going through a major life event. "I know." I lift a finger in the air. "Let's break out of this place. I have my car here, and we'll tend to important matters instead of listening to an old guy talk about hotel stuff."

The door to her stall opens even further, and her red face seems to accept that this is our only option, and she nods gently.

A line stretches on my mouth in support for her before I search my bag for the key to my car. "Here." I hand it to her.

"Please… don't tell him why we're leaving."

I zip my lips with my fingers. "I won't," I promise.

Okay, it seems the waterfall tears want to form, but I remain defiant and hold them in for her, and she snatches the keys and walks away. This is a big moment for her, and she must be scared. There isn't a woman in her life, but somehow the universe decided it should be shared with me.

Once I can't see Lori, I let out a deep breath that I think I need because I'm surprised we both survived that scene.

Gathering myself for a few ticks, I head straight back to the table.

Holden looks at me with concern and seems to be searching for Lori. "Where is my daughter?"

I lean down with one hand on the back of his chair and the other on the table to ensure I'm only in his earshot. "I think this is a perfect guys' night. Lori and I will be leaving."

"She hasn't even had dinner yet?" Holden doesn't sound pleased.

I smile tightly to him. "Trust me, okay?" I mumble under my breath. His brows lift, not impressed. "Holden, we're leaving." I'm firm in my tone that only he can hear.

He examines my face, only to read the message in my eyes that I'm putting my foot down and he has no choice but to accept it. "Sure. I'll bring home a doggy bag."

I stand and give the table a wide smile. "Forgotten homework, right?" I lift my shoulders.

"It's Saturday," Harry points out.

Geez, can anyone at this table just let it go?

"John, although brief, it was nice to meet you. I'm sure we will cross paths again."

He stands and sets his napkin on the table. "Of course. I'll be sure to get your details from Holden."

I smile in appreciation and turn, only to lock eyes one last time with Holden who has an unusual stare that's new to me.

It's fine. He should enjoy his dinner because I have a feeling he might freak out later.

I FIDDLE my thumbs as I lean over the kitchen counter when I hear Holden and Harry arrive home.

"Head upstairs, and I'll say goodnight soon," I hear him tell his son, followed by feet thumping up the stairs.

I dread what's coming, but Holden will figure it out. My eyes lift when he slowly saunters my way, half pissed and the other half lost.

"You owe me a few explanations. That was one abrupt exit for an important meeting. What has my daughter done now?"

I grab the bottle of wine that I had opened and drag it my way, but then second-guess myself and slide it in Holden's direction and pour him a glass, as he will need it at the ready.

"She started her period," I mention as I close the bottle.

Holden's eyes flutter, and he seems to be registering the information. "Excuse me, she what?"

Okay, disbelief it is.

"Holden." I circle around the island to be close to him because a counter seems too much distance for us. "You know what I said."

He grabs the glass and takes a gulp of wine before setting it down and hissing a breath as he claws his hair. "The time has come."

I nod in understanding. "It seems it has."

He blinks a few times, taking in the fact that his little girl is growing up. "I knew this was coming, I just wasn't expecting it now. I'm kind of unready and surprised here."

I touch his arm to ensure he connects his eyes with me. "Then imagine how she's feeling."

"What the fuck do I do? I'm not prepared. Do I need to go upstairs and talk to her? Throw her party to welcome her to no longer being my little girl?" He's all over the place, as expected.

My hands skim up to square his shoulders to me, and I squeeze the curve of his muscles to assure him. "I took care of it, and if you need to add buying supplies next month to your grocery list then so be it. That's life."

He attempts to escape my hold. "I should talk—"

"*Noooo.*" I shut that down right away. "Just let her have some space tonight, and tomorrow it's a normal day. She wanted me to tell you, and I have."

Another sigh leaves his lips. "Okay, normal day. Yeah, I can do that. I can totally do that." He peps himself up.

I look at him with skepticism. "Really?" My tone is flat. "You're eyeing the wine bottle wondering where you put the whiskey. I can read your mind."

At last, he scoffs a sound of calm. "That's right… Want to have a drink with me?"

"I want my doggy bag actually. Lori and I just ate ice cream, and I need my Alfredo."

His face drops. "Oh shit, I knew I forgot something."

"Tell me you didn't." Ugh.

A grin stretches on his face again. "Nah, but messing with you is a relief right now."

I swat his arm, only for him to catch my attempt. His hand wraps around my wrist to hold up with warmth in his eyes.

"Lexi…"

"Yeah," I rasp.

"Thank you. I'm happy… that you're here. I would have been lost."

"It's nothing."

He crooks the fingers of his other hand and captures my chin before tipping my nose up to give him a perfect canvas. His lips lowering onto mine feels different.

Overpowering yet tender.

It isn't lust but instead a moment with significance behind it.

Holden presses down to suck my air before his mouth seizes my upper lip, softening the kiss. A light feathery feeling floats through my body, sending sensitive ripples from my toes all the way up.

Breaking away, his teeth scrape along my bottom lip. I feel it in my bones that this isn't a normal kiss. When he nuzzles my nose with his, it dawns on me that this is slow. The kind of kiss that leaves you entranced for days.

He reluctantly backs away, still keeping his finger under my jaw. "Truly thank you. You're..." he whispers, and although he doesn't finish his sentence, it feels as though we are on a new line.

A slow chip to a layer that we said we wouldn't cross.

After all, we both know what our attraction only is, right?

HOLDEN

I kissed her like it matters.

I know I did.

But it's not a complication. Is it? Now I need to focus on Lori who is about to come down the stairs for breakfast. I remind myself to stay calm and collected. Play it cool. Lexi is near, casually sipping her tea, and Harry pulls out a donut from the box.

The sound of Lori's steps approaching feels daunting, but I've mentally been preparing myself for this all night.

She looks at me warily, but I decide to jump right in. "*So…* it's morning." I have no clue why I just said that, but if it sounds like I'm nervous, it's because I am.

Lexi gently touches my elbow. "I think she knows that."

Lori grabs a donut from the box. "Why do we have donuts? Normally we have donuts on Saturdays."

"I know, but two days in a row is fine. I went this morning to Jolly Joe's to pick them up, they're fresh." Because I couldn't sleep. I clap my hands together. "You know what? Today we'll make peanut butter and jelly cheesecake."

Harry perks up. "Awesome, donuts and cake in the same day."

"Well, the cheesecake needs to be in the fridge overnight, so not exactly all today," I correct him.

Lori stares at me blankly, waiting for whatever blunder might come out of my mouth next.

"How about tomorrow? I'll just let school know that you'll be off for a few days."

The flare of fury erupts on my daughter's face. "Stop acting weird." I try to get us back to normal morning routine, and I drink my mug of coffee. "I'm a woman now, okay?" She's defensive, and I nearly choke on my hot brew.

Lexi intervenes. "Well, I think Harry and your dad can make that cake and you and I can get out of the house while your dad… *adjusts*." She gawks at me as a warning to get it the fuck together.

Harry's eyes dance between us all. "Why is everyone acting strange?"

I pinch the bridge of nose, miserably failing at this morning. "Doesn't matter, buddy."

Lori bites into a donut with glaze, her favorite. "You know now. I'm fine. Let's move on. I want to just lie on the couch anyways, I feel ugh."

I swallow, hating myself right now. A woman's monthly supplies don't scare me, but when it comes to my daughter, I'm a basket case.

"Sounds like a plan. I'll join you. Grab some nail polish and snacks, I can grab you a blanket, and we'll probably binge on some bad reality television," Lexi offers.

It grabs my attention when it dawns on me. "Don't you have the flea market today?"

She shrugs. "It's okay. There's another one next weekend."

My lips twitch from her thoughtfulness, and she recognizes it.

"Thanks, Lexi," Lori says softly and throws Lexi a look that seems to be a sort of understanding that only they have. I guess the name houseguest went out the window.

It occurred to me a few times that there isn't a woman in Lori's life to prepare her for the years ahead. My mom and sister are a few hours' drive too far to play a role. I just never figured out an answer of how to deal with a daughter and only her dad in her life.

I guess Lexi paid me back more than a favor.

———

LEXI'S MOUTH gapes open as she watches Harry and me prepare a cake. "You really swirl strawberry jelly into the cake, that's a heaven of cream cheese and peanut butter?"

"It's the best." Harry is in his element.

I carefully swirl the jam with the blade of a knife. "It's delicious. The graham cracker crust is essential, though. We tried it once with chocolate cookie crumbs, and that was just an insane tastebud explosion on that one. We all mutually agreed that we needed to take it down a notch and go traditional with this recipe," I explain.

Despite the start of the day, it's been relaxing spending time with Harry and Lori, although quiet. Lori nods her head in agreement with my assessment and has a new glow on her face that might even connect us more. The snark went down a level.

And then there is Lexi who observes us all with joy. Maybe she's doubted me and parenting, but today she seems in awe.

"I feel, as the houseguest, that I should get the first piece once it's done." Lexi is dead serious, and Harry and I smile.

"Nuh-uh, I always get the first piece," Harry is quick to inform her.

She brings her hand to her heart. "Then I shall not break tradition."

We're going into the final stretch as I slide the cake onto the wire rack in the oven. Once it's out, then we have hours of cooling off the cake before it goes in the fridge. "Okay, negotiations over then. What are we doing for actual dinner? Stir fry?"

Lexi raises her hand. "I could try to make Sloppy Joes… or rather, find a can of it. But seriously, I can make it from scratch."

"Yes, can we have that?" Harry asks me.

"Yep. Lexi has to prove her cooking skills," I agree.

Our eyes catch, and we're becoming even more relaxed around one another, with Lori and Harry too. Why isn't there a red warning flare in my head yet?

————

AFTER CLEANUP of delicious sloppy joes and with the cheesecake now in the fridge for overnight, I do what I know I shouldn't. I find myself knocking on the guest room door.

It's only a few seconds before Lexi greets me at the door in a tank and pajama pants. "Hey there, stranger. Is this the part when you tell me that someone has food poisoning?"

I chuckle. "No. It's the part where I yet again thank you."

Her demeanor leaves her sarcasm behind. "You did good, Holden. I imagine it can't be easy."

My lips roll in because I agree with her but also appreciate her support. "Yeah, but you were there. Unplanned. But you were there. That's maybe the real favor that I needed. So, thank you for writing that IOU on a napkin way back."

I feel like we both have a giddy look on our faces because this conversation calls for emotion that can't be hidden behind jabs and teasing.

"I wouldn't consider it a favor."

I step closer, but she doesn't budge nor back up into her room. It's better that way since my son and daughter are upstairs. But it doesn't matter where she stands because I cup her face and bring her lips to mine, an instant murmur from her mouth before she kisses me back. We won't get to strip off a scrap of clothing right now, but I still want to kiss her.

It's not even from a debt that I owe her. It's because it isn't a debt to her at all.

We light a fire when we drown in our simmering sexual tension, but there is more to her that is underlying and deserves attention. The combination of attraction and personality opens a weakness within me.

I should run. Close the door and move on.

But her forehead rests against my nose when our mouths part, and she stays put. I smell her flowery hair, and my heart quickens. Lexi should retreat, but she doesn't. There is a wind around us; it should blow us in all directions, but it takes us only in one.

"Hey, Lexi," I whisper.

"Hmm."

My words are lost when all I can think about is asking for a weekend, just us. But something stops me.

"Nothing. Just good night and sleep well."

"I will." She smiles softly as she creates space. "Actually, tomorrow, can we meet? I mean at the Dizzy Duck?" My eyes nearly bug out, and she giggles. "Bad host of the house, I was purely indicating that I wanted to show you a few rooms that I'll finish tomorrow morning."

"Sure. Just find me when you're ready." I tense when I realize how our brains are wired and where our imaginations are going. "The meeting, about rooms and designs."

"Bedrooms. Not just rooms. Guest bedrooms," she replies with a husky tone, very well aware that we're both acting odd. My only response is to groan as I pivot to walk away.

When I hear her door close behind me, I'm relieved, because tomorrow means that I'll be closer to her again. Me and her.

14

HOLDEN

Lexi is a mix of enthusiastic and proud. She also appears like a jumping bean due to her eagerness for me to inspect her creation. With her hand on the handle, it feels like she's opening a door to a new kingdom.

I'm not sure it's a kingdom without us. Especially when she's in a flared skirt that ends just above her knees.

"I really think you are going to love this. It's the largest suite at the Dizzy Duck, and it's by no means a cheap stay. Ready?"

Her mood is infectious which is why my face is beaming. "I am."

She nods her head. "Great. Here we are."

The door slowly opens, and I guess all those house shows I watch in my spare time feel a little more realistic. I walk a few steps in and then freeze. I need to take a moment to assess the room that is a complete opposite to what it was before, and I'm in awe.

Lexi observes me, with her hands in tight fists against her chest. She's about to burst if I don't say something.

"This is… fantastic," I exclaim.

The natural dark wood floors have replaced the carpet, and instead there is a threaded area rug. Everything in this room is white except accessories and pillows that are the pop of color. The dark blue blends well. A free-standing tub has a tray across it with a candle holder resting on it for effect.

Stepping farther into the room, my eyes focus on different areas. The chest at the bottom of the four-poster bed, the different heightened candlesticks along the mantle of the cozy fireplace with two rocking chairs nearby.

"Like a magazine, right?" She finally lets out her excitement.

My eyes can't stop exploring, but I slow down my track when I land on my destination which is Lexi who is now twirling once as she takes in her surroundings.

"That was the goal," I reply. "It's exactly what I was hoping for and more." Already my mind has marketing plans, and I'm eager to get this room available as soon as possible. I could probably raise the price too.

"I was hoping you would say that." She rushes to me and grabs my arm to ensure she can direct me to where she wants me to examine. "Did you see the table by the window with a feathered pen and glasses with a classic bottle for port? And then there are little things like a hockey rubber duck with a Spinners jersey for Lake Spark's favorite pastime, next to the towels and shampoo. The curtains along the massive window and French terrace really removes the cookie-cutter hotel feel. Out on the terrace we ha—"

I spin to grab her wrist and pull her close. She seems caught off guard as she peers down to my hand then back up. "Everything is great… really," I assure her.

It's honesty, and I also need to cool her down a bit. I won't need any more coffee today, that's for sure. Her hyper state has rubbed off on me.

"I'm happy about that," she quietly answers.

I ease my grip. "Where is the furniture from that antique barn place?"

"I'm using that for another room. Remember? Every room will be unique."

I scoff. "Unique." Just like her. Lexi doesn't seem to grasp that it's her I mean.

She steps away. "Everything is coming along so well. Moving ahead of schedule probably," she continues to babble.

Oh, I know why, I really know why.

"Lexi." I think I need to rein her in a bit. She remains oblivious to my attempt. "Lexi," I repeat.

"I can imagine this will be a prime honeymoon destination, and with matching bathrobes and a welcome basket, then it's…"

"Lexi." Now my voice is tight, and it catches her attention, except she avoids my gaze. I notice that her breath is heavy. "Are you speaking a mile a minute because you're alone with me?"

She chortles. "Trust me, you don't scare me. It's just…" Her head tilts gently. "I'm not sure," she admits.

My journey begins with walking to her while she backs up. "You probably feel how I did last night when I wished you good night."

Lexi licks her lips. "We do seem to align on thoughts."

Closer, but it's not fast enough.

"I must insist on one more thing in relation to your design process." My eyes are hunting her.

"What might that be?" Her voice is thick with curiosity, especially when the back of her knees hit the end of the mattress and she braces her hand on the bedpost.

My arm circles around her waist in a flash to pull her tight against me. "We need to test the bed."

Our mouths meet for a kiss that has more urgency than last night. Not as tender, not as soft. It's a hell of a lot more demanding and reverent.

She squeals when I lift her onto the mattress, creating a dent against the duvet. "Hey," she scolds.

I'm already traveling to her hips with my hands but freeze at her warning. "Yes?"

"What will housekeeping think if they come in here and see a rumpled bed?"

A gruff chuckle rumbles in my throat while I hover over her, causing her to lie on her back. "That's why we should just use the bed all afternoon. Make it worth their time. Besides, I pay them, and they signed papers for discretion of all guests. I get a free pass."

And who the fuck cares? Because I'm desperate for her.

She hums due to my answer, and we kiss as she kicks off her shoes. Her fingers drag the fabric of my shirt up my back, and every inch of my body that she touches spirals me into a man that is about to rip clothes if I can't get us naked fast enough.

Somehow, we get there and I'm naked, and all she has is her turquoise bra that needs to find the floor. I kiss her along her shoulder, dragging the straps down, trying to fight the magnetism to plunge right into her because her thighs align with my hips and her knees point to the ceiling. The mere touch of her thigh against my cock is a dangerous game for us.

Lexi lifts her shoulders enough to enable me to sneak behind her to unclasp the bra.

I imprint the image of Lexi underneath me with hair splayed against the duvet and a gleam in her eyes of hazed desire.

Maybe I should take her slowly? That's what I'm wanting, isn't it?

To distract that thought, I stand, ensuring her legs stayed glued to my middle, and I grip some of her hair, pulling her up to inform her that I'm in control.

"The last twenty-four hours, all I've wanted is to fuck you."

Her smile indicates that I have no chance of being in control. This is her show, because right now she is slaying me in every way possible.

"Well, Holden, what a funny coincidence." She falls back and her legs loosen until she urges me to return to her, only she fools me and presses her big toe into my chest to keep me at bay. "I've been wanting the same thing. Now before you get comfortable, we need a condom."

"Obviously. While I handle that, how about you get those hands of yours wrapped around the bedpost as you stand, and I'll take you from behind."

She salutes me, and we both do what we need.

With condom sheathed, I bring her back to my front, and she jolts from my force. My lips scrape along her neck, my breath creating a wildfire against her skin. Lexi's arm wraps up behind my neck, with her body now stretched, and she searches over her shoulder for my mouth. Our lips meld together for a long kiss that confirms that whatever we do, we'll walk away as two people who can handle our boundaries.

Lexi hums into my mouth when my palm flattens against her belly then travels down to land on her clit that I circle with my long finger.

"You're soaking. Is that all for me?"

"Yes," she rasps.

Growling into her neck, I want to punish her for creating a man that is determined only for her.

"Those hands of yours better hold on to the post, Lexi," I warn.

Always the obedient one, she does as I say, and I guide her hips back to ensure prime position.

A few strokes of my cock in her arousal and then I'm sliding into her pussy.

"Fuck, Holden." Lexi does her best to scoot back to bring me deeper inside of her while she tightens around my length.

"Be a fucking good girl and face forward."

I press down at the bottom of her spine for a better angle, bringing my hands underneath her to squeeze her breasts and twist her nipples a few times. Everything is heightened, which is why I slam into her harder and faster, her body jolting on every thrust.

"See? The bed isn't even moving. Your designer picked a sturdy piece of furniture."

That comment earns her my palm on her ass in one spank. "Your wicked mouth, Lexi," I taunt. "But I guess it isn't punishment since you enjoy it."

"I do. In fact, I think I earned a few more."

This woman. I move faster, harder, deeper. Sweat breaks out as her body heats and her breathing changes. I spank her once more, just making us like this. Thrusting together with equal temptation to get us to an orgasm because there is no stopping this ride that we're on together in this moment.

The post gets held tighter because Lexi's body is bouncing every time I hit her deep, then I lift her off just enough that only my tip remains before I plunge into her body.

I grunt because we're out of control now. No possibility to slow down. Nor would we want to.

My release comes first, even though she's close. A dizzy spell hits me which is new for me, but then again, Lexi probably has the ability to change my blood supply. I moan and sigh when the very last drop is out, but I continue to pump her slowly and bring my fingers to flick her clit to help her, and it's not long until she's coming around my cock.

We're both completely gone when she falls onto the mattress, and I join her to steady my breath.

"We need to try harder. All scenarios to ensure the bed really can't break," I joke.

Lexi wipes her hand across her forehead. "Let me recover a minute or at least a few seconds."

"You consider your timeline while I head to the bathroom to take care of this."

I force myself to leave the bed and walk to the bathroom.

"Now housekeeping will really know what we did," she calls out.

My smirk only intensifies with perhaps a sense of pride because I don't think I'm afraid about people figuring out that I have a claim on Lexi.

Shaking my head from my apparent new philosophy, I join her back on the bed where she seems to be searching for clothes.

"No, you don't." I shackle her wrist with my hand and drag her back to lying down. "I've literally added another notch to my bedpost."

Lexi snorts a laugh. "Fair enough, that joke was waiting to be said."

I bring my hands behind my head and stare up at the ceiling. "Comfy bed."

"Only the best."

My arm shapes around Lexi, and she inches close to me on her side.

"Give me a few minutes then I need to lick that pussy of yours."

"Seriously, we had our quickie, and now we need to get out of here because this room needs new linens, even though there are no guest reservations."

I roll to my side with mischief on my face. "When you say it like that, then it makes me want to do it even more."

Her grin stays fixed. "Don't you have work to do?"

"Probably, but I would much prefer having an afternoon of sliding into you." Not even that. I could spend an afternoon just staring at her while she's tucked into my body.

"I need a nap," she deadpans.

I laugh to myself. "Not a bad idea either."

Lexi places her hand over mine and guides it along her curves. "Maybe sliding into me before a nap would be a perfect compromise?"

With that I drag her on top of me with full intention to give us this.

———

BLINKING MY EYES OPEN, I'm drowsy. My blurry vision fades when I see Lexi sitting on the side of the bed throwing on a shirt.

"Running away?" I sit up and search for my watch which is lying next to an old rotary phone where you need to spin the dial, an extra touch, I guess.

She throws me a glare. "We've been in here for three hours because we really did fall asleep."

"I guess the bed passes all the tests then."

"Except if it can handle the weight of three." She flashes her eyes at me,

I leach forward and tackle her back to her position on the pillow next to mine. "That doesn't need to be tested," I affirm.

"Anyhow, I'm going to run and grab a cookie on my way through the lobby on my walk of shame when I tell the front desk that they need to send housekeeping here."

I grin. "Let me handle that. I'm sure your excuse would be creative, though."

"As opposed to yours?"

"Stuart won't ask questions. He's a pro. Discretion is key for my staff."

She sputters a laugh. "I'm sure there is a fine line crossed when you have to clean up your boss's afternoon activities that involves sheets."

I ruefully drop my head.

The sheet still hangs around my waist which draws Lexi's attention low, or rather she's unable to move out of this bed,

"Well, this has been a fun afternoon," she says. I nod in agreement with her. "Don't forget that Harry wanted you to check his tablet. It was malfunctioning during his stock update."

I can tell that she thinks we're all crazy.

"Ah, the economy is malfunctioning, so it might not be his piece of technology at all."

"He really is a smart kid."

Pride and fondness come over me. "The math club is starting up again, so he will be in his element."

Appreciation floods me too. Lexi asks about my kids because she's generally interested. They are not a deterrent to her.

"That's good because he will need to count how many pieces of cheesecake have been stolen because peanut butter and jelly cheesecake is hands down the best thing in my life in the last few weeks."

I feign a scowl. "Sorry for not making you come on a regular basis."

Her smile stretches. "Oh yeah, thanks for the reminder."

We both seem to settle back to sinking into the mattress and take in the air around us that's filled with lust.

"But seriously, the last few weeks have been fun." *Fun*, huh. I'm beginning to hate that word. "I guess I've been so busy in a life of wanderlust and then the spontaneity of every project that it's refreshing to just be steady and having a chance to really observe life floating by."

"Doesn't sound half bad."

Lexi presses her lips together and ponders for a second. "I guess so. Nearly makes me want to put down roots and settle. My parents would be thrilled with that."

Holding her closer, it dawns on me that I haven't really asked. "I keep forgetting who your father is." I smirk to myself.

She points at me. "Good. Most men try to get into my bed because of my sports connection. You're way past your prime game days, so I don't need to worry."

I shake my head. "Great way of explaining that. Love being reminded of my expiration date."

"Oops, sorry. It just makes you hotter." She soothes my chest with the print of her fingers.

We both begin to shuffle. "I'll take that." I spot my clothes on the floor and yawn as I leave the bed.

"Really need to talk to the owner. There are no snacks in this room," I comment.

"The owner was busy today." She smirks.

"That he was." I grin proudly.

Lexi and I acknowledge this moment while she ties up her hair. "I was going to run to the grocery store. Now that I'm comfortable with your kids not poisoning me at breakfast, I can finally buy yogurt and not live in fear. Need anything?"

"You're not scared of them," I state.

She shrugs. "Why would I be? They're kids and great kids. If I run into the PTA mom at the store, I will even run my cart into her for them."

Lexi makes everything sound so simple. It's comforting, it's new, it's… hopeful?

Don't do it. No, Holden, don't go down this road.

DO. NOT. DO. IT

"Hey, Lexi, uhm, Lori and Harry are going to stay at my parents' up north. Forgot to mention." They live just far and close enough all the same.

That hint doesn't count, does it? I can still back out.

Lexi holds onto the post as she slips on a shoe, pausing for a quick second. "That's… an interesting piece of information."

I scratch the back of my head. "Yeah, so we'll have the house all to ourselves."

Damn it, man, don't suddenly have nerves when I'm perceived as the man with a heart of steel.

"Wait… so, we're alone… the whole weekend… together." It dawns on her, and she even gulps in this adorable way.

I work the buckle of my jeans. "Something like that. Maybe we can find an antique store or farmers' market, hiking maybe." Okay, ready to spit it out. "Maybe do adult things like dinner or wine, in case we need to leave the bed."

Lexi has an odd look as she stands then brings one hand to her waist as she tips out her hip. "I hate hiking," she flatly informs me. "But, uhm… the other things are appealing."

We both walk to one another to meet in the middle of the room, as if we are walking on a balance beam. Once we're close enough, our eyes meet to be certain, and her face softens. From an automatic response that's formed recently around her, the back of my knuckles caress her cheek and her fingers play with my shirt.

"Other things it is," I whisper.

"Yeah… just to be sure I'm not confusing things. You mean, like, kind of spending the weekend together as more than friends with benefits?" She isn't nervous, she is well aware what I said, but she wants to hear it.

"Exactly."

We smile at one another, both blushing. Something new floats between us because we have a fresh horizon.

Because I completely did what I said I wouldn't.

I'm asking for more.

15

LEXI

"Big plans?" Summer asks as she appears next to me. She was in town on errands and saw me.

I stare at Piper's lingerie boutique on Main Street. The owner designs her own creations and just so happens to be married to a football coach that everyone raves about. My head cocks gently to the side as I contemplate for what feels like twenty minutes but is probably only two.

"Not sure it's a great idea. Oh, what the hell. Why not? We have an entire weekend to shake things up, after all." I speak my subconscious thoughts more than directing my sentence to Summer.

She grabs my arm to break me from my daze. "Weekend?"

I wince. "Holden's kids are away which means we're alone. Avoiding one another could be an option, but he kind of suggested… maybe we can grab dinner or have wine together. Stepping up our game."

Her eyes blaze open. "Damn it, I knew I should have picked up popcorn at the grocery store," she teases. I give her an unimpressed look. "I warned you that this could get complicated, except sometimes complications unravel into perfect relationships. A chance you could run with."

I shake my head. "I think it's better that I just see this weekend as purely that. Two people who enjoy one another's company. Besides, he has kids and his hotel. I'm not sure a relationship is what he wants. Otherwise, wouldn't he have had one by now? He has options."

"Sometimes you have to wait for the right someone to drop from the sky."

My sight returns to the window. I do see a white number including garters. White is perfect; it reminds us that I'm an innocent soul who has no intention to complicate his life. Except the low plunging line of the lace bra leaves little to the imagination but an A+ for effort.

"Don't think."

I sigh. "What the hell. I've always been fearless." That thought instantly causes my heart to dip slightly. "He has great children who are excellent at causing trouble which makes them all the sweeter. I would never want to insert myself into his life where it affects him or them in a confusing way."

Summer's closed smile begins to stretch. "Lexi… the fact that you're even considering that is a sign that you can't help but imagine what the future might hold. You want to explore something and with care. So let him lead the way." I smirk to myself, and she notices. "Outside of the bedroom, Lexi. Outside," she clarifies with a tight smile.

My body relaxes and an ease hits me from her sound logic. "You're right. I'll just relax because there isn't really any pressure or anything. This is a big adventure."

"Great. You listen to me. Now, I think you're in luck. Piper has a sale this week." She winks before leaving me.

My feet take the lead and head over to the door to go on in.

———

I BEGIN to smile to myself when my hand turns the knob of the front door, and I let go of any nerves. There is no reason to feel this way. If

Holden can be calm, then so can I. We're always on the same level in everything we do, and right now is no different. That's the lucky thing about us; the ease. We keep one another on point.

The sound of someone shuffling around in the kitchen informs me that Holden is already home. He must have finished early with the staff meeting at the Dizzy Duck. It doesn't matter. It's officially the weekend now.

Slowing my pace, I observe him unloading the dishwasher. Who knew a man doing chores would be sexy as hell. I like that not many people have seen that, under his well-taken-care-of appearance and strong presence when he enters the room, he has a domesticated side. It makes me feel sort of special that I've had a front-row seat. Is that odd?

His eyes bolt open when he notices me. I stride to the island counter with a sly look on my face. My nails begin to tap the marble as we greet one another.

"So, this is the weekend it seems," I begin, maybe even challenging Holden.

"The clock does say that." He wants to laugh, I can see it.

My gaze swirls around the kitchen, wondering what our plan of action is. But then I know I'm being ridiculous. "Did Lori and Harry get to your parents' okay?"

He nods as he closes the dishwasher. "Yeah, they live up near Madison, so we meet halfway to make it easy. They normally see one another every six weeks or so."

"That's great. I assume you grew up there?"

Holden shakes his head before he takes a few steps to open the cupboard and grabs two wine glasses by the stems. "Not exactly. Actually, I grew up near St. Paul in Minnesota but by chance my parents wanted to move to Wisconsin to be closer to an aunt who lives there. They then formed a social circle and realized they would be close to their grandkids, and they set down roots."

I accept the wine goblet that he hands me. It's the size of a bowl, but I know we will have white wine which I don't mind at all. "We can start on wine, but probably by eight, I'll have you on shots."

He chuckles. "That's quite a party."

I shrug as I hold out my glass while he pops the cork. "Why not? You can let loose; the kids are away, and you can even be a devil by sleeping in for once."

"Why not." He grins.

My glass becomes full, and we clink our glasses before taking a sip. "Ooh, crisp and not sweet. Smooth," I note.

"It's the Blisswood brand. Midwest's finest."

"I've noticed their wine is on every menu in this town, not to mention the giant display in the supermarket. Right next to the Grizzly Dash maple syrup collection."

He tips his glass at me. "Lexi, you know they are all connected to Lake Spark, and a riot will start if any other brand attempts to take over." I giggle at his answer. "Besides, the Grizzly Dash syrup made special-label mini bottles for our hotel guests."

My hands come together. "I love that touch. Stuart also informed me that the Dizzy Duck has special ticketed seats for Spinners games, only for VIP guests. See? These things set the inn apart. Not only for people who want to leave Chicago for the weekend but also anyone who is looking for a getaway near or far."

Holden appears proud. "You can stop with the flattery and maybe park business to the side."

I nod a few times. "You're totally right." My lips tuck into my mouth, feeling the next part of our night is about to hit us.

Especially when he leans over the counter, not having a care that he must use his arms to slightly lift himself over to reach me. I do the same, and we meet halfway where our mouths gravitate, until our lips press together with a quick swipe of our tongues tracing one another's lips. It's a quick kiss, but it still scares me slightly. Fast kisses are the kind reserved for couples, or at least they are in my mind.

"I believe you promised me something else. Such as food, no hiking, maybe more food," I list.

"Thanks for the reminder, and I'm happy to report that I picked up some Italian dishes from the deli at the general store. We can just throw it into the oven."

"Solid choice for my calorie intake. Bonus points if dessert is included."

He throws me an enticing look. "Depends if having you on your knees with my dick down your throat counts?" His brow arches because he's playing with me, or not, but it's in jest. "Unlucky for me, you can have leftover peanut butter and jelly cheesecake that I hid in the freezer and am defrosting now so it will be ready."

I point my finger at him. "Perfect plan."

We take the next half-hour to prepare dinner and set some plates out on the dining table. Not taking any notice that we're speeding through our bottle of wine, and not because we need to for courage, it's more due to the fact that we seem to unwind with good wine and conversation.

Sitting down, we both take a few bites. I'm in love with the eggplant parmesan. "I wish I was a better cook. I'm just thankful takeout exists."

Holden looks at me peculiarly. "That's all you really eat?"

"Of course," I sputter, only to hold up one finger. "Wait, not entirely true. My mother is a great cook. She makes a mean brisket, which sounds like the last thing in the world that would be someone's favorite food, and it's not my number one on my dishes list, but when she makes it then I'm there."

His eyes flash. "Ah yes, your parents. I keep forgetting about your dad."

"Maybe because your career is miles behind you. He coached so many players over the years, and I'm not sure he has favorites."

"That I believe. You're not very close with him," he notes.

I cut another bite of my food. "Yes and no. When we're around one another, then yes. When he is away and especially during hockey season, then no. Yet, he still feels that he has a say in my future life as a wife and mother. I guess that's a dad thing."

"I don't even think that far ahead when it comes to my kids. I need to focus on now."

My hand finds his, and I plant it over the back of his hand resting on the table. "That's the perfect answer. Besides, you have to survive the next bake sale at Lake Spark Academy. I even got a flyer when I did drop-off the other day. They were handing them out."

His other hand pinches the bridge of his nose in agitation. "*And* here comes a financial donation. Not going to walk into that den of wildlife."

A loud laugh escapes me. "It's… refreshing, the whole settled feeling, yet little things bring aggravation for a moment or two. Sure beats the constant travel without much regard for the future, because who knows what the universe will throw at you."

Holden flips his hand with his palm now open to collect my hand. "The universe will throw something at you even if you are standing in the same place."

My head lolls to the side, and I tip my nose up as my lips quirk out. His philosophy makes sense and sends a clap of thunder to the center of my chest. He has a valid point.

"Never thought of it that way, yet it's logical."

He releases my hand to grab his wine. "I'm not even sure why I seem to have wisdom tonight."

I pick up my fork again. "Probably because you don't get many chances to talk about it with someone, I mean a woman, or maybe you have, and it just didn't work out." Yikes, I'm prying for info.

Holden has a gleam in his eyes as he leans back in his chair. "No woman who I actually talked with, admittedly. It's kind of been blank physical fulfillment, except I don't even think it was fulfillment. You have to have the whole package of bedroom and out-of-bedroom interaction, including conversation, to have fulfillment."

His words catch me in a moment. My suspicions are right, and it seems we are crossing paths. "Why am I sitting here having good conversation with you?" I'm serious.

He scoffs to himself before his mouth changes form to a pleasant look. "It seems you've drawn me into wanting it."

Now my pulse quickens. "Holden." I focus on the table but then decide there is no need to hide. "I-I feel it too. But this is my warning to you…" His eyes search mine with great interest. "Only sex is one thing. But I don't do well with crossing the line from sex to beyond. I go all-in once a line is crossed. My ability to separate it is nearly non-existent. The last few days, I can't help but remind myself that you have a different dynamic that is new to me. Your age, kids, and a commitment that I'm not sure you have interest in giving. Not to mention, I'm your houseguest which adds some extra complication to our cocktail of current life."

His lips quirk out, and the waiting for him to answer me is nearly overbearing. Even when his mouth begins to make a sound, I'm anticipating his words, even though I'm aware that I have to accept whatever he says.

"Lexi, I hear what you're saying. I do. And all I can say is I have some strange new inkling that I wanted to spend the weekend with you. Maybe it's selfish," he explains with a softness in his tone.

I take a deep breath and abruptly stand, pushing my chair behind me, then circle around the corner of the table to Holden. His tongue darts to the corner of his mouth, his eyes glued to me with a desire that mirrors my own. He's letting me lead the scene, but his demeanor is eager.

Between him and the table, I lift my leg to cross over his lap to square my body to his. I slowly lower myself until I'm straddling him, with his eyes peering down then back up to mine. I can feel his cock harden against my panties, with my skirt now bunched around my waist and my arms resting on the curve of his shoulders. The feeling of his hands firmly gripping my sides intensifies everything I want in this moment.

"Focus on now, Lexi, and we'll see where this weekend takes us." His voice is a simmering warning. It's also a key to open a door if it's locked.

"I agree."

I lower my mouth to trace his lips, ensuring they don't touch but skim to tease him. His hands work behind me at moving his plate.

"Don't tease, Lexi," he warns. Using his strength, he lifts us then sets me on the edge of the table, with his glass of wine spilling and neither of us caring. "Now lean back on your hands and take it like a good girl when I fuck you with my tongue before I flip you to fuck you from behind while I yank your hair."

My entire body flares, with arousal soaking my panties.

I nod once as our eyes hold. Then he kisses me as I fall back to my propped arms.

All thoughts of complexity float out of my mind, even when he nearly rips my panties as he drags them roughly down my legs, a growl escaping from deep in his throat. He parts my legs in one swift move and stares at my bare pussy, his entire face hungry.

"I need to fuck you so damn hard here before I take you upstairs to my room."

A strike to my center. I've never been to his room. We've only ever fucked on neutral ground, but now he is crossing us over a line.

HOLDEN

I don't care about the spilled wine, nor the fact that clothes have created a trail as we moved upstairs, arriving perfectly naked at my room.

It was a few licks on her luscious pussy, but then I felt a need to transfer us. Probably, the fact that the living area is not just mine, it's my kids'. Maybe one day we will share it with someone else, but right now doesn't seem right yet. But the true reason, if I'm honest, is I want to lay Lexi down in *my* bed. No woman has crossed that line since I moved into this house. It's far too intimate, yet here I am with an eager desire to have Lexi in my bed.

That's the reason why I throw her onto my bed, only for her to reach for my arms to tug me down to join her. We find our way to the middle of the mattress, and I sit up as Lexi swings her legs around my waist because it must be her position of choice today. She's straddling me again, this time with her glistening pussy rubbing against my bare, hard cock.

Her eyes float around the room when we settle into a little silence.

"This is your room, it appears." She does that cute thing where she slows her speech and states the obvious.

I tuck hair behind her ear, causing her to focus on me again. "You are very wise," I whisper. "I guess it's new for us." My room is large, with a king-sized bed, a lot of gray happening in the simple decorating. A man's room, I guess.

She splays her hand against my chest. We don't say anything more because something so small seems to signify a lot. The simple act of letting her into my room that I normally keep private says enough.

Our lips find their way to meet, and we kiss. A sensual kiss that brings our bodies pressed together and my arms wrapping tighter around her waist, as if tight isn't even enough.

We pull away, and her eyes gleam with sentimentality. "Hi," she whispers.

"Hi," I echo.

She smiles almost shyly, but I'm putting an end to that. I adjust our bodies and roll her back with her head now near the end of my bed, I encourage her to tilt her hips up, giving me ample opportunity to go slow with her.

Parting her thighs open, my tongue finds her clit again, and instantly she gasps. Lexi's limber, and I appreciate that she can hold this position until I have her trembling. I circle her clit and keep my eyes focused on her face and hands that have found her breasts to fondle with. She's even more damn beautiful because she freely does what she craves.

I'm not sure the cause of how drenched her thighs and pussy are, because since I set her on the dining table, I've both licked her and turned her on purely with the tease of what we're going to do. Now I'm adding a finger to her pussy, and she needs my cock.

"Baby, you must be aching and craving my cock to fill you." I watch her eyes hood closed then open while she thrums with pleasure. I add another digit, and she twists her nipples between her fingers, her hips beginning to circle, eager for more. "Tell me what you need."

"I need you. You make me feel so good," she grates out.

I pop my fingers out of her pussy and shove them straight into her mouth. "You're sweet, Lexi. Delicious, and you're making a mess of your thighs. I've done this to you, and I have every intention of being inside you."

"Please," she begs.

I rumble a sound of pride while I reach for my nightstand to grab a condom. She follows my cues and comes to sit on me again in the middle of the bed. Our eyes lock, and I don't need any words; she slides down onto me. Deadly slow, with every inch taking us deeper into our own world. Her hair falls behind her shoulder as she looks up, and her breasts present themselves to me for my teeth to drag around her nipple and my hands to mold against the shape.

She drags her pussy up then bears down on me with force that buries the tip of my cock as deep as possible inside of her.

Her breath becomes labored. "You feel so good," she whispers.

My hands roam down her spine until I grip the cheeks of her ass in one slap. Her body jolts, but then approval through her smirk informs me that she didn't mind. Using my hands on her behind, I guide her rhythm. She loops her arms around my neck for support, and we seem to be moving closer and closer. Our bodies have nowhere to go as the emotional element of sex only intensifies the ability to become one and move in sync.

That's what has happened. Hasn't it? I care for Lexi, she brightens my day, and when I close my eyes, I don't see her gone.

I refuse to label this, but I'm allowed to have this time with her.

We're both overheating with a sheen of sweat forming on our bodies. Through our heavy breathing, we still manage to kiss deeply. We slow down our thrusts, and our foreheads touch as we both soak in a few seconds of one another.

"You're so fucking beautiful when you aren't afraid," I whisper.

Her eyes flick to mine. "What should I be afraid of?"

My lips twitch, but I don't respond. Because I'm not sure of the answer. Did I mean her sexual confidence or what's transpiring between us?

It doesn't matter. I pull her flush to my body and begin to piston up inside of her, needing to hit that spot that makes her see stars.

She's losing control, and she brings her mouth to the curve of my shoulder to caress and nip.

Our speed picks up with her hand between us toying with her clit. We both moan, and when we finally reach our destination, I'm positive I black out from a mind-blowing orgasm. All her doing.

————

"I SHOULDN'T BE YAWNING," I declare as my mouth stretches, with Lexi in my arms in my bed.

Lexi begins to mirror me. "Don't say yawning. When you hear the word then you automatically yawn." Lexi places her hand on my bare chest. "Old man." She snickers.

"Watch it there." I look at my clock. "Fair point, maybe. It's not even nine and we're drowsy in bed."

"I think we know why."

"Har, har. We were supposed to watch a movie or talk over a bottle of wine. Didn't you have the idea of shots?" I list.

I could get used to the feeling of her lips kissing my pec. Always delicate but without thought. "We can always bring the bottle here, but I feel like that might ruin this sacred surrounding. Tomorrow, we have the whole day. Besides, I kind of like your bed. It's comfortable, there are great pillows, a hot guy, high thread count sheets, and big windows over there."

I tickle her, and she squeals. "Hot guy, huh?"

"Don't get cocky on me. But seriously, I don't need to leave this bed. I'm tired too. I mean, unless you want me to leave this bed." She sounds unsure.

I laugh under my breath. "I'm not kicking you out," I clarify.

"Okay, but I'm a cuddler."

"Then I'll spoon the hell out of you."

"And I wake sometimes in the middle of the night," she adds.

"I'll slide into you and fuck you back to sleep."

She hooks her leg across my body around my hips. "Do I have to sleep naked, or do I get one of your shirts?"

I grin. "You have a lot of questions." Lexi looks up to give me a love-to-tease-me look. "But to answer. No scraps of clothing allowed in this bed."

"Hmm, I was afraid of that." She frowns, but then her entire body perks up. "I guess being at your service at all times will have to do."

My arm sweeps her in closer to me. "Don't say things like that to me."

"Fine." We both simmer in our joint embrace in silence until she breaks it. "Your jersey isn't here."

"Nah, I keep that on the wall in my home office. I kind of need a space with no reminders of the outside world."

Her nails tap against my skin. "Huh… I don't even see photos of Lori and Harry in here."

"I love them, but this space needs to be a blank room so I can gather my thoughts."

"That's actually… a perfect thing to have."

My eyes close because tiredness begins to take over, but I still listen and talk. "That means a lot coming from a professional designer."

"No work talk. Tell me something new. Why don't you have a dog? That makes children's lives happy."

I'm wide awake again and burst out a laugh. "Because we killed Pebbles the fish way back after two days at home. Doubt we can handle a dog."

Our fingers entwine and move together, creating their own shapes. "I had Diamond growing up. A Dalmatian who was pretty cool. Used to sit on my bed when I would do homework or sneak out my bedroom window. She was even exactly where I left her when I returned home. I'm positive she only kept quiet because she wanted my bed to nap on."

"That's ridiculous. Do you ever want to have another dog?"

"I think so. I need to settle somewhere first. Before I was traveling all the time, so it wasn't ideal. Now that life is less hectic with less travel, it seems that a dog is getting closer on the horizon."

I begin to ponder in my thoughts. "Okay, focus on projects, no plans of traveling, less hectic, anything else?"

"Why are you making a list? Something brewing in your head?" She's amused.

But her observation strikes a chord, and I move to my side to face her. "How do you manage to assess my thoughts?"

A sly smile creeps on her lips. "Because our minds think alike. Isn't that kind of scary?"

"Terrifying," I deadpan.

Lexi's expression turns serious, and she cups my face in her hand, with her thumb tracing my bottom lip. "I know the feeling," she whispers. "Isn't it a strange realization when a strong click that you share with someone has been blinded by the fun you have with them? Turns out the connection isn't just on the surface."

She explains it well. Too well.

"Tell me something that will make me walk away from you, completely uninterested," I request softly. I'm spiraling again, no control of my thoughts or feelings.

Her fingers stroke my hair, a calming smile faint on her lips. "I'll maybe tell you in the morning, but right now, I think you need to find your way back inside of me."

My fingers trail down her body to find her pussy that is wet again. She's trying to distract me, and it's working.

Waking up when Lexi begins to stir in my arms, I blink my eyes to see the sun peeking through the curtains. We kept true to our suggestion of waking in the night and I spooned her from behind. Now I have every intention of having lazy morning sex with her.

She rolls out of my hold, and I reach to yank her back but fail.

"Holden." She shoos me away. "I need breakfast, and I'm sure there is a carnage of wine over your table."

I rub my face to wake up. "Forgot about that."

She's already out of bed and heads directly to my closet to get lost in, only to return a few seconds later, pulling on one of my old Spinners shirts, and it drowns her but is still hot as hell. "We can come back to bed after breakfast. Or… we could actually do something non-bed related. I was thinking we could head to the ice rink."

My face puzzles. "I'm always up for the rink. Didn't really expect you to say that, though."

She splays out her hands. "I'm full of surprises."

That she is. "Give me a few minutes and I'll be downstairs."

"I'll grab the toaster pastries that are full of artificial goodness. If you have those weird cinnamon ones, then I'll be concerned."

I pretend to be serious. "That's a classic."

"Or we can just pick something up at Jolly Joe's."

"Good plan," I agree.

It's a few minutes later when I arrive downstairs to find Lexi still in my shirt, dancing around the kitchen as she puts dishes away from last night. I don't think she realizes I'm there as she's belting out George Michaels' "Father Figure."

Clearing my throat, she startles. "Have some daddy scenarios that we need to talk about?"

It's not even nine and we're already into our daily rhythm of back and forth.

Lexi waves a finger at me. "Hmm, I don't think so. But I'm all for some chains and floggers."

My eyes grow bold. "Shut up. No seriously, shut up. Every time I know you're serious about your sexual wishes, it only makes me become more curious about what I can do with you."

She salutes me. "Yes, sir."

"Seriously, get in the car in ten minutes, otherwise we have no hope of leaving this house." I'm growing frustrated with her lack of inhibitions, purely because I want to instantly put them into practice.

Her face goes neutral. "Agreed."

We make it out of the house and pick up bagels and coffees on our way to the rink. I wasn't really expecting her to suggest this, but I'm game.

Lake Spark is lucky that the Spinners' training center here also has a small public rink. It's where Lori has her lessons. Fortunately, it's not busy either, considering it's a Saturday. We should probably give it an hour or two before it picks up.

Lexi and I tie our skates on, and I follow her onto the ice.

"Here we go. Non-inappropriate activities here we come," I say.

She throws me a glare.

And soon I know why.

Lexi skates away, and she doesn't have one wobble. Instead, her speed picks up and then her body circles before skating more. It seems as though she's warming up. I just slowly skate in observation. Then stop in amazement when she jumps off the ice in a turn. It doesn't stop. Leg up, twirls, another turn in the air.

No fucking way. She's not at all an amateur.

I give up on skating since I much prefer the show. She slows down with a smile and skates around me as if I'm a target.

"What's the story, Lexi? I've heard mention that you used to skate. Yet, this talent you still seem to have, you did nothing with it."

Lexi shrugs and tries not to look at me. "It's nothing. Besides I gave up when I was a teenager. My mother wasn't a fan. Felt I'd be better off going to college."

"And your dad?"

"He wanted to go all out on the skating front."

She brings her leg up while her body lines into an L shape. "And me? I guess fate ran its course."

I take a few glides, and she skates away a little, as if I need to chase her, and I do. But then we both reach out and grab one another's arms which knocks us to the ice. Nobody is hurt, though, and we burst out laughing.

We lie on our backs and stay there while our hysteria fades away. Staring up, we just freeze, but she reaches out her finger and invites me to link with mine.

"You still have skills," I point out.

Lexi sighs. "I still practice sometimes for the old feeling. It's been a while, though."

"And how does it feel?"

"Liberating." She sounds at peace.

My head angles to study her face that looks content. "How come you haven't watched Lori, out of curiosity? She loves figure skating."

Lexi meets my gaze and hesitates. "Simple. I wasn't sure how much she hated her new houseguest and didn't want another reason for her to."

Creases form on my forehead. "That's a silly reason."

She shakes her head in disagreement. "Also… when you're her age, the last thing you want is for someone to steal your limelight. Skating is her thing, so let her shine in it. I didn't want to take that away."

My entire body wilts from her thoughtfulness and the way she ignites wants and feelings that I imagined were always locked away.

I don't care who is watching or the feeling of ice on the other side of my clothes. I lean on my side and kiss her softly on the lips then look down at her.

"You keep surprising me. In every best possible way. I'm not sure what to do."

She lifts her head up to kiss me once more. "Me neither."

We both lie back down, splayed out like two octopuses. Not a concern in the world that a few other skaters are circling the rink.

It's a minute of our hands laced and relaxing breathing as we stare at the ceiling.

Until Lexi laughs to herself.

"What's funny?"

"I lied to you."

My eyes snap in her direction, fear now flooding me. Of course, it's too good to be true.

But her smile, it's coy yet promising.

"What did you lie about?"

She hurries and scrambles to standing on her skates, and she offers me a hand to yank me up, which is kind of pointless as I'll just take her back down due to my size. I don't take her offered arm because I would rather have an answer.

"I didn't tell you that I know."

"As in?" I need a clue.

Lexi licks her lips, and her cheeks tighten from a cheeky smile wanting to break free. "I know you turned the water off on purpose, always knew."

She laughs and skates away. Leaving me sitting on the ice grinning to myself.

Because even from day one, she still stayed.

HOLDEN

Tequila. A bottle of tequila rests on the rug near the turned-on fireplace downstairs. I spill some from my shot glass onto my hand as we sit on the floor. A few shots might do that to you.

We both chuckle as we let loose. It's been quite a day and here we are post-dinner—well, a charcuterie board. Lexi brings out a side of me that I haven't felt in years. Sure, I would kick back with a few drinks with friends. However, the constant laugh while we're doing it seems to be different. It's more uplifting, with my cares of the world turned off. And even more of a change is that there is a woman in my house who is more than a platonic friend.

"Last one," I say.

Lexi nods and tosses her empty glass to the side, and it lands on the rug. "Agreed. We have to think clearly." She points a finger at me.

"What? That you are a bad influence?"

A cheeky proud smile stretches on her lips. "Yet you, oh so wise old guy, follow me willingly?"

My brows lift, and I give her a warning. "Seven years. Only seven years older," I remind her then slide all signs of alcohol to the side. It gives me ample space to tickle her and guide her back onto the floor. We both quickly lie on our sides and rest our heads against propped elbows while we stare at one another. "I'm having fun."

"Good. You should. Take it down a notch on the stress level. You're allowed to do that."

"So it seems."

Our eyes are glued to one another, and after a few ticks, a gentle look floods her face. "We might be tipsy but still we know that tomorrow this is a thing of the past. I should probably go stay at the Dizzy Duck after tonight."

"Is it the alcohol? Or did I just hear you say that you're leaving my house?"

She shakes her head. "Our dynamics have changed, and I don't think this is a good idea."

Sobriety hits me at rocket speed. My lips press out, and I debate for a few seconds. "How is this different to you staying here while we fucked on what was becoming a regular basis?" My free hand lands on her hip and rubs back and forth. I can't not touch more of her.

"It's a little more than physical now, don't ya think?" Her face turns puzzled.

She's right. But I'm too selfish. "What if I refuse to let you leave? I'm beginning to think my kids wouldn't like it either. You can still stay in the guest room."

Lexi sighs then rolls to her back, with frustration clearly growing. "Holden, I am completely on board with Harry and Lori being in the dark. But this. Where is it going? At some point, one of us will want more, and I have a feeling it's not you. Impending disaster is probably looming over us."

An inclination inside me has me ready to be far too honest. "Lexi, you're... I can't describe it, but you are different. I always turned off the possibility to go anywhere with anyone—"

She cuts me right off. "Exactly. You don't even allow yourself to have anyone in your life that could be more. You seem to have thrown away that you're allowed to be in a relationship and be a great dad too. Which is why I think me leaving my captivity is the way to go."

My hand on her hip drags her closer to me. "Will you let me finish?" She rolls her eyes, yet that just makes me even more certain of what I want to say, because her ability to be blunt all the time is a positive to me. "I told you at the start of the weekend about going with the tide. Here we are. What if I'm saying that I'm curious to see if, yeah, I can have what I've been missing, and it seems you're actually that key since you're on the other side." A suave smirk hits my lips as I know I've surprised her.

Her head cranes up with her face skeptical. "Really?"

"Yeah."

"Not tequila doing this to us?" she double-checks.

I squeeze her hip to add a signal that she needs to get with the program. "Nah, this is me. Even if it was the alcohol, people normally speak honestly anyhow, they have no fear suddenly."

Her eyes blaze, and Lexi seems to soak in everything that I just told her the last two minutes. "Then kiss me."

Now I grin, my fingers raking into her hair then gripping the back of her head. "I'll do better than that. I'll take you right here because off-limits locations to fuck you senseless have been abolished."

Her smile is pleased. "Okay, I'm convinced. Now please show me."

I dive right in to kiss her lips.

———

It's Monday morning and Lori and Harry are silent as they eat their cereal at the counter. That's not unusual for Harry, but the fact that Lori is on time and actually eating breakfast is new. Kind of scary, to be honest. Eerily unusual.

"Uh, I'm going to head to the inn to check the delivery of new lamps." Lexi holds up her to-go mug of smoothie she made. "Thanks, guys, for not adding any extra ingredients."

"We could have added laxatives for all you know. You don't taste those," Lori deadpans.

We all swing our attention to Lori. "What?" I check if I heard her correctly.

She shrugs. "Relax. It was a joke."

Lexi releases a smile. "You have some dry humor, but thank you for confirming."

Lori offers her a faint smile that only seems directed at Lexi.

I glance at the clock on the oven. "Okay, team, five minutes until we need to head out." My kids groan but pick up their speed, their spoons full of cereal. "I will walk you out, Lexi. The switch for the garage is acting a little funny."

"Thanks."

As soon as I close the door from the hall to the garage, I break Lexi's attempt to hit the switch. "Lexi."

She looks over her shoulder. "What? This seems to work fine."

The door is already slowly rising. "Of course, it does. But I needed a cover to kiss you good morning."

Lexi greets me with a knowing smile. "I figured. But I like to make you work a few seconds extra."

My arms loop around her waist, and I pull her until our middles touch. Our lips meet for a slow sensual morning kiss. A few days ago, I probably would have called this sappy. But now? It seems I want my day to start this way. Especially since I don't get to enjoy a shower or morning sex with her. Maybe we can role play that later at the Dizzy Duck.

She purrs a sound as our sensual kiss deepens. It's one long kiss to begin the day on a strong basis. When we pull away, we take a few seconds more to admire each other before she shakes out of my hold.

"Down, boy, I do have to get to my job. Plus, I make Stuart's day by having a morning cup of coffee with him. He's trying to ask someone out that he met at the supermarket. It's kind of cute."

I chuckle. "Phew, had me worried he's a contender."

"God, no. I'm not even sure he knows how to use a key for handcuffs."

She pats my shoulder then is quickly heading toward her car. Lexi is the type of person that always wants to start the day with a smile. It does ease me. I have no qualms that when I head back inside it might be chaotic, but it's looking a little less stressful lately.

But that thought vanishes as soon as I return inside and turn the corner of the hall to the kitchen; it isn't quiet.

"No, Dad has to take me to my music lesson, not to your fufu skating lesson." Harry is standing his ground against his big sister and seems annoyed too.

Lori is unimpressed. "No, he is taking me to figure skating because someone in this family actually has talent. Besides, I have a competition coming up."

My hands come up, trying to calm them. "Alright, relax. We probably have three more weeks before we get another nanny. Or at least that's what the agency said. For now, can we just balance it out? I'll ask Lexi to help so everyone can get to their afterschool activities."

"It's not an activity, it could be my career," Lori says, defensive.

Bringing my hand to my heart, I'm ready to apologize. "You're completely right." Blowing out a breath, I twirl my finger in the air indicating to wrap this all up. I give Lori zero pressure when it comes to skating, but if she envisions a career, then I'm not going to knock her down.

Somehow, we all make it to the car in record time. On the road, Harry is occupied in the back, while Lori is in the front messing with the Bluetooth.

"Can we try to find a middle ground on the music? I bet you would find some bands that you actually like that I grew up with too."

Lori throws me a glare as she sits back, satisfied that she won the music battle with a pop song. "Not today." She crosses her arms, and I give up in defeat, but it's after a little silence that she speaks up again. "Did you fix the garage door?"

Her question causes me to quickly glance to my side while I keep my hands steady on the wheel. "Yeah, just needed a little wiggle." I swallow my lie.

"Sure, it did." She sounds skeptical.

But she doesn't press, instead turning her attention outside, but I can't help but notice in the side mirror that her lips twitch into a closed-mouth smile to herself. Almost as if she has a thought that makes her glad.

I don't try to interpret it because the warmth of her face is something that is far more important because she doesn't do it often.

———

I WAIT for my coffee at Jolly Joe's after school drop-off. I hate school drop-off. The moms always give me an over-the-top smile, even if I don't leave my car. They stand on the sidewalk with a cute little wave or drive up beside me and ensure we catch sight of one another through the windows. My awkward smiles are beginning to hurt my face. But these are the things we do for our children.

Stone and his fiancée Harlow walk into the place, the little bell ringing over the door. They instantly catch sight of me, and it feels like their looks are entertained.

"What are the odds?" Stone grins as he lands right next to me, pretending to read the menu.

"Not really. You know I swing by after the morning school run," I highlight.

Harlow clears her throat. "I attempted to divert his attention to other topics, but it failed." She steps forward to order with the lady behind the counter.

Stone turns to me with that grin still smacked on his face. "But while I'm here, we should catch up since you've avoided me the last week. Then, our boy Stuart—"

"You hate Stuart. You try to have me fire him every week." My tone is flat.

Stone slaps a hand on my shoulder. "Well, I look at him a bit more positively since I did a cookie pickup yesterday for Harlow, and Stuart shared some fun information."

I take a step forward to grab my coffee order that is ready. "And what might that be?"

"Shall we take a seat? This might be a few minutes."

Sighing, I give up. Plus, I could use an ear now. We find a booth by the window, and Harlow joins us. They both sit across from me with bright smiles.

"Stuart informed me that you seem awfully happy lately, and Lexi seems quite chipper too. Any coincidence?"

"You know that answer."

Harlow seems ecstatic. "Is this the part where you move on from the only-benefits plan?"

My cheeks puff out while my finger taps the side of my to-go cup. "Yeah, okay? Yeah. We seem to be doing more than that."

"As in? We need more intel to advise you correctly." Stone thanks the man who brings their coffees and a plate with a cinnamon roll.

"We spent the weekend together when Lori and Harry were away. Now we are, ya know…"

Harlow and Stone wait patiently, both with arms crossed on the table and their backs straight.

"Lexi and I enjoy one another. She makes me laugh and doesn't seem to mind the kids, either. In fact, I think with every antic they pull she likes them even more. It doesn't feel as though she's out of place when they're around. I can't seem to shake that we're more than a fling," I admit.

Harlow's face lights up like a Christmas tree; she writes romance books, after all. "The realization phase has hit you. Go for it." Her palm comes up to face me. "Go for it. You've sworn off relationships in the past, but she's the gamechanger, and if she has a great connection with Lori and Harry, then even more reason to keep exploring this thing."

My eyes land on Stone with a plea. "Calm her down."

He gently touches his fiancée's arm. "Go a little easy, even if you are 100% correct." His sight sharply turns to find mine again. "Holden, for fuck's sake, you seem happy."

"Which is why we are going to see where things go."

"Perfect. As long as fear doesn't become a barrier, then this could be something special."

I smile to myself. "That's the thing. I'm not sure there is any fear, other than it scares me that there is no fear, you know what I mean?"

Harlow sips her coffee and remains elated. "That's your sign then."

I snicker a sound and throw my hands up. "Everyone here is speaking logic, congrats to us."

Stone and Harlow hold up their coffee mugs and meet them in the middle for a toast.

"Fast or slow, you have a chance at a relationship worth everything," Harlow announces before we clink our mugs.

Stone sets the little spoon for his coffee to the side. "Now just don't fuck it up when it comes time to tell the kids," he casually mentions.

Because one day, when the time is right to share the news, then they could be the dealbreaker.

"These cookies are so damn good." I nearly moan as the gooey chocolate chip cookie bends easily in my hand.

"There is something about Dizzy Duck's welcome cookies that is like a psychedelic experience," Harlow says with her mouth full.

We're sitting on a couch in the lobby of the Dizzy Duck. The finished lobby, if I may add. Harlow is someone I recently met. But she's around the inn a lot, as she and Stone stayed here for a bit while their home was getting renovated. They are a perfect couple, and it's nearly infectious to see.

I put my cookie back on the napkin then set it on the coffee table in front of us. "I really need to figure out what it is about the recipe," I mention.

"Nah, they're only excellent because someone else bakes them." Harlow nods then looks at me funny. "Uhm…" She's trying to keep a smile in. "I saw Holden the other day."

Ah, I think I know where this is going.

"*And?*"

Her smile breaks out. "He's close to Stone and me. I consider him a good friend, and maybe I shouldn't be talking to you about him. But my mouth won't stay shut because he seems different. I think it's great that he is opening up with someone. I've even heard his kids have calmed down a bit. Seems that you are a good influence on everyone."

I shrug my shoulders, brushing off her proclamation. "Nah, just a distraction for most. Something new."

She shakes her head. "Except, you know that you're no longer just a distraction to Holden."

A feeling of pure joy explodes inside me. "I'm not sure that I should be talking to you about this, but I believe so, and if I'm honest, he isn't to me either. I'm just not used to a connection with someone like this."

Harlow gives me a look of understanding. "But you like it?"

"Love it."

"Then maybe as time goes on the bond will only get stronger. You're up for that?"

"Is this an interrogation?" I volley but lightheartedly.

She laughs then scans the room before her gaze falls on me again. "Maybe or maybe not. I just love to see two people with a clear connection letting it grow. It doesn't seem to scare you that he is a bit older or has kids, right?"

I think about it for a second, because nobody has confronted me in this way, but I have no hesitation either. "No, it doesn't. Should it?"

"If it isn't an issue for you then not at all."

Reaching forward, I pick up the remainder of my cookie. "But you know we're kind of keeping everything on the downlow, right? I mean, I'm almost finished here at the Dizzy Duck, although it never really crossed my mind that he is kind of my boss." My head tips to the side, and I wince. "It's more we have a few factors, so we need to be sure before being more open."

Harlow sputters then throws a thumb over her shoulder to the empty reception desk. "Trust me, reception is well aware what shenanigans are happening between Holden and you. Staying ambiguous can only last for so long. Plus, what the hell? You're staying in his house?"

My finger whips up. "Only until the water is fixed at the guesthouse he rents out… which he might have turned off on purpose."

She roars with laughter. "Ha! No way is that ever happening. Besides, then you would just become his neighbor. Want my advice?" She slides a little closer to me, prepared to speak softer.

"I think you will give it to me anyhow."

"Just continue the living situation as it is, then when it's clear there is a serious next step in the relationship, you're already where you need to be. Besides, you've already tested the co-habiting with his family. Don't need to practice on that part."

My lips purse out, acknowledging that her plan is worth pondering. I just want to repeat the obvious. "First we just need to be… us."

Harlow begins to stand, while she throws the strap of her purse over her shoulder. "All positive thoughts. Now, if you will excuse me, I have a Zumba class to attend. Cookies and Zumba is just how I roll."

I raise myself up and off the couch too. "That sounds like a slogan for a t-shirt."

"Totally, right? See ya soon."

We both say goodbye as I walk to the reception desk, slightly unnerved when Stuart has a day off. It's just not the same. Jane puts in the effort, but she seems to fret about little things, as if she's scared that she will be fired any moment. Before I can be polite to say hello, a hand that I've become familiar with touches my elbow.

"I believe you need to update me on the last of the guest rooms and the timeline for completion." Holden sounds way too playful, even though his sentence is a fact.

Turning, I'm faced with his smoldering gaze. "Is that so?"

"Completely."

"You're going to have to wait. I want to make a few calls."

"I'll live."

I cross my arms over my chest while I give him a wry smile. "Oh gee, I was greatly concerned."

He steps closer and that thin layer of sensitivity creates a wall between us, and I believe he knows that. "Caring, as always."

"You should really be more professional here," I tease him.

But then our moment of flirtation is subdued, and we just stand in the presence of one another, still synced together and unable to part.

He drags a knuckle across his jawline. Holden always has a little bit of short stubble on his chin, and I love it. It only adds to the flaming look he has.

"Thanks for handling school lunches this morning. I'm kind of thinking they prefer yours over mine."

I lick my lips. "I do make a mean cashew butter and jelly sandwich."

He stifles a laugh. "Maybe tonight after they go to bed, we can open a bottle of wine?"

"I would like that."

We're frozen with one another, feet planted on the floor. "I heard we've both been cornered by our friends over our latest developments."

"Oh, we have." His body completely relaxes from the humor of all this.

"The moms at school have already been assuming for weeks, but if they ever receive a fact, then I'm positive they'll be grabbing the pitchforks. Don't really care. I still get to fuck you, not them."

Holden breaks out in laugh. "I... I love how you always present life in a positive way, minus pitchforks."

I feel like I'm melting. I don't need to kiss Holden or have sex. Just being in his presence weakens everything inside of me.

"I should probably get to those calls." I make it not even half a step before Holden touches my arm to ensure I can't pass. "Is there something else?"

His face changes to a shade of vulnerability. It only ups the ante of connection because it's a side I'm aware not many people see. "You're still satisfied with what's going on between us, right?"

I just want to throw my arms around him and kiss him. "Do I

look like someone who isn't? I am completely happy and satisfied," I assure him.

Relief floods his face. He's just as scared as I am in this exhilarating rollercoaster that we're on. But his relief twists into something else. His eyes send a straight line over my shoulder, and he freezes.

"Why do you look like that?" Now fear hits me.

Holden clears his throat, almost nervous. "There is someone here for you."

"Like who?" I only turn halfway and a startled shriek bursts out of me. "Daddy?"

My father stands a few feet from me in a windbreaker and long khakis. It doesn't matter because his outfit most definitely doesn't match his cold glare directed at the man now behind me.

"Coach Moore," Holden greets my father.

"Holden," he replies, a little too firm for my liking. His eyes float between Holden and me.

Maybe Holden gets a hint or he just wants to escape, but he is quick to say, "I'll leave you two to catch up. Good to see you, Coach Moore. Feel free to grab lunch or drinks in the restaurant or patio, on the house. Maybe I will join you later to talk about old times."

"Good to see you too, I think."

My head spins between them until Holden smiles tightly and leaves us be.

I prepare myself for my father's unexpected arrival. I do my best to form an excited smile. "Daddy, this is a surprise." I walk to his open arms for a bear hug, because although we sometimes have odd moments, that soft spot as Daddy's Little Girl is always there.

"I wanted to surprise you while we have a little break on the team schedule, even if this town doesn't have the right team when it comes to hockey." Of course, the Spinners are his rivals. "And you've been too busy for time with your old man. Your mother sends her love, but she has her book club meeting that happens only once a month."

"I forget that she's still doing that. Ever since I was a little girl," I reflect. It takes me a moment for my bearings to return. "Come on, let's go grab a drink out by the lake. The weather is great."

"Sounds like a plan. You have to show me some of your work first."

I interlace our arms and begin the tour. In the end, I only explain the lobby and show him a few touches near the private party room. Mostly because it's still a little frenzied with a few contractors scattered around, and housekeeping is busy working their daily rounds. But in all honesty, I wanted to speed up to our conversation.

We grab two iced teas and a bowl of nuts from the bar and go outside to sit at a table on the patio.

"Everything looks great. I'm proud of you, Lexi."

My father's praise causes me to smile. "Thanks, Dad."

His gaze turns firm in my direction. "Must be fun staying here while you're busy with the project."

An ice cube falls out of my mouth. "Did I not mention... I'm staying with Holden. In the guest room since the guesthouse had a water issue, and there was a leak here, but they still need a few rooms open for guests..." I quickly sew together a sentence.

My father's eyes darken. "How convenient." Not one ounce of sincerity is in his tone. "It was only a few years ago that he was on my team, and I coached him. He had a lot of drama in his life. Kids, divorce, a lot of attention from women and the press."

A need to defend Holden hits me in a boom. "Well, his kids are great, maybe misunderstood, but they are kids with a warm heart. Plus, Holden's not in the media anymore, and I'm sure Holden from years ago is not the same man as now."

He rests his arms on the table. "Except now he's sleeping with my daughter."

My face drops. "Daddy!"

My father shakes his head and grabs a handful of nuts from the bowl. I feel as though I'm about to be lectured as if I'm no longer an adult.

"It was obvious the moment I walked through the door that something is going on."

"I-I…" I don't lie to my father unless I'm sixteen and sneaking out to a party. "What if I am? I'm an adult."

Leaning back, his cold look gives me no clue of what he must be considering. "You're right. Doesn't mean I can't voice my opinion. You're younger than him, he has kids, and his life is quite different to yours. You travel and look for adventure."

Anger is flaming inside of me. "What if being with Holden *is* an adventure?"

A near sinister laugh hits my ears. "What if you're infatuated?" He takes a moment to admire the lake view and maybe calm a smidgen. "I'm just watching out for you."

I twist my hair and plump it on the top of my head to tie into a bun. "I get that. But, please, just let me figure out my life on my own."

"He doesn't even have the decency to speak with me about this."

Throwing my hands up in the air, I'm exhausted. "We're new. Going slow. We're being sensitive to his family situation," I explain. Watching them is more a picture of a family than I had growing up.

My father's eyes grow big. "Moving into his house? That's not going slow."

"Not that it's your business, but we weren't this way when I moved in. He needed a little help with his son and daughter since the nanny quit."

He scoffs a sound of further disappointment. "You're a nanny now?"

The humor in how this must all sound brings a smile to my face. "No. I'm not the nanny," I grumble. "Now, can you be the dad that I've always remembered who would let me be and discover the world for myself?"

"Daddy bear has to come out when you're dating an older man who I happen to know quite well." He is half serious, which makes it all the more endearing.

Throwing him a pout, the kind that causes him to remember the days when I would skip around with piggy tails, his entire body falters.

A sound of hopelessness fills the air. "Fine, Lexi, I'm not one to tell you what to do with your love life. I can only warn you and hope you don't get hurt."

"Thank you." I pick up the bowl of nuts and offer it to him. They're his favorite, slightly salted with a few sugary coated peanuts thrown in.

"Any other shockers I need to prepare myself for?" he queries.

I shake my head. "Not that I can think of."

"Great. Will you do me a favor then?"

"Of course."

My father rubs his face. "Text your mom about this. Because if I have to tell her, then I'll have to listen to her shriek for half an hour straight."

Warmly, I smile. "No problem."

The next half-hour, we talk about the team, a vacation he is planning with my mom, and possibly redoing their BBQ area in their backyard. My father has an uncanny knack to continue conversation, even if a thousand thoughts are running in his head.

By the time we are hugging goodbye and walking through the lobby, I take notice of the clock on the wall. It's nearly the end of the school day, which for some reason now makes me wonder how Lori and Harry's day went or what homework they have.

It's also the time when Holden walks through the lobby because he needs to go pick up the kids, as he is doing exactly now. The faceoff between my father and Holden is instant.

"I'm expecting you to contact me for a talk. My daughter isn't hockey." My father's voice has a lot of bite to it, and it causes my body to jolt and my brow to raise. I'm not sure if I should chortle or be scared. He storms off before I can solve it, or before Holden can reply.

Holden strides my way, his face pained. "Figured it out, huh?"

"Oh yeah. Call it my father's instant assessment of situations."

He rakes his hand through his hair. "Well, almost feels like we should just throw up a billboard at this point."

I step forward and touch his chest with no care in the world about our surroundings. "It's okay. We will take a little more time for Lori and Harry."

A bitter laugh hits him. "If they don't hear it from somewhere else or figure it out for themselves."

I lift my shoulders. "I don't know what to say. It's your train to drive."

He leans in to kiss my forehead. It's chaste, but to the world, obvious enough that I'm his woman and he's my man.

"Need to get the kids. We'll talk later."

I reluctantly remove my hand and nod in understanding, watching him walk away and wondering what is the next step in relation to our families and should I be scared?

19

HOLDEN

The calendar on my desk taunts me with the days ticking by. After a couple of weeks, everything is complete at the Dizzy Duck, and although fantastic for business, it does mean one thing. Lexi won't have a reason to be waltzing into the Dizzy Duck on a daily basis as if she owns the place. Making demands of what she needs, all while delivery men smile and Lexi shows kindness to the staff that adore her.

Leaning back in my chair, I tap the wood, very well knowing that my concentration for the day has gone to shit. It's been a week since her father showed up, a week of a weighty awareness that this small town has a tiny bubble of gossip that may no doubt reach my kids before I do.

The sound of my door cracking open causes me to smirk. Lexi doesn't even bother with knocking, and even if we weren't sleeping together, I'm positive she wouldn't knock anyhow.

"Holden, the magazine called, and they want to take photos of the inn a few days earlier than planned. We can make it work, I just will need to order two rounds of flowers, and we need to up the ante on little trinkets to hand out. We'll need to do everything now…"

She looks up from her little notebook that she carries around and stops in her ramble to notice me.

I'm always amused by her adorable fits of speed talking. My elbows rest on the arms of my chair and my fingers steeple together.

"What's up with you? You seem grumbly," she adds as she strides my way, approaching me as though I'm her target, ready to relax me.

"Not grumpy. Just lost in thought."

She clicks her fingers. "Well, snap out of it. I only have fifteen minutes until I'm supposed to pick up Lori and get her to her lesson. Her coach has been sick for the whole week, and to my surprise, Lori asked me if I could… monitor, help, give tips…" She's doubting what to say, but Lexi seems fully invested.

I spin my chair slightly and reach out for her wrists which causes her to flop her notebook on my desk. I give her a tug until she lands on my lap in a perfect fit. "Thank you for doing it." She shrugs, because to her it's nothing, which is why a simple smile graces her lips. "You've kind of become a staple in the not-a-nanny-but-a-houseguest role."

Lexi gently smacks her palm against my chest. "How are you doing with that? You better have not put that nanny search on hold. Although, I'm positive that a pre-teen does not want a nanny, nor needs one. You really should consider other options, otherwise you'll only have more angst to deal with, and I'm positive she's switched your normal coffee with decaf just to test you." Again, her long-winded sentences return. Lexi does that when she's invested in things.

I bring my hands up to cup her face then quickly crash my lips onto hers to quiet her… and also because her lips look luscious today with a pink gloss. It does the trick, and she eases instantly with a purr and her wrists resting on my shoulders. In truth, these kisses bring us both back to a stable foundation here on earth. Sometimes we're stronger together.

Pulling away, I lick my lips to taste her. "A shame we only have fifteen minutes," I say in a near-rough voice, desperate for more in this moment.

Her eyes pop out. "Really? Fifteen minutes is stopping you? I'm sure that's not an issue."

I laugh and quickly peck her mouth once more. "It will have to wait. I kind of want to talk to you about something."

A slight fear forms in her eyes. "Oh…"

To ease her worries, I smile at her. "It's nothing bad, except we seem to be avoiding the detail of what to do once the inn finishes…" Lexi's chin lifts up, waiting for me to say it or to give her own assessment. "It will kind of feel like a step back if you move out. Which is crazy, as we probably should go back a few stages that we skipped over. It's just…"

"Yeah, of course, I totally get it." She nervously tucks hair behind her ear and her eyes avoid mine.

"I don't really want you to leave, and I'm not sure Lori and Harry would want you to, either. They've become accustomed to you."

Her eyes whip back to me. "But if I get a few projects around Lake Spark that I've been asked to do, then I can take the guesthouse with working water, but it's not… You know, if we're moving too fast. We are moving fast."

"The guesthouse? It's not the same."

Lexi's lips begin to curve up, but she can't quite commit. "I'm not sure what to say…"

I begin to rub her arms that fell from my shoulders, coaxing her to continue. "The truth."

Her eyes blink a few times. "The thought has crossed my mind… the slight sadness of leaving. Even if I'll be banished to the guest room downstairs."

My finger is quick to shush her lips. "Then it seems we have a predicament." She nods in agreement with my finger never parting. "Lori and Harry should probably be clued in on this change between you and me." She bobs her head again, nearly mesmerized. I break out in a wide grin. "It's settled. I will tell them tonight, maybe alone is best. This is a change they've never had before. I've never had a girlfriend in the picture really."

Lexi laughs. "Really? I should probably dive into that mystery a little more, but fuck it. Holden, we are at a point where my feelings for you are an attachment that will be difficult to break. Everything we are doing, I hope it's because you feel it deep within you that we're going somewhere on the long-term. Because the last few years I've been floating around life, one place after another. But I'm ready to settle down in a way, and that's an adventure in itself."

To cement my agreement, I kiss her. Long and firm. Promising too. "That's what I wanted to hear, Lexi." My thumbs follow the curve of her face. "This is new to me, but it feels right."

Her smile breaks out, and she gives me a quick kiss before bouncing up, leaving my lap. "Then we're on the same road. It's clear. Which is great because I'm out of time right now."

"To pick up my daughter, which hits me somewhere unknown within me. You're special, Lexi."

She winks at me. "I couldn't agree more."

I shake my head because she can take soft moments and bring us back to our normal day in a split second, and that's what I need, because pondering in my thoughts for too long sometimes leads me in all directions.

———

Lexi went to have dinner with Harlow and Summer to give me some breathing room to talk to Lori and Harry who are staring at me while we sit in the living room.

I uneasily scratch the back of my neck, wishing I had rehearsed this a little bit instead of choosing to wing it. "It's good that we can spend a little time together. Nothing like pizza."

"On the couch. You never let us have pizza on the couch. This is a little weird," Harry highlights my rule.

Meanwhile, Lori sits with arms crossed and her face neutral. "Probably because he is trying to butter us up."

"Oh man, is this the part when you say that I can't get a dog for my birthday? That sucks." Harry flops his piece of pizza on his plate, his garlic stick falling off onto the couch, which is the least of my worries right now.

My head tips gently to the side. Huh, I forgot about that request. It also seems that this conversation really is normal to him. But Lori's eyes? They're waiting for me.

"The thing is, as you know Lexi has been staying here, and with the inn almost done and the water fixed in the guesthouse, then it means…" Now Harry's attention is grabbed. "I've asked her to stay… here."

"And why is that, dear father?" Lori's face shades to one I'm very familiar with since it's a mirror of my own when I'm waiting for her to confess her past tricks. She thinks she has the upper hand right now.

A sound escapes the back of my throat, now aware of Lori's play. "Because we're together."

My daughter has a satisfied smile at her win and drops her arms. "No shit. This conversation wasn't obvious at all," she muses with sarcasm.

"Really? Like, you have a girlfriend? That's a little…" Harry contemplates.

It's a little worrying, as my children's opinions matter to me. They will always come first in my life, that's how parenting works, how I want it to work. There is no other way in my book. My attention turns back to Lori.

"Care to elaborate on your no-shit expression?"

"Which you won't care about my use of language because you're probably freaking out about my opinion." Damn, this daughter of mine keeps me on my toes, and in other circumstances, I would be a little proud she has my genes. "You think I'm an idiot? As if you cut your neck while shaving. It was totally a hickey."

"That was weeks ago."

"And your over-the-top concern what we might do to her at breakfast was another clue. Then there is the ridiculous cover of checking on cars and garages." Lori sits back on the sofa, grabbing a pillow to hug because this appears to be a casual discussion.

My eyes tear away from Lori to my son. "You okay there, buddy?"

He hums a noise and brings his finger to his chin to contemplate. "I guess it's fine. I do like her. This means we have to see all of this cuddly stuff, don't we?"

"That's kind of how relationships work," I highlight to my son.

"Fine. But this doesn't mean she gets to eat all of our cheesecake when she wants. We all get equal shares. Speaking of which, we really need to talk about your stock portfolio. Lexi let me explain to her why she should invest the other day. She may be richer than you one day if she invests the way I tell her."

I snort a laugh because I can envision Lexi's perplexed face as she listened to him. But it seems business as usual with them, not bothered about my news.

Which brings me back to the apple of my eye, and she notices. "Now I have someone to take me bra shopping, I need one of those."

My hands claw the arms on my chair, with my entire body tightening and my face attempting not to show my total freakout that my little girl is no longer a little girl. "Oh yeah, I'm sure she'll help with that," I nearly squeak. Deep breath. "But why didn't you tell me you knew about Lexi and me?"

She shrugs her shoulder. "I wanted to see how this ship would sail, and here we are. I'm fine. It's cool. You can even focus on her more and let me have my space."

I groan at this girl's ability to wrap me around her finger and keep me at her mercy. "Delightful." Another deep exhale. "Is this conversation done? Any questions?"

"All good." Lori stands and flicks her hair. "Off to my room to call my friends to tell them that this conversation has happened. They had timeline estimates and now need confirmation. Bye."

I can't even with her. In my peripheral view, I see Harry has cheese strung along from his mouth to the plate, only to have it break and land on the couch cushion.

Guess we're all going to be alright.

20

HOLDEN

L exi gives me a peculiar stare as we stand in the reception room of a country club outside of Chicago. Lake Spark may be a hockey town, but sometimes sponsors like to get away from the ice for a children's charity and find neutral territory for athletes from all teams to come together for a cause. These events can be fun. Still, my team at home are not impressed, which is why Lori's stare is more a near scowl—but still cute.

"I'm not sure this counts as a family outing?" Lexi chides but then touches my arm and completely relaxes and smiles because she's joking.

I snicker. "I can't get out of it. It's a sponsor that I still have a contract with. It's why I still appear at sports functions. At least it's a family-themed event and you got to watch me attempt to golf one hole, no?"

"*And* you should just stick to hockey," she mumbles but then stands tall. "My dad is here, and I spoke to him for a little bit. I'm surprised I didn't need to chain you up and drag you here because of that. How could you not want to fake a sickness and get out of this?" Lexi refutes.

"I'm aware." I sigh. I need to face him eventually. After all, with my kids now in the loop about my relationship status, then it's a step into the not-casual-dating category. I owe Coach Moore a chat. I missed the traditional train to ask for permission to date his daughter, but I can still make an effort.

I study my kids for a second. Lori scans the room while Harry is already beelining it to the snack table. My face turns pleading when I face my daughter. "An hour or two tops, then I promise we can do something just the four of us."

"Does fun include shopping?" Her tone is flat.

"Not exactly." But the four of us, for sure. Since everything between Lexi and me is out in the open, everyone seems a little happier. Lori in particular seems to have bonded with Lexi, which is refreshing to see since Lori could use a strong female figure in her life to look up to. It also brings Harry and me closer because the pranks have died down and I don't have to spend time defusing fires.

Lexi plants her hands on Lori's shoulders and guides her in a new direction. "Come on, I hear there are cute junior hockey players visiting this event, and we can go look at them over there." Lexi flashes her eyes at me as they leave.

Still, I manage to hear them as they walk away. "Does it matter? I see the Spinners practice at the rink all the time," my daughter reminds Lexi.

Ruefully, I shake my head as a guy calls my name. I turn to see Trey, an old buddy from my team.

"Hey, if it's not Mr. Entrepreneur himself." His hand comes up to shake mine. A strong hold because it's nearly a side hug.

"Hey, Trey. Long time no see. How's life treating you?"

He hitches a thumb over his shoulder. "Pretty damn awesome. Kim is over there talking to a few of the other wives. She's holding baby one, and baby two is on the way. Gotta have those kids close together in age. Complete the diaper phase in one big swoosh." Trey shines, and it's great to see.

"Congrats. My kids are around here somewhere."

"They must be big now. I still don't know how you managed to play hockey on little sleep. Respect." He squeezes my shoulder. "Miss the team life?"

I place a hand on my waist. "Nah, it was a great life. A little wild at times. Eventually we settle down, or at least I wanted to. I need the energy too, for my kids. It's like the first years are chaotic, then you get a break age six to ten, and then it goes back into the unruly phase where you want to grit your teeth far too many times to prevent words you shouldn't say from leaving your mouth."

Trey chuckles. "Thanks for the warning." He nudges my arm. "And… might have noticed that you didn't come alone today." He raises his brows. "Man, the coach's daughter? Didn't see that one coming. But does it count when you're no longer on the team and have retired? Surely, his cold glare coming straight for us is a signal that it isn't a big deal. Even if you and Lexi look pretty damn good together."

"I am lucky. Easy on the eyes, younger to keep me rejuvenated, and an absolutely great personality."

He smiles to himself. "Hope luck is on your side because Coach Moore has arrived to talk to you." Trey winks to me and then gives the man behind my shoulder a smile. "Hey, Coach, we still have it in us. See how our team came together to golf? A reflection of your fine leadership. It's just some of us forgot about certain rules pertaining to your daughter." He's proud of himself as he pivots and leaves. Trey has a good heart, and everything he does is in a positive jest. Maybe he even just lightened the blow because I turn to face the man that I need to speak to.

"Coach Moore," I greet him.

"Holden." His tone is stiff, and he indicates that we should step to the corner out of earshot, which I feel is probably a great idea.

Nervously I smile, reminding myself that I'm a grown man who was always determined and fearless. "I've been wanting to reach out and talk to you. Life has been a little busy with the Dizzy Duck and my kids."

"Not to mention my daughter. You seem to be busy with my

daughter." His cold demeanor is nearly scary as shit, but in the corner of my eye I see Lexi giving me an encouraging thumbs up.

"Listen, you can doubt my intentions or believe I'm not the right fit for Lexi, but I won't hear what you have to say about it. All that matters is that Lexi and I believe that we're something worth building on." I'm firm in tone, my stance strong.

His eyes survey my body up and down. "I'm concerned about the experiences you have. You've been through a lot, when Lexi has lived one big carefree journey, even if it means ignoring the negatives. If you two are strong and have a future, then even if you're nowhere near there, it still must've crossed your mind that one day she will want her first and hopefully only marriage, probably a baby too. Anything about that scare you? Because you've already experienced both, except the wife who is long-lasting. Would you do it again for my daughter?"

I take a few beats because everything he says is a stark reality that maybe I haven't thought about this all enough. Still, it's not a scary warning that I should run away either. Lexi is younger, and of course one day will want things that are already part of my life story.

"Yes, sir. I've thought about all of that, yet here I am."

He lifts his chin, debating if I'm worthy. One thing that is different to our dynamic than any other normal relationship is that Lexi's dad was my coach and through that we learned how we both react to situations. He knows if I'm being honest or not.

"Lexi raves about your wonderful children. Good kids normally means that someone in their life is a strong influence. They've had you, which indicates that you're responsible. That counts for a lot in my book. You know I value strong family dynamics."

My hands splay out. "Then look no further. You also know that I can support Lexi too."

Coach chortles. "Now you're sounding like this is a marriage talk. Don't get ahead of yourself."

My body relaxes, as he just made a joke, that's a good sign at least. "What will it be? Skepticism or an attempt to accept us? You know I'm not one to settle for anything less than a win."

He glances over to the other corner where Lexi suddenly appears to keep herself busy with something else, having clearly been observing this scene.

His lips stretch slightly. "This is taking a little bit to wrap my head around. You broke my token rule to stay the hell away from my daughter. Which means you are even more persistent in getting what you want. I'm assuming you're not doing this for kicks, and my daughter's blatant joy right now is because of you."

"Hopefully so."

He sighs. "Fine." He deflates. "She's an adult and can make her own choices, even if it means that upcoming family dinners might need to defrost my opinion a little."

My lips press tightly together, debating what else I should say to plead my case. "Thawing of opinions it is," I concede.

We stare at one another for a long few seconds, standing our ground and wanting the same thing—for Lexi to be happy. I offer my hand; he hesitates, but we shake. An agreement between two men.

That's another checklist item done.

When he walks away, I sigh in relief as Lexi nearly skips to me, overly joyous, and she claps her hands together.

"See? Not so bad. I made him promise that he would go easy."

I rub my face in doubt. "I guess it could have been worse. Remind me to sit on the other side of the table at Thanksgiving."

"A perfect idea."

I wrap my arm around her shoulders, and we begin to walk through the room to find my little heathens that I love beyond the world.

"We should head outside. There are some games for the kids. Then I can also sign some stuff for the children from the foundation."

"Sounds like a plan."

After a few more chitchat conversations with a few people, we move outside. Harry and Lori run ahead of us to the candy-apple making next to the face-painting tent. Lexi and I keep our fingers gently linked as we walk. I spot the area where my former teammates are signing things for the children who anxiously wait with glee, and I'm happy this event makes their day.

"I want to give some time to this, so if everyone can be a little patient a little longer," I tell Lexi.

She nods then tips her head in the direction of a face-painting stand. "Of course. I totally need to get a unicorn painted on my cheek anyhow."

We both lean in for a kiss. God, it feels good not to have to sneak around. We're in the open with no worries in sight.

That's how it should be.

———

LORI THROWS some popcorn at her brother while we're all set in our places in the living room. Harry and Lori on the other ends of one sofa and Lexi and me on the other. We all have a blanket and snacks as we watch a movie. I should be a little stricter with what Harry watches, but I agreed to PG-13 since it was his choice to pick, and he wanted to watch an action move.

Lexi rests her head against my shoulder as she snuggles into me. Never thought I would see this scene where someone else joins the three of us for casual family time. Nor did I expect to have a woman in my arms who isn't just instant gratification behind closed doors.

This feels like a right fit for all of us.

My phone vibrates on the side table next to the couch, and I feel compelled to answer it to ensure that everything is fine at the inn, as I haven't checked in all weekend. My screen only shows me an alert related to news… on me. Probably not the brightest idea, but long ago I set up alerts about my name in the news. It was more to ensure Lori and Harry wouldn't have to be blindsided by anything from others, although I do my damnedest to keep them out of the public eye. Another reason that I appreciate Lake Spark Academy; they take these kinds of things seriously, especially as there are other high-profile parents too.

Swiping my screen, I'm not sure I want to smirk to myself or be kind of pissed.

"What is it?" Lexi asks as she notices my interest on my cell. Her eyes travel down then move in different angles. "Is that us?"

"Yeah, seems it is. I forgot there was a photographer at the charity event yesterday."

Holden West in a Relationship with Former Coach's Daughter.

The photo only shows us holding hands, but it shows enough to make assumptions.

Lexi pops her lips. "At least it's a good angle," she quips.

It's been a hell of a long time since I've appeared in any photos this way, but I guess I don't seem to mind.

"Ooh, someone is going to get some glaring eyes on them at the next school drop-off." Lori seems excited.

"Yep, my life's goal," I joke.

Lexi yawns. "Just roll with it."

"It's fine. Nobody will care tomorrow, and there are no photos of Lori and Harry."

Stretching her arms, Lexi gives me the clue that she's tired. "Guys, are we sure we're close to the end?"

"Five minutes," Harry informs us.

"Okay, I can cope with that," Lexi promises.

But it felt like a long five minutes, even for me. The movie dragged, and after picking up kernels of popcorn that seemed to have scattered everywhere and folding blankets, everyone was ready to call it a night, as tomorrow is a school day.

Every night lately, it's been the same routine. Harry and Lori to their rooms. Harry to check his financial portfolio on his tablet and me promising to actually talk to my financial advisor. Lori scrolling her social media on her phone, and me reminding her to turn her phone off. They both make their way to sleep on their own, and it works.

Lexi? It's a humorous scene every damn time. I lie on the bed waiting for her, and she hesitates in the doorframe of my bathroom, doubting what she should do.

I offer the same easy and assuring smile every night. "Come on, woman. I'm getting impatient."

"Are you sure this is a good idea?"

Shaking my head, I'm not sure how many times I need to repeat this. "Yes."

She takes a few more steps, slowly adapting to the idea. "I mean, it must be a little weird for them to know that I'm in *here*."

That's why I'm waiting as a man ready to pounce her. "Trust me, Lori and Harry don't seem to notice or care."

Lexi twists the ends of her tank top because regular sleeping with one another entails normal pajamas now, just in case we have any family mishaps. "What if they're scared to say something? It must feel odd that suddenly there is a woman sleeping in their father's room."

I pat the bed, inviting her in. "I think we've been over this a thousand times. Now get in here."

Finally, she drops her shoulders and nods in agreement. "You're right. I'm being silly." I lift the duvet, and she slides underneath. "I mean, I know how to be quiet anyhow." There is her assertive spirit returning.

"Damn straight you can, now pass me a condom so we can get a step ahead on this train."

Her mouth forms an O shape, and a sound croaks out of her mouth. "It's okay. I'm on the pill, and I want to feel you completely, and I'm positive that you want that too."

I take hold of her body and drag her on top of me, our eyes connecting with a new significance. There is something about this that only binds us closer.

"Lexi, if you're truly comfortable with that then there is no going back, because the first taste of the way you feel will be the only way I'll ever take you again."

She lowers herself and murmurs against my lips. "I want you to come inside me."

I'm completely hers, and it's true… there is no going back in all aspects of us, because she's completely mine too.

21

LEXI

My toes dig into the mattress while Holden's eyes gleam and cascade down my body for inspection. There is something about a woman wearing white lingerie with garter belts and stockings; it brings innocence when we're the opposite. The fact that I'm sitting on the middle of the bed in the luxury suite of the Dizzy Duck Inn is even more special, I think.

I crook a finger to invite Holden to join me. "Surprise," I whisper.

A sly grin appears on his face as he steps forward while he unbuttons his cufflinks. "I thought we were having a meeting about last-minute touches for the opening in a few days." His knee dips into the mattress while he approaches me.

My palms smooth next to me over the duvet. "All the more reason to enjoy this room before others get to. Consider it my present to you for reaching a professional milestone in your life."

With his shirt now on the floor, his lips find mine, and I lose my balance only to land on my back. Holden joins me on his side, breaking our kiss, and his eyes strike below to watch his fingers feather along the lines of the lingerie.

He hisses a sound, very satisfied with this situation. "I

completely approve of this outfit, and I completely approve of what you're going to do while wearing it," he warns.

"Oh yeah? What might that be?" I rasp.

His kiss on my lips feels stronger; it's the type that draws out my breath every time and also a kiss to remind me that, for the next few minutes, his mouth will be elsewhere. I'm correct when his lips begin to slither down my throat, skimming my skin, with my entire body curving up to offer him more. Sensitive ripples float through me like a wave, and the ache between my legs begins to make me feel impatient.

"I plan on inspecting every inch of this lace." Oh yeah, I asked him a question. His lips cover one nipple while his hand squeezes my other breast for attention. "The lace covers far more than I prefer, but it's so damn sexy on you."

"Mmhmm." I close my eyes when he travels below my bra, and I feel his hand sliding up my thigh to explore the edge of my stockings. My panties are already soaked because he's drawing on my navel with his tongue, pausing near the band of the garter to taunt me.

Snap. His fingers flick the thin straps holding up my stockings. "I think these might need to stay on when your legs are wrapped around me," he murmurs against my skin.

"Holden." I begin to beg as I'm desperate for a touch on the spot that will give me only a tiny bit of relief, eager for more.

A moan hits me as his fingers skim over the drenched lace between my legs and along my pussy. I'm mad now that I'm even wearing panties because I want his bare touch. I want all of him. Always.

"You are dying for my cock, clearly."

His fingers slip under the fabric for one long sweep through my arousal, but that's all I get as he abandons my pussy to bring his fingers up, ensuring that I'm watching him, with his eyes possessive as he sucks and hums, the sound of his fingers popping out of his mouth. "Sweet as always."

I nod once, mesmerized by his ability to lead and dominate us without my body or mind wanting to challenge.

He captures my lips for a soft kiss, his lips tracing mine side to side, and I know he wants me to taste myself on his mouth. "I taste good."

Holden laughs under his breath. "Damn right you do, but I want you to taste me."

I know my cue, which is why I urge him to lie back, and he obeys. My best sultry look appears on my face as I swing my legs over his hips to straddle him, with my hands working on his pants to open and slide them off his legs.

The moment my tongue darts to swirl around the tip of his cock, we're both nearly gone. I always love the sound that he makes when I begin to take more of him into my mouth. Wrapping my lips to suck, my eyes flick up to watch his face with that pleasured smirk. I release my own moan into my filled mouth. Our senses heighten when I bring him in deeper near the back of my throat, and his hands claw into my hair to guide me to ensure I give it to him the way he likes. Pumps that get harder, then slow, then harder. Every time he escapes my salivating mouth, I lick along his length before I repeat my actions.

But unless we are only doing a quick blowjob when we steal a moment, he always pulls me off his cock because he prefers to come inside me.

Holden scoots to the headboard. "On my lap but face forward."

"I think I like the sound of this," I tell him as I take action to get in place.

"You should."

My back is to his body, but we are tightly bound together, his hand roughly parting my thighs to ensure he has an open canvas before he tucks his hand into my panties from the top and instantly circles around my clit, bringing his other hand to cup my breast.

"You like that? Playing with your clit." His voice is thick and raspy in my ear, sending new tingles to my pulsing nub of nerves.

I cover his hand on my breast and bring the free fingers of my other hand to my untouched nipple. "So good. You always know where to touch me." My voice is heavy and my breath changes.

His movements on my pussy become more frantic, with one finger inside of me and the other rubbing my clit up and down, nearly punishing me for being so aroused.

"I think we've played enough." Both his hands abandon my body, and he drags my panties quickly off before he squares my hips to lift me slightly to ensure his cock has room.

The moment he aligns his tip, he plunges me down onto his length, and we moan together. His hard cock is snug in my body, and I need him deeper. I bounce on him, and he thrashes up inside of me. Neither of us want slow right now. We want our incinerating desire for one another to indicate the way.

Our moans sync, our bodies sync, and something else between us syncs too, but I can't pinpoint it.

But it becomes clear when he directs me off his cock and cues my body to lying on my back. In no time, he's over me and back inside of me, deep… but slower. My toes rest against his ass to keep my thighs wide. One arm gets pinned to the bed while our eyes connect.

A new gust blows in my body, but it's surrounding my heart—no, it's taken over my heart. I swear the sentiment that's flaring inside of me is mirrored in his eyes.

Our lips meld, and we move together as our foreheads touch. Both clearly about to fall in the same place.

———

"WELL, THAT WAS…" I pant along with Holden as we rest on the bed, trying our best to come down from our high.

A breath sighs from his mouth. "It was."

Neither of us can find words to describe it. "Different?"

"A little beyond our usual savage tactics in the bedroom," he attempts to lighten the reality of the axis of our relationship changing.

I roll off the bed, holding my index finger up. "Hold that thought. I need to take care of something."

After cleaning up, I open the bathroom door and suddenly seem shy as I walk back to the bed. "Hi." My voice is etched with gentleness I'm not used to.

"Hi," he returns the sentiment.

Sliding back into his arms, we stare at the ceiling and there is silence, but it doesn't feel uneasy.

"We have to stop this," he mentions.

My head whips to look at him but remains set against the pillow. "What do you mean?" I must sound concerned.

But then the corners of his mouth hitch up. "Me asking housekeeping for a discreet favor because we keep using this room for our escapades… although worth it."

I smile in relief. "After tomorrow, we are passing on the torch to couples who will have a romantic night at the Dizzy Duck Inn."

Holden squeezes me tight against his body. "It's okay."

My lips press together and roll into my mouth. I've never been one to refrain from speaking my mind, but now I am. "Excited for tomorrow?" I cop out and talk as if it's an average day.

He chortles a laugh. "You want to talk about mundane subjects when we should be discussing this hot-as-fuck outfit you're wearing?" Holden looks down at me to capture my gaze.

I lift my shoulders. "I was saving it for a special occasion, and I felt that the mundane topic you just mentioned is actually kind of a big deal. You're really going to have a finished inn that is ready to shine."

"Because of you. I sure as hell didn't pick out paint colors or take down moose heads."

My fingers crawl up his chest. "It was one moose, and I'm not exactly sure why you didn't do it before."

"It was a statement piece that got people talking when they arrived."

"Solid tactic." I begin to stir out of his arms. "Now if you'll excuse me, I'm freezing and need to get out of this."

Holden sits up, disappointed, but then slants his head. "I guess we need to leave this room eventually today." His eyes pin on me with that devilish grin forming. "Can I have one picture of you like this? For my eyes only?"

I glance away, both honored and entertained that he would ask that. "How do you want me?" I agree.

He stands up and walks to his pants lying carelessly on the floor to grab his phone. "We can do several so I have options."

"Now this is a photoshoot?"

His eyes draw up from his phone. "Well yeah, I need you standing up, lying down on your back and belly, on your knees too. Would you squeeze your tits together once?" he quips, but I'm going to give it all to him anyway, which is why I'm crawling back onto the bed.

"Here you are, sir."

Holden stalls for a second, his eyes glowing with a shade that I can only describe as fragile. A thought seems to cross his mind, and I don't believe it has to do with dirty pictures.

"I like this surprise." It floats off his lips.

Our eyes linking together only confirms my suspicions. The thought in his mind has everything to do with us, but beyond the bedroom.

———

I EXAMINE the lobby once more as various guests chat while trays of champagne and nibbles travel through the room. My fingers wrap around my wrists to keep busy, causing the fabric of my long-sleeved black dress to move. The lines of the dress follow my curves, and Holden fully approves, judging by the once-over I got earlier when everyone was placing the final touches here before guests arrived.

After discussing with the event planner, I asked that we have a few options that are a homage to the history and design of this place. How she mixed pioneer with 1920's flare, I'm not entirely sure, except I see champagne in classic goblets. I'm too nauseous to eat, but the corn-inspired food looks delish. The pride I feel for my work, I want to be validated. The other day when the press did a walk-through for photos and to ask questions, it seemed positive. But now close family and friends, plus the Lake Spark mayor, are here. They will kill me if I got it all wrong. This is a place of history for the town. It's special to all for so many reasons.

The line of my lips moves from straight to curved when I see Lori and Harry next to the snack table. Of course, they go straight for the pecan squares. Lori even seems invested in the night, with a smile on her face.

"You did great," my father mentions as he stands by my side with whiskey in hand. He quickly stopped by, even though the team needs to be in San Jose tomorrow. My mother already had a girls' trip planned with friends in California.

My head turns to the side with elation from his comment. "Thank you. That means a lot to me. Also, that you managed to stop by, even if really quick."

His lips snag up. "Sorry about that, but hockey season calls."

I shrug my shoulders. "I know, it always does." I think I've become accepting of that fact. When I was younger, I didn't quite understand his absence due to his marriage to hockey, but it now makes sense.

"I wish I could stay for the toasts and grill your boyfriend a little, but that will be for another time." He's actually teasing me.

I chuckle at him. "More accepting now?"

"A higher percentage than last time." His mundane tone represents truth yet skepticism all in one, and I throw him a pretend glare. "I said hello to him and congratulated him on the opening. Even shook his hand. We're progressing."

"Best present of the day," I reply dryly.

My father leans in to kiss my cheek. "As long as he doesn't break your heart, then we'll be okay. Might even let him cut the turkey at future holiday dinners." I give a side hug, pleased with his comment. "Congratulations, sweetheart. Sorry I have to run."

"Thanks, Dad. I'll see you soon."

He squeezes my shoulder once in passing before he moves in the direction of the entrance.

My eyes scan the room yet again, but it doesn't take long for someone else to say my name.

"Hey, Lexi," Harlow's voice breaks my daze.

My eyes sideline to her. "Hey, nice to see you here."

Her welcoming face returns the sentiment. "Well, since my boyfriend has invested in this place and wants to do nothing with it, then I have to make an appearance." She's half sarcastic.

"Have to get his money's worth, right?"

"Totally. I love everything about the design of this place."

The compliment causes my face to brighten even more. "You had the whole tour of everything, including the bedrooms?"

"The master suite, oh my, gorgeous. I'm jealous of whoever books that," she gushes.

"Thanks, Harlow. It's nice to hear that. I mean, I've had a few new clients reach out even here for Lake Spark, but it's even better to hear from friends and family or at least, you know, from Holden's circle."

She looks at me amused. "Yeah…" She sips from her wine glass. "Heard that ship is sailing into calm seas. He also seems extremely happy. I've also noticed his eyes keep tracking you down. Saw it when Stone and I briefly chatted with him, and well, right now, he seems to have a hard look that's a cross between possessive and sentimental. *And* he's walking over here. Ciao."

My entire body thrums with excitement because it's a type of bliss unknown to me when someone in your life appears blatantly happy and it's your doing. Plus, he is extremely hot when he's wearing dark jeans with a white button-down and blue blazer. I could melt purely from seeing his image. Even though he strolls my way, it surprises me when he stands next to me to lean in to whisper in my ear. Everyone in the room can see us, and we very much appear as a couple, especially when he places his palm on my lower back to keep me close.

"Everyone is raving," he reminds me.

"I think so too. Oh hey, why is the principal of Lake Spark Academy here? Figured she would be last on your invite list."

Holden chuckles low. "Because it's strategy. First off, she's on the list of the essential Lake Spark people who consider themselves crucial to the running of our small town. Plus, I need to schmooze her for my kids."

I snicker a laugh. "Very smart."

"Want to get some air before I give the toasts?" he suggests.

"Sure."

He tips his head in the direction of the hall to the bar. It's the closest room with a door to the back of the inn for a view of the lake and the patio. We step on the stones from the patio to the bench swing that gives us a little more privacy.

Facing one another, with the sound of the party distant in the background, my heart beats fast.

"Lexi…"

What kind of conversation is this going to be?

"I love you." It just bursts out of my mouth without thought.

We both realize what words are now in the air, unable to be forgotten.

Maybe that's why Holden stares at me, frozen.

Which only makes my body weaken from fear.

22

HOLDEN

Lexi's eyes twinkle, and although petrified about what she just said because she doesn't think I was expecting it, it was honest, and I'm not surprised. There was a shift yesterday in bed with one another. The air is heavy, but it feels as though we can only lift up.

Still, I blow out a long breath, and my eyes swim side to side.

Her lips part open. "I-I'm sor… No, I'm not. It just rolled out of my mouth." I stand there just listening with my entire posture and face blank. "It's just, I can't control this giant ball that keeps rolling and rolling, taking me into this future, that crosses my mind." She's talking fast again; my nervous Lexi is back.

"Lexi." I state her name, attempting to break her chain of thoughts spewing out of her mouth.

It falls on deaf ears. "I'm sure you don't, you don't, you know… feel. But I can't hold it in. I have feelings for you. They're strong, and I feel connected to you and your family. It's warm and caring. So it slipped out of my mouth, and we know my mind and mouth have little control—"

"Lexi," I attempt to stop her again as the line of my mouth stretches up. Her chest is visibly moving up and down. "Lexi? Is the third time's the charm going to get your attention?" It does, as her eyes rocket up to meet mine. I step forward, and my fingertips embrace her elbows to ensure she can't run. "I love you."

Her face falls with relief before completely brightening with a smile. "You do?"

I nod. "I would say so, since I asked you to come out here to talk because it was getting kind of unbearable."

"This is crazy, right? Everything we do seems to be big steps ahead. Yet, looking back, it all makes sense, and we haven't missed any."

My grin is in full force. "Crazy sounds about right. Now, can you shut up for a hot minute? I believe we have something to do." I step closer and dive my mouth down to cement our new state.

That's what this kiss is. Lexi has this uncanny capability to break down my walls, causing me to believe that I'm allowed to feel things that haven't been on my radar in years. I'm not ignorant to the practical fact of that. I'm in this new state because of her. I want it to be her. It is her. Now she's mine.

Her arms circle around my neck and my own loop around her middle to pull her flush to my body. She sighs in relief against my lips, not wanting us to part. "We have this click, the kind too overbearing to ignore. And you shouldn't because it will only get better," I tell her.

How can it not? She molds into my life, with Lori and Harry included. Most of all, I'm alive in the way that brings constant excitement for what the day ahead will look like. It will always be an adventure. That's a pretty damn good way to live.

"It kept building inside of me, this feeling. Maybe it's because I've intertwined in your life, houseguest upgrade included. But none of that would have happened if you and I didn't have a flare between us that grew into a fire." She nuzzles my nose, completely content with melting into my body and ready for what time will bring to us.

I cup her head, my thumb circling her cheek, ensuring her eyes gaze up at me. "Sound like we're aligned. Does this mean I get another gift like yesterday's show?" I tease her, and she pinches my stomach to cause me to flinch. Lexi knows that I'm playing with her.

But we calm, and she burrows her cheek into my palm while she calmly inhales. "I love you," she repeats in a rasp.

"I love you too."

We stay firmly in place, not wanting this moment to end, but it has to.

"We'll have a long night ahead in bed, but right now, I have toasts to do."

She creates space, with understanding seeping across her face. "Of course."

A quick kiss and then she pivots, only for me to yank her back for one more fast, decadent kiss.

Watching her walk away, I examine her sway and notice that it has extra pep to her movement, and hopefully that's my doing.

This is a big step for us, but it's our direction.

Now that the knot that was inside of me all day is untied, I can focus on the rest of the night with ease.

Walking back inside, I mentally switch gears and remind myself about my speech. Everyone has been waiting for it since they arrived before sunset so they could see the inn in two different lights.

Returning to the noisy lobby, everyone seems in good spirits. When I see Lori and Harry talking with Harlow, I know they're in good hands. They look freaking adorable. Lori in a simple blue dress, yet she picked it out herself, and Harry in a blazer minus the tie. They didn't even grumble when I asked them to dress up.

"No pressure but make this a long-run success. I hope to get my money's worth," Stone jokes.

I flash him a sly smile. "Funny. At least you showed up. Nash is still MIA. He may not care, but he still has 10% of this place."

Stone shakes his head. "It doesn't matter. You have 70%."

My head bobs. "True. Besides, I'm not surprised. Happy with the end result of this place?"

His eyes brighten. "It's phenomenal. I'm scared tourists are going to flock here in droves, more than the usual. I don't want to have to wait longer at Jolly Joe's for my coffee."

My brows rise. "Problem solved. The Dizzy Duck has a new coffee machine, and we switched the beans. We now have the best coffee around. Be nice to Stuart at the front desk and he might even grab you a cup whenever you demand."

He smacks me on my shoulder. "Thinking of all the tiny details. Now go give that speech so you can take home that future bride-to-be I saw you making out with."

"Marriage isn't on the radar, but yeah, we're something more than what began," I clarify.

A cheeky grin is glued on his face. "Well, I'll be damned, totally didn't see that coming when you decided to sleep with her." He's completely sarcastic.

I shake my head then decide to let him wallow in his correct prediction.

On my way to the fireplace, in passing I snatch a glass of champagne from the tray a waiter is holding. Arriving at the lit fireplace, I quickly run through the simple fact that despite what everyone may think, I absolutely… did fuck all to prepare for this speech about to happen in three seconds.

An old man who must be a friend of the old owner is sitting on the sofa in my vicinity. "Do you mind, sir, if you clink your glass with the fork on your snack plate? I need everyone's attention."

"Of course, young man." It seems to brighten his day that he gets to do the honors.

The sound of glass being used as a bell begins to cause the noise in the room to subside. Then everyone's eyes are on me.

Clearing my throat, I gather a few thoughts, about to wing this. "Thank you for giving me a moment to say a few words. I just wanted to first of all welcome you to the Dizzy Duck Inn, a staple in Lake Spark for many years. When I heard that the former owner, Mr. Nix, who is here with us tonight, was planning on selling, it caught my attention. After all, what is a pro-hockey player to do once he retires?" It earns me a few chuckles from the room. "Having visited

Lake Spark several times due to the sports complex here, and well, the population being overrun by professional athletes, then it seemed fate stepped in.”

My eyes catch Lexi's in the back of the room, watching me intently, and it gives me the courage to come up with more words. “The inn was already a little gem, but it was time to freshen it up for a new chapter.” I tip my champagne glass up to the bricks above the fireplace. “Which is probably why some of us might be mourning the farewell of Caesar the moose's head that was hanging up there. I promise, he is living a better life somewhere… in a closet… or the bottom of the lake. Not quite sure, but he is happy.” More laughs from the room. “Anyhow, I hope you all got a chance to walk around and see for yourself; the inn is ready to welcome guests. It wasn't possible without a few key people. For one, my partner in the inn who prefers to stay anonymous yet reaps the benefits of partly owning an inn.” The room enjoys this, more laughter. “Any contractor who came in to use a hammer, because I cannot.” I glance to my kids. “My children who are creative in everything they do, whether it gets them grounded or not.” Lori and Harry softly smile and the shade of pride on their faces nearly makes a tear form in my eyes.

But then my eyes swing to Lexi whose smile hasn't faded, and it gives me the strength to rid any potential waterworks. “Then there is Lexi, the mastermind behind all of this. It was her doing that you're sitting in a perfectly designed lobby or walking into suites fit for a king.” *Or me as her king.* “She walked in here ready to conquer, not afraid and diving right into everything. This is truly what will make the Dizzy Duck the hotel that everyone wants to put their name on the waiting list for.”

Summer nearby watches her friend with pride, tipping her glass in her direction as her husband, Zac, has an arm around her waist.

“Lexi tends to blow into your life, ready to change it… Thank you.” I don't mean the inn, which is why her lips twitch, because she understands my undertone.

I hold up my glass. “Okay, that's enough speech time. If

everyone can hold up your glass and say cheers." The room erupts with the sounds of cheers, clinking a few glasses of people in the vicinity, before the room quiets down as everyone sips from their glass.

With the room revving up again with soft music in the background, I walk to my kids and instantly receive a hug.

"Can we go now?" Harry asks.

"Let me think about that," I pretend. "Uh, no," I flat-out answer, and he grumbles.

My eyes land on Lori who appears content. "This place is kind of cool now."

"I would hope so."

"Does this mean Lexi is leaving since everything is done?"

I'm quick to assure her, "Nah, something tells me that she will be sticking around." Because I love her.

Perfect coincidence, Lexi arrives and plants her hand on my shoulder to rub once. "What's going on, gang?"

I wink at Lori. "Nothing. Just chatting about corn muffins."

"Well, that was a great speech," Lexi praises.

Without thought, I kiss her cheek as a thanks.

"May we have a picture of you two?" one of the photographers asks, who's been working the room all day. We've already had the essential owner and designer photo in front of the inn this morning.

What's one more. "Yeah, sure."

I pull Lexi to my side, and we look at one another. I tuck her even closer and her hands fist my blazer as she looks up at me and I look down. Clearly, we have affection for one another.

"You know, it never crossed my mind that you were my semi-boss. Should that concern me?" she jokes so only I can hear.

"Nah, but I will continue to boss you around anyhow," I reply. She giggles, and it vibrates through my body.

We completely forget that there is someone taking our photo.

23

HOLDEN

"Ouch," Lexi yelps, because I just smacked her ass in passing to grab a water bottle from the fridge.

"My hands have a mind of their own," I lie.

It took a few days after the party at the Dizzy Duck to have exhaustion disappear. Not that it stopped Lexi and me from fucking that night after the party. Something about the strong feelings involved and the need to be impeccably silent in the house only heightened the experience. Made it better, and the bar was already high.

But now it's a week later, and Lexi searches the kitchen with my face in her neck. I want to touch her indecently, and she's still trying to get accustomed to my kids catching us, even though I know the clues when to stop. "Harry could walk in at any moment and be grossed out. Let's not do that to him today. He already isn't looking forward to being dragged to the regional skating competition."

My lips quirk out. "You're right. We should probably get going." Lori is already there, as she practiced once more with her coach.

"Sure."

"Harry," I call out and hear a grumbled noise from upstairs.

Lexi is busy checking her purse, but she's a good multi-tasker. "I heard from the mayor, and he actually wants me to change the interior of his house now that he and his wife are heading into a new chapter with grandkids and have more need for guest rooms."

I walk to her to wrap my arms around her body from behind. "That's good. Keeps you around Lake Spark and available to occupy my bed," I tease.

"Funny," she replies.

The reality is that this solves a few of our concerns. There are only so many places to redesign in the area. One project at a time, I guess.

"Give me your credit card." Lexi indicates with her hand to hand it over. "I was going to take Lori for a spa day tomorrow post-competition."

My face screws up. "You do realize I own the place, so a card will not be needed."

She gives me an overdone smile. "I know, but it just sounded more fun to say it." Lexi pats my cheek and walks away to grab her phone. An elated smile hits my own lips.

I glance at the clock on the oven. "Come on," I yell again, and scrambling feet sound a few seconds later, scurrying down the stairs.

"Do I really need to go?" Harry grumbles.

I narrow my eyes at him. "Depends. Do you want me to take away your tablet or…"

"Fine," he groans.

"Good. Because next week when you have the science fair, then Lori will tag along for that."

Harry stomps away to the garage, and Lexi attempts to keep her smile to herself. Just a usual Saturday morning for us.

The car ride to the ice rink is a breeze. No need to drive slow, as not a duck or deer in sight near the road, and no complaints of hunger since we had donuts and eggs for breakfast. This is our new routine, and it's perfect. The way it should always be.

Today, we've all gathered our energy for a new milestone, Lori's big day.

We got settled in our seats and endured the skate routines of the girls ahead of my daughter on the program, but then my girl shone. Not one little mistake, every jump landed, and her spins stable. I guess I don't get to watch her enough, because in a way, this all surprises me, her talent. I believe in it, just never saw it in live action. She's been working hard for this, and when she skated off the ice after her stellar short program skate, I whistle and clap having watched my little girl amaze the audience.

Lexi squeezes my arm tighter in complete excitement. "She rocked it. I bet she'll get a high score."

"Otherwise, I'll fire her coach," I deadpan but don't mean a word. Lori could get a low score, yet I would still think she's amazing. It's a junior regional competition, but in a few years, she can move into senior, and that's fast approaching. Only if she wants it.

The applause for her performance wears off, and we anxiously wait in our seats behind the boards for her score. Even Harry is invested in this afternoon. Lori sits with her coach, and then again, we find ourselves cheering, because when the numbers appear on the board behind the ice, we have more reason to celebrate.

I can't wait to see her after the competition. We'll have to have a special dinner or something.

The rink grows quiet as the next girl appears on the ice. We're going to have to watch the rest of program until we know who in the end is going on to the next round of competition. Plus, Lori has to sit with the rest of the skaters from her club to show good sportsman-ship, which I fully support.

My eyes travel around to observe the crowd, finding it humorous and understandable when I see parents clenching one another with fingers crossed. We're at the age when decisions between parents and daughters need to be made if this will be a hobby or a serious sport to follow.

Harry next to me breaks out his book because that's what he does to pass time when he's bored.

"Hey, maybe show a little more respect to those on the ice and pretend to be interested?" I suggest.

My son looks up with a scowl. "You got me here, I invested full attention to my sister, now let me be."

Lexi's face screws up, and she gives me an understanding pained look. Harry is not in the best of moods, and we shouldn't push.

"Okay then," I give up in defeat.

Lexi reaches over to squeeze my arm. "Not long to go," she reminds me.

I wobble my head gently, internally reminding myself of our schedule today. My eyes scan the rink and the people sitting in the rows before us. A little boy runs from the entrance of the lobby to our section of the stands, and past a woman. I can only see the side profile of the stranger, except she's too familiar, and I squint my eyes to get a better view.

But then something causes me alarm. Or rather someone.

It can't be.

I do a double take because the woman with light hair I notice standing next to the boards is someone unexpected.

This can't be happening.

No fucking way.

Lexi must notice my demeanor change from enjoying this afternoon to utter disbelief and anger. Her fingers touch my elbow from concern, but I barely feel it as my mind is about to combust from the thousands of thoughts running through it.

"Are you okay?" She lowers her voice as she leans in to me and not to scare Harry.

My eyes snap to her. "Just stay with Harry, I need to take care of something. Keep him occupied," my whisper is hoarse.

Even though confusion floods her eyes, she agrees, her head gently nodding. "Of course."

"I'll be right back, buddy. Just going to check on something," I tell my son.

"Sure." He shrugs.

I nearly bolt down the steps to where my dread is confirmed.

My fierce possessiveness for my kids kicks in, which is why I have no qualms about quickly and discreetly grabbing my ex-wife's arm.

"Ouch. What are you doing, Holden?"

With a fast pace, I drag us out of the rink to the lobby which only has a few people, and they're not taking much notice.

I let go of her arm. "Michelle, what the fuck are you doing here?"

She seems taken aback. Even though I know her ability to throw on theatrics and fake any emotion, there is a hint of authenticity shading her face. "I've come to see Lori."

My nostrils flare, and I pinch the bridge of my nose. "Like fuck you are. You happily gave me sole custody and haven't been in Lori *and* Harry's lives for years."

"People change."

I shake my head. "When it involves Lori and Harry, then you're actually going to have to tell the truth, because I won't let you waltz back into their lives only to leave."

Michelle steps closer to me with a sly line on her mouth. This can't be good. "Like I said, I came to see Lori. She's at that age when she needs a mother in her life."

My eyes bug out. "Oh… because all the years before didn't matter? And you keep forgetting that there isn't just Lori but also her brother. How did you know she would be here?"

She shrugs. "A little digging."

I glance over her shoulder to ensure nobody is in earshot. "Cut to the chase, Michelle."

Her eyes dip down, and she seems to be taking a breath for courage. "I saw a photo online of you and your new… girlfriend." She slowly claps her hands together. "Bravo for scoring a younger woman," she seethes, but then her own tone seems to surprise her.

"Don't even get me started. If that's the reason you returned, then that is a shitty reason," I grit out through my anger for this moment.

Michelle holds her palm up. "No." She sighs. "I'm not trying to… What I mean is that I really came for Lori."

I shake my head, still in disbelief that I'm even stuck in this moment. "Suddenly?" My eyes don't blink as I remain suspicious.

"Yes," she shoots back. "She is a beauty on the ice." I'll give her the credit where it's due, and there is a tiny ounce of admiration in her sentence.

Standing taller, a new wave of protectiveness comes over me. "Michelle, you signed that I get full custody and that you wanted zero visitation, even when I offered for the sake of Lori and Harry," I remind her.

"Look, I made a mistake, and I want to rectify it." She sounds sincere to any stranger, but I know her too well, and behind all these words is a flawed logic swirling in her head. "I want to see my kids."

"Not if it's only to abandon them again."

"I won't." She will, I can see it in her eyes.

My entire body tenses. "I need you to leave. They cannot see you until we talk about this further, otherwise you are completely disrupting their lives. If you are serious about everything you just said, then you would know that there is a better way to approach this. But here you are out of nowhere, not being responsible or practical." Her eyes grow anxious. "Now tell me, why the fuck are you here?" I force out.

That ridiculous over-the-top astute leer returns. "Fine. It's simple…" She steps closer, appearing as if she has the upper hand. "Why do you get to have a happy ever after with a woman and my kids? People change, and I also deserve a life fulfilled. And after the shit you pulled—"

I nearly fall back from her twisted perception of history. "You mean, when *you* signed a legal document after *you* abandoned your kids and demanded a shit load of money. It's not just Lori you left but also the son that you never seem to mention." My fists form at my sides, doing my damnedest to keep my rage inside.

"I'm not okay with a woman being in your life since you've held off on that for so long. I have a right to see my kids, and it seems that I need to look into legal options to bring us back to court."

An inferno enlarges my eyes, and I snicker a sound. "Oh boy, blackmail. Should have seen this coming."

Michelle's smile is faintly fake. "I'm concerned for my children, and I'm sure a judge would like to evaluate that."

"What in the world would you even do if you got visitation? Actually try to be a mother? Unsettle their lives?"

"This is me being a good mother." She honestly believes that.

I rub my forehead. "Still delusional, great." I look up to the ceiling to gather an idea of what to do. "Just out to ruin our happiness or is there something else on your agenda?"

"Even though you probably owe me for emotional damage, I'm here because it's time to reconnect with them. Seeing you and your new family just gave me the push to do what has been on my mind for a while now. I have the courage now to do what I've been debating."

"You mean to blackmail me into seeing the kids, or is it money that you want?"

She doesn't answer.

My finger comes up to the air. "Ah, there it is. Money too. You think that I'm just going to fall to your requests?"

She brings her finger to her chin. "Probably. I'm definitely staying to congratulate my daughter."

I'm quick to reply. "No. Do not do that. You will play with her emotions."

"All the more reason she needs me, don't ya think? She's at a sensitive age. The judge will see it that way too. Lori is now old enough to make her opinion known, and the judge will want to hear that."

A groan escapes me. "Leave now and I will meet you tomorrow to discuss this. Can you at least do that?"

Michelle ponders for a second. "Fine. But we better speak tomorrow."

"I'm assuming you're not staying at my inn, as you are on the do-not-allow list." I wish it was sarcasm but sadly not. "So, my guess is you're staying one town over. If you have the same number, then I will text you tomorrow."

She brightly smiles. "Good." Michelle instantly turns and flicks her hair nearly the way Lori does herself.

My entire body continues to want to break down, unable to fathom what the hell to do. The fear in me is strong about what will happen to Lori and Harry.

A calming hand touches my back. "Everything okay? The results are nearly in."

My eyes lift only for a second to acknowledge Lexi. "It was my ex-wife."

Lexi seems unsure of what to say. "Oh… W-what did she want?"

Sharply, I turn to give her my full attention, even if my face is firmly stoic. How do I say that my ex-wife saw a photo of us and now she is attempting to uproot my life?

A fatherly instinct kicks in that I have two kids in there who need me calm.

"We'll talk later, okay?"

Her look tells me she grasps the seriousness of all this. At the same time, she's innocent but the catalyst to a problem.

24

LEXI

Holden is broken.

I see it. He did his best when we drove us home, but I could tell he was about to break into pieces. Holden kept looking back in the rearview mirror to observe his children, and right now, he is spending extra time to get them to sleep. He normally gives them space and says a quick good night as they're old enough.

Standing in the shower, the hot water loosens my muscles as I analyze my concern. We haven't had a chance to discuss what happened yet. I'm trying not to make predictions, but an uneasy feeling fills my body.

With the sound of the shower door opening behind me, there is no need to glance over my shoulder, my sense of him near has been in full force lately. His fingertips fall to my hips and begin to twist my body to face him, and I do, looping my arms around his neck, my eyes fixed on his face with pain flooding his eyes.

"Tell me what's wrong," I softly plead as the steam warms us.

Holden shakes his head gently that he's not ready to talk; instead, he steps to trap me between the wall and his body in a tight embrace, with his hand sliding up my leg between us. I'm sure he needs comfort.

"I'm on my period," I remind him.

"Shh, I don't care. I need this."

It's a lighter day, and we're in the shower. I'm surprised, and it's new to us, me. But I want to help him grieve whatever the situation is. He desperately needs relief.

I don't answer and reach between us to guide him to my pussy.

The moment he slides into me, senses overload me. It's different both physically and emotionally. Our eyes lock as he begins to move deep within me, our bodies tightly bound together. I let him lead the way because he can take whatever he requests right now. I want to give that to him.

My mouth seals against the shape of his shoulder, burying my whimper and feeling his lips below my ear as his breath and grunt brings more tightness to my nipples. His thrusts turn faster and harder into me. I wrap my leg around his middle to give him more space to rock into me. It won't matter if I come or not, he just needs something to calm down.

The sensual emotions between us build as he moves faster, running toward his release until he reaches his point, and he fills me while he strongly pants, syncing with the pulse of his heart. His head falls to the crook of my neck, and I lower my leg and begin to draw circles on his back.

I've never seen a grown man so fragile. I'm positive we will collapse onto the floor, but instead, we stand for minutes, holding one another with the sound of water in the background. When we do exit the shower, we stay quiet while we dry off. Holden throws on a robe to give me an extra minute to prepare for bed and clean up a bit.

When I enter his room, I see that he must have collapsed onto the edge of the bed to sit, with a lack of energy left in him. I'm quick to crouch down, my eyes drifting up to grab his attention.

"She wants to be back in their lives," he informs me simply.

Maybe that was floating in the back of my mind as a possibility, but for some reason, this doesn't blindside me.

I grab hold of his forearms to ensure our eyes meet. "What are you going to do?"

"I'm not sure. First solve if she is telling the truth. I'm 99% sure she's lying and just wants money. But still, maybe there was a flicker of honesty in what she said too. I think I owe it to Lori and Harry to at least hear Michelle out. Also talk to my lawyer, keep Michelle away from the kids until this is all figured out. They can't have their hearts broken. She already left them years ago," he explains then stands to pace the room with his head hung low. "There is a chance that this will also bring us back to court which is a mess in itself."

I slide onto the mattress and sit patiently to be the sounding board he needs. "I'm sorry. This can't be easy. I wish I could help."

His eyes snap up to observe me, with a snicker escaping his from his mouth. "That might be a problem."

My face puzzles. "Why?"

"She saw a photo of us, and that's one reason why she appeared out of nowhere to blindside me."

My heart sinks because contributing to his current state is the last thing I would want. I want the opposite, to support him.

Words are lost in my throat that now feels strained.

"I'm sure there are other reasons too. She loves money, after all." He attempts to quell any fears brewing inside me, but it sounds too weak for me.

"I don't know what to say or how to wrap my head around this," I admit.

A long silence hits us again as my face remains blank.

He steps back in my direction. "Let's sleep. Maybe I'll have clearer thoughts in the morning."

I nod once. "Probably the best idea for now."

———

DURING THE NIGHT, we barely slept, and even if I tried, I could feel Holden lost in his head. Could it be that when I briefly closed my eyes to capture light sleep, that even while sleeping I still felt him near and knew he was awake?

No amount of holding one another feels like it's leading us to any resolution.

But still, I manage a little shuteye, except I wake to find Holden aimlessly staring out the bay window as he stands with his head against the glass. He's clearly exhausted with no ounce of sleep had.

I sit up and grab my robe at the edge of the bed. Quickly, I walk to him and stand behind him to touch his hanging arms.

"You must be tired," I whisper.

"It doesn't matter. I needed to get my thoughts in order."

I hum a sound of understanding. "I can imagine."

He steps out of my hold and leaves me like an unexpected breeze. When I have the opportunity to study his agitated face, my center point in my stomach begins to twist with fear.

"I should have been wiser," he begins. "I've been careless by letting you into my life, into Lori and Harry's lives."

My attempt to walk to him is stopped when he holds his hands up indicating not to step closer. But I will say what I need to anyhow. "We can figure this all out together. I won't let you do this alone. I care for Harry and Lori too," I assure him. I'll stand firm on that.

"Lexi, we've been doing everything backwards. Living together, saying feelings that might not be true…" He stalls because my entire body freezes. I want to believe he's just pushing me away and trying to hurt me. "I mean, one day you'll want a husband and a child of your own. You're still young, and we haven't talked about it. I just assumed probably."

My fearlessness and conviction to my beliefs hit me in a flash. I walk to him to grab his arm, as if I can beg. But he only shakes me off. "I know what you're doing, but I'll still be here for you because I love you. You don't have to do this all alone."

He goes even further to the other side of the room, and I keep my feet planted in place. To anyone who might walk in, it would appear as if we are in two separate corners in a boxing match, except no physical pain will happen except in our hearts.

"Lexi, I'm serious. I've made a mistake, and I realize that now." Holden can't even look at me, yet his voice is excruciatingly firm.

I raise my voice. "I'll erase this conversation, because you can't be thinking clearly after being blindsided by your ex-wife and protectiveness for your children because you're a great dad—"

"I need to do this alone." Our eyes meet, and his are a razor to my heart, his eyes dark.

Tears begin to burn, but I won't let them escape. He needs to realize that I will put action behind my words. "I won't let you do it alone. That's how relationships work."

He shakes his head in disagreement, now ignoring my presence, walking to his dresser and fumbling in his drawer. "Not when our relationship is a mistake. We're just two people who have great sex and got lost in lust."

A swoosh of change finally hits me, and his wall is too big and strong. Holden has made up his mind.

Those tears that I've been squeezing tight fall. "If you really feel that way, then I'll pack up my bags now and leave. It seems like I have no choice. You may break my heart now, but I'll still hold on to hope that Lori and Harry will be okay and you'll be at peace with your decision."

He ensures his back is to me, as though he doesn't want me to read his facial expressions. "It is my decision," he reiterates.

I wipe away a tear and take a moment to gather myself. "Well then… goodbye."

Holden storms to the door to leave me to gather myself. But his hand stalls on the knob, and he stands there for a few beats.

"When it comes to you, Lexi, a realization struck me last night…"

"What would that be, since you already made your list of our failures together known," I snipe with bitterness.

Another long pause keeps him stalled as he sighs, but then he opens the door and gives me one last look.

"The moment we kissed is when I should have run."

25

HOLDEN

My fingers tap on the table, as what feels like the devil just arrived. Michelle sits across from me in a restaurant in an old log cabin outside of Lake Spark amongst the woods.

"Here we are." My enthusiasm is non-existent.

She reaches out to touch the back of my hand, and I don't give her a chance by ripping my hand away. Her face falls, and I have no ounce of sympathy. This is a woman who left her kids not because she had an issue that would put Lori and Harry in danger, she didn't need to go away and find herself before returning a better person. It was purely her selfishness to walk away without a backward glance or any hint of remorse. And as a bonus on top, requesting a hefty settlement too. Lori and Harry were young, they barely remember, but it was damage enough.

"I want to see Lori and Harry again. They have a right to see me."

"Nope." My tone is firm. "I make the decisions. That's how sole custody works."

She sighs, and the waitress interrupts us at the wrong moment, but also, I'm thankful.

"Coffee, black," I order without giving any attention to the lady with an apron.

"Same." Michelle presses her lips together and waits for our standoff to continue.

We stare at one another, and I try to remind myself that I owe a chance to Lori and Harry's mother even if it hurts.

"Give me an opportunity. I can see them once even, with you present," she requests with sincerity but not enough for me to be fully convinced, as I was once married to her.

"Then what?"

She shrugs her shoulders. "Maybe I can take them alone somewhere. Pioneer Park is in Lake Spark, they must love that."

I snicker. "Harry has other interests, and Lori is nearly a teenager, she's too old for people in costumes sewing quilts. You yourself argued yesterday that she's at a time in her life when she needs a strong female." My face must appear extremely coldhearted.

Probably because within me, I'm more than aware that Lexi is the strong woman that Lori has become attached to. The type of role model that Lori needs. Nor does Lexi forget about Harry, ever.

Most of all, Lexi is the woman who kindles my heart and made me believe that I could have it all. Now I've broken her heart and severely wounded my own. But my children's mother reappearing must be a sign that this whole situation happened because I'm not allowed to have it all. Fate can play the cruelest of games. As soon as you get something great, then you get knocked by something bad. If I look back in my life, I've never had the balance. I'm not going to drag Lexi deeper into my life if we won't be possible need to protect her not only from my batshit crazy ex's games, but I also need to protect Lexi's heart.

"Holden," Michelle's sharp tone breaks my thought. "You owe me this or I take us to court."

My head juts up, hesitating. "You do realize your time limit to challenge our agreement has passed, right?"

She shakes her head. "But visitation is not impossible, we didn't sign away parental rights. Plus, I can still see them or contact them without you—"

I'm quick to cut her off. "No. If you want to contact them, then we have to discuss that, even if we have to do that in court. You say you care for them, but this approach is a shitty way to show it."

In court, this would be scorching and completely difficult for Lori and Harry too. My hands are completely tied in this impossible situation, and I'm not entirely sure why it never crossed my mind. There was always a chance that this could happen. But I never saw someone so determined to leave their kids in favor of money and a life of jet-setting and boyfriends.

The cracking of my heart is different to last night with Lexi. My children always come first.

"Okay." My eyes glint to examine her words and behavior. "If I agree?"

Hope glazes her eyes. "Then I want to see them tomorrow… without *her*."

I chortle to myself because this predicament really feels like I'm at the gates of Hell. "That won't be a problem, as Lexi's…" Do I admit that I've ruined a strong and loving relationship with so much promise all because of Michelle, who feels like a signal that nobody gets it all? On one hand, it will ease her argument. But on the other, satisfaction gives her power. "It's not an issue."

Michelle seems surprised. "Well then, one less thing to worry about to lead us to a peaceful resolution."

My knuckles form fists, and I'm trying to bite in all my anger that wants to unleash. I need to get this discussion over with before I burst. "Let me talk to the kids. If they don't want to see you, then I don't think we should push this."

"They don't even know me, and they deserve to know me," she defends.

I glance away, trying again to keep my rage in. "Tomorrow, Michelle. That's when you get to prove yourself that *maybe* we can explore this conversation more."

"Fine. But I mean it, Holden. If you don't give me any chance, then I will find a way to ruin you." She stands, her words hostile.

I gently shake my head, not surprised at all. "That's a shocker."

Watching her walk away, a chill hits me. This can't be my life right now. Everything was within my grasp, but it's clear that I'm simply not made for a life with everything that could possibly make a person happy.

———

WALKING through the hall at the Dizzy Duck, my attempt to keep myself busy before school pickup will fail, I know it will. I'm reserving my energy for my call to the lawyer and talking with Lori and Harry.

But this day only sinks me deeper into despair because I feel Lexi's presence. I don't even need to look up. She became a natural magnet to me when it comes to my senses and instinct. But I do look up because her steps have slowed.

At first, we're both silent. Even without sleep, she appears radiant, in a skirt and heels. She's holding a swatch while her eyes dance side to side.

"Hi." My voice is soft.

"I was just leaving. I forgot I left a few things here for designs." She holds up the swatch ring, clearly wanting to ignore me or be anywhere but here.

When she attempts to walk away, I grab her wrist then the other to keep her in a strong hold. "Wait." I'm not sure what to say, other than I need to touch her one last time.

"What, Holden? You said enough. Your message was clear."

We're both fuming, and she's so close within my grasp. "It's just…" What words do I use?

Her eyes widen, she's growing impatient. "Yes?"

I'm being a coward. Not saying the true reasons behind my need to part ways with her.

When she breaks my hold on her, she catches me off balance

when she shoves me. "You are a coward." Ah yes, I forgot she has a talent to read my mind. We both scan the area, and we're all alone, as nobody really comes this way unless they're staff. "What the fuck did you think would happen?"

"Lexi…" Do I argue or attempt to explain?

Her finger darts out to poke my chest. "Even a smart man knows full well that when you bring someone close into your life, interweave them into your circle with the people who you hold dear. When you kiss and whisper 'I love you' or your entire body is aware that when that person says they support you that you know it's true. It's not a surprise that you are heading toward something longstanding. And now you suddenly want to tell me it isn't?"

"Lexi, I…"

"You don't need to say anything because maybe I even understand. I think you believe this will help your current situation, and I'm the easy answer to soften the blow." Her eyes begin to water, and I hate how she is probably right.

"Lexi, I'm not meant to have everything. That's the reality." I run my tongue along my mouth because I'm nervous around her, wanting so many things with her, but I can't give her any.

She waves her finger in front of her with clear fury apparent and her chest rising and falling from her emotions taking over. "What the fuck did you expect to happen when you light a fire? This flame between us. *We* are what happened. Willingly crossing the line between fucking and having something more. And you…" She tries to gather her words because her lips quiver from the pure destruction that I've caused her.

"Lexi." I want to comfort her, calm her, selfishly make sure she'll be alright to make me feel less of an ass who blew up our bliss.

She steps back with her palm up to indicate that I shouldn't step in her direction. "Don't you dare get close to me," she barks. "You know, I've also never had this connection with someone. At least I didn't get scared and ruin a good thing."

"You don't understand my situation, you don't have kids. You still have life to experience." My tone is weak. I rub my hand across my jaw, trying my best not to look at the image before me.

"Do. Not. Throw that card at me," she grits out.

At this point, I'm waiting for her to slap me because I deserve it. Lexi can be feisty, but right now she's shattered.

Her hand lands on her waist. She looks like she's going to pounce on me, but she has a point to make. I scratch my cheek, waiting for her revelation. "I'm going right now, and the most fucked-up thing about this entire situation is that I'm going to inform you of the obvious. Work out your shit, Holden. Because even though I should be the one to run…" Her strong tone begins to diminish. "I'll still be waiting."

Our eyes can't part, and the air cuts around us. I'm sure I even gasp because I know she's speaking the truth.

Watching her walk away and turn the corner, I slam the wall with my hand and scream to myself.

———

It's not because of my witch of an ex-wife, it's because a stone hit me to slow down. Which means, Lexi will never get what she deserves. Cutting her loose is the only way.

"You look like shit."

My eyes snap up to my daughter due to her brazen tone, as she just slid into the front seat after I picked her up from skating. "Aren't we honest," I say, my tone flippant.

"Well, you do," she justifies. "It's like one day without Lexi and you've turned into a grumpy old man." My kids haven't heard the news about Lexi and me yet, only noticed that she wasn't at breakfast.

I don't bother turning the engine back on; instead, I decide it's time to bite the bullet. Harry is at a friend's house, and Lori will probably comprehend the news of her mother in a different way.

Swallowing, I nibble on my bottom lip, wanting to be tactful. "There is something I kind of want to talk to you about."

"No," Lori exclaims, with her face falling. "You and Lexi? Did something happen? She's really cool, Dad."

My head falls back to the seat while I curse to myself internally. Which bombshell do I deliver first? I slant my body to face Lori better. I'm dreading every second of this conversation.

"It's your mom." I wait for Lori to react, but she just stares blankly, blinking a few times. "I wanted to talk to you first before Harry. You're more of an adult than I would like right now."

"What about her?" I almost can't hear because she speaks so softly. Suddenly my child with a strong personality looks like a ghost.

I sigh. "Hypothetically, what would you do if she showed up wanting to see you and Harry?"

Lori takes a moment to digest my sentence, but then something snaps in her mind, and she immediately shakes her head repeatedly. "I wouldn't want to see her. And I don't think this is hypothetical at all."

Closing my eyes, I gather my strength yet again. "I understand your feeling, but she's also your mother, and maybe it matters to Harry. She says she wants to be serious."

"Do you really believe what you just said?"

My head drops low. "I don't think I have much of a choice." Legal action is not something my daughter needs to know. "Maybe one day you will look back and wish you saw her."

Lori crosses her arms. "Well, I don't want to see her. I barely remember her, and I've forgotten her." She's adamant, and as much as a parent sometimes needs to guide their child on the future, I'm not going to push this. Right now, Lori and Harry are carefree children who deserve to stay that way.

I bite the corner of my lip while I sit as fragile as Lori right now. "And what do you think Harry would want?"

She sneers. "She's probably as good as dead to him. He never even knew her."

Sighing, I pause for a few seconds. "Do you think I should ask him? You two have a strong bond."

Lori shakes her head no, just as she did before. "I don't think you should ask because I don't even call her Mom, and Harry barely mentions her… ever. I want her to go away."

Oh how I want that too.

Her face is heartbreaking because I can see that she truly means every word leaving her mouth. "I… I will try." Is it a lie? Or am I not trying hard enough?

She slouches into the seat and turns away from me to gaze out the window. "Promise me, she'll go away."

I squeeze my eyes closed with my entire body tense. "Maybe I shouldn't have had this conversation with you, but if there was any ounce that you would want to see her then I owed it to you to ask."

"Well, now you know, and we can forget this conversation," she snipes, and I'm not sure if it's me or her mom that she's angry at.

At this moment, I don't dare mention about Lexi and me. One step at a time.

"Okay, Lori," I promise.

Starting up the car, I drive us away in silence, wondering how many more mistakes I can make in the span of 48 hours.

Because I'm walking through a maze and failing miserably at discovering the end.

26

LEXI

Opening my suitcase that I threw onto the edge of the bed in Summer's spare room, I sigh. Zac is away at a medical conference, so we're all alone for a few days. Still, I debate if I should even unpack anything.

"Here. Have some water," Summer offers when she strolls into the room. She hands me a bottle while she too observes my predicament. "You're just going to live out of a suitcase?"

I take a sip of the drink then flop onto the mattress next to the bag. "I'm not sure. I feel like Holden will come to his senses, but then again, he trampled on my heart, so that's my sign to leave Lake Spark. *Except…*" I sigh. "I already accepted my next project, and I think my new addiction to Jolly Joe's coffee can't simply be ignored." I must sound miserable.

Summer stares at me with a glint of amusement as she crosses her arms. "Do you truly believe he is going to beg for you to come back?"

I bite my inner cheek and ignore the dullness in my belly. "Maybe I want to imagine it far too much that I'm blinded by the obvious."

She grabs a nightgown from the top of the pile in my luggage and holds the lace up by her finger as she inspects it. "Does this even cover anything?" Her face screws up.

My brows rise because this is the last thing we should be discussing, yet it's still a nice memory with Holden. "I think that's the point."

She stutters a laugh and drops it back onto the clothes. "I want to root for you two. I'm sure you're right, that he's pushing you away due to his current situation, although…" She bobs her head side to side. "It's a shitty way to do it. *But* sometimes in life we need to let go because it isn't meant to be." Her eyes fill with sorrow, and I wonder if she's speaking of herself in her current marriage.

I throw my closed bottle of water behind me. "This hurts too much. You could be right. No more chance for us." A cry bursts up through my body to hit the back of my throat and sting my eyes. A wound he caused that makes my lips quiver. "I'm sure as hell not going to chase him or try and speak to him again any time soon. He has to figure everything out, and if he didn't mean what he said, then he must make the next move. But that's the problem…"

Summer walks to lean against the dresser. "Go on."

"It could very well be that Holden meant every word." I scoff a sound and fall back onto the mattress. "What a naïve woman I've been."

Summer sighs. "It will be okay, either way."

I wipe a tear away. "Why does it have to hurt this much?"

"Sometimes love hurts us."

My attention causes me to shoot up onto my elbows. "I guess I've never looked at it from that angle. Still doesn't make it any less painful. When he first broke it off, his conviction was strong, but yesterday at the hotel it was less. Still, I'm hopeful, even if he doesn't deserve it."

"Maybe space will help. But why are you so adamant to wait for him? He ran away when things got tough." It keeps sounding as though she is speaking to herself.

A faint wry smile brings a line to my mouth. "I've always treated life with such ease. But now, I see what I've been missing, and

Holden surges into my life and I see everything through a different lens. I didn't know I was waiting for that. Now? My instincts scream that I shouldn't let go. That's what you do when you love someone."

"Don't confuse attachment with love," she highlights.

I swing my legs off the bed and stand. "I hear you. But I feel it in my bones that we are the real thing. It's so twisted, but I will wait a long time if it means he comes around." I search for my sweater that I tossed somewhere in my anguish.

Summer slants her shoulders up. "As long as he can fix the wound that he caused, then maybe you have the outlook that more of us should have." There's that sorrow again underlying in her voice. I really need to make sense of what's going on with her, but right now, I'm selfish and need to deal with my situation.

I find my sweater on the floor and bundle up. "I can't think of it any other way, otherwise the pain will only grow and be hard to fade away. Actually, our relationship moved fast, but the pain might last longer if this is our end."

Her eyes widen. "You really are optimistic."

I lick my lips and puff out my chest, attempting to gather strength to ensure I don't mope around. "Don't worry, I'm raging with anger, but this fucked-up sympathy inside of me has me unable to run. I can only imagine what he's going through. And saying he doesn't love me or that we were a mistake stings like hell." She looks at me, unsure, while I point my finger to the door. "I cried all night. But right now, I need a break from the waterworks and to go get a damn coffee at Jolly Joe's."

A renewed energy hits me, and Summer grins. "Well, before you go, I wanted to tell you some happy news." I smile and patiently wait. "Zac and I are having a baby." She appears happy.

I squeal in delight. "Finally, some great news in this shitty day. This is wonderful." I jump up to give her a hug.

"I think so. It feels like life is happening quick, but this is a gift." She glances down at her flat belly.

"It is." And maybe one day, I'll have a baby, too. With Holden's eyes and his humor and his nose…

Lexi, stop.

"Well, I just wanted to let you know in case I throw up at some point. But I'm nearly at the end of my first trimester, and it hasn't been bad."

"Well, I'll be there to clean up any puke if you do."

She nods in appreciation. "Okay, I'll let you be so I can focus on some work. Just don't wait forever, Lexi. Nobody deserves that heartache."

I nod that I understand, but I can't go down the rabbit hole of rehashing all of my feelings. I gently touch her shoulder in passing as I leave. Maybe she understands more than I could imagine, and she is wiser than me.

———

OKAY, my confidence that everything will resolve was a fucking lie. Or that's what I feel as that swirling sadness and anger hits me again somewhere between parking my car and walking down Main Street. My head hangs low, and my misery returns, as if my rant earlier didn't happen.

"Lexi?" a young faint voice says, and my eyes snap up to see a beautiful 12-year-old with sass walking my way. She's missing a smile, though.

"Hey, Lori." I search the area, concerned that I will run into Holden again. But there's only a group of her friends from school heading into Jolly Joe's.

She quirks her mouth and tucks her hands into her jeans pockets. "Won't you come back?"

My nose rises because I'm not entirely sure what their dad told them. "Uh, I'm not…"

"He didn't say anything, probably because, well, someone showed up. But you haven't been around, and I'm smarter than my little brother."

Ah, Holden has spoken with Lori about her mother. "It's kind of complicated."

"He's being an ass."

Her blunt statement causes my head to perk up from surprise. "You're not afraid to be bold, huh."

Lori rolls a shoulder back, and her eyes peer down. "I don't want to see her and still my dad is walking around moody."

Indicating with my head, I suggest we sit down on the bench nearby, and she follows me. "If only it was that easy." I'm sure he didn't get into the specifics with her. "Sometimes adulting really sucks." I sigh and try to level with her age.

"Yeah, I can clearly see that." Her flippant tone brings a half-smirk to my face. "Just, please, can't you talk to him? You're just having a disagreement, and someone has to say sorry, right? You'll be there when we order pizza this weekend."

I glance away. "Lori, it's… I want to be honest, and time will tell."

A long silence floats in the air. "Please, Lexi, can't you talk to him? Maybe he'll listen. He can deal with my mom and fix whatever it is with you."

My eyes snap in her direction and see her hope. I touch her arm. "I-I... My only answer is to give him space. There is nothing else."

"Okay, but you'll be back tomorrow? Surely, that's all it will take for you both to be happy together again. I've never seen him this happy, well, until he lost it a few days ago."

My heart breaks more, and I do my best to keep my tears at bay in front of her. "Lori, I do appreciate that you felt the need to talk to me." I spot one of her friends at the door of Jolly Joe's, and she calls Lori's name. "You should go to your friends, okay?"

She nods in agreement and stands. "Just…" Lori can't finish her sentence.

But still, I give her a knowing look.

I should have seen that Holden making my heart crack would affect more than just me. If only he could see that mistakes can be rectified.

27

HOLDEN

I rub my hands together before I groan into my palms. I'm sitting on the bench swing outside the Dizzy Duck near the dock, looking at the serene lake that doesn't reflect my current mood. I have a headache of my own doing. It's also risky sitting here because everything here reminds me of Lexi.

Stone is sitting next to me, also staring out at the lake. "This is kind of weird, right? Sitting on a swing together?"

"Then leave," I snipe.

"Whoa there, don't take your aggression out on me due to your current life turmoil," he volleys back. I've brushed him up on everything that's happened, but now I feel like he's about to lecture me with that the wise logic that he believes he has.

"Look, Lori doesn't want to see Michelle, Michelle forgets she even has a son, and I sure as hell don't want to see my ex-wife again. My lawyer better hurry up with this call back. He was looking into options," I explain.

"Did you forget the other matter?"

I sideline my eyes and meet his neutral look. "No, that's on my mind non-stop. Breaking up with Lexi wasn't the highlight of my week—or life, for that matter." It's fucking incinerating.

"Yet you did it. I'm not sure why since she would only help you," he reminds me.

I run the back of my finger along my jaw, and my eyes whirl side to side as I try to push my theory out of my head. "I don't think I can think clearly, and why sink her down into this situation with me. A perfect life isn't for me, and she deserves one. This week was just a sign of that. Why put Lexi through misery by sticking around if eventually my contentment breaks because I'm unable to balance amazing kids, great work, and Lexi, who gets her own category."

Stone sputters a sound. "That is the most fucked-up thought. Get it together and realize that it doesn't have to be that way."

I rub the back of my neck in pure agony due to the days past. Time to admit the truth to my friend. "I'm scared shitless, okay?"

He smirks. "We kind of all figured that out, but kudos for saying it out loud and avoiding an expensive therapist."

I glare at him, not entertained. "It is what it is."

He tips his head to the side and makes a sound of doubt. "I don't exactly agree. There must be a reason you feel that way. You sure as hell were fearless back in your pro days."

"I had a very busy life until Michelle kind of ruined that with months of mediation with lawyers and unreasonable demands, but I was willing to do anything for Lori and Harry."

Stone snaps his fingers. "Bingo. You do everything for them but never yourself, and because of that, you're letting a difficult divorce stop you from actually getting what you deserve."

Just like dominoes toppling, every brick that quickly falls in my head leads me to another realization, another connection of thoughts now becoming clearer. A sort of epiphany that begins to fuel one thought: I need to turn around this future.

I inhale a sharp breath, nearly ashamed that I let this happen. "I can't go back in time," I say softly.

He smiles to himself and leans back with pride. "But you can change the future, and that, my friend, is my amazing advice that you're going to follow."

Stone is so sure of himself, and that cockiness causes me to smirk weakly. "Not sure the damage with Lexi can be fixed. I was beyond what she deserves. Not at all showing the love that I have for her."

It's a few seconds before he slaps a hand on my shoulder. "You don't know until you try."

I slant a shoulder up to my ear, trying to comprehend this conversation and form a plan of action. "You're right. I just wish I didn't first have to conquer the ex-wife who is intent on breaking my kids' hearts yet again. I can't even manage to say *our* kids. Hell, in that short time, Lexi has been more of a mother than they've ever had."

Stone stands. He mentioned earlier that he needed to meet Harlow so they could babysit his niece. "Then beat Michelle at her tricks then calm the hell down, before you find Lexi to fix both of your broken hearts. Every heart can be mended." He brings a hand to his chest. "Damn, I'm on fire today with this sappy advice. Owe that to my soon-to-be wife."

A soft smile spreads on my mouth at the happiness in his life that I'm desperately intent on getting back.

———

AM I really standing in a parking lot about to do this? After a long call with my lawyer and documents sent by courier, here I am. Maybe it's the worst mistake of my life or one day Harry or Lori might hate me. But this is me protecting their interests. I'm the adult here, and this is what feels to be the best solution for us all.

Michelle stands by her car with her arms crossed, waiting for me to speak.

"Lori doesn't want to see you, and I'm not going to force it," I begin.

Her face is blank, but I see the glaze of her eyes that she doesn't seem surprised.

"Harry doesn't remember you, and you haven't actually mentioned his name once, as though you've forgotten about him."

She stands tall. "That's because a daughter needs her mother more."

I shake my head gently. "Not true. But we've managed just fine since you left."

"Did you even ask him?"

"He's ten years old and doesn't remember you at all. Not once has he mentioned you, since you were never in his life. Harry only knows that you weren't around, and he never asked again because he's been a kid with a strong head on his shoulders from the moment he could walk. It's in his best interest that he doesn't know about your unexpected appearance unless you provide proof that you want to make an effort. I'm making the choice to see you for him."

Irritation is seeping through her deep exhale. "He has you, and Lori has me."

I rub the back of my neck in utter disbelief. "As in separate them when you would visit?"

She shrugs. "Maybe. I don't know how to approach this."

I pinch the bridge of my nose, feeling the rage forming. "Fuck this illogical thought of yours. Be honest and tell me that you truly want. You're really going to tell me that you will make an effort with them, and if I were to offer you money beyond our settlement from years ago that you wouldn't blink an eye and would refuse it because the kids are more important?"

She seems to be prolonging her answer because I know it's not good. "Fine. You're right, I can't."

A sound escapes me because my instincts are unfortunately true. "Let me guess. You did reappear to cause chaos and try to get money in return?"

Her body relaxes from her charade no longer needed. "I did think about seeing them again." Her voice is delicate, and this I do believe. "But you can also make this go away."

"Thought so. Especially since you recently went through divorce number three." I glance down at the papers in my hand. "So, let's solve this right away." I hand her the documents. "You never showed interest in the kids, and I'm not going to chance you returning, as they still have quite a few years until they are legal adults."

She examines the papers, but she doesn't seem to have any feeling. "Voluntarily relinquish parental rights." She holds the sheets up, unimpressed.

"Yeah. You can sign the form, or if you're not sure, go to counseling before you sign the form to ensure you've thought this through, or we could have a judge approve, if you want someone to hear why I'm doing this. I know it's a big decision." I do have sympathy for that.

"Even though it would be voluntary, I will still pay you one last sum. If you ever had any ounce of love for them then I think you know this is the way."

Her arm drops low as the papers hang from her hand, and we stand here for a long few seconds. "Does this mean… that one day someone can adopt them to be their mother?" I don't think she's being vindictive in this moment. She may have a few narcissistic bones too many but right now she's trying to understand, truly understand, what this all means.

My shoulders slant up as my face remains serious. "Hasn't crossed my mind. If you mean Lexi… we're going at our own pace, and I haven't thought about it, but she cares for them as her own." And I need to get us back on the road. "But would it be so bad that one day Lori and Harry might have an even stronger family unit?"

Michelle thinks to herself, with her eyes reeling side to side before she sighs. "Maybe I'm just a horrible person and you're right." She's actually seriously reflecting on herself.

I rub my eyebrow, remembering that sometimes people need a little compassion, and our marriage may have gone wrong, but she was part of my life and gave me Lori and Harry. "Even horrible people can turn their life around. But after nearly ten years away with no contact with the kids, then I think when you look deep within yourself, you can make a decision that maybe you aren't as horrible as you might imagine... It's okay to say that you never wanted to be a mother."

She nods gently in agreement and appears thankful that I've calmed and am attempting to show understanding. "Okay." Her shoulders slump. "If I do this then…"

My lips curl because why am I not surprised. "Last page." I look away from this because I knew deep down that getting something in return would be the only way to seal the deal, even if in the bottom of her heart she feels it's the truth.

"Fine."

My head whips up now, astonished how fast she answered. "Wow. Proof for your presence in Lake Spark."

She tosses the papers on the hood of her car. "I'll sign."

"Okay. But you can think about it, too. I know it's a big decision. Probably a good idea that we don't stretch this out. I'm giving you a deadline to make the choice. Won't keep any of us in a limbo."

"Agreed. I'll be in touch soon," she responds and stalls for a second before swiveling away to avoid prolonging this discussion any longer.

It's heartbreaking for Lori and Harry. They just don't know it because I'm carrying the brunt for them.

But the heartbreak I'm carrying inside for Lexi, both her heart and my own, is shared with her, and I need to gather my plan of action to rectify that.

———

SPREADING the cream cheese mixture into the cake pan, I hate to admit that I'm not making my signature peanut butter and jelly cheesecake for my kids. It's because I need a distraction, as tomorrow, after an attempted night of sleep and going through all the reasons that life could actually be full on all fronts, I need to find Lexi.

Holding up the spatula, I debate licking it. Normally, I don't do that, but I guess trying new things and views begins now. But I laugh to myself, because before the spatula can hit my lips, my son comes racing to the counter.

"Hey, you're making the cheesecake. I bet it's for Lexi and not me."

My brows furrow because I haven't yet spoken to them about

Lexi, only kept it vague, and thank the heavens, because now I don't have to explain what I'm doing. Well, first I need to win back Lexi, but I won't relent.

"What do you mean, buddy?"

"She was busy with her friend, that's why she hasn't been around lately."

I attempt to hide my relief at his theory. "Yeah… this might be for her." If I can convince her of my true feelings. I hand my son the spatula to lick as a peace offering for baking his favorite cake and not having notified him.

"Dad, I finished my homework, now can I please have my phone back?" Lori yells as she walks down the stairs.

Life is feeling back to normal, except with one giant piece missing.

Lori has a bounce in her step. "Oh hey, it's cake baking. What's the special occasion?"

My eyes travel between my children. "Just wanted to…"

Lori gives me a peculiar smile. "I saw her today in town." Instantly, I know she means Lexi, but I like it a lot that Lexi still seems to give Lori attention, even if I may have ruined a good thing. "I think she'll… like it." The corner of her mouth hitches to give me a sort of secret assurance before she grabs an apple and takes a big bite.

And that gives me promise.

Why oh why does Lake Spark do this to me? I think as I stare at the general store. There's a sign on the door that says they've closed early due to a staff meeting. It throws a wrench in the works for me to buy a bottle of wine and drown in it. I know drinking alcohol is not the best way to cure the misery that I'm mired in, but I've cried enough today, the numbness overbearing.

There's Catch 22, but right now that feels like too far of a walk. Jolly Joe's doesn't serve alcohol, and I'm not sure whose home wine supply I can steal without them asking how I am and then I'd break down in tears.

"Damn it," I growl to myself. My only option right now is the Dizzy Duck, and I should avoid that place like the plague… except… it's late, and a school night which means Holden won't be there, since that's the time he's with Lori and Harry who I already miss.

Ugh, I'll take the risk and go for it. Maybe Stuart will be at the front desk or Jonathan behind the bar. They're good company, and they don't really talk to me as they seem to lose their words if I'm around. Talking to a wall could be good. Okay, the Dizzy Duck it is.

It's a ten-minute walk to the Dizzy Duck, and when I walk in, there is only Jill tonight working in reception, but she's friendly and smiles at me. The line of my mouth snags in an attempt to return her sentiment. I spot the plate of chocolate chip cookies that are always available for guests in the lobby. Walking by, I grab one then stuff it into my mouth as if I'm a savage, because I don't care that my mouth is full or that I'm leaving crumbs. Straight to the bar I go and greet Jonathan.

"Hey, Lexi, I'm surprised to see you. It's been a while since the re-open." He places a clean wine glass back on the rack. "What can I get you?"

Sliding onto the stool, I cut to the chase. "White wine. Wait, no… go straight for something stronger. A vodka tonic, please." I slump over to rest my head on my hands. "Don't forget to add a slice of lemon," I order.

I am *not* the best version of myself right now.

In my peripheral view, I see that there's a hockey game on the television. A line on my mouth twitches. Hockey. It's my dad's team, and I always forget to tune in, but after years, it's impossible to watch every game. Hockey; it's also the reason I first met Holden. A flicker inside me hits, and that only causes me to sigh.

"I'll be right back, need to get more ice from the back," Jonathan informs me.

My eyes bug out. "Hurry. Can't you see I'm a woman who is desperate?"

He tries to suppress his humored look, and I just snarl to myself. My nails begin to tap the wood of the bar as I contemplate what to do going forward. I'm supposed to stay in Lake Spark for my next project, and I only want to stay at Summer's place for so long. Plus, my chances of running into Holden are too statistically high.

Tonight, though, I will just drown in my sorrows while I try to take my mind to a happy place of thinking about refurbished wood and hanging lights.

Jonathan returns with a small bucket of ice. "Back. Okay, let's get you that drink."

"Let's." My tone is flippant.

His brows furrow as he gets to work on my drink. I stare aimlessly at the floor while I wait.

"Here you are."

I turn my head, and he sets my napkin down, and I do a double take because something catches my eye. There is black writing on the napkin. From a dark pen, and my eyes focus to read the writing.

I owe you an apology and a future.

"An IOU on a napkin. Just like all those years ago." My head whizzes to search the bar area, and I spot Holden as he slowly saunters to me. I hate to say it, but his swagger is already weakening me. My jaw drops, but I'm speechless as my eyes follow his every step until he slides onto the stool next to me.

"I don't believe this seat is taken," he conveys to me. There is satisfaction shading his gentle smirk that he's stunned me a little.

Once again, my eyes circle the nearly empty bar area. "It would seem so," I whisper.

"I'm sorry," he begins. I give him my full attention. "I've made a lot of mistakes lately, and you're one that I want to fix, because you're right, we could be everything."

The speed of my heart picks up.

My eyes stay locked on Holden. "Will you hold off on that drink, Jonathan?" I don't bother turning my head, as I'm still in disbelief.

Holden's mouth snatches up slightly. "He already left us alone about thirty seconds ago."

"Guess I didn't notice. I wasn't expecting you here, which is why I came to bless this place with my presence," I explain.

"Lori and Harry are at sleepovers with friends. I kind of needed some space to figure out my shit, and it just so happens I was here, ready to find you, but it seems fate gave me a break and here you are."

I wet my lips, gathering my emotions, then finding words. "You hurt me," I state blankly.

He scoops my hands up in his. "I'm aware. I just believed complete happiness wasn't meant for me."

I chortle bitterly. "That belief is the biggest lie of the century. Everyone is allowed to have it all if they want."

Holden squeezes my hands and his head tips slightly to the side. "I needed to discover that myself, it seems."

"Shitty way of communicating that." I do make my disappointment apparent, yet I will listen for as long as I need to.

He exhales a deep breath. "I didn't mean what I said, any of it. I'll keep apologizing even if it takes eternity."

"Eternity is a long time." My neutral tone doesn't change as I study his eyes, soaking in his honesty.

"Well, that's kind of what I want, and since you mentioned that you would still be waiting even though I don't deserve it, then I'm hoping you would be along for the ride." A line draws across his mouth.

Lightness begins to flow through me. "I think…" I bob my head side to side. "You might have to grovel a bit more. Probably for a while, but my heart won't tear away from that future that I desperately want with you."

He lifts my hand to kiss the back of it, with his eyes raking up to ensure our connection doesn't break. It makes me smirk because it's such a classic gesture, a saccharine move, yet it breaks another piece of sadness from the last few days away.

"Is the issue with your ex-wife solved?" I wonder.

Holden glances away for a few seconds before swinging back with an impartial face that I can't read. "Very much so. I got closure too. She signed away her parental rights."

My jaw drops, as that's such a big milestone for any parent. "That's… a lot."

"It's sad but the right move. No potential return that could hurt Lori and Harry," he explains.

A long breath draws out from my body. "I'm relieved for you." I press my lips tightly together, as I owe it to myself to confront any doubt I may have. "But you can't be sitting before me just because the issue with your ex-wife is solved. If that was the reason you pushed me away, then… it was a weak reason. I refuse to be reunited with someone just because they let something like that get in the way."

His finger instantly lands on my mouth to hush me. "I shouldn't have let it all affect me, even though it was scary to have any potential harm to my kids. However, the reason that I pushed you away is because I felt maybe the situation was a warning that it was all too good to be true. Because, Lexi, *you* are too good to be true. But lucky for me, you entered my life. Life feels complete when you're with me, with my kids, in our house. Finally, I have it all, and it's scary as hell because does anybody get that lucky? For a few days, I thought it wasn't what I was allowed."

Tears build in my eyes. Everything he says helps me understand his mind frame lately, and it's full of promise. "I've been miserable without you. I'm missing you and everything in your life, it's as though I'm not complete. It makes no sense because our speed is fast but so right."

Holden brings his hands to cradle my face. "It is right, and I just need you back, desperately. Because I fucking love you so much."

A smile stretches on my lips. "Me too."

"We're a team, like you said. You didn't give up on me and stayed feisty the way I like. I want us to move forward, and I promise never to doubt our life again."

I nod up and down. Maybe I'll be hesitant to trust the coming days or weeks, but it's only because I need to shake off the fear of losing him and the pain of the last few days. "Forward it is."

He crashes his lips down onto mine but kisses me slowly, gentle yet sensual and completely loving. I accept all of it because with him is where I belong, and I promised to be waiting because I believed he would find his way back to me.

Our lips part, and we both have giddy looks on our faces, ready for our next step.

"Move back in?"

My mouth slides side to side. "Yeah." I smirk to myself. "I mean, I did accidentally leave behind a bra in a drawer, and that was going to be awkward trying to get it back anyhow."

He feigns doubt. "Did you now?" His voice rises an octave. "That is the oldest trick in the book."

"Completely."

That repartee I love returns to us, and I'm relieved and curious if I will fall in love with him all over again, because the first time was already amazing.

"Lori and Harry let me bake a peanut butter and jelly cheesecake last night that wasn't for them. Harry thought it would convince you to come back."

My face completely brightens. "I love that. What do they know?"

Holden's shoulder lifts. "That we were taking some time apart, and they both instantly told me they didn't agree with my choice. Lori even told me that I suck at emotions."

A giggle escapes me. "Was that before she flipped her hair and stormed upstairs?"

"Obviously."

"Harry and I have some catching up to do, too. He needs to update me on my stock choices." My smile is pure contentment.

"He did mention something about that."

I stand between the seat and Holden, bringing my arms up to drape off his shoulders. "Don't ever run away again."

He pulls me close, a jolt that sends fire through me. "Can't. You've locked me down."

Kissing him, goosebumps bubble on my skin and an uncontrollable need to take more of him, away from here.

"Want to get out of here? I might have checked that our favorite room is free," he murmurs against my lips with pure trouble in his tone.

"Someone is presumptuous." I grin.

Holden stands too, and our bodies glue together for another kiss that's a warning for the night ahead. I love it.

"Does it fucking matter? Even if you didn't want to take me back, I would have found a way to get you to the room and convince you that we're meant to be."

"Hmm, that might have been a better experience," I tease him.

He yanks me in the direction of the exit, but I resist. "Wait, I need something." I reach behind me and sweep the napkin off the bar top. Holding it up, I show Holden. "A memento that we need to keep."

He smiles in agreement.

———

CLOTHES SCATTER to the floor within seconds of closing the door. But we don't even manage to make it to the bed because we fall to the rug, laughing when one of us trips on his belt that fell somewhere in our frenzy. We explore one another with our hands as our lips stay melded to one another as we kneel. We're in this crazy frenzy of wanting it all at once.

The moment his fingers sneak between us to circle my clit, I'm already shuddering from an orgasm that will hit me soon. Holden always knows how to touch me, the map of my body he long ago discovered and imprinted in his head.

His skims down my neck, nipping a few times as he strokes my pussy. "So fucking ready for me," he mutters against my collarbone. He brings his soaking fingers up to twist my nipple, and he latches his mouth onto the other.

"Please," I croon. "Inside of me now."

He answers by guiding me back onto the floor and parting my thighs with my knees up. "I need to come inside you." He slips inside of me, taking me deep on the first thrust, my entire body buzzing with anticipation and desire. Surrendering to Holden leads us on this session of clinging to one another, his cock hitting that spot and his tip going as deep as possible. I'm snug around him, squeezing a little extra, with my arousal covering his length.

"You're mine," he whispers in my ear.

"I'm yours," I rasp back.

We move together in sync, and I don't even care that our bodies are roughly mounting against the rug.

It only takes a few minutes until we both collapse, seeing stars.

Holden stays in me, his ear resting against my chest where my heart feels like it might explode.

A droll smile ghosts my lips. "I'm positive I might have bruises tomorrow." I laugh. We have every reason to be happy right now.

He kisses the top of my breast. "Sorry."

"I'm not. It's kind of funny."

Holden looks up at me with skeptical eyes, only to notice my overjoyed face. "We didn't even make it to our favorite bed."

I rake his hair with my fingers. "Meh, we now know the rug I chose is perfect for all activities."

He chuckles. "Let me get you something." The moment he pulls out, I feel a loss and want him back. But the logistics of sex on a rug that isn't ours is crucial right now. Holden returns with a towel and cleans me up. "On the bed."

My eyes turn into saucers. "I know you used to be an athlete but surely your recovery time after what just transpired can't be that quick."

He shakes his head ruefully then offers me his hand to yank me up. "To actually enjoy the bed. We can even sleep here tonight. That's a first and a cause for celebration."

I snort a laugh. "Oh, because our making up is not at all important," I say sarcastically as I find my way under the duvet with Holden.

"We can go back and forth like this for eternity." His smile is something new to me; he's truly happy and at peace. My head finds the center of his chest to rest on, and he kisses the top of my hair. "Speaking of eternity, do you ever want to get married?"

My eyes turn bold because he said that so easily. "Oh." I bite my bottom lip. "I guess, yet again, we might have missed a tiny detail or two in terms of discussions we probably should have had." A sound of humor rumbles in the back of his throat. "But yes."

He squeezes me close. "Okay. I'm on board. Kids?"

Something inside me twists. He already has two kids, so maybe he doesn't want to relive having a baby around, but honesty is essential. "Yes, one baby."

"I can do that. Or rather, I would love it. To see you pregnant with my child." God, I love the certainty in his voice.

"All the checkmarks complete… Oh, wait."

Holden gives me a peculiar look. "Yes," he draws out.

"I want a dog too. That would be fun."

He rolls his eyes. "Have you been talking to Harry?"

"Hmm. Would you still say no if I did?"

"For now, yes. I can barely keep them in order. Adding a dog would just bring more disarray."

I shift my position to straddle him, and I bop the tip of his nose with my finger. "You know that I will still come home with a dog without your approval."

He grips my hips to yank me down. "And that's why I love you."

"Thought so." Then we kiss because we have all night to be tangled in the sheets while the moon shines in.

––––––––

HARRY AND LORI stare at me as I slide my suitcase down the hall from the garage.

"Can't my dad be a gentleman and do that?" Lori questions as she observes the scene.

I continue to kick my suitcase as it moves a few inches since it's on wheels. "He can, but he's busy grabbing another bag from my car."

"Duh, leave it there and he'll carry it later. He's supposed to be strong. Otherwise, why does he bother with his protein shakes?" I love the wit and attitude of this almost teenager.

"Come on, Lexi. I've been waiting for you to come back. Now I can eat my cake." Harry turns to nearly stomp to the kitchen.

I'm slightly taken aback but not surprised, he's a kid. "Thanks for showing your true excitement that I'm back and that it's more fun than cake," I call out. "Never mind that we have my stock profile to talk about and you're holding my financial future in the palm of your hand," I add.

Lori grows quiet, and that just means she's about to share some of her wisdom that is far too clever for a girl her age. "Finally, my dad can be happy… it loosens him up." That's sweet, and I give her a soft smile. "It's perfect, really." My heart melts more. "Now he won't freak out when he finds out that there are boys meeting our group when I go to the movies on Friday." My own smile drops while hers just rises. "Thanks, Lexi." She nearly skips away.

I blow out a breath, already trying to think of a way to calm this blow to Holden; better yet that Lori just charmed me and now I need to form a team with Holden. To think that I got him to agree to buy her concert tickets for her birthday. Chaperone duty here I come.

But a few minutes later, I enter the kitchen with Holden, and Lori comes to hug me, then Harry, before they hop onto their stools. As if it was an everyday occurrence, and my heart is completely soft for them.

We all assess the peanut butter and jelly cheesecake that's waiting for us to cause some serious carnage on the snacking front. I interlace Holden's arm with mine and lean my head against his shoulder.

"I love you," I whisper.

Holden continues to look forward. "That's good to know since I just carried all your stuff upstairs and will never ever carry that stuff down again since it's dead weight. But yeah, I love you too," he teases me.

My eyes follow the line from Holden to the kids already using their fingers to grab crumbs.

And this scene is perfect.

It feels like home.

EPILOGUE: HOLDEN

---

15 MONTHS LATER

"This is the worst idea in the entire history of civilization," Lexi chastises me.

I continue to look intently at the movie screen with my jaw tight while everyone rustles into their seats in the cinema, waiting for the movie to start.

"Lexi," I grind out a warning, letting her know that I'm not impressed by her words. She throws a piece of popcorn at me, and I reluctantly drag my eyes away to ten rows up ahead.

"Holden, everyone knows when the parents of a group of thirteen-year-olds discuss having a chaperone to the movie theater that you absolutely, 100%, under no circumstances *ever* volunteer to be that parent. Yet, here we are. Every. Single. Time."

My attention completely snaps in her direction. "First off, Mrs. Overthrew the Parent Committee President—"

She waves her finger in front of me. "Don't you dare. Kate McClearly had it coming, and I'm the best damn parent-board president there is. Everyone loves me." Her loud whisper squeaks. "I started the moms-who-wine club. Thank. You. Very. Much."

I want to smirk with pride, but I need to focus on what the actual fuck is going on right now. "Don't you remember what you were like when you were thirteen?" She winces because I'm completely right. "Besides, that little punk sitting next to her doesn't seem to care that I can watch his every finger. He's unaffected."

Lexi gives me that sexy eye roll and is well aware there is no taming this tiger.

"They are a group of like eight teenagers. All the other parents just carpool, drop off their kids, and go have dinner somewhere, then pick them up again. But *no,* here we are eating popcorn that tastes kind of weird." She studies the box of popcorn.

I lean back in my seat and sigh a breath. "Maybe you're right. We need to nail this down because Harry will be here in a year or two. It's just... the lights? They go off. Then maybe it's a scary movie where hand squeezing needs to happen or it contains scenes that I sure as hell don't need my daughter watching with a guy that seems intent on kissing her."

Lexi shakes her head at me. "Chill out, seriously. She already hates us for this. So good luck dealing with that when she comes home tonight. We're not stalking them when they all go for after-movie hot chocolate, are we?" Her concern is apparent.

"Well... I mean, I kind of—"

She grips my arm to stop me. "I'm putting my foot down. If you do that to her, then you are not getting sex tonight. In fact, I'll even go to bed in lingerie and nope, no action."

The older man behind us clears his throat where he's sitting next to his wife, clearly having heard. I give him a curt nod before focusing on my target again.

Licking my lips, I interlace my fingers with my wife's as we sit there. I know I should calm down, but my daughter is beautiful, witty, smart, and from what I hear, boys even in the eighth grade are lining up. No way am I going to sit at home and wait for her to return.

"How about you promise to fuck me just so I can relax?" I attempt to ask seriously.

Lexi's face floods with disbelief, and I vaguely hear the old man clear his throat again. "How do you suggest we do that here?" She loops her arm with mine to pull me close as the lights dim. "Will I be able to leave you alone for like two minutes later? I've been dying to pee for what feels like forever but needed to rein you in a bit upon arrival."

I kiss the top of her head and regain some fucking composure, let Lori be, and focus on my wife cuddling into my arm. It's been years since I've been in a movie theater.

After cooling off after five minutes and being convinced that the group of teenagers with hormones raging are actually watching the movie, Lexi risked a run to the ladies' room and then came back with chocolate with mint filling.

"Of all the options, you pick that? What a bad choice," I berate her.

She gets comfortable back on her chair again. "Sorry if I'm making bad choices today. My husband must have rubbed off on me," she loudly whispers her sarcasm.

"Don't throw me attitude now. I had to deal with that for fifteen minutes from our daughter before we left the house." Because my kids have Lexi locked into that role, even if it's not official.

In the corner of my eye, I can see that Lexi is smirking. Those facial expressions of hers always calm me, which is why we do enjoy the rest of the action movie, and I only spy on our daughter a few times.

I even give them space when the group heads to Jolly Joe's for a November hot chocolate with whipped cream. We stay seated on the bench down the street, bundled in coats and scarfs.

"Aren't you proud of me?" I smile brightly at Lexi.

She swoops her hand under my chin to guide my eyes to hers. "Very." Lexi kisses me, a soft warm kind that still feels sensual.

"Are you sure I can't convince you to shower with me before bed? I've been a good boy," I murmur into her hair as she nuzzles me.

Her fingers crawl on my thigh. "Maybe… if you can get me a hot chocolate with marshmallows and a candy cane." Her tone rhapsodizes but underneath she's serious.

"Oh, come on," I raise my voice. Now I'm annoyed and sit up straight. "All night, I get the third degree, and *now* you want me to actually go invade their space?"

She shakes her hands as though she's flustered. "I'm sorry, but that popcorn sucked."

"It tasted fine," I counter.

"But I'm kind of hungry and those chocolate things didn't cut it."

I stare at her blankly. "Because you pulled a rookie move and got chocolate with mint."

Lexi shrugs. "So? I would go myself, but truthfully, my legs feel like I can't walk after that Pilates class this morning nearly killed me."

I stand and take a few paces. Walking to Jolly Joe's right now will be similar to a man getting eaten alive by sharks, except it's purely through glares of disdain from our daughter and her friends.

Dragging a hand across my face, I gather some strength. "Fine." I sound completely unenthused.

She tries to give me an innocent happy smile, but she knows that I'll make her pay later, which in retrospect just thrills her more.

I begin to walk away. "Whipped cream on top?" I call out over my shoulder as I begin my journey to hell.

"No. By the way, I'm pregnant." Her monotone statement doesn't faze me for a second.

My feet freeze instantly, and I blink a few times. Did I hear her right? Turning on my heel, I face Lexi casually sitting on the bench with her arms stretched out along the back, her smirk completely honest.

"What did you say?" I don't blink.

"I'm pregnant," she repeats, with her smile warming as she waits for it all to sink in for me.

She caught me off guard, which was probably her intention.

A smile spreads on my mouth, and I stride straight back to her and kneel down, sliding her hands into mine. "We're pregnant?"

Lexi's lips quirk out. "That we are, Husband."

We haven't been trying with intention or thinking about it non-stop, but we did decide to see where things go when Lexi went off birth control. The baby will have quite an age gap with his or her brother and sister, but it makes it all the more fun.

My lips meet hers for a kiss that is mixed with love and happiness. "This is so much better than getting that puppy that drives me insane," I whisper against her lips.

"I hope so." She laughs, and her smile must hurt from how happy she seems.

Pulling away, I narrow my eyes. "Wait, do you really want hot chocolate?"

Lexi pretends to debate. "Nah. But the popcorn was disgusting, the chocolate mint was a bad choice, and along with the need for the bathroom, they were probably the hints I was wondering if you would pick up on."

I flex my jaw side to side. "Ah, maybe they were."

"This morning, you were occupied with tonight, so I didn't tell you. But I don't know, I didn't want to hold out until tomorrow's breakfast at the Dizzy Duck." Sunday brunch is our family tradition, dog included, as he just chills by the fireplace in the lobby and guests love it.

Blowing out a long breath, I am so ecstatic with this news. Maybe it was never on my mind to have more kids, but with Lexi, it was clear as day that we should have a baby. She'll be so relaxed and still keep us all in line.

I kiss her again and again, her cheek, jaw, neck, everywhere that would be appropriate for a bench on Main Street.

"I love you so much," she tells me, the streetlight causing her eyes to glint with a twinkle.

"Me too." I kiss our intertwined hands.

She peers over my shoulder. "You're happy?"

I nod. "Of course, what kind of question is that?"

"Good, because Harry isn't at his friend's house. They seem to be over there where they are about to light firecrackers on the street, and the old lady walking with her hot drink looks pissed." Her face looks strained and cautious.

My head draws a line from her eyes to where she's pointing to see my son is messing around with a friend from math club.

Because our family has a difficult time enjoying a calming day, and that's kind of the way we like it. Or I keep telling myself that every breakfast when chaos exists and my wife just calmly sits there while reassuring me with a wink, because later she'll swing by the Dizzy Duck like old times to get sassy with me as she sneaks her hands up my shirt.

I don't dare say life is perfect, but it's pretty damn close.

It's true, and I repeat it to myself right before I puff out my chest, gather a breath, and prepare to face my son.

But I don't get far.

The sound of a couple arguing causes me to pause.

Lexi squeezes my arm as we both dart our sight to the other corner of Main Street where we see Summer.

She's been through hell in recent months. Her husband passed, and she's used working at the Dizzy Duck as a distraction and appears strong. That was until her late husband's brother, and the Dizzy Duck's 10% owner, Nash, showed up.

Summer yanks her arm away from Nash's hold. "This shouldn't be happening," Summer protests, and she looks fired up.

Nash steps closer to her. "You know that's a lie."

Lexi and I glance at one another, very well aware that nobody should be witnessing this...

SHOULD HAVE BEEN

1

SUMMER

This isn't the way it was supposed to be.

That's what I think, as my feet dangling over the lake water as I sit on the edge of the dock. This spot to perch is only fitting. It reminds me of *that summer*, after all.

The summer where I was stuck in a corner between the Nix brothers. Zac, my closest friend, who was without a clue that his brother Nash was more.

And here I am seven years later after having my heart broken… twice. But broken in two very different ways. That's what the Nix brothers do to a human. Or at least me.

The two brothers were always complete opposites. Zac was slim and not as tall, still attractive to most, even if he often had his nose in a book, whereas Nash was and still is the guy who has a bit of muscle and a look that is cocky and tense. His glances could slice the air in half, if that were possible. Maybe that's why hockey was his calling. He was Zac's Irish twin, only ten months older. But old enough for Nash to go into protective big-brother mode, which was my undoing.

Now my husband is gone.

Zac Nix is gone.

Our marriage wasn't what it seemed, but we cared for one another all the same, and we created a child from our hearts, which means I'll always have a piece of him. A ping hits my heart. He left us five months ago, and now I have a seven-month-old baby.

Cancer is a bitch, and the path he left behind wanders around corners too sharp.

Luckily, footsteps break my morbid thoughts.

"Hey, Summer, I saw you from the window by the lobby," my friend Lexi informs me.

I glance over my shoulder to be greeted with a smile and the backdrop of the Dizzy Duck Inn. The place where people escape Chicago for a weekend getaway. Even now, when the leaves begin to turn and the charm of lake swims and sailing fade away.

"Hey." My tone must sound somber to her.

She drags her shiny blonde locks up into a messy ponytail and sits down next to me.

Lexi nudges my shoulder. "Big day."

It causes a crack of a smile to break out. "No shit. I've had my playlist on repeat for the past three hours while I was handling payroll in the staffroom. How is the lookout going?"

She winces. "Sorry. I'm not on my A-game with my detective skills today. School drop-off was an adventure this morning. Holden and Lori might kill one another soon." A fond smile hits her face.

She's perfect for Holden, who runs the Dizzy Duck Inn, and Lexi is perfect as a stepmom too, even if the school moms get snooty at her for the age difference. I can only imagine that rearing a thirteen-year-old and an eleven-year-old doesn't come easy.

I give her an amused look. "Did we not establish that today we have priorities? Holden can deal with teenage angst for the team. I needed you to be Sherlock today."

"Well, you already know…" She's dreading to remind me.

I wave her off. "That he checked in? Yeah, I heard someone mention. But damn it, I need more clues or at least a giant bucket of ice cream from Jolly Joe's."

"Gosh, our local Lake Spark establishment never fails us. Cures everything. Did you hear the bubble gum ice cream is back?"

My nose squinches. "Disgusting. If I want bubble gum flavor, then I'll just grab the children's medicine from the pharmacy," I attempt to joke.

"I know, right?" I appreciate her effort to distract me.

This is a big day. My entire body is unsettled, and my heart isn't ready for this either.

Zac, a doctor, so meticulous, left behind a house that's mine, a child so perfect, and assurance that my support network of friends won't leave me to be alone. He also passed on without ever learning of the secret I carried.

I focus my gaze on the pines surrounding the other side of the serene lake. Blowing out a breath, I can't keep it in anymore. "Tell me I'm not heading toward a car crash that I've already been in?"

Lexi opens her mouth, a sound scraping out, only to close her lips as she considers her answer. "I'm sure it's fine. Everyone needs a former hockey star to argue with. Besides, Nash is Bo's uncle."

I laugh to myself. "Really? Could have fooled me. Nash Nix has a shitty way of showing it."

"Want me to come over later, see how it all goes?" she offers.

"Nah, I have a new bottle of white in my fridge. We're good. Besides it's almost twelve, so no need to doubt when to open the bottle." I don't even really drink except for the occasional dinner. But desperate times, desperate measures, right?

Lexi rubs my shoulder. "Good philosophy to have. You've got this."

"Thanks." My voice thins.

She begins to scurry up to leave me. "If you need anything at all, just send me an SOS."

"Will do." I sigh.

My eyes shift down to the ripples in the water beneath my sneak-ered feet; there must have been a tiny fish that jumped. As a kid, I would imagine there were pirates on the lake, with treasure along the bottom. A ridiculous notion considering we aren't far from the corn fields that surround us, once you escape the hills surrounding the lake. I only ever shared that secret with one person, and I'm not sure why. We shared many secrets, actually.

Some more earth-shattering than others.

And now that man is walking around Lake Spark.

Okay, find another thought, Summer.

My job. Yes, my job. I love my job managing the staff at the Dizzy Duck Inn. Brings me joy, and damn, the stories of what happens there can make anyone grab a seat and wish they could watch while eating popcorn. Thanks to Holden, I get to work around my schedule, too. Which has been a saving grace when balancing a baby and mourning a loss, even though I'm finding normalcy again.

This doesn't seem to detour the pit in my stomach.

Nash.

Occasionally, Nash would sweep into our life, or rather Zac's, at random moments, and despite time passing, they always picked up where they left off. Nash was so busy with his hockey life, after all. I scoff, because for someone who is all steely and confident on the ice, he avoids me or any situation where he had to face Zac and me as a couple. If our eyes ever met, then he would only take a few moments before he would ensure his eyes snapped in a new direction.

Damn it, Zac. What have you done? Leaving me.

Because I already feel the dread and fear, purely for the fact that Nash is in Lake Spark today to speak with Zac's lawyer about his testament. The part of his will that I have no clue the contents.

I've handled Zac's death well for the most part. Despite the anger he caused in me that I don't want to think about now, we had the chance to say goodbye, and he was insistent that it shouldn't be a sad moment. He promised to be winking at me from up in the sky. But I can't help feeling that he didn't tell me something.

He was a good soul, so kind and fun, but sometimes he would be lost in thought when Nash's name was mentioned, because he missed his tight bond with his brother that they once had.

Shit. Younger us really fucked up life slightly.

My nails begin to tap the wood that I'm sitting on. There is no way to sweep away the image of where Nash is right now. Probably strolling on Main Street, with the baking club ladies sitting on a bench all ogle-eyed. I bet he's flashing them a suave grin to rile them up. Right before his eyes catch sight of the new nurse in town that might be of interest, and the mere thought causes a cold shiver to run down my spine.

Summer, come on. Get it together. You have moved on like a storm heading east.

But then I feel him before I even hear the soft steps. My body stiffens, and I'm too late to take a calming breath.

My body feels like I've eaten a hot tamale, and I climb up to face Nash who takes over my vision. His gleaming brown eyes and his face with short stubble are unreadable, but it's still damaging. The maroon t-shirt hugs the curves of his broad shoulders, and his light brown hair is short as always.

Our eyes meet in a tense standoff, and words lodge in my throat. Nash doesn't bother examining any other part of my body because his piercing eyes have trapped me.

"Did you find your treasure yet?" That deep voice wraps around me.

I may fear him because it's due to him that I have a different path in life. And despite nearly hating this man… my heart thrums.

2

NASH

"Well?" Summer finally manages to say.

Those are her first words? No hello?

Summer's eyes blaze open, and a thin line draws on her lips that are a shade of pink with a glaze of lip balm. Realizing that I'm glancing at her lips, I snap my sight up to study her brown eyes and the way her dark blonde hair forms a trail around her face, hiding the small scar on her forehead.

Shaking my need to soak in the image of her and the fact my chest constricts, I stay firm in my stance and decide to get right to it. Where do we pick up, anyhow? "I met with the lawyer."

"No shit. Not really news." Sass? That's the emotion she's choosing to give me right now?

But it causes the corner of my mouth to tug slightly from amusement. "I've been made executor of Zac's will." The document that we were told to wait to open.

It should have been an old game collection he left me or asking me to put money aside for Bo's college fund. Or he could've left me his stocks, but my brother always had thoughts that he kept to himself. It's just the logic behind this request that has me muddled, with no clear reasoning in my brain.

Summer stands tall, with her arms crossed around her chest, and with that t-shirt, it causes her breasts to lift, which I notice because I'm apparently an immoral person when it comes to this situation.

Creases form between her brows. "He never shared that with me."

I nod subtly once and swallow because the start of our roller-coaster of what-the-fuck moments is about to begin. "And also..."

She gawks at me. "Care to elaborate?" Summer has her feisty A-game on today.

"He requested that I move in... with you... for six weeks."

Her body completely freezes.

She's shocked, and quite frankly, so am I. This is not the news I imagined I would be delivering today.

A croak escapes Summer's throat as her mouth cracks open; she seems to be digesting the news.

"No," she states firmly her delayed response to my bombshell.

"Yes," I sigh.

"No," she repeats.

"Yes," I volley back.

Look at us, already quarrelling. She throws her hands up into the air. "Why the hell would he request that?"

I scan the area and wonder why it is so quiet today at the Dizzy Duck. I should probably take more interest in my tiny investment. My parents sold off the Dizzy Duck under the contingency that a small part was kept in the family. Since Zac had no interest, I kept 10%. Two other hockey guys completely took over the place, and I already knew them well enough.

Pinching my nose, I'm reminded that the only route of escape is turning my back on Summer. I mean, maybe jumping on a rowboat could be an option, but that seems kind of extreme. Hesitantly, I take a few steps in her direction to close our distance. Closer is my undoing around her.

"It's his request," I recap.

"I'll contest it," she says tightly.

I glide my tongue along my inner cheek, doing my best to stay calm. "Really? Of all the things, that's what you want to waste your time on? You know your desire to honor his wishes will only stop you from picking up the phone to call a lawyer anyhow."

Summer rolls her eyes while her shoulders drop, knowing damn well I'm right. "Are you going to follow it?"

Scratching the back of my neck, I go over the thoughts I had running through my head on the drive over. Zac was my little brother; I always felt a protective nature over him, but now he has asked me to take care of what he held so precious and close to his heart.

But it's Summer…

"My hockey career finished a year ago," I highlight.

I never played for the Spinners, the team that practices here in town, my career mostly took me to Michigan. Not to say I haven't spent many hours on the ice here in Lake Spark. "Besides, I have a tiny stake in the inn, too."

She chirps a laugh. "Now you want to take interest in the inn? That's rich, considering you didn't seem to have a lot of time for your family before."

I step forward, feeling a charge of regret and anger. "That's not true," I defend. But I'm not sure why I'm attempting. I've been a little more than absent over the past few years.

Summer stands with her hands in fists hanging at her sides. "Really? At the funeral you hid in the back. When Bo was born, you didn't even visit." Nor could I watch Zac and Summer together after they eloped or while they held their son together. "Just like you didn't when Zac was sick. How many times did you visit him then?"

My palm soars up to calm her. "More than you realize. Damn, Summer, you know I saw him a few times in private."

Just not enough.

She scoffs at me. "Away from my watch, right?" Her voice is soft and subdued, her eyes dropping low.

A long silence floats in the air as we both relay the facts of history in our head.

"He loved you." More than I could, or at least that's what I tell myself to dull the pain.

She strikes her glance up to me with tears pooling in her eyes. "He did love me, and I loved him… but you know it's not…" She hesitates doesn't finish her sentence.

It's Summer. She and Zac were close friends since they were probably thirteen. She always looked out for him when they were teenagers. And for that, she held a high position in our hearts.

In high school, she ignored social hierarchy and was kind to everyone. Zac had been sick, in and out of the hospital for cancer treatment more times than I care to count, and every single time she showed up with the right movie or care package to make him happy. They were always friends, until recently.

The only thing Summer has ever done wrong is…

Stopping myself, I divert my thoughts away from facts that nobody knows except her.

"We're both in a situation we never planned on. You're a widow now and—"

"Don't you dare say it, Nash." She walks past me, and I follow her trail before she turns back to me, frustrated. "What? Am I not playing the part of a grieving widow enough? Do I look like someone who needs a man to sweep in and save her?"

I bring my hand to my hip while I swipe the other across my stubbled jaw. "It's his request," I reiterate.

Way to go, Nash, saying that for the thousandth time.

"You were his wife, he… I also spoke with my mom."

She eases a smidgen. "I'm in contact with Walter and Gail, update them a few times a week via text about Bo. I guess they need space to mourn, and that's why they're staying at their vacation house in North Carolina."

My lips twitch from the fact that they are hurting, too. Zac, the favorite son. They always had a better relationship with him, I can't deny that. "They want to stay there for a change of scene, and they've decided to sell their house here and want me to handle that."

Her mouth forms an O shape. "And… they are worried about you. You're alone in taking care of their grandson."

Her sound of anger hits my ears at record speed. "Don't," she barks out. "They wouldn't try to take him from me, would they?"

I'm quick to clarify. "Absolutely not. It's just… they also want me to ensure that you and Bo are okay."

She tosses her arms up in the air. "Can everyone in your family get a grip? My family too. My brother checks in nearly every day in place of my parents who are always MIA. I'm fine, not made of glass. I've mourned, and I refuse to feel guilty for finding a routine again."

It's a long pause because I'm mulling over if I believe her. "They care. I ca— Watching out for you is what your husband would have wanted."

Her eyes shoot to mine. "Nash, I don't want to talk about my marriage or my late husband."

But he got you, and you had a baby with him.

"You two were always going to be something."

She begins to pace back and forth. "That makes it easier for you, doesn't it?"

That boil begins inside of me, and only she can cause it. "This isn't about me."

"It is. Because you know Zac and I always cared for one another—"

"He was madly in love with you," I state the truth, and it was my downfall too.

She laughs cynically to herself. "Maybe so, but he and I…"

"What? Just roommates who shared a bed?" Now I sound like a jealous son of a bitch.

Her jaw drops, as it should because my sentence came from the offside, even for me.

"You would think that, wouldn't you," she snarls.

"No point in arguing this. We have a wish to fulfill."

She shakes her head once, twice, with astonishment flooding her face. "You're really going to do it, aren't you? Move into the home Zac left me. You feel some sort of guilt and now here we are."

Now I'm fuming, and I step toward her, towering over her petite frame with her eyes sliding up to meet mine. She smells of mango, a peculiar smell, but that's always been her shampoo… always.

"It's not guilt."

Summer jabs her finger against my chest, her stare carving into me. "It is. Because you're the one who let me go— You changed the path."

I'm quick to grab Summer's wrist, and her breath catches. I swear my chest is about to burst from the spike of my pulse, and I do at least 100 reps on the bench press on a daily basis to raise my heart rate. "Now isn't the time to rehash events," I warn her.

Crap. Are we having a confrontation for the whole world to see? The guests on the second floor must be getting a show.

A sly smirk begins to form on her beautiful mouth, and it concerns me but sucks me in all the same. "We'll have to eventually if you plan on living back in Lake Spark."

"But not today." Our eyes are in a tight latch again, and the air seems to evaporate around us. This is why I've stayed away. "Does it matter anyhow?"

"Nash, what have we been thrown into? What has your brother done?" Her voice grows delicate.

"Damage, without even knowing it," I rasp.

The joke's on us, it has to be.

"He always loved games." Everything softens inside of her. "Gosh, remember how he insisted on playing the old-school version of that video game where the kid is a paperboy for like a week?" she reflects and has a small wry smile.

My entire body eases. "Such a geek like that. He should have been dating, he had the looks. Instead, he could master every single card game and boardgame, too. I do remember that he nearly lost it when you informed him that there was a second version of the game. And remember how he had those ridiculous drawings?"

We both chuckle softly, and the air around us lightens.

But then her eyes abandon me to glance down to see my hand still wrapped around her wrist. I drop my fingers away like a burn to the skin then clear my throat, and we both step back to create some distance.

She clears her throat. "Fine." Her tone is curt.

"Fine what?"

"If you suddenly feel like you owe something to Zac, then move your bags on in and get to know your nephew." She doesn't sound thrilled, more deflated. "That's the *only* reason. To honor Zac's wishes because he loved Bo, and he wants you to know your nephew. For Zac and Bo," she clarifies.

My tongue darts to the corner of my mouth. I could scream that Zac owes me more. Alas, right now, it's about Summer who just received the bombshell she was never warned about.

"I'm moving in." That's my answer.

Against all better judgment.

"Honorable," she snipes as she shuffles her feet and walks a few paces with her back facing me as she looks at the water along the side of the dock.

I go from zero to a hundred around this woman. Tormented, angered, then hopelessly at her mercy; if only she knew. "It will be good for Bo, and you'll get a little relief."

A bitter noise rumbles from her throat. "Relief? You've got to be kidding me. You've stormed back into my life on a full-time basis."

Staring up at the sky, I then bow my head from exhaustion. "Like you were with my brother on a full-time basis?"

Her head darts in my direction, with her fumed expression cannonballing into me. "Listen." She clenches her fists in pure anger. "Let's be super clear from the get-go. We all were close at one time. You and me? We were supposed…" Summer can't muster the words, and I don't want her to.

The pain drips from every word. "But you were a coward. Your brother and I were friends. He did feel more, and I loved him differently. I wouldn't change the fact that our marriage…" She keeps doing that, as if she realizes what she is about to say but she doesn't want to. "Zac got to experience a marriage and fatherhood," she simply states.

Only because I let him have you.

I close my lids tightly, only to open them, wishing I could turn the clock back. "Don't say anything more."

"Fine." She's not impressed.

I can't even respond, which she takes as her cue to end this conversation. Summer pivots and grumbles as she leaves. "See you at *home*."

I can't help feeling that something isn't right. She's holding onto something she doesn't want me to know.

3

NASH

I lean against the reception desk inside the hotel. The man behind the desk whose name tag reads Stuart is busy swiping the tablet. I'm waiting patiently, but I crack a smile when Holden walks in my direction.

"Hey there, I heard you were back in town." He pats my shoulder and joins me at the desk.

"Where did you hear that?"

He scratches the back of his neck. "I have my sources."

I grin. "How bad is it?"

"Yeah, okay. I might have heard the other day when my wife and Summer were chatting about your mysterious impending arrival back at Lake Spark."

"Ah… and considering I just saw Summer, should I give it ten or twenty minutes before Lexi phones you with the latest news?"

Holden slants his head to the side and quirks his lips out. "Meh, it's school pick-up time, so probably twenty-five minutes."

Despite my absence in almost everything around this town, I know Holden and Stone, the other investor, well enough.

Holden's face turns serious for a moment. "As much as I'm not impressed with your lack of involvement at the Dizzy Duck, that was always what you wished for, and we agreed on it from the start. That means we don't need to have any awkward business conversations. I can just ask, how are you holding up?"

"I'm doing okay. It's my brother's uncanny knack to turn his passing into a time of… well, I'm not sure, but he made mourning easy until now," I explain.

"Okay, that's you all checked out," Stuart, the receptionist, interrupts.

Holden's brows furrow. "You just got here. I kind of thought that you would at least check on the place that you have some stake in?"

I hand Stuart my key, as the Dizzy Duck stuck to classic keys instead of upgrading to keycards. I glance at Holden. "No, I will be around more for the next few weeks. I'll discover what I've missed and understand how you've made this place better than my parents ever would have."

He grins and pats my shoulder. "Now that's what I want to hear. We can have an informal meeting with Stone and catch up, plus go over some ideas for the coming months."

"Sounds like a plan, and it will keep me busy I guess." I shrug.

Holden's smile fades, and his face turns puzzled. "Wait, what? You're staying longer term? Why aren't you staying here?"

"I have a new place that I'll be lodging at."

"Where might that be?"

I can *almost* find humor in all of this. "Turns out my brother's request is that I move in with Summer for a bit. Ensure she and Bo are doing okay."

Holden has no words as he looks at me with a blank face, his brows raised.

With my knuckles curled, I bump his arm. "It's okay. Say nothing. You're doing far better at taking the news than Summer did. And I'm too hyped up on adrenaline to even contemplate how this day is going."

"Cookie?" Stuart asks as he holds up a basket, oblivious to the tone of our conversation. I forgot he was in earshot.

"Not the time, Stuart." But they are great chocolate chip cookies that guests get at arrival and departure, even at turndown service. I reach over. "You know what, give me a cookie." I slant a shoulder up. "For the road," I justify.

"Damn, that's a little crazy," Holden finally comments.

I take a bite of the sweet goodness. "I know, right? My brother conspires even from beyond. Kind of never thought he had it in him, but alright, on this ride I shall go. I'm sure Summer and I can keep enough distance between us. We'll just get into a routine, honor my brother, ignore our past, pretend all is well," I list with a full mouth, treating this moment far too casually because that's how I'm adjusting to shock.

"I don't even know the background of..." His eyes swim side to side. "Doesn't she kind of hate you?"

My lips roll into my mouth, and I tip my head to the side in contemplation. "Probably." Because there are no labels when it comes to my history with Summer, everyone just assumes we dislike one another.

Holden looks relieved with my answer. "Anything I can do?"

I shake my head. "Nah." I hold up my cookie. "Just save me when the shock wears off," I plead.

"You got it," he says as I brush past him.

But then I stall when I get a few steps further and pivot on the balls of my feet.

"Hey, Holden." I'm not sure I want to hear the answer of what I'm about to ask. He stares at me, waiting. "Summer... how has she been holding up?"

He scratches his chin. "Oh, I guess she's doing better than we would all expect. Keeps herself busy. Focuses on Bo. You know... she's been eager to move her life forward." His shoulder raises then drops. "I'm not sure if it's a cover or not, nor do I have any idea what it's like for her when she heads home. But here at the inn, she manages to smile."

Relief hits me. I'm not sure I could handle another answer. I've always stayed away to save us all, and if I were to blow back into town needing to rescue Summer, then I'm not sure I would have it in me to keep things on a neutral level with her.

"Thanks. Well… I, uh… I should go."

His eyes seem to study me, and he nods once. If it's understanding that he is offering, then I'll take it.

———

KNOCKING ON THE DOOR, I'm still wondering why I'm standing here about to embark on a request from my brother.

The door opens, and Summer's scowl greets me, but for a few ticks our eyes hold in silence.

"I'm here. Can I come in?"

She steps to the side and holds the door open. "Surprised you asked since this is now your home, too." Zero enthusiasm seeped through those words.

I mosey past her, and already I'm observing the setting as we walk into the living area. Examining the room, it's cozy and airy. The wood of the shelves is painted white, and the floors are a light pine shade. A contrast to the dark pines surrounding the house as seen through the double doors in the living room.

"And here we are. Nash knocking on our door and waltzing on in to uproot our lives."

"That's what you think. I'll always be the villain in your book." I give her a steely stare.

Rage brews inside of her, and I see her face etched in annoyance. "It's because this request is near insanity. When I got married, you sent a damn waffle maker with a note."

"It's a classic wedding gift," I defend coolly.

She's not amused. "When Bo was born, you sent a stuffed proboscis monkey and a note. Who the hell sends the ugliest freakiest choice when a normal monkey should have sufficed."

I shrug, and I'm doing my best to shove down a smirk. "It's different."

"And now you want to upgrade to moving in? I'm surprised you didn't just drop a note with one sentence through the mailbox to inform me. It's more your style," she says dryly.

Feisty Summer. It doesn't happen often, except when she's around me.

I don't answer, instead pinching the bridge of my nose and bowing my head down.

"Now if you'll excuse me, Bo is waking up."

By the time I lift my eyes, she's already whizzed away.

Slowly I walk around the living room, and my eyes pause when I see the basket of baby toys in the corner. I've seen Bo once now, at my brother's funeral. What a shitty uncle I've been. I know that I need to rectify that.

The patter of steps down the stairs draws my gaze up to see Summer walking into the room holding Bo who looks wide awake, holding the monkey.

"Oh, look at that, someone enjoys his freaky monkey." I smile confidently and raise my brows at Summer.

She rolls her eyes and bounces him on her hip, choosing to ignore me. "This is your uncle." She sighs. "He's moving in." Her tone is impassive, and she picks up his little hand to wave. "I know, what a surprise." Tone still unchanged.

I step forward to touch my nephew gently, and the corner of my mouth hitches up. Bo makes a sound that is promising for me.

"Hey, buddy, you probably don't remember me, but I'm your uncle." I grab his loose shirt delicately. He's wiggly in Summer's arms, so he acts as a barrier between her and me.

But still, my eyes flick up and catch Summer soaking in the scene, as if she's been waiting for this. Maybe so, I'm blood-related to this little guy who is smiling at me, and that lightens the feeling in my chest too.

Summer clears her throat. "Uhm… he probably needs a snack, so we should go do that."

I step back. "Of course."

A few minutes later, my nephew is staring at me with marvel in his eyes. He smiles a lot, especially when he's sitting in his highchair squishing banana between his fingers. Bo is going to be the spitting image of my brother, I can tell.

"So, buddy, looks like you and I are going to be hanging out more." I hold my clenched fist up. "No? No fist bump?" I joke as I sit next to him at the kitchen table.

"You two will get along well. He doesn't respond with words, so you'll be in your element, spewing out sentences with nobody to debate you." Summer brings the rim of her tea mug to her lips, but I can see the smug grin that she's trying to hide.

"Cute." A contrite smile is pasted on my mouth. She's angry at me for staying away for so long, and I don't blame her.

"Uhm, so…" Awkwardness begins. "I'm going to head back to Chicago for a day or two to gather some things and wrap up some meetings with my agent."

Lines form on her forehead. "I thought your hockey days are over."

"They are, but I still have a few sponsor commitments."

Her head tips slightly to the side. "Right."

"Just let me know which room I'm moving into."

An amused look greets me. "Subtle."

Shaking my head, I'm now completely drained by her attitude. "I'm not trying to figure out which room you decided to make a baby in, if that's what you are wondering."

Shit. That came out cruel and envious.

Her mouth gapes open, yet she contains her composure. "Unbelievable. You really are a piece of work."

"Not sure I'm the only one."

Summer's cheeks puff out. "I don't have time for this. I have laundry to do and a bottle of white to drown in when Bo goes to sleep tonight. But for your information, you can take the guest room across from Bo's room. It's never been used."

I'm not sure if that brings ease or is more oil thrown on the fire as I puzzle together the history of sleeping arrangements in this house, even though Summer has only been living here since around the time my brother passed. But it's the mere thought of them that…

Summer marches to Bo, ignoring the fact that she's pushing me out of the way, practically on top of me as I sit, and she reaches to unbuckle Bo from his highchair. Her body stretching too close to me drives my body haywire in epic proportions.

"Come on, cutie. Let's go play in the living room." She throws a glare over her shoulder. "My son is the cutie, in case you need every detail to be explained."

"Spirited as always." My tone is flat.

She props Bo against her hip before she grumbles and walks away.

I rub my face with my hands. I have to get a grip. We won't be able to live together like this.

I've always watched Summer from afar to lessen the sting. But now she's way too close for my resolve.

I heave a sigh and slide off the chair, knowing I'm going to have to face her one more time today for good measure. Plus, I need to walk through the living room to get to the front door.

Walking into the living room, I stop in my tracks when I see Summer sitting on the floor, her hair down and feathering her arms. She's making noises at Bo, and they're both giggling while she wiggles his captured foot. She was always meant to be a mom. She's a natural, and this is an image of two happy souls. Despite what's happened, they deserve this moment.

Even if Summer doesn't want to admit it, she's hurting from my brother's passing too. And Bo? Well, he'll never remember his father. My heart aches for too many reasons, but I won't let Summer be the reason this time. I owe it to my brother to be the man who watches over his family.

My eyes slide to the side, and something captures my eye. Taking a few steps, I pause when I notice a photo of Summer, Zac, and Bo, the three of them together when Bo must have been a few weeks old.

They're a family in the photo with affection on their faces. But the photo next to them, it's clear. No need to see it up close.

The three of *us*. My brother, Summer, and me.

Long ago.

When this mess all began.

And it all comes back…

NASH

Don't torture yourself. You knew they would be here, and still you decide to join when you saw them. Damn it, Nash.

I slow my walk as I approach Summer and Zac sitting on the edge of the dock. My brother's legs dangling and Summer sitting cross-legged half turned to face him. They are deep in conversation, but Summer's eyes slide in my direction, then she does a double take. Her eyes are laced with fear and delight that I'm here.

My brother shoots his gaze up and an instant beaming smile forms.

"Oh hey, I thought you would be at the rink." My brother scoots over to make room for me to join, and I sit on his other side cross-legged to face Summer as my brother leans back on his elbows.

"Finished early. It's the off season. I was just focusing on practicing skills and concentration. Can't work too hard," I explain. It's been five years since I went pro, but it still feels good to come home in the summer.

My brother shrugs it off. "I was just telling Summer about a BBQ

I want to throw later. Remember in high school, when our parents would be complete idiots and leave us alone on the weekends? They kept giving us prime opportunities for parties and stuff," he reflects.

Zac is right, someone should have given them the parenting-a-teenager playbook.

One person's stupidity is another person's gain, right? It meant at the end of my senior year, it gave me ample opportunity for a stolen moment with Summer that stayed in my mind, but we left it in the past.

Until a few months ago.

"Anyway, I think we'll all go easy tonight with a few friends and throw some burgers on the grill. Nothing like the way you normally celebrate a game win," my brother explains.

Last season I only celebrated with Summer because we happened one night. My little brother's best friend who has always occupied my thoughts. It was a kiss in the making, a pop of the tension bubble between us, and it quickly turned to more. We kissed once when we were younger, but this was zero to a hundred within a minute.

It should have only been a hook-up, but I've been addicted to Summer ever since.

We've just kept it quiet, as we weren't sure how Zac would react. Maybe it was our logic that we would only be a fling and he would never need to know.

But it's no longer what we imagined.

Summer clears her throat. "I'm sure people just want to hang out. No need to break out the shots."

"I'm sure that's how Nash rolls between games. Girls are always all over him. They must buy him shots." My brother's words agitate Summer, and I can tell because of the way she nibbles her bottom lip to hide her disdain at the thought.

"How were your classes this morning?" I divert the conversation and stare down at the wood. My brother is taking extra classes because he's in medical school and is about to start clinical rotations.

Summer laughs. "You're too smart for me," she teases Zac.

Zac looks between us, then his eyes land on Summer. "You guys won't be laughing when I'm a doctor and you both need me to save you."

"Whoa, I'm never trusting you, even if you have a stethoscope around your neck," she pushes back in good humor, and it makes him grin more.

My eyes catch Summer's, and my brother is oblivious. It's been happening a lot the past few weeks. We get to have a few seconds of connection before one of has to tear our sight away, and this time it's me when Zac pushes off the dock.

"I have to head in. Need like an hour more of study time. I'll hit the store on my way home."

When Zac stands and looks down, he takes a moment to look between us. His expression is peculiar; I don't recognize it, but when he smiles softly again, then ease hits me.

"See ya." I tip my nose up.

"Later, Zac."

He gives Summer an extra smile. "Don't look too hot tonight, otherwise Nash and I will be too busy playing bodyguard."

Her face blossoms red, but she plays it cool. "I'll do my best to suppress my superpowers." She salutes him.

By the time he's out of sight, my full attention is on Summer who will not be having anyone's fingers but my own touching her tonight.

I admire the way Summer's lips twist when she blushes, and the way her eyes attempt to escape my watch is one of the most beautiful things I've seen. Her head tips to the side as she examines me, waiting for me to say something.

I place the palm of my hand on her thigh below the hem of her jean shorts, not caring that we're on the dock at the Dizzy Duck Inn on a warm summer's day. I lean in to steal a kiss. I need her lips on mine. The way I've needed her every time we manage to see one another. During the end of the season, she would tell Zac she was visiting a friend from college, but really, she was with me when my game schedule would allow.

She always melts under the command of my mouth, always

following my cues, as if I will lead the way and be her protector. Her trust in me runs strong.

No matter how hard I kiss her, her lips always remain soft and silky. Even when I'm inside of her going hard, she still captures my mouth so delicately.

Right now, she scoots closer to me, causing our knees to touch to ensure that we are inseparable.

One more second. That's all I get before we need air. Pulling apart, my hand stays put on the back of her neck, with my thumb caressing her cheek.

"Nash," she tuts. "Anyone can see."

"And? My parents own this place. We've also agreed that Zac should probably know, we just need to find the right moment."

She nods her head in complete agreement. "*Finally*. I've begged you for weeks to tell him."

My jaw flexes at the uncomfortable reminder. "It's just... you two have been friends forever. He thinks I look at you like a little sister."

Summer's eyes widen. "Well, I'm sure he will change his view when he discovers you fucked me in the family pool house the other week, and then we agreed that our theory is true and that we're quite good at it together. Hence, why we fuck like crazy."

Summer, my spitfire Summer. I need to thank someone upstairs.

I chuckle and glance up at the sky then back to Summer who is smirking. "You have such a mouth."

She gives me a funny look. "Like you're one to talk." Her smile stays fixed as her eyes squinch from the sun, the breeze off the lake blowing her hair behind her shoulders. "You're leaving soon," she reminds me. Hockey season is not a friend to any relationship.

"We'll make it work." I shrug.

Her blue eyes sparkle at my insistence, and she interlaces our fingers, with her eyes set on our hands as if she is taking a mental picture, but she doesn't answer.

I guide her to turn toward me. "Let's not discuss it any more today. When I'm away, I'll still be possessive of you. You're like a hockey puck I won't let anyone touch."

Her head falls back when she cracks a laugh. "Oh my gosh, you did not just compare your gorgeous fuck to a puck."

"Summer, language," I chide to tease her. We begin to walk back toward the shore, and I nudge her shoulder with mine. "Come on, we have a window of a few hours."

And we take advantage of it. A few hours later, I'm looking in the mirror as I run my fingers through my hair. It's apparent by my flushed look that I've just had sex, and a small smirk of pride hits the corner of my mouth as I slide back into my boxer briefs.

It's a little crazy that I'm back in my family home, but my parents are gone to their house in North Carolina. I have plenty of money to get my own place for the summer, but I just want downtime and the familiar, away from city life. And this room has memories. A first kiss with Summer, and now a few years later, I step back into the room to see her sitting up in bed with her feet on the floor as she attempts to clasp her bra closed.

I dive on top of the bed on my side and take over to help her, then I gently kiss the curve of her shoulder.

An unusual silence fills the room until she breaks it. "Nash, I feel something strong. I know that I'm in—"

I cut her off instantly and plant my finger on her mouth, not wanting to hear the words. "I feel it, too."

She twists her body to glance down to me. "You have me. Every part, and don't you dare break it." Her lips skim my bottom lip.

She means her heart.

5

SUMMER

I adjust the few flowers that I just set on the grave.

"I know, I know. I'm being a complete, well…" I ponder to myself and even roll my eyes. "A bitch, if I'm being really honest. But your brother is returning it in full."

Speaking to Zac's grave seems to be a weekly occurrence for me. But it's never tears, no. Oh no, he would never have that.

"Every time, I want to lay it on the table. And I know I should, but… I'm scared of his reaction."

The truth is too easy.

"It's the same as you, I guess. You never told me you loved me until you were sick. Before then you chickened out, and I didn't feel I needed to press. Anyhow, Bo will be excited to have Nash here. He also thinks O-shaped cereal is the greatest thing on earth, so perhaps his standards are low. You know, Bo still loves to look at the photo on the mantle of you, Nash, and me. We were so young and naïve then, weren't we? Oh, and did I tell you that we had a guest at the Dizzy Duck who screamed to her husband that she wanted a divorce? We all know, because it happened in the restaurant… where the husband and his mistress were having dinner. These are the kinds of things that keep me moving."

My eyes draw a line up to the sky, admiring the clear blue, then I return to the gray stone. "I wonder if you're mad at me up there for never telling you about me and Nash before you died. You probably get all of the best secrets up there, don't you? I have a feeling I should brace myself. What are you up to?"

I trace my fingers over the lettering on the stone. "Until next time." I smile to myself.

Leaving the graveyard, I take a deep breath. It's odd, but I always feel calm after visiting. It's quiet here. I don't follow any religion, but if there is something in our afterlife, then I would like to think everyone here has found solace.

Deciding to take the long walk, I wander along the lake and then up Main Street. A freshly brewed coffee is in order, and when I walk through the door of Jolly Joe's, with the bell dinging, I inhale the smell of the place as my eyes take in the 50s-style diner and hope someone picked a good song on the jukebox.

It's still early enough in the day, which means the smell of coffee and cinnamon rolls runs strong. It's so silly, but they place little jelly-beans in every single cup of coffee because apparently it brings luck.

"The usual?" Mary, behind the counter, asks. She's worked here for as long as I can remember.

"Yes, please. No cinnamon roll today." I smile.

"Sure thing, kiddo. By the way," she begins as she holds up a mug, and I know where this is going. Now is the time to plaster on a fake smile. "I heard Nash was back in town."

Yep, there it is.

"He is." My smile is strained.

"Hmm." That's how she manages to respond? I would say I got off easy, but she seems to be examining me and forming an internal theory.

Ignoring her, I slide into a booth and remove my scarf. I texted Lexi on my way here to see if she was in town, but I didn't hear back.

I have to smile to myself as I sit here. It's nostalgic, and you always know what you'll get. I thank Mary when she places the coffee in front of me and look up in pleasant surprise when I see Harlow, another friend, stepping through the door.

"Hey there, can I join you?"

"Please." I sound relieved because it means I won't have to listen to Mary share her observations.

Harlow smiles politely at Mary in passing before joining me at the table. Harlow is married to Stone who owns part of the Dizzy Duck, and she's also an author.

"I've been craving an orange roll since two am this morning," she groans.

My face forms lines. "Two am?"

She tucks her light brown locks behind her ear then looks down at her belly. "This thing won't let me sleep."

I chuckle at her. "Thing. You mean baby?"

"Baby, thing, does it matter? I can't sleep, and I still have another two months to go."

"It's a special time." I raise a shoulder.

She waves me off and captures Mary's attention then points to the orange rolls on display.

"So, how are you? I heard a special guest checked into the Dizzy Duck, only to check back out." She flashes me a look.

That's what I appreciate about my friends. They don't treat me like I'm fragile. I've made it clear that I want to have normalcy in my life, and they follow my lead; hence, why she can tease me about a fact that shouldn't be funny at all. Yet, if I were in her shoes, I would do the same.

"I'm surprised the mayor hasn't put up a billboard yet to welcome Nash back. But yes, he rolled into town and now apparently gets a key to my house, too." I take a long sip of my coffee.

Harlow's eyes bug out. "Why?"

"It's Zac's wish to have his brother move in for six weeks."

"Huh, he didn't talk about this at all before he passed?"

I shake my head. "No. Don't think he would have, actually. From what I gather, it's a sort of brotherly tribal thing, you know, step in when the other cannot. I'm just surprised that Zac would think I need a protector."

She taps her flawless manicured olive-green nails on the table. "I mean, you all used to be friends, right?"

I huff a sound. "Something like that…"

A friendship too far, perhaps.

So many things where I should have put my foot down, but I didn't, especially three years ago, and recalling it still brings mixed emotions.

I nearly tumble onto the chair at Catch 22, the restaurant on the lake that's half casual and half sophisticated. I'm late.

"So, so, soooo sorry." I'm panting after hurrying from my car to here where Zac is waiting. "There was a family of ducks crossing the road, and you know how I get. Have to stop for ducks. I mean, who doesn't in Lake Spark? Did you hear that there is a coyote that's been rampaging through people's garbage at night?"

He smiles wryly as I ramble, and he waits patiently for me to stop. When I set my purse on the empty chair at the table, he takes it as his cue to speak. "You are a noble citizen. And we all had the extra section on our drivers test in regard to stopping for Lake Spark wildlife."

I smile brightly. "See?" I grab the glass of water and take a quick sip. "I'm happy you picked this place for our weekly brunch. I want to try the new chicken salad."

That's us. We see one another on a regular basis. One another's ride-or-die.

"I'm going to head right into it. I have to ask you something."

His sentence grabs my attention. "Shoot. What's up?"

Zac swipes his fingers across his jaw as he hesitates. "You and Nash."

I nearly spit out the ice cube in my mouth as my body freezes. His name gives me this reaction every single time, yet I attempt to be unaffected.

"What about him?" The room feels cold. "If this is about Nash

living in his own world, then just, you know, let it go, or you can reach out. I'm sure you both will renew your brotherly bond."

The thorn in my side. Nash breaking my heart then distancing himself from Lake Spark altogether. I know he has an investment in the Dizzy Duck, it was their parents' stipulation when they sold the place.

"It's not that. Although, I wish we were at a better place. He has his hockey career." A pit in my stomach always forms when we talk about him. "Nothing ever happened between you and him, right?"

My heart sinks. A lie is a lie, but for some reason, Nash and I decided long ago that it's better for Zac. Not even sure why I went along with it, but I keep my feet firmly planted for stability against the lie that is about to spew from my mouth. "No, of course not."

Relief fills his eyes. "Sorry. Of course." A half-smile breaks out. "I mean, at the random family functions when he graces us with his presence, you two look like you might kill each other. And to be honest, I wouldn't like it if you two had some history. In fact, I would hate it. I'm too protective of you, and my brother isn't always great news when it comes to the female population."

Oh, I know. Preaching to the choir.

"I know you've clarified this many times, it's just lately..." He rolls his shoulder back then subtly shakes his head. "I'm being crazy."

That's why we haven't told him. No need to crush him. I'm not blind, I know Zac loves me in a different way, he's just never openly admitted it, and still, it hasn't affected our friendship.

Swallowing, I remind myself to bury Nash deeper inside of me, as he surfaces too much in my thoughts when someone brings him up. "Anyhow, was that all, detective?" I manage to bring back my bright and cheery voice.

Zac seems to chuckle under his breath, and his eyes circle the room as he seems to be finding words. "You know I would do anything for you, right?"

"Of course. And I return the sentiment in full." I beam.

"Then I have the world's most extreme favor to ask." His face shades to pleading.

My eyes narrow as I try to figure out where this conversation is going. "Okay, and…" It draws out.

"It's more that I need a favor to ensure that everything is set for a life insurance policy should…"

"Did the doctor say something?" My heart sinks for the second time in this conversation, but this time it's all devoted to Zac. Fear fills me at record speed. He's been healthy for years, but it doesn't surprise me that there could always be a recurrence or it leading to something else.

He doesn't need to say any words, his face says it all. "The thing is, I have this long list of things that I wanted in life but…"

I stare at him blankly. "What's on the list?"

"You… Marry me."

———

Harlow waves a hand in front of my face. "Uhm, are you okay?"

My eyes flicker. "Oh yeah, totally."

Not really. Did I do the right thing? I married my best friend. I couldn't say no because of an overbearing feeling of caring for him while he was ill. I was naïve to think that he was supposed to get better. I wasn't supposed to feel that I wanted a child and that he would be a great father. Zac was optimistic he would be okay, until he told me when I was very pregnant that he didn't have long left.

Harlow sinks into the booth. "You know if you need a break or something, just send Bo our way. I'd be happy to take care of him if you need rest or…"

I look at her, unimpressed but still with a humored smile. "I'm sure you mean if Nash and I need to have a serious discussion?"

"No," she lies, her voice uneven, then she takes a second before she gives in. "Totally," she says bluntly.

That causes the corners of my mouth to tug up. Twirling some hair around my finger, I do my best to sink into my current life status. "I should have thought about this more. I mean, not just agreeing that he could move in."

"Maybe. But if it's in his will, can you even do anything? How do those things work?"

A short laugh escapes me. "I'm still processing the request a little more. Instead, my mouth didn't connect with my brain, and I found myself agreeing to it."

She shrugs. "Maybe that's a good thing. Our brains are the last to catch up. Besides, wouldn't you want Bo to be around his family?"

I hold my mug up to her. "Exactly that." Harlow waits for me to continue because she can tell that I'm about to rant, and I do. "We will just have to set some rules, go over schedules, and he will need to learn that we work around Bo's needs. And he has to work on his baby-caring skills. Do you think I can leave him alone with Bo yet?" I bring a finger to my chin, also recognizing that they had an instant connection. "Of course not, silly thought. He probably doesn't even know how to change a diaper. Oh, and he absolutely better not leave dirty dishes in the sink."

Harlow taps her nails on the table. "You might need to slow down. I think you first need to make him a spare key," she points out.

"Ugh, this is not happening." I collapse onto the table with an innate need to bang my head for show.

Harlow gently pets my head. "Unexpected things can bring sadness, but they can also bring the best things in life," she mentions softly.

I raise my head to look at her.

Because what she says is crazy, ridiculous… and probably true.

———

COULDN'T HE USE A DOORBELL? But *noooo,* let's just knock.

It stirs up some therapeutic nonsense that someone offered after Zac's passing. I vaguely remember the words that knocks means right decisions, positive change, a message from a spirit, a soul mate…

Huffing out a breath, I open the door with gusto.

"It's me… again." Nash has an uncomfortable look on his face.

I crane my neck and tip my nose up to search for his luggage. "Changed your mind? There are no suitcases."

Nash steps through the threshold without a care in the world. "In my car, and I'll get it later."

Closing the door, I follow him to the living room where he plops himself onto the couch as if he owns the place.

"Where's Bo?"

"Sleeping. He does that a lot in case you're wondering. Speaking of which, what is your experience with babies on a scale of one to ten?"

"Probably a two." He doesn't seem bothered. At least he's honest.

"And how do you want to handle the schedule? Are you just going to come and go as you please?"

He kicks his feet up on the coffee table, bringing his crossed arms behind his head, and I stomp right over and strip his feet off back onto the floor. "I'll work around you guys, handle everything I need to while I'm in Lake Spark."

"Fine." I pick up a baby blanket on the floor and begin to fold it to keep my hands occupied. "Dishwasher and garbage, those are your chores."

Nash chuckles. "Didn't realize I would have a sticker chore chart. Do I get ice cream at the end of the week if I'm good?" He's mocking me.

I throw him a tight smile. "Funny."

He leans forward and rests his elbows on his knees, his hands hanging between his thighs. "Seriously, do you need anything? The house all good?"

I take myself down a notch to bring neutrality to the room. "It's fine. I've only had this house since right before Zac passed. He was insistent that he buy it, and in a rush, too. We didn't have a lot of time once he found out that he was terminal. In fact, in the end, he didn't even sleep here since I moved in while he was in the hospital. Still, I'm sure his spirit is here."

Nash seems to register my meaning. "He wanted to ensure you and Bo were taken care of."

I toss the blanket onto the arm of the sofa, giving up on folding it properly. "That's him. He kept saying to me *'Don't worry, Summer. I've made sure that you have everything you'll need, I promise.'"* The pure thought causes my lips to curve.

Perching on the sofa arm almost exhausted, I reach up to find the charm of my necklace to twist between my fingers.

"Everything made sense in his head," Nash notes.

"So it seems." I bring my charm to my mouth, a habit.

"What is it?"

At first, I don't understand, but then I see Nash with his eyes set on my fingers.

"This?" I hold it up and affection warms my face. "It's a treasure chest." Nash seems surprised, and his eyes widen slightly. "Zac got it for me."

To me it's normal, but Nash's eyes are lasered in on my chain, and most of all, I can't help but notice his eyes have darkened. A shiver runs down my body all the way to my toes.

"A lucky guess on the charm since I never mentioned my ridiculous theory of the mystical lake. He got it for me after we…"

I don't finish the sentence because I can already see that Nash is lost in thoughts, or worse, memories.

6

NASH

"We're going to miss your presence during hockey season. We're still holding out that you'll get traded to the Spinners here in town." One of the guys from the ice rink holds his cup up amongst the chatter. The kitchen is buzzing with a few of Zac's friends as we talk around the kitchen island with drinks and chips with dip.

"We should have just made this a goodbye party to our town's royalty." My brother sounds almost annoyed.

Summer nudges Zac from where she's leaning against the countertop next to him. "Don't be a grumpy old man."

My brother's eyes flare up at her, unimpressed by her comment.

I step forward and pat my brother's shoulder. "Come on, little brother, let's go check if the BBQ is ready to grill the burgers."

Zac sighs. "Sure. I could use some fresh air."

Summer gives me a nervous nod but stays put, and my heart heats in anticipation of this conversation, and the endgame is that I can kiss her in the open right after it's all done.

My brother needs to know.

When we're outside, the music from inside simmers down, and despite two or three friends perched on the steps on the other side of the pool, it's quiet enough.

My brotherly senses ring an alarm bell because Zac just doesn't seem himself, or at least not the same guy as earlier today.

I squeeze his shoulder and guide him to sit down on a chair. "Everything okay? You seem a little off tonight."

He shakes his shoulders and adjusts his neck as if he can rid the tension. "It's fine. It's just…" He's agitated for sure. "It's Summer."

My brows rise. "What about her?" Does he already know?

Zac sighs. "Tonight's the night, tonight's the night that the truth has to come out."

"Look, Zac, about Summer and—"

"I'm going to make my move," he interjects.

My entire body jolts from surprise. "W-what do you mean?" There is an edge in my voice of concern and fear.

"You've seen the way I look at her. I know you have. You keep examining us with your eyes. You've got to see it, that she and I could be more."

Nausea hits my stomach. "I… don't know."

He leans back into the chair, sulking. "Of course, you wouldn't know. At the snap of your fingers, you have it all. I don't think she and I were meant to be friends. Our connection is too strong and only gets stronger as the years go by."

I swipe my hand across my jaw, now stuck behind a difficult rock. "What if she doesn't want that?"

My brother seems to contemplate, and even he doesn't know. "It's… she's been different lately. I feel like it's a sign that I can be honest with her. Do you think she's seeing someone?" Swallowing, words get stuck in my throat, and I can't answer. "I think I might kill the guy that gets to kiss her."

"I never knew you felt this way about her."

"She never gave an indication that maybe she would be interested, so I kept it all in. But, for sure, she's been so happy lately, and it has to be…"

I clench my fist, doing my best to come up with a game plan for this turn of events. "What if I said I kissed her?" What the fuck just spun off my tongue?

Zac frowns yet doesn't seem concerned. "You wouldn't do that to me. Nah, you're just throwing hypotheticals at me. Besides, you're leaving for your hockey career, and that would just leave Summer here all alone. Not to mention, you would never let a girl come between us." He eases as if my sentence was crazy, but his facts are correct too, and a hint of doubt begins to hit me. "High school sucked, I was home a lot sick. Then college and medical school are stressful as hell, but maybe now I get to have something great in my life. For once, I can be the guy who is luckier than you."

My stomach fills with nausea. If I admit the truth now, then he will be shattered. And he's already had a few bad years. What have I done? I had no clue he was interested, except deep down, I probably did but kept it locked up.

"I mean, with you busy with your hockey career, we don't see one another as much. But Summer? We seem to bond closer," he continues, but my ears seem to be buzzing.

I'm his big brother. I've watched him suffer, and I feel guilty that it wasn't me. He seems excited and happy. Even though I know Summer isn't interested, they will be together more than I will with Summer, that's what my professional life does. I don't want him to be alone. Because even if he makes a move, Summer will laugh it off and get them back on track as friends.

Except if she's with me? He'll resent us both, and he'll be miserable.

Everything inside of me twists.

There is a long silence between us. My brother stares at me, and maybe he is reading my mind or he's completely oblivious, but it feels as though an unspoken warning seems to be sent from him.

And that's enough for me.

———

MY LIPS PART from the bruising kiss between me and Summer as we sit in the front of my car. Our noses nuzzle, and I wish I could take more.

"Don't do this," she whispers.

"You shouldn't have followed me." I'm desperate to get as far from her as possible. I barely drank, a few sips really. Getting away from the party and the house is the only way I might breathe tonight.

I shake my head, bracing myself for the struggle not to touch her as I sink back into my seat. "We can't make this work."

Summer sighs. "That's a lie. You're telling me that you spoke to Zac and now you say that we have no future. What aren't you telling me?" She's begged me to explain, but all I can do is break up with her and use a lie.

"I've thought about it more, with my hockey schedule and you living in Lake Spark. Zac just pointed out the obvious. There is no realistic way for us to work. You'll be miserable and so will I." I do my best to avoid her eyes.

She turns, with her sight landing on me as her head stays put against the headrest. I always love the way the light from my dashboard reflects off her beautiful face.

She turns away from me to look out the window, doing her best to stay composed.

"You can blame me, Summer," I rasp. I can't tear my eyes away from her as I watch her crumble. "I'm doing this so in the long run your heart doesn't break even harder."

An unamused sound leaves her lips. "So just do it now, is that it?"

I start the engine with every intention of taking her home. We need to part ways because the air around us is insufferable right now.

Unbearable silence fills my car as I drive us away from my house.

"You'll change your mind in the morning when you realize how much of a mistake this is," she tells me softly.

"I know you. You have a kind heart. Nor do you want to be that girl that gets between two brothers. Tell me that isn't true?" I challenge.

Her face bows down, and she goes quiet for a second. "You're right."

"It's why you will let me walk. You have to let me walk away."

"You'll change your mind."

My heart is ripping into pieces. "I won't, Summer." I feel my throat strain, as I don't want to talk but I have to. I swallow. "Sometimes we have to let go, and that's what we need to do. We had a few great months, but we need to just..."

The sound of her sniffling is torment. My entire body tenses, and I want to escape the vehicle.

But I can't because I feel the wheel of the car shift, and my hands lose grip as we swivel.

It happens so fast. And it isn't until we crash and the airbags deflate that I realize I must have lost grip of the wheel. I can't process if it's a tree we hit or something else, I'm not sure, because there are a thousand thoughts in my head.

I don't even worry about myself, even though I feel an ache somewhere. But when I glance to my side, my heart drops when I see Summer has blood gushing down her face.

———

I watch from the doorway of the hospital room with my arms crossed, leaning against the doorframe as the nurse finishes bandaging Summer's head. An airbag and a broken window caused Summer to need stiches that the doctor said will probably scar. There's bruising on her body, plus abrasions on her chin. Not to mention, her arm is probably going to ache for days. Are we lucky on the car crash front? We aren't on any other front.

Or at least me. Because of guilt.

Someone bumps into my shoulder, ignoring me, and it doesn't take long for me to see it's Zac. He storms straight to Summer and pauses for a moment as he looks at the nurse who gives him a smile as she gathers her things and gives them space.

Zac sweeps Summer's hand between his two palms. "Fuck, I was so worried. When Nash called, I nearly went out of my mind."

Summer groans as she attempts to sit further up, and my brother is quick to touch her arms to encourage her to slow down. "Sorry if we ruined your BBQ, hope you saved us some leftovers," she attempts to joke, but her voice is groggy.

"Not funny. I guess Nash was taking you home. Thankfully, he was there to help you." Zac glances back to me, and I can see the concern in his face. "It's miraculous that she's not in more pieces. We're lucky that you're okay and we can focus on Summer getting better."

Over his shoulder, I see Summer gawking her eyes at me. She wants me to say something, but I can't. It's my fault she's lying here. I broke her heart, and the anger within me caused me to lose focus on the road. All because I don't act normal around this woman.

"Relax, Zac, Mr. Future Doctor. I'll be fine. They want me to stay overnight for observation, but tomorrow I'll be good as new," Summer attempts to calm him.

My brother's eyes whip to Summer. "Not so easy. I want to check your vitals."

"You're a soon-to-be doctor if things go well. I think she's fine," I remind him. Partly, because I don't want him to study all the ways that Summer is in pain right now… because of my doing.

"I'm going to ignore him." Zac perches on the edge of the bed and holds Summer's hand tighter. "Summer, I would hate life if you weren't in it. You're everything to me."

She can't look at him. And my focus on Summer is boiling emotions inside of me. All I do is cause her pain. This has to be a sign, another reason that I made the right decision.

Zac is about to melt down because he cares more for this woman than anything. He loves and pines for her, that I'm sure of.

The thought already spins in my mind.

"We should probably let Summer sleep," I suggest softly.

"I'm not leaving her. They must be checking for a concussion."

A sound escapes Summer as she attempts to shift again. "Really, it will be fine. Nash was my superhero."

My brother circles his thumb on top of Summer's hand. "Doesn't matter. You're precious goods to me. Probably Nash, too… well, when he doesn't disappear for long periods of time for the hockey season. But you get my drift," he attempts to make a joke.

However, he's right again.

Summer's eyes soften to me, pleading, and maybe she already grasps my thoughts.

I'm no good for her. She deserves better. Around me, her life gets turned upside down.

Water begins to swell in the bottom of her eyes.

"Nash," she warns and pleads, her voice uneven and quiet.

Our eyes hold, and it hurts, but sometimes you have to close a door.

Maybe she's lucky.

Her scar that will be visible on her head will be nothing compared to the deep scar that I'll carry on my heart.

7

NASH

I can't tear my eyes away from the charm trapped between the pads of Summer's fingers. She just explained how she ended up with the necklace as if it's no big deal. Of course, she has no clue.

"I don't wear it every day, but still, it's special. I keep thinking maybe I should add my wedding ring to it." She splays her hand out in front of her to examine her fingers. I notice her fingers are bare; it causes me to wonder, but it makes it easier for me to return my attention to the necklace.

My throat bobs as I try to suppress the memory because I've had enough memories today. "It's pretty."

Summer gives me a peculiar look. "Uh, thanks." The air turns stiff, and she must feel it too because she stands up. "I'm going to grab a water, want anything?" Wow, she's being hospitable to me.

Gently, I shake my head as she patters past me, and unfortunately, my mind drifts to why she has the necklace.

"I want to get her something really nice. She's special, and after getting married, a ring just doesn't seem enough," my brother explains as we peruse the jewelry store.

I'm not sure why I'm doing this to myself. They eloped out of the blue, and I do my best to see them less and less. I've barely spoken to my brother, but Zac is in Dallas for a medical conference, and since I have a game here, we managed to squeeze in a quick lunch. And now I'm being dragged to a jewelry store.

"How is she?" I pry, with a sting inside of me.

Zac doesn't bother glancing up as he studies the contents of the glass case. "Good. She's been my rock and seems content with work and living in Lake Spark still."

I'm happy for her... and him. This is what was supposed to happen when I locked my heart from Summer. I still feel like I probably left pieces in my trail, even if for the long run it's the best for everyone. Doesn't mean she doesn't cross my mind more than she should.

"There it is." My brother taps on the glass with his long finger. "A charm necklace. Perfect for someone you love."

"Because she loves you too." I'm not sure why I need the clarification so quick.

He stalls and draws his gaze to me. "Of course." Why didn't that feel more confident? It's a long moment before he occupies himself with the contents under the glass. "I bet she would love the flower."

Peeking over his shoulder, I examine the choices, and then my eyes lock onto one particular choice.

"Can I have a look at the flower charm?" my brother requests to the lady who scurries our way.

"Of course." She unlocks the back of the display with a key that was around her neck on a lanyard. "Everyone loves these. At Christmas, we have presents and trees."

Pretending to look at my watch, I pat his shoulder. "I'm going to head out. Need to get ready for the game." And I don't want to watch you buy Summer jewelry, because you're in love with the woman who should have been mine.

He gives me a healthy smile while the jeweler sets the tray in front of him. "Sure thing. It was great seeing you. You have to come back to Lake Spark more often. We all miss you."

"Maybe."

I turn to walk away and manage a few steps when I hear the jeweler speak. "It was the flower you wanted to look at, right?"

"Yes, the flo—"

"Zac," I cut him off. It takes a moment before I glance back and flex my jaw side to side. "The treasure chest. You should look at the treasure chest."

He looks over his shoulder, perplexed. "Why?"

I lick my lips, remembering the most ridiculous secret that Summer shared with me once. "I don't know," I lie. "Just… the treasure chest is a nice pick."

Now I'm in Summer's house with my brother dead and a necklace around her neck that I knew would make her happy.

Rubbing my hands over my face, I'm beginning to wonder why I'm putting myself through this. I should just ignore my brother's request and move on.

But it's Summer.

And a baby that's my nephew.

If she truly needs someone to help her like everyone suggests then I'll never forgive myself, because before my brother would protect her, and now there is only me.

Summer saunters back into the living room, oblivious to my mind having just gone down memory lane.

"You don't get a choice. I'm just ordering pizza, going to steal a slice, and then I'll give Bo a bath, bottle, and everything. By the way, he can try soft foods in little pieces, just stay away from honey. I guess you'll learn quickly. Also, he likes going for 'swims.'" She uses air quotes. "At the Dizzy Duck. I know it's technically a spa pool, but Holden doesn't mind. The water is perfectly warm too. The other thing is Bo still wakes once a night, so be prepared for that." She's rambling again.

I grimace. "You're going to keep using his routine as our talking point, aren't you?"

She heaves a sigh because she's been called out. "Yeah," she answers bluntly. Summer climbs down to the floor and crosses her legs, getting comfortable as it seems she is willing to talk.

"We're out of our depth, Nash," she admits.

"We always were," I reflect.

"You're leaving in six weeks? Zac wanted six weeks."

I rub the back of my neck as I give a long exhale. "I don't know, probably. I can't think clearly."

Summer picks up a toy block that was on the floor within reach and begins to toss it between her hands. "You're bound to get close with Bo, so whatever you plan on doing, just remember you need to follow through. Don't just be an uncle for six weeks, play the long game."

I hold my palm up. "I understand."

She shakes her head in disbelief. "I don't trust you. We just need to look at history to know that you won't commit, and you always find a reason to stay away. But Nash..." Her warning turns sharp. "This isn't me. It's Bo, an innocent baby who is oblivious to life's heartaches. So don't you dare run away again."

I lift my nose slightly. "Are you really just talking on behalf of Bo?" I challenge, because underlying, she could mean her too.

She grumbles, clearly annoyed or wanting to escape the truth as she is quick to scramble to her feet. "Discussion over."

I have my answer.

———

A FEW HOURS LATER, Summer and I haven't really crossed paths. Only when she showed me how to handle a diaper and bottle did she actually construct a sentence around me. When pizza came, she gobbled down a slice, and we again focused on Bo who makes a mess when tomato sauce and melted cheese are involved. Then again, he can't eat the crust yet.

Still, despite dinner, I'm searching the fridge, not exactly sure what I'm looking for. I'm restless and on edge that I'll run into Summer.

My theory is proven correct when I hear the soft patter of footsteps approaching the kitchen. Sighing, I close the fridge and prepare myself to see the beautiful woman that's tormented me for years, and it's all my fault.

Flicking my eyes up, I see that Summer slows her step, and her face shows caution, yet it's gentle. Why does she have to wear an off-the-shoulder t-shirt that displays the curve of her bare shoulder?

"Hi."

Folding my arms against my chest, I lean against the counter. "Hi," I reply.

Her fingers twist the hem of her shirt. "I'm not sure what to say to you when Bo isn't around. You and I have an edgy relationship to say the least."

Glancing to the side, I do my best to gather composure. "Well…" I click my tongue in my mouth.

A long silence feels as though we could take a knife and slice it.

Summer rolls her eyes. "Great talk." She's not impressed, and I'm unsure if it's us or me. Frustrated, she turns to pick up a dirty bottle with aggravation. Her insistence to use glass baby bottles is not the best of ideas because as she twists to head to the sink, she drops it and glass shatters on the floor. "Shit."

I'm quick to take a few steps and lean down at the same time as her. She's already picking up little pieces which makes zero sense as she will need a dustpan and brush for sure. Her movements are as sharp as the shards of glass.

Placing my hand on the back of her palm, she stills. "Slow down," I whisper. At last, her eyes swing up to pin her face in my view, but she says nothing. I can't help it. That little scar, it's part of her for life. "Does it hurt?"

She understands what I mean. Her lips press together. "No."

Licking my lips, I drop my head down and pick up a big piece of glass. "Who the hell still uses glass baby bottles?" I attempt to make a joke, but she's in no mood.

"A normal person who just decided that life is already a little fucked up, so might as well add a fragile baby bottle that's a pain to carry around as it leaks. But hey, points for me for finding the funny little things in this living arrangement," she counters.

Here we go.

"Why are you always so feisty?" I wonder.

Her death glare is a bullseye to my chest. "I'm only this way with you."

"Lucky me."

She's quick to keep this debate going. "It's not my fault my mouth has a mind of its own around you."

I smirk. "I know, I remember your mouth."

Her eyes turn into saucers because I just reminded her of the fact that our bodies mold together with perfection, and we know exactly how to make one another see stars.

"Nice. Smug Nash is making an appearance tonight." Her sarcasm isn't appreciated.

"How about you just accept that I'm here." My voice has an edge.

"I'm trying," she grits out as our eyes stay locked.

"Could've fooled me." I whistle a sound.

Her tongue swipes along her teeth. "Are we just going to go back and forth?"

We both take a moment to sigh, and we collapse into sitting on the floor, completely exhausted from our little tit-for-tat.

Vulnerability kicks in. "I just want to do the right thing. I've only ever done what everyone needs."

She deflates and scoffs to herself. "What a lie. Then, you were only what I needed."

It surprises me that she admits that, and it twists my stomach. "But you're what he needed, and in the end, you have a son," I remind us.

Summer seems to grasp my theory, and she gulps a breath. "Can we just not talk about this anymore?"

"Agreed." I pick up a large piece of glass. "I'll clean this up."

"I can do it."

Now I have to laugh. "Let's not go down another spiral of arguing over stupid shit."

She bobs her head in agreement. "You're right."

Our eyes meet for a brief second. "Can I just do what I want to do? I'll take care of you. I'll clean this up. Anything else? A leaky pipe. Mowing the grass. There must be something."

Anything to occupy me from wanting to take care of her in other ways.

Her head tilts slightly to the side. "I mean… I guess the sink does have a drip."

"I'm on it," I promise.

The moment that she rolls her shoulder back and seems to ease sends a whoosh of relief down my body. "Actually, I really could use some help…" Her finger twirls in the air. "Babyproofing, the crawling phase will hit us at any moment."

Reaching out, I touch her wrist. "No problem. I'll be a pro at it and earn myself another point on the baby-experience scale."

Her eyes flood with appreciation and proof that I'm chipping away a piece of our wall. Summer nods once before her eyes drop down to soak in the view of my fingers connecting us. After a moment, she begins to teeter up. "Thanks. Uh, if you're okay with this," she indicates to the floor, "I'll go finish some laundry and things. I guess… I'll see you tomorrow."

"Sure."

We both seem to blow out a breath at the same time.

———

UPSTAIRS, I try to adjust to the fact that I'm in a guest room that has empty drawers and a closet. It's a nice room, a log cabin meets modern feel with a quilt on the bed. Zac and Summer seem to have good taste in interior design.

Summer kept to her word that she would be busy with Bo, and I've heard enough squeals from a baby with the sound of water running to calm any nerves.

But it is a momentary pause, because when the upstairs grows quiet, anxiousness reappears with a vengeance.

Summer's on the other side of the wall, sleeping, alone in bed, with her heart in pieces. She's strong, but even warriors need breaks.

Walking, I stop and reach up to plant a palm against the white wall, wondering what she's like on the other side.

Is she sleeping or lying with her gaze stuck on the ceiling because we're breathing the same air under the same roof, and that alone can cause an earthquake.

8

SUMMER

I'm more agitated than I should be today. While Bo slept like an angel, I barely slept a wink. Knowing Nash is on the other side of my bedroom wall will not be great for the lines under my eyes.

"So, how's it going with the brother-in-law? I'm beginning to wonder if you think he's from hell," Lexi asks casually as we walk down the hall of the inn toward the event room. She sometimes visits Holden during the day, but lately she's been decorating the place for fall and Halloween, as she's an interior designer.

My eyes slide up for a mere second then focus again on my list of upcoming events. "Fine. Barely. Okay. Whatever."

She stunts a laugh. "Sounds peachy."

I sigh and give up on trying to work and drop the list, and it hangs by my side in my clasp. "I'm trying to adapt to this whirlwind that my late husband seemed to have insisted he throw my way as a parting gift." Cynicism is my coping method.

"Makes sense. It's just you seem completely, well, almost… I can't pinpoint it, but it's a mix of good and bad." She reviews me then extends her palm up. "I mean, you have total right to feel every emotion under the sun lately."

I throw her a glare because she knows not to treat me like delicate goods. She gawks at me at the reminder.

"Sorry," she apologizes before she presses the button on her watch. "Shit. Sorry to cut this short, but I need to meet the PTA moms for planning a fundraiser."

Ah, I needed to hear that because it makes me burst out with a laugh. "I can't believe you actually had a campaign to be voted head of the PTA."

"There's no shame in using cupcakes and bottles of wine to sway the vote," she defends.

"It's just... I can only imagine what they all think of you. The hot younger stepmom who infiltrated their circle."

Lexi shrugs. "They needed a new direction. Their former committee president wasn't upping her game in school events and was being a total bitch to half the population."

That whole situation has been fun to see. She loves Holden's kids like they're her own, because sometimes a parent comes in many forms. It causes a thought in my head, wondering if Nash will have this sort of feeling with Bo one day in the absence of Zac. The moment I process what I just imagined, I shake it off.

"Oh, hey." Harlow approaches us, and she looks as though she's heading to the gym.

"Bye, you guys, gotta run," Lexi greets her and scurries away.

My smile remains, and Harlow looks over her shoulder and her thumb directs toward Lexi who is turning a corner. "Another kid crisis?"

"Something like that." She hums a sound in understanding. "What brings you here?"

"Wanted to walk on the treadmill and use some tiny weights to stay in shape." She glances down at her protruding belly. "Besides, Stone wanted to meet with Holden and your new houseguest apparently. A Dizzy Duck executive meeting."

I stand in attention. "Oh."

Crap. I must look uncomfortable with the information that she's brought to light.

"Is that a problem?"

I bite my bottom lip as she observes me peculiarly.

Assessing the area, I decide mornings are sometimes too quiet here. That's the tranquility of Lake Spark, right? Guess it's a good time for a sounding board. "Hey, can I ask you something?"

"Of course."

I draw my tongue along my lip and tap the nails of my free hand against my dark fitted jeans. The perks of working at a boutique hotel is we can wear what we want within reason.

"Have you ever, I don't know, thought or known something, and as much as you want to keep it to yourself, you know you shouldn't? But if you do, then it can kind of turn the tide of daily life?"

Harlow exhales deeply and offers me an empathetic look. "I have." I'm an idiot, of course she has; past life events that she doesn't share often because they are just plain horrendous.

"What did you do?" I ask.

"Well, I wanted to keep it in more than anything. It took a while, but then I shared it with someone."

My neck elongates. "And?"

"It all became easier. Life became easier."

My entire body eases from the reality of what I already knew but needed confirmation on. "I was afraid you might say that."

"Then what's stopping you?"

"A further complication that it could cause," I reply.

Her eyes still appraise me, and she reaches out to my shoulder in comfort. "But will it really?"

"Haven't figured that out yet," I admit.

"Deep down you know. A moment will present itself."

"Maybe so."

I know so.

———

"HERE, LET ME DO IT." I take over the mouse for the laptop from Stuart as we stand behind the receptionist desk. "Just click here then pull up the reservation screen." My actions follow my words as we attempt to tackle the new software.

"I don't think that helps," he points out.

I grumble and begin to jab the mouse button repeatedly to no avail.

"Go easy, will ya?" Holden says as he approaches the desk.

My eyes dart up to find Holden with a smile walking next to Nash who has an unreadable expression.

I grumble slightly. "Sorry. I'm just…" Nope. Not going to admit that I'm tired. "Forgot to grab my cup of coffee," I lie.

Nash clears his throat. "I can grab you one if you want."

"I don't need you to save the day," I mutter with annoyance, but then everyone darts their attention to me because they heard.

"Well… that's our cue to leave you two. Come on, Stuart, I think a new box of wine bottles arrived," Holden suggests, and in my side view, I can see Stuart give an odd look and nod in agreement.

It takes a few seconds, but then Nash and I stare at one another, and we're both unsure who should say something first.

It's me. "I forgot that you suddenly have an interest in the hotel." At least my normal voice is back.

"Yeah, thought I would have a meeting with Holden first thing after a run."

I swallow. "I would say that I noticed you gone this morning, but I'm used to having no house guests, so it was a normal morning," I fib. I actually assumed it was avoidance.

"Right, I forgot to ask about the childcare situation with Bo when you're at work." Nash runs his hand along the back of his neck.

My cheeks rise as I laugh silently to myself. "You did mention that your baby skills were a two out of ten, so I'm not surprised." It causes him to ease. "My neighbor's eighteen-year-old daughter mostly watches him since she's taking night classes at the community college."

"Okay. Uhm, just let me know if you need me to watch him."

I'm now entertained. "Are you sure? Because you sound unsure."

He licks his lips that I remember as powerful. "It's why I'm here, isn't it? I want to help. I'll just need to pick up a few baby-whisperer abilities. That's all."

I tap my nails on the desk, debating what to do. I need to make this easier on us, except it probably won't. In fact, I'm about to lead us down a dangerous road.

I skim the lobby with my eyes and see that there is one older guest who is enjoying his cup of coffee while reading a financial newspaper as he sits in a comfortable chaise lounge.

Tucking a few loose strands of my hair behind my ear, I take the plunge. "Perhaps we can talk outside?" I suggest.

"Sure." Nash seems invested in wanting to have a discussion which is a start.

I close the laptop on the desk, perhaps with a little too much gusto. Nash lifts his arm out, indicating that I should lead the way. I offer him a polite half-smile, and he follows me in tow.

Just like the other day, we find ourselves on the inn's dock. And again, we face one another in an odd silence. I glance down at my foot as I draw a half circle on the wood, and I cross my arms.

Nash stuffs his hands into the pockets of his jeans as he rocks on his heels. "We always seem to end up here… past and present."

Our eyes meet with recognition. "Seems so." We linger in a moment that feels too heavy on my chest. "We should probably get over this awkwardness if we're going to be around one another more."

Nash nods once. "I agree."

"We have both been thrown into an unknown realm that Zac set us in."

He scoffs. "He was your husband. You would know him best."

That sets me off like a cannonball. "You really are going to keep throwing it in my face, aren't you? That I had a husband and have a son. And it's with your brother, too."

"Sorry." There is remorse in his tone, and he rubs his forehead.

"I'm not sure that's true." I mosey on past him with my back now facing him. "You're the one who walked away all those years ago. You had me first then let go."

"And you walked straight into his arms." Now he just sounds bitter again.

I pivot, and my head whips in his direction. "*You* paved the road, Nash." Anger is now building up. I walk straight to him and push him because I'm furious at the heartache he gave me. "Maybe Zac never realized, but you're the one who pushed me away because of loyalty to your brother. I know I'm right."

"At least someone got their wish." His words are barely audible but not quiet enough. "He got you. The whole reason I let you go. He got the wife who he loved because you moved on from me."

I growl in frustration. "You wanted this!" I jostle him again.

He tenses, and he too is aggravated but does his best to keep it in. "Summer," he cautions.

I step in again, and he steps back. "No. I won't walk around as though I've done something wrong by becoming a wife and a mother."

Nash looks away. "A part of me always thought that you wouldn't return his feelings, but still, we couldn't hurt him. I just didn't think you two would ever happen. But he actually got to put a ring around your finger."

My shoulders puff up, and I do my best to square off with him. "Nash, you have no clue, do you?"

His brows rise. "What? That you were his wife and had a baby with Zac? It's pretty obvious."

My hands form fists as my tongue swipes across my teeth, gathering my strength for this conversation. "I loved him but in a different way."

He shakes his head, not believing me.

"Nash, I wanted to make him happy while he was sick. He asked, and I didn't say no because that's how much I care for him, but that doesn't mean that I was madly in love, you idiot."

His entire body stills as if a bullet just hit him, and for a few ticks, he evaluates my words. "Say that again."

"Our marriage wasn't what you thought."

Nash voluntarily steps back, and my feet follow as I face him, but it causes him to stumble… right into the water.

"Nash!"

The sound of water splashing and the sight of Nash's head appearing above water as he slows his strokes has me instantly near the edge.

I lean down and offer my hand which is ridiculous, as he's too strong for me anyhow. "This wasn't how this conversation was supposed to go."

"Really? Wouldn't have thought." He's sarcastic but reaches up for my hand.

In a flash, he curls his hand around my wrist and yanks me, causing me to lose my balance and plunge into the water with him.

What the hell? Now I'm furious all over again.

I flail my arms until I find stillness. My nipples are hard as pebbles, and I'm already freezing. I'm completely soaked, and my makeup is probably melting down my skin.

"Are you crazy?" I yell. "It's the end of September and the water is cold."

"Oh yeah? Then why did you cause me to fall in?"

I'm stunned. "Are you serious? You tripped!"

"Because you just casually mentioned something quite key to this little set-up my brother has thrown me into." Nash sounds livid.

"Ugh, I'm reminded why I think that I might hate you."

He swims closer to me. "Maybe I hate you too, except you know, that I never could, and I'm sure you know the sentiment."

"Fine! I dislike you with a strong dose of anger."

He pushes water toward me. "Ditto, Summer."

I splash water at him, frustrated. "Well, now you know. I married Zac when he told me he was sick and he had a wish. He was my best friend, something felt right about it. I cared so deeply for him, and I knew he loved me. I'd already been feeling alone for some time, and then he asked. I was overwhelmed."

Nash's nostrils flare. "Why didn't you clue me the fuck in about your marriage situation?"

"Really? That's your concern? You weren't at the top of the list of who to inform. Because if I recall, you sure as hell weren't dropping by for weekly family dinners or expressing an interest that you would come crawling back to me."

"I had hockey, and I had to stay away from y—" He cuts his statement short.

I growl as my legs whirl underneath the water. "Well, I made sure that happened. Besides, some things made sense between Zac and me. We were friends who made one another happy. Just not…"

Deeply in love.

"And Bo?"

"Sue me. We did something a few times, and maybe it was even an unspoken compromise because I've always wanted to be a mom. We ended up with a great child, your nephew."

Nash blinks as everything sinks in, literally.

Now that he knows this, everything is more dangerous between Nash and me.

We shouldn't be around one another. But right now, our bodies are nearly pressed together because I take hold of his shirt.

"Why the fuck did you have you to tell me this?" He nearly sneers.

"What?" My voice squeaks as I look up the sky because now I think Nash is crazy.

"This tidbit of information might have been useful." He's flippant. "Especially when deciding to stay here."

Because it makes it all even more complicated.

I shake my head and shove water his way. "No shit."

He continues to swim in place, clearly agitated. "You are not on the list of people who make me feel okay right now."

"I'm sure your list is non-existent on a normal day."

"Fuck," he barks. "I had the tiniest inclinations that your relationship might have been something like this. I just didn't want the fucking confirmation." He slams his hands on top of the water causing more ripples on the surface.

"What the hell does that mean?" My voice raises an octave.

Nash's eyes laser in, and he looks at me as if I should solve the riddle. "It might make it hurt even more."

I shake my head. "If you rewind the last five minutes, then you would realize we've established that it's *you* who led us all down this path."

"The past few days you let me think that your marriage was…"

"We started on the wrong foot because you're still a cocky asshole sometimes."

Nash growls then wipes droplets from his face. "The house?" His cheeks rise, and he's trying to keep his temper down.

"Oh, you mean which room I made a baby in?" I mock him, and it only makes him more dismayed.

"Summer," he grits out a warning.

I glance away then slide my eyes back to him. "I only moved in with Bo when Zac was in the hospital. So to answer your very inappropriate question from the other day, no. No, there is not a room where I made a baby in my house. The bed is new, too, you asshole. And while we're at it, no. No, I never told him about us. I made a promise, and I tend to keep those." I'm nearly livid that we're discussing this topic.

Nash stares at me blankly. "Okay," he replies with zero indication of what's running through his mind.

"Oh gee, does my answer appease you? I really want to throttle you right now."

He peers down and back up with a faint chuckle. "Well, you could if you want. Look where we are."

I take a moment to let the surroundings remind me of my setting. "Shit. Why are we still in the water?"

"Because you felt the need to explain important facts here," he says, irritated.

I growl. "Ugh, I need to find a way to live with you. This is ridiculous that I'm in the lake."

He smirks at me, and it's so smug. I remember that look. The one he would give before his mouth would move lower on my body. "What's even more ludicrous is that we can stand here."

"What?" *Oh.* It's a bit of a reach, but still, my feet touch the bottom of the lake and my head is still above the water.

Then it happens as we both stand. A calmness overtakes us as we stare at one another. A moment where even I can let my mouth ease into a small smile. It's not every day that you can clear the air in cold water. The corners of his mouth stretch up because he must feel it too.

Nash's hand comes out on offer. "A peace offering? No more jabs at one another?"

I think for a moment then sigh. Bo shouldn't be dragged into Nash's and my history. "Yes."

Reluctantly, I slide my hand into his. The connection hits with a jolt and an anger that the water on our skin is an extra layer between us. It rushes through my body, the patter of my heart and the warning that a truth may alter the moments that I'm alone with Nash.

But I won't think too hard as I walk up the slant of the dark sand on the shore.

We both look up to see that we have an entire audience.

Holden's face is puzzled. "Uh… you guys okay? I thought about throwing in the life vest, but when we all heard you two screaming that you hate one another, we decided you have some issues to work out."

While Nash continues his slow walk with a satisfied grin, I look at Holden and a few other staff members with embarrassment.

"How much of that did you hear?" I wonder.

"Nothing except the hate part. Kind of concerning," Holden tells me, pretty amused by all of this.

I hold my hand up, and my breath is heavy. "I think this…" I twirl a finger in the air, "is my cue that I might need to leave early today. I'm freezing, and I think…" I blink, trying to adapt to being back on land.

Holden holds his palms up. He's trying to suppress a laugh. "Say no more."

"What? What was that?" Nash cups his ear with his hand, pretending to try and listen. "Pick up milk from the grocery store since we now have a truce and I need to up my baby-whispering game from a two? You got it."

A rumbling sound rolls up my throat.

Was this a turning point for us? Arguing in the water to have transparency about our current situation…

…except our situation just became more complex. We now have a new kind of tension.

9

NASH

I sit quietly at the kitchen table with a beer bottle in hand, doing my best to run through the facts that I've learned. Truthfully, I don't know how to process it all. I don't doubt that Summer and Zac had their own kind of relationship. One that, if I'm honest with myself, gave my brother solace before he passed.

It's just, now I'm under the same roof as Summer and wondering what happens when we bury the past and start on a fresh page, if we can.

The sound of feet walking down the stairs doesn't snap me out of my subdued mood. Hearing Summer's steps slow doesn't change the feeling, either. Still, my eyes flick up to watch her delicately enter the kitchen as she dries her hair with a towel.

"Hi."

I take one sip of my beer. "Hey."

Our eyes meet, and it feels like we have reached a gate with each of us on opposite sides. Summer swipes her hair to the side, and her small scar confronts me the way it always does when I least expect.

"So… that was that." She's trying to approach the subject.

It causes me to smirk slightly to myself. "What can I say? That dock does stupid shit to people. Some weird possessed sacred piece of wood over water."

"That's one way of looking at it." She slides onto a chair and pulls her knee up to wrap her arms around her leg. "I'm sorry."

"For what, Summer?"

She seems to brace herself. "That we ended up in Lake Spark. There was probably a better way to have discussed this all."

My shoulders lift. "It is what it is."

"Some days, I don't even know how to process the last two years. It's a lot."

My lips wrap around my beer bottle for another sip, but beer is doing fuck all to simmer me down. "You did what you felt was right, and you have a son that makes you happy."

Warmth washes over her face. "He does." It's a long moment of silence as our sight stakes the other. "You and I called a ceasefire."

"So we did." And I have zero clue how non-angry us will be.

Her eyes seem to wander around as her fingers tap on the table. "We should probably break the ice again… between us, I mean."

I laugh to myself. "And how do you propose we do that?"

"Hmm…" Her eyes catch on something. "How about we play a boardgame?"

Now I have to smile at her absurd suggestion. "A boardgame?"

"Yeah. We have a bunch. Remember, your brother had a whole collection? We also have the old-school game system, but that's in a box somewhere."

She stands and eagerly finds her way to a cupboard against the wall. There are a bunch of candles on top of what looks to be a refurbished antique dresser. She opens the door, and her finger taps her chin. "I know. We can honor Zac by playing one of his favorite games. That boardgame where it's like medieval times. There are like three different boxes, I guess for new levels or new kingdoms or something weird like that."

A chuckle booms out of me. "Oh man, I think I know where this is going. Open the lid and I'll have my answer."

Her face is etched in curiosity, and she peeks down as she opens the game. "Oh no, hell no." Now my head lolls to the side, and I grin to myself. "It's like a gazillion pieces. Cards, little figures, is that more figures but in different sizes?" She tips her head to the side to examine the contents. "This must take like an hour to set up."

"So that's a no?" I press.

Summer looks at me, horrified, before she closes the box again and sets it back in the cupboard. "We should probably stick to cards. That's simple."

Then my body stills again. "Cards," I state, and my lips roll into my mouth.

It registers in her head. "Right. Cards." This can't keep happening. "We always used to play with Zac when we were teenagers…"

I say nothing.

"And when I was upset that my parents were divorcing during my last year of high school and I showed up to see Zac, my best friend, he wasn't there, but you were…"

I stand and take a few steps when I see a shade of pain, though it's not because of me. It's because it makes her think of Zac, except laced with conflict. I touch her shoulder with my fingertips. "It's okay, he won't be angry if you remember memories of you and me, or at least, that's what I choose to tell myself, now."

Her face softens when she looks at me, and she nods once in understanding. "I didn't want to be alone. My brother was already about to finish college."

I interrupt her. "Your brother always hated me, I'm sure of it."

Summer snickers a laugh. "Keats? Well, maybe." That's a yes. Her face softens, with her eyes tipping up to meet my gaze. "Your parents were away, and we played cards. We kissed for the first time, and you held me while I was upset, and we slept in your bed. It was a blip, easy to forget and never act on again, a little secret but doable. Then years later, we discovered we were wrong."

I remain composed. "Despite what happened down the road, it's a bittersweet memory, and I'm not sure that's so bad."

Her pressed lips stretch in my favor. "You're right." But it takes only a few seconds for Summer to create space and begin to busy herself. I watch her as she ties up her hair, the slope of her neck taunting me. "You know, I think I forgot to get more oatmeal. Bo likes that with a little jam. I should find my keys and go to the grocery store."

"Oh, yeah, totally," I answer dryly.

She begins to walk in the direction of the living room but stalls and snaps her fingers in the air. "Shit. The neighbor will drop Bo off soon. I should probably…"

I step forward. "It's fine. I'm here, and surely, I can handle that." It's clear that she needs some air and a moment away from the house.

She gives me an appreciative smile. "Okay, let's consider it your trial on baby skills, except there can be no error."

My cheeks rise from her humor that is blossoming back. "Noted."

"Won't be long."

I nod and watch her walk out the door. Except, in a little while, she'll walk right back in.

———

"SERIOUSLY? It's an entire toy with many popping animal options, and you just want to focus on the lion for the hundredth time?" I tell my nephew as he sits up, continuing to press the button with the animal appearing before he closes the square again. Every time his giggle causes me to smile wider.

I've never really thought about kids in my life. It's not that I'm against it. It just never got that serious with any woman that I've dated. My brother always wanted a wife, kids, dog, and a home that was more than just a house. Me? I guess I was still figuring it all out.

Bo lets out a yawn, and I feel like it's a cue that at last the toy can take a rest. "Come on, buddy. Someone mentioned that you sleep a lot, and I'm not sure you're supposed to sleep before dinner, so let's just chill a little, okay?"

I pick him up in my arms and carry him to the sofa. Getting comfortable, I rest him against my chest, throw my feet up on the table—even though Summer hates it—and grab the nearby remote control to turn the television on to head straight to the sports channel. "A little hockey highlights to prepare you for your future."

My companion doesn't answer, and when I look down, I see him struggling to keep his eyes open, with his lids hooding closed.

It must be a little later when my eyes slowly open, and I realize that I must have dozed off, and I feel a warm weight against my chest. Glancing down, my nephew is asleep even with the TV still on as background noise. In my peripheral view, I notice Summer watching as she leans against the frame of the wall where the living room joins the kitchen. Her arms are clasping her long sweater tightly, and her ankles are crossed; it doesn't feel as though she just arrived.

Lifting my head, I do my best not to move so my nephew doesn't wake. "Hey, how long have you been there?"

Her mouth tugs. "Long enough." It translates to she's been observing us. "Seems you upgraded from a two to a four on the baby-experience scale."

My stunted laugh is scratchy and groggy. "Good to know."

Summer quietly walks to us and leans down to coax him awake. "As much as Bo is in his zone in dreamland, I'm going to wake him up to ensure he sleeps during the night. Otherwise, none of us will get shuteye."

Her hand snakes under him and against my chest to try and lift him up. The space between all of us is far too close. Summer's long hair feathers my arm as she scoops up Bo. The moment she is standing with her son resting his head against her shoulder and her hand swirling on his back, I feel alone.

She begins to sway as he stirs. "He's a cuddler. It's nearly impossible to just lie with him, you'll always join him on his nap."

I sit up and stretch. "I have now experienced the proof."

"I didn't think about dinner when I was at the store," she mentions.

I grimace. "Probably because you didn't go to the store."

Her eyes travel the room to avoid me and hide her pressed smile. "Very true. A drive around the lake it was."

I stand and choose not to begin an inquest on how her time for air was or if it helped. "What do you want for dinner?"

"Oh, I'll probably just make a sandwich or something."

My eyes narrow. "Is that really dinner?"

With Bo now more awake, she bounces him gently. "Well, I normally don't cook. I don't really have time, and it's just easier since I'm alon—" She ends her admission because Summer probably thinks I'm going to judge.

"Alone?" I finish the sentence for her.

"Something like that. Just seems silly, that's all. Besides, I'm so busy with Bo that I think I forget half the time," she confesses, but as soon as she realizes, a sound pulls from her throat. "I mean…"

I raise my palm to calm her. "Relax. I'm not judging you or taking this as a point that you need someone to watch out for you like everyone seems to want," I partly lie. I'm not going to use this as ammo, but I'm not thrilled with the fact that she takes care of herself last. Bo is resilient and happy, but that doesn't mean that Summer can't follow suit.

Summer rolls her lips in, aware that I'm right.

I clap my hands together. "I've learned to cook…" Her eyes widen, and she seems impressed. "No other option when I was playing pro. Had to watch the nutrients. Anyhow, we'll save your taste-testing for another night. I'll run to the deli to pick up some meals they have. Pasta, chicken?"

Summer's eyes flutter. "Oh, I…" Then her stance turns confident. "Sure. Thanks." Her genuine smile looks good on her. It's honest.

"No problem."

"Do you think you can stop by the drugstore? They were out of Bo's bath soap, it's this special kind of natural stuff I get. They ordered some more the other day, and it should be in now."

I salute her. "I will complete my mission."

"Thanks."

"Sure."

Our eyes struggle to break apart. It's these long lingering moments that are not good for us. No wonder she fled earlier to get air.

———

I'M WAITING PATIENTLY while the older man behind the counter searches in the back for Summer's order. My eyes wander around as there is something quaint about Lake Spark in that everything is a throwback to another era. My sight lands on the wall of jars that are filled with candy that you put in a bag then they weigh at the end. It always made my grandmother give us stories about when she was younger. Zac and I would always listen then wrap her around our finger to get caramel toffees. Young us were charmers and were such a team.

"Summer Nix?"

For a moment my heart flurries from the sound of that name and how my last name sounds good on her. But then my heart drops when I have to remind myself that she has the name because of my brother.

I scratch the back of my head. "Yeah, that's her." He hands me the bag with a post-it attached, and I clear my throat. "Uhm, yeah, thank you."

"No problem." He smiles brightly at me, and I give him a curt nod.

I'm quick to leave, and when I'm out the door, my phone vibrates in my pocket. Balancing the bag and swiping my screen when I see it's my mom calling, I answer.

"Hey, Mom," I say, unsure if today she is doing better than the others. My parents are also finding a routine again since Zac's passing. It's just, I can't help feeling that when they talk to me, it stirs everything up. I'm the other son. The one who is alive and for the most part well. It's especially my dad who is quite cold with me.

"Hi, Nash. Just wanted to check in." She sounds as though today is a good day for her, which is a relief.

"No need to check in," I remind her as I continue to walk toward my car on Main Street.

She lets out a breath. "How is she? Bo?"

Ah, that's why she's really calling. "They're… they're fine. Bo seems happy. He's a baby, after all."

"That's nice. He's growing fast from what I see from the photos that Summer sends. We're planning a time to come up and visit. And Summer? How is she holding up?"

A sting hits my body. How do I say she's thriving if I'm not quite sure it's the truth? I'm sure as hell not going to say that she's keeping herself so damn occupied that I'm beginning to think she's running herself thin. Or that me being in Lake Spark only stirs things that shouldn't be touched.

"She's doing the best she can for Bo." That's not a lie, at least.

"I'm happy to hear. You be sure to help them out while you're in town. Your brother would have wanted that. He held Summer and Bo so close to his heart."

I swallow because my parents have no clue the dynamics between Summer and Zac. Let alone when I'm thrown into the equation.

"I know, Mom."

"I'm actually calling because I need you to check on the house. The realtor wants to take photos next week as we prepare to put the house on the market. But I would like you to run through to see if anything needs to be fixed or seems out of place."

A grin curves on my mouth. "Would it matter? The size of the house makes up for anything that could be wrong. I'm sure it will sell fast." Kind of a shame, too. It's a great house full of memories.

"Maybe you're right. Also…"

"Yes?"

She stalls for a second or two. "Your brother left you a box. He had set some things aside before… well, he wanted to ensure we saved some things for Bo. I guess he found stuff from when you guys were younger. I set the box in the den before we left to head south."

Yet again today, I pause in my step before I reach my car. "Oh. I didn't realize he did that." Probably because I vanished after he passed.

"He loved you a lot."

"Zac was special." That's why I let him have his gift that ended up being his wife and giving him a son.

"Mmhmm."

I sigh. "I'll check on the house, maybe on my way home. Have to run some errands."

"Thanks, sweetie."

Ending the call, I close my eyes for a second to adjust to the fact that I saw him less in recent years when he needed a brother more than anything. Yet, my brother did a kind gesture by leaving me mementos when he deserved more from me.

Still, I get in my car and throw the bag of baby shampoo on the front seat. It's early, and I figure we have another hour before it's dinner time. Or rather, Summer can eat after Bo goes to bed, so she doesn't need to rush dinner.

My drive around the lake with changing leaves doesn't do much for clearing my head. Nor does arriving to my childhood home. After parking, entering the security code, and walking into the hall, I do a quick assessment of the place. I know they still have a cleaner visit every other week and a lawn service for the yard. There isn't much to check on, as everything is the way it should be.

That may be a stretch. The house is missing people inside who are happy, far from aching.

Remembering that there is a box waiting for me because our lives are in mourning, I enter the den where memories trickle into my thoughts. The way Zac would game or have friends over to watch TV and plan BBQs. He and I would watch movies. Summer would join us, and there was always popcorn being thrown. They were always good times.

I spot the box on the sofa, and I'm not nervous to open it. Maybe I should be. Lifting the lid off, I instantly snort a laugh. My eyes are greeted with a game system and collection of his old-school games. Summer wasn't wrong about it being in a box somewhere. There is also a trophy that our friends got us because we apparently committed the best prank on the history teacher on Halloween. A pack of cards that we would always play when we would visit our grandparents. A plastic Easter egg because we got roped into manning the Easter egg hunt at the Dizzy Duck when I was sixteen.

I pick up more things from what would appear to be a box of junk but is anything but. One by one, a flood of happiness washes over me. His notebook of drawings, feeling like it's a piece of art even though it's mostly nonsense. I toss it to the side.

Everything is out when I notice one last thing at the bottom of the box. An envelope of photos with the seal broken, and I have a peek at the few, mostly family photos and Zac and me at a party together. One more that's Summer, Zac, and me. Different to the one on Summer's living room mantle. I turn the pictures for dates. Memory lane suddenly steals my breath, with my entire body experiencing its own clap of thunder.

A date is a reminder of how time passes.

I wave the photo against my palm. I'm not sure now is the time to recap to myself that time passing can also equate to wearing off and making room for a revival or change.

And for now, I just want to get on with my day.

I set the food on the kitchen counter. It's just rotisserie chicken and a few sides from the deli. Figured, there would be leftovers for tomorrow. A quick glance at the oven clock and it's already time for when Summer must be almost done with Bo's nighttime routine, so I decide to let her know that dinner is ready since the chicken just came out of the rotisserie at the store and is still warm.

I jog up the stairs but halt when I arrive at the top because I hear a sniffle. Teetering on my feet, I slowly approach Bo's nursery, and with the door partly ajar with only the nightlight on, I can see that he's asleep.

Summer? She's standing over the crib and watching him, wiping her tears away.

She must hear me because her head lifts gently in my direction, and she quickly smears a tear with the back of her hand along her cheek then takes a few paces to the door, silently stepping out, only to turn her back to me to pull the door closed.

My hand comes up to rest on her shoulder. "You okay?"

Her body melts into my hand that suddenly feels heavy.

"Fine. Just dust or something."

I encourage her to turn around and face me, and even though I succeed, her sight hangs low. "If that's what you want me to believe then I'll play along, but something tells me this happens a lot."

"Can we not make a deal out of this?" she quietly requests.

I blow out a breath. "If that's what you want, even though bullshit isn't my style."

Her puffy eyes give me attention. "It's not a daily occurrence if that's what you're thinking."

"Of course not, you dust the house every other day."

She appreciates my attempt to turn her sad moment around, but the quarter of a smile quickly wilts, her chin trembling instead. Summer steps forward, and my body reacts by bringing my arms up and engulfing her as she dives her face into my chest.

A hug.

That's what we find ourselves in.

She creates the barest of inches between my chest and her mouth, only to mumble, "I'm not sure if I'm sad that Zac is gone or… you're back, and I wonder too much what it all would've been like if our road were different long ago between you and me." More tears fall. "Does that make me a horrible person?"

I think I needed to hear her say that. I'm not alone. From instinct, I'm quick to wrap my arms around her and pull her tight to my body. Every bit of distance that I've attempted to keep between us over the years vanishes, and it feels as though a key turned.

"Don't ever think that." I kiss the top of her head, wanting with everything in my body to protect her from another cry that may escape.

"It hurts," she mutters before burying her head once more into my chest.

This is where she is supposed to be. That makes *me* the horrible person, because it's all I can think about. That she's supposed to be in my arms when she's in mourning for my brother.

But now isn't the time to explore my confliction.

"Today you forgot to dust it seems."

She chortles because apparently that loosens her down a level. "It was laundry day. I was too busy putting your ugly proboscis monkey stuffed animal in the washing machine," she quips.

Now I smile out all of my emotion. "You still have your wit, it seems. Come on, you need to eat. We're not really debating that, either."

Our eyes meet and they say enough.

Turns out we may just be able to support one another together.

A far cry from arguing in the lake.

10

SUMMER

The heaviness of sleep begins to fade as I stretch my body, my eyes blinking open. It takes a second or two, but then I realize where I am. In my bed, except I'm lying on top of the duvet with a throw blanket over my body. The setup causes me to sit up and attempt to recall how I got here.

The only thing that makes sense is that Nash must have carried me up here. I only remember sitting on the couch while he put away dishes. I must have fallen asleep. I rub my eyes to wake up further.

A little gesture begins to cause chaos inside of me. If I ended up here, then it means I was in *his* arms. For a moment, I let down my defenses yesterday, and a natural hug found my body far too close to his. The idea of Nash carrying me to my bedroom shouldn't affect me, but it does.

I hear the breakout of Bo's cry beginning to form. Our clocks are aligned, so I know that he is waking, too. I swing my legs out of bed, my feet touching the rug. I'm still in my tank top and jeans from yesterday, but I'll worry about that later.

Walking groggily into the hall, a peculiar sound occurs; Bo hasn't reached his full-fledged crying status.

My eyes open wide when I reach the doorway to his room.

Immediately, my sight strikes up to the ceiling, trying to gain composure.

"Hey," Nash greets me.

He's pulling Bo up and out of his crib. Albeit, shirtless. What's worse is that I don't think he is even lacking a shirt on purpose. That just makes this all the more endearing.

Internally I curse to myself before getting a grip. "Hey. Looks like we can upgrade your baby skills from a four to a five." I meander into the room and reach my arms out to take hold of my son, but Nash makes no effort to hand him to me.

"It's good. I think I can handle making oatmeal if you want to change."

Subconsciously, my eyes slip down to examine myself, and I cross my arms as if I can shield myself. "Yeah, sure… uhm, thanks?" My voice is uneven. "I mean for taking me to bed." His eyes widen. Shit. "I mean not *to bed*, just bed, my bed, setting me in bed so I can sleep." Phew, I think I saved that.

He tries to suppress his melting grin, but I see it all the same. "I got what you meant the first time."

I blow out a breath, thankful that we can move on. "Just thanks. Okay?"

"No problem," Nash says as he swings his body side to side, and Bo seems to take interest in grabbing Nash's chin.

"And, yeah, that would help if you can do the oatmeal. I normally make it then bring him to the bathroom so I can shower and he chills in his bouncer," I explain.

I take a few steps to Bo's dresser and pull out some clothes and a fresh diaper then pause when I pivot to look at Nash with doubt. "Maybe I should get him dressed."

Nash chuckles. "Nah, I have to learn."

Skeptically, I agree. A few seconds' pause is mindless. Well, that is until it bursts out of my mouth about logistics last night. "How did you carry me up the stairs?"

He gives me a proud look. "Summer, I've played hockey most of my life. If I don't have the ability to carry you, then I think they were paying millions to the wrong person," he jokes.

It causes me to smirk. "If you say so."

Our eyes remain locked for a moment before I leave him to be with my son who is cooing.

The moment I'm out of the room, I lean against the hallway wall and sigh, acknowledging that there has been a shift between Nash and me. And it's scary.

———

WATCHING Nash skate is somehow soothing, with his hockey stick in hand, oblivious to me. Is it the sound of blades on ice? Or simply knowing that he'll be surprised I'm here.

Truthfully, I'm not exactly sure what possessed me to drive here, but my feet are planted to watch as I hold Bo in my arms. When Nash looks up for a millisecond, he does a double take, surprised that I'm here, as he should be. I raise Bo's wrist to give a little wave to Nash, and a faint line on his mouth slides up.

Nash slowly skates our way until he's at gate from the ice.

"Hey. Wasn't expecting you to be here."

My eyes circle the arena. "Well, me neither, but here I am. You mentioned earlier about coming here." My face must show that I'm pleased to be here; no jabs are planned to leave my mouth in the next few minutes.

Nash uses his stick to toss up the puck until he snatches it away and shows Bo. "Maybe you'll like hockey one day," he says to my son before his eyes dart to me as he waits for an explanation.

"I just wanted to… well, everyone is right, maybe." There I said it.

His face screws up in confusion.

"Maybe I do need a little help," I admit. Nash listens patiently. "Can we just forget I said anything." I'm backtracking and press my lips together and rinse the thoughts in my mind. But Nash's eyes study me, and his face is neutral. "Fine." I roll my eyes, caving. "Maybe we can just… keep it between us?"

"We're good at that," he remarks simply. My lashes bat as I recognize the truth in that. "But yeah… we can."

Appreciation floods my face.

"Anything for you," he mutters. I don't think he expected me to hear, but my breath hitches all the same.

"Lie of the century," I rasp. *He left.* "But let's keep this a normal conversation. Besides, there are seven-year-olds about the descend onto the ice. We can keep it classy and get an award for this perfectly normal conversation." I straighten my posture as much as I can with a baby propped on one hip.

The corners of his mouth twist. "Sure."

"Okay, well, uh… see you at home." He looks at me strangely, probably because I'm being awkward. Even when I turn to leave only to backtrack, I find him waiting in the exact spot with the exact same facial expression. "Actually, I thought about going for a coffee or ice cream with Bo. Maybe…"

Now he just grins. "I would like to tag along?" He helps me out because my invitation just spewed out of my mouth without thought.

"Yeah, something like that. Or like that." It drags out of my mouth.

He chuckles as he lowers his hand to unlock the gate. "I'll see you soon then."

———

DEBATING, I'm not sure if this is the right move. It's just Bo, and Nash is his uncle. I can't keep Nash at bay. This is good for Bo. Hence, why all three of us are wandering down Main Street to Jolly Joe's for ice cream.

"I'm surprised it isn't colder. The weather for fall seems to be okay," Nash remarks.

I continue to push Bo's stroller. "You may have jinxed us."

The fall decorations of Lake Spark overpower the scene. Pumpkins, hay bales, a weird-looking scarecrow, plus fakes leaves in shop windows.

"Are you decorating the house for Halloween?"

Shrugging a shoulder, I remind myself that is another item on my to-do list. "I guess I should at least get a pumpkin or something. Trick-or-treaters are ruthless here."

A brimming smile is pasted on his face. "Oh, I remember. Prime prank time."

"Speaking from experience." I give him a pointed look, very well aware of his younger antics.

"Don't you want to take Bo to a pumpkin patch or something? Isn't that a photo-op necessity?"

I move my head side to side in contemplation. "Solid point. I'll figure it out."

He nudges my shoulder with his. "There's a pumpkin farm down in Bluetop, at the Blisswood winery. We can go there one day."

We.

I'm wary of the term, as much as it warms my heart. "Maybe a good idea." We arrive at Jolly Joe's, and Nash is quick to open the door for me. "One scoop of blueberry and one scoop of rainbow sherbet per your usual? The ice cream of senior citizens."

Nash seems surprised. "You remember my ice cream flavor choice?"

"Of course, I do. How many times have we been here?"

A fond smile shades his face. "Probably too many to count, Ms. Chocolate Cherry Shake."

My mouth turns to an O shape. "Seems you remember, too. It's a classic flavor," I protest.

We find our way to a table, and I get situated as Nash prepares to order at the counter. "For the little guy?"

"I don't really let him have too much sugar, but they say the vanilla bean here has the least amount, so perhaps a small scoop of that."

"Got it."

Finding a table, I decide to leave Bo in his stroller and hand him a soft book with different activities, it should keep him occupied. My eyes drift to Nash ordering with his suave smile that he gives everyone. I hate that it's the little things that bring back memories that makes me twist inside.

"So, you watched the game?" Nash wipes a hand through his sweaty hair while he holds his helmet to the side, with the background noise of the arena. His face is red, and he still causes my middle to swirl. I was up in Michigan to visit a friend from college and Nash left tickets for us.

"Well, I'm here, aren't I?" I tease.

He's nearly bashful and glances away while he licks his lips. When his sight returns to me, I think we might be melting. It's been a few years since we both acted on a spark, because who knew a simple kiss could cause years of attraction to grow. The seldom times that we saw one another since, we left it as a magnetism between us that we never acted on. But tonight feels different.

"What are you doing after?"

"My friend and I were going to probably get a drink."

A devilish grin hits his mouth. "I need to change, but I'll text you a place where we can all meet."

I snicker a laugh. "Something feels like this isn't an innocent 'let's go for ice cream' suggestion."

That grin is my undoing. "It's really not. But I think you knew that when you came here."

"Earth to Summer." Nash waves a hand in front of my face, and it snaps me back to reality, brushing thoughts of how our secret months began.

I forcefully form a smile. "Yeah, sorry, just… remembering something for work."

Nash slides into the booth, not entirely convinced, and thanks the waitress for following with the ice cream and shake. "You have work tomorrow?" he asks me.

"Yeah. You're going to meet with your parents' realtor?" He nods in answer. "Sounds like we're busy then. Bo will be with the babysitter, so everything is on schedule."

"Cool."

I try not to look at him in a different way. It's just odd to be sitting here as if life is normal… and the three of us are together.

"I forgot to ask you how your brother is," Nash says. Yep, general everyday conversation.

"Keats is doing well. Checks up on me far too much, but hey, who doesn't?"

My brother is older than me by a few years and just moved a few towns over after living in the city. He's on the legal counsel for the Lake Spark Spinners. We're close, as our parents kind of live in their own world, divorced and now living with new spouses who don't get our approval.

Nash watches me intently with understanding. "That's good to hear."

"Your mom mentioned in the group chat that she enjoyed seeing a photo of you and Bo together."

He beams an honest smile. "Yeah, took it when you were getting ready. Figured, it would make them happy." His attention turns to Bo who is busy chewing on the corner of his book. Nash leans over to take the book away. "Come on, buddy, let's trade that for some ice cream."

Nash slides the small cup of ice cream his way and grabs the small spoon. I must be motionless as I watch everything unfold in front of me. The way he flawlessly offers Bo a small bite and then waits before scooping up another. No experience with babies my ass, he must have lied.

I have to wonder. "Did you ever want kids? I mean, with whomever you might have dated… in the past." My face flushes with uncomfortable warmth. I shouldn't be asking this.

It causes Nash to plop the spoon back into the bowl. "No bullshit, Summer. You asked that, and you're not sure why, except it's more than curiosity." His face is serious. "To answer your question. No. Why? Because there hasn't been anyone remotely close to y—" He stops short of what I'm well aware he is about to say.

My chest wants to burst, and my throat closes. He's right. I wanted to hear him say that there wasn't anyone else. Maybe I wanted him to suffer for pushing me away all those years ago or maybe I wanted him to confirm that I'm not crazy in my theories. Either way, the truth is now out in the open.

We both sit here, trying to understand what to say or do. Ease hits us when Bo squeaks a noise and steals our attention, immediately causing both of us to laugh. He managed to get his fingers into the ice cream.

"Uh-oh, we have a misfit in training." Nash slides the bowl away while I grab a napkin.

"Must run in the family." Our eyes connect in recognition.

Because Nash has always done things in his own way.

Which means he will do the same now that he's back in Lake Spark.

———

"THIS IS PRETTY GOOD," Lexi informs me with a full mouth as we sit by the turned-off fireplace in the inn's lobby.

I hold up a small wrapped candy. "I think so. I mean, we have the welcome sugar cookies now shaped in pumpkins and ghosts. Now we also have homemade Halloween candy with Dizzy Duck Inn wrappers."

"A perfect touch."

"Yeah, completely." I drop the caramel back into the bowl. Lexi swallows her candy, and the way she's studying me is unnerving. "What?" I wonder.

"Are you okay? You seem distant. Not in a bad way, just distant in a different way."

A long exhale leaves my lungs. "I don't know anymore. It's more Nash reappearing in my life."

"Hmm. Is it not going well with him following Zac's wishes?"

I press my lips together. "For Bo, it's fine. For me?" My head tips to the side. "Not so much. He's stirring up too much."

"About Zac?"

My mouth crosses from one side to the other. "No… Nash and I."

Lexi surveys the area to ensure we're all alone, and despite nobody in sight, she still scoots closer to me. "What about you two, exactly?"

"We were together once. Long before Zac."

She offers me a comforting look. "I kind of figured. You just never talked about it."

My shoulders lift to my ears. "Kind of hard to. I married his brother. But Nash coming back stirs up a pot of memories, remorse for even thinking some of things that are running through my head…" I begin to list.

She touches my arm. "If you mean Zac, well, he isn't around to judge," she delicately reminds me.

"I don't know what he can judge me for, except it feels like something. A tide is changing. I could say it was Nash and me fighting, but in truth, it moved as soon as he returned. And I don't know what to do." My lips begin to quiver because everything inside of me hurts, wants, and hopes all in one.

Lexi offers me a hug and soothes my back with her palm. "Maybe this is what you need to move on. We all mourn in different ways."

I begin to play with the ends of my hair. "Perhaps so. I'm just scared shitless that a door to the past might be reopened. I'm not sure it's the right thing to do."

I always feel appreciation when my friends listen without judgment. I've never shared the full story of the dynamics between me and the Nix brothers, but they would be blind not to see that there is something far too deep. A wound that I'm wondering if it could ever be healed.

The two wounds they caused. Or was it me?

"There isn't a timeframe for when you can move on. Or explore what needs to be. Maybe that's what you need? Clarity, and that only can happen in a way that works for you."

My lips quirk out, and everything inside of me is one big hurricane brewing. "You're right."

"Good, because Nash just arrived with the other owners who use inn meetings as an excuse to just have a good time," she nervously states with a droll smile.

We both stand, and she heads straight to her husband. Stone walks to the reception desk to ask something, and Nash stays put. But I don't say anything; my chest visibly moving up and down is enough of a message.

"How was your meeting? Or rather time at the ice rink? I can only imagine it was all productive," Lexi teases her husband and pats his chest.

Holden circles his eyes between all of us, with the stiffness between me and Nash gnawing away at our current loss of clarity. "Not productive at all except for getting some tension out. Funny how skating and hockey pucks can do that."

She yanks his arm slightly, well aware that his observation is only multiplying the strain in here.

My only option is to escape when Nash doesn't say anything, instead he wipes his thumb across his jaw. "I'm going to leave you all. Need to check on one of the rooms. A guest had a special request before they arrive," I explain.

I dart away before anyone can say anything.

My powerwalk doesn't seem to be fast enough because when I'm upstairs pulling a key out of my pocket to unlock the door, I feel him near even if I don't see him.

"Go away, Nash," I request, although I know that it falls on deaf ears.

He steps closer. "I don't think I can. I think that you are avoiding the obvious."

I refuse to meet his gaze. "Humor me," I tell him dryly.

"The shift between us since the other day, it's changed things. Neither one of us has figured out what."

Fumbling with the key, I choose not to answer.

"Summer, it's impossible. Always has been between us. Except now it's anything but and that scares the hell out of me, which means it scares the hell out of you. Tell me I'm wrong." He reaches out to grab my arm when I get the door open.

My heart flips, my throat tightens, and a turmoil of emotion barrels up inside of me. I can't face him, I shouldn't face him.

But I do.

A mere glance and then I do it.

My hands plunge forward and grip his shoulders as I slam my lips onto his, a world of memories hitting me like a drug.

Instantly, he wraps his arm around me with pure reverence. Our lips don't need to explore, because they are meeting again in a fierce return. Hard, crushing, and tender, yet fast all the same.

We tumble into the room, our mouths not parting, instead tilting to get more. Our tongues greet one another in a reunion. I swear my body reacts as if no time has passed between Nash and me.

It's so fierce and desperate. I'm not sure who is murmuring and who is leading. The air I breathe is Nash's again. No thoughts of the time between us interfering. He kisses me just as he did when I was his.

Why aren't our mouths more hesitant? Why is my entire body easing into Nash just as a piece fits into a puzzle?

Then we slow, with his hands sliding up to cradle my face. Our lips soften, they chase, they part, they return. We stop. Our foreheads touching and our bodies still connected, I soak in this moment.

Wondering if this is the circle that leads back to a starting point.

Nash. Oh, Nash.

You came back wanting to fulfill a promise, caring for me. That was the request. I'm not sure taking my heart back was part of that.

It's simple. I want to stay. But something still inside me is enough to cause me to flee.

"Nash, this can't or can or, I don't know… just, I have to go."

I begin to escape, but he pulls me back. "Summer."

My eyes strike up to meet his that are full of devotion to his new plan. Still, I need to breathe in air that isn't drenched in Nash's presence. "Nash," I plead.

He nods subtly in understanding and quickly gives me a kiss on my forehead as a parting gift right before I leave.

Because I'm running away from the inevitable.

SUMMER

I rush through the hotel until I'm outside in the crisp autumn air. It's nearly a march that gets me to the dock. Hearing my name being called causes me to groan and look up, with my hand cradling my neck as if a gentle massage will do something in this moment.

"Summer, wait!"

Of course, Nash would follow me. How could I think that I would get off so lucky? A moment to process isn't in the books today.

"Go away, Nash," I sneer.

It only adds fuel, and Nash continues his quest to arrive right in front of me. He extends his arm to touch my elbow, but I yank my arm away with a scowl.

"I was going to give you space, but I can't. We should talk about this." He's adamant.

I scoff a laugh to myself. "I don't even know where to begin." My eyes move in all directions as I become aware of another fact. "How the hell do we keep ending up on this dock?"

Fuck him for smirking. "Maybe this time we won't end up in the water." My death stare causes him to sober up his humor. "This was always a spot for us, long before. It seems it hasn't changed. What better location to talk than here? The guests get live entertainment, too." His attempt to make me laugh falls flat.

I charge forward and grip his shirt in pure frustration. "Now is not the time for jokes. I'm about to have a meltdown. No, *I am* melting down."

Nash remains composed and encircles my wrists to keep my arms in place. "Why is that?"

It's happening again today. That wave of an uncontrollable blur of feelings cannonballing through me. "Because I feel guilty. It's crazy, but I do. I should still be mourning, not making out with my dead husband's brother. It feels like I'm still sneaking around behind his back."

My words must hit Nash hard as he instantly recoils, letting my wrists fall. "Damn it, Summer. That thought has to snap out of your head."

I shake my head. "It confuses me."

"No shit. Your mixed thoughts caused you to kiss me."

"I wanted to see if that fire is still between us," I almost shout then realize what I just admitted and halt.

Nash snickers. "You really needed to test that? That's a bad excuse."

I grab my hair as I sink through a hole. "Is it? Back then, you let me go. You moved on as if I was a mistake. Why wouldn't I have my guard up?"

His face turns dark, his eyes seething with a mix of anger. "You want to know something, Summer?" I look blankly at him because it wasn't a question. "That necklace that you sometimes wear? The one hanging around your neck?" My eyes drop down, and I clasp the treasure chest. "I told him to get it. He was determined to buy you a flower or some shit like that, and I told him he should get you the treasure chest, a lucky guess I said. I left before I could see if he heard me or not. Seems he did. And you know why I told him?"

I swallow, wanting my heart to stop the spark that might explode. "Don't tell me," I breathlessly implore.

His eyes inform me that he won't listen to me. "Because you never fucking left my mind."

My eyes sting with tears. "You're making this worse."

He steps to me and slides his hand along my cheek to the back of my head, giving me no choice but to face his resolve. "I'm supposed to be in Lake Spark to make it better."

"Everything hurts," I simply answer.

His thumb wipes away a lone tear falling down my cheek, and he pauses for a second when his sight locks on the view of my scar. "It doesn't need to." His whisper scrapes his throat.

My cheek nestles into his palm. "I'm not sure what that looks like yet."

Nash gives me a comforting look. "Me neither, but I want to find out."

My heart is gravitating toward him. I'm conflicted about whether I should feel guilty or not.

"I need to get out of here."

The corner of his mouth lifts. "Are you sure you don't want to push me into the water?"

He always knows when to attempt to calm me. "Shut up, Nash." I'm not in the mood.

His hand falls away, and I give myself a moment to study him, wondering about his intentions now that he's back.

It's clear as day, he has no qualms about what he wants, and at least that's honest.

———

SITTING on the couch in the living room, I have music on and pour myself a glass of wine then set the bottle on the coffee table. Bo is asleep, and I'm aware that Nash will be returning home any moment. I'm sure he found every excuse under the sun to stay away for the last few hours. My small sip turns into a less-than-elegant near chug. It's been that kind of day.

The key turning in the lock immediately heightens my blood

pressure because it's Nash returning. Clearing my head only brought me a tiny ounce of transparency. If there weren't the factor of being a widow, then without a doubt I would explore the magnetic friction that Nash and I have.

If I look back through the years, I shouldn't have been so blind. We had a loosened knot that only needed to be retightened. Loyalty was in the way, and now there is a ghost between us, and this dynamic is new to me.

I glance up when I hear the door close, and Nash slowly walks my way with hesitation, yet his piercing eyes are still far too powerful.

"I was wondering if I needed to send out a search dog or something." I smile nervously.

"Nah, just wanted to give you space and figured you would be in good company with a bottle of white." He indicates with his head to the bottle on the living room table.

"Seemed only fitting. Want a glass?"

"I'll grab a beer." He disappears into the kitchen, and after the sound of the fridge closing, I hear the snap of the bottle cap. Nash is quick to return with a bottle, and he swaggers his way to the couch to sit down on the opposite end of the sofa, a solid no-man's land between us.

I thrum my fingers on my thigh. "Uhm, you can put on the sports channel or something. I know pre-season games are over and the season is starting."

He smiles to himself. "Very honorable of you, but I wanted to ask… is it better if I stay at the Dizzy Duck? I know my brother wanted me to stay here to ensure you're okay, but I might be making this worse for you."

"No," I raise my voice, then calm. "I mean, it's fine. I don't want you to go. It's good for Bo, and I'm not sure…" I avoid meeting his eyes, and I stare at my bare ring finger. "I don't think staying at the Dizzy Duck would matter. You're still in Lake Spark. Still close enough to do damage."

"Damage. Great." His tone is edged.

My hand rockets up to relax his thoughts, and I scooch over on the couch to bring up my legs and bare feet to cross and half face him. "No, I mean… It's just, I would still be a hot mess of feelings, so might as well get a baby-oatmeal maker out of the deal."

Relief hits him. "Okay then."

"As… well, as long as it's okay for you. It's not just me having issues here, right?"

His jaw juts out as if he's wondering where I'm going with this. "Is that so?" He's messing with me. Or is he? "Maybe when I first got back, but it's becoming too obvious what to do. I can handle that… I've accepted that."

He slides over a little, and our space is closing even more. Heat rises under my skin, and my face must appear flushed. "Summer, I'm not going to feel guilty. I've come to the conclusion that maybe my way of mourning is to be near you. To be *with* you."

My eyes dip low, and I see my charm necklace hanging and floating in the air, and I use it to divert us. "It seems the Nix brothers have a thing for giving me jewelry. A ring and a necklace." Because it was really Nash, wasn't it?

"I'm angry he was the one who gave the necklace to you, if that's any consolation."

My skin burns from the contrast of thoughts due to that admission. "You shouldn't say things like that."

Because I might agree.

Our eyes linger again, the air nearly suffocating. Nash's finger bolts out and hooks under my chin to draw my attention to him, with his fortitude written all over his face. "There's something I've wanted to do since I've been back."

The room is beginning to spin as every ounce of anticipation inside me surges, and I attempt to keep it down. "I don't think I want to know," I rasp.

Nash leans in. "And I don't care."

My chest panics that he is going to try and kiss me, but his lips bypass my mouth and do something much worse. They brush along the scar above my eyebrow. My entire body melts when Nash gently kisses it.

"I'm sorry," he murmurs against my skin.

I'm not sure how to breathe anymore, as the room seems to be fading around us. "Nash."

"I did this to you… and I'm the selfish guy who not only thinks you're beautiful but who is slightly satisfied that every day you are reminded of me."

As twisted as it sounds, the possessiveness that he has ignites something inside of me. His hands stay firmly planted to hold my head when he withdraws slightly.

"Every time I look in the mirror, there is no escape from you," I confess in a whisper.

He follows the path of his fingers as he lifts a part of my hair, then he places it behind my shoulder. "You're allowed to let your walls down if that's what you need."

Every part of my body is reacting. From my head to my toes and all parts in between, including my sensitive area that longs to be touched.

"Tell me to get up and leave," I plead, with my throat feeling dry.

His mouth quirks out, and Nash's eyes remain persistent with his beliefs. "I'm selfish, remember? You were mine first, so you know I won't tell you to run."

I nod gently, aware that the inevitable is happening.

Slowly we both lean in to let our lips meet. It's a softer kiss than earlier today, sensual and longing spilling out. I hate as much as I love how our mouths perfectly fit.

Our tongues delve in with their tips gently tickling each other, making me want more. Nash cradles my head between his hands to kiss me deeper, to hold onto me so I won't fall. In truth, I already did within.

A murmur fills my throat, and I grip his arms, wanting to ensure that I stay completely in place because I don't want to escape this time. Our mouths part only to find one another again, this time more fervent and insistent. We are past going slow.

I feel my body naturally lead and guide Nash to sit back, and I adjust my legs until I'm straddling him, with our mouths still intact for a kiss, except his hands drop to my waist, his fingers sneaking under the fabric of my tank top. He slowly drags my shirt up, and I want more, too. My hands search between us for his shirt, and I begin to tug as I want it gone. He abandons me for a second to whip his shirt up and off. Meanwhile, I finish the job of getting my own shirt off, leaving me in a bra.

My head falls back as Nash's mouth brushes down my throat to my collarbone that he kisses gently. I place the palms of my hands against his bare chest to create a little space. I check in that we're really going to do this. It appears that all our fears have vanished. With urgency, we return to our exploration of one another. Nash's lips graze my cleavage while his fingers work the clasp behind me. Instantly, my breasts peek out, and his mouth begins to tease my nipple. Everything in me is painfully throbbing for his touch.

Dampness from my pussy seeps through my yoga pants, and I swirl my hips against him. Nash always liked to lead and could read my body, always giving me what I needed. It seems now is no different. He guides me back until my head lands on a cushion, and he hovers over me while we kiss.

But my lips feel vacant when he sits up on his knees to pull my yoga pants down while I raise my legs. His eyes are on me, hungry.

"My beautiful Summer," he whispers. The pants find a home on the floor, and his wicked eyes warn me as his mouth coasts up my legs, slowing on my thighs for a few soft kisses and giving me agony in anticipation.

"Nash."

He teases my thighs with his lips, drawing lazy patterns. His fingers slide up and rub against my panties. I'm not ashamed how soaked I am for him, and he's pleased as he moans in response. Slipping under the fabric to glide along my pussy, he finds my clit, and my entire body tilts up in response. Nash's palm splays against my stomach to calm me, and I'm rewarded with his mouth kissing me over the fabric on that sensitive spot.

"Don't stop." I breathe out my torture.

He pauses for a second. "I never wanted to." Then he returns to worshipping me.

Except his sentence had more meaning. He never wanted to leave and stop us all those years ago… but loyalty got in the way.

My eyes close, taking in the overflow of desire, feeling my panties disappear, and the sound of Nash's zipper filling my ears.

"Tell me I can take you like this." It's not a question, more of a plea.

I lick my lips. "I have an IUD. And I know you would never…" It doesn't matter about logistics now. He would never hurt me physically.

"I want to get lost in you again," he mutters as he parts my thighs open and kisses me by my knee.

I'm already lost in him, this, everything.

The moment he enters me with just his tip, we both moan together. It's been too long, and our tension incinerates as he pumps deeper until I'm full and stretched. Every move causing tremors through my body.

"Summer." His warm breath tickles me, and his mouth caresses my breast as he gently thrusts inside me.

My nails scrape his back to bring him deeper. It sets him off, and our pace changes to a hurried need to let go together. With our eyes connected, it's intense as our bodies become one with him inside me, which is why we let go.

I've needed him.

It's all clear to me now.

I've missed him. That I already knew.

When we settle into an embrace in our afterglow, with Nash tossing a blanket from the back of the sofa over us and my head resting firmly against his chest, there is another thought that hits me.

I was supposed to end up back in his arms.

But why does my heart twist so much?

12

NASH

My fingers trail along Summer's arm as we lie on the couch with a throw blanket loosely draped over her. All the more reason why I need to keep her naked body warm and close to me.

"This has to be our last time," she whispers weakly as her eyes follow her fingertips tracing my chest.

"Then why are you still in my arms?"

"Maybe I want to get every moment I can," she answers.

I inhale the scent of her hair, a familiar calmness coming over me. "I'm surprised you haven't run away yet. But here you stay." Her lips brush along my chest, and she settles again with her cheek resting against my body as I begin to stroke her hair.

"It's hard to… It feels like we are picking up from the last moment I was in your arms like this. Except there's time between us, and I'm not sure if it haunts me or not."

"Let go, Summer. Speak without thought. Otherwise, you'll be miserable."

"I don't like being alone," she laments.

I squeeze her tighter. "You're not. You don't need to fight it. I'm not going to run away."

"You did last time."

My body stills for a second due to the reminder. "Things change. Life changed."

She gave a gift to my brother. My nephew is in the picture. The challenges seem vague in the future for us, but that's better than nothing.

Our fingers gravitate toward one another and intertwine to move our hands together. "It feels like we've come full circle if I'm honest. It was you, then not, and now I'm back to you. The hole in my heart for many reasons is beginning to diminish slightly, barely."

"That's a start."

We lie here in silence in an embrace that is more than comfort; it's right.

"I remember you and I being like this for hours. Nobody knew. Now it seems to be a repeat, except I haven't figured out if the stakes are higher."

Inside of me there is a fight to shake her and tell her it's all going to be okay. In truth, this is a whole new realm for all of us. Both Summer and I want to honor Zac and the time since he has passed. Except for me, my timer is up. Does that make me a bad person?

Am I just swooping in because I have my chance to have Summer again? We haven't even figured out if my brother is the ghost that will haunt us or guide us. I'm just choosing the latter.

"Remember when you and I would order in food so we would never be apart? Just you and me barely clothed and talking?" she asks.

"I wouldn't forget something like that." We would lie in bed for hours, and I would take her too many times to count.

"We were in our own world. That's what I want now." Summer lifts her head to bring her gaze to mine. "I need to process what's happening between you and me. Is this what consolation is, or do people get a second chance in the saddest of circumstances?"

What she says is wise. We could both be blinded by lust, even if I'm confident that I won't let go this time.

"I'll give us that," I agree.

Her sigh for once sounds comforting. Summer's letting go, even if just for tonight.

"I should probably go to sleep. I need to be at the Dizzy Duck early," she mentions yet doesn't make an effort to move.

Nor do I encourage her to leave our island on the couch. My eyes roam the room, purposely avoiding any photos on mantels, and I'm relieved that the box of blocks is an easy distraction. "Summer."

"Mmhmm." She sounds drowsy.

"I'm sorry I didn't show up when Bo was born."

I wasn't a man. I couldn't put my pride to the side, instead wallowing in what I didn't have.

Summer adjusts her body again, and her fingers grip my jaw to guide my gaze to hers. "It's okay. You showed up eventually."

She isn't mad at me now, but I know she was, and maybe now it's just washed away.

Something has been stirring in me lately, and I should tell her. "I'm not here because I feel like I owe it to someone to be here for Bo. I *want* to be here for him."

Her mouth shifts to a faint smile. "It seems you just went from a five to a six on the baby scale."

"I need to work on my diaper changing, is that it? Is that why I'm not excelling at a faster rate to a ten?"

She chuckles faintly. "Probably. Now I think I need to leave this sofa purely because my side is beginning to ache. I'm impressed that we both fit here like this."

"We're kind of one body right now." And it's the only fit that will be the right size.

"True. Still, my hip is going to hate me tomorrow."

That's reasonable, which is why I shuffle with her to sitting up with the blanket carelessly covering her breasts. We both take a moment to stretch before Summer stands and gazes at me peculiarly. "Do you think you can sleep with me?"

My eyes grow big. "I was supposed to return to my room?" I'm teasing her because it probably was an option in her head.

"I shouldn't answer that," she admits right before she peers up with her eyes vulnerable. "I don't want to sleep alone. Not tonight."

"Then I'll follow you."

Her eyes gleam with appreciation.

I grab my boxer briefs and tell her to go on ahead. Picking up the beer bottle and wine glass, I bring them to the kitchen counter and will worry about them tomorrow. When I'm upstairs, I do a quick check through the door that's ajar to Bo's room, and I hear white noise and see the glow of the blue nightlight that projects stars. It's cute. I head to my room, grab a shirt, and check myself in the bathroom. Settling in for the night sounds good right now.

Arriving at Summer's room, I remember she mentioned the timeline of moving into the house which already erased one equation of this whole situation. Summer is on her side under the covers, now in a cotton t-shirt.

"Hey," she greets me shyly.

I saunter to the bed and then slide under the blankets to join her. We face one another and lie on our sides. "You're still warm," she grins.

"Uh, should I be ice?" I wonder.

"No, it's just I remember sleeping with you and you radiated so much body heat that you had no choice but to take your shirt off."

My tongue runs along my bottom lip. "It will probably happen again, if that's okay?"

Her hands rest under her cheek and her smile feels earnest. "It is. So just hold me," she requests.

I scoop Summer close, encasing my body to hers. "You never need to ask."

"Then maybe I never asked enough," she states softly.

Quieting her, I seal her lips with a tender kiss, refusing to recall why she couldn't ask.

———

OF COURSE, I woke to a cold bed because Summer slipped out without detection this morning. I'm not surprised, but that doesn't mean I'm not going to confront it.

Which is exactly why I'm leaning against the front desk in the Dizzy Duck with my ankles crossed and snacking on a pumpkin-shaped sugar cookie, thankful that I didn't get the ghost-shaped one because that would be too fucking relevant.

"I don't know, I'm kind of thinking that the whole traditional Christmas gala has to return. It's stuffy, and my parents loved it. It was kind of a competition with the Lake Spark Country Club, but the Dizzy Duck Inn had a bit more holiday festivity. You know? Like, a resemblance to the setting of that game Clue but with a holiday theme," I explain to Stuart behind the front desk.

He listens with interest. "You mean, like a murder mystery kind of night?"

I snap my fingers. "Ooh, that's a good thought. I think that historical museum over in Everhope does one of those. We need one a bit closer, and it seems that we have a place. I should run that by Holden and Stone." I roll my shoulders back with a cocky tone. "I should have given this place more attention the last few years. I'm full of great ideas."

"Hey, Stuart, do you know when the coffee repair guy is coming? That machine Holden ordered way back keeps breaking down. It's becoming a nuisance," Summer asks as she focuses on a few papers in her hand.

"Kind of like me?"

Her eyes shoot up. "Shit," she mutters to herself, clearly being caught out and aware this was going to happen.

I give Stuart a warning glare to disappear, and he gets the message.

"Avoiding me is classic," I inform her.

She rolls her eyes. "Can we just leave it?"

Approaching her, I tsk my tongue. "No. So either we talk here or I'm happy to carry you to the dock since you tend not to shut up there."

Summer seems irritated. "Nash, now isn't the time—"

I shove my half-eaten cookie into her mouth and her sound is muffled. "I need you quiet."

She wipes the back of her hand across her mouth as she chews and swallows the cookie. "What the hell, Nash," she barks.

"You're freaking out, I know you are."

"This is happening so fast. You're back a week and I'm sharing a bed with you. I should feel guilty or... it's only been a few months since..." She is quick to scan the room and sees we are alone. "A few months as a widow. Am I dishonoring him by ending up in bed with you? I don't know the timeline for these things."

"There isn't one," I blankly remind her.

Summer jabs a finger into my chest. "Why aren't you feeling the same way? This must be a slap in Zac's face. Don't you feel guilty?"

"No." I'm direct. My bluntness causes her eyes to spear me with surprise, as she wasn't expecting me to say that. "Not today, at least." Which makes me an asshole, I'm sure.

She blinks as she tries to contemplate my answer. It's a long silence. Idling in some ways, too.

The tip of her tongue darts out to lick a crumb away. "Damn, the seasonal cookies are good." She shakes her head, realizing she's slightly off track. "Nash, I'm..." She heaves a breath and straightens her posture. "It just feels..."

I cross my arms. "I'm waiting, otherwise that dock is calling our name, and throwing you over my shoulder is no issue for me."

Summer provides me with a pointed look. "Fine. My sentence as a non-flustered human is that this thing between us, it just feels... gravitating, impossible to ignore. But a fucking clock is taunting me; I should be taking longer to mourn."

"Language, Summer," I goad her to try and get the faintest of smiles from her. But then I step closer, realizing the magnitude of her thoughts. "Don't run away. We'll figure it out together. I'm also on the same timeline of history as you."

"Everyone doesn't stare at you the same way," she hisses softly. It kills me that she appears to fear shame.

"Summer, who cares what people think? You have a backbone. Don't let anyone but me get to you."

She exhales a deep breath as she soaks in my words. "Okay."

I touch her shoulder delicately. "Okay, you're saying it to get rid of me now, or okay because you are agreeing?"

She's exhausted by me, but her smile developing means she doesn't mind. "Okay, I am agreeing." She still sounds a bit stubborn, and I'm still not 100% convinced.

"Can I also hold you while you sleep again tonight? Maybe tomorrow too?"

Her tongue darts to the corner of her mouth, and she contemplates for a second. "Well… considering last night, then it would feel kind of… empty sleeping alone. So, yes."

I grin at her response, as it is the only answer for me.

Her hand shoos me away. "Now go. I need to get back to work, so can you just…" She ushers me in the direction where I need to go, but I don't budge.

I have to throw in my smug card. "I partly own this place. I'm sure I can ensure you don't get in trouble if you want to grab lunch as two people trying to figure out life together."

Summer looks away, but her light demeanor remains. "Not today. I really do want to work to ensure I finish on time to let the babysitter go."

"Want me to do that? Rumor has it if I add pick-up duty to my roster, then I might move up from a six to a seven on the baby scale."

Summer chuckles. "Get out of here. And no, I'll do it."

All the complications between us seem to fade away for these few moments. "Hey, Summer, I was…" My thumb draws a line from my mouth to my stubbled chin as I hesitate to ask, but I take the plunge anyhow. "Maybe we can do that pumpkin patch thing this weekend. It would be good to get out of Lake Spark for a day. Just you, Bo, and me."

"That could be…" She stops herself from protesting.

But another issue dawns on me. "You, uhm… you're not afraid to get in a car with me, are you?" Last time she ended up in the hospital.

She glances away then back. "No, Nash. I'm not. The accident was literally that."

"We had been arguing before," I remind her.

"Yeah, because you ended things." That's a cold splash of water, but then her entire face softens. "Everything happens for a reason, even if we don't want it that way."

I swallow, accepting her answer, even if I'm not entirely free of my guilt. "I just wanted to check. I mean, I would understand if you are."

Summer's eyes grow into large circles, clearly now humorously annoyed. "Can we close this topic? You had an idea for this weekend."

I relax a little. "Yeah, a getaway."

"A good idea. For all of us, the three of us." Summer nods and leaves me be.

The three of us. She didn't mean anything by it. Just a simple answer.

But it tugs somewhere inside of me.

Stepping into someone's shoes. Or getting a renewed chance.

Fuck.

I'm going to throw every ghost cookie, no matter how perfectly delicious, into the garbage. I have enough reminders as it is.

13

SUMMER

hange.

That's what the fall season is a sign of.

My head rests on the back of the seat while Nash drives his SUV. I have to smile to myself because I doubt he intended for this car to become one with a sleeping baby in the back. I'm really not sure why he is sliding into the whole uncle role so easily, but he is.

Nash glances in the rearview mirror. "That kid is like a mystical baby creature or something. He's never really fussy, is he?"

I scoff a laugh. "He is. When he was born, the first month was hell. Didn't really want to sleep. Now looking back, I'm kind of grateful that he didn't. It meant Zac had more waking moments with Bo."

Way to go, Summer. Just cut the air in half again.

"I'm sorry I keep bringing up your brother." I observe Nash who stays focused on the road.

"It's okay. You don't need to be closed off about it. He is ultimately Bo's father."

I hum a sound in agreement. "That I know you support. I just don't want us to be reminded of the conflict inside of us."

"Really, it's fine. Besides, if I'm honest, it has crossed my mind today. He would have loved to have done this with Bo. Now I'm stepping in and it isn't quite the same." Nash's voice when he goes soft and exposed is more than a comfort; it lifts light inside of me as we share an understanding.

I extend my fingers to touch his arm gently. "I think we've gotten this out of the way, so let's focus on having a good day. I know the Blisswood farm is more than a winery, but someone mentioned they have a great pumpkin season with cider, too."

"It is. Their connection to Lake Spark also scores bonus points for choosing this place to visit. Sometimes, you see the brothers making a delivery in Lake Spark. They also have family there, too, as someone married Hudson Arrows's son."

"Everyone knows who is who in town." I check once more to see Bo beginning to stir. "Uh-oh, the Little Baby Creature Thing as you sometimes call him is awakening." I find it adorable the way Nash was at first unsure of being around kids, but then he glides right into being a pro at it, and I know that's going to happen today.

"Is he going to be cranky until he gets a snack?"

I nod a few times and reach for my bag on the floor by my feet to search for a soft baby cookie. "Most definitely. That's why I always come prepared." I hold up the cookie with pride, and that half-smile of his stays permanent.

"We're almost there. Like do we need one classic pumpkin or are you going to take it a notch up and we buy a few?"

"I guess as many as your arms can handle."

He chuckles. "Fair play."

Bo gives me a few blinks before he yawns, and then a smile begins to curve on his chubby little cheeks.

"Remind me to get him a Halloween costume. The Dizzy Duck has a staff party coming up, which I'm sure you know since your executive meetings are at the ice rink and very informative where lots of work gets done." I flash my eyes at him before I stretch my body to the back and hand Bo his snack.

"Whoa, whoa, whoa. It's team building, and we do discuss the Dizzy Duck."

I doubt this tremendously. "Really?"

Nash tips his head to the side and grins to himself. "Okay, we mostly listen to Holden complain about the expensive coffee machine breaking and how we are currently using a French press for coffee."

I interrupt and point my finger at him. "Which the guests actually love and feel it's a classic touch."

"Tell that to Holden. But really, the Dizzy Duck is successful without me. There isn't much to discuss."

I'm not sure how I've been so ignorant to the fact that Nash is only supposed to be in town for a short time. Suddenly, a small dose of fear swims inside of me.

Luckily broken by the car coming to a halt in the parking lot.

"Here we are. I get the stroller out of the trunk, right?" Nash asks, oblivious to my thoughts.

I unbuckle my seatbelt. "It's probably better if I use the baby carrier."

"Cool. I'll get him out before he can cause any more crumb damage to my car."

That is such a Nash thing to say, and it does the trick, as all negative thoughts fade away.

We get everything settled and Bo strapped to the front of my body. The weather is great today, with sun and temperatures in the high 50s, but it feels warmer. The farm is gorgeous, well taken care of, and I understand why it's often a weekend hotspot.

"I know the wine is good, but since they do have two rooms for their bed-and-breakfast, then we should be wondering if we're cheating on your business investment and my place of employment," I tease.

"We're good," he assures me and zips up his jacket then yanks my arm, carefully since Bo is in his carrier. "Come on, we have a hay maze to conquer."

I laugh because it's so silly but also perfect. "I like that idea. If you get us lost, then you have to do dishes for a week."

"I'm being sentenced to a chore chart again?" This is the banter I need.

When we enter the maze, I'm already completely lost, and we haven't even turned a corner. "Remember in high school we would all head to the haunted hayride at Pioneer Park outside of town? It's like the only time of year that they don't cater to the kid population."

"That ride was scary shit. After, there was always some crazy party at someone's house that would get out of hand," Nash recalls as he debates which way we go at the fork in the road.

I playfully slap his arm. "You always went as the same thing. No costume at all."

He throws me a cocky look. "Because I didn't need to dress up. I would wear my jersey and I was set."

"Just like reality. I guess fake blood on your jersey wouldn't really be different to your hockey games."

Nash twirls his finger in the air. "Let's backtrack for a second. You were a cat in fishnets with a skirt way too fucking short for my liking."

I cover Bo's ears and smile humorously. "Watch the language around this little guy… and I'm surprised you remember."

He looks at me as if I'm crazy. "I'm not sure any guy that night forgot."

I grin proudly to myself as we continue our stroll and approach a scarecrow. "I'm going to have to find a mom-appropriate costume for my son's first Halloween."

Nash snickers. "You rock the hot-mom thing, wear what you want."

Who would have thought our playful comments wouldn't spook me today. It feels normal, way too quickly. Leading us down a path, I feel him follow in tow.

"I can take that sentence in so many different ways." I'm having a good time, and we're flirting, too. "Priority is figuring out a costume for this little guy." I bounce Bo as his hands reach out.

"I'll do it. Let me be in charge of costume duty… for him, I mean."

My lips quirk out as I mull it over. "It should be a big thing for me to choose, but in all honesty, I don't have the brain power right now, and I'm curious what on earth you might come up with."

"Great."

We arrive at the end of the maze to face the pumpkin patch, and we both breathe in relief. "Oh, thank you, pumpkin lords. Hay is exciting for only like a minute," I pretend to speak to a higher power.

Nash nudges my shoulder with his. "Nah, you loved it. You could walk aimlessly around."

I stand taller and think about it. He's right, I'm kind of relaxed and not overthinking for a few moments. "You have a point," I confirm. "Now pumpkins. What are you benching these days that they used to pay you millions for?"

He smirks at me and my humor. "Summer, we could easily pack the trunk full, but I'm going to say that five feels like a good number for your doorstep."

"I agree," I say and begin to unbuckle the carrier to take Bo out. I turn him around and lean down so he can touch a pumpkin, and that immediately makes me smile. In the corner of my eye, I notice that Nash is admiring the view and takes a photo with his phone. "How could I forget that we need photos?"

"Don't worry. Your superhero is here. Now come on, both of you pose." I listen to my command and face the camera, doing my best to get Bo to cooperate.

This is what we do for what feels like hours but is probably only twenty minutes. "I think we've studied the field enough and are ready to make our choices," I announce.

Nash looks at me, impressed. "Didn't realize we were doing a draft pick for pumpkins. Let's make sure they sign their entry-level contract before they reach my car."

That causes me to laugh hard, nearly making my stomach hurt, and when my laugh calms, I have to ask. "Missing the hockey life already?"

He seems to ponder it as he moves a pumpkin out of the way. "I do, actually, but my focus was getting lost anyhow."

"You had a lot going on in life, it's understandable," I sympathize.

"Maybe, or maybe I was just losing heart in the game. I don't think I miss the social life outside the rink, either."

I consider what might be going through his mind. "Then what awaits you?"

"When I arrived in Lake Spark I didn't know. Now? I'm beginning to wonder if my brother is giving me hints to what exactly life will be."

My eyes snap to the ground to avoid our eyes meeting. "Right. Six weeks and then…"

Nash steps forward and lifts Bo from my arms, and Bo coos. "Actually, I kind of forgot that timeline. I'm too stuck on what's going on between us and how it's kind of… healing, helping, I'm not sure. Seems to be my way of coping, too."

Immediately, my sight zaps to look up, and Nash's face is stoic, but it's because he knows he's delivered a new fact to me. "I kind of thought…"

"That I would sleep with you, try to be an uncle, and leave?"

My eyes drift down, nearly ashamed of the thought. "It was the plan. Not the sleeping-together part but the request from Zac part to stay only six weeks."

"Maybe plans change. It's hard to think past tomorrow. I arrived in Lake Spark not at all thrilled with his wish, because you and I were not on the radar, and I didn't know how to process. We both were not thrilled and showed it. Now? It seems you and I are a lot more than two people dreading a request. I feel too compelled to explore this, but we can both acknowledge that we have two very different approaches of how to handle this situation."

Stepping closer to them, I feel a whoosh travel down my body. "I think I needed that clarification. The timeline factor."

A firm line forms on Nash's mouth, and he focuses his attention on Bo. "One day at a time, right, buddy?"

A second or two then I switch our focus. "Get in position," I tell him, and my hand slips into the pocket of the carrier still loosely buckled around me to grab my cell. "We need some photos of you two. Your parents will lose their cool if they see this. The number of heart emojis your parents send with every Bo picture has made me wonder if they know how to use any other emoji or just insist on pressing the same one a million times." I crack a smile because it's so true and also sweet.

"Geez, they still do that stuff? When I was playing hockey, after every game they would send me the emoji of a flexed muscle and a hockey stick, then repeat that pattern about a thousand times in one message. So don't worry, they have two more emojis in their portfolio." Nash has a warm smile glued to his face as he kneels down and holds Bo on his knee as my son reaches out for a pumpkin.

"It's not every day a parent can say they have a professional hockey player and a doctor as sons. I'm sure they were starstruck even with their own kids. Now stop stalling and give me a photo that is holiday-card worthy."

Nash ruefully shakes his head and glances down at Bo, and that's the shot. I need no more. There is love there. Bo is calm, and Nash seems invested. It's all apparent through the camera and also to me.

It's an overbearing wave of consolation.

I snap a few more photos just in case, until a hand on my shoulder causes me to bring my attention to an older woman who seems to be the grandmother of the little girl running up ahead.

"Do you want me to take a photo of you three together?" she offers.

"That's kind of you to ask. Sure." I show her the button on my screen and scurry to Bo and Nash. Leaning down and balancing on my toes, I touch Nash's shoulder for support. My other hand grabs my son's little hand, and I guess we are all smiling when the old lady takes a photo. I can't see because we all face the same direction, but I feel our elated faces.

I smile and walk back to the older woman. "Thank you so much."

"No problem. It will be a lovely picture, you're a cute little family," she compliments.

I pause for a second and soak in her words. "Thanks."

I glance over my shoulder back to Nash who is throwing goofy faces at Bo who in return is grabbing his nose. Reminding myself that it's okay to have a day to feel like myself again and be hopeful, I throw on a smile, take a deep breath, and place my cell back into the pocket.

"I think we need to load the pumpkins and grab some cider, maybe a few bottles of wine, and while we're at it, I think I saw lemon bars somewhere," I list.

"Someone just got bossy." Nash winks at me.

"That's normally your department." I clearly forgot to filter out innuendo, and now Nash has a devilish grin. My face warms, and I'm well aware that I'm blushing. "Let's just find cider, okay?" Move us along. That's my plan.

We managed to get more photos when we saw a swing by the pond and had a delicious lunch, too. The Blisswood farm doesn't really have many animals, but they let us see the horse when they discovered we're from Lake Spark, and Bo looked at the horse with wonder.

I don't think Bo will sleep on the way back to Lake Spark, but that's okay. Nash and I take a moment to rest before we start the drive, and I take this as an opportunity to catch his fingers and entwine them with mine.

"Thank you for today. It's been a while since I've gotten to kind of turn off," I admit.

Nash brings my knuckle up to his lips for a kiss that is near saccharine. "You need to go easy, Summer. You're allowed to take time when you need it. Beyond the circumstances, I can only imagine just being a mom is tough work. Guys that I used to play with looked like hell when they had a baby at home. I mean, a few even had to sleep in separate rooms away from their kids just to get proper sleep before a game. You're doing it all alone."

"I'm going to give myself a little more compassion, but distraction is also my thing."

I elongate my body and bring my hand to touch the side of his head as I kiss his lips. We're not in public in Lake Spark, nobody can judge me for being in my own little world with Nash. He returns the kiss in full, and it causes me to murmur because it's so perfectly tender, and I wanted it like this, which is why I initiated our lips finding one another. My thumb rubs a circle on his gruff cheek when I pull away with our foreheads touching.

"I've missed this. Being with you as if the world can stop. Kissing you when I want," I convey to him.

"Me too, Summer. Me too." He kisses the tip of my nose.

A break of a cry begins, only to build.

"You totally jinxed us earlier by saying he never cries." I pull away with a wide grin.

Nash chuckles as he starts the car, and I reach back to set the pacifier back in Bo's mouth.

Today felt like a family day, and that's always good for the soul.

———

With my long t-shirt on, I flop onto the bed where Nash is waiting. It's nice having someone in bed, ready to welcome you with open arms. It's been a very long time since I've had this with a strong flame underneath. My marriage was cuddly, but it lacked the fire. But now Nash is here, and he always had the match.

Straddling him, he grips my hips as he sits up. "You're too beautiful," he murmurs when his lips lightly press into the curve of my neck.

"You've mentioned once or twice, Mr. Ages Well."

Nash growls where my throat meets my collarbone. "Stroking my ego when we're in bed together is a very risky move."

My forearms come up to rest on his shoulders, with my hands linking behind his neck. My pussy is right on top of his hard shaft, and this sheet around his waist has to go or it will just end up a tangled mess.

"I remember all of your risky moves, Nash." My voice is sultry, and I'm so turned on in this moment that I'm about to beg.

Our eyes check in with one another, a mirror of simmering determination. "We both seem to remember." It's a scraped whisper from his throat.

Something inside of me is about to explode, and it's a battle between my pussy and my chest. It's only made worse when he tosses me off and ensures I land on my back, with his body floating over me.

"Arms above your head, Summer." His eyes are piercing me and his voice sweltering. Here is demanding Nash. The Nash that is a reminder that his steely exterior sometimes transfers over into the bedroom.

I obey without question, and I'm rewarded with his hand skimming up my thigh. "I appreciate that you came to bed with no panties. It gets us to our destination sooner."

My entire body curves up into him to build friction. "Where might that be?" I coo.

"My mouth on your pussy right before my cock fills you up."

A moan escapes me from the pure thought. "You're wasting time it seems by talking right now."

That causes him to dare me to taunt him again. "I have no problem flipping you to your stomach to take you right away."

My knees butterfly out, offering myself to him, and the moment his fingers touch my pussy, I'm desperate for him.

Passion is our thing. It's why we could barely be in a room together for years. Patience seems to have paid off, and I ignore every thought of why that is.

Because today I got to see that now can be better if I take steps to move on.

14

NASH

I'm kissing her again.

We're in the same bed again.

And the way Summer's cheeks are tight, with her swollen lips gently pulled up, it seems she can experience a moment when she is less numb again.

Summer's eyes draw down to me as my mouth trails below her belly while my splayed hands push the thin fabric of her shirt up until my palm rests between her breasts. My mouth? There is only one direction where I plan to go, and she eases me down by weaving her fingers through my hair.

My lips pause and I peer up. "Arms, Summer," I prompt her again.

A sound escapes her mouth to make me aware that she's toying with me. She knew I would remind her of what I want. She ceremoniously stretches her arms over her head again, and I continue my journey, landing right where I want.

My tongue flicks out to sweep across her clit, and we both marvel in the instant electricity that intensifies between us. Her taste on my tongue makes me eager for more, and my dick is ready to plunge inside of her.

Hooking my arms underneath her knees, I widen her and dive in again to lap her up and down a few times until I circle her clit again then suck. Her body jolts from the sensation, and pride roars through me that her body is mine to play with.

"I'm addicted to you all over," I murmur to her and scrape my lips along her inner thigh, with her silky skin imprinting on my lips.

"Nash, I need you," she purrs as she props her upper body up on her elbows, enabling her to receive a better view of me.

My eyes feel stormy. Summer is mine, only mine, and I'm scared I might reach so deep inside of her that she will scream, but today was a special day. Or at least, it felt that way. A glimpse of what I once dreamed then let go of when she was no longer mine, and apparently, I didn't need to let go, only hold on and wait.

I drop her legs because my body now provides the stability to keep her open since I'm quick to drift over Summer to steal a kiss, a quick one that I receive before her hand comes up to caress my cheek. Our eyes seal together, with nothing from the outside world able to break this moment.

Between us, our hands meet to pull down my boxer briefs, and she wraps her hand around my length, causing my eyes to close for a few seconds to enjoy Summer having me in her hold.

"Please, Nash," she begs, already guiding my shaft to where she needs me.

"Summer, I warned you. Hands above your head. Your body is mine, and I'll ensure we both get what we need." My fingers lock around her wrists to rocket her arms straight back up to where they need to stay. Her fraught body displays her perfectly round breasts with tight hard nipples, and naturally, I need to tease her with my fingers and tongue. A tug and a twist, and her hips rise as she attempts to get me inside of her.

"The moment I'm inside of you, we need to keep you quiet. I'm not going to go slow or easy. I'm going to take and take until you're filled with me, understand?" I caution her.

She nods up and down once with a sly grin.

I sit up on my knees to yank her hips closer to me, and as soon as I find my position, I enter Summer's snug fit and follow her body up until she's underneath me. Slamming into her, both our bodies quiver from the force. I pump into her a few times, and Summer wraps her legs around me, using me to hang on. Maybe I should worry more about hurting her, but our eyes confirm that like this is for us. We have years to make up for. It was the fucking longest full circle of my life, and with every thrust into Summer, I let her body know that it's mine now. Only mine, and I have no plans to let that go.

My mouth covers hers as her moan can no longer be kept quiet, with the mattress moving when I take over her body fully. Maybe she'll ache tomorrow, but as long as she doesn't tell me to stop, I'm going to ensure she's aware that I have a claim on her.

We move in rhythm, and as my speed quickens, she uses my shoulder to muffle her sounds as I grunt. Her teeth sink into my skin in a playful manner, but it keeps every part of Summer connected to me.

Even when we start to shake together, we both stay as one.

I like that she doesn't go straight to the bathroom to clean up. I'm still inside of her, and it feels territorial.

"Is this us making up for lost time? Or just eager to fuck one another's brains out," I wonder as my breath begins to cool off. Gravity takes over, causing me to slip out of her and land on my back next to her.

Summer rolls to her side to give me an amused glance and pats my chest. "Nah, you've never really done fragile or treated me like I was once a virgin, so don't you worry, you're sticking to tradition."

She's funny, this one. "Okay, in that case, you'll be waking up with me fucking you from behind."

"Such a hardship," she teases then returns to her back to look at the ceiling.

I peel the duvet up and over us. "Younger us were a little wild at times."

Summer snorts out a laugh. "You mean handcuffing me to your bed or kitchen escapades?"

"Excuse me, Miss Go Down on Me in the Shower, even when I was running late for practice."

"Well, it was fun. Besides, I'm happy you have the memories, because windows of opportunities are not in our favor with a baby around," she highlights.

I tilt my head to the side and bring Summer close. "It doesn't seem to bother me. I'm not used to all this domesticated stuff. Yet today wasn't what I thought it would be, and I doubt tomorrow will be, either. We're supposed to be like this, you and me."

"Perhaps. I think we're still getting used to life being not this a few weeks ago and now here we are. A cosmic boom."

I begin to tickle her, and she giggles. "Enough sentimental crap. If you want a cosmic boom, then get on your hands and knees so I can take you from behind." Summer actually listens and begins to stir in my arms, and my cock is already twitching for her.

But alas, that window of opportunity she mentioned seems to hit us right on cue.

We both pause and wait for Bo's crackly sounds to intensify.

Summer growls. "See?" she whispers loudly to me and begins to scoot to the edge of the bed.

I tug her arm to stop her from leaving. "I'll go."

She squinches her eyes. "It's fine, I'm used to—"

Ignoring her, I move to stand. "That's exactly why. Enjoy staying in bed, you dirty girl. I would say clean up, but I kind of have plans for you later."

Summer sighs and squirms to get in a comfortable position. "I shall be waiting. And thank you. Bo is already used to you, so it shouldn't take long to get him back to sleep."

I throw on a shirt, and I'm calm, needing no pep talk. This parenting thing isn't so bad. I think I'm a natural or want to be for them. That's a good thing too, because this is the whole point of me being back in Lake Spark. To help with my brother's widow and his son.

And apparently to stay.

———

MAYBE WE'VE SETTLED into a routine. That's what the past week has felt like. My nephew slides an entire bowl of yogurt off his highchair tray onto the floor, and I give him an unimpressed look which only makes him giggle.

Luckily, the babysitter knocks on the front door, and I'm quick to leave Bo in his happy mess to go answer the door for Dana, our babysitter.

"Morning, you're in for a real treat today with Bo. He woke up full of mischief."

She smiles brightly. "That's okay. Makes it more fun."

We make our way back to the kitchen, and I take note of the time on my watch. I was hoping to run a few errands and also knock on Holden's door to see if there is anything I can do. Bo for sure keeps me busy, but in terms of professional work, it seems I have an itch to find something to occupy my time.

My eyes swipe up to Dana who is already making funny voices with Bo as she picks up the bowl.

"I can do that," I offer.

"No worries. Is Summer around? I wanted to ask if I can take a day off next week since I have midterms."

I wave it off. "It's fine. I'm here." The babysitter gives me a peculiar look, or hesitation. "Really, I can be in charge," I assure her, and she has an unnerving smile. I guess she is used to only Summer as her boss, even though she's already seen me a few times.

The thumping down the stairs informs me that Summer must be dressed and ready for her day. We used the snooze button a few too many times for other activities.

Walking down the hall, I meet her at the bottom of stairs.

"I'm so late." She's frantic as she ties her hair up.

"You're fine. I know your boss," I attempt to joke as I slide her coat off the hook by the front door.

Her eyes bug out, and she's displeased. "How many times do I had to tell you that I hate that joke?"

I place my hand on her shoulder to ease her. "But seriously, slow down."

She's already buttoning her coat, ignoring my touch. "I just don't want anyone to think that I'm distracted and dropping the ball. The sympathy card needs to be burned; I hate it."

Leaning down, I swoop up her scarf that she dropped. I swing the fabric around her neck and pull her to me, giving her no choice but to catch a breath. "You're fine. I may have only been back for a short time, but even I know that you still have time to grab a coffee to-go at Jolly Joe's."

Her stern look with her eyes narrowing is cute, but I'd rather she throws that look at me when I have her on her knees later. For now, I yank her closer to give her a kiss. "May I kiss you good morning to calm you?"

Summer relaxes for a beat and hooks her arms around my neck. "That's not what we're doing. The whole 'have a good day, dear. Don't forget I'm making you lasagna for dinner, so be home on time, dear.'" She throws on a theatrical voice.

"Wait for me naked in bed by eight with your mouth ready, dear," I mumble into her forehead as my lips are planted on her skin.

She pinches me for that remark, but she still lets me kiss her, and a deep one, too.

That is until a sound causes her to flinch right off me, and she straightens her coat. My eyes sideline, and I see Dana holding Bo.

"Uh, I was just… going to change Bo." The poor college kid appears to be a deer in headlights. She wasn't expecting to walk in on this.

"It's… it's fine. Nash was helping me with my scarf," Summer explains, flustered and avoiding eye contact with anyone.

A stiff silence hits all of us.

"I will be home on time today since I know you're preparing for your exams." Summer is quick to kiss the top of Bo's head before she bounces her eyes to study all of us. "Okay, bye." She nearly bolts out the door.

I smile tightly to Dana. "I'm just going to…" I point outside.

Dana nods once and doesn't seem to judge and continues with Bo upstairs.

Turning on my heel, I'm quick to catch up with Summer outside where she drops her key fob by her car door and is completely agitated.

"Are you okay?" I cup her elbow as she straightens her body and takes a deep breath with her back to me.

"*No*, Nash. I'm not okay." She turns to face me with complete helplessness. "I meant what I said. How you and I are behind closed doors is for us. In the real world… well, I'm still a widow whose husband has only been gone for a few months."

Pinching my nose, I look past her shoulder to consider my words. "Summer—"

"Nash." Summer peers shyly up at me. "We've hidden our relationship before, we're pros at it."

My eyes grow bold. "That's not the same. Things are different."

She bobs her head side to side. "Under the radar. It's not crazy. We talked about this."

"I understand, but back there was the babysitter who I think could care less."

She now appears fuming. "Do you not remember how small Lake Spark is? It takes one whisper and the whole town will know that I'm sleeping with my dead husband's brother. I mean, what the hell will your parents even think if they find out?"

My lips roll in as I digest her words, and I hold my palms in front of my chest to indicate for her to calm down. "I hear you, I do. Just don't let this ruin your day."

"You're far too relaxed about all of this, but even I know that you want to honor Zac's memory, even if we don't in private."

Her words hit hard. If only she knew how deep we're in.

I swallow any response because I don't have one. "I think we're both on the same page, just coping differently. Now breathe, Summer. You don't have to be perfect."

Her nostrils flare from her hitched breath as she soaks in my words. "I'm sorry. I didn't sleep much last night."

My brows rise and then drop. We both realize why, but this isn't a time to flirt.

"I'll see you later. I really need to go, and I keep reminding myself one day at a time, and today this is where we are," she states as she pulls the handle on the driver's door.

I smile faintly.

Inside, I want to punch something, because I hate that despite what's transpiring between us, she feels a turmoil that's hard to ignore.

———

"Cut the crap. What the fuck have you done?" I say to my brother's gravestone.

It's my first time here since the funeral a few months back. I'm not sure why I haven't visited since, but I can't hold it in anymore.

"Is this some game that you decided we could all play as a parting gift?" I struggle to keep my rage at bay. "There is no way you had me return to Lake Spark under the ruse of watching out for Summer and Bo. I'm just not sure Summer really grasps that. Quite frankly, I'm going to let her figure it out herself. It's the safest way."

Fumbling with loose grass, I sigh as I calm. "I'm attached. To Bo, to Summer, to Lake Spark and its near cult-like fascination with fall. Even the Dizzy Duck, which I had zero interest in before, is suddenly appealing. You were lucky. Lake Spark, the wife, and a son. If only I had realized that, maybe I could have been lucky, too." I toss the grass to the side. "I feel guilty even thinking that. She was always supposed to be yours, but now I realize that it might not be true. I can't have that thought, because otherwise, there would be no Bo. When I came back to Lake Spark, I thought you sent me into this scenario to taunt me with what you had. But is it a taunt if I get it?"

Because that's the kind of man that I am—selfish.

"I'm sorry. This road that you're sending us on? It's not your ridiculous video game of throwing newspapers into people's windows... which by the way, I played all the way through one weekend when you were away with a friend, *and* I beat your high score… It's just… you're playing with us. Except… only I'm aware of the rules to this game it seems."

My sharp breath informs me that I'll only go in a circle. I've said my piece, and now I just need to wait.

———

TOSSING A PUCK BETWEEN MY HANDS, I lean against Holden's office door, listening to him repeat that everything is under control at the Dizzy Duck.

"Nothing that you need help with?"

Holden seems exhausted from me as he leans back in his chair and chews on a pen. "Just listen when we talk numbers and throw in a few good ideas."

My eyes squint as I study him and realize Summer's conundrum. "You're being extra sensitive and sympathetic to me, aren't you? Don't want me to feel compelled to do more?"

Holden's jaw flexes side to side, as he's aware he has been caught out. "Don't kill me for trying to be a decent human. Summer already makes me question if acting business as usual is normal."

I throw the puck in the air then catch it. "Maybe it is. Just let us figure it out."

"Us?" His face is puzzled.

"I mean the whole mourning someone close to you thing," I correct, and although true, it's not what I meant, and Holden isn't blind, nor will he press.

Holden drops the pen onto this desk and brings his hands behind his head to lean back into the chair. "You know Lake Spark Academy is looking for a new hockey coach, maybe that's something for you."

I laugh instantly. "Coaching teenagers?"

Holden doesn't change his demeanor. "You do realize that most of them end up on great college teams or even straight to major and minor teams when they're eighteen, just like you did, right?"

Throwing the puck his way, he catches it with one hand. "Why would you suggest it if I'm only supposed to be here six weeks?" Possibly because it's obvious that I will be staying longer.

He chuckles under his breath. "Sure." He doubts me, which means he's well aware of my current situation.

"See ya." I decide leaving is the best option, and it causes him to smirk.

I head straight to the lobby, even though I know that Summer is probably already on her way home for Bo.

The lobby is quiet, one of the joys of having a boutique hotel that caters to adults. Everything is always tranquil.

"Hi, Nash, fresh cookie?" Stuart offers from the basket behind the counter with his signature wide smile, as a guest in a suit with their back to me is busy signing a paper.

"Is it ghost-shaped?" I ask in passing as I continue my pace.

"Yes."

"Then fuck no," I call out my response.

I'm nearly one foot out the door when I'm interrupted.

"Aren't you going to say hi, Nash?" I hear.

Oh shit, I know that voice.

I reluctantly turn to see our new Dizzy Duck guest setting the pen down on the counter then grab a cookie from the basket. He turns, clearly happy that he caught me off guard. By the look on his face, he still seems to have me low on his list of favorite people.

"Keats," I greet Summer's brother.

He casually takes a bite of his cookie. "Yep. Thought I would surprise my little sister and see that she's hanging in there."

I rub my forehead, feeling a headache coming on strong. My mind is already contriving how his presence will freak out Summer even more considering our current predicament.

15

NASH

"It's been a while," I say as I drag my thumb across my jaw, unsure of what else to say.

Keats has a smirk laced with confidence that makes even me uneasy, and I've had my fair share of rumbles on the ice. "It has, since you vanished as fast as a breeze after the funeral. Not sure you even spoke to anybody, including my grieving sister."

I take a sharp breath, tamping down the urge to snap back. "Summer didn't mention that you would be in town."

He hasn't blinked once due to his unwavering thoughts. "She isn't aware that I'm here. I thought I would visit to check up on her and my nephew. If I told her my plans, then she would just protest and say she's fine," he explains, and it feels as though we are already in a stare-off.

"I'm sure she'll…"

"A word." Keats indicates with his head to follow him as he brushes past me. Dread hits me, as nothing about Keats feels promising when it comes to me. He turns when we are out on the veranda with rocking chairs. "She mentioned that you moved in temporarily."

"I did. It was Zac's request."

He scoffs. "I'm sure it's only causing more turmoil for my sister."

I stand tall, and my nose rises slightly to square off. "Why would you say that?"

He seems humored by me. "The thing is… Summer and your brother were always close. They made sense and had a good marriage with a beautiful baby. You? You're like a tornado rolling into town and uprooting my sister's life. So, I don't care what the fuck was in your brother's mind about this little arrangement, but I can guarantee that Summer is not getting space to process and grieve."

Gently I shake my head in disbelief. "What is it that you hate about me so much? You've made no effort to hide it."

Keats's eyes grow into saucers in surprise. "You were a cocky asshole already when you played varsity hockey, but that's not the issue. I'm not an idiot. Ever since the car crash when *you* were driving, my sister could barely muster your name for the past few years, and now suddenly you appear in photos of Bo with pumpkins. So yeah, sorry if brother bear is here to check up."

Licking my lips, I can understand where he's coming from, which is odd, as it's not exactly in my favor. "You're kind of being an ass considering it's my brother who passed."

Keats pauses for a second, a small dose of regret showing in his eyes. "I'm… sorry. I'm just worried about Summer. She's always been one to appear okay on the outside while breaking on the inside."

I couldn't agree more, and I hate that she and I are an unsettling feeling of right and wrong. Swallowing, I do my best to be careful with my words. "I'm doing my best to look out for her. To ensure she and Bo are okay."

There is skepticism written all over Keats's face as he leans against the pillar and crosses his arms. "I'm seriously wondering how that's working."

Glancing up, I'm still uneasy of what exactly Keats's theory may be in his head, but I'm going to bury it and do what is best for

Summer. "I think it's a good idea that you let Summer know you're in town, and I'm sure you must be excited to see Bo, too."

"Very true." He tugs up his sleeve to peek at his watch. "Since you're living with my sister, then I'm sure you can confirm that Bo still goes to bed around seven, which means I need to get a move on to see them."

My jaw tightens. "Schedule confirmed."

Keats strolls away slowly, patting my shoulder in passing. "I'm only being an ass because it's my sister on the line, and I worry about her." There is honesty in his voice, which I do appreciate.

Still, just as he has doubts about me, I have misgivings about his presence.

––––––––

Bo sits on Keats's knee, and they stare at one another. "You're getting big too fast. Slow it down."

I'm observing from the sofa with a beer in hand. Summer does seem happy as she sits on the floor near them. "Or you're just not visiting him enough, Mr. Bigshot Lawyer?"

Her brother gives her a pointed look in jest. "I'm not complaining about that title."

"Sure, but I don't see any women trailing behind you, so you may need to work on a few qualities," Summer teases.

Keats quirks his lips at Bo. "Did you hear that? Your mommy is being mean."

"That's the whole point of being a sibling, to watch out and call you out when needed."

Keats's eyes sharply dagger my gaze. Summer's innocent sentence has way too much meaning.

Clearing my throat, I divert us. "The Chinese food should be here soon."

Summer skims a quick look at me before returning to wiggling Bo's feet playfully. "It's the easiest, plus you don't need to cook."

"Sounds like you two have a routine down to the T."

Summer slides her eyes between her brother and me, uncertain how to answer. "Kind of happens when you're living together." She shrugs.

"Well, I'm here for a few days while a crew finish renovations at my house in Everhope, so I can help you out if needed. Stock up on Halloween candy or something ridiculous. Do you need me to check out that sink you were complaining about?" her brother offers, even though he's probably the last person to be able to fix a sink. His life is law and overworking.

"Oh, well, Nash already fixed the sink and bought all the candy we need when we were at the store." Summer smiles, still unaware that her brother wants to roast me.

"All is well," I direct my sentence to only Keats, as Summer focuses on Bo.

His cheeks twitch with his eyes darkening. "Seems so."

"It's really great that you're back in Lake Spark for a visit. It feels like it's been forever since I've seen you," she mentions.

Keats bounces Bo on his knee and plays with his little arms. "I'll be around more as I will handling legal for the Spinners. Anyhow, you know I'm always just a phone call away, and I should have visited more, but you were kind of persistent that having space to return to normalcy has been helping."

Summer looks in my direction for a millisecond. "I thought so," she says softly.

A silence overcomes us as we all accept the fact that Summer had it all wrong.

Keats thinks she's admitting to needing more support.

And I believe it's because she needs me.

Keats wanders his eyes around him then picks up the stuffed monkey. "This is the weirdest monkey ever."

"It's a proboscis monkey," I clarify.

Summer snorts a laugh. "Nash got it for Bo when he was born, and Bo won't sleep without it."

Yet again, Keats shoots his eyes between Summer and me.

Luckily, I'm saved by the doorbell. "I'll get that."

"We'll head into the kitchen," Summer says and already begins to shuffle on the floor.

I head to the door and answer to collect the bag of food. I double-check the receipt stapled to the paper bag to ensure that we have the right order, thank the delivery man with a tip, and make my way to the kitchen where Summer is buckling Bo into his chair.

"Mashed avocado?" I ask her, and she throws me an appreciative look as I set the food on the table. Like our normal routine, I grab an avocado from the fruit bowl and get to work on getting Bo's plate ready.

"Oh, can you get his bib? I think the blue one is clean," she requests.

Picking up the bib by the sink, I raise it in the air. "Got it."

I can't help noticing that Keats is studying us intently as Summer and I work together in our new rhythm that is our evening routine. It's a minute later when we're settled at the table.

"Make yourself useful and unpack the boxes," Summer goads her brother.

They've always been close in their own sort of way. As much as Keats's sharp stare is unnerving, he's making Summer appear lighter today. She's smiling more than normal.

"How's Everhope?" I'm putting in the effort to make conversation.

At last, Keats seem to ease. "I think I like it. My house is almost ready, and right now my neighbor's house is empty, so I have extra privacy. Someone won't be moving in for another few months. There is a lot of space in my house, too. A few bedrooms too many, and I'm desperate for a houseguest with a baby. Hint, hint."

Summer is busy loading her plate and doesn't look up. "You've mentioned a few times."

"You already turned down my offer to move out of Lake Spark for a change of scene," he reminds Summer.

Her tongue darts to the corner of her mouth. "I have this house, and Zac would have wanted me to live here. I can't run. It won't change that he's gone."

The air evaporates from the room, and the only sound is in the background, Bo making muffled noises with his spoon.

I bring my hand to rest on the nape of my neck, realizing that when I least expect it something slices into me. It seems that this is one of those times.

"Summer." His voice is near authoritarian because he noticed that Summer's mood dropped. Keats places his hand on her arm to comfort her. "It's okay. It will get better." She rips her arm away from his grasp and abruptly stands to leave the table and flee the room.

Keats immediately sighs and realizes his error. "I should go fin—"

"No. I'll do it," I cut in, and my palm indicates for him to stay put. To my surprise he seems to agree.

Leaving Bo and Keats in the kitchen, I don't need to search where Summer is as I know she's upstairs, probably pacing in front of Bo's room. That's her spot when she's upset. I skip steps to get to her faster, and despite her back to me, I already know when she turns that tears will be pooling in her eyes.

"Summer."

"Nash." I don't even get a chance to view her face before she buries into my chest with my arms looping around her.

"He was just trying to help."

Her quiet cry is killing me, and her puffy eyes that slides up to me don't help. "I know. He's always done everything to be there for me. I just feel guilty because the only thing that seems to be helping is..." She hiccups a sniffle. "You."

I soothe her back and bring her to my chest. Her favorite pillow, even if it's soaked in tears. Kissing the top of her head, I'm conflicted, too. "We're figuring it out," I assure her.

"He wouldn't see it that way. It's a constant battle of following what everyone expects but wanting to scream that there is another way that's helping me. Gluing tiny pieces together. It's fucked up too, because it's only been a few weeks since you've been here, and we were quick to fall into one another's arms."

My body tightens, reminding myself that I'm in this with her, and we'll unravel to where we are supposed to end up. "Summer, you just have to… Our little world, remember that, okay? For now, that's what helps, and in time it might make sense."

Summer reluctantly nods and grips my shirt to ensure she can't let go with our eyes, confirming that we need one another.

The sound of steps startles Summer, and she steps back to smooth her hair.

"Sorry." Her brother is holding Bo and seems to struggle with words. "Bo seems to need a new diaper."

Summer wipes away a tear with her wrist. "I'll just take him straight to bed. It's time anyway. Besides, I'd rather do that than listen to you grill me about why I'm crying."

Keats hands over the baby to Summer with sympathy etched on his face. "I was going to let you off the hook tonight. Plus…" His eyes brush a quick glance in my direction. "It seems you don't need me for that."

Protectively, Summer holds Bo tight to her body and kisses his cheek. "Just go downstairs and eat before it gets cold."

"Stop being a pain in my ass and not eating your dinner. It's not even peas, it's a warm eggroll calling your name," he rebuffs.

Keats is fond of her, and their back-and-forth is something that Zac and I used to have. Maybe a twinge of jealousy hits me that Summer still gets that with someone.

We both let Summer escape, and Keats and I share a look of understanding.

We even sit in silence while we attempt to eat. I guess we'll be adding more leftovers for tomorrow.

"Be honest with me. You and Summer are more than room-mates." His eyes remain fixed on his fork, playing with his food. "It's obvious."

I collapse in my chair because apparently my body was tense walking on eggshells.

He continues, "Here's the thing. If it helps her smile again, then fine. But just remember that it's easy for her to be confused right now. Once the cloud clears, then what?"

Biting my inner cheek, I'm doubting whether I'm in the hot seat or being offered an olive branch. "What if she is the one also clearing my cloud?" I challenge.

It grabs Keats's attention, and he doesn't blink as our eyes meet. He doesn't answer me. Instead, he stands. "Tell Summer that I'll see her tomorrow morning for breakfast at the Dizzy Duck."

"Okay," I promise.

"Just her and me." His tone is short.

I stay quiet and give him a weak salute as he walks past me, before both of my hands come to my face, and I laugh bitterly to myself.

———

WE SIT in the middle of the bed with Summer's legs wrapped around me as she sits in my lap. I can't stop caressing her cheek, her scar, her hair, brushing kisses everywhere I can without breaking our embrace. We're naked and tied up with a blanket around our middle; it seems like we've been here for a long time, and perhaps we have.

Summer drops her head to my shoulder. "Tell me something happy."

"Hmm, where should I begin?"

"A memory."

My lips stretch as I recall one. "You used to love these chips, sour cream and onion. It was after one of my game days at the end of the season, and we were going to watch a movie on my couch. I think we were making out or something, but when you laid back, there was a bag of your chips, and you completely flattened them. Your back was covered in that sour-cream-and-onion smell. It was all over my sofa, and it took like weeks to get that smell out. Your shirt was completely ruined and had to go into the washing machine." I chuckle under my breath.

She smiles against my skin. "Then you gave me one of your

shirts to wear and… it was the same one you gave me when I was eighteen. You didn't even realize."

"I guess I didn't. Just habit, maybe."

Her lips drag along the curve of my shoulder. "This is a horrible idea. Memory lane keeps us swirling back to the idea of a different road."

My fingers draw lazy circles on her back. "Fine. Holden suggested I apply to be the new hockey coach at Lake Spark Academy."

Immediately, she giggles a laugh. "That's funny," she sputters out. "I just can't see you hanging around your old stomping ground and dealing with high-strung parents. Besides, would you even pass the background check? You literally pulled a prank every week when you were there."

"Hey, filling the principal's office with a bubble machine was a smart idea… we just underestimated the soap residue not coming off wood so easily."

She squeezes and shakes my shoulder. "You got away with so much shit. No way were they going to get rid of you. They needed your skills to win regionals."

"When you have a gift, use it," I say cockily.

"I made a cake and dropped a beer bottle cap into the batter. Only realized that after it was in the oven."

I laugh. "Oh yeah, in high school. We decided it was either break the cake open or eat it and see who got the lucky piece. You ended up with the bottle cap slice."

"It was a good luck charm and saved my ass from my parents discovering it. I think Keats had a party or something. I'm not sure, but we said whoever got the piece was lucky."

"You are. It just seems blurry right now."

Summer's lips press together, but she doesn't answer. I shouldn't have said that. It's all wrong.

I take her with me when I lie back down. "You're going to be okay tomorrow with your brother?"

"It's fine. If things feel like they're going south, I will just shove a croissant into my mouth."

"Just stay clear of the pumpkin-shaped platter." Her face turns perplexed. "It means there is an edible ghost shape somewhere in the vicinity."

She seems to think that I'm being ridiculous, and I am joking, partly. Summer bops my nose with hers. "Aren't you cute."

"Some of the time. Others would say that I'm grumpy or an ass the rest of the time."

"That's okay. Only I get to see your other side, which is good, as it involves a lot of commands and lack of clothing." Her sexy look is going to get us in trouble, but her eyes soften. "You have a side that surprises me as much as you. You're not the same anymore. Just seeing you with Bo I realize that."

I wrap my arms firmly around her. "And when it comes to you? Am I the same?"

It's a long silence then a sigh. "No. We've been dealt a hand in life that has made us resilient, and it only works if we have one another. It's as exhilarating as it is scary."

"Tunnels. You go in one side and leave the other. Sometimes you don't know what's on the other side."

Except I do. And if Summer is scared, then she might be petrified.

16

SUMMER

Throwing a piece of croissant at my brother, I'm reminded how Keats has always been the brother who can still alleviate a bad day, even if he has ideas in his head that he will never change his mind about.

His gleaming brown eyes accompanied by his grin cause me to wonder why my handsome brother's parade of women hasn't yet led to finding the one.

But I have a feeling that this breakfast won't be about him for even a second.

My brother winces when the piece of croissant hits his chest. "Chill out, Summer." He smirks as he grabs his cup of coffee. We're sitting by the window of the Dizzy Duck's restaurant for breakfast. I'm not starting work until later, so it's refreshing to just sit here without obligations.

"You asked me how I am again. Not the how am I as in the answer is good, but the *how am I,* as in am I having a breakdown yet."

Keats gawks his eyes at me. "And? It's not a crime."

I puff out an exhausted breath. "Can we talk about something else? I want to say it's great seeing you, and it's great for Bo, but I'm sure the underlying reason of why you're here will only piss me off again, and my eggs haven't even arrived yet." I rip off another piece of croissant as I sink back in my seat.

"Fine. I needed to use some vacation days."

I snort a laugh. "You don't take vacations and probably already woke at the crack of dawn to work on your laptop."

"Maybe I've changed."

"Doubt it."

He tips his cup in my direction. "Bad cover, huh?"

"Could have thought of a few better reasons."

He sighs and is about to say something, but Jane, our waitress, appears with our plates of eggs and bacon. We both thank her, and when she leaves, Keats seems ready to pick up where he left off.

"I promise I'll focus on Bo talk in a minute, but first, I need to talk about something." He doesn't even look up as he sprinkles pepper on his eggs.

I give up and set my fork on the edge of the plate, shaking my head as I'm defeated. "Say it."

Keats examines me for a few seconds. "Nash," he states simply.

A breath gets trapped in my chest before I let go. "What about him?"

My brother's eyes impale me to let me know that he is serious, with zero ounce of humor about to come my way. "He's more than your house guest."

A weak laugh leaves me. "Of course, he's Bo's uncle."

Keats gives me a pointed look, clearly not believing me. "I'm not blind."

My eyes circle the room, ensuring that nobody is about to hear that my brother is going to tell me his unwelcome wisdom.

"He was just comforting me last night, it happens sometimes." Keats still isn't buying it. "I'm not going to talk about this with you."

"Oh, you are." His tone is firm, and my eyes nearly pop out. "You're vulnerable, and I don't want this to blow up in your face when you process your emotions at a later date."

"You don't get to say what I need to cope," I counter.

Keats throws his napkin onto the table and slides his plate to the side with a jostled sound of his fork before he rests his elbows on the table. "Exactly, I don't. If you would let me finish, then you might also realize that I accept that your current life chapter is up to you about how you want to deal with it."

"Just not with Nash," I bite back.

A smirk begins to stretch on my brother's mouth which surprises me. "To my own disbelief, I'm not saying that."

My neck gooses up, curious what point he is trying to make. "Then what are you saying?"

"I want to say he's taking advantage of your sadness right now, but on this visit to Lake Spark, you seem a tad brighter, and that's new. And..." His tongue glides along his teeth before he scratches his neck, preparing himself to finish the sentence. "I have to find some compassion that he lost someone too, and it seems you are also helping him find his way."

My eyes narrow in on my brother, and my body tenses because this isn't Keats. I'm fairly confident that his coldness toward Nash didn't fade overnight. "Why are you being empathetic?"

He snickers while he quickly glances out the bay window to the calm lake with orange and yellow leaves surrounding the trees that outline the water. Then his sight lands right back on me with a nearly smug look. "The thing is... I've always seen it. Not just now. It's always been there."

My shoulders sag, and I shake my head gently, informing him that I have no clue and am waiting for his explanation.

"You and Zac made sense. But the Nix brothers have always had something in common. Zac and Nash looked at you the same way, madly in love with you." My eyes drop at his admission. "But you only ever had the same look for one of them... Nash."

Snapping up my eyes, I'm surprised by his observation, but internally, I've always felt it. It's just I never expected someone to say it so bluntly.

"Why are you telling me this?"

Keats reaches across the table to touch the top of my hand.

"Because I also know that your loss is now turning into turmoil because of that simple fact. You think you're not following the rule book. Too soon, wrong person, not honorable, and all that other shit that gets put in our heads."

My throat tightens by his views because they are spot on. "It's only been a few months and…"

He pats my hand before he returns to sitting up straight. "Trust me." His brows knit together. "That crossed my mind."

"Then imagine what other people might think." The building of frustration and guilt begin to swirl up inside me.

"I'm not here to say that's going to be okay. I can't. However, I do think someone needs to tell you that's it's okay to eventually move on, and maybe that's now or not. Just… you are."

Widening my eyes to keep tears down, I appreciate his encouragement. "I'm not sure what to say. I wasn't expecting the conversation to go this way."

He chuckles and adjusts his plate in front of him. "Trust me, yesterday I wouldn't have expected it either. It's just, you are my kid sister, and whatever sliver it may take to ease your pain, I'll allow it."

I laugh. "Allow it? I swear to God, this whole honorable-brother philosophy that everyone in Lake Spark possesses is making me question the water here."

"So what? It has me sitting in front of you, telling you that you can do all this in your own way. Being sad for life isn't what Zac would have wanted."

A warmth fills my heart because he's right. I just don't remind myself enough.

I pick up my fork and begin to play with my eggs, and I'm going to be honest. "I just don't know how to handle all of this except to say that Nash is helping." A faint smile cracks the lines on my face. "It's crazy. Sometimes I wonder if Zac did all this on purpose. But that would just be… I'm not sure what it would be."

Keats gives me a knowing glare. "Is it far-fetched?"

Hmm, that hypothesis is so obvious, but still, I'm not ready to commit to the theory.

"Can we move on from this conversation? A sunnier topic, perhaps?" I implore.

Keats beams at me. "You've earned that after listening to me."

"Geez, thanks," I state dryly, and it causes him to chuckle.

"I think I'll leave later today. I'll take Bo to the park and then head out. It seems I don't need to stay a few days to babysit you, and you're doing alright. You have someone stepping in for me."

A warm wry smile naturally appears. "I think so, too."

"Good. Because Bo spit up on my expensive shirt, and I'm not sure I'm in the mood for a repeat and a need to replace my wardrobe," he jokes.

Now comfortable, I get to work on my plate of food. "Please, oh please," I beg with my hands in prayer, "let me find you a girlfriend. Maybe on one of those apps or see if taking out a newspaper ad will help. One day you might have a child, and then you'll never care about any shirt, you'll see. And if kids aren't for you, then at least you'll have a relationship, and I don't need to learn a new name."

"Watch it there. I can rewind this entire breakfast if you feel like you want to take us back to an uncomfortable discussion," he teases.

I ruefully shake my head. "Shut up and pass me the salt."

I've been lucky. The past few days between Nash and my brother, I've been distracted, as if life is almost whole again. That's a promising start.

Over the remainder of our breakfast, we change topics to his work and our holiday schedules to puzzle a time to get together. It's only when Nash slowly strolls into the dining room, eyeing us, unsure of the atmosphere, that I'm reminded I need to work soon.

"Hey," I greet him.

"I was with Stone, checking on something for the Dizzy Duck, and thought I would stop by." Nash stares at Keats with caution which now nearly makes me laugh.

It's only a solid ten seconds of silence before my brother pulls out his chair and stands. "Well, I think I need to get a move on. Just let the babysitter know I'm stopping by to hang with my nephew for an hour."

I stand too and nervously play with my hair. "Of course."

Keats and Nash give one another a nod, and when my brother offers his hand to Nash, confusion floods Nash's face, but he reluctantly shakes his hand. A strong shake, a shake of truce, and it's kind of touching.

"Take care of her," my brother warns Nash.

"You don't need to tell me," Nash reminds him softly.

"*And* that's my cue to break up this little strange initiation." I do my best to use a cheerful tone.

Their hands drop, and my brother gives me one last knowing smile before stepping to me for a quick hug. "Remember what I said," he whispers.

I nod in understanding.

Nash observes from the sidelines as my brother walks away. We both watch Keats's every step until he vanishes.

"What the fuck was that? Did I miss the apocalypse?" Nash is mesmerized after the last minute, then he directs his stare to me.

"My brother just gave me a little insight." I hope that my lack of a frown eases Nash, especially when I touch his arm. "Maybe later we can talk? I need to check in with the event planner for someone's wedding this weekend."

His hand mirrors my gesture and grazes my arm for a quick touch. "Of course. You're all good?"

My smile is authentic with no need to cover my internal demons. "I think so."

———

Leaning against the kitchen counter with a glass of wine in hand, my eyes follow Nash's path as he enters the room and heads straight to the fridge. He put Bo to bed tonight.

"Have I mentioned lately that your baby-whisperer skills have been upgraded to an eight?"

Nash peeks out from around the open fridge door. "Oh yeah?" He's proud.

"Uh-oh, I just boosted your self-image."

He closes the door with a beer bottle in his hand, then he slides the bottle opener that was lying on the counter off, snaps the cap, and throws the cap somewhere near the sink, which he most definitely will be picking up later. Arriving next to me, he joins in leaning over the counter and looking in the same direction toward the wall where a picture of me hangs, taken one fall day. It was spontaneous, but I think the way the light catches my eyes and glimmers on my skin makes me confidently beautiful.

Somehow, similar to many family photos in this house, everything became part of the background, and I forget to look. Today, the remnants of other times give me a few moments of self-reflection for my body to relax.

"We never got to talk about your brother. Is he always so brazen or just when I'm around?"

I grin as I nudge Nash's shoulder with mine. "Actually, he gave me a little perspective, and no, he took you off his list of who to hunt down. Not sure he was praising your graces, but it was close enough."

"Really?"

I nod once. "He knows about us. Or at least, his own notion of us. To my surprise, we talked, and he gave me a little hope that I don't need to feel so guilty as long as this is right."

Nash's eyes nearly bug out when I side-eye him. "And do you believe in what you just said?"

The balls of my bare feet turn on the smooth wood to rest my back against the counter. "Maybe a tiny bit."

Nash moves to stand in front of me with my legs between his as we stand, and both of his hands rest on the counter to frame my hips, giving me a chance to leave. But I don't want to. The heat between us and the subtle hint of a cardamom-pine cologne hits my senses.

"I'm happy if his unexpected visit gave you a little peace of mind."

My lips quirk out, and my fingers find his shirt to play with. "I think I'm going to let go of a little guilt. Otherwise, it only prolongs the sorrow, doesn't it?"

Nash releases one of his hands and runs his long finger along my cheek. "I believe so."

"I can breathe a little more easily after talking to him. I thought he would judge me, and maybe he was, but in the end, he made me feel that I'm finding my own way, and I shouldn't be scared about others' expectations of what I should feel."

"Summer, it's true."

Collecting his finger in my hand, I bring it up to my lips for a soft kiss. "It's still not entirely clear what we're doing, Nash. But I'm choosing to go to sleep with a little less remorse, and that already lifts me a little more."

Something I say sets him off because he scoops my head into his hands at record speed, and his mouth lowers to capture my lips in a firm kiss filled with reverence. "I needed to hear you say that." Nash kisses my forehead then pulls me in tight to his chest.

My mouth tugs as it seems we are standing in the same place and not just literally.

I pull away, and our eyes dance in recognition of where we are in life. There is a glint in Nash's eyes that holds me. I can't tear away from them, even when he hoists me up onto the kitchen counter with clear purpose for what he wants.

"Summer," he rasps.

I press my finger against his lips. "Shh."

The corner of his mouth hitches up before he continues his journey, leading me to lie on my back as his mouth travels down my body, stopping just above that sensitive spot. Instead, he kisses my belly and then again.

"Screw my shh plea, I need to tell you that doing this on the kitchen counter is wildly inappropriate considering there are baby bottles and cereal crumbs scattered around the counter," I joke to break our moment into bliss.

"Tsk, tsk," Nash tuts. "All the more incentive to take this wildly inappropriateness onto the floor." In a flash, he picks me up, and we fall to the floor, and I giggle as we stumble. But he wastes no time and gets me on my back with his teeth dragging my shirt up, tugging a few times, his stubbled jaw rubbing against my skin and causing a sensitive ripple in my body.

I moan purely from watching him and his persistence. He must notice. "You might have back pain tomorrow. I need to keep you on the floor for a while so I can go slow and take you the way you deserve since you've knocked down a brick or two."

As tempting as that is… I push him off me, and he sinks to sitting with his back to the cupboard door. I end up in his lap with my legs around him. "That's only if you manage to get me off of you," I challenge him, and I sweep my shirt up and off.

This is a mixture of fun and passion that continues to grow between us. There is a reason I don't look at the pictures around the house anymore.

Because Nash re-entered my life, causing me to be blinded of the border between past and present.

With her hands on her hips and eyes wide, Summer stands in the living room like a superwoman. She's surprised, but it's already making her beam a smile.

"This is the costume choice?"

Bouncing Bo in my arms, he gives me no animation because he's probably wondering what the fuck I've done to him.

"He's a little hockey player," I explain proudly.

"I gathered that with the booties that look like skates and a jersey, and is that a helmet? Wait, is that like a plush hockey stick?"

Glancing down, I admit that I knocked this out of the park. The onesie jersey might be a pain in the ass if we have a diaper drama.

Summer walks to Bo and instantly makes little noises with him, the type where she raises her tone and has a melody.

"I think everyone will think you are the cutest baby, yes you are." She pretends to bite his skate, and he squeals.

"Does this upgrade me on the baby-qualification scale?"

Summer pretends to contemplate with her finger on her chin. "Hmm, let me think. You did pick his costume and now know how to make his bottle… If you can make his mom relax by coming a little more during the night, then that might get you those extra points."

My jaw drops, because even if she's toying with me, she just crossed a line. "Whoa there, my ability to relax you has a higher point average than my baby-scale record."

She has a sultry appearance on her face, and I like that a lot. "You're right. I'll give you a 9.5. Now we should head to the Dizzy Duck staff party."

"What are the chances that I can pass off the baby and sneak off with you?"

Summer nearly frowns. "I think as much as I'm taking my fears down a notch… I think we need to—"

"I agree. Relax," I assure her.

"Good. Now let's go stuff our faces with food so we don't need to worry about dinner later."

I attempt to grab Bo's attention. "See? Your mom is a smart lady."

It's a half-hour later when we get to the Dizzy Duck. Staff are busy out back enjoying a buffet and carving pumpkins. The weather is perfect today. An afternoon that only requires a light jacket. A few clouds, but I always felt autumn isn't a sunny season.

Summer gently cups my elbow as we arrive and takes Bo from my arms. "I'm going to catch up with Lexi and Harlow, plus they are near the caramel-apple-making station, and that's kind of my priority today." It makes me happy that she's already loving her day.

I mosey my way to Stone and Holden who are standing on the patio near the bench swing and a bit away from everyone, looking out at the lake, both with drinks in their hands. They greet me as I join them.

"Shouldn't we be more social?"

Holden partly turns his shoulder with a feigned attempt to check. "My kids are chill, so no, I'm not going to interrupt my moment of solitude," he states dryly before taking a sip of his beer. His pre-teen and teenager can get a little rambunctious at times.

Stone takes a long sip from his beer then makes a noise, informing me that it's a good IPA. "The women are gossiping, and there's a baby present. We're all good."

I chuckle at their answers. "Alright."

Holden tips his nose in the direction of Summer holding Bo. "Cute costume." While he means it, I sense the undertone.

"Something you care to share?"

Stone and Holden exchange awkward glances, and it seems Stone is the one to take the plunge. "He is cute, really. It's just… the arrangement between you and Summer. We're all trying to get used to you stepping into Zac's shoes… and…" He sounds uncomfortable as he scratches his cheek, and his eyes plead with Holden for a save.

"Fuck it." Holden hangs his beer bottle low with his fingers. "Is there something more going on? There. We said it."

My body constricts, and suddenly I'm having déjà vu as this keeps happening lately, and every time I grasp where Summer is coming from. "What's it to anyone if there is?"

Again, they seem to look to one another for encouragement. "It's not our business as long as Summer ends up in a better place. You kind of missed the immediate aftermath of your brother passing and watching Summer try to cope before jumping into acting as though nothing happened." That reminder is not appreciated because it twists me. "Don't get us wrong. It's great seeing her in better spirits. It's just sometimes everything happens so fast that you don't realize until after."

My eyes bug out and my lips pop out. "Not your business but still offering your thoughts. Thanks." I'm not exactly impressed.

"Don't lose it. That's our view, and we can move on. We care for Summer, that's all."

"Way to go on making this a festive staff celebration," I say sarcastically.

Stone slants his head to the side for a second. "To be fair, the party favors are kind of above par."

A contrite smile grows on my mouth. "Aren't you two adorable."

They smirk to themselves. "We are. Now, we are happy that you survived Keats and also Summer doesn't have a fake smile on her face for once. Which reminds me, did she tell you about our guest yesterday?" Holden asks.

"No." It's nice that we can switch gears.

"This guy who is worth millions called the front desk at like one in the morning. You would think he wanted a whiskey or something. Do you know what he wanted?"

Stone takes a guess. "A hooker that doesn't exist in Lake Spark as we are a wholesome town?"

"Nah, he wanted a cheese sandwich cut into animal shapes and a glass of milk."

Stone and I sputter out a laugh. "What?"

"Yeah, and he even wanted a straw in the milk."

"The night receptionist told us about it the next morning in the staff meeting," Holden explains.

"I think when my parents owned this place it was mostly marriage breakups for the world to see. Oh, they had one guy who snuck in a fifty-pound lizard, and it got loose."

"Your parents also had that ridiculous moose on the wall," Stone reminds me. Luckily, last year they ditched the dead animal for a different interior design.

Fondly, I smile. "Old school."

"No offence, our new direction of the Dizzy Duck just ups the standard." Holden is proud of this place, as he should be since he puts in the most hours.

"By the way, speaking of guests, did you run into the principal from your kids' school again?" Stone pries.

"Nah, thankfully. I have angels now since Lexi entered the picture with her stepmom-extraordinaire skills."

I wonder if I'm entering the picture as more than an uncle to Bo. Not sure why that thought comes to my mind, but it's a credible question.

"Well, I did. She asked if I want to coach the hockey team," Stone explains.

"I'm sure you declined, with your writing schedule." Holden grips my shoulder. "Besides, if Nash sticks around then the job is his."

Shaking my head, I press my lips together. "Not happening."

If I stick around? I need to address that at some point.

"I'm telling Dad that you're texting Justin Russo." Holden's son is loud enough that we hear him snipe at his sister.

Holden recoils. "My clue that peace is broken." He groans and turns, while Stone and I follow as we should probably check on everyone. Besides, I'm getting hungry.

Summer and I meet halfway to the buffet table. The way the breeze blows in her hair gives me a view of her entire neck which is beautiful. Necks are underappreciated.

"Want me to go on duty?" I offer.

She already begins to hand Bo off. "That would be great. I'm dead serious. I need to make a candy apple and down a pumpkin-spiced expresso martini that I hear is rumored to be floating around."

I chortle from the fact that she's not one bit joking. "I might be carrying you both home later," I note.

She waves me off. "Nah, I'm a perfectly responsible adult."

Her high spirits wilt to a frown, and I notice she's looking over my shoulder. I follow her line of sight and instantly relate to where her mind just went. There's a boy who is dressed as a doctor.

And I'm the asshole who chose the hockey costume instead of the doctor option at the store. Bo's dad, the doctor.

"Next year. A perfect costume for Bo." I mean it when I say it.

Summer meets my gaze. "I'm fine. Maybe it's good that sometimes we get little reminders just to ensure he isn't forgotten. For Bo."

She attempts to bring her smile back, but it's weak. "There are sweet potatoes in the buffet. That would be perfect for Bo."

"A gourmet meal is coming his way," I promise.

The glimmer of appreciation in her eyes for the support is only intended for me, we just flow. Summer is about to step closer to show affection to me but stops herself when her eyes circle, and she reminds herself where we are.

It doesn't matter. She's having a decent day, and that's all that matters.

———

"You're kind of tipsy," I tease Summer as she giggles.

Bo was fast asleep in the car, and I took him straight to bed. Now, I'm downstairs on the couch with Summer and enjoying a drink to kick back and relax.

Summer indicates with her fingers a small size as she sits on her knees and faces me. "A tiny bit. It's been forever since I've enjoyed a cocktail."

I'm entertained. "It's been a while since I've seen this. What does tipsy Summer do again?"

"Eat lots of Halloween candy."

"We'll have nothing left."

"Uhm. I used to strip for you," she recalls.

My lips quirk out as my bottle rests on my lap. She did. That was the thing. We were explosive together. So much so that I feared at times it was only that. But then it was clear.

Summer was more.

She *is* more.

"What else do you remember?" I prod, fully invested that we're in replay mode.

Summer springs up from the couch and offers her hand to me. "You would dance with me."

Setting my beer bottle on the side table, I grin. I have no qualms, if she wants a man that will dance with her, then that is what she'll get.

I smirk as she begins to lead the way, her arms floating as she takes my hands.

"There's no music," I highlight that fact.

Her face softens. "I don't think that matters."

Taking hold of her hands, I bring them to my chest, causing our distance to close as we both begin to sway with our eyes entranced.

The last few minutes of fun and banter vanish as something profound overwhelms the air, nearly creating a catastrophic tension.

It takes no words to acknowledge that. Summer slides her hands around me to hold on as her head lands on my chest.

"You always surprised me. Every time in your arms, I felt more protected than the last." Her tone is neutral, no longer tipsy and thoughts in her head sobering her up.

Kissing the top of her head, I wrap my arms around her as we continue to barely sway. "It's still the case, Summer. I just…" *Let you go*.

"Don't leave me, too." With her somber tone, I can't figure out if she's asking for a promise or telling me a fear.

My breath catches as I come to terms with a reality that I need to make clear. "I'm not going anywhere, Summer."

She doesn't look up nor change her tone. "I forgot that the clock had six weeks on it when it comes to us."

I begin to rub circles on her back. "Did I not make myself clear at the pumpkin patch? I'm breaking the clock. I'm staying."

It causes our eyes to find one another like a magnet. "I've lost my best friend. He isn't coming back. But you? I've lost once, and I won't survive twice."

My hands are quick to frame her face, forcing her gaze to connect with mine. "I promise you. I'm already two steps ahead of you. I won't let you break," I promise her.

"I'm counting on that." The vulnerability is apparent, it's written all over her body.

"Remember? You're my puck." Please bring that smile back again.

She sputters a laugh. "The puck that you fuck. How could I forget."

It does the trick. I won't let her wallow or sink down a spiral because she's sad or scared.

"I said some stupid stuff then," I admit.

The corners of her mouth sweep slightly up. "And I loved it. We would laugh a lot… I don't want us to be a mess of emotions this time around. We can still laugh, every day I see that more."

"Me too, Summer, me too."

"Can we go upstairs?"

I don't answer her, my droll smile is enough.

We head upstairs, and once we're in her room, there's a shift.

We both find our way to the middle of the bed, on top of the duvet, on our knees, facing each other but watching our fingertips imprint against one another.

"I think the cloud we've been thrown into is beginning to vanish," she comments.

It doesn't take a scientist to be aware that this entire situation of how we ended up here was out of our hands, or at least, this chapter of life. Even if I never let her go, my brother would still be gone.

My mouth lowers to hers, our lips mold, and it's that tender part of me that I only have with her. Our tongues swirl against one another.

"We'll make it to other side of the cloud, I promise."

Then I slowly guide her back until we're lying on top of the mattress, taking time to just say nothing, instead letting our fingers explore.

Her eyes flick up to tie us together with an invisible string. "You've been making a lot of promises lately... but this time I believe you," she whispers.

This is the man I should have been. I recognize that. It's different now.

Because I have more promises to come.

18

SUMMER

I'm not sure why I'm sitting at Catch 22. Not when I have the Dizzy Duck and Jolly Joe's as the lunch options in town. Instead, I decided to meet Harlow the extra 15-minute walk from Main Street. Sometimes it's nice to have a change of scene, and their chicken salad sandwich is to die for.

"We are too lucky with this fall. I'm sure I just jinxed myself and now we'll have snow for Thanksgiving. I've only lived here for a short while, but I'm now accustomed to the fact that Illinois weather likes to play tricks on us." Harlow swirls her straw in her iced tea. I'm sure she is missing her Florida sun, but we make compromises when it comes to love, and that's what she did for Stone when she moved here.

"I really love this season. Crunchy leaves and pumpkin pie, you can't go wrong," I reminisce and throw a fry in my mouth. It's been a few weeks since Halloween, but autumn is still here. "How is the bambino?" I indicate to her growing belly.

She glances down and rubs her belly. "Like her father. Waking me up in the middle of the night."

I shake my head at her humor but then pause for a tick. "I was actually wondering something…"

Her shoulders slant up. "Sure."

"Uhm, maybe you and Stone need a little baby practice."

Harlow's eyes squint at me. "Uh, should I be offended?"

I laugh and realize my entry was not my strongest. "No, I'm trying to ask if maybe you and Stone could watch Bo for me?"

She's chewing on her burger and speaks with her mouth full. "Yeah, totally. What, like, for a few hours?"

I wince, and I'm wondering if this is where I face my first judgment. "No, actually…" I glance out at the lake, happy we are inside as it seems beautiful but a little windy. "Maybe overnight?" I gulp.

Harlow slowly places her burger back on her plate, now attempting to connect the dots. "As in…"

My eyes focus on the fry that I'm now toying with. "I just need a night without interruptions."

"I would love to help, you deserve a quiet night." She smooths her napkin on her lap, and her lips press before she sighs. "I don't think it's only because of you, though. Nash…" she drawls.

A long breath leaves me. "Yeah," I admit. She nods and waits patiently. "I know it's soon, but I just want to have some time alone with him. We've reconnected, and I think we owe it to ourselves to have some alone time."

She ponders for a second. "Sure," she chirps out and raises her burger to her mouth as if it's no big deal.

"Sure?" I study her, and it seems that her mood is breezy.

Harlow shrugs. "Yeah, I'm not going to be judgmental if that's what you were thinking. It's your life. As long as you feel it's a good idea, then it doesn't matter what I think."

My brows furrow. "Do you think something?"

"Hmm, you know… at first, I wasn't sure what it was, can't label this situation, but then it kind of became apparent that your lake swim might have opened a door to something between you two. Should you give yourself more time to just be yourself and alone? Maybe. But it's not my place to judge."

My face relaxes from her explanation. "Thanks. I guess it's what I needed to hear today."

Her straw makes a slurping noise. "Although, do you think you two could fall into the water again? I missed that scene, sadly." Her monotone has me concerned that she's probably serious.

It causes me to smile. "Probably not. I'm trying to draw less attention, and to be honest, that lake was a lot colder than it looks. I still freak out there are toads or something like that, too."

"I know, right? The mystery of Lake Spark's water wildlife."

I'm happy that a normal conversation overtakes us, and I'm having another day that feels promising.

We ask the waiter for the bill, and I pay since Harlow's doing me a favor. As we walk to our cars, we talk over her baby shower that is in the process of being planned.

"Okay, drop off your little gentleman when you want. Make Stone set up that portable crib thing, I want to see if he passes his nursery-construction skills." I love that she has an upbeat personality. I've heard that her beginning with Stone was not necessarily like that. We've all come a long way, I guess.

"I promise. Thanks again."

My smile doesn't seem to fade.

———

IT FEELS strange walking through the Nix family home. Of course, I've been back as an adult when Zac was alive. But visiting the house since his passing? No. I follow Nash as he checks the pool cover outside. We've added an errand to our day without Bo.

"This real estate agent is a pain in my ass." He moves a few more leaves from the blue cover as he leans over the side of the pool. "Of course it's not broken. If she just cleared a few of autumn's little sprinkles, then she would see everything is attached."

A laugh breaks out of me so fast as he stands. "Autumn's little sprinkles?"

He gives me an *oh, really* look. "What's wrong with that?"

I touch his arm "Nothing. It's cute."

Nash steps closer to tickle me. "Don't worry, I'm anything but cute."

Giggling, I do my best to shake him off. "Stop it. Wouldn't two people falling on a pool tarp break it? I mean, you and I are horrible around water."

He creates space with a wry smile and his eyes glint. "Maybe…" His thumb brushes along his jaw; I love when he does that. "As teenagers we had so many parties here," he reflects fondly.

I look around, taking in the place that was nearly my second home for so many years. "This place has a lot of good memories."

"Yeah… yeah, it does. But it's time for my parents to move on. A change of scene. Besides, they don't need a five-bedroom house."

We begin to walk to the sliding door to the kitchen, and I tuck my hands into my coat pockets. "This kitchen is great, though."

Nash swoops up my hand as we enter and slides the door shut with his free hand. "You used to bake cookies for us here."

"You guys would be on microwave duty for my popcorn intake when we would all watch movies."

"Ah yes, the family room of chilling." We stroll in no particular direction, just letting our feet lead their way out of the kitchen and down the hall.

We walk past the family den and pause for a second before we continue our journey, when Nash tugs on my arm. "Come on, we need to check upstairs too. Apparently, there's a window stuck in my parents' room."

Nothing in my mind seems to protest, it's only when we reach the top of the stairs and Nash gets to work on the agent's request and leaves me alone that a click in my mind turns on.

Sauntering down the hall, the corner of my mouth twitches when I see Zac's room. He showed it to an unaware Bo when he was born. Bo got the whole tour, and I teased that Zac's room was always so over-the-top clean as teenagers that I was always scared to even enter. It helped his study aura he believed. My fingertips tick a few times against the handle of the open door, feeling a squeeze in my heart. I will always have feelings for him in a different manner, and missing him will probably hurt forever.

Turning on my heel, I follow the carpet until I stop in front of Nash's old room. While Zac's room squeezed my heart, this room blazes it. Leaning against the doorframe, I cross my arms to soak in the scene.

It doesn't resemble the old days, when he'd had a few hockey trophies from high school on a shelf, and even though it's the same bed, it's a different duvet.

With the blinds open, the afternoon sun brightens the room, but my mind only imagines it at night when lamps were on.

I'm startled when a hand gently touches my shoulder.

"Sorry, didn't mean to scare you there," Nash states softly.

"It's okay." I can't rip my head away from the room. "Just going down memory lane, I guess."

"Right." Nash understands.

My head zips in his direction. "I mean, I was here quite a lot when I was married, and obviously, we had a few awkward family holiday dinners here over the years."

He tries to suppress his grin. "You mean, me avoiding making eye contact and barely saying a word to one another while someone asked if I could pass the green beans?"

My cheeks tighten from his perspective. "Something like that."

"I'm happy you got to lie in that bed once with me."

In an abrupt move, I offer my hand, and when our palms join, I lead us straight to the bed where we both plop on top of the mattress and stare at the ceiling from on our backs.

"Whoa, didn't think you had in you to initiate this here. I mean, how do you want me? On my back or on my knees?" He's teasing me, and I playfully hit his arm.

"Mr. Funny today," I remark. "But since Bo is with Harlow, then we don't need to rush anywhere."

Nash wiggles on the bed to get comfortable. "So true."

I sigh. "Your parents texted me that they're visiting for Thanksgiving. They want to do one last dinner here. For Christmas, they are staying south."

Nash smacks his lips together before his mouth parts open. "My mom mentioned that tiny fact."

I turn my head, and my cheek flattens against the blanket. "I'm not sure what to do."

He jostles to his side with his arms sprawled out along his body and over his head. "Me neither. My dad and I are slightly strained, and my mom, I'm not sure what sets off her emotions these days."

"They'll figure it out." My melancholy tone doesn't help the dullness of that aspect.

"Honesty is probably the way to go."

"That we've become close because you've helped me with Bo and we live together," I answer.

Nash's fingers dart out to stroke my cheek. "Except you and I actually started on this very bed."

My hand covers his, and I rest against our joined hands. "We did. Then we took a few years to let it be more. And now a few years more to be…" I have no clue how to answer.

"I'm not letting you go," he reminds me in a whisper.

"You've mentioned."

He leans in to brush his lips along mine. "Sometimes we need to untangle feelings for it to be clear."

It's as if thunder is rolling in my chest as I'm taking a chance, until sounds from my lips are the clap after lightning. "I love you, Nash, and that may be a problem."

Nash captures my bottom lip between his until he lets go, the fear not tamed inside of me after I said it. "Summer, I love you. We were idiots for not saying it back then, but maybe the words were waiting for us now, after a long road."

I bring my head to his, and our noses nuzzle. "I might have buried it for a while when life took me in a different direction, but that isn't the case anymore."

He sweeps up my hand to hold the way he does when there is a strong reverence that takes over him. He's always been this way for his whole life. "It's always been bubbling at the surface for me."

Another kiss, and I trace my thumb over the lines of his face. "Not everyone will see it this way."

"But today nobody is looking," he whispers.

Our feelings are confirming, with no regard in my head for the consequences of what this will bring to our lives. If they are consequences at all.

———

MY ARMS ENCIRCLE Nash as he balances his focus on stirring the pot and sideways over his shoulder at the hockey game on TV between the Spinners and Dallas.

"Don't burn the house down."

"Damn it." He's not impressed, and he doesn't mean me. The hockey game must not be going in our favor.

Stepping back, I wonder if this is a lost cause. "Uhm, I'm naked and wet," I say, even though I'm in sweats.

Nope. No reaction.

"I'll get on my knees for you right here."

Still no.

I pinch his shirt and guide his attention to me. "Really?"

"What?"

My eyes grow large. "I don't mind the hockey, you know that. We can even watch after dinner. But now?" My hands splay out. "No kiddo in sight, and I believe in time management."

He grins and wraps his arms around me, pulling me flush. "Sorry. I do love the way you arranged for us to have some alone time. It kind of surprised me, but I think it's great."

I smile, feeling accomplished. "Say more."

"You're beautiful."

"More."

"I plan on making love to you."

"Hmm, might need further explanation on that one."

Nash squeezes me once. "All night. Different positions. Start with spooning and sometime during the night you'll ride me," he deadpans.

I chortle from his response. "I think I could agree to all of that." My arms snake around his neck as I almost hang off him.

His fingers dig into the sides of my thighs, and he hoists me up, setting me on the counter. "I could get used to this."

Our eyes hold as my lips press together. "I had it in my head that we could eat dinner and watch a movie like old times' sake. I guess we have plenty of opportunities in the future for that."

With purpose, Nash grazes my body as he stretches to turn off the stove knob. "Plenty," he rasps.

"One day we will walk down the street hand in hand. That will be new for us. It was never in our cards before," I point out.

Nash bends his knees and nuzzles his face into my belly. "I need to take you, Summer." He sounds desperate.

My face must confirm that I agree, as in one swift move, he has me thrown over his shoulder and carries me in the direction of the stairs.

I squeal and attempt to grip the back of his shirt. "Couldn't carry me the romantic way?" I'm flippant.

He bites into my buttocks before he slides me over his shoulder to change positions to cradle me as he walks. "Better?"

My smile nearly hurts my face. "Yeah, much better."

I'm still surprised when he manages to carry me up each step without a single sign of struggle.

When he lays me on the bed, I'm positive that I'm melting.

"Every scrap of clothing needs to come off. Not negotiable."

No hesitation from me as I begin to strip, as does he. My breath is already picking up, and we seem to turn into a frenzy of two frantic people.

The feeling of the mattress against my back doesn't cure the cold in the room. My nipples have turned into stones, and Nash's starving eyes have noticed. My body begins to warm when Nash holds his weight above me. Body warmth, right?

"You're mine, Summer." His kiss simmers against my lips. It's hard and locking me down.

My hand slips between us. I don't want any foreplay, I just want him inside of me. Gripping his shaft, I bring him to me, playing with him to wet his tip around my clit, and the moment he begins to enter me, we both groan from the pleasure.

"It seems that I'm yours," I whisper in his ear as he pumps fervently inside me.

Wrapping my thighs tighter around his waist, my eyes hood closed as I sink into the feeling of his lips skimming my shoulder. My moans grow labored, as every time he hits me to the hilt inside me, I swear I'm discovering new colors.

"I'm going to take my time and ravish you later," he murmurs against my skin. "But I'm addicted to you, and it makes me far too determined to make you come."

I chuckle under my breath. "That's in my favor, so I wholeheartedly agree."

"Well, I do have your heart, so that would make sense." I can hear the humor in his voice right before he pulls out of me and flips me to my stomach. His lips follow the trail of my spine, with his breath spreading a wildfire through my body. "I love you." His words tickle my skin in the most heavenly of ways.

He doesn't wait for me to answer before he abandons my back to kneel between my legs, and he takes the liberty to pull my waist and tilt my body until my ass is just off the bed but my upper body still down. His fingers explore my pussy, and I'm excited how he is going to take me right now.

"If you're about to fuck me until I tell you I love you again, then you better get a move on." Teasing him is a dangerous game, but I'm feeling happy today.

He slaps his palm across my ass with just the right amount of force to cause my skin to sting. "That mouth of yours is wicked today."

He takes two fingers to rub my clit, causing me to want relief from the ache between my legs. I glance over my shoulder to see him inspecting my pussy, and it doesn't make me self-conscious. Even when his fingers vacate me and I'm left hanging until Nash's finger dips inside of me, exploring my walls.

Nash has approval written all over his face, and his right hand grips the base of his shaft to give himself one stroke, then he's finding the spot he wants. Inside me.

Leaning over as he begins to thrust, his lips journey back up my spine in a tantalizing slow way, his fingers entwining in my hair to yank slightly to ensure he can amply capture my lips for a kiss.

"Tell me, Summer. Who do you belong to?" He speaks against my lips, still inside of me.

"You," I breathe out.

My answer satisfies him, and he begins to fuck me with more determination as he returns to a better position, and his hands now push my lower back down with my face squished against the pillow and his grunts sounding in the room.

Clawing the duvet, I hold on for an explosion to transpire between both of us.

And that tiny hint in my brain flashing that it might not just be in bed… I turn it off.

19

NASH

Throwing items into the grocery cart, I'm not exactly sure what I'm doing. First, that I'm even in the grocery store, and second, is this my avoidance tactic for the next few days? Which I'm sure I'll be called out on since I know that my mom will handle the shopping for Thanksgiving. Hell, even Summer uses the grocery store as her ruse when she needs to escape.

A coo draws my attention to Bo who is sitting the cart seat with a coat I fluffed in to prop him up.

"Bet you only want the animal crackers to gnaw on, don't you?"

No reply.

I spot the oatmeal, and even though I'm aware that Summer stockpiled a few boxes at home, it won't hurt to have one more. She might kill me. I'm here while she'll arrive home soon from work to face my parents' arrival. They insisted on making Bo their first stop before heading to their house.

"Be on your best behavior in the coming days, buddy. We need you to distract everyone." I ruffle his hair. An indistinct sound is the response that I get. "I'll take that as an agreement."

My feet tread along like a soldier in mud, prolonging every

second. I do want to see my parents. Of course, I do. Even if there is friction between my dad and me.

Seeing their grandson is the ultimate light in the past year. What I'm not eager to experience is Summer on eggshells and our nerves of indecision. We don't want them to know as much as we want them to know. Summer and I have no clue what their reaction will be, but even we know that my parents hearing of the possibility is better if it comes from us directly.

Still, how we present this is an unknown.

For a second today, I thought of visiting Zac's grave again, but it was only a millisecond, and I was watching Bo today. I don't think even Summer takes him to his dad's grave. And it's not my place to decide that.

Pulling up my phone, I see that time is not on my side. No more procrastination. I have to face everyone.

I stroke the back of my hand across Bo's cheek once. "You're about to get a lot of attention. A saving grace really. The truth is, I'm scared. Your mom thinks they will judge her, but it's probably me who will face their wrath."

But I can't break. Summer and my brother are counting on me to make it all okay.

———

OPENING THE FRONT DOOR, I hear the tail end of a conversation about what my mom will cook for Thanksgiving. Dropping the bag of groceries on the floor by the bottom of the stairs, I hold Nephew in my other arm. I take a few strides into the living room.

Then it happens.

My parents have smiles of happiness with a hint of sadness when their heads turn.

Summer's eyes catch with mine as she sits on the edge of the sofa arm. She must have been facing the brunt of chit-chat for who knows how long.

"There is my little bear." My mom's arms are already

outstretched to take over as she stands. She looks a bit more refreshed than a few months ago. No longer frail, she must be returning to her bi-weekly trip to the salon for her nails and hair, and she's back to wearing slacks and turtlenecks with jewelry.

"Here he is." I grin and rub Bo's stomach, right before my mom snatches him out of my arms.

My father joins my mother to look down at their grandson. "Already turning into a little gentleman." Dad is just the same, stoic and wearing a polo shirt. His steely demeanor means that I've never quite figured out what he's been going through since Zac died.

My mom glances up and has a warm smile on her face. "Don't you just turn into a puddle of goo every time you see this little guy," she asks me with eyes bright.

I swipe my hand behind my neck. "Well, I'm still standing, so I guess not a puddle."

"You're just getting way too big." She's already rocking him side to side on her hip.

My eyes shift to my father who has taken a step back. His eyes have a glint in them, and as per usual, he is hard to read, but our eyes meet for a chilly recognition.

The moment is broken when Summer clears her throat. "How was the grocery store?"

"Fine. Bo loves it," I tell everyone. "Which reminds me, I should get the bag of stuff into the fridge."

"I'll help." Summer sounds way too eager, but my parents don't seem to bat a lash. They are completely in the Bo zone.

Summer and I make the quickest exit in history, and I swipe up the bag on that journey. When we're in the kitchen, I set the bag on the counter and begin to unpack. Summer helps but bubbles a laugh as she holds up a box of oatmeal.

"Don't see any items that need the fridge." Her brows rise, as she's well aware that she called me out.

"Trust me, I debated if pre-chilled wine was the way to go but decided against it. Can't have them thinking that we need a shortcut to downing some alcohol percentage."

The soft smile on Summer's face puts me at ease, and she turns to rest her back against the counter and crosses her arms. "They haven't cried yet," she mentions delicately.

On the opposite side of her, I mirror her pose. "That's good."

"Your parents only asked about the Dizzy Duck and how it's funny that I trust you to take Bo alone somewhere. More in a joking way."

My nose lifts up. "Maybe this won't be as emotional as we thought." I sound hopeful.

Summer quirks her lips out, and it's clear she doesn't quite believe me. "At some point a reminder will hit them of who is missing at Thanksgiving dinner."

I don't like hearing that realization, so I widen my eyes and survey the kitchen, deciding a snack plate for the room is in order. "You already got them drinks, right?" Avoidance of the upcoming holiday weekend is where I seem to be heading. "Maybe some cheese and crackers? I think we have olives somewhere," I jabber away as I search for crackers.

"Sure. I think they will only stay a little longer then grab dinner themselves somewhere. They must be tired from their trip."

A long sigh leaves me as I break the seal on a canister of nuts that I found in the cupboard, completely giving up on crackers. "Summer..."

She subtly touches my wrist from behind. "Nash."

"Why does it feel like the next few days are going to be hard, and it might have nothing to do with us?"

There is a brief silence. "It's the holidays. Life events or not, holidays do funny things to families."

"True." We stand in silence as I finish a plate of snacks with a bowl of nuts in the middle. I hold it up, ready to serve. "Let's get back in there."

"Yeah, I already hear Bo getting fussy."

"My parents have that effect on people." I snort a laugh.

Arriving back in the living room, my parents are sitting on the couch, praising Bo for merely blowing a bubble. "I could just eat you up, yum, yum, yum." My mother is on the overboard train, but it causes Summer to grin wryly.

"Thought we could use a snack that's not the baby," I announce and set the plate down on the coffee table.

"A good idea. Perhaps you and I can have lunch tomorrow at the Dizzy Duck?" my father suggests. "I want to see what's been done with the place since I handed over the reins." Instantly my head retreats in surprise that he wants lunch alone with me, and that humors him. "What? Thought we avoid one another the next few days?"

I don't blink, and my entire body is uncertain, but it's an olive branch that's more the size of a twig, and I will explore that. "You didn't suggest golf, so that's already a bonus." I adjust my neck. "Sure, we can meet tomorrow."

The room grows eerily quiet, and my mother notices. "Sounds like tomorrow is all set for you two. I can watch Bo, and Summer can have a bit of a rest."

"Oh, that's okay. Nash has carried a lot of the weight around here, so I'm actually all rested up," Summer informs everyone, and she seems to notice that my mother glances sidelong at my father. They have a secret language.

"That's wonderful. Then Summer and I can grab coffee and head to the grocery store for our Thanksgiving list." My mother's smile feels sincere enough. "It will be the last holiday in the house. The realtor mentioned that there is an interested family, and they will likely put in an offer after the holiday weekend."

Somewhere inside of me, I find that disappointing. Memories swept away, but then my eyes move to Summer, and I'm reminded of them all over again, except this time new memories trickle in.

"Sounds like we all have plans for tomorrow," my father announces.

That odd chill swirls in the room again as we all exchange glances.

Summer reaches out to collect Bo. "You know, I think I'm going to get his dinner ready. I try to get him in bed by seven."

"Okay, dear." My mother smiles.

"I'll do bath time later," I say just like it's our usual day.

Lines form on my father's forehead from my readiness to help. I dial it down to the fact that me with a child is a far cry from my reckless nights as a hockey player. "Well, sounds like you both have a busy hour or two, so we'll leave you and see both of you tomorrow."

"Good night." Summer smiles.

It's a quick round of goodbyes and hugs for Summer and Bo before the air clears, and then it's back to being Summer, Bo, and me. The three of us.

The unusual emotion that flows through me causes me to wonder if I stopped breathing, which isn't even logical.

"I'm not sure what I was assuming the welcome would be. I guess I have only seen your parents a few times since the funeral." Summer lifts a shoulder. "They probably need a night to let it all sink in that they're back in Lake Spark."

I study Summer for a good long beat, and I don't want to burst her bubble as she seems to believe her words.

But I don't.

MY HANDS SPLAY OUT. "So that's the Dizzy Duck in present day," I say after the end of our tour and walk toward a table in the corner by the double windows for lunch.

There wasn't much to show since my dad was here a few months ago. Still, his attachment to this place will never vanish, and that's understandable.

"Well, now it's time to check out the menu," he tells me as he sits down, and the smile on his face isn't a lie.

Joining him by sitting across from him at the table, I'm feeling more confident that this might be a bearable lunch. "Seasonal specials, right? Maybe I can ask the chef if he can make a few of the upcoming holiday courses that will start next week after Thanksgiving. We were waiting for the decorations to come up."

"Nah, it's okay. I'm sure it will just be chicken roulade with cranberry compote."

It causes me to chuckle. "A classic, eh."

My father's mouth curves a tick into a grin. "Something like that."

He thanks the waiter for dropping off our drinks that we ordered on the way in. My brows furrow slightly on his choice of whiskey, considering it's 11:50am, but then again, I ordered an IPA beer with a solid 9.57% alcohol.

He takes a long sip then sets the glass down and slides it off to the side. "How is she?"

Here we go. I haven't even finished pouring my beer bottle into a chilled glass yet.

"Summer is doing well. Just focusing on Bo and returning to life in a healthy, natural way."

He hums a sound. "That's good. That's good," he repeats then taps his fingers on the tablecloth.

His mind is somewhere else. He's my dad, and over the years I've been qualified to understand his body language.

My eyes dip down as I debate how to break the ice, but I decide to take a hammer to it. "Just say what you've been trying to."

He smirks because he knows I've just read him like a book. "Your mom and I have different views on this situation."

"Situation?"

"The fact that Zac wanted you to move in for a little bit. Your mother would like nothing more than for you to stay with Summer. It's better than some other man stepping in."

I sigh and slouch back into my seat. "What if she didn't need a man at all? Why is everyone fixated on the idea that Summer needs a superhero?"

He snickers at me. "Because your brother had the grand idea. In truth, maybe it makes a little sense. But only for a temporary moment. You'll be leaving Lake Spark eventually, even if you already are past the six-week deadline."

"I'm staying."

My father appears taken aback, as proven by a lack of quick response and his need for another sip of whiskey. "I hope that means you'll be taking more interest in the Dizzy Duck."

"Not more than now."

"You're going to find your own place and stick around to be an uncle?" he prods for further details.

Confidence overtakes me, and I roll my shoulders back. "That's the right thing to do, and I want to. Bo is a cute little kid."

My dad's lips roll in as he contemplates. "You didn't answer the moving-out part. So, let's be clear. He's Zac's son and don't you forget that." His sharp tone has me narrowing down his thought path.

"I'm not moving out for now."

He nods subtly, only half believing my statement. "You and I haven't had the best of relationships in the past few years. It was your choice to create distance, and I can only imagine why. Now is as good a time as any to improve that, but I swear to the heavens that if you're waltzing in only to disrespect his memory, then we have no hope."

Leaning forward, I puff out a breath and rest my elbows on the table. "Cut to the chase. You don't mean Bo."

"Damn straight. Summer is vulnerable, and if you feel you need to take advantage of your late brother's wife and should something be happening that goes beyond living together, then so help me, a bridge between us just broke."

Anger swirls inside of me. Then again, what was I expecting? This isn't surprising. Eventually, he'll have to deal with it. There is no way they will break a relationship with Summer since that would entail not seeing their grandson.

Am I being selfish lately? Probably. But there is a reason. It will make sense. One day.

The waiter dropping off a breadbasket and a plate of butter shaped as a turkey doesn't seem to defuse this conversation as this stare-off is no different to the times he informed me that I should put in more effort to visit when I was playing hockey. A damn contradiction in this very moment.

"Shouldn't we just focus on tomorrow? It's Bo's first Thanksgiving and Mom's first holiday without Zac."

My father inhales a deep breath, taking a moment to calm himself. "You're right."

I have zero appetite right now. Plus, I'm wondering what Summer is facing at this very moment with my mom.

"Enjoy your lunch. It's best you and I take a breather." He nods at me, and my response is taking my knife and stabbing it straight through the butter turkey.

———

SUMMER and I stand in the shower, with the warm water spilling down our bodies.

"Really, your mom didn't bring anything up. She just seemed completely in her element with Bo, and she kept mentioning how she's happy that you're around," Summer assures me.

I grab the bottle of shampoo, even though soapsuds are already dripping down my body. "Tomorrow may not be so fun."

Summer takes the bottle from my hand and sets it back to the side. "In the end this is about Bo. We all need to put our differences aside."

"You're not the one they will be pissed off with when they find out we're together."

She snickers a sound, not impressed. "Right." Her T is tight. "I'm the damsel in distress." Summer is now annoyed because that's the last thing that she ever wants.

My fingertips touch her shoulders to calm her. "This is on me, and that's fine."

Summer wants to protest, but she stops short. "One day at a time, Nash. Now relax. Tomorrow is tomorrow." She begins to slither down my body with a mischievous smirk until she is on her knees, her playful eyes watching my facial expressions. "Let me calm your nerves."

My instinctual reflex around this woman causes my hand to smooth her hair. "Fuck, Summer."

"In my mouth? Yes, please." She plants her hands on the frame of my hips then her tongue darts out to lick my tip.

"This is how this is going to go? I get to fuck your mouth before your pussy for who knows how many hours. We'll both arrive tomorrow tired." I hiss when her mouth wraps around me.

Summer's sound is muffled because her mouth is full of my cock. My head falls back and rests against the tiled wall, taking in every lick and suck. I swear in a moment I'm going to yank her up, flip her around, spank her ass, then plunge right into her. Playful Summer in the shower is a gift from the heavens.

Her lips bind tighter around me, dragging out every pump which only brings another groan out of my mouth. I thrust into her mouth a few more times, holding her head to guide her, and when I'm getting too damn close, I pull her off.

"On your feet, Summer," I direct.

Summer's sexy face agrees with that request. Turning her until her back is flat against the wall, I raise her arms up and around my neck.

"Tight around my waist, Summer." My order is met with Summer obeying by sliding her leg up with the power of her thigh, winding me closer to her body. With one hand on the wall overhead, my other quickly swipes her pussy a few times before I plummet into her, with our moans as one.

"I needed this," I whisper into her ear as the sound of water and our bodies slapping echoes in the bathroom.

"We needed one another it seems. And not just now. Yesterday and tomorrow, too."

My teeth scrape along the base of her neck.

If only she knew…

20

SUMMER

I'm nervous. How can I not be?

Always, I knew and wanted that Zac's family would be involved in Bo's life. There was no question about that. It's just, I wasn't anticipating their other son being the one who is part of my life in a different way. The way that I'm not sure his parents would appreciate.

Waking up, I came to the realization that I'm foolish to think Nash and I can hide.

So here I am in the Nix residence kitchen on Thanksgiving Day.

"It looks delicious," I say to Gail as she cuts up the corn bread and places perfect little squares into a basket lined with a cloth napkin.

"Thank you. Always one of my favorites to bake." Her smile is wonderful to see. I'm sure this can't be easy for her, a holiday without Zac. I also feared it. That was until Nash made life a little less broken. Gail stares off into the living room. "I'm going to miss this house. So many memories." Her sight drops back to the basket. "But I can't handle another Illinois winter at my age, plus we have so many friends at the golf club in North Carolina. It makes sense. I just expect you to visit." She gives me a pointed look.

I toss the salad with a lack of effort. "Of course, we will."

"You and Bo will love it."

Right. We as in Bo and me.

We both glance to our side when we hear Bo laughing, Nash raising him up in the air as he enters the living room.

"He sure is good with him." Gail seems pleased by that. "Wasn't expecting it, to be honest. I'm happy Zac made this request. Also, that Nash seems to be staying longer. Handling his responsibilities and stepping up."

Her words draw an unexpected bewilderment from me. "You mean with Bo." My statement comes out weak, because really, I'm prying into where her mind is at.

"Sure, dear." She folds the napkin over the bread.

"I should probably go check on Bo," I mention. Mostly because I need to adjust to her comment, wondering what thoughts are brewing in her head.

Circling around the kitchen island, I mosey on over to Nash and begin to coo with Bo as I snatch his foot. "There's my little turkey. Ready for your first Thanksgiving?"

"He is. I already had him check the football schedule for today and hockey schedule for tomorrow," Nash explains as he props Bo on his hip.

Lowering my voice, I have to ask. "How is it going with your dad?"

Nash sighs. "Not so bad. We make small talk over sports."

"Good. Your mom seems fine, so perhaps dinner will go by like a breeze."

He laughs under his breath. "Miracles do happen on holidays."

The next few minutes, I leave Nash to watch Bo, and I return to the kitchen to help. Sliding a casserole dish out of the oven, I inhale a whiff of sweet potatoes with marshmallow now melted on top. "Yum. Sweet goodness on a source of a healthy superfood."

"Alright, dear, I think we are ready to head to the table. Oh…" She snaps her fingers into the air. "Forgot to grab the highchair from the garage."

"No worries. Nash already set it up."

Gail does it again, she stalls for a millisecond before continuing her task. I don't think about it, as I have oven gloves on and am desperate to get this dish to the dining table. We both scurry back and forth, ensuring our dinner is complete.

Sitting with Nash on one side and Bo on the other, I'm not sure that I feel protected.

"Let me just get Bo sorted before we start dinner," I note to everyone at the table. Nash's dad is swirling scotch in his glass, and his mom is pouring wine and doesn't seem to mind the slight delay.

"Okay, so are we trying the green bean casserole or already giving up that Bo won't eat it?" Nash's eyes scan the array of food options, and he begins to add a few items onto Bo's plate. "We can try a little bit of the sweet potato casserole, right? Marshmallow won't kill him." He glances quickly to my side. "For sure, we're going to mush some stuffing and mashed potato."

"Yeah, exactly."

But then I see our audience sitting across the table.

"You two really have a tempo with one another," Gail says somberly, but there is a twinkle in her eye that's maybe hopeful.

I side-eye Nash and see that he's sinking into the magnitude of the next few hours. The heavy feeling that doesn't seem as though it will fade.

A secret floating around us.

"Uh, a toast before dinner, or will we just dive on in and eat this turkey big enough for twenty people?" Nash's fingers skim the wine glass in front of him.

"A toast sounds like a very good place to start." My father-in-law, Walter, holds up his glass. Following suit, I hold my glass up. "To family. For those we miss and those that are here." His voice trembles, and everyone bows their heads, probably trying to hide the crack in our hearts. "He would have wanted us to enjoy this day. For Zac."

It's a long few seconds that break when our shining light saves us; my son decided that now is the right moment to throw a little sweet potato, which causes all of our faces to soften. "He seems in agreement. Cheers," my father adds.

We all take a sip, and when dishes begin to be passed around, I'm grateful that an overload of calories will keep conversation neutral.

"You know, I think the Spinners and Pittsburg will have a good match tomorrow on the ice," Walter begins.

"Really? Maybe. The Spinners' new coach is more promising than last season, I guess." It's nice seeing Nash and his dad interact in this way.

"You must really miss it," his mother adds as she sets the bowl of salad down.

Now I have to laugh. "You know, a few people in Lake Spark have been trying to convince Nash here to become coach at Lake Spark Academy."

Everyone chuckles at that thought, except his mom who is grinning ear to ear. "That would be wonderful. You would be here permanently. Could really help with Bo."

Nash's laugh dies down. "Nah, I'll be sticking around anyway for Summer and Bo."

His innocent sentence is the match to the powder keg. I feel it in my bones because Gail and Walter give one another a look, clear as day that they've been discussing my current living situation.

Walter sets his napkin down with the air now needing a chisel to free us from this ice. "It's time for honesty."

My fear has become a reality, and I close my eyes shut tight before opening them with a tear in the corner of my eyes. Even Nash squeezing my hand under the table has no effect on my feeling of falling off a cliff, wondering if the parachute might work.

"You two are together, aren't you? Not just for Bo, either." His father's serious look confirms what should have been obvious from moment one. Gail and Walter already knew this scenario was coming.

"Yes," Nash doesn't hesitate.

Immediately, I attempt to defuse their thought. "I-i-it's not what you..." I stagger.

"Think." His father finishes my sentence.

"We happened, and I'm staying in Lake Spark." Nash is firm and far too calm for me.

Walter abruptly stands, his chair screeching, and he towers over the table as he points his finger between Nash and me. "This is completely disrespectful. I'm disappointed in both of you. Not even time to mourn and already you're both sharing a bed."

"Walter! That's enough." Gail grabs his arm.

"What the fuck did you think would happen when Zac set me up on this request?" Nash now joins everyone in this little face-off that makes me feel like a horrible person.

"I'm not trying to disrespect a memory, I promise." My murmur to myself isn't so quiet, as everyone whips their gaze to me.

The air thickening graces us with only a moment of quiet. "Don't put this on her. Put it on me."

"Oh, I will, Nash. You're acting selfish, reckless, and most of all, basically erasing your brother." Walter is livid.

"Stop it," his mother implores. "Maybe this is a good thing. He's Bo's uncle, and I would much rather Nash step in than perhaps some other guy with no family connection. Nash won't take Bo away from us."

My rage has been unlocked, too. Standing up, my hands are clenched into fists. "I would never take him away from you. Bo's your grandson. And I'm here, you don't need to talk about me. Nor do I need someone to sweep in and help me."

"No. You just needed someone to warm your bed." His father's menacing tone causes my jaw to drop.

Gail gasps, and Nash slams his hands onto the table. "Fuck that. You know that's not true."

"We're all grieving. Maybe this is their way, Walter," Gail attempts to justify, and now it becomes clear. She wants this. Everything to stay in the family, as if it's a path of honor. In some twisted tradition, she believes Nash should be the one in my life.

Walter shakes his arm away from Gail. "Are you blind, Gail? Nash has probably been waiting, and he didn't waste any time."

"It was Zac's request!" Gail responds.

"Because Summer causes our sons to think irrationally, always has."

Nash snickers, not impressed with his dad's choice of words. "You're fucking out of line."

"You watch that tone, young man," he snipes.

"Really? Because basically calling your son's widow and the mother of your grandson a Jezebel is keeping it respectful?" He's flippant.

I've had enough, and my arms come out as though I need to be a referee. "Stop it! If you want me to feel guilty then congratulations, you have." My tears spill down my cheek, and I turn to unbuckle Bo from the seat as he fusses.

"You don't need to feel guilty," Nash reminds me.

"No?" I bring Bo to rest on my hip. "I just need to be judged, because apparently, I can't see what is so obvious. Clearly, I'm being careless with the situation."

Nash steps forward and touches my shoulder to ensure our eyes meet. "You're not doing that, either. You and I are right where we're meant to be, I promise. Love after loss, right? We just happened to find one another again."

My heart is in his hand, but the audience is throwing stones.

"Again?" his father squeaks out before grabbing his scotch glass. "Why am I not surprised. I don't even want to know the timeline of that in relation to my dead son."

Nash directs his fuming gaze to his father. "Not the timeline you think. So just please stop." His mom is shaking her head, his father emotionless gulping another sip, and I'm staring helplessly when Nash finds my eyes to keep me in a stronghold. "Don't let them bother you."

"I need to process this shitshow of a dinner," I admit.

"Don't go. We haven't even gotten a photo of Bo eating turkey." Gail seems frantic, in denial, and somehow thinks this dinner can be sewn back together.

We all look at her. "Trust me. You don't want a photo right now.

So that's not happening." Nash's monotone voice brings disappointment to his mother's face. But his embrace on my eyes returns.
"Don't run alone. Not when we can do it together."

Gently I shake my head. "Every dart I feared they would throw,
they just did. Let Bo and me go, we'll talk later."

To my surprise, but then again Nash has always been brave, he
steps forward to kiss my forehead. "We'll be okay. One day at a
time."

My shoulders sink low, my body defeated, as I leave them all be,
feeling as though I've destroyed their family the moment I entered
their lives.

21

NASH

atching Summer flee is as excruciating as facing my father who decided to cross the line on many fronts.

"What the hell was that?" I gesture with my hand to where Summer and Bo are now nowhere in sight. "Whatever your opinions, why on earth would you say all of that shit to her?"

My dad pinches the bridge of his nose and seems to have a wave of remorse. He takes a moment to gather his bearings, and then his eyes flick up to meet mine. "Okay, I was maybe a little too candid. My views are still the same."

"Summer will never want to see us again," my mom chides my dad. "She's Zac's widow and the mother of our grandson."

"Exactly. My son's widow. Last year it was Thanksgiving here with one of our sons, and now this year it's Thanksgiving with our other son." My father relays his opinion.

I shake my head as my hands clench in the air before sliding down the back of my neck, doing everything in my power not to reach for my father in pure fury. "Leave her out of this. It's me you have the problem with."

He takes hold of his scotch glass again. "Damn straight. You couldn't resist comforting her and taking advantage of the situation."

"Oh my God." I look up to the ceiling only to align my nose back down. "We're going in circles. Summer and I... we just connected, always have. We're both hurting, except... not with one another." My heart pinches because maybe to the outside world it might appear that Summer and I disregard anyone except each other.

"You know my thoughts are not far away from the truth."

"I'm going to leave you two alone," my mother says, getting up from the table. "I don't want to hear any more of this. Am I surprised you and she happened so quickly? Yes. But I'm by no means blindsided." She's disappointed with my father and me in our behavior, and she has every right to be.

We both watch her nearly march away. My chest moves visibly up and down as I count in my head to try and calm down. It's useless.

"Why the hell did you say all those things?" I grit out.

My dad crosses his arms. "Someone needed to. You need to grasp the reality of this situation. You're ignoring reality."

"What? That you pretty much just called your daughter-in-law an indecent woman?"

He licks his lips and pauses for a second. "You're right, and I'll apologize to her later."

"Damn straight you will. You don't even deserve the forgiveness that I know she will give you because she's a good person, so kind that she gave Zac everything he ever wanted."

"What does that mean?" My dad's eyes freeze on me.

Rubbing my face, I'm already exhausted from all of this. "Nothing." Only that she married and made him so unbelievably happy, even if she harbored different feelings. "You know I did everything I was supposed to. I gave up Summer, and he got her just like he wanted."

He cranes his neck and his chin tips slightly up. "Is that so? The reason you kept your distance in recent years. You couldn't overcome your pride to remain close with your brother?"

I want to respond with a denial, but... I can't, simply because it's true.

"Why don't we just get down to it and realize that Summer and Bo are not part of this. At the root, it's your disapproval of me."

My father drops onto his chair, deflated, and swipes a hand across his jaw. "You're right." Honesty is brutal, and it seems that it's about to barrel at me. "I'm angry that your brother isn't here—"

"Because the wrong son died?"

He shakes his head. "What kind of father would I be if I were to think that? So no, I don't believe that."

"Then what is the issue?"

His deep sigh in a way turns the axis of tension in the room. "I do think it's too soon for all of this to transpire. I worry that neither one of you are thinking clearly. Forgetting the repercussions if it doesn't work out or how you will fit into their lives."

Biting my lip, I hate that he's making me boil. I don't want to listen to him, even if he has points that I've chosen to ignore.

"I think you've both forgotten a few steps. It's your responsibility to ensure they're okay."

My nostrils flare, and I close my eyes tightly then open them. "What about me being okay?"

My father's lips quirk out. "Exactly. All the more reason that you and Summer are not a good idea right now. You're both trying to return to normalcy."

"Except normalcy is with her," I justify, and I'm not sure why it sounds as though I'm pleading for his understanding.

"Nash, I think we both need a breather from this conversation. I believe you're being disrespectful by you both moving on so quickly, not fully grasping the situation. That's where I stand. I need space, and I promise I'll apologize to Summer tomorrow." At least, he sounds calm and sincere. The first time in the last fifteen minutes.

Gently nodding my head, I agree that this is the best plan, too. "Fine."

Storming out, I beeline it outside, slamming the door in the process. Immediately, I see Summer finishing buckling Bo into his car seat.

"Come on, let's get out of here."

"Please," Summer agrees as she slides into the front seat.

When I'm in the car and turning on the engine, I still feel hyped up.

Summer holds up a bag. "Your mom gave us the food she still had in the kitchen." She sounds melancholy. Her shoulder lifts. "Apparently, we need an entire pumpkin pie."

I begin to back the car up, looking over my shoulder. "She's the least of our problems."

"I know. We're doing exactly what she wants. It's your father who basically thinks I'm the worst person in the world."

Focusing on the road, I remind myself that it's prime deer-crossing time. "He'll cool off. If it's any consolation, it's me he's really mad at. Thinks I'm trying to replace the missing puzzle piece in your life."

The stone-cold silence has me concerned, especially when the only sound I begin to hear is a stifling attempt not to break out in a cry.

Shit.

Of course, it's true.

"Is that what you think? I jumped in to replace him?"

In the corner of my eye, I see her gently shake her head side to side. Noticing a spot up ahead, I pull off the road, remembering the night I crashed the car with Summer in it.

The crash that happened because I broke her heart.

And here we are, in a car, with tears in her eyes all over again.

"Maybe it's true. We're in a fog and not thinking. It could just be lust or we're confusing this moment in life with reality." Summer wipes a tear away.

My entire body burns inside. I could end this pain for her in one moment, but I won't. We have to reach the destination on our own terms. "I believe we're living reality."

"Nash, everyone is thinking what we ignore. It's only been a few months and…"

Reaching over, I catch a tear descending her cheek with my thumb. "Who cares what anyone may think."

Her snicker takes me aback, and she looks at me, with the dashboard light shading her face in a light blue hue. Just as it did all those years ago. Beautiful and sad. She was the Summer I let go then. But she won't be the Summer I let go now.

"That's kind of rich, don't you think? Back then, you cared about what Zac thought so much that it destroyed us. Now it doesn't matter?"

Yet again, someone is calling me out on what I should be thinking about more.

"I-I guess…"

"Because we no longer have something blocking our way?" she highlights that fact.

Shamefully, I nod my head. "Summer, this isn't how today was supposed to go. We knew they would find out, and we were aware that it might be uneasy."

"That was a lion's den, Nash."

Finding her hand, I trap it between my palms. "You're not any of those things my dad said. He's just… dealing in his own way since Zac left us."

She exhales. "I'm aware. It's more his points about us that maybe rub me the wrong way."

"How so?"

"What is the plan? You move in? To the house that your brother bought? What about Bo? Do you raise him as your own? Or as your nephew? Can there be a difference? You and me? Are we going too fast? We never had closure, you and I. We were a car crash followed by years of silence. Maybe this is our closure."

I don't have answers. All I realize is that when I saw a moment to have her, I didn't let go. Maybe I should have given her more breathing space or just thrown her the magic sign that I've been holding onto.

"We'll figure it out."

"Don't keep saying that." She raises her voice but then glances to the back where Bo has fallen asleep. "My world is spinning," she whispers. "I'm in a car with you, and it doesn't feel like last time. I see it in your eyes. You won't let go this time."

"I won't," I promise.

Her lip trembles while she wipes away another tear with the back of her hand. "Why do we keep ending up in these places?" She attempts to smile. "A car or that ridiculous dock."

Letting go of her hand, I choose to hook my finger under her chin to guide her gaze to me. "Want some good news?"

"Yes."

"The cookies at the Dizzy Duck are now shaped as snowmen."

It causes her to giggle and cry at the same time. "That is good news."

Leaning down, I capture her mouth for a kiss, not caring about the salty tears. I just need to ease her. My heart wants to wrap around her and lock her in.

It's so painfully obvious to me right now.

My brother left her in pieces when she became a widow, and now I'm bringing her to pieces because of confusion of what is right. That's two times broken in a short time. It makes sense why this is so difficult for her.

It should be for me too.

But I'm too strong and greedy.

The moment our lips part, she places a soft kiss inside my palm. "Tomorrow, I think I'm going to see my brother since he finally unpacked all of his moving boxes in his new house."

"Okay, we can do that."

She shakes her head. "No. I want to go alone. I need a little breathing space."

My stomach drops with fear that she's running away with regrets, but at the same time, she needs to get perspective. She deserves that. "Sure, are you taking Bo with?"

"If it's okay, I'll leave him with you. Your mom wanted to spend time with him."

Her kindness is in full swing. That's just Summer. Her heart is soft for others and hesitant around only me.

"You know I love you, right?" I remind her.

"I do, because I love you too. I'm just a bit of a wired mess now."

I kiss her again on her mouth, eager to shake her until she believes that everything will be alright.

But true love is when you let someone find their path to you on their own terms.

Which is what I will give to her.

22

SUMMER

How did I end up here?

In the Dizzy Duck Inn reception on the day after Thanksgiving, bright and early at 9am. Nothing is going according to plan today. Then again, it hasn't been for months.

Staring down at the pile of papers, I can't believe I forgot to sign off on the invoices that need to be paid by Monday. My mind has been muddled lately to say the least.

Staring at my name on the paper, I still sometimes wonder how a name could inflict so much emotion. I'm carrying the last name that has changed my life.

Sliding the papers into a yellow envelope, I write a quick note so Holden knows the contents. Now I can get on my way and drive to my brother's. My plan is to stay there until late afternoon.

Sighing, I turn to leave the lobby, but I hear someone call my name.

My eyes search and find an older lady who is smiling brightly at me. "Mrs. Nix?"

I point to myself. "Me?" She nods, and I step forward. "Is it my mother-in-law that you're after?" After all, what does this old lady want with me?

Her smile remains. "No, dear, you. You live in my house now."

"Oh. You must be Mrs. Grace?" I never met her, but I heard about the friendly lady.

"Yes. I'm staying here while I'm in town to see my granddaughter. I do hope that you're enjoying my old house."

"What's not to love."

Her eyes bow for a second. "I'm sorry about your husband."

My lips purse out. "Thank you. "

"He was a special man. You know, when he heard I might sell, he first came to me almost two years ago, asking if I would sell early. I thought it was the most heartbreaking thing."

My head perks to the side. "How so?"

"He told me how he was dying and wanted to ensure that you would have the house and everything you would need."

"W-what?" It makes no sense. He only found out he was terminal a month before Bo was born. Everything happened so quickly. "It can't be. He was sick but not that sick then."

Confusion paints onto her face. "Huh. I clearly remember him telling me how he didn't have much time. He pleaded with me to sell because he thought it would be a house that you would want. I wasn't quite ready, even though he pulled on my heartstrings."

"But I only moved in much later."

She shrugs. "Well, I only decided later."

"Are you sure you have the timing right?" It simply can't be. Zac wouldn't have kept that from me.

Mrs. Grace seems to grasp that she's sharing new information with me, and she gently touches my shoulder. "Forget what I said. I'm just happy you live in my old house. It's a perfect little place."

I nod with an attempted closed-mouth smile. "Uhm, I need to be somewhere, but it was lovely meeting you." Swallowing, I do my best to digest her information. "Have a lovely holiday weekend."

"You too, dear."

Fleeing, I find myself behind the wheel of my car, paused and wondering what the hell.

"I've made sure that you have everything that you'll need, I promise."

Shaking my head, I'm even more happy now to get the fuck out of Lake Spark.

———

W‌ANDERING through Keats's home to the kitchen, it's clear this restored old house is far too big for him. Despite the farmhouse kitchen that brings a bit of lightness, this place screams bachelor pad, down to his tray of whiskey tumblers and crystal decanter near a restored fireplace.

"Juice or water? I actually went to the grocery store this morning," he informs me as he disappears behind his fridge door.

Sitting at the island, I twiddle my thumbs as I tell him a water.

He reappears with a bottle for me. "I'm happy you came, though without my nephew, but still a relief that you feel this place is a refuge. I just wish it was under better circumstances."

My lips twist as I play with the cap of the water bottle. "I wanted some air to clear my head, and since you said you wanted to work yesterday and let me enjoy time alone with the Nix family, then I have no choice but to drive here. And trust me, I didn't enjoy the time alone."

Keats reaches out to soothe my arm with his hand. "I'm sorry. I wish things were better. They didn't take it well that you and Nash are something, did they?"

"His father, absolutely not. Gail seemed okay. She wants to keep me in the family, even if that means switching sons. I'm getting confused if I've ruined their family or if they ruined my life. But after unraveling it all, I'm well aware that they didn't destroy my life and they probably didn't mean their words."

"Nah, they don't hate you or anything. They're just sensitive considering the last year. But to be honest, the parents are not bothering you. It's something else. Or rather someone."

Clawing my hair with my fingers, I growl a sound of frustration.

"I love him, but I fear I've been blinded." My hands slide down to rub the back of my neck. "Everything is spinning so fast that I'm not sure I'm looking the right way," I admit. The clouded judgment isn't just a theory, I'm now an example of it.

"Summer, I was convinced that's what you and Nash are. But you smile around him, seem more yourself. It's more a question of if you're truly ready to move on."

Licking my lips, the question in my head confronts me again. "That's when the guilt cycle begins to turn. I've never really moved on from Nash, just tucked him away. It's a horrible thing to say out loud because I had a husband, but I loved him too, just in an altered way. Not many people would realize that, nor am I going to correct them. Zac wanted a wife, and he got one, so I won't let the world know that it was anything different."

"You never explained it fully, but you're my kid sister, and it was always my sixth sense."

"The thing is… to everyone it must appear that Nash is sliding right in where his brother left off, but I don't see any other way. It's a wall about what the future may look like. I'm just stuck in a moment."

Keats tips his head in the direction of the couch. "Come on. This conversation deserves a more relaxed setting."

I half smile in agreement and hop off the stool. Walking to the living room, I glance out the window to see the gray sky and notice the neighbor's house. "It's empty. Your new neighbor hasn't moved in yet?"

"Why? Want to move closer to me? You know I would love it."

"Ha, ha. You've offered many times for Bo and me to move in here for a bit, but we're staying in Lake Spark."

My brother flops onto the sofa. "The neighbor better move in soon, otherwise I swear a family of raccoons might take up occupancy. Now back to you, and no more small talk." He narrows his eyes at me.

I salute him that I shall listen. "The wall, right?" I check to remember where we left off, and he nods to confirm. "I don't think I see any other paths with Nash, but responsible me reminds myself that we are skipping a lot of steps."

"Well… he does live with you."

I roll my eyes. "Which feels like that might be a strange story, too. I think I just need to hear it one more time from someone that I'm allowed to be happy, and it just so happens to be with Nash."

"The guy annoys the shit out of me, but he loves you. If he makes you happy then it's okay."

"Maybe I should slow us down, you know? Suddenly, Bo has more than an uncle in the picture. Nash is so much beyond. We have to tread carefully."

Keats stares at me blankly. "Bo chews on his foot. He is fine."

I crack a smile at his comment. "As true as that is, I wouldn't want to do anything that will affect him. Nash is… great with him. None of us expected that. Maybe I didn't want that. I was counting on him leaving after six weeks, yet he didn't leave at all."

"Sounds to me that you get to have everything you wanted. A friendship and a son. And now the guy who I'm fairly positive you wanted all along. Now you just need to come to terms with it."

My eyes grow as I sigh. "You're supposed to be solving this situation for me. That's kind of crazy too. Your romantic life needs improvement." I pinch his arm.

"We're focusing on you today," my brother deadpans.

"I'm kind of surprised how calm you are. Considering my life is imploding, I thought for sure you would go brother bear on me."

"Meh, as much as I want to punch a few people, it's a holiday weekend. I'm being considerate. Besides, Nash hasn't *actually* done anything wrong. It's you and what's inside of your head that's the problem. The pin will drop any moment, I feel it."

I have to smirk at his optimism. "Did you really just have a few drinks with friends last night after work? Are you sure they didn't slip anything into your food?" I joke.

"Funny." He slides his eyes to the side then back to me. "Take the afternoon to breathe and lightning will come. Now don't fucking ponder any more right now, I want to take you for lunch or at least try this coffee place in town. I would say it's part of my marketing plan to get you to move here, but I think you would much rather still refresh and start your life anew in Lake Spark."

My brother cares so much, and it makes the corners of my mouth hitch. "You're probably right. In fact, I know you're right. Just need a little more time to clear my head."

Keats stands up and offers me his hand. "Coffee it is then."

Chipping the brick away. It takes time. I'm not there yet, but the brick wall is getting smaller.

————

ARRIVING BACK TO MY HOUSE, I see the lights on upstairs which tells me that Nash is home and probably getting Bo to bed. I was expecting that. I just wasn't expecting Walter to be waiting in his car on the street.

This was bound to happen at some point, but still, I slide out of my seat with a little dread. He exits his car and walks toward me. Closing my door, I take a few steps to meet him halfway.

"Summer."

"That's me." I avoid looking at him and examine the area instead. The outside lights are enough for us to read one another.

He clears his throat. "I owe you an apology. A big one."

My shoulders sag, and my mouth quirks out. "I think you also said what you think."

"Maybe so, but I could have worded it better, and I was out of line. It's just hard to figure this all out. They're both my sons and very different in all ways. Except they share one thing in common, and that's… you."

My gaze snaps in his direction, and he must sense that he caught me off guard. "I believe you realize that, too."

Crossing my arms around my body, I inhale a long breath only to let it fall out. "I don't want you to think that I'm a horr—"

He holds his palm up in protest. "I don't, so no need to say it."

"How long have you been waiting?"

"Nash was with Gail all afternoon, and he mentioned you would be back later. I arrived here and he was already upstairs. He hasn't realized that I'm here."

I chortle a laugh. "Maybe that's for the best. I want to remain on good terms with my neighbors."

Walter seems to find that amusing. "Probably a good idea."

A long pause lingers around us.

"Again, I'm sorry. I might not be forgotten, but I just wanted to let you know that I'm sorry."

"Consider it forgotten and move on." My personal crime, giving forgiveness so easily. I do it a lot. Especially with men from this family.

"You make it too easy on us. You know if you just held your ground a little more then maybe it will be easier to move forward."

Now I laugh to myself. "I think I'm offended by that comment but to hell with it. We can sweep the last forty-eight hours away and just… tomorrow, you and Gail can spend more time with Bo before you head back."

He nods. "Thank you." He begins to leave, but a thought comes to me.

"Uhm, an unusual question. It's just the timeline in my head is blurry, and things happened so quick when we realized that Zac wasn't going to get better. Only two months and then he was gone. Right, two months?" Not a year.

Nash's dad scratches his cheek. "Yeah, Summer. Your memory serves you well."

"A silly question, I'm sorry. Just… have a good night."

I'm not sure if the air is eerie or hopeful or just plain strange. At least I got an apology, and it did feel as though he felt remorse. I kind of have enough issues as it is to let it bubble in my head.

Settling back home, I set my coat and purse by the door, take my shoes off, and go upstairs. When I reach the top of the stairs, I can already see that Nash is tiptoeing out of Bo's room, clearly having just put Bo down.

"Hey," he whispers.

"Hi. I guess I just missed it."

Nash steps to the side. "Have a look."

I walk on the balls of my feet to keep quiet and then peek through the half-open door to hear a little snore. My little heart, forever he will be.

Warmth of a hand on my shoulder causes my head to turn to Nash. "A good day?"

"He was fine. You?"

"I'm tired."

Nash scoops up my hand to guide me to my bedroom, or is it our bedroom? What a muddle of logistics. "Want me to leave you be?" he checks in, because it seems he's reading my thoughts.

"Tomorrow we'll talk. For now, let's go to sleep. Hold me under the covers, Nash. That's what I need," I coo, wanting to say nothing, and instead, comfort is what I want now.

He nods in understanding, and as he tows me toward the room, I glance over my shoulder to the room of white noise and nightlights then back to Nash.

"Don't worry, Summer. I've made sure that you have everything that you'll need, I promise."

It floats in my head, pushing me to the finishing line.

23

NASH

Waking, I feel Summer sitting on the edge of the bed. She's reaching behind to fasten her bra, and I drag my body up to sitting to help her. It flashes in my head, how I always used to do this.

Then and now.

"Here," I say as I close the hook and inhale the mango scent from her shower gel. She fell asleep quickly last night after causing me to burst out laughing when she said my father apologized, until I realized she wasn't joking. I was relieved, as that just meant one less thing to worry about. Still, Summer seemed worn out, and I just followed her cues and let her close her eyes in my arms. Whatever is on her mind or mine, it didn't seem to ruin our deep sleep. "Morning."

Summer barely glances over her shoulder with a look of appreciation then swipes the sweater that she had set on the bed. "Good morning. Didn't mean to wake you, thought you could sleep in."

Rubbing my eyes, I feel the haze of sleep fade away. "It's okay. I would rather we talk and spend the day together."

That remark earns me a smirk. "If you don't mind, I'm just going to spend the day with Bo. I want to make up for yesterday not being here, and Harlow suggested we meet for coffee."

She's avoiding me. It isn't rocket science.

"Sure. Want me to get Bo dressed?"

Summer is already standing and zipping up her jeans. "It's okay, he's just in his crib playing around with his stuffed monkey."

"That little dude can scare away all of his bad dreams."

Her closed-mouth smile feels promising. "Doesn't change the fact it's a freaky little thing."

She quickly leans down to give me a peck on the lips. "We can meet later."

I grab her wrist before she can escape. "Are you avoiding me? Is that what this is?"

Her lips press together. "Maybe. I just want a little more time to clear my head, you know? Plus, you probably need it too."

Reluctantly letting her wrist free, I don't debate her. "Okay."

The good news as she walks out the door is that she doesn't seem to be as down as yesterday, but the bad news is that she still needs time.

My eyes drift to the drawer where somehow, I've occupied with my things in such a short period. Items in a drawer that hide a solution she doesn't realize.

Shaking my head, I throw the sheet hanging around my waist off. I'll head to the ice rink to wear off some tension. It's been a week since the Dizzy Duck management meeting on the ice. Today, I just want to skate alone.

———

AN HOUR LATER, I'm on the ice, but I don't get my wish to be alone.

"Seriously, I thought Lori was going to throw her phone at me. She flipped out, and Lexi just watched like it was some reality show," Holden explains as he slowly skates next to me.

I have to laugh. "Who the fuck tells their teenager that they're in charge of taking the group of friends to the movie theater and that they are staying to chaperone? If I were her, I would have thrown a lot more. Let them be and make sure they're home by eleven."

We pass the puck gently between us with our sticks, well aware that there are a few other people on the ice, including a few kids. "Trust me, when you're a dad, you'll understand the protective overboard nature." Holden immediately pauses when he realizes his choice of words. To be honest, I don't even know how to interpret it. "I mean, it's not that you're not a da— You're an uncle, but you're…" He winces, as he must feel as though he is sinking into a melting pile of ice.

"It's fine. I'm not even sure how to label this. Of course, I'm protective of Bo, I just need to figure out how to navigate the role without replacing a piece, you know? It's one of the reasons why Summer has been freaking out lately. Not helped by my dad being a complete jackass."

"That bad, huh?"

My head cocks to the side slightly, but I don't need much time to evaluate. "A shitshow, to be honest. Summer went to visit her brother yesterday to escape. Now, we haven't really spoken since the other day." I lift the puck with my stick and begin to toss it in the air. "It doesn't seem to be bad for me, but I'm not sure."

"It will come around." Holden gently touches my arm to prevent me from skating forward. "And hey, about the parent thing. Maybe slightly different, but Lexi treats my kids as her own. The parenting dynamic comes in different shapes but something feels as though it isn't the greatest issue."

I begin to skate in a circle around him. "It's not. For fleeting moments, I remind myself that I'm a greedy asshole and should probably give Summer space, nor should I have led us down this path. I mean, what kind of brother am I? Stealing his wife after he's barely been laid to rest. But then… everything indicates that I'm right where I should be. I'm already confident about that. I've just been waiting for Summer to catch up. I don't want her with me for the wrong reasons. But my patience sometimes runs thin."

"What's the next step?"

"She wants to talk tonight. That's a good thing, except... I might have something to make everything go away..." Because I've been hiding something from her all along.

Holden seems puzzled. "Be honest with her. Don't do something stupid. I learned my lesson the hard way." We skate toward the exit, and Holden groans. "Shit. Principal Johnson. How can I not escape that woman? Even when my kids are well behaved. She must be visiting her daughter who is back from college."

I glance to my side. "You have horrible luck."

Then he gets a devious look on his face. "Nah, I think it will change. I'm saying hi then mentioning that you're sticking around and that you two should chat." He winks at me before skating off, not giving me a chance to protest.

I smile tightly when Principal Johnson approaches the exit of the ice, ready to pounce with her over-the-top grimace. "What a lovely surprise. I've mentioned that Lake Spark Academy is..."

What the hell, I have some time to kill. I might as well humor everyone for the next thirty minutes.

———

SOME WOULD SAY the holiday lights at night on Main Street and the shop windows lit up are magical. Except seeing Summer pacing back and forth on the corner of the street causes my heart to clasp around a speck of fear, and I dip my fingers into my pocket to feel the crinkle of glossy paper.

She asked me to meet her here since Bo is with Harlow and Stone. Summer was on a walk then sounded adamant that I come to meet her here. The house is too confronting, perhaps, and the dock has been overused for our life confrontations.

Summer's eyes draw up from the ground to face me as she shakes out her hands. "The thing is, Nash." Oh, okay, she's going straight into this. "I'm not some toy that's been tossed around between you and your brother. Sometimes it feels that way, and I'm not that woman. You are every red flag that I've been warned about.

You could run away at the first hint of a challenge. Or realize you're confused too in a time of mourning." Her impassioned words are causing her breath to stagger, and her body is anything but calm.

"Summer, are you sure you want to talk about this right now?" As I move forward, she takes a step back, clearly adamant that we will continue this conversation in public.

"Yes. I need to get this out now. For the last few weeks, I've been beating myself up about how life is transpiring, except… it's with you, and that's a missing piece that I've been waiting for." Her face shifts, and I see the blaze in her eyes. "You know, your brother lied to me, to all of us. He knew he wasn't going to make it long before we did. I just discovered that little fact, but it makes sense now. It's as though he was playing a game of chess." There is anger in her voice.

My jaw flexes side to side from her revelation as dots begin to connect in my head. "What do you mean?"

"You and I?" She throws her arms up in the air, and the glint of her treasure necklace catches the light just right as she begins to walk away. "This shouldn't be happening, Nash," she nearly yells.

Following her, I grab her arm to ensure she faces me again. "You know that's not true."

I'm still fighting for her it seems. It's as though I'm staring at a wall, debating if there is a crack or not.

A tear falls down her cheek. "Which is exactly why… you're right." The certainty of her words catches me by surprise, with a swoosh of air wrapping around me. She isn't fighting. "I want you. I want this. No more running. No hiding. I won't feel guilty, and I'm allowed to have this, us," Summer lists, overwhelmed with emotion.

Instantly, I step closer to her and touch her shoulders, ready to pull her close. I couldn't care less that probably half the street has heard us or that we have an audience.

My own breath is heavy as I'm melting with Summer. "I've been waiting for you to figure it out."

"How so?"

I squeeze my eyes shut then open. "We've returned to one

another because of us. The situation gave us that opportunity, but it's our feelings that have us standing here together, wanting it all." I gesture to the street, and I swear Holden and Lexi are lurking across the street watching this confrontation between Summer and me. "I've been lying to you."

Summer's breath catches and concern floods her face. "What do y-you mean?" she stammers.

"The thing is, I came back to Lake Spark, and the moment I saw the opportunity to make you mine again, I selfishly took it. Then, I had a sign that it was okay. I just… didn't tell you. I wanted you to find your way to me because *you* wanted me. Not because you got a nudge."

Summer glances to the side then back to me, her tongue sweeping across her bottom lip. "I think we got that as we lived together. It's like he was plotting for a while." She nervously laughs as if it's a joke.

But my stomach drops because it is no joke.

Shoving my hands in my pocket, I debate what is the right thing to say right now. "I love you, and we're right where we should be. You're with me on this, right? We're together, and you're comfortable that we're happening and have a future for the right reasons?"

She nods, with honesty written all over her face.

"Plotting isn't a far stretch. We may never have told my brother about us, but he couldn't have been blind, and he left this for me to find…" Sighing, I take the photo from my pocket and hand it to her.

Summer's gaze drives down to the photo to see the three of us from all those years ago, then she flips it over. It feels as though I'm reading it with her, and both of our minds catch up with our hearts. Her eyes strike up to meet mine, and we share a similar look. An inescapable emotion, and our sight drops again to the back of the photo.

"It seems we all knew that you and I would end up where we always should have been," I state softly.

Maybe it's the doodle he drew of her necklace or maybe it's

simply his writing. But the words vanish all worries because her mouth quivers yet forms a soft smile as she reads aloud.

"*'For someone who loves treasure, I ensured she got her crown jewel. I was her first husband, but you'll be her last.'*"

She looks up. "And that's why he told me… 'Don't worry, Summer, I've made sure that you'll have everything you need, I promise.'"

24

SUMMER

Nash lays me down on the bed, his body over me and his eyes intent on staying locked with mine. This whole evening is a shock but only a soft one. Underneath everything, we always knew that the cards were set up. Just now, we've accepted it.

His brown eyes have a glint that's new, a reflection that's changed. The feeling of his stubbled jaw brushing along the line of my face brings a smile to my face.

"I love you." His words drag along my skin before his teeth scrape my bottom lip.

My body bucks up and shapes to his form. I need him inside me to the hilt, our breaths mingling and our bodies never untying tonight.

I chase his mouth and capture him for a kiss. A deep kiss that lingers and plays, before our eyes follow patterns together. "I love you," I whisper.

Nash takes a moment to let me go and lifts his shirt up. He leans down to help me with my own, but I beat him to it, but I do allow him to slide my jeans off and every scrap of clothing that remains on my body. I'm not sure why but the sound of a buckle coming undone only heightens my desire that's building far more quickly than we might like. But we have all night to do this over and over again.

I do my best to rub against Nash for friction because I'm becoming unhinged and can't lie still. He knows it and grins right before his tongue swirls around my nipple, with his hand skimming and leading my arm up against the mattress over my head.

A moan falls off my tongue, and the sensation of the tip of his cock sliding between my thighs lands exactly where I want him to, on my clit, which only causes more desperation.

"Nash, please."

He doesn't use words to respond, instead shifting his body, and he trails his lips down my body until he stops right above my pubic bone where his nose nuzzles side to side to make this moment an agonizing wait.

"We have all the time in the world, Summer." His tongue arrows out to lick an indistinct pattern against my skin.

Every pulsing sensation that I could possibly have swims in waves through my body. "Yet, you couldn't get me up here fast enough."

He chuckles with that deep velvety tone. "Forgive me for wanting a moment to cherish this body that is mine."

"Nash," I gasp. "Then mark me inside."

That remark only earns me his chuckle, turning to a devilish smirk, his finger skating between my slit for a swipe. It should be a crime when the pad of his finger taps my clit for a few beats. My body is on fire, and I do my best to tilt my body to guide his cock to enter me.

But then he kisses my neck as he leads his cock straight to where I want it. The groan we share when I feel him fill me up still doesn't bring even the slightest release to the ache between my legs that keeps building. Not even after a few thrusts and more moments of moving together.

When he is as deep as he can get, with nowhere to go, we pause. I should be screaming, but I don't mind because our eyes meet for acknowledgment that everything will be okay. The spark between us remains as always, it can't fade.

"Seems we get forever." It barely escapes my lips, but everything about those words warms my heart. I'll photograph the look on Nash's face in my head and cherish it forever. He agrees and is as happy as I am.

His grin begins to form "Well… I don't plan on making this moment last forever. I kind of need to fill you up, and I'm nearly about to explode."

Naturally, I clench harder around his cock and tighten my legs around his waist, and I hiss. "Tsk, tsk, someone was adamant that we could even go slow right now. What happened to my captor?"

Teasing him only causes Nash to pump inside me harder and faster again. "He's reminding your soul that I'm the only guy you'll ever be sharing a bed with."

It's no longer a prospect which is why we meet for a bruising kiss that isn't sensual but good all the same, and I smile when our lips part.

We both race toward complete bliss in bed.

But for our life too.

———

He's the perfect pillow and his fingers the perfect feather on my back. Nash and I haven't left the bed, even though the sun came up about an hour ago.

"You're okay with me staying here or would you eventually want to move?"

I roll my eyes again. "Yes. I'm fine with you staying here on a non-temporary basis, and for now we don't need to think about other houses. My brain can only process cleaning up toys in the living room and searching for that damn proboscis monkey that keeps getting lost." The feeling of his chest vibrating with a rumble of a laugh is a calming moment.

We've been talking about a few things since we woke up. A few topics Nash keeps bringing up on repeat; I guess he needs certainty of what I meant last night. Everything still holds true. I'm comfortable and certain.

"I kind of forgot to tell you one more thing," Nash tells me.

My head perks up from that sentence. It's been a lot of life changes in the last twenty-four hours. "Oh, uhm…"

The fear that my face must portray only cracks him up, and his hand soothes my arm. "Relax. Just wanted to prove to you that I won't run away nor be a pain in your ass and bother you at work every day—although, I am ten percent owner—and I'll keep myself busy beyond baby talk and toddler-proofing."

"How are you going to do that?" I'm clueless.

His jaw moves side to side, and he winces. "I kind of…"

"What?"

"Agreed to help coach the hockey team at Lake Spark Academy."

My body halts as I let that sentence melt into my brain. It's like a ding in my head, and my laugh is beyond bursting, it's a volcano. My laugh is so powerful that it causes Nash to be kind of annoyed. "Really? Like, *really* really?" I flop to my back, feeling tears forming because my stomach is hurting from my laughter.

"Yeah, really." He moves to his side and looks down at me. "I can do it," he protests.

"Sure you can." I pat his arm because he's adorable.

"Calm it down, will ya?"

I swallow my last chuckle. "You're right. My apologies. I do think you will be good at it. Just the full circle of life is hitting us in one big wave. Except this one? My hockey guy returns to the birthplace of his wildness to try and tame teenagers. This is going to be… a little epic."

"Ha, ha." He tickles me and now my face hurts from smiling.

But then the room calms, and it's a heavy silence.

"Uh, Summer…" He swipes his thumb across his morning stubble.

A ting hits me, but I stay poised. "Bo."

He nods once.

I reach up to comb my fingers through his hair. "You'll be as good a father to him… but we'll always remind him that you're his uncle."

Fondness floods his face. He doesn't need to say any words, we're both on the same line when it comes to that. Deception has no part when you're living in honesty and memory.

It takes a moment for us to snap out of our serious moment, but I know just how. My finger lands on Nash's mouth to shush him. "No marriage talk now, mister."

Because he'll bring it up again.

He bites my finger playfully. "Fine."

I hum that I'm in a peaceful state. Nothing is heavy around my heart anymore.

As flawless as waking up like this is, we also have to hustle our way out of bed and get a move on. I begin to wiggle, and Nash takes it as our sign.

"How could we forget that we have a little guy to pick up?" he says as we both leave the warm sheets.

"We didn't forget. We just chose to discuss important matters… and perhaps, steal a few extra minutes of sleep." I ramble that sentence out because it's completely true.

Nash is already walking to the bathroom with a grin.

My eyes wander the room, and a shiver hits me that causes me to feel cold then instantly warm, and my lips quirk from that, and I step comfortably forward in the direction of the bathroom, to a door.

Doors open.

"Thank you again. I know it was only supposed to be a few hours, and then, well, that plan changed and—"

Harlow calms me by sputtering a laugh, with her hand on her belly, as we sit in the lobby of the Dizzy Duck Inn. "Oh, honey, I never thought you would be gone for only a few hours." She glances down to Bo in his stroller. "Mommy was being silly, wasn't she." Her baby voice doesn't need any improvement; she's going to nail the mom thing. "Then when Holden and Lexi texted about the fireworks on Main Street between your mommy and uncle, then you and I just got cozy for the night, didn't we?"

My son giggles and grabs his feet in the air. He doesn't seem to have missed me.

"I guess it was obvious."

"Well, I mean, all of us are already aware, it's just you two kind of kept it under the radar, so we were never sure how to act. Are you openly together so we can all calm down?"

I smile and stare at my son. "All good on the public front."

Harlow pretends to wipe her forehead. "Phew. Lexi was planting mistletoe all around the hotel. Little booby traps so we could see you two attempt not to kiss when you really want to kiss, but then you do kiss and question it, only to kiss again," she babbles, and it's her romantic heart at work.

"It's fine. Make a map for where I can find the hanging plant," I gladly declare.

The sound of two men laughing brings my gaze to my right. Stone and Nash are joining us, and it seems they must have been discussing anything but the running of the Dizzy Duck Inn.

"Ready to nosh on some brunch while my parents debate a Virgin Bloody Mary or not?"

I snort a laugh and stand. "That's not even in question."

Next to Nash where I should be, his elbow runs along my arm as he slips on the diaper bag and makes a funny face at Bo.

"Have fun. The croissants with local jam never fail at our fine establishment," Stone jokingly reflects.

"Yeah, it's the broken coffee machine that's shit," Nash points out.

Shaking my head, it's nice to be lighthearted today. "No more Dizzy Duck critique." I begin to push the stroller.

It's a quick round of goodbyes, then Nash and I make our way to the dining room.

When we enter, we spot his parents in the corner. It's their last day here before they head back south. Their demeanor is different to a few days ago, no longer tense but still resigned.

They too will find harmony; maybe not today but soon, I'm sure.

Nash and I are thinking clearly.

We have a future.

No sin is involved because there never was to begin with.

Maybe it's the flick in our eyes that meet his parents' or the fact that we know we have Harlow, Stone, Holden, and Lexi as unexpected spies who are not so casually sipping on mimosas at the bar, pretending not to watch.

Everything is hopeful.

Which is why Nash and I look to one another with a smile then interlace our fingers to hold hands.

Because we're together.

EPILOGUE: SUMMER

SIX MONTHS LATER

"**A**re you sure you're going to be fine? I mean, that big shot lawyer guy from Colorado is staying this weekend," I explain as Stone and Holden stand in front of the reception desk. They stare at me, unfazed, with their arms crossed.

In fact, Stone is casually drinking from his to-go cup of coffee. "Oh, whatever will we do if a fire starts and the Lake Spark fire department is busy saving a deer somewhere," he deadpans. He probably thinks I'm being ridiculous.

My head cocks to the side from his demeanor.

"Go. Go on your much-deserved day off," Holden assures me.

I nearly snort a laugh. "Seeing my brother isn't exactly a holiday. There's a fifty-fifty chance that Nash and Keats will get along."

Holden quirks his lips and thinks to himself for a second. "I think they'll be fine. You have a kid to distract them."

A proud smile hits me. "Yeah, Bo is the best ever, isn't he?"

"I mean, let's not go overboard. My little guy is going to be the best little superhero in the making," Stone highlights. He's glowing like a proud father does.

Stuart clears his throat; I always forget when he's around. Peeking around Stone and Holden, I see Stuart staring up from the tablet at the desk. "Could you do one more thing for me before you go?" He rolls his shoulder back and seems afraid to ask.

Poor kid, Stone still makes him nervous. "Sure," I reply, my smile still intact.

"On the dock, there seems to be a guest who wants to complain about the rowboat."

I grumble to myself. "Really?" I answer dryly. "That's what I have to deal with before I go?"

"We would offer to step in, but we have places to go and people to see. Enjoy your free day, Summer," Holden states as he and Stone propel themselves from the desk. Stone gives me a little nod and smiles as they walk away.

"Cookie?" Stuart's upbeat tone is back as he holds up the basket of welcome cookies.

My brows knit together. "What shape?"

His eyes dip down, and he examines the basket. "Uh, we're back to the traditional chocolate chip. Oh, there is this odd-shaped one."

My hand finds my hip that tips out. "Odd-shaped one? We are serving our guests deformed cookies?"

Stuart shrugs, and I'm quick to snap the cookie from the basket, completely unenthused. I look at the cookie then do a double take. My head lolls softly to the side. Huh? Is this…

"I think the dock issue is waiting," Stuart reminds me, and now I realize that he has been setting me up.

The cookie I'm holding between my two fingers isn't an odd shape.

It's a treasure chest with icing.

My frustration with work vanishes. "Thanks. I better get a move on."

The pace of my walk is nearly a skip through the Dizzy Duck until I stop at the door to the back patio. My hand stills on the handle as a rush of blood pumps through my body. Slowly opening the door, I'm greeted with the vision that I'll never get bored of.

Nash is standing on the dock, holding my son's raised hands, his nephew. Bo is strong but can only walk with our help. Any day now that will change.

I make my way to them, wrapping my arms around my body to keep me warm from the gentle breeze, and the moment my feet touch the dock, I'm aware that I won't be leaving as the same woman.

Holding up the cookie, I grin, because Nash has a suave look that shows satisfaction to his plans. "Nice cookie request." Ceremoniously, I take a bite.

His smirk knocks every nerve inside my body to red alert that Nash will make me happy. "Beats those damn ghost shapes," he replies.

I step closer, my eyes meeting his for a few ticks before I lean down and offer Bo the remainder of the cookie.

Nash lets his hands go and encourages Bo to sit. "Why don't we just have you chill there for a bit, huh, buddy?" Nash rustles Bo's hair as my son grabs the cookie from my hand with vigor and is quick to go to town on it.

When Nash and I move to stand, our foreheads bump. "Ow." I rub my head as we part.

Nash chuckles. "Of course, that would happen. We are on the mystical dock."

"The dock." It's barely a whisper from my parted lips.

"Our place."

"Our place," I repeat.

He narrows his eyes at me. "Just going to repeat my words?"

I'm mesmerized because every fiber in my body is aware of what he's about to do. It's my instinct. "That depends."

The gleam in Nash's eyes seems as though he's happy with that answer.

I snicker when he begins to lower to one knee because I knew two minutes ago how this scene would go. It doesn't faze him as he continues his quest, taking hold of my hands and peering up at me.

"Summer." His tone is firm, almost as though he's trying to keep me in line. "You and I have had a long and winding road. Turns out it was leading us to where we should be. Maybe we should have been more then, but we can't change the clock, and here we are now. It's true. I'm supposed to be your last husband."

Tears are beginning to bubble. It's in an odd second, yet right that he references that sentiment from his brother. It doesn't matter because it's true.

"But in order for that to happen, you have to marry me." His sly smirk turns to a fully warm grin.

Now I have to chortle and smile. "I don't hear a question there." No way am I going to make this easy for him.

"You can't question facts." Nash's wink only solidifies my difficulty to ever break this smile.

Lowering to a squat, we come face to face, with my fingertips spread out against his cheeks. "Then it seems we can't challenge that." I love interacting with him this way.

"Exactly," he rasps.

"You know, marrying me comes with some very serious perks." I drop my knees to the dock.

"Oh yeah?" he says, playing along.

I nod once. "Free cookies."

"I partly own this establishment. I already get free cookies."

I tsk him to shut up. "Fine. Remembering the past and being at peace. A great kid."

"Who will have a brother or sister soon."

My eyes widen as my arms link around his neck. "Soon? You might need to wait on that little request."

"What else?"

"Hmm, depends on the ring," I tease him.

"Look in my jeans pocket."

I smirk slyly as my hand dives into the pocket in a way that brings us close, and if we had no audience, then we would probably have clothes off soon. Our lips brush as I slide the ring out of his pocket. Glancing to my side, I hold up the ring. Beautiful and simple. Perfect for me.

I pretend to ponder. "I mean, I guess this works." Nash yanks me closer to kiss my lips, and our teeth touch because our lips are still tightly in a grin. "That list," I murmur against his lips. "You'll also get a wife who will make every shower enjoyable as I will completely be on my knees to take you—" Bo's squeal breaks our attention.

Our foreheads continue to touch as we move to study Bo. "I know, right? Your mommy has such a foul mouth."

Bo holds up his hands with crumbs and icing stuck to his skin. He's grabby because he wants more cookies.

"So, were you in on this too, kid?" I ask my son.

His response in to say, "Mama."

The feeling of my fingers being dragged causes me to look down, and I watch Nash slip the ring on.

"I'm kind of surprised it didn't fall down and between the boards because that's just our style on this dock," he quips.

My hand soars up, and I stretch my fingers to appraise the ring. It's simple, Bohemian, and suits me in every way.

"Not too shabby," I say.

Nash yanks me tight to his body and kisses me with a delicious warning. "You're going to drive me crazy forever, aren't you?"

"And you don't mind."

He swipes a few strands of my hair away, and we get lost in one another's eyes for a few seconds before another kiss is shared between us.

But the clawing at my ankles updates me that someone is getting restless. "Okay, we get the hint. You're happy about this, want more cookies, and you're ready for your car ride to your other uncle." I scoop Bo into my arms and pretend to bite his nose which earns me a few giggles. "You're going to be the cutest little ring bearer, yes you are." My mom voice is out in full.

"Alright, let's get you two in the car. Champagne will have to wait for later because we have a schedule to keep, and you have no sweater on."

I suddenly remember that I have nothing covering my arms, and that causes a shiver from the realization. Then another one runs through my head. "Wait, champagne later? Does Keats know?"

Nash releases a short laugh. "Did you really think I was going to show up at his house with a ring around his sister's finger and face his wrath? Yeah. Yeah, he knows. Seemed neutral about it."

It makes me laugh, as I can only imagine how that conversation went, but then my laugh softens. "And your parents?" Gail never had an issue with Nash and me, and Walter has slowly come around.

Nash touches my shoulder to put me at ease. "They're fine." My smile begins to etch on my lips again.

"Let's go then. Seems everything is in place."

"It is."

Our delicate voices and our eyes catching are the perfect confirmation that we are exactly where we should be. Where we always should have been.

THE CAR RIDE was needed to gather my strength for balancing the testosterone between Keats and Nash. As he drives, we've been sharing pure puppy eyes and giddy looks. We're nearly over the top, and I'm sure it will make my brother scowl a few times.

"Here we are." Nash sighs as we turn onto my brother's street.

I chuckle. "Enthusiasm to the brim," I retort.

"Don't get me wrong. It's just… we haven't really stayed in a family member's house since we've been together. I'm not sure Keats should be our trial." We decided to stay overnight, makes it easier if we want to enjoy wine.

I rub his hand where it's sitting on the middle console. I find this entertaining. "We'll be fine. Besides, I think he still has work to do, and it will be just a chill dinner. A BBQ maybe."

Nash's eyes seem focused through the front window of the car as he slows down. When he tilts his head and eyes squint, it causes me to wonder what's happening. "Uh, looks like your brother is going to be *on* a BBQ."

My eyes snap forward as we come to a stop in front of his house. He's in the front yard with a woman our age arguing with him, and Keats seems to be dishing it right back.

Hesitantly, I unbuckle my belt and open the door to hop out. They seem unaware of our arrival.

"You. You are the one who dragged me to that party," she seethes.

"Really, Esme? Pretty positive you got an invite too, and it just so happens we ended up driving home together."

She points a finger at my brother. "You are the worst neighbor. You are such a mind fuck."

I stand there in awe and feel Nash arrive by my side. I'm not sure either of us blink, too engrossed in the scene.

"Do we interrupt them, let them know to tone down the language before I take Bo out?" Nash wonders.

"I'm not sure. I kind of want to see how this plays out."

Nash's eyes and my own nearly pop out when my brother steps forward and so does Esme. Ah, I know this scene. A reminder of Nash and I pre-reunion, which is why I smirk.

"It's not my fault you voluntarily came home with me and then we—"

"Whoa," I speak up and wave my hand. "We don't need to hear more."

Both Keats and Esme whip their sight to us, suddenly aware of our presence.

Nash just smirks, clearly enjoying my brother's shock or embarrassment, I'm not sure what it is.

"How long have you been standing there?" Keats asks, frozen.

"Long enough for me to enjoy this weekend's *roasted* BBQ." Nash has a cheeky smile—because he won't let this go—right before he turns to open Bo's door with vigor.

My fingers give a little wiggle wave. "You must be the neighbor. I've heard about you. Not exactly in your favor," I admit with a tight smile. "But you seem to be handling my brother… kind of… maybe."

"Summer," Keats grits out a warning.

"What?' My voice rises an octave as I shrug. "Clearly she returns the sentiment, and it's not my problem that we showed up to your lovers' quarrel."

"We are not lovers," they both say in unison.

Nash just chuckles under his breath. "Sure, you aren't."

What an eventful dinner this is going to be.

www.ingramcontent.com/pod-product-compliance
Lightning Source LLC
Chambersburg PA
CBHW060557300726
48975CB00005B/1350